1939–1979 [...] rday, over tea and jam at Seweryn Pollack's house, we were discussing the odd way in which time seemed to be flowing, creating a simultaneous twofold impression of a protracted present and a past that was cut off, as if every 'yesterday' were at the same time a 'once upon a time' in which our reflections and shadows remain imprisoned. In memory, we seem to be our own ancestors, and not such distant ancestors, either, from two years, twenty years back. How do we differ from the *émigrés* – probably only in that their memory of the past is identified with Poland: they have been not only dispossessed of time but of place as well. When feeling nostalgic for a weeping willow by the road, what they are longing for is themselves under a willow before 1939 or 1945 or 1968 – for the landscape of their youth, and not for the countryside or cityscape itself. After all, we have that landscape, every day, and don't we long for it, too? One longs for what is absent. And it is we who are not here, we who are gone: we as we were in the past.

Kazimierz Brandys
A Warsaw Diary 1978–1981

Winter is yours. Spring will be ours.

Graffiti on the walls of Warsaw,
winter 1981–82

Sue Gee

SPRING WILL BE OURS

Mandarin

For the family – the living and the dead

A Mandarin Paperback

SPRING WILL BE OURS

First published in Great Britain 1988
by Century Hutchinson Ltd
This edition published 1989
Reprinted 1989
by Mandarin Paperbacks
Michelin House, 81 Fulham Road, London SW3 6RB

Mandarin is an imprint of the Octopus Publishing Group

Copyright © Sue Gee 1988

British Library Cataloguing in Publication Data
Gee, Sue
Spring will be ours.
I. Title
823'.914[F]

ISBN 0 7493 0039 6

Printed in Great Britain
by Cox & Wyman Ltd, Reading

Contents

Part 1

The Lighthouse Keepers

Part 2

My Country

Part 3

Winter is Yours

Acknowledgements

I am grateful to the following for permission to reproduce extracts: the BBC Written Archives Centre for news bulletin material, and particularly to Neil Somerville and Jeff Walden for help in research; Chatto & Windus for *A Warsaw Diary* by Kazimierz Brandys; Century Hutchinson for 'Refrain' by Karol Wojtyla, in *Collected Poems*, translated by Jerzy Pieterkiewicz; Piast Publishing Company and the American Institute of Polish Culture for the translation by Monica M. Gardiner of 'The Lighthouse Keeper' in *Selected Tales* by Henryk Sienkiewicz; the Polish Solidarity Campaign for extracts from *PSC News*; Mrs Myfanwy Thomas for 'Rain' by Edward Thomas.

I am indebted to many books, but in particular to *Righteous Among Nations* by W. Bartoszewski; *The Secret Army* by Bór-Komorowski; *The Polish August* by Neal Ascherson; *A Warsaw Diary* by Kazimierz Brandys; *God's Playground: A History of Poland* by Norman Davies; *Polish Revolution* by Timothy Garton-Ash; *The Civilian Population and the Warsaw Rising* by Joanna Hanson; *Warsaw* by Stanisław Jankowski and Adolf Ciborowski; *The Canary and Other Tales of Martial Law* by Marek Nowakowski; *Courier from Warsaw* by Jan Nowak; *The Polish Challenge* by Kevin Ruane; *The Poles* by Stewart Steven; *The Polish Ordeal* by Andrzej Szczypiorski; *Death in the Forest* and *Nothing But Honour: The Story of the Warsaw Uprising 1944* by J. K. Zawodny.

Any errors in this book are entirely my own. But for guidance, discussion and advice, I should like to thank most warmly my publisher, Rosie Cheetham, and my agent, Jennifer Kavanagh; Mr Jerzy de Berg and Mr Krzysztof de Berg; Dr Józef Garliński, for corrections to Chapters 2, 3, 4 and 5; Marek Garztecki, Solidarity representative in the UK; Giles Hart, of the Polish Solidarity Campaign; Joanna Szula and Gera Drymer, of the Polish Refugee Rights Group; Wiola Hola; Tadek Jarski and Ryszard Sliwa, of Solidarity with Solidarity; the Imperial War Museum; Hanna Kazanowska; the Scottish painter Helen Lee, for a painting; Danusia Mayer; Krystyna Mayer; Anna Paczuska, of the *Labour Focus on*

Eastern Europe collective; the Polish Library; Captain Milewski of the Polish Institute and Sikorski Museum; the Polish Underground Movement Study Trust; Grazyna Sokołowska; Maria Sokołowska; Dr Keith Sword, of the School of Slavonic and East European Studies; and Sue Vincent, for photographs and anecdotes. To Kate Neville-Smith and Margaret Raw, my gratitude for giving Jamie such happy times; and to Betty Nunn, for typing beautifully, at top speed.

Finally, there are people without whom this book could not have been written. My deepest thanks go to Hanna Mayer, who began it all, and helped all the way through; and to Hazel and Antony Wood, the best of friends, who so generously gave me a room of my own, and endless encouragement. And to all the family, and especially my mother, and Marek and Jamie, who give me everything: my love.

Notes on Meaning and Pronunciation

Tata is Polish for Daddy

Andrzej – And'jeh*
Babcia (Grandmother) – Babcha
Dziadek (Grandfather) – Jadek
Ewa – Ay'vah
Jan – Yan
Jerzy – Yier'jeh*
Tomasz – Tomash
Wojtek – Voytek

The two letters sz are pronounced sh.
The word ending –cz is pronounced –ch.
The Polish w is pronounced as a v.
The Polish letter ł is pronounced w.
Polish surnames ending in –ski, –cki take the masculine and feminine
endings –i and –a, thus Jan Prawicki, Anna Prawicka (pronounced
Pravitski, Pravitska).

* There is no exact English sound or transliteration corresponding to the
soft buzz of –rz, or ż.

Part 1

The Lighthouse Keepers

Prologue:
London, December 1981

In the light from the platform, in the lights along the track, the rails gleamed, wet with frost melted by the last train, already beginning to freeze again, crystals glistening. In the watery yellow lakes of light along the embankment he could see stiff grass and weeds, rime-encrusted, winter's graveyard, then darkness. His breath streamed into the cold as he paced up and down, past the damp wooden seats, the posters, the graffiti.

In Warsaw, in Gdańsk, in Kraków and Bydgoszcz, in cities and obscure small towns all over Poland, they were creeping out at night with hoarded paint, and secretly printed, thin posters, as they had done in the war. Then, they had scrawled an anchor out of the letters PW – ⚓ – you could do that at lightning speed and run, leaving the message: *Polska Walcząca*. Fighting Poland. Now, the anchor swung from beneath the S of Solidarność. To chalk or paint that on a street corner wall, to scribble swiftly: Winter is yours, spring will be ours – just to do that, they were risking everything.

Here, there was nothing to risk, no freedom to lose or fight for, and they played with aerosols, spraying the wall with obscenities, the phone numbers of prostitutes. No – sometimes there was something else, another two letters: NF. Once, a swastika. He had tried to cross that out, but it was done in thick black spray, and was impossible. Let it stay – let them find out here what it was like to live in an occupied country, to wake to find the phone lines cut, hear of arrests in the night, see from your window the tanks, crawling down the street.

He was at the foot of the steps leading up to the bridge, the ticket office and the Christmas lights in the shop windows beyond, and he heard voices. He turned abruptly, walked for the hundredth time back towards the end of the platform, and the warning: Passengers Must Not Go Beyond This Point. The last train of the evening was due in a few minutes; then they would close the barrier at the top of the steps, and no one else would come down.

He had been here for perhaps an hour. The raw air had seeped into his shoes, his coat and gloves; his feet and his face were almost numb, and he was glad. Over there, they had been herded into camps by the thousand; they stood stamping frantically in the snow, interned like criminals, like cattle, all the energy and hope of the summer of 1980 crushed and spat upon. Why should he be spared?

The line hummed, and he heard behind him the rattle of the southbound train. More footsteps came pounding down the steps, doors slammed, the train moved slowly past him and swung, carriage by carriage, into the distance. The last alighted passenger walked away; on the bridge, someone was drunkenly singing 'Jingle Bells'. Then there was only the sound of the traffic, and no voices. He stood looking along the gleaming rails, and saw again the thousands of figures, stamping behind snow-covered barbed wire, and himself outside it, free, undeserving of freedom, belonging neither with them, in a doomed country, nor here, in a country of exile.

Above him the barrier creaked, and was slammed shut. The neon strips over the platform flickered and went out; then the light in the ticket office. A few stinging flakes of snow began to fall into the blackness – it did not feel as if it were going to be a generous fall but perhaps, by tomorrow, the heath would be blanketed. He walked slowly along the platform, hearing his own steps as if, already, they did not matter, or were made by someone else who did not matter, and he made out the telegraph pole, and the outline of the notice. When he reached it, he used it to hold on to for a moment, to feel his way on to the slope of concrete leading down. It was only a short slope, and then he could feel gravel and frozen earth, before he stumbled over the first rail, and out on to the track.

1
London, 1958

When he was almost five, they moved to a long dark street in Clapham. Three-storey mansion blocks, with dark green paintwork, lined either side; indoors, the paintwork was brown, and the stairs were covered with linoleum. Every time the tenants went up and down, the banisters trembled. There was a notice pinned to the front door of their block: No Banging.

It took the whole afternoon to move them all into the two flats on the top floor. His grandparents were to be on one side of the stairwell; he and Mama and Tata and Ewa on the other. Linoleum covered not just the stairs, but the narrow corridors and the floor of each room; all day, it was discovered, and for much of the night, you could hear footsteps, chairs scraping, the clack of brush against skirting board, heavy saucepans bang on to heavy stoves. And voices, but to these he did not pay much attention.

There was another noise. A mighty rhythm of hissing and puffing, lit by an orange glow and sparks. He stood on tiptoe in the empty room at the back and gazed through dusty glass at the network of tracks, at the huge, black, beautiful engine and the men inside; at the gleaming green coaches, the cloud of steam. The tree-lined streets of Streatham disappeared: a half-remembered sunny afternoon, the walk from Ewa's school, and they were gone.

He would live here always.

'Jerzy?'

Leave me alone.

'Jerzy!'

'Yes, Mama?'

Rapid footsteps echoing along the corridor; the half-closed door flung wide.

'All alone? There is tea in the kitchen. Come and sit down.'

'Yes. Look, Mama.'

Her thin skirt against the side of his head, her hand on his shoulder. A sigh.

'Yes. It will be very noisy. Come along now.'

Hand in hand; more echoes; everyone round the varnished table; lifted on to his chair. The same chair.

'Mama?'

'Yes?'

'Where shall I sleep?'

'With Ewa.'

'I should like to sleep at the back. Please.'

'Perhaps.'

That night he lay in his bed in the room at the back, filled with unpacked cardboard boxes; a blanket was pinned over the window. Movement in the bedclothes on the other side of the room.

'Ewa?'

'Yes?'

'Do you like it here?'

'I don't know. I don't think so.'

'I like it.'

'Good. Go to sleep now.'

'Goodnight.'

'Goodnight.'

He waited, listening until he was sure she was asleep. Then, when a new clanking and hissing came from the track below, he crept on bare feet to the window and pulled aside a corner of blanket. For as long as they were there, he watched the dark shapes of the driver and of the firemen, bending and stoking, feeding the red belly of the engine. Chilled, he tiptoed back to bed when it had gone; beneath the linoleum a floorboard creaked. He must watch out for that. Under the blankets he rubbed one cold foot against another.

From somewhere in the flat came the low voices of his parents and grandparents; doors closed; downstairs, a baby cried, then stopped abruptly. He slept.

Brown paint; pale light. In the days since the move, Anna had washed every door, every window frame, and skirting board. Dust and grime was lifted, but the colour must stay; there was not a penny to spare for decoration. To relieve her eyes she paused every now and then to gaze through the freshly washed windows at the autumn sky. September's departing sunlight was unable to break through continuous thin cloud, but there was no rain, just the great pale flatness, over the railway line and the rooftops of unknown houses.

The wireless played *Music While You Work*. She sat in the kitchen, slicing potatoes and carrots. The children were in the front room, playing – Ewa had a cold, and was off school today; there was more space for them here, and Dziadek and Babcia could feel secure, living two steps across the landing. There were other Polish people living in the street – the housing association evidently found them reliable tenants, and though the rent was higher than Streatham it was just affordable.

'But don't expect me to pay all the bills as well,' Jan had said, the Sunday morning after they arrived. He was tired after carrying all the boxes up three flights, and a night broken by the trains. Anna said nothing; he would have to find work once Jerzy started school. Her English was quite fluent now, certainly adequate for everyday use, but even so, the thought of having to use it all the time was terrifying. And she would have to start all over again, to explain all over again:

I have my mała matura, *my Polish A-levels. I studied for them in secret, in occupied Warsaw, where if I had been discovered I would have been arrested; quite probably, if that had happened, I should not be here now. But I was not arrested, although many other things happened to me then. I took some of the exams in the transit camp in Italy, in 1945, the rest in the resettlement camp in Herefordshire in 1946. No, I have no English qualifications. When I realized that I could not return to Poland, I began to train as a nurse; I knew hardly any English then, but I managed, sitting up late with dictionaries and textbooks. And then I got married, I got pregnant, I gave it up . . .*

A whistle blew, and further down the track a train drew breath and prepared to leave for Victoria. Anna dropped the vegetables into the black saucepan, filled it with water and set it on the stove. Then she went to the window and watched, as if from a great distance. Already, she was able to blot out most of the noise at night, though she was still awake at once if the children called. She yawned, turned away when the train was past, and began to lay the table. Half a loaf on the breadboard criss-crossed with lines; a saucer of margarine. Three mats, three white soup plates, the Woolworth's spoons, two apples. For herself she did not mind, but the children must have one each day.

She went into their room to fetch the mending she had put aside that morning. Jerzy was in there, face pressed to the window; he did not turn round, and jumped when she touched his shoulder.

'What are you doing?'

'Nothing, Mama. Just watching.'

'I thought you were with Ewa – I didn't hear you in the corridor.'

17

'I was with her. But I came here by myself.'

She stroked his hair. 'You must have tiptoed. Like a little mouse.'

He smiled.

After lunch, Anna switched on *Listen with Mother*. Ewa could understand almost everything she heard on the wireless now: Jerzy was beginning to pick out quite a lot. 'Are you sitting comfortably? Then I'll begin . . .' The mellow voice of Daphne Oxenford filled the kitchen; the children sat, elbows on the table, chins in cupped hands, listening while Anna washed up.

'Simple Simon met a pieman

Going to the fair.

Said Simple Simon to the pieman:

Let me taste your ware . . .'

'Mama? What does he mean: "taste your where"?' asked Ewa.

She shook her head, rinsing the plates. 'We'll have to look it up.' How could she possibly get a job?

'Said the pieman unto Simon

Show me first your penny,

Said Simple Simon to the pieman

Sir, I have not any . . .'

The singer was called George. He had a deep voice which sounded as if it should be in a church, even on stage. Anna had a sudden vision of him all dressed up by himself in the studio – Jerzy thought he lived in the wireless – singing nursery rhymes very loudly.

'Mama? What are you laughing at?'

'Just a thought.'

After the story, and slow, sleepy signature tune on the piano, which they all liked, Anna sent them for a rest on their beds, then cleared the front room, putting small cars, farmyard animals and dolls neatly into cardboard boxes, all ready to come back to after their walk. It was important that they should have fresh air and exercise each day. She swept the floor and then she allowed herself, as always, fifteen minutes' rest, lying down on the double bed. For a few moments she thought, exhausted, of nothing at all. Then she turned on her side and looked at the photographs on the varnished chest of drawers.

In sepia tones, from a gilt and plastic Woolworth's frame, her mother gazed at her. She wore a soft white blouse; her hair was cut short, her brown eyes enormous. The photograph had been taken in Warsaw in 1930; Anna was four then, her brother Jerzy six. He laughed at her from another frame, from another year, much later,

18

sitting with their father under a silver birch tree, on a sunlit river bank.

There were many memories of Jerzy and Tata; two particular ones of her mother. Occasionally she allowed herself to relive them.

Anna closed her eyes and saw a great expanse of snow.

Dark clumps of fir trees broke up the glittering whiteness; distantly, far up the mountains, were tiny figures on skis. Anna did not know why she was not with them, how she came to be standing alone under a tree, staring at the empty slopes. She began to cry, and the sound of her own sobbing on the cold silent air frightened her still more. Then, with a great, wonderful swooping movement, her mother was beside her, snow on the tips of her skis, on her dark hair and gloves.

'Mama! Mama!'

'*Maleńka* – little one – here I am.'

She was clasped in a warm, delicious hug of heavy tweed, fur brushing her cheek, the smell of snow breathed in deep.

On a Sunday afternoon in the spring of the following year, Anna stood outside her father's study door, listening to the murmur of voices.

'I am sorry, Tomasz,' her mother was saying. 'I don't like to worry you . . .'

'But of course you must tell me. Anyway, I can see how unlike yourself you are these days. So tired . . .'

There was a long sigh. 'Always so tired. Sometimes I can hardly get out of bed – and when I go for even a short walk with the children, I'm almost crawling by the time we get home.'

'Poor Ewa. Perhaps you're anaemic – we must send you for a blood test.'

'Yes.' A pause. 'It's not just the tiredness. I – I keep having these silly nosebleeds. Quite often I forget to tell you about them, but I suppose I must have one almost every day. And I don't know why, but I seem to bruise more easily, or something. I keep finding bruises in places I can't remember hurting myself at all . . .'

'Do you?' Anna heard her father's chair pushed back as he got up from behind his desk, piled high with medical textbooks. She loved looking at them when he was out on his calls, carefully tracing the diagrams with her fingers, smelling the leather bindings.

'Let's have a look at you, my darling. Where are these bruises?'

Silence. Anna pressed her ear to the crack of the door, imagining her mother undressing, her father's gentle touch.

His intake of breath was just audible. She waited, suddenly frightened: what was wrong with Mama? Then a door opened at the end of the passage: Aunt Wiktoria was coming. She fled.

Two clear memories only: of the day she was lost and found, and the day when she knew, somehow, that her mother was lost to her for ever. Anna had half-understood a number of facts from her father's textbooks. It was not until she was much older, ten or eleven, that he told her he had been studying the symptoms of leukaemia during the weeks that her mother grew so unwell. Anna listened gravely as he told her of the Sunday afternoon when he examined her, and understood why. She never let him know that she had heard the terrifying silence of his discovery.

'Mama! Mama!'

Ewa and Jerzy were awake. Anna swung herself quickly off the bed and went to their room on stockinged feet.

'Such a noise!'

'Can we go out now? Can we go to the common?'

'Yes, in a little while.' She sat on the edge of Ewa's bed and shivered. Streatham had been cramped, but the heating had been included in the rent. It would be difficult to heat this flat, with the draughty corridor.

'Did you sleep well?' she asked.

Ewa stretched. 'I had a funny dream – about Tata . . . I can't remember.' She reached for her book, the cartoon antics of the goat Matołek. 'Can I read until we go out?'

'Yes.' Anna forced herself to stop shivering. Jerzy was getting out of bed, his feet bare. 'Your socks, *Maleńki* . . . '

Half an hour later they were walking down the grey streets, the children's coats buttoned up to the neck. The weather was changing. Litter blew along the pavement and the trees shook chestnuts over the path across the common. Dogs barked as their leads were unclipped, and Ewa and Jerzy ran ahead, kicking up piles of yellow leaves.

Every Sunday they went to mass, and afterwards they had lunch with the grandparents. Jerzy thought that before the move they had all gone to mass together, always. Now, quite often he and Ewa went with Dziadek and Babcia by themselves. Sometimes Tata met them afterwards, on the common, and they went with him to watch the toy boats sail on the pond. He never came with them to church.

Mama used to, but not any more; when he thought about it Jerzy was a little puzzled; he had thought she liked it.

He liked it. In his grey coat and shorts, shoes stiff with polish, he walked beside his grandfather, holding his hand. Dziadek wore his dark coat now it was getting cold, and his black leather gloves. Babcia had a nice grey coat for Sundays, and wore a hat.

If it rained, they took the bus. Otherwise, they walked all the way down the main road to the church. It was an English church, Babcia explained, but permission had been given for Polish mass to be held there at one o'clock. She and Dziadek smiled and nodded to the families they knew, walking down the path, but never spoke as they took their grandchildren through the half-open door. It was time for silence.

Jerzy drew a deep breath of wax and incense, flowers and dampness, as they entered the church and crossed themselves before the Virgin, the Queen of Poland. Candles burned at her feet, and when the coughing and shuffling and rustling of prayerbooks had settled, and the priest began to speak, Jerzy somehow felt that the man's voice was not exactly a human voice at all, but something quite mysterious, coming out of and belonging to the flames flickering in the darkness. He hardly knew that he had this feeling, but it was there, always. After a while, he would start to think of other things: of his Sunday talks with Dziadek, of lunch, of the trains – he knew several of the regular journeys now.

Occasionally there were prayers for Poland in the service, and Jerzy knew they were important, and tried to pray too. Through half-closed eyes he watched Dziadek and Babcia go to the altar rail for Communion, and wondered what it was like up there, so close to the murmuring priest, taking the host on their tongues in the candlelight. Was it really Jesus they were eating? Ewa would have her First Communion soon; perhaps she could tell him then.

After mass, people stood talking in dark knots outside the church, and the priest moved among them, smoothing down his brilliantined hair. The chidren were allowed to scamper, but not too much. Then came the walk home, and inside the green door they pounded up the echoing stairs in their loud Sunday shoes.

'Mama! Mama!'

She stood at the door to the flat, smiling at the grandparents as they went through their own front door. Inside, the children put on their slippers, and she took them into the kitchen and gave them a hot drink.

'Did you see Tata on the common?'

Sometimes they said yes, and that he'd taken them to the pond, and she looked pleased, and asked them about the boats. Or they said no, they'd looked for him, but must have missed him, and then she said nothing. They all went into the front room, to draw with their crayons, and wait for him to come home.

Soon afterwards, every Sunday, Jerzy got up and said: 'I'm going to Dziadek now,' and his mother nodded. 'Be good.'

There was very little light on the landing between the two flats, only what filtered up through the thick starred glass of the window in the hall, far below. He stood on the shadowy square of linoleum, and knocked on his grandparents' door. When it opened, it was filled with Dziadek, smiling in welcome, and behind him it was even darker, and always felt quiet, though Babcia was preparing lunch. His grandfather led him into the front room.

After the darkness of the landing and corridor, it seemed to be filled with light. Later, when all the family was there, clatter and conversation would obscure what Jerzy somehow thought of as the real room; this time, always, it felt as still and light and silent as if it were under glass. Crimson and blue tapestries hung on the walls; Babcia made those, in the evenings. Lacy net curtains were at the windows, and when the sun shone their patterns fell on to the carpet. There were a lot of stiff green plants, and photographs of him and Ewa. Before the gas fire stood an unyielding brown sofa; on the mantelpiece a large clock ticked into the quietness.

He wandered over to the window, lifted the lacy curtain over his head, and stood looking out, across to the window opposite, and down at the street, far below. The woman in the window waved to him: she was English, and had a lot of visitors, mostly men. There were children playing in the street, kicking a football up and down, along the pavement, against the dustbins, shouting to each other. They couldn't see him, right up here.

'Come and sit down, *maleńki*.'

On the table was spread the newspaper from yesterday, *Dziennik Polski*, the *Polish Daily*, which Dziadek didn't have time to read on Saturday mornings, because that was when he taught at Polish school. When Jerzy was a litte older, he would go there, like Ewa. Until then, this was his private school. Next to the paper was the shiny red exercise book, neatly open at this week's page, with the sharpened blue pencil beside it. He and Dziadek sat side by side on the high-backed chairs, and slowly he copied the words for today: *rzeka*, river; *rząd*, government; *żołnierz*, soldier; *bitwa*, battle.

'Tell me a story, Dziadek.'

'What story would you like?'

'The one about the night you crossed the frozen lake on horseback.'
It was one of the best.

'It was the winter of 1917,' Dziadek began, 'and my unit was moving to a new front. All our artillery was drawn by horse, and the road we should have taken to reach our destination was blocked by a great snowdrift. In any case, it was a long way by road to the village we were making for, and we were all cold and tired and hungry. We came to the edge of a great lake, completely covered with a thick sheet of ice . . .'

Behind every word which Jerzy carefully copied, over and over again along the lines of the exercise book, he could see pictures: a huge dark starlit country where men with frozen moustaches galloped over snow; from the photograph album, the wooden house where Tata had been born; summery pictures of picnics under rustling trees; a prison cell. He knew that Dziadek had been in prison for a long time, but he didn't know exactly why, just that it was during the war. His medals came from the war – was it the same war as Tata's? Tata had a medal but he didn't wear his, just kept it in a little box in the table drawer. Once Jerzy had heard Mama and Babcia talk about how Tata's jaw had never properly healed – that was something to do with the war, too.

'And so,' Dziadek was saying, 'what could we do? We nailed spikes to the shoes of our brave horses, and they stepped on to the frozen lake, and slowly, slowly they hauled all our cannon across to the other side.'

'By the light of the moon.'

'By the light of the moon.'

Jerzy gave a sigh of satisfaction.

There was a knocking at the front door and he heard Babcia hurry from the kitchen, and the voices of his family. Tata was there! He helped Dziadek clear the table, so Babcia could lay it with the white Sunday cloth.

'Tata!'

He ran into his father's arms, was picked up and lightly kissed, put down again.

'You have been good?'

He nodded, watching his father turn back to Ewa, smiling. The table laid, they could enjoy at last the best meal of the week. Babcia made meatballs in a rich gravy, with stewed beetroot and potatoes with dill. For dessert they had apple compote, and afterwards, while the grown-ups had their glasses of tea, he and Ewa were allowed to get down and take slices of *babka* into the kitchen, and do their drawings.

Soon it would be time to make Christmas cards. Today Jerzy began to draw a brave grey horse, with spikes on his shoes and a shining moon high above. When the three o'clock train to Folkestone roared past, he was at the window, redirecting it to Warsaw.

At half-past seven in the morning, Jan and his father left the mansion block together. It was dark and cold; in the misty light from the street lamps their breath hung on the air, and they didn't talk much as they walked down the road to the underground station. There, when his father had bought his ticket, Jan stood at the top of the long flight of concrete steps to the platform and watched him go down. He wore a heavy black coat, a homburg and leather gloves; he made his way down slowly, his back straight; towards the bottom he reached for the handrail. Then he turned, raised his hand to Jan, and walked off along the platform, his metal toecaps loud on the concrete. It was cold even down there, with an acrid smell of stale cigarette smoke. Someone was whistling; far down in the tunnel a signal light gleamed red. There weren't many people: the rush began nearer eight; now, it was women office cleaners with their hair in rollers, West Indian men travelling to London Transport bus depots, factory workers. For a few moments Jan stood watching his father pace up and down among them. Then the light in the tunnel changed to green, and the northbound train rattled out and stopped. The sliding doors drew apart, his father got on with the other passengers, and they closed again; the train moved into the next tunnel, taking him towards Tottenham. Twenty years ago, Major Prawicki had commanded a division of the Polish Army. Now he worked on an assembly line, in a factory making surgical instruments.

Jan went out of the station, past the neon-lit window of the ticket office and on to the main road. At the kiosk he bought the *Telegraph*, then walked under the railway bridge and on past the closed-up shops. He could wait for his bus here, but he preferred, unless there was smog, or it was pouring with rain, to walk on a good quarter-mile, past the clock tower, so that he could wait opposite the first stretch of the common. Even though it was winter, even though it was dark, he could see beyond the diffused pools of light from the street lamps the outlines of the trees, and the gleam of the still water on the pond. He liked the exercise, and he liked it here, listening to front doors open in the tall houses behind him, the chink of milk bottles taken inside, watching the downstairs lights switched on. Footsteps hurried along the pavement, the queue behind him grew. He watched the clouds roll away above the trees on the common, and a couple of people appear, walking their dogs. Sometimes, on Sundays, he met his parents and the children, coming back from mass, and went with them to watch the toy boats with their white sails drift across the pond; he should do it more often – it was the only time he had with them, except for Sunday lunch, but if there was anyone he knew in the Polish Club he liked to stay and have a drink and a game of chess. What was the harm in that?

The lighted windows of the 118 drew near, and Jan got on. He paid his fare, opened the paper and turned to the chess problem. He had half an hour before he got to Streatham, to the engineering works, and his board in the draughtsman's section. He didn't mind the work too much: considering the state of things when he came here in '46 he wasn't doing too badly. He was nineteen, then, with barely any English, just enough to get by on from the classes they'd run in Italy: in the first few days he'd wondered why so many places were called Ostermilk. In the freezing East Anglian camp, in the worst winter the English had known for forty years, he'd joined the Polish Resettlement Corps like everyone else, and the welfare workers had nodded when he tried to explain that his education in Warsaw had been broken off under the occupation. His skills had been in making hand grenades, building barricades . . . The welfare workers had understood the facts, but not what it had felt like.

But they were okay, they organized proper English classes, suggested draughtsmanship, found him a place on a course. He hadn't done so badly, but he could have done better, he knew. It had all happened too fast: marrying so young, when he hadn't even finished his training, the babies coming so quickly. Ewa an accident; Anna needing him to be a responsible family man when he was hardly out of his teens. That was one reason why he'd avoided too much responsibility at work: he could be training for management now, if he wanted, but he did not want. He liked the company of the few other Poles there, but he did not want to be supervising them. Certainly, he did not want to supervise English workers: he'd met and heard about enough hostility in the early days, when the press had forgotten the Polish heroes of the Battle of Britain and Monte Cassino, and was full of stories of how the Poles were taking English jobs; a lot of the trade unions had thought of them as fascists. Fascists! He'd like to have seen them in Poland in the years after the war. Now it was the turn of the West Indians: how was the bus conductor enjoying himself over here? Brixton was full of them; they were beginning to move into their street, too.

Rook takes bishop . . . They were almost there, and the bus was filling up. It stopped, and a crowd of passengers got on. Jan looked up, saw the sky quite light now, saw a boy moving down the aisle who reminded him of someone. He was tall and fine-featured, with fair hair; sixteen or seventeen, wearing a navy school raincoat, and a school tie. Jan watched him move in the crush towards the front, and raise his arm to hold on to the rail as the bus changed gear abruptly in the traffic. Something in that gesture, in his face . . . He *was* a bit like Paweł. Jan put his hand to his jaw, and saw again Paweł raising an imaginary rifle joyfully above his head in the hour before the Uprising began. He saw him, weeks later, in the last agonies of the Old Town, and a sharp slither of pain drove beneath his gum.

The paper and the chess problem fell to his lap. Jan, on the journey to work he made every day, looked again at the fair-haired boy in the raincoat and recalled another journey, through sewers. He stared out of the window, beyond the pebbledash and mock Tudor frontages of Streatham.

Jerzy was ill. On Thursday morning he looked feverish, and would eat nothing at lunch. Anna made him some tea and when he woke after his nap he seemed better. By five, after quarrelling with Ewa, he was scarlet-cheeked and tearful. She put him to bed with a cold flannel on his forehead, and stayed until he fell asleep.

She read to Ewa in the front room by the fire, though of course it was much cheaper to have her in bed with her dressing gown on and no need for a heater. When she, too, was asleep, Anna made supper for Jan, did two hours' ironing and went to bed.

Some time after midnight she heard Jan's key in the lock. She lay and listened to him walk heavily to the kitchen and scrape back his chair. A little later she heard the rush of the bathroom taps and the toilet flushing. Then the bedroom door was pushed open. She lay motionless as he undressed in the dark and sank into bed beside her.

'Anna?'

She breathed deeply, clenching her hand next to the wall.

'Anna?'

She was tired, she was tired.

He turned away.

Wide awake now, knowing how long it would take to get to sleep again, she lay staring at the wall. A bright December moon was still high in the sky, and through the curtains a thin line of light fell across the picture rail. After a while, Jan began to snore, and Anna unclenched her hand and pulled her pillow down close to her. Slowly, with difficulty, she drifted towards sleep.

'Mama! Mama!'

She sat up, saw Ewa in the doorway, nothing on her feet, no dressing gown, hair tousled.

'Jerzy can't breathe.'

'What?'

'He says it hurts.'

'All right, I'm coming. Go back to bed and keep warm.'

'He says it really hurts.' She stood uncertainly.

'Sssh!' But there was no fear of waking Jan now. Anna slid off the end of the bed, reached for her dressing gown and hurried down the corridor, holding Ewa's hand.

Jerzy was leaning back on his pillow, pale and dark-eyed, panting in short, shallow breaths.

'What is it, *maleńki?*' She sat down beside him, and took his hand. 'Your chest?'

He nodded, gasping. Anna turned to Ewa. 'Go and put the kettle on, can you do that? Quickly.'

Ewa scurried to the kitchen. Anna sat watching Jerzy's bony chest heaving in shorter and shorter spasms. Had he caught a cold, a chest infection? She shivered in her dressing gown.

'The kettle's on,' said Ewa, back again. 'What shall I do now?'

'Nothing, just pop back into bed. Thank you, *kochana*. Now keep an eye on Jerzy for me while I go and look in the medicine cupboard.'

'Mama . . .' Jerzy's hand wavered towards her.

'It's all right, Ewa's here. I shan't be a minute. Good boy.'

The bathroom was very cold. She went quickly through the cabinet until she found the Friar's Balsam, poured some into a bowl and hurried to the kitchen. The kettle was steaming; she poured hot water into the bowl and took a deep breath. Lovely, comforting smell.

Back in the bedroom, she held Jerzy's damp head over the bowl, under towels. Across the room, Ewa was giggling.

'He looks like a ghost.'

27

The towels twitched, irritably.

'Poor little ghost. He'll be better soon.'

But it took a long time for Jerzy to stop gasping, and fall back on to the pillow, and by that time Ewa was sound asleep. Anna sponged his face, gave him a drink, tucked him up.

'There now . . . you snuggle down.'

'Thanks, Mama.'

She kissed him and crept back to bed, where she slept uneasily. Jan woke her at seven.

'What's going on? There's no breakfast – I'll be late.'

'Sssh! Jerzy's not well, a bad chest. We were up half the night.'

'I didn't hear anything. You should have woken me.'

'Never mind. But can you phone the doctor as soon as you get to work? Ask if he'll come and look at him this morning – I don't want to take him out to the surgery.'

'All right.'

'Thank you.' She hurried to the kitchen, and began to prepare breakfast. The sky beyond the windows was dark with rain; when she went to look at Jerzy he was still asleep, his face clammy.

It rained all morning. Anna waited until half-past twelve, but still the doctor did not call, and at last she left Babcia in charge while she went out to the phone box in the next street. The windows streamed with condensation.

'Dr Watkins' surgery.'

'Hello . . . I am sorry . . . I expect visit, but doctor is not coming . . .'

The receptionist sighed. 'What name is it, dear?'

'Prawicka. Mrs Prawicka. My husband telephone this morning . . .'

'Just let me check the list of calls. Pra . . . would you spell that for me, dear? And the address? No, the doctor's not got you on his list.'

'But . . .' Anna could not believe that Jan had not phoned. 'It is my little boy, Jerzy. He has chest pain, temperature . . .'

'I'm sorry, dear, but I can't get in touch with the doctor now; he's on his rounds. Can you try and bring your little boy to the evening surgery? We open at five. If he's really not well enough to come, ring again, and we'll see what we can do.'

At half-past three, Anna collected Ewa from school. At half-past four, she left her with her mother-in-law and dressed Jerzy in trousers, two jumpers, coat, scarf, hat and gloves. She put him in the pushchair, covered him with a knitted blanket and set off down the wet, lamplit streets to the surgery.

The waiting room was crowded and smelt of damp clothes and, faintly, disinfectant. A small gas fire sputtered and popped; a young girl with combs in her hair and scarlet lipstick sat next to it, reading *Woman's Own* and swinging a foot. Anna took one of the last two wooden chairs and held Jerzy on her lap; he leant against her, thin legs dangling, heavy head pressed against her collar. She rocked him as they sat, not really aware of doing so. Every few minutes the door opened and someone else arrived, registered with the receptionist and stood against the wall, and the air grew damper and warmer, and Anna felt herself begin to nod.

Her head filled gently with a soft cloud of wool; distantly she could hear the low voice of the receptionist and, intermittently, the ping of the surgery bell. Jerzy breathed heavily; she pressed her face against his woollen hat and closed her eyes.

'Mrs Prawicka? Mrs Prawicka?'

She jerked herself awake and slid Jerzy to the floor. He swayed, tearful. 'It's all right, we have to see doctor now.' She led him on unsteady feet into the surgery.

'Hello, young man, and what's the matter with you? Sit down, sit down. Mrs . . . Prawicka, isn't it?'

Anna nodded, and sat, overpowered as usual by Dr Watkins' indifferent joviality.

'He has temperature . . . last night he can't breathe . . . lot of pain. My husband phone for visit this morning, but . . .'

'Well, well, let's take a look at him, eh? Come on, up on the couch, young man, I want to have a little listen to your chest with this thing. Know what this is?' He waved his stethoscope; Jerzy shrank. On the high narrow couch he squirmed and cried when Dr Watkins tried to lift his layers of clothes.

'Now, now, no need for any of this . . .'

'It's all right, Jerzy, doctor is going to make you better now. Just let him . . .'

'No, no!'

Eventually Anna calmed him enough for Dr Watkins to run his hands quickly over his chest and listen.

'Mmm, bit of a wheeze there, touch of asthma, I should think; bit of an infection.'

Jerzy slid off the couch; she tugged down his vest and jumpers.

29

'He's rather thin,' Dr Watkins went on. 'You . . . er . . . you managing all right?'

Anna blushed. 'Yes, thank you.'

'Good, good, I'm sure you are. Well, now, I'll give you a prescription.' He pulled his pad towards him on the desk. 'M & B, these things are called – he might have a bit of a reaction, but they'll clear it up. Keep him in the warm. How's the rest of the family? All well? Good, good.'

He scribbled on the pad. 'Here we are, you can get this at the chemist on the corner.' He smiled at Jerzy. 'Soon be starting school, I expect, won't you?'

Jerzy stared at him.

'Yes,' said Anna. 'He will start in January.'

'St Mary's?'

'Yes.' She buttoned him into his coat.

'Excellent. How's his English coming along?'

Anna blushed again. 'I am teaching him a little.'

'Well done. Don't want him too far behind when he starts. All the best to you now.' He smiled at Jerzy again, and struck the bell on his desk. 'Bell. This is a bell. Can you say "bell" for me, young man?' Jerzy stared. 'Never mind. Off you go now, and be good.'

Anna bundled her son out of the room and into the pushchair. She changed the prescription at the chemist and hurried home, tucking Jerzy back into bed with a hot-water bottle. In the bathroom, she burst into tears.

She tried to imagine saying to Dr Watkins: 'My father was a doctor, you know. He was highly respected. If it had not been for the war, I should have gone to medical school.' She heard him answer: 'Splendid. Splendid.'

Jan came home after eleven.

'What happened?'

'What do you mean?'

'The doctor. The phone call . . .'

'The doctor. Oh, God, I forgot. I'm sorry. I'm sorry. Don't look at me like that.'

The house where Polish school was held stood back from the road behind a laurel hedge. It was a large, square, late Victorian building, one of many on a broad road between Clapham and Wandsworth. The ground between the hedge and the front door was scuffed mud and thin gravel, and there were narrow paths on either side of the house to a large plain garden at the back. The house had been bought by members of the Polish Educational Society, and during the week it was used for meetings and discussions; but on Saturday mornings the children of twenty or thirty families met in the classrooms.

It was the best day of Ewa's week. Dziadek walked at his usual regular pace down the road from the bus stop, carrying his briefcase, but she ran ahead, and pressed the china bell beside the front door, almost always the first to arrive.

'Dzień dobry – good morning, Ewa.' Pan Mazur, the caretaker, swung open the door and she stepped inside, her feet echoing on the bare floorboards as she crossed the hall. A wide uncarpeted staircase led to the shadowy upper floor; down here, there were two classrooms on the left, with a cloakroom, and on the right a narrow passage led to the kitchen, and Pan Mazur's flat. Ewa spun on her toes and breathed deeply, smelling the particular mingling of wood and chalk, polish and dust and, from the kitchen, coffee.

On the wall plaque facing you as soon as you were inside the front door, the white Polish eagle glared in profile from beneath his crown. Sometimes Ewa went to stand beneath him, gazing up at the white feathers on their red background – the national colours – at the proud cruel beak and eye. Lech, the legendary founder of Poland, chose him as the nation's emblem because a rare, beautiful white eagle had appeared in the sky one day when he was travelling alone – she had learned that here. And the eagle wore a crown because the people of Poland would never recognize that he had lost it, when the Russians came. Sometimes, if Pan Mazur had disappeared, and Dziadek not yet arrived, Ewa would close her eyes and stretch out her arms like wings beneath the plaque, standing on tiptoe, poised to soar above the world. Then she would hear Dziadek's step on the path outside and go quickly to the cloakroom and take off her coat and scarf. Soon, the other children began to arrive and, within the next ten minutes, other teachers, their parents.

Ewa's classroom held sixteen small double desks and chairs, and a large raised teacher's desk beneath the blackboard. Three tall windows divided the wall on the left; through them you could see only the path and privet hedge separating them from the house next door. The wall on the right held a hissing brown radiator and an enormous map of Poland – 'przed-wojenne – pre-war, children, pre-war'. Ewa had stood beside Dziadek many times, watching his pointer move from place to place: Lwów, now deep in Russia, was where he had been born – 'a great walled city'; Wilno, also taken by the

31

Russians; Warsaw, where Mama and Tata had been in the Uprising against the Germans in 1944 – though they didn't know each other then; Kraków, where the castle of the Polish kings stood, near a beautiful church, all blue and gold inside. The Black Madonna lived in Częstochowa, and hundreds of pilgrims went to visit her each year. In Poland it was so cold in winter that the men's moustaches had icicles on them; in summer the peasants made hay in boiling sun, and the children rode home on the very top of the waggons, with geese waddling after them. Ewa had seen them, in a book.

Some of the books at school came all the way from Poland, and some came from the teachers' homes and had to be very carefully looked after because they, too, were *przed-wojenne*. Sometimes, parcels of books arrived which made Dziadek and the other teachers angry, and they sent the parcels back unopened. When Ewa asked why, Dziadek said that they had been sent by the Polish Embassy in London, by the communists.

There was another place on the map which he had pointed out to the children on a bright summer morning two years ago, when all the teachers had arrived grim-faced, and some of them crying; Poznań, in the west, where the *milicja* had fired on ordinary working people, rioting in the streets because they could not afford the food prices in the shops: more than fifty people had been killed. Ewa found it difficult to fit these two pictures of Poland together in her mind: the place where everyone at home had grown up, and the place which wasn't their home any more, and where they could never go back.

At nine-fifteen the class assembled. Ewa sat next to her friend Myszka; like her, Myszka wore her hair in plaits, but her clothes were nicer, somehow – they seemed softer, and fitted very well. Her father was a doctor, and she had a doll with four changes of clothes. '*Dzień dobry* – good morning, chidren.' Dziadek stood smiling beside the teacher's desk.

'*Dzień dobry, Panu.*'

'This morning, as usual, we shall begin with our history lesson, then you will study the Polish language with Pan Dábrowski. After break you will have the pleasure of Pani Dábrowska playing the piano for the dancing class upstairs. We shall conclude the morning with our Christmas carols. Now, will you please get out your exercise books and pencils.'

There was a rustling and murmuring, the woody smell of pencils being sharpened, neat little curls of shaving trimmed with yellow falling into the ink gutters at the top of the desk. Thin winter sunlight

32

lit the polished brass vase of Michaelmas daisies on the teacher's desk, and Dziadek surveyed the upturned faces before him. Each Saturday, at this moment, Ewa felt the delicious sense of belonging, of readiness and purpose. Neatly she spread open her exercise book, and wrote down the heading which Dziadek dictated.

'The Reign of Zygmunt I Stary, 1506–1548. I shall spell Zygmunt . . . You all have that? Now, you will recall that last week we spoke a little of the reign of Kazimierz, 1444–1492. I should like one of you to refresh our memories with the main events of those years. Yes, Maciek?'

Maciek Sokolowski, eight years old, built like a grasshopper, with a pale, earnest face, reminded the class of the Peace of Toruń and partition of Prussia, of the founding of the printing press in Kraków, and the establishment of the two-chambered *sejm*.

'Excellent,' said Dziadek. 'Now, will you please write: When Zygmunt I Stary came to the throne, he had lived for many years in the court at Buda . . .'

After geography, and the morning break, Pan Dąbrowski arrived. He was a short, square man with a head like a bullet, and he instructed the class as though in a military camp.

'Good morning. Sit. Books on the table. Open at page thirty-six. Stanisław Malinowicz, please stand and conjugate the verb *pamiętać*.'

Always, the children felt a tremor of insecurity as the kindly shape of Pan Prawicki, Ewa's grandfather, disappeared, and Pan Dąbrowski arrived. Once, he had lost his temper with a boy who had not done his homework, and hit his hand with a ruler, but that was a long time ago, and perhaps there was no real need to be uneasy. They bent over their exercise books and copied down today's vocabulary.

From the floor above, the first bars of a Chopin nocturne drifted down the stairwell: Pani Dąbrowska was enjoying herself, before the dancing class. Ewa paused in her copying of the word *weidza*, knowledge, and gazed out of the window. The music and the moment were inseparable: all her life, from the radio, from the concert platform, from a half-open window on a rainy street, those melancholy bars would instantly transport her to a morning in December, when she was eight years old, and sitting in the warm classroom of Polish school in Clapham.

At break, in good weather, they all went into the garden, but the leafless tress and bare flowerbeds were uninviting now, and it was too cold. They drank their bottles of milk in the hall, and ran about.

Then, at twelve o'clock, Ewa and Myszka climbed the stairs with fourteen other children, and entered the huge bare room reserved for the dancing class. Chairs lined the walls; over the plaster mantelpiece hung a vast mirror spotted with mildew. The piano, with Pani Dąbrowska overflowing on the stool, stood in the corner by one of the tall windows, where the pattern of bare branch and rooftop stretched into the distance under a leaden sky.

Pani Dąbrowska clapped her hands. 'Good afternoon, children. Will you please take your partners, and we shall go over the steps of the Krakowiak folk dance. Piotr and Myszka, would you be so kind as to step into the centre of the floor for us? No giggling, *please!*'

There was the soft dry movement of feet in socks on floorboards, as the children copied the steps to the tapping of Pani Dąbrowska's little stick on the top of the piano.

'*Dobrze, dobrze* – good, good. And so now with the music . . .' She settled back on to the stool like a hen upon her eggs. 'And a *one*, two, three, four, *one*, two, three, four – very nice, Ewa and Stanisław – *dobrze, dobrze* . . .'

And the children rose and dipped around the room as the winter sky grew darker, and Pan Mazur slipped in quietly to switch on the lights and stand for a moment, watching.

At the very end of the morning, the two halves of the class came together again, and all the teachers stood round the piano, leading the Christmas carols. Afterwards, walking with Dziadek in the cold street to the bus stop, Ewa's head still hummed with singing. Her feet tapped along the pavement, but in her mind she was still in the brightly lit music room, and the words of the last hymn, chorused by thirty voices, rose into the air and followed her all the way home:

Oh, God, in your power and glory
For centuries you have watched over Poland.
Before your altar we beg you:
Return a free homeland to us . . .

Wigilia. Christmas Eve. Traditionally, they must all be at the table with the first evening star. Anna stood at the window of the front room and gazed at the sodium-orange, starless London sky. She drew the curtains and took a last look at the room; in a few moments she must collect the children from the grandparents, where they had been since midday.

Two white candles stood in saucers in the centre of the table, laid with the embroidered cloth. The tree was on a low stool in the window, the presents hidden in the kitchen. The best present of all

34

was locked in the bathroom, after spending the night with Dziadek and Babcia: by a miracle he had been concealed from the children since his arrival yesterday afternoon. They could not afford him, Anna knew, but he would bring so much pleasure, and he needed a home. She went to the mirror over the fire, saw a thin intense face with dark shadows under the eyes stare back as she put on her lipstick. Then the key turned in the front door and she turned to see Jan, holding flowers.

'Here.' He crossed the room and awkwardly put them in her arms, forced early daffodils wrapped in cellophane and tied with white ribbon. '*Wesołych Świąt*. Happy Christmas.'

'Thank you. Beautiful . . .' She carefully undid the wrapping, and bent to smell them, then raised her head to look at him.

He smiled, touched her hair. 'Very pretty. Very tired, Anna . . .'

'Yes?'

'We will try . . . I will try . . .'

'Thank you,' she said again. 'Shall we call the children now?'

The daffodils, in a cut-glass vase borrowed from Babcia, stood between the two lit candles, now the shimmering heart of the room. Pale with cleanliness and excitement, Ewa and Jerzy stood by the fire as Dziadek took from a small dish on the table a wafer of *opłatek*, the host, made from embossed rice paper and sent from Poland by Mama's Aunt Wiktoria. He passed it to his son. There was one for each member of the family, to break and exchange with each other, wishing all that was good for the coming year, and then to eat.

'Look!' Ewa whispered to Jerzy. 'Mine has angels on it.'

'And mine has the crib,' said Jerzy, gazing at his square.

Then his mother was standing before him, holding out a piece broken from her own, and saying: 'Well, *kochany* – darling – I wish for you the toy you most want, and a wonderful surprise, and health as you begin your first term at school. I hope you make many friends there, and study hard and grow up strong.'

He took the piece of wafer and solemnly placed it on his tongue. It began to dissolve, tasting of nothing.

'Thank you, Mama. I wish you a very happy Christmas . . . and . . . what is the surprise?'

'Aha.' She winked. 'Wait and see.'

When they had all exchanged the host, and kissed each other, they went to the window and drew back the curtains. The sky was a hazy orange, still, but a tiny point of light was just visible above the rooftops.

'An aeroplane,' said Jan.

'The first evening star,' said Anna. 'And now for goodness' sake let's eat.'

'The table looks beautiful!' said Ewa.

Babcia ladled out the bowls of *barscht*, clear beetroot soup with dried mushrooms floating like dark fish below the surface.

'Excellent,' said Dziadek.

When his mother opened the door to fetch the second course from the kitchen – a dish of baked carp – Jerzy thought he could hear a whining sound from somewhere.

'Tata?'

'Yes?'

'What's that noise?'

'What noise?' But all the grown-ups were exchanging glances and smiles. 'Wait,' said Tata. 'Wait and see.'

Fifteen aching minutes later, Anna said: 'Let's have dessert after the presents. I can hardly wait myself.'

They left the table and all sat round the fire. 'Close your eyes, children,' Anna said softly, and they closed them, waiting for the year's moment of magic, when Dziadek stepped outside the door and they heard the distant tinkle of a bell. 'The reindeer sleigh,' said Anna, and they could hear the door open again, and a rustling.

'All right, children,' said Dziadek. 'Open your eyes. Let's see what Father Christmas has brought you.'

They gazed at the little heap of presents beneath the tree.

'The surprise!' Jerzy begged. 'Where's the surprise?'

'Close your eyes again.'

From along the corridor came the sound of claws scratching linoleum, a panting, and – 'Mama! Mama!' They were across the room, hugging him, huge and dark and soft, with lolling tongue and nervous eyes.

'Gently with him, children. Let him get to know you.'

'Good boy,' Ewa murmured, and patted his back. 'Good boy.'

'What's his name?' asked Jerzy.

'We must choose one,' said his mother. 'Come on, boy, come here by the fire.'

She patted her chair and the dog moved slowly across the room and stood, trembling.

'Where did you find him?' Ewa asked.

'In Battersea Dogs' Home – it's a place where lost dogs, or unwanted dogs are kept.'

'Lots of dogs?'

'Hundreds.'

'Why did you choose this one?'

'Look at him,' said Anna, reaching out her hand. 'How could I not choose this one?'

He padded closer and stood by her lap as she stroked his head.

'Burek,' said Jerzy. 'Let's call him Burek. That's a good dog name.' He moved towards him and put his cheek against the great dark head.

When all the presents had been opened, they gathered round the tree for carols.

'When the lovely Lady?' asked Anna. 'Shall we have that one first?'

'Oh, yes,' said Ewa. 'We had it at school, didn't we, Dziadek?'

'You can lead us, then.'

'When the lovely Lady rocked her Son,' Ewa sang, and they all joined in:

When the lovely Lady rocked her Son,
Full of joy she sang to him:
'Lulla-lullaby, my little baby,
Lulla-lullaby, my lovely little lord.'

Softly, little breeze, softly, little wind from the south,
Blow softly, for the new lord is sleeping.
'Lulla-lullaby, my little baby,
Lulla-lullaby, my lovely little lord.'

Down in the street, voices were calling; a taxi drew up; doors slammed.

'The shepherds came to Bethlehem,' suggested Babcia, and they sang:

The shepherds came to Bethlehem
Merrily playing to the Child on their lyre
Glory in the Highest,
And Peace on Earth . . .

It was almost ten when Anna tucked Jerzy and Ewa into bed and kissed them goodnight. Ewa was holding her new doll: she had two dresses and petticoats and a winter coat and hat, with matching gloves and scarf. Anna had made them all. On the locker by Jerzy's bed stood a small black engine with three green coaches, and a signal which went up and down when you pressed a tiny lever.

'You like what Father Christmas brought you?'

'Yes, Mama,' said Jerzy. 'And Burek is the best. How did he fit on the sleigh?'

'He must have got very cold,' said Ewa. 'Can we take him for a walk in the morning. On the common?'

'Of course. We will have to take him for a long walk every day. Go to sleep quickly now. Happy Christmas.' And she went down the corridor to join the other grown-ups.

'Ewa?'

'Yes?'

'There's a train coming soon.'

'Sssh! It's too cold to get out of bed – and there won't be trains at Christmas.'

'There are a few. I want to watch the Night Ferry, that's all. I've got my socks on.'

'Well . . . just that one. Then you must go to sleep.'

He slipped out of bed and padded to the window, tugged aside the curtain, and waited. In the distance he could hear the strong, steady breathing of the Night Ferry train, moving close, down the track from Victoria. The Christmas ferry to France. 'Come and look, Ewa – it's such a beautiful one.'

She pushed back her bedclothes and came to stand beside him. He held his breath, and it roared towards them, the sleek silhouette of the engine with its glowing heart, and the huge coaches. People were asleep in there. There was a rush of steam, and a deep throaty whistle pierced the night. Then it was gone, gathering speed down the line, off to the dark Kent coast, and another country.

On the second Monday in January, he left the house with Mama, tightly holding her hand. Ewa walked on the other side. Every morning, until today, he had stood at the window of Dziadek's and Babcia's flat, watching his mother and sister hurry down the road to catch the bus to school, waving as they turned the corner. Now he was going, too.

He had often been with Mama to collect Ewa in the afternoons, so it wasn't as though he was going to a place he'd never seen. And Ewa would be there, after all, and would look after him in the playground. But it was very cold, and his stomach was full of butterflies. On Saturday Mama had taken him to buy new shoes; they felt stiff and uncomfortable. He did like the grey sweater she had knitted especially, with his own nametape on the neckband. Jerzy Tomasz Prawicki. It was inked inside his shoes as well.

At the corner they stopped and turned. Babcia was high up at the window, waving and smiling. Beside her, Burek's dark head and ears were just visible – Mama would take him out when she got home; he couldn't come on the bus. It felt very strange, seeing part of his family far away up there. He waved, and tried to smile.

'Quick!' said Mama. 'I can see it coming.'

They panted towards the stop.

The bus was crowded, and there were a lot of schoolchildren. He watched them teasing each other, not understanding the jokes. Last night he had been drilled by Mama and Ewa in some important words which he must remember. *Toilet. Yes. No. Thank you. My name is Jerzy. What is your name?*

'It's *easy*,' Ewa had said. She spoke English as well as anything, now. He would. He would, too.

'Come on,' Mama was saying. 'This is the stop.'

He followed her and Ewa down the aisle, bumping into satchels and bags. In the street, the other children ran ahead, shouting. He could not see their mothers anywhere.

Mama's arm was round his shoulder as they reached the school. A high wall ran the length of the playground, and the tall iron gate was bolted open. Through it he could see hundreds of English children, scarves flying as they ran up and down, calling each other's names.

'That's my classroom,' said Ewa, pointing to a window on the first floor. 'I feel a bit funny, coming back.'

'Ewa . . .' said Mama.

'And that's your classroom, Jerzy, downstairs. Come on, I'll take you inside.'

He stared at his feet.

Mama bent down and kissed him. 'It's all right, *maleńki*. You'll soon feel at home here. Of course it's a bit strange today, but . . .' She stood up. 'I'll see you here this afternoon, and you can tell me all about it. Now off you go with Ewa.'

She had left him, before he even had a chance to say goodbye. Mutely, he followed Ewa through the gate, across the playground and up the steps to the front door. They went into a long, noisy corridor; a large boy pushed past them and went out into the playground, ringing a bell. Jerzy put his hands over his ears.

'Quick!' said Ewa. 'That's for Register – we all have to be in our

39

classes now.' She tugged him down the corridor and stopped at a half-open door with glass panels. 'This is Class 1 – it must be you. Oh yes, there's Miss Chambers.'

A tall smiling woman came towards them. 'Hello, Ewa. Is this the little brother? Lovely. Hello, dear. What's your name?'

He understood, but could not answer.

'It's Jerzy,' said Ewa.

'Yer-jay. Very nice. Not as easy as Ewa, but never mind.' She smiled again. 'Run along now. Yerjay will be quite all right with me, won't you, dear?'

'Bye!' called Ewa. 'See you at break.'

He watched her go, and then other children arrived, each one greeted by Miss Chambers. She left him by her desk, standing quite still and staring at the floor. There was a ragged splash of ink on the boards; distantly observing it, he noticed its resemblance to a steam engine, and closed his eyes. He would travel on it, far away – anywhere, as long as it was not here. He never would be here.

2
Warsaw, 1939

The apartment house in Praga had a chestnut tree in the courtyard. From the window of their bedroom, Anna and Jerzy could almost touch the leaves; in late spring a rustling breeze sometimes sent a few white flowers drifting into the room, leaving a thin dust of pollen, a scattering of waxy petals on the desk. Now, after weeks of hot weather, the tree was just beginning to turn yellow; Anna left the rucksack open on her bed and stood watching the slow fall of one leaf then another on to the cobbles, the occasional drop of a spiky chestnut case.

The apartment was full of quiet, end-of-the-week sounds. The outer door to her father's surgery, at the far end of the shadowy corridor, opened and closed; through his half-open window, which also faced the courtyard, she could hear his murmurs of greeting and inquiry. In the kitchen Teresa and Marta, the maid, were listening to the news on the wireless and preparing supper for tonight: the family was going to have lunch with Wiktoria, Tata's sister, across the river; it was her Saint's Day. Anna heard Marta chopping vegetables, the rush of water from the tap, the oven door open and shut, plates and glasses taken from the cupboard and set on the dark green tray. The door to the sitting room was ajar; sun from the casement windows facing the street fell in a thin line on to the corridor, and the tapestry *kilims* on the wall which Mama had made when she and Tata were first married. Jerzy was practising: he ran up and down a scale repeatedly.

'You're supposed to be *packing*,' Anna called. The scale rose and fell again, then stopped, and he was standing in the bedroom doorway, pulling a face at the litter of shirts and shorts and socks on his bed.

'Give me a hand.'

'Honestly,' said Anna. 'Anyone would think we were going away for a year. You know Tata told us to travel light.'

Yesterday evening they had sat in the sitting room after supper, the map spread out over the walnut table. 'We shall take the train

41

right up here, to the north of Wilno,' said Tata, 'which is here, in the north-east . . .' His finger led their eyes up the worn map from Warsaw, across plains, past lakes, through Białystok. 'As you will recall from your history lessons, Wilno is one of the most beautiful and important medieval cities in Poland.' He raised a dark eyebrow. 'You do of course recall it.'

Anna giggled. 'Yes, Tata.'

'Good. And then we shall paddle our dear old *kajak* all the way through these lovely lakes, here . . . down to the river Zejmiana . . . here . . . and all the way on to the river Wilia. It is particularly lovely countryside – we shall travel by river all the way to Wilno, and there we shall catch the train back to Warsaw.' His finger skimmed down winding tributaries, and brought them safely home. 'By which time you will be fit! We shall paddle and swim and walk – you have both been disgracefully idle all summer.'

'Yes, Tata.' Jerzy and Anna winked at each other, and then there was a rattle of cups from the corridor, and they looked up to see Teresa in the doorway with a tray of coffee.

'Ah – thank you, my dear,' said Tata, and folded the map, nodding to them to pull back a chair for her and rise.

Last month, while Jerzy was camping with his Scout troop, and Anna with Guides, Tata and Teresa had had a little holiday by themselves. Anna didn't know why Teresa was not coming with them now, and she didn't like to ask, partly because she wasn't used to questioning any decision Tata made, and partly because she wouldn't want him to think she wanted her with them. She did not exactly dislike Teresa: she was simply, even after three years, an intrusion, and she tried too hard.

Tata still kept the photograph of their real mother on his desk in the surgery; there was another in their room, on the chest of drawers: Mama with Anna on her lap, Jerzy standing beside her, already, even at two, very dark and serious and still. Anna sometimes thought now that at fifteen he looked like the pictures of Slavic scholars she'd seen in an old book of Tata's – thin, with cropped hair, high cheekbones, wide-set eyes: when he was reading, or playing the piano, he was lost. Quite different from Andrzej, his best friend. Andrzej was big-boned, fair-haired, athletic, a bit of a daredevil. Anna liked him, but she was also shy of him: when he came to the apartment she smiled, and went off with her drawing book.

The photographs of her and Jerzy, as small children, with Mama and Tata, were everywhere, for so long so much a part of her life that they were in its background, like the stories Tata told them, of the days when Mama was alive. In the foreground were school, and Guides; her friends Natalia and Jadwiga; her drawing. Every now and then there moved in and out of her thoughts, like a wraith, her secret sense of . . . displacement, as if she were not quite whole, and therefore did not quite belong anywhere, even with her friends, even in the family. Most important in her life was Tata, to whom she had tried a few weeks ago to talk about this strange feeling. He had been writing notes in his surgery after his last patient had gone; she somehow found it easier to mention it when he was half-preoccupied.

'Tata?' She sat on the leather couch, her legs swinging.

'Mm-hm?'

'I have this funny feeling sometimes . . .'

'Mmm?' His pen moved across the page, his balding head bent low. He needed glasses.

'Don't you need glasses, Tata?'

'Possibly. I am trying to refer Pani Treszka to a consultant. What feeling?'

'Oh, just . . . sometimes I feel as if there's a bit of me missing, that's all.'

'Your head, perhaps?' He finished writing and turned the page over on to the blotting pad, smoothing it, looking across at her quizzically.

'Oh, never mind.' She slid off the couch and went to stand beside him, her arm across his shoulders. 'Is Pani Treszka very ill?'

'No, but you know that I should not tell you if she were. One does not discuss one's patients with ignorant children.'

'No, Tata.' She smiled and leaned against him, feeling utterly safe. 'Perhaps I'll be a doctor one day – not quite so ignorant.' That was all she really wanted: to be as clever, and useful, as Tata – or Mama: she'd been a doctor, too.

'What are you trying to tell me, darling?'

But the feeling of strangeness had melted; she patted Tata's balding head. 'I can't remember.'

The front door banged: Jerzy was home from the *gimnazium*, secondary school; it was the start of the summer holidays. What did anything else matter?

He was calling from the corridor. 'Tata?'

'In here.' The surgery door opened, and he came in. They were together again.

And now the summer was almost over, and they would be together

for two whole weeks. She looked at Jerzy rummaging through the clothes on his bed, stuffing shirts into his rucksack – hardly a Slavic scholar now.

'Hopeless . . .' she said. 'Let me.'

'Thank you. I did ask.' He perched on the other end of the bed, watching her folding and stacking. 'I suppose we'll need sweaters.'

'Of course. Have you got a clean one?'

'I think Teresa . . .' He swung off the bed, pulled out a drawer in the chest and a deep blue sweater from within it. 'Yes, she did. Good for her.' He examined a sleeve. 'Darned, too.'

Anna felt a twinge of guilt in her relief that Teresa was not coming. Then the door from the surgery into the apartment was opened, and Tata called out: 'Is everyone ready?'

The wireless in the kitchen was turned off. 'Almost,' called Teresa. 'I'm just going to change.' They heard her coming out and saying something to Tata in a low voice; he did not answer, but they went into their bedroom and closed the door.

Jerzy looked at Anna and raised an eyebrow. 'What's all that about?'

She shrugged. 'I don't know.' She looked down at her cotton skirt and sandals. 'Do you think I look respectable enough for Aunt Wiktoria?'

'Don't ask me.' He looked at her critically. 'You look fine – it's just the face that's the problem.'

She threw a shirt at him.

The door from Tata's and Teresa's room was opened.

'Come on, you two,' called Tata, and Teresa hurried in. 'All right? Are you packed? Anna, dear, do you think . . . should you wear a dress?'

The tram swung along the bridge across the gleaming Vistula. Ahead, the outlines of the buildings on the west bank were hazy in the heat: the medieval houses of the Old Town clustered near the Royal Palace; the nineteenth-century warehouses on the waterfront; in Napoleon Square, the sixteen-storey skyscraper, the only one in Warsaw, where the offices of the Prudential Insurance Company were housed. Riverboats hooted beneath them; gulls wheeled in a cloudless sky. Over the bridge and through the Old Town, they caught another tram. It hummed past spacious parks and down broad avenues where on the orders of Mayor Starzyński trees had been planted all along the centre.

This was elegant Warsaw, the Warsaw where well-heeled families came in from the suburbs to shop for clothes, to spend the evenings in expensive restaurants and at the theatre; the Warsaw where the Polish intelligentsia browsed in the university libraries, and went to concerts, the opera, cabaret. In Żoliborz, the district in the north of the city, there were more parks, large villas stood in well-kept gardens, and new, low apartment blocks were bordered by trees. Many of the people strolling down Jerozolimskie Avenue or Marszałkowska lived in Żoliborz.

There were other districts where you saw a different Warsaw. In Stare Miasto, the Old Town, pastel-painted, red-tiled medieval houses, tall and narrow, clustered along narrow streets and alleyways, overlooked cobbled squares. It was picturesque, parts of it were very fashionable, the pride of the city on the banks of the Vistula. But it was also densely populated, overpopulated, perhaps a hundred thousand people crammed into the few square miles, and many of the pretty houses, with their freezing attics and sprawling damp cellars, bred squalor and disease.

Bordering Stare Miasto was the ancient Jewish district, which stretched through the west of the city. Anna had hardly ever been into this foreign land, where cramped, overcrowded tenements housed enormous families of pale-faced Hassidic children. They ran out of the courtyards on to the long streets in ill-fitting shoes with flapping soles; their earlocks swung beneath their little caps and shaved heads. The little girls wore headscarves, and patched dresses. They called to each other in Yiddish and stared at the non-Jewish Poles who came into their district. Anna had been stared at, on the rare occasions she had gone through there with Tata or Teresa, in her nice cotton frock and neat plaits, and felt like a foreigner herself.

Tata had a few Jewish patients, but they weren't living here, they were professional, members of the Jewish intelligentsia. Most of his patients were well-to-do Poles, but he had always been available to see others not so fortunate, for nothing, or a token fee. In the days when he and Mama were first married, they'd lived and worked on this side of the river, and he still had families from those days for whom he was 'our doctor'. He visited patients in Stare Miasto, and occasionally in the bleak, impoverished suburbs of Wola and Ochota, on the other side of the city, where some of the houses were no more than wooden shacks, and the roads unmade. He came home to Praga with stories of children the same age as Anna and Jerzy who were ill and undernourished, living in crowded, cold, damp rooms – 'and

45

don't ever forget how fortunate you are,' he told them. Anna worried sometimes that he would catch some awful illness on these visits, and die, like Mama, but she never said so.

It was hot in the tram. She gazed out of the window, watching people greet each other in the open-air cafés, and settle down under the long sunblinds for lunch, and she turned and saw Teresa looking at the dress-shop windows and wondered if she were going to be taken on a last-minute shopping expedition, later in the afternoon.

The tram drew up at the intersection of Marszałkowska and Hoża. where Wiktoria lived, and they got off. A flower-seller stood on the pavement, buckets of carnations, tall scented stock and gypsophylla at her feet. The building behind her cast a deep cool shadow.

They stood for a moment, Teresa in her pale linen dress and jacket with her arm through Tata's, lightly, as he looked carefully over everything.

'Carnations?' she suggested.

He smiled, half at the flower-seller. 'That would be very nice.'

They walked up the long street, the pavements beneath the shops and high apartment houses black with shadow, the centre lit by the sun. Aunt Wiktoria's apartment was on the third floor of a block entered directly from the street through wrought-iron gates. They climbed the worn stone stairs and rang the bell.

'You're panting, Tata,' said Jerzy as they waited.

'Nonsense.' He straightened his tie and looked at them sternly.

'Poor Tomasz,' said Teresa. 'You work too hard.' She stretched up to brush something from his lapel; Anna looked away. Why was she always touching him?

Then the door was opened wide, and Aunt Wiktoria stood smiling at them all. 'Come in! Come in! I was just caught on the telephone . . . are these for me? Beautiful, now let me just find a vase . . .'

She led them into the main room, which like their own doubled as dining and drawing room, and where the table was laid for lunch with silver, and linen napkins, the polished glasses winking in the sunlight. Anna flopped down on to the sofa; Jerzy went to look at the bookcase. There were newspapers on the table by the window; Anna watched her father cross over, pick up the one on the top and scan it quickly, holding it close.

'You *do* need glasses, Tata.'

He didn't answer; she saw him and Teresa exchange a look and then he put the paper back on the pile, but turned over.

'Here we are.' Wiktoria returned from the kitchen with the flowers in a vase, and put it on the table. 'Thank you all so much. Now – I expect everyone is dying for a drink. Tomasz, perhaps you could . . .'

'Of course.' Tata went to the sideboard and opened the bottle of vodka which stood there.

'Jerzy, are you drinking now?' Wiktoria asked.

He turned from the bookshelves. 'Please, Aunt.' He wandered over to the pile of newspapers, and picked up the one on the top.

'And Anna?'

'A little, please.'

'Perhaps with water,' suggested Teresa, sitting in the armchair. 'Jerzy, dear, come and sit down.'

Wiktoria was handing glasses.

'*Na zdrowie*,' said Tata, raising his glass to her. 'Cheers. Happy Saint's Day.'

'*Na zdrowie*,' they all chorused, and Jerzy put the paper down again as Wiktoria nodded, smiling. She was a tall, big-boned woman, with dark hair and horn-rimmed spectacles which hung on a chain round her neck. Their severity, when she wore them, was quite belied by the eyes behind: she seemed to Anna always to be laughing or smiling, although when they were children she had taken no nonsense from them. She had never married; Anna didn't know why, and it didn't seem important: she was secretary to one of the professors in the University Medical Faculty where Tata and Mama had trained, and had more friends than anyone else they knew. Anna reached into her satchel for the drawing she'd done for her, and pulled it out just as Jerzy asked abruptly:

'Is there going to be a war?'

The question, and the silence which answered it, seemed to fill every corner of the sunlit room.

'Is there?' said Jerzy.

'It is possible,' said Tata slowly.

Anna stared at him. All through the summer there had been talk on the wireless about Germany, and the Nazi Party, and Danzig, but she hadn't really listened, and Tata and Teresa hadn't seemed to pay much attention. She didn't usually see the newspapers, they went straight into the surgery; perhaps the one this morning hadn't come, or Tata hadn't had time to look at it. But Teresa had been listening to the wireless . . . was that why they had shut their bedroom door? What did Danzig matter? She knew, without knowing why, that it

47

was important, like Wilno, where they were going on holiday . . . They were going on holiday! How could there be a war?

'It is possible,' Tata said again, 'but we are all praying that it won't happen.'

'But . . . but even if there is,' Anna said, frowning, 'you wouldn't have to go, would you?'

'Well . . .'

'What?' Surely he wouldn't, he wasn't in the army, was he? He was just an ordinary doctor.

'I am in the Reserve Corps,' he said, 'like most professional men. If Poland were to be invaded, I expect we would all be called up.'

He had known all this all summer, and he hadn't said anything? He and Teresa had had a secret like that from her and Jerzy? She could feel a great lump of misery begin to fill her throat, and turned away.

'Anna . . .' He came to sit beside her, and put his arm round her. 'I am telling you the truth, because it's better to do that, isn't it?'

She could hardly speak. 'Why . . . why didn't you tell us before?'

'Because it may not happen, after all. Why worry unless you have to? We wanted you and Jerzy to have a happy summer. And tomorrow we're going on holiday.'

'Still?' She blew her nose.

'Of course.'

'But Tata,' said Jerzy, still standing by the window, 'will I have to go?'

'Do you imagine you are old enough to join the army, you poor ignorant boy?' said Tata, and began to sound like himself again. He got up, and looked at Wiktoria. 'And now, perhaps . . .'

'Of course. Lunch is quite ready – Teresa, my dear, would you be kind enough . . .'

The two women went out to the kitchen.

'All right now?' Tata asked Anna.

She nodded. 'Yes, thank you.' But unease gnawed at her. 'I'm just going to the bathroom.'

In the corridor she heard Teresa's and Wiktoria's low voices from the kitchen. She stopped, her hand on the handle of the bathroom door, and listened.

The British and the French . . . allies . . . the Anglo–French agreement . . . pledged to come to Poland's aid . . . invasion . . . Tomasz might not have to go . . .

He might not have to go. That was all she cared about. She went into the bathroom and closed the door. Inside, she looked at herself in the mirror, and splashed water over her burning, angry face. This time tomorrow they would already be on the train out of Warsaw.

'Look, Tata, quick!'

From the *kajak* Jerzy pointed to the river bank: in the meadow beyond, a stork stood motionless amidst the rippling grass. Tata stopped paddling and they rested, watching. The bird raised its head, then picked its way slowly through the field; Jerzy shifted a little, and the *kajak* rocked.

'Careful!' said Anna, and the stork suddenly lifted its wings and took off, flapping awkwardly and low over the field at first, then, gaining power, steadily rising into the morning sun and away to the woods beyond.

It was ten o'clock, already growing warm, though on the river they still needed to wear jumpers. They had been travelling for just over a week; pitching their tent and exploring the countryside around for a day or two, then moving on, a journey of sunlight and water. The river meandered between deep banks planted with silver birch trees; sunflowers nodded over every corner of a field or patch of vegetables they passed. In the afternoon heat they stripped off and swam past clumps of reeds and rushes, or paddled over broad flat rocks on the river bed, where the water flickered. Grey church spires and the red-tiled roofs of distant villages marked the horizon; when they walked inland on baked mud paths and unmade roads they passed clusters of cottages under dirty thatch. Barefooted children stared from doorways; the single rooms inside were dark.

In almost every field a horse stood irritably flicking flies in the heat; men in shirtsleeves and women and children in kerchiefs moved through the corn and hay with scythes, bending and swishing, piling and tying. In late afternoon or early evening, the waggons moved slowly out of the fields and back to the villages, the children swaying on piles of hay six or seven feet high. Ragged lines of geese followed, honking; hens ran squawking to the verge.

In the larger villages Tata bought bread, potatoes and sausages, smoked bacon and yellow apples. He and Jerzy and Anna gathered sticks as they made their way back to the tent, and laid a fire, sticking the potatoes in at the bottom.

'I wish we could live like this always,' Jerzy said that night as they sat round the embers. He poked them with a stick; ash sighed through the charred branches to the ground.

'One always thinks that on holiday,' said Tata. 'By the end of next week you will be impatient for your piano, your friends. You'll have had quite enough of your dull old Tata.' He stretched, and stood up; twigs snapped.

'Light the lamp, Tata, and stop talking nonsense,' said Anna. 'Let's go and read in the tent.'

The tent was awkward to handle, heavy old canvas with stiffened guy ropes, but roomy enough for the three of them. Tata had had it for years – he thought his own father might have used it in the last war – and he and Mama used to go camping in it in the twenties, when they were first married. Anna and Jerzy had seen pictures of them in the album he kept in his desk: laughing at each other into the camera, striking poses, or caught unawares: Tata – he had more hair, then – gazing into the distance with a cigarette or Mama bending down to pack more into the rucksack, showing slim calves above ankle socks and summer shoes. Tata still had the heavy black box camera; he'd used it all holiday.

It was growing dark. Anna picked up the water can and saucepan, and shivered: though they had camped well back from the river bank, she could feel the chill rising from the water. Jerzy stamped out the last of the fire.

'Come on, you two!' Tata called, and they turned and saw the pale yellow glow of the paraffin lamp through the canvas, and his shadow, as he sat down and reached for the book.

He looked up and smiled as they pushed apart the entrance flaps and went inside. 'Here – ' he picked up the rug beside him and passed it to Anna. 'I told you to bring two jumpers, didn't I?'

'Yes, Tata.' She pulled the rug round her shoulders and sat down, leaning against his shoulder. Jerzy flopped on to his sleeping bag.

'Come on, then, where've we got to?'

He had been reading to them for as long as they could remember. When they were small, and especially after Mama went to hospital and Wiktoria was looking after them, he came every night and sat on their beds in turn, reading the fairy tales and nursery rhymes they still had on the bookshelf in their room. When they went to school he continued, although as they got older and his practice more demanding it was sometimes only at weekends; but it had never stopped. Long after their friends had outgrown being read to, Jerzy and Anna continued to listen. Much of last year had been spent reading *Peasants*, the quartet of novels which made up Reymont's great hymn to rural Poland. For the holiday, they'd brought with them a volume of short stories by Sienkiewicz, reading one, or part of a long one, each evening.

'Now . . .' said Tata. He slipped out the cracked leather bookmark and peered at the title of the next story. 'This one is called "The Lighthouse Keeper" – it's based on a true story, I think.' He shifted a little, settled back against his rolled-up sleeping bag, and began to read.

'It so happened that the lighthouse keeper in Aspinwall, not far from Panama, disappeared without leaving a trace. As this occurred during a storm, it was supposed that the unfortunate man must have gone too near the edge of the island rock on which the lighthouse stood, and been washed away by a wave. This was the more probable, because his boat was not found the next day in its rocky niche. The post of lighthouse keeper therefore fell vacant . . .'

'Can you see all right, Tata?'

'Perfectly, thank you, Anna. You can move a little to the left, perhaps, so that your shadow does not obscure the page entirely . . .'

She moved, lay down, closed her eyes and listened.

'The task of finding a new lighthouse keeper devolved on the Consul of the United States who lived in Panama, and it was a task of no small difficulty . . . Life in a lighthouse tower is an extraordinarily hard one . . . it is a claustral life, and even more than claustral, for it is a hermit's life . . . It is, therefore, not surprising that Mr Isaac Folcombridge was in great perplexity where to find a permanent successor, and his joy may be imagined when that successor most unexpectedly appeared that very same day. He was a man already old, seventy years or more, but hale, erect, with the movements and bearing of a soldier. His hair was quite white; his complexion was as sunburnt as a creole's, but judging from his blue eyes he belonged to no southern race. His face had an oppressed and sad, but honest expression. Folcombridge took a fancy to him at first sight.

' "Where do you come from?"

' "I am a Pole."

' "What have you been doing up till now?"

' "I've led a roving life."

' "A lighthouse keeper must be fond of staying in one place."

' "I need rest." '

Tata cleared his throat. They lay listening as the interview continued. The old man, Skawiński, showed himself in his papers and testimonials as a courageous soldier who had fought in any number of campaigns throughout Europe and against the South in the American Civil War.

' "Do you know anything about life at sea?"

' "I served three years on a whaler."

' "You've tried different occupations?"

' "It's because I never could find peace anywhere."

' "Why?"

The old man shrugged his shoulders. "Fate."

' "You look to me too old for a lighthouse keeper."

' "Sir!" the candidate burst out in agitated tones. "I am very tired and battered about. You see I've gone through a lot. This post is one of those I've most longed to get. I'm old. I need rest. I need to be able to say to myself: You are going to settle down here now, you're in port. Oh, sir! this depends only on you . . . I've had enough of all that wandering."

'The old man's eyes were so beseeching that Folcombridge, who was kind and simple of heart, felt touched.

' "Well!" he said. "I accept you. You are the lighthouse keeper."

'The old man's face lit up with an unspeakable joy.

' "Just one word: for the slightest negligence in your duty you'll be dismissed."

'The old man was rowed out to the lighthouse. That night he stood on the balcony close to the mighty lantern, and stood gazing out over the sea, secure and at peace.

'His misfortune had been that as often as he pitched his tent and lit the fire on his hearth to settle down for good, the wind tore away the tent pegs, scattered the ashes of his fire, and brought himself to ruin . . . it seemed as though all four elements persecuted him . . . He believed that some powerful and avenging hand was pursuing him everywhere, by land and water . . . Yet he had the patience of an Indian, and the great and quiet resisting power that springs from rectitude of soul. During his service in Hungary he received several bayonet thrusts because he refused to seize the strap shown him as his means of safety and cry: "I surrender."

'At last he was overpowered by one thought only: the thought of rest. It took complete possession of the old man, and absorbed all other desires and hopes . . . now, suddenly, in the course of twelve hours, he had obtained a post that seemed chosen out of all others in the world for him. . . .

'One hour followed after another, and he was still on the balcony. He gazed; he drank his fill. The lens of the lantern flung into the darkness a mighty cone of light, beyond which the old man's eyes were lost in a distance that was pitch black, mysterious and terrible. Yet that distance seemed to be running towards the light. Long, jagged waves rolled out from the darkness and, roaring, reached as far as the foot of the little island, and then their foaming manes were visible, glittering, rose-coloured, in the light of the lantern. The tide was fast coming in and pouring over the sandbanks. The mysterious language of the ocean was approaching from the deep, ever stronger, ever louder . . . A storm growled in the distance. On the dark heaving waste a few little green lamps flashed, hanging on the masts of ships . . .

'Skawinski went down to his room. The storm had begun to howl. Out there men on those ships were battling with the night, with the dark, with the waves; but inside the room it was quiet and still . . . there was only the rhythmic tick-tack of the clock that seemed to rock the tired old man to sleep.'

Anna heard the dry sound of pages turned, her father's steady voice filling the tent as he read on.

'Everything with which the lighthouse keeper comes into contact is huge, without concrete or definite form. The sky is one element, water the other; and between those immensities one solitary human soul . . . The old man lived in the company of the tower, the lantern, the rock, the sandbanks, and solitude . . .

'His tower guarded him against all evil. Indeed, he only left it at intervals, on Sunday mornings. Then he put on his long blue official coat with silver buttons, hung his crosses on his breast; and he carried his milk-white head with a certain pride when, as he came out of church, he heard the creoles say to one another: "We've got a proper lighthouse keeper!" But he returned to the island immediately after Mass, and was glad to return, for he still felt some lurking distrust of the mainland. On Sundays, too, he would read a Spanish newspaper that he bought in the town, or the *New York Herald*, borrowed from Folcombridge, searching through them for their scanty news of Europe. Poor old heart! In that watchtower and in another hemisphere, it still beat for his country . . .

'Homesickness had passed into resignation. The whole world now began and ended for the old man on his little island . . . Moreover he was becoming a mystic . . . ceasing to exist as a separate personality . . . becoming ever more one with that which surrounded him . . . in the end it seemed to him that the sky, the water, his rock, the tower, and the golden sandbanks, and the swelling sails and the gulls, the incoming and outgoing tides, were all one great harmony and one mighty, mysterious soul; and he was submerged in that mystery, and felt the presence of that soul which was living and at rest. He sank into it, he was cradled by it, memory fled; and in that captivity of his own separate existence, in that half-consciousness, half-sleep, he found a peace so great that it almost resembled death.'

For Anna, listening, the darkening woods outside the tent had slipped away, as the mainland and the world had done for the old man in his lighthouse. There was only the light and warmth from the lamp, and the smell of paraffin, the sound of Jerzy occasionally changing position on his sleeping bag, their father's voice, leading her into the deepest, half-forgotten places of her childhood, when she had lain in bed and been soothed by it to sleep.

He paused for a moment and she opened her eyes, saw Jerzy lying on his stomach, his head on his folded arms.

'Is he asleep?' she whispered.

'No,' muttered Jerzy. 'Go on, Tata.'

He turned back to the book once more.

'One day after the boat had brought water and a stock of provisions, Skawinski, coming down an hour later from the tower, saw that besides the ordinary load there was another packet. On the outer cover of the packet were United States postage stamps, and the address, "Skawinski, Esq.," written clearly on the rough canvas. His curiosity greatly excited, the old man cut through the canvas and saw books. He took one in his hand, looked, and laid it down again. Then his hands began trembling violently. He shaded his eyes, as though he could not trust them; he thought he was dreaming; the book was Polish. What could this mean? Who had sent the book to him?

'At the moment he had forgotten that quite at the beginning of his career in the lighthouse he had read one day in a *Herald*, borrowed from the Consul, of the foundation of a Polish Society in New York, and that he had immediately sent the society half of his monthly salary, for which as a matter of fact he had no use in the tower. The society had sent him the books as a token of gratitude. They had come in a natural way, but at first the old man could not grasp this idea. Polish books in Aspinwall, in his tower, in his solitude, were to his mind something extraordinary, like a breath of old days; a sort of miracle . . .

'He sat for a minute with closed eyes, and he was almost certain that when he opened them the dream would vanish. No! The packet on which the afternoon rays of the sun were shining lay distinctly before him, cut open, and on it the open book . . . It was poetry.'

Anna closed her eyes again as Tata read aloud the lines the old man had read aloud, there on the narrow lonely shore of the lighthouse rock: they were verses by Adam Mickiewicz, who with hundreds of other Poles had lived in exile in Paris after the 1830 Rising against the Czar.

'Lithuania, my country, thou art like health.
How much to prize thee can only be told
By him who hath lost thee. All thy beauty today
I see, and I sing, for I pine after thee . . .

'Holy Virgin, who dost guard Czestochowa bright . . .
As by a miracle thou grantest me, a child, return to health
So thou shalt grant us to return by a miracle to our land.

'The old man uttered a loud cry, and flung himself on the ground. Forty years had passed since he had seen his country, and God knows how many since he had heard his native language; yet here that language had come to him of its own accord; it had crossed the ocean, and found the lonely recluse in the other hemisphere; that language so beloved, so dear, so beautiful! In the sobbing which shook him there was no grief, only a suddenly awakened, infinite love, beside which all else was as naught . . .

'Twilight had blotted out the letters on the white page; a twilight as short as the twinkling of an eye. The old man leant his head on the rock and closed his eyes . . . Long red and golden trails were still burning in the sky, and on those shafts of light he fled to his beloved land. The pine woods roared in his ears; his native rivers gurgled . . .

'He saw wide fields, green unploughed strips dividing them, meadows, woods and hamlets. By now it was night. At that hour his lantern was used to shine over the darkness of the sea; but he was now in his native village . . . he saw it as though he had left it yesterday: the row of cottages, with faint lights in their windows, the dykes, the mill, the two ponds lying over against each other, and ringing all night with choirs of frogs. Once, in that village of his, he was on sentry duty at night. That past now suddenly rose before him in a series of visions. He is again a lancer on guard . . .

'Wait a little, and you will hear the corncrake calling in the darkness and bitterns booming in the reeds. The night is calm and cool, a real Polish night. In the distance the pine forest murmurs with wind – like the waves of the sea. Soon the dawn will whiten the east; yes, the cocks are crowing already behind the edges. Each takes up the other's voice, one after the other from cottage to cottage; suddenly the cranes, too, cry from high up in the sky. . . . Oh, beloved, beloved land!

'Hush! The watchful sentry hears footsteps approaching. They must be coming to relieve the guard.

'Suddenly a voice rang out over Skawiński's head.

' "Hi, old chap! Get up. What's the matter with you?"

'The old man opened his eyes, and gazed bewildered at the man standing before him. Remnants of the visions of his dreams struggled in his brain with reality. Finally, the visions grew faint and vanished. Johns, the harbour watchman, was standing in front of him.

' "What's all this?" Johns asked. "Are you ill?"

' "No."

' "You didn't light the lantern. You are going to be dismissed from the service. A boat from San Geromo has been wrecked on a sand-reef. Luckily no one was drowned. If they had been, you'd have been tried for it. Get into the boat with me. You'll hear the rest in the Consulate."

'The old man turned pale. Indeed, he had not lit the lantern that night.

'A few days later, Skawiński might have been seen on the deck of a vessel going from Aspinwall to New York. The poor old man had lost his post. New ways of a wanderer's existence had opened again before him. Again the wind had blown the leaf away to cast it forth by land and sea, to make sport of it at its will. During those few days the old man had grown very shrunken and bent; only his eyes shone. But in his breast he carried into the new roads of his life his book, which from time to time his hand grasped as though fearful lest that, too, should be taken from him.'

There was a silence, then the soft sound of the book being closed and put down. They lay without speaking; when Anna opened her eyes she could see the dark shapes of moths and insects bumping blindly against the canvas outside, struggling to reach the warm yellow glow of the lamp. She thought of the great cone of light from the lighthouse lantern flung out over the black night sea, of the old man, exiled, losing himself and his soul in the dissolution of sky and water, until the strange parcel of Polish books arrived, and he remembered who he was.

'Tata?' said Jerzy.

'Mmm?'

'He forgot to light the lamp . . .'

'Yes.' Their father stretched, ran his fingers over his balding head. He was looking rather drawn. 'A very sad and beautiful story. And now I think it's time we went to sleep. We'll move on tomorrow.' He pulled on his jacket. 'I'm going outside for a minute, Jerzy. Coming?'

Anna listened to their footsteps as they went to relieve themselves; she undressed rapidly, and pulled her jumper over her nightdress. Then she huddled inside her sleeping bag.

Jerzy put his head through the flaps and came in. 'There's a wonderful sky.'

She sat up, and shifted in her bag to the opening. 'Oh, yes!' An explosion of pale stars was splashed across the blue-black above the trees: she gazed at them, and felt herself shrink, like the lighthouse keeper, in the vastness of the world.

'Where's Tata?'

'He's gone for a walk – I think he wants to be by himself for a bit.'

'Oh.' She withdrew quickly into the tent again, and wriggled into the sleeping bag, up to her neck. Jerzy pulled on pyjamas and jumper, slid inside his, and they lay for a few minutes in silence.

'Anna? What did you think of the story?'

'It made me want to cry.'

'I don't understand it . . . does he really mean Poles care too much about the past? That we neglect the present?'

'But of course he cared – he'd lost everything.'

'I know.'

Anna lay gazing up at the moths outside, still buffeting themselves against the canvas, searching vainly for a way to reach the light. Tata had been out for quite a while. Their tent, which had felt so warm and safe, seemed suddenly a very small and defenceless place, pitched in the emptiness of the woods, beneath the night sky, and the uneasy feeling which had gnawed at her all summer stirred in her stomach like a dark snake uncurling from sleep. *Did you think I had gone away? I am always here.* She shivered.

'Jerzy?'

'Mmm?'

'Is Tata all right?'

'I think so.'

She turned over, and heard the faraway hoot of an owl. It spoke of hollowness, of being alone and afraid. What was Tata thinking about, out there? There was another noise, a sudden tearing cry, and they both sat up; Anna grabbed Jerzy's arm.

'What was that?'

Twigs broke outside the tent. 'A fox,' said Tata, appearing through the entrance. He winked at them. 'My poor city dwellers, how well you would do if you had to live like this always.'

They laughed. 'Phew,' said Jerzy, and they lay watching him undress, bumping comfortingly against the sides. The cry came again, but from further away.

'It's horrible – it sounds like something from hell,' said Jerzy.

'Well it isn't,' said Tata, and blew out the lamp. 'Goodnight, you two.'

'Goodnight.'

'Goodnight.'

Anna lay in the darkness, listening. The fox did not cry out again, but the owl called several times, lonely, unanswered.

She sat on the river bank, sketching. It was mid-afternoon, hazy and warm; birds sang in the birch trees behind her. Her eyes flicked up and down, up and down, from sketchpad to glinting water; on the far side of the river a pair of moorhens swam jerkily in and out of the reeds. There was a faint splash as a fish broke the surface, then silence. Watching the ripples, Anna was conscious again of the feeling she couldn't put properly into words, or explain, even to Tata. She was isolated, perhaps even unreal – as if she were dreaming her own life. Sometimes she wasn't properly inside herself at all, but a cold observer – like now: a girl of thirteen in old cotton shorts and shirt, her hair in plaits, sitting by the river and trying to draw the sunlight on the water. If that was her, who was watching? Perhaps someone else was dreaming her life, and when they woke up, that would be the end.

Tata and Jerzy had gone for a walk to the village, to stock up again. This morning had been lazy, getting up well after nine, swimming, taking photographs of each other, splashing about and laughing. Last night's unease, about Tata, about herself, had been forgotten: she was carefree and untroubled. Why, now, should she begin again to question, to ask things which seemed unanswerable: who was she? Why was she who she was?

She got up and began to walk restlessly along the bank. The leaves on the birch trees rustled. Then she heard footsteps coming quickly through the woods, twigs snapping underfoot, but no voices, and turned back to see Jerzy, carrying the rucksack, with a strange sort of look about him, a mixture of excitement and apprehension. Tata was beside him, tapping a newspaper against his leg as he walked, doing it automatically, as if he had some kind of tic. He, too, looked different. He looked grey.

Anna felt her legs go suddenly weak as she ran towards them, calling: 'What is it? What's happened?' Even as she asked, she knew what it was, heard Jerzy asking a week ago: 'Is there going to be a war?' and Tata's slow reply: 'It is possible.'

The railway station at Wilno was in chaos, the platforms crowded with people clutching suitcases and hastily tied bundles of clothes – holiday makers, like them, frantic to get home to Warsaw and find out what was happening. There was no timetable, and the station master and porters had no idea when the next train to Warsaw, or anywhere else, might be running. Jerzy and Anna were exhausted: by paddling non-stop, they had made the three-day journey to Wilno in just under two; they'd come into a marina just outside the city, and then had to spend precious hours dismantling the heavy, cumbersome *kajak*, packing it all up, lugging that and the tent, and their luggage, all the way here. They'd eaten the last of their food this morning – Tata had thought they might be able to buy something in Wilno, but all the shops were closed and on the station there was not even a barrow.

Everyone was waiting for a Warsaw train; Jerzy stood next to a trembling peasant woman whose son and his family lived there now. Tata spoke to a group of soldiers in uniform, carrying heavy kitbags. One of them had a cousin living right across the country in western Poland, near the German frontier. He had managed to telephone. 'You know what he told me?' he said bitterly. 'The bastards came through on motorbikes. They just flung up the barrier and came through, as easy as opening a gate.'

It was almost two hours, and late in the afternoon, before a train arrived, clouds of steam billowing into a reddening sky. At once, there was a rush for the doors, and Anna almost choked in the crush as a man behind her shoved forward, his suitcase pressing into her ribs. 'Come on! Come on!' Then Tata bent down from the step and hauled her up beside him, and Jerzy managed to scramble up and into the corridor. There was no chance of a seat: pressed against the window, Anna was jammed between Tata and a heavy-faced man smelling sourly of sweat. The train began to move, and further down the corridor a baby started howling. Anna shut her eyes. Please God make this not be happening, she thought bleakly, and willed them all back by the placid river, with nothing to be afraid of.

The train was unlit. Occasionally they could see a distant light somewhere in the black landscape, but they were too far back to get any of the glow from the engine, except when they rounded a bend. After a while most people stopped talking, and they travelled in silence except for the sound of breathing, or a cough, or shifting feet as someone moved in the crush. It was hot, airless. 'Tata . . .' Anna whispered. He put his arm round her and she put her hand in his jacket pocket and held on. By the time they reached Warsaw they were all so stiff it was hard to move at all.

Central Station, too, was in darkness, except for a light in the ticket office, by which they made their way in the crowd to the street outside. The trams on Nowogrodzka stood empty on the rails.

'Come on.' said Tata quickly. 'We'll have to walk.'

'Oh God,' Anna said. 'Teresa . . .' She thought of her alone in the apartment, wondering where they were.

'We'll try to telephone.' But the only working phone they passed had a long queue, and they hurried on. The pavements on Jerozolimskie Avenue were covered in broken glass; great ugly holes gaped in the windows of shops and offices. There were few people except other passengers from the station, and almost no traffic.

'Hey!' Jerzy said suddenly. 'There's a taxi!' He dropped his rucksack and darted out into the road, waving and calling. The taxi pulled up and he flung open the door and called back to them. 'Quick!'

They ran up and threw the tent and rucksacks on to the back seat.

'Praga?' asked Tata, pushing Anna and Jerzy inside, and the driver nodded. 'We'll try. Ten złotys.' Tata climbed in to the front seat and banged the door, and they drove off through the unlit streets towards the bridge.

'Tell us . . .' said Tata. 'We've just got back from Wilno.'

The driver reached for his Mewa cigarettes, on the ledge above the wheel. 'It started first thing on the first – they bombed the racecourse down in Mokotów, about five in the morning.' He lit a cigarette and drew a deep breath. 'I've been smoking twice the usual. You might be safer in Praga, but . . .'

Tata asked about their street.

'I haven't heard anything, I expect it's all right. You know the English and French have declared, don't you?'

'Thank God.'

'On the third: you should've seen the crowds outside the British Embassy. You couldn't move on Nowy Świat – they were singing "Warszawianka", and "God Save the King", waving flags, throwing flowers . . .' He took another puff.

'Does that mean it'll be over quite soon?' Jerzy asked.

The driver shrugged. 'I haven't seen an English plane yet. But if anyone thinks Warsaw's going to surrender . . .' He looked at Tata. 'Are you reporting tomorrow?'

Tata nodded. 'And you?'

'I already have – I'm just waiting to hear where they'll send me.'

Listening in the back, Anna stared at the dim lights on the dashboard, and clenched her hands on the seat. The cigarette smoke wafted towards her and she coughed. Tata turned round. 'All right?'

She nodded, a pool of nervousness flooding her stomach. They had reached the bridge: a siren wailed, and there was a sudden burst of gunfire. Anna grabbed Jerzy's arm. 'What's that?'

'Anti-aircraft fire,' said the driver. 'Don't worry – we'll be all right.' Then the sky was lit by a flare and as they raced over the bridge the whole of the Vistula gleamed. 'We're across!' the driver yelled, and Anna and Jerzy lifted their heads and turned to look through the back window. The black shape of a plane circled once, then flew slowly downriver, searching.

Anna found herself shaking. Jerzy put his arm round her and she felt him trembling too.

'Well done. We're almost there,' Tata was saying to the driver.

'Think I'll make this my last fare – I don't like staying inside, it feels as if I'm doing something useful out here. But my wife will be worried sick.'

'And mine also,' said Tata. 'This is the street – thank God they haven't touched it. We'll walk now; you get home.'

'I'll take you to the door. What's the number?'

'Thirty-four.'

He pulled up outside the apartment house, and they got out

quickly, looking up to the two big windows of the sitting room. The curtains were closely drawn. Tata paid the driver. 'Goodnight. Thank you.'

He nodded. 'All the best. You get to bed, young lady.'

Anna smiled weakly. 'Goodnight.'

He drove away, turning into a side street, and Tata felt for his keys. Inside, they walked quickly up the stairs. There was no sound from the ground-floor apartments but from behind their own door they could just hear the wireless. Tata turned the key. They went in, saw a low light from the sitting room, and at once Teresa was in the hall.

'Tomasz!' Anna and Jerzy stood watching as she ran towards their father and into his arms. For a few moments they held each other, and Anna realized that she had never before seen them give each other anything but the lightest kiss on the cheek. Then Tata gently drew away, and Teresa looked at Anna and Jerzy and burst into tears. 'Come here.' They hugged her, and she said: 'I thought you'd never get back. They're bombing railway lines everywhere . . .'

'I think we might have made one of the last journeys,' said Tata. 'Are you all right?'

'Oh, yes, just so worried. You must be very hungry. I'll make something at once.'

They followed her into the kitchen. 'I'm starving,' said Jerzy.

'It's been difficult to shop. Only a couple of places were open at all yesterday, but I've managed to stock up a little.' Teresa was slicing a loaf, spreading plum jam she'd made earlier in the summer. 'Here – have this while I make some soup.'

'I'm going to wash,' said Tata. He went out to the bathroom and then they heard him go into the surgery and close the door. The faint ting of the telephone receiver being picked up sounded in the hall.

'Reporting,' said Jerzy, helping himself to another slice of bread.

Anna sat at the table and watched Teresa stirring the pan on the stove. 'Perhaps he won't have to go yet,' she said. 'He might not have to go at all – if the British and the French send help soon, he might not have to.' Teresa went on stirring.

After a while they heard the telephone ting again, faintly, as if the receiver were being put down with care, and they waited. Silence. Then the surgery door clicked open and they heard him walk down the corridor.

'Well,' he said, standing in the doorway. 'I leave tomorrow morning – for the hospital in Brześć.'

'Tomorrow?' Teresa left the stove and came across to him, putting a pale hand on his sleeve. 'Really, tomorrow?'

'I'm afraid so.' He put his arm round her, and smiled at Anna and Jerzy. 'I don't imagine it will be for very long. And you two are to look after Teresa for me until I come home.'

'Where's Brześć?' asked Anna.

Tata rolled his eyes. 'All your geography lessons, and still you know nothing.'

'It's somewhere in the east,' said Jerzy.

'Near Russia?' Anna asked.

'Quite near the Russian border, yes.'

'Oh.' She thought for a moment. Tata would be safer there, wouldn't he? Surely the Germans would never get that far.

'And now,' he said, 'I think we are all very tired. Let's have some supper and an early night. The soup smells wonderful.'

As they ate, they could hear more bursts of anti-aircraft fire.

Teresa described how she had woken on the morning of the first and switched on the wireless as usual. 'It was like a play,' she said. 'I couldn't believe what I was hearing. They called for great care in using arms, to save them as much as possible.' She looked at Tata. 'We are horribly ill-defended.'

He nodded. 'I'm afraid it's true.'

In bed, Anna and Jerzy lay listening in the dark. They could hear Tata and Teresa moving about the apartment, turning out lights, putting dishes away, switching off the wireless, and locking the front door. The evening sounds they always heard.

They both appeared like shadows at the door. 'Goodnight,' said Tata. 'Sleep well – try not to worry.'

'Goodnight, Tata. Goodnight, Teresa.'

Then they went out to their own room, and closed the door.

It was very early in the morning when they woke to find Tata standing between their beds, already dressed in his uniform and carrying his leather suitcase.

Anna sat up, confused. Pale grey light was filtering through the curtains, and it felt cold. 'You're not going already?'

'I've got to, darling.'

She began to cry, still half-asleep. 'Please don't. Please.'

'I'm sure it won't be for long,' he said. 'Please be brave.'

Jerzy was out of bed, pulling on his dressing gown. 'Come on, Anna, let's see him to the door.'

Teresa was in the hall, washed and dressed, her hair brushed neatly, her eyes red. She smiled thinly as they joined her: Anna swallowed. Then Tata turned to hug each one, and went to the front door. He fumbled at the latch, then laughed. 'It's still locked.'

'Good,' said Jerzy. 'I hope you've lost the key.'

'I wish I had,' Tata said. 'Unfortunately . . . Teresa, dear, get it, will you?' She went silently to the kitchen, came back and unlocked the door herself. 'There,' she said. 'Now you can go. Come back very soon.'

'I will. Perhaps you could wave from the window?'

They ran to the sitting room, and waited, listening to his footsteps going down the stairs, and the front door bang. They saw him going down the street, which looked damp and cold, turning to wave, a tall, kind-faced man in a uniform which already made him look as if he belonged to an army barracks, and not with them. He smiled up at them as they waved back, and blew them a kiss. Then he walked away.

Within days the bombardment of Praga was so heavy that Teresa decided they should try to get across the river to the city centre, and stay with Wiktoria. Marta left to join her own family: they all cried as they kissed her goodbye, and stood at the window to watch her go, too, but running, not like Tata. Then Teresa packed one large suitcase between them, and the last of the food: not a single shop was open, now; they had flour, half a kilo of sugar and a bag of potatoes. She tried to phone Wiktoria but couldn't get through.

'I don't imagine things will have been any easier for her,' she said. 'We'd better take everything we have.'

Since Tata left, Teresa was the only one to have ventured out, and that was three days ago. They left the apartment house early in the morning, hurried down the street and turned into the main road. Then they stopped, and for a moment Anna lost all sense of who or where she was. Jerzy whistled. 'Phew . . .'

Half the street was filled with rubble. The fronts of several houses had been completely blown away; in the rooms, pitifully exposed, broken furniture was flung up against walls; in one block a bath hung crazily from twisted pipes into a gaping hole. From beneath a heap of bricks Anna saw something bloody and horrible obtrude, and grabbed Teresa's arm. 'What's that?'

'I – I don't know.' Teresa's face was a sickly yellow. 'Come on.'

The Kierbedzia Bridge was crowded with people running, carrying suitcases, bags of food, staring children. All through the city they passed bombed buildings, trams hurled from the rails, boarded shops and cafés; in one street a group of old men and women was digging frantically into the rubble, calling the same name over and over again: 'Ryszard! Ryszard!' On another corner a woman stood with a baby in her arms, the apartment house behind her shattered into two ugly halves; she looked at them blankly as they hurried past.

Aunt Wiktoria's apartment in Hoża was not far from the main telephone exchange; so far, though that seemed a likely target for the Germans, the street had suffered no damage. Inside the building, they climbed the stairs to Number 4 and rang the bell. There were voices from inside. 'Who's with her?' Jerzy asked.

The door opened and Wiktoria, wearing her dressing gown, her hair unbrushed, stared at them. 'Oh, my dears . . .' Behind her they could see through the open door to the living room three or four people huddled on the floor in blankets. 'Come in,' she said, and led them to the kitchen, closing the living room door as they went past.

The kettle was on the stove. 'I was just about to make tea for everyone. Put that case down, Jerzy, and get your stepmother a chair; she looks dreadful.'

'Nonsense,' said Teresa, and began to sway.

'Quick!' Jerzy and Anna rushed to help her sit down, Wiktoria pushed her head on to the table and waved at the sink. 'Get her a glass of water.'

After a few moments Teresa raised her head and Anna held the glass to her lips. They were chalky white. She sipped, then nodded weakly. 'Better . . .'

Wiktoria put a pot of tea on the table and set out a number of thick glasses. A pale young girl appeared in the doorway and nodded to them all.

'Danuta,' said Wiktoria, 'is from Poznań, the daughter of a dear friend. If she stays in Poznań she has no hope at all. Danuta, my dear, this is Teresa, my brother's wife, and his son and daughter, Jerzy and Anna. Sit down.' She began to pour out the tea. 'And I'm afraid that this is all I can offer you.'

An elderly couple came in. 'Danuta's parents,' said Wiktoria, and introduced them all again.

'We've brought some food,' said Jerzy. 'Flour, and – '

Wiktoria cut him off. 'If you had come earlier, my dears, I should have given you my own bed. As it is, I have to tell you that every blanket I have is already being used and that you cannot possibly stay. However – ' She got up and took a bunch of keys from a hook on the shelf by the stove. 'Your cousin and his wife managed to get away in the first two days. With any luck, they are now well inside Romania, and their apartment is empty. You must go there – it's only a couple of blocks away, on Żórawia. Tell me about Tomasz. When did he go?'

She was like him, Anna thought, sipping hot weak tea and listening to Teresa describe Tata's hurried departure. Tall, well-built, made you feel safe. She wished they could stay.

Another woman joined them, and the kitchen began to feel crowded and uncomfortable. They got up to go. Wiktoria refused to take even a few potatoes. 'We'll manage,' she said at the door, kissing them. 'Just let's pray the British send help soon.'

Their cousin lived in a large block near Three Crosses Square, and not far from Central Park; from the sitting room window they could see the yellowing trees. At the back, the windows of the kitchen and bedroom overlooked the garden shared by the whole block, planted with shrubs and roses round a small lawn. There was no one out there, and the grass needed cutting. Many of the blinds were drawn: it felt suddenly very quiet, and strange, to be in an empty apartment belonging to people fled to another country. In the main bedroom, clothes spilled from the chest of drawers, and the wardrobe door swung open. There was no food in the kitchen except a bag of dried beans at the bottom of a cupboard. 'Good,' said Teresa, her voice sounding very loud, 'we'll have bean soup.' Jerzy pulled a face, and went back to the sitting room; they heard him switch on the wireless and went to listen. Mayor Starzyński was appealing for order in the city: he sounded calm and encouraging, as though no one had anything to fear, as long as they were sensible. Tonight, said the announcer who followed him, the Polish Ambassador in London would be making a broadcast to the whole nation, from the BBC.

Jerzy found a pack of cards in the sideboard, and they spent the rest of the morning playing rummy. Teresa baked potatoes for lunch; as they sat down to eat they heard the scream of low-flying planes and Jerzy rushed to the window.

'Come away!' Teresa was on her feet.

'It's all right.' He was craning his neck. 'They're quite a long way off.'

They went to the window, saw two planes hover briefly like malignant birds and then a sudden fall of black rain and a dreadful roar

66

as buildings beyond the park spewed flames and rooftops into the air.

'It's like a film,' Jerzy said under his breath, and the planes flew steadily on.

That night they sat huddled round the wireless, listening to the gentle, cultured voice of Count Edward Raczyński, speaking from London.

'Attacked by the enemy,' he said, 'Poland is heroically resisting the armies of the invader, evoking the admiration and the most profound feelings of sympathy of the whole world . . . Twenty-five years ago, when the first cadres of the Polish Army marched off into battle, so as to bear witness to the continued existence of the Polish nation amidst the conflagration of the world war, we were fighting for liberty and for our right to an independent existence. Today, each of us feels as strong in a conviction that in this hour of trial we must pass the test of history. The future of the Polish nation is at stake . . .'

Outside the curtained windows, somewhere in the city, came fierce bursts of anti-aircraft fire, and then an explosion, as another building fell. Anna gripped the arms of her chair. The voice of the Ambassador buzzed with static.

'The Polish nation will pass this test, which will lead to victory. We have linked our destiny with the destinies of Great Britain and France, bound not only by written alliances and treaties, not only by fundamental interests of security and the defence of our state, but also by common ideals which Europe cannot allow to be trodden on . . . On land, on sea, and in the air, we march shoulder to shoulder today.'

'But where *are* they?' said Jerzy impatiently. 'Where's the RAF? Where are the French?'

'Sssh!' Teresa was leaning forward, turning up the volume.

'As the representative of the Polish Republic in London, I affirm that on the part of leading British statesmen I have found during this difficult period the most complete comprehension of Polish interests, and the unchangeable traditional fidelity to the given word . . . Into the scales of war, Great Britain has now cast all the forces of the empire. She is determined to fight on Poland's side until victory is achieved.'

'I hope Tata is listening to this,' Anna said. 'They'll have a wireless, won't they, in his barracks?'

'I expect they've drafted him into the hospital in Brześć,' said Teresa. 'He might not have time to listen.'

'But it's a wonderful speech, isn't it?'

'Shut up!' said Jerzy. 'You've just missed something – he's reading a message from Chamberlain.'

'We in Great Britain are watching with profound admiration the heroic struggle of the Polish forces against the enemy invading their land. Great Britain and France have entered the war with the determination to aid with all their power the resistance of Poland to aggression. They are strengthened by the knowledge that they are fighting for things that are greater than the interests of any one country – for honour, for justice, and for the freedom of the world. Those who have taken up arms in such a cause are assured, whatever sacrifices they may be called upon to make, of victory in the end.'

And then Count Raczyński was wishing them all goodnight, and through the buzzing wireless came the first few tender bars of Chopin's *Polonaise*. Outside the curtained windows, the bombs went on falling.

'Today, Warsaw defending the honour of Poland has reached the climax of her greatness and glory.' That was Starzyński's last, hoarse wireless message to the city. Warsaw, almost the last place in Poland to surrender, finally did so on the 28 September. They heard it on the wireless, but they did not need to hear. By then, whole streets of the city were ablaze or in ruins. Nowy Świat, one of the most important arteries, was destroyed; every hospital had been bombed; epidemics were raging. There was no gas, no electricity, no mains water for drinking or fire fighting, almost no food. Not a single British plane, nor any kind of military assistance, had been sent; two hundred thousand had died. The government had fled across the Carpathian Mountains in the south-east to Romania. And on the 17th, Russia had invaded eastern Poland. Holed up in their apartment on Żórawia Street, Teresa and the children heard this on the wireless some days later and were stunned. When the news of the surrender came, and they made their way, famished and apprehensive, to Wiktoria's apartment, she met them in tears.

'I can't believe it, I can't believe it . . .' She sat trembling on the edge of a chair in the sitting room, hungry and debilitated, all her assurance gone. 'To think it is only twenty years since the last war,

68

the last occupation. Twenty years of independence – and now it's all gone again. What will they do to us now, I wonder?'

'What do you think will happen to Tata?' Anna asked, because she couldn't bear not to.

Wiktoria bit her lip and shook her head, repeating everything like an old woman. 'I don't know, I don't know. Some of them are coming back, I believe – the Russians can't take every man alive a prisoner, surely?' She blew her nose. 'You must get back to Praga, all of you, and find out what's happened. If Tomasz does get home, and finds it empty . . .'

'Is it true that Hitler's going to hold a victory parade?' Jerzy asked.

'God knows . . .' She began to cry again.

Teresa stood up. 'Well, we shall not be here to see it,' she said. 'Do you want to come with us, Wiktoria?'

'How can I?' She gestured weakly at the room. There were whole panes missing from the windows, a film of plaster dust over every piece of furniture. 'I'm not leaving just so that the Germans can take over my home – anyway, my friends are still here. We'll – we'll manage, I suppose. Go on, go back quickly now.'

'We'll keep in touch.'

Wiktoria nodded. 'Yes. Yes. Keep in touch.'

They walked all the way back to Praga through a shell-shocked city, bodies sprawled on the pavements by great mounds of rubble, thousands of makeshift graves in the streets and squares. They passed a large *gimnazium* school where a cavalry unit had been stationed and saw dead horses in the playground, heads askew on glossy necks, tongues lolling, eyes rolled up in terror.

The Kierbedzia Bridge was still thronged with refugees. 'Why do they keep coming?' Jerzy asked, panting.

'Perhaps they don't know yet. Perhaps it's worse everywhere else.' Teresa's eyes were searching. 'Do you think your father – ?' Every now and then a knot of uniformed men, dirty and dishevelled, appeared in the crowd, returning home.

'Do you think he's in Praga?' asked Anna. 'Do you think he might be?'

'I shouldn't really think so. Not yet.'

All the way back she thought: make him be there. Make him be there.

When they reached their street they saw that it was covered, like almost everywhere else, in broken glass and rubble. Their house and all those nearby were still standing, and largely untouched, but they looked dead, eyeless and abandoned in a pale afternoon sun.

They got inside, climbed the stairs, and Teresa turned the key of their own door: they stepped into a cold dark hall. 'Tata?' Anna couldn't help it, even though she didn't really believe there'd be an answer. They walked down the corridor and shivered; the sitting room floor was covered in a silvery mass of splintered glass. In the bathroom, when Teresa turned on the taps, there was a deep shuddering cough in the pipes and a trickle of brown water leaked into the basin, then stopped.

Anna went into the surgery. Books were sprawled open on the floor; a drift of papers, covered in thick dust, spilt out from boxes. Panes here were mostly broken, too; so was the glass in the cabinet of instruments on the wall, and in the picture of Mama on the desk; a few dry leaves from the chestnut tree in the courtyard had blown through the holes in the window. She lifted the black telephone receiver, and heard nothing. So they couldn't even phone Wiktoria now, and Tata wouldn't be able to call them, either. On the blotting pad stood the black box camera they'd taken on holiday. She put down the receiver and picked up the camera, leaving a clean white square in the dust.

Months later, she took the film to a Polish photographer to be developed, and she and Jerzy sat in their father's empty surgery and stared at the prints. From under the silver birch trees he smiled at them in black and white. There were pictures of Anna and Jerzy in the boat, in swimsuits, laughing and fooling about in the water. It seemed to her then absurd that they could not have known – had she thought, once, that she was dreaming her own life? The whole of her past, of Tata's and Jerzy's past, looked now like a distant dream, as insubstantial as light and air, a family drifting downriver like Alice in Wonderland, innocent, uncaring; something that might or might not have happened a very long time ago, before the terror began, and everything changed for ever.

3
Warsaw, 1939–1941

Inhabitants of the General Government!
Victorious German arms have, once and for all, put an end to the
Polish State. Behind you lies an episode in history which you should
forget forthwith; it belongs to the past and will never return.

Inhabitants of the General Government!

The Führer has decided to form a General Government as part
of the territory of the Polish State, and to place me at its head.
The General Government can become the refuge of the Polish people
if they will submit loyally and completely to the orders of the
German authorities and accomplish the task set them in the German
war effort. Every attempt to oppose the New German order will
be ruthlessly suppressed.

> Hans Frank, Governor General
> Kraków, 12 October 1939

Hans Frank was Hitler's lawyer. A large, fleshy man, in the years
before 1939 he had visited Poland on a number of occasions, well
dressed, smiling. Now, appointed by Hitler as Governor General, he
was installed in Kraków, in Wawel Castle, ancient palace of Polish
kings. The swastika fluttered above the city; from here, Frank ruled
the 'General Government', a large central and southern area of the
country. On the west, it was bordered by Polish territory seized into
the German Reich. On the east, along the river Bug, it was bordered
by Polish territory seized by the Soviet Union. Under the terms of
the Nazi–Soviet Pact, secretly signed by Ribbentrop and Molotov in
August, Poland was held in pincers.

Kraków, beautiful university city, was now the capital; Warsaw
had been stripped of her historic, heroic role, and there, on 26
October, Dr Ludwig Fischer, lean and grey-haired, became District
Governor.

Soon, the walls of the city were plastered with notices and proclamations, in German and Polish. When the decree announcing the
'refuge' of the General Government went up, so did a poster showing

a Polish soldier in rags, bent over a wounded comrade. His bloody fist was raised against a background of the ruins of Warsaw beneath a lurid sky. A picture of Neville Chamberlain hung there, and the caption read: ENGLAND, THIS IS YOUR WORK! Anna saw a copy of the poster, pasted up in the main shopping street in Praga, and felt sick. She thought of the sunny afternoon in Wiktoria's apartment, hiding in the bathroom and listening to the grown-ups talking about how if there was a war the British and French would come and save them. She remembered listening to the wireless with Jerzy and Teresa, to Count Raczyński reading the stirring message from Chamberlain, his assurances of victory. She didn't know what to think about the poster – she knew it was called propaganda, and that she should ignore it, but nonetheless it confused and frightened her.

In October, the first snow began to fall. A few days later, frost gripped the city, and the temperature plunged into an abyss of cold. Figures in black picked their way slowly through the streets, past snow-covered mounds of rubble from the siege. Peasants from beyond the suburbs drove through with their carts piled up and turned to stare at the German patrols on every street. Coal vanished, reappearing on the black market at terrifying prices. It was strictly forbidden to venture into the forests outside the city and forage for wood, but people went, or stayed in bed all day to keep warm, boarding up the holes in the windows with cardboard. The mains water was still cut off: almost all the pipes had been destroyed during the bombing, and long, shivering queues formed at the frozen pumps in streets and courtyards. Some electricity was restored, but there were frequent power cuts. On milder days, people walked to the farms beyond the suburbs – Teresa and the children went to the fields in Bródno – and searched the hard ground for potatoes, turnips and cabbages. Most of the farmhouses were empty, the farmers captured by the advancing German troops, their wives and children fled. Machinery stood unoiled and neglected, the animals had gone. There was little to be found in the way of food, but occasionally people stumbled on rusting guns and rifles, hastily buried by Polish Army units before they were taken prisoner. Even in Central Park, weapons had been buried. Few people dared to dig them up and take them home, but the places where they lay were carefully noted.

New notices went up: all wireless sets were to be handed in to collecting points all over Warsaw. To own a wireless, even to be found listening to one, was punishable by death. It was also punishable by death to go out after curfew. In the long, freezing winter evenings, people were trapped in their bombarded homes; they sat in the dark, eking out candles, isolated and afraid.

Early one morning Anna woke to hear something being smashed. For a few moments, dazed and sleepy, she thought it was a window breaking; then she realized that the sound was coming from right inside the apartment, from the sitting room. She scrambled out of bed, and ran down the corridor. The banging and smashing grew louder; she could hear Jerzy swearing.

'What on earth – '

Inside the sitting room, she found him with a hammer, sweating. On the floor at his feet lay pieces of Bakelite, brown mesh, wires and glass valves.

'Jerzy!'

'If they have it, they have it in pieces,' he said, kicking the mess into a heap. 'Do they think we're going to let them confiscate *our* wireless, and have them and their fat wives sit listening to it?' He marched out of the room, and came back with a cardboard box. 'Come on, give me a hand.'

They knelt down and scooped it all into the box. Anna picked up a broken piece from the front, with half of the company name snapped off. Tele – Telefunken, it had been. A German set. They'd all been so pleased when Tata brought it home two years ago. She dropped the piece on to the heap.

'Right,' said Jerzy. 'I'm off.'

'Do be careful,' said Anna, following him to the front door. 'I mean – don't say anything to upset them.'

'Oh, but I want to upset them! I'm looking forward to this.' He went out of the door and down the stairs, whistling.

Within weeks, secret listening stations had been set up, monitoring the broadcasts from London and Paris. The first underground paper, *Polska Żyje*, Poland Alive, began to circulate. Soon, through the underground *komunikats* – news bulletins mimeographed on wafer-thin paper, distributed and instantly destroyed – everyone knew that a Government in Exile had been formed in Paris, under the leadership of President Raczkiewicz and General Sikorski, Prime Minister and Commander-in-Chief of the Polish Armed Forces abroad.

From all over the country, disguised as railway workers and peasant farmers, men travelled south to the frozen Carpathian Mountains and attempted the dangerous and punishing journey across them at night. There were German dog patrols up to forty miles deep into the frontier territory, and escapees were arrested if they were caught, and later sent to Auschwitz. But thousands reached Romania, and from there made the long journey to France, to join the Polish forces.

Those who remained formed themselves into what was to become the most powerful resistance movement in occupied Europe. There was an entire civilian administration, the *Delegatura*, the Government Delegate. Responsible to the Government in Exile, the *Delegatura* secretly ran a judiciary, schools and hospitals – all the functions of the state, ready to assume power as soon as the war was over.

There was, too, an underground military resistance, organized in clandestine cells all over the country. The Union of Armed Struggle, as it was first known, was responsible to General Sikorski in Paris, and directed from Warsaw by Colonel 'Grot' Rowecki. His deputy was eventually to be General 'Bór' Komorowski.

'Anna, Jerzy! Wake up – there's a letter from your father.'

They woke in the kitchen, where they all slept each night on mattresses next to the tall tiled stove. Teresa in her dressing gown, was holding a small grey sealed card.

'Where's it from?' Jerzy leaned across and peered at the postmark as she sat down beside Anna. 'Kozielsk . . . where's that?'

Teresa shook her head. 'We'll have to look it up.' She carefully slit open the card, and they read:

30.11.39

My darlings,

I am in good health. Write to me often about everything. Are the children going to school? I hug and kiss you with all my heart.

Tomasz

'He's a prisoner?' asked Anna. She looked again the Russian lettering on the front of the card.

'Yes – but at least we can write to him now.' Teresa looked suddenly calmer than she had for months. 'Let's have breakfast.'

They sat at the table in their overcoats. Breakfast was black bread, available only on rations, which Jerzy had queued for an hour to get the day before, and weak ersatz coffee.

'Disgusting,' he said. 'What the hell do they make it from?'

Anna swallowed and grimaced. 'Do you think it's acorns?'

'It's barley,' said Teresa. 'Go and get the atlas, Jerzy.'

He returned with it from the sitting room and they pored over

Russia, searching for Kozielsk. 'Oh, here it is,' Teresa said at last. It was deep inside Russia, east of Smoleńsk.

'What do you think he's doing?' Anna asked. 'Do you think he really is in good health?'

'He wouldn't tell us if he wasn't, would he?' Jerzy said.

'But his writing's quite strong, isn't it?' said Teresa.

'He won't get a letter from us until next year, now,' Jerzy said, tearing off another hunk of bread. 'I can't imagine Christmas without him.'

'I can't imagine Christmas at all,' said Anna.

Last year, at *Wigilia*, they had all gone together to midnight mass. This year, the curfew made that impossible. Wiktoria came to stay with them, and they all went to mass on Christmas Day morning, in a church which had escaped any damage in the bombing.

It was bitterly cold, but the church was packed; the unheated aisles were clouded with breath, and when they knelt to pray the scraping of boots and shoes echoed on the icy stone. A single tall candle burned on the altar, from where the crucifix and all the tapestries had been removed: Anna imagined the priest hiding them somewhere deep in the crypt, perhaps even daring to keep them in his own apartment – anywhere, as long as the Germans could not take them away. Throughout the service people's eyes wandered upwards, to look at the shattered stained-glass windows, roughly patched with pieces of wood. After the mass, and prayers for the souls of those who had died in the siege, the priest said: 'Let us have a few moments of silent prayer for those dear to us.'

Kneeling between Jerzy and Teresa, Anna clenched her hands. *Please, please let Tata come home to us soon.* She struggled to imagine her father as a prisoner, could not even begin to imagine what his prison might look like. A fortress? A row of huts? Then she had a sudden image of lines and lines of men in heavy coats, stamping up and down in the cold, being shouted at, and she began to cry. *Please look after him.*

'And now,' the priest was saying quietly, 'perhaps you would all like to join me in the National Anthem.' Still kneeling, they began to whisper:

'Poland is not yet lost,
As long as we are alive,
We will take back with our sabre
What the enemy have taken from us . . .'

At the end, when they slowly stood up again, almost everyone was crying.

'Did you pray for Tata?' Jerzy asked as they came out, stiff with cold, on to the steps.

'Sort of,' said Anna. 'Did you?'

'I tried. I don't know if . . . if I really can believe any more.'

On the corner of the street a group of German soldiers was watching the congregation come out, blowing into their hands.

'Hope they freeze to death,' he said loudly.

Teresa and Wiktoria came up behind them. 'Come on, children, quickly.'

By January, they had all lost so much weight that their clothes hung loosely and hunger and the monotonous diet were fraying their nerves. Rationing had been introduced two weeks before Christmas, but there was little to buy with their cards. There was no fruit, few vegetables, only potatoes, potatoes. Teresa made potato soup, baked potatoes, potato cutlets and *placki* – potato cakes fried in oil, for there was no butter, though later the Germans introduced margarine. There were pulses, there was pasta; they ate endless bowls of soup. Each day they took it in turns to queue for the coarse dark bread which was now the only loaf you could buy.

'It makes you fart,' said Jerzy. 'Only the Nazis could make bread that makes you fart.'

Occasionally they were able to get *słonina* from the butcher – pieces of salted bacon fat with the rind still on, and that did add flavour to the soups and dumplings. Anna dreamed of oranges, and juicy apples. She was getting spots. Restless and uneasy, she longed to be back at school, but even by February the gates were still closed.

In the first week of March, they had a visitor.

It was still bitterly cold, and they still spent most of their time in the kitchen. This morning they were using the last of the coal, the stove was almost out, and it wasn't much warmer in here than in the sitting room, where the windows even now were partly boarded up. Putty and glass were like gold now, impossible to find except on the black market, and barely affordable then. Jerzy was in the sitting room, practising half-heartedly in the semi-darkness; from the kitchen, where she and Teresa were peeling potatoes, Anna heard the doorbell ring once, sharply, and Jerzy break off, and go to answer it. She looked at Teresa, who pursed her lips, shrugging.

'I'd better go and see.'

Anna followed her out, and found her headmistress standing in the hall. She was panting a little beneath her coat and scarf; wet snow dripped from her boots.

'Pani Jawicz!' Anna stood uncertainly, then hurried across to her. If Pani Jawicz were here, stout and ordinary, she could be ordinary again. Perhaps school *was* starting – thank God. The boredom, the dreariness, of being shut up here!

Teresa was offering to take her coat, but it was a gesture only.

'Thank you, my dear, but I'll keep it on, this cold is terrible.' She smiled at Anna's eager face. 'How are you all managing?' She followed Jerzy down the corridor to the kitchen, where they all sat round the table like old friends. 'Ah, that's better. Now tell me – have you any news of the doctor?'

They told her about the postcard, the few lines.

'We write to him,' said Anna. 'I write all the time, to this Kozielsk, but he never writes back.'

Jerzy got up and riddled the stove.

'Tch, tch, tch.' Pani Jawicz was shaking her head. 'Such a good man, and you are not alone, my dears, we have many, many pupils in the same situation, waiting for news from their fathers.' She leaned across the table and patted Anna's hand. 'You need something to take your minds off it, and besides, we cannot let you all sit about, learning nothing!'

Anna smiled, feeling better than she had for months. 'Is school opening up again?'

'Not . . . exactly. You don't know what's happened to the schools?'

'What? What's happening?' Behind her, Jerzy had stopped raking the few remaining coals. He came over, and pulled out a chair.

'They have been permanently closed,' said Pani Jawicz. 'In the primary schools, the German "authorities" ' – she pulled a face at the word – 'have forbidden the teaching of anything except arithmetic and the German language. As for the *gimnazium* and *liceum* – pupils of secondary age are to learn a trade, nothing more. You should be working towards your exams, both of you, but there is no question of your going back to school for that.' She paused. 'May I ask what you were reading last summer?'

Jerzy and Anna looked at each other. 'Tata was reading us short stories by Sienkiewicz,' Anna said slowly. 'When we were on holiday. And I was reading *A Tale of Two Cities*.'

'And did you finish them?'

'No.' The Sienkiewicz volume must still be somewhere in Tata's study – perhaps it had never been unpacked from his bag.

'That's a pity,' said Pani Jawicz, 'because from now on they are banned.'

'*Banned?*'

'Sienkiewicz is banned. Mickiewicz is banned. You may take it that all Polish authors – and, I expect, all English ones, too – are now strictly forbidden. Almost all the textbooks at school have been impounded. It is forbidden to display pictures of any national hero, either – last week I spent the day in school taking down all the pictures: Chopin, Marie-Curie, Piłsudski, Paderewski, . . . I had to take down the map of Poland, too – you remember that large one in the assembly hall?'

'Yes.' Anna had sat underneath it scores of times. She thought of it being taken down, and handed over to some Nazi bureaucrat, leaving a dusty oblong on the wall. There would be shapes like that all through the school – the walls were filled with pictures from Polish history.

'And naturally,' said Pani Jawicz, 'I had to take down the flag behind the dais.'

'You gave it to them?'

'I . . . put it away,' she said, with an almost imperceptible smile. 'So – you understand the situation. Education – Polish education – has been crushed. Officially, Anna, you may train as dressmaker. Or perhaps a cook. You would like that?'

She slowly shook her head, feeling a great lump in her throat.

'And you, Jerzy – ' Pani Jawicz turned to him. 'An electrician? A plumber? A mechanic?'

He shrugged, looking at the tablecloth.

'They have closed the universities, the medical schools, the academies,' Pani Jawicz said bitterly. 'In Kraków, we understand, the professors have been imprisoned, perhaps even – ' She broke off. 'So. You work, or you train for a trade. However – Jerzy, please, come and sit down, my dear, I haven't come only to bring bad news.' She lowered her voice as he came over and pulled out a chair. 'Naturally, we are not putting up with this. We are setting up a network of schools – TON, we are calling it: Tajna Organizacja Nanczycielstwa, the Secret Schooling Organization, responsible to the Education Department of the Delegatura. All our staff are joining, so you will have the same teachers, Anna, for the same subjects – Pani Sokołowa for Latin, and so on – but you will be taught in their own homes. You will study in a small group, a *komplet* of perhaps five or six girls, and you will go to a different address each time, and arrive one by one. You understand why? You understand that you must be absolutely scrupulous in never discussing it, where you are to meet next, or who with, except in the teacher's house?'

Anna looked at her. It felt extraordinary to have Pani Jawicz, whom she was used to seeing on a dais at assembly, firmly addressing the whole school, seated here at their kitchen table, talking almost in a whisper. Through a gap in a broken pane where the stuffed newspaper had come loose, a thin icy draught was playing on her neck, and she shivered.

'I've frightened you?' Pani Jawicz asked kindly. 'You mustn't be afraid, you must be brave. I'm sure that's what your father would want, isn't it?' She turned to Teresa. 'Of course, Anna must have your permission to continue her education in this rather bizarre fashion.'

Teresa half-smiled, biting her lip. 'Yes – of course. I am trying to think what my husband would say. I'm sure he wouldn't want her to miss her studies, but – ' She took a deep breath. 'It sounds very dangerous. It is a great responsibility for me to agree to it, you understand. If anything should happen . . .'

'Teresa!' said Anna. 'Please! Tata asked about school, didn't he? That was the one thing he asked about. I *know* he'd want us to go.' What would she do if Teresa said no? Sit cooped up up here peeling potatoes? Go to some horrible trade school and train to be a skivvy? 'Nothing will happen, nothing will happen! I'll be so careful, I promise.'

'But it could happen,' Pani Jawicz said slowly. 'You must realize that, Anna. I don't want to frighten you, but I must be clear: if we are discovered, we will be arrested, there is no question. However, I'm sure, as you say, that you will be extremely careful, and if everyone is sensible then there is no reason why you should not study for your exams, and eventually sit them, so that when the war ends you will be able to go on to university.'

'Medical school.'

'Medical school. So – ' She turned to Teresa again.

Teresa gave a long sigh. 'Very well. But if there is any sign that you are in real danger, you stop immediately, Anna, you understand?'

'Yes, yes. Thank you. Oh, thank goodness! When do we start?'

Pani Jawicz smiled. 'Next Monday. You will go to Pani Sokołowa's apartment in Białołęcka Street – you know where that is, of course.'

'Yes.' It was one of the longest streets in Praga.

'Good. Number fifty-nine. Take an exercise book if you can, or paper at least – we are very short, as you can imagine. If you see any of your classmates on the way, ignore them. Each of you will arrive at a different time – you will be there by nine-fifteen, please. Pani Sokołowa will give you all something for lunch, and you will leave by two. You have taken all that in?'

'Number fifty-nine Białołęka Street,' said Anna. 'Thank you.'

'Good, good. So – now there is only Jerzy to organize!' She smiled at him encouragingly. 'I believe Pan Korczak will be coming to see you tomorrow, to tell you of the arrangements for the *liceum*.'

Jerzy was picking at a piece of loose thread in the tablecloth; he did not look up. 'I'm not going back to school.'

'Oh? And why is that? Surely you are not afraid?'

'No!'

'I see.' Pani Jawicz rose heavily, exchanging glances with Teresa. 'Well – I shall leave you to discuss it in private. Or with Pan Korczak tomorrow.' She moved towards the door.

'Jerzy!' Anna hissed. 'Get up! Don't be so rude!'

He pushed back his chair and went to hold the door open, but he didn't speak.

'Thank you.' Pani Jawicz went out with Teresa, and down the corridor to the front door. Anna and Jerzy could hear them talking there in low voices.

'Jerzy?'

'What?'

'Come and sit down. What's the matter with you?'

'Nothing!' He came over and kicked the chair leg against the table.

'What do you mean, nothing? Look at you!'

The front door closed, and Teresa came hurrying back.

'Jerzy . . .' She put her hand on his shoulder. 'What is it, dear? What's troubling you?'

He shrugged, exaggeratedly, so that her hand on his shoulder became awkward, and she took it away, sighing.

'I should have thought you would have jumped at the chance to go on studying. As Anna says, so long as you are not in real danger it is certainly what your father would want.'

'But he doesn't know what it's really like now, does he?' Jerzy snapped. 'He doesn't know how we're scrimping, and hungry, hungry all the bloody time? How are we supposed to live, if none of us is working?'

'Well, of course I shall have to find some kind of work . . .'

'Doing what? Why should you work for us? I'm – I'm the man of the house now, aren't I? I should be working, not creeping off to school!'

'You're still a boy,' said Teresa. 'You're only fifteen, Jerzy! And what do you think you're going to do?'

'You're not going to work for the Germans, are you?' Anna demanded.

'Of course I'm bloody not!' Jerzy yelled. 'How can you even ask?'

'Well what are you going to do, then?'

They were all on their feet and shouting now, all on the verge of tears.

'I don't know yet!' Jerzy was banging his chair back and forth against the table. 'I was talking to Andrzej yesterday, in the bread queue. He feels the same, and he seems to have a few ideas. I don't care if I have to be a plumber, or sell coal, or mend windows, but I'm not going to sit around hungry any longer. I'm going out to see Andrzej now, all right?' And he stormed out of the kitchen, slamming the door.

Anna and Teresa avoided each other's eyes, and then they looked at each other, and sat down.

'Dear God . . .' said Teresa. She put her head in her hands. 'If only Tomasz – '

'Don't,' said Anna. 'Don't.'

They sat in silence. Eventually Teresa looked up and said carefully: 'Andrzej . . . the one with fair hair, yes? They're in the same class at the *liceum*?'

'Yes. Jerzy's always looked up to him.'

'And is he sensible? He won't lead Jerzy into trouble, will he?'

Anna shrugged. What was trouble, now? 'I don't think so. I like him.'

'Do you?' Teresa smiled weakly. 'Poor Anna. Poor Jerzy.' She took a deep breath. 'Well – I have an idea, too. Will you come and look through my jewellery box with me? I should like you to help me choose something to barter.'

'For food?' Anna frowned at her. 'Are people bartering now?'

'Everyone talks about it in the queues. What else can we do? Come and help me choose something you think your father wouldn't mind too much about, I think perhaps my amber might still be worth something. And if it isn't – well, we shall have to part with the best dinner service, shan't we? Or – or anything, I suppose.'

She got up, and Anna followed her out of the kitchen and into the freezing bedroom, where her father no longer slept.

At dawn, he stood waiting in the deserted railway yard. The cold was intense; as he fumbled to undo the buttons on his jacket to get out the shovel his fingers hurt so much that he almost cried. Carefully he propped it up against the wall, then, unable to stand still, walked beyond it, out to the platform. Snow-covered broken tracks stretched in the half-light into nowhere; they were empty except for a couple of abandoned coaches, where a door hung open and he could see the seats inside flung on to the floor. Above, the signal box had a gaping hole in its roof and side, and the wooden stairs were wrenched at an angle away from the doorway. He peered up and saw the skeletal iron levers snapped and twisted. They might come in useful for something, but he wasn't going to go up there now, alone. Where the hell was Andrzej?

He walked to the end of the platform, watching the last stars fade and the sky grow paler behind the scrubby trees on the embankment; then he paced back again, and heard a rattling in the yard. Quickly he rounded the wall and saw Andrzej with the wooden trolley, standing by a small white heap in the corner.

'You're late,' he whispered.

'I know. Sorry. Look, it's here.' He nudged the heap with his foot and as Jerzy went over he saw wet, gleaming pieces of coal shift silently on to the snow.

'There's quite a bit.'

'Yes,' said Andrzej. 'I told you. Where's the shovel?'

He picked it up and swore, dropping it again. 'It feels like ice.'

'Why didn't you wear gloves?'

'I couldn't find them.'

'Idiot. You keep watch, then.'

Andrzej bent down, picked up the shovel and began to lift the coal on to the low trolley. It had taken them the whole of last weekend to make it, borrowing wheels from a neighbour's old pram, and wood, nails and a hinge from his uncle. From the far corner of the yard, Jerzy watched him, keeping half an eye open for any movement on the dim, unlit road. There was no one.

The trolley was piled high, and there was still a good three or four loads left in the coal heap, by the look of it. He walked across to Andrzej and said: 'Shall we come back tomorrow?'

Andrzej nodded, passing him the shovel. 'We'll have to. There you are – I've warmed it up a bit.' He grinned. 'Come on.'

Jerzy tucked the shovel back inside his jacket, and Andrzej picked up the handle of the trolley and began to drag it across the snow.

'What about the tracks?' Jerzy said suddenly. 'And our footprints?'

'Oh, shit.' Andrzej stopped. 'Go on, go back.'

He jumped on and scraped with his foot all the thin lines left by the wheel, and the prints of their heavy boots. Andrzej had reached the road; the trolley, piled high, began to sway awkwardly – they had made the handle too short, he could see, now – and a few pieces of coal fell out. He ran to pick them up, and they turned and walked as quickly as they dared, dragging the load past the dark sheds and houses until, as the sky ebbed into morning, they were in reach of Andrzej's street.

They hid the trolley in the courtyard outhouse, where they had built it, then climbed the stairs to his apartment, shaking with cold and relief.

'Must be worth an absolute fortune,' Andrzej said, as he unlocked the door. 'All we need now are the bags.'

Białołęcka Street was very long, and many of the houses were eighteenth-century, built of wood. On Monday morning, as Anna walked slowly along, an early spring sun was melting some of the hard-packed snow along the pavement to crystals, and two or three people were out with shovels, scraping it into the gutter. A woman nodded to her, but did not smile, and in any case Anna was feeling too uneasy and apprehensive to dare to ask how far along number 59 might be. She walked on, looking every now and then at the doors and gateways fringed with snow, until two blocks ahead she saw a thin dark-haired girl in a navy coat: Natalia! Anna stopped. Natalia paused outside a low, modern house, looked quickly round, then went to the front door and rang the bell. In moments, she disappeared inside.

Anna looked at her watch. Five past nine. She walked on as slowly as she felt might look normal, her knees suddenly like water. There was not a German on the street, but what about the side roads? Was anyone watching her?

Number 59 was a clean-lined, pale-washed house with balconies on the upper floor; it reminded Anna of the villas in Żoliborz, the residential suburb on the other side of Warsaw, where much of the building had been done in the mid-thirties. It was so unlike her own old apartment house and the wooden ones nearby, and the weather was suddenly so mild, that for a moment she felt as if she had stepped outside the occupied city altogether. Then, as she went up to the green front door and rang the bell, not daring to look round, all her nervousness returned.

Footsteps came running down the stairs inside and the door was quickly opened. Pani Sokołowa smiled, said, 'Good morning, Anna,' as if she were back at school, and shut the door. 'We are upstairs.' Anna followed her up a flight of low stone stairs to a white-painted door and they went into the apartment.

The sitting room was light and airy, and very cold. Three girls were sitting in their coats round a table: Natalia, Basia Oliwa and Helena Kapek. They looked up as Anna came in, and Natalia patted the chair beside her.

'Come on.'

'Thanks.' Anna went quickly to sit next to her, and the girls all smiled at each other. fleetingly, on edge.

'There,' said Pani Sokołowa. 'Now we have only Jadwiga to join us, and then we can begin. I'm making some tea, I expect you could all do with it.'

'Please.'

'Yes, please.'

She went out of the room again, and the girls could hear the chink of glasses and teaspoons, reassuring sounds, as if they had all come for an end-of-term treat. They looked at each other, hesitantly, the first time they had been together since the end of the summer term last year, and that was in another lifetime. Behind them a clock ticked irregularly.

'Doesn't it feel strange?' said Natalia. 'Were you frightened, coming?'

'Yes,' said Anna. 'I saw you ahead of me, and I was afraid if I walked slowly I'd be noticed. But oh, I'm glad we're here, aren't you? What's it like at home?'

'Hateful,' said Natalia. 'My father still hasn't come back, we haven't heard a word, have you?'

'Just a postcard. From somewhere called Kozielsk.'

'You're lucky. Mama watches for the post every morning, and cries when there's nothing. I know she does, though of course she pretends she's got a cold.'

'My sister's ill,' said Helena. 'She's got something wrong with her kidneys, and we can't get any medicine. My mother cries a lot, too.'

'Oh dear, that must be dreadful.'

Then the doorbell rang, a long, urgent ring, and they all jumped, and heard Pani Sokołowa hurrying out of the kitchen and down the stairs.

'Isn't she brave?' Basia whispered. 'Suppose it's the Germans?'

'Sssh!'

They sat on the edge of their chairs. Then the door of the apartment opened, and they could hear Jadwiga, loudly apologizing; she came in, panting, her hair a wild bush around her head.

'Oh, isn't this *horrible?* I never thought I'd be so glad to see all of you again!'

'We thought you were the Germans,' said Helena, giggling.

'What, all of them?' Jadwiga pulled out a chair and sat down.

'Now listen, girls,' said Pani Sokołowa. 'We must have a proper arrangement for the doorbell, there was no need to ring like that, was there, Jadwiga? It's all right, you've said you're sorry. But two short sharp rings from now on, yes? Buzz-buzz. Then I shall know it's one of you.'

'Buzz-buzz,' said Jadwiga, wiggling her fingers like antennae, and they all shrieked with laughter.

Pani Sokołowa shook her head. 'I suppose I must make allowances,' she said, and went back to the kitchen.

'Buzz-buzz!' whispered Helena, helplessly.

'Sssh!' They held their hands to their mouths.

Pani Sokołowa returned with a tray; she handed round glasses of tea, and wreaths of steam rose comfortingly above the table. 'It's very weak,' she said, 'but I have a friend who managed to get a little for me yesterday, and I wanted you all to have it.'

'Thank you.'

'Thank you.'

She pulled out her own chair, and sat down, cupping her glass in her hands, and gazed round at them all, a fair-haired, pretty woman, who hadn't long been married – one or two of the girls had gone to her wedding, last spring. A photograph of her husband, in his university gown, stood on the desk at the window. Glancing at it, Anna remembered hearing that he, too, had been taken prisoner in the Reserve Corps, early on. So Pani Sokołowa was living alone, now. That must be miserable. Strangely, she had put on weight – her face was fuller, and . . . and she was pregnant, wasn't she? How could Anna not have noticed that before?

'Well, now,' Pani Sokołowa was saying. 'We have all been having a rather difficult time. I'm very glad that we can meet like this –

you're all bright girls, and if you make up your minds to work hard, and to overcome these circumstances, there is no reason why you should fall behind. I hope you all understand that there will be no dropping of standards? I shall be preparing you for the *mała matura* in two years' time, and I shall expect as much from you as always. I know the other teachers feel the same.'

Jadwiga pulled a face as long as a horse. Anna spluttered. Pani Sokołowa appeared not to have noticed.

'Before we begin this class,' she went on, 'I had better make sure you are all properly informed about the present . . . situation. You know that everyone of fifteen and over must register for work? You are fortunate to be too young yet, but next year it will apply to you, if things haven't changed, so be prepared to have some kind of cover. In the meantime, do you all know about the . . . the classification that is going on? It is not very pleasant. Anyone who can show that they have German blood within three generations may register as *Volksdeutsche* – I believe there are certain privileges, or exemptions, which attach to this status.' She pursed her lips in distaste. 'I don't believe that this applies to any of you?'

No one answered.

'So. There is also the question of Jewish blood.' She lowered her voice, and spoke looking straight ahead. 'Are you all aware of the dangers to the Jews under the Nazis? Again, I'm sure that this does not apply to any of you, but there are, of course, plenty of Jews among the intelligentsia – if any of you have friends, or . . . or family with such connections, you will understand that you and they must be on constant guard.'

No one spoke, no one looked at anyone else. My God, thought Anna, if any of us had anything to hide, we wouldn't dare to tell, not even here. We daren't even trust our best friends, our teacher. At least I don't have to worry about any of this, we're all pure Pole in our family; perhaps there was some Russian blood on Mama's side, but that's all right, isn't it?

And then she thought, with a sudden lurch of her stomach; but what about Teresa?

'To tell the truth,' Pani Sokołowa was saying slowly, 'simply to be Polish is to be in danger now. I expect you are all aware of that. However, I know that you are all brave, sensible girls, and we shan't talk any more about it. Now – have you all managed to bring something to write on? And pens? Good. I believe Pani Jawicz explained that we have no textbooks, that they have all been impounded. So I shall dictate the verbs I should like you to learn this week, and we shall start with the third conjugation.'

There was a rustling of pages turned and smoothed down; overcoat sleeves were pulled up, and the girls bent their heads. The familiar, soothing sound of Pani Sokołowa's dictation voice, carefully enunciating Latin verbs and vocabulary, filled the room; the unsteady clock ticked on.

Writing in gloves was awkward, but the room was so cold that there was no choice, and even wearing them Anna's fingers felt stiff. The concentration, however, was wonderful – she was able to block out everything that had happened in the last six months – even that last, terrible thought.

Pani Sokołowa dictated steadily, for perhaps an hour. Suddenly, there was a crumpled, moaning sound, and they all looked up to see Basia dissolving into tears.

'Basia! What is it, what's the matter?' Pani Sokołowa rose quickly, and went over to her.

'I'm so *hungry*,' Basia sobbed. 'I'm sorry . . . I just can't think about anything else . . .'

Pani Sokołowa put her arm round her. 'Poor girl, did you not have any breakfast?'

Basia shook her head, still crying. 'We've run out of bread, and last night there were just a few dumplings, but my brother ate them all . . .'

'Selfish brute,' said Jadwiga, and they all laughed, uncertainly.

Basia blew her nose, and smiled. 'He isn't really,' she said. 'He just gets so irritable when he's hungry . . .'

'So does Jerzy,' said Anna. 'He's horrible.'

'No he's not,' said Natalia, and Anna looked at her in surprise.

'Everyone's hungry these days,' said Pani Sokołowa. 'I think we'll have an early lunch, I could do with it myself. Now, perhaps one of you would like to help me bring it in, and the rest of you clear away your books. The bathroom is just down the corridor, on the left.'

They put away their exercise books, chattering as if the bell had just gone at school.

'Don't you worry, Basia,' said Jadwiga. 'My cousin has this peasant woman, from somewhere outside Otwock – she's wonderful, she brings in eggs and bacon, and my cousin supplies Mama. I'll bring you in some tomorrow, if I can.'

'Thanks.' Basia smiled weakly, very pale.

'The Red Cross are sending food parcels, aren't they?' asked

Helena, coming back with a tray. 'That's what my aunt says, anyway.'
She set out spoons and plates.

'You tell your aunt to let us know the minute one arrives,' said
Jadwiga. 'God, the thought of a bar of chocolate! The thought of
anything – do I actually look like a potato, or just feel like one?'

'Here we are,' said Pani Sokołowa, with another tray. 'Pea soup.'
She passed round bowls, put down the breadboard. 'We had the gas
restored in this block last week, thank goodness. Help yourselves.'

'Thank you.'

'Thank you.'

The soup was thin but piping hot; they dunked crusts of dark
bread.

'Pani Sokołowa?' Anna asked hesitantly. 'May I ask you
something?'

'Of course.'

'Are you expecting a baby?'

'Yes,' said Pani Sokołowa briefly, and did not smile.

'When?' Jadwiga asked bluntly, and then Pani Sokołowa did smile,
but shaking her head. 'In June. It is something I should be looking
forward to, but I'm afraid that without my husband . . .' She sighed.
'Never mind, perhaps by then he will have returned.' She did not
sound as if she thought it likely, and Anna put down her spoon,
thinking of Tata. She would write to him this afternoon, and tell him
about *komplety*. Oh – no, she couldn't, could she, it would be much
too dangerous. Well, she'd hint, and he could work it out. He'd be
so pleased to know she was studying again.

When they had finished eating, they cleared away, and Pani Sokołowa
gave them all a translation, a single sheet of paper she had copied
from the *Aeneid*, which they passed round, translating in turn.
Everyone was rusty and awkward.

'Very well,' she said, when Helena had stumbled through the last
sentence. 'You all have plenty of catching up to do. Verbs and
vocabulary by heart, please, for Wednesday. We shall be meeting at
Pani Lasocka's apartment.' She gave them the address, and a time
of arrival for each of them. Beyond the windows, the morning's
spring sunshine had disappeared.

'Go home quickly, now,' she said. 'One at a time – well, perhaps
two is all right, I suppose a stream of girls one by one looks odd. Off
you go.'

'You come with me, Basia,' said Jadwiga, pulling her to her feet.
'I don't want you fainting on the way.'

Anna and Natalia followed, ten minutes later, leaving Helena, who lived nearest, to go home alone. The sky was darkening to snow clouds and the packed snow along the edge of the pavement was beginning to freeze again. They hurried down the street arm in arm.

'Do you think Guides will start up now, as well?' Anna asked.

Natalia shrugged. 'They might, I suppose. I hope so. Or perhaps it's too dangerous, perhaps that would have to be secret, too.'

An unlit tram moved slowly down the centre of the street, and then the snow began to fall. They said goodbye on the corner, lightly kissing cold cheeks, and Anna ran home, shivering.

The snow melted, the trees came into bud again. With the warm spring weather, Anna found herself feeling calmer, settled at least into a routine: *komplety* three mornings a week, studying in the afternoons, writing to Tata. After a while, though, these letters became difficult. She couldn't write about *komplety*, she couldn't write about Jerzy, keeping odd hours, doing odd jobs, she couldn't write about Teresa – she couldn't write about anything that was actually happening.

I miss you terribly, and only hope that you are safe and well. Come home soon . . .

How many ways were there of saying that? She went on saying it, because they were, after all, the only words that mattered. After supper, she dropped the letters into the postbox at the end of the street, and walked slowly home. Now that the evenings were growing lighter, it felt dreadful to be so restricted about going out, even before curfew. Teresa's anxiety was like an illness.

'Can't I go back to Guides?' Anna pleaded with her. 'Everyone else is going – Natalia, Jadwiga, Helena . . .'

'But you are not,' said Teresa. 'I'm sorry, and please don't look so sulky, but *komplety* is enough.'

'It isn't for me!' Anna said crossly.

'Well, it will simply have to be! Do you want to be here, when your father returns, or do you want to be under arrest? For heaven's sake be sensible.'

Anna sighed heavily, and went to fetch her sketchpad.

In June, the *Nowy Kurier Warszawski*, the German propaganda newspaper, jubilantly announced the fall of France. For days, no one could talk of anything else. If Paris could fall . . . The news was terrible, but in one way at least it brought a perverse comfort. In the early weeks after the seige last year, there had been a lot of bitter talk about the pre-war government: they had been ill-prepared, short-sighted. Talking like that made people uneasy, and even though they knew that without real outside assistance no single city could have resisted for long the bombardment Germany had given her, there still lingered a secret sense of shame. Now – if mighty Paris could fall, Poland's swift defeat did not feel quite so humiliating.

Soon, through the *komunikats*, they heard that the Government in Exile – led by General Sikorski, who had been in opposition at the outbreak of the war – had escaped from Paris and flown to London. Over the next months, in *komplety*, the girls were told that the Polish forces were now based mainly in Scotland, and that the many Polish airmen in the British RAF were now fighting in desperate air battles against the *Luftwaffe* to help prevent an invasion of Great Britain.

Walking to school one light summer morning, Anna saw a man ahead of her, walking with the slow, dazed step of complete exhaustion. Men returned from the western front, demoralized but free, quite frequently now: Anna had seen them before. This man wore a heavy army coat, perhaps because he was too weary to carry it, a coat which reminded her of Tata's, and which hung loosely, as though he had lost a great deal of weight. She quickened her step, called in a sudden, burning rush of hope, 'Tata? Tata!' He stopped, and turned, and looked at her, from a face whose features were thick with fatigue; then he shook his head, apologetically, and walked on, into a side street where a bird was singing.

Anna stood, waiting until the trembling in her knees had subsided, and she was able to walk properly again. Then she went on, to the house on Białołęcka Street, and in Pani Sokołowa's sitting room took out her translation and sat down. Later in the morning it came to her, with absolute certainty, that Tata would be there when she got home. Distantly she was aware of Pani Sokołowa's dictation, of reciting verbs and showing her work; all the time she knew that the ghostlike figure she had seen this morning was a herald: that when she rang the bell that evening, Tata would answer it, and nothing would matter any more.

Pani Sokołowa released them at four, and she ran all the way home, past the broken tram limes, running until she had a stitch in her side, but didn't stop. At the apartment door she leaned, panting, on the bell. The door opened, and Teresa stood there, holding a bunch of letters.

'Is Tata here?'

'No – did you think he was? Look . . .'

She held out an envelope, and Anna saw her own writing, and the address of the camp in Kozielsk. Stamped right across it were the words *retour – parti*.

'Return to sender? Gone away. But why? Where is he?'

Teresa shook her head. 'I don't know. No one knows. Wiktoria telephoned this morning – she's had all the letters she wrote since April returned.'

She looked suddenly much older, the dark circles under her eyes deeper, as if they would never go away now. At the same moment, Anna realized, in the midst of her own flood of misery, that Teresa seemed no older than she was herself – as frightened, as bereft.

They clung to each other, and the letters fell to the floor.

It was cold again, the leaves falling all along the avenues, piled up high by the street sweepers and sent drifting again by the wind from the river. The air smelt of water and bonfire smoke.

In their kitchen, Anna and Teresa sat at the table, turning over the white cards: one for each of them, stamped with a black, uncrowned eagle. A circle hung from his talons, enclosing a swastika. Inside, above their names, their race and their dates of birth, Teresa, Jerzy and Anna each stared at the camera. Teresa had fetched the cards that morning, and gave Anna hers without a word, when she came back from *komplety*.

'Where's Jerzy?'

'He's gone across the river, with Andrzej, I think. He said he might not be back until this evening.'

'Oh.' Anna looked at her photograph again, and put down the card. Who was Anna Kurowska? If she were stopped in the street, what could anyone tell from that face – was she a victim, or someone to be reckoned with? Teresa looked frail in her photograph: covertly, Anna scanned the features. What could anyone tell from Teresa's face? She was fair, or at least mousey; there was nothing in her features to indicate that she might be Jewish. But that didn't mean that she wasn't.

'Teresa . . .'

'Yes?'

'I'm sorry – this sounds ridiculous . . .' Anna tried a casual laugh; it sounded horribly false. 'I can't remember your surname,' she said, and felt herself blushing. 'I mean, before you married Tata.'

'My surname? It was Pawlik,' said Teresa. 'Why?'

She didn't sound in the least suspicious. Pawlik – well, that

91

sounded perfectly Polish. But probably some Jewish names did, they couldn't all be called Kaufman, or Jakobson, could they?

'Anna?'

'Yes? I remember now, of course I do, I wonder why I forgot?'

'I wonder why you want to remember,' Teresa said slowly, and Anna felt her cheeks burn. She picked at a loose thread on the tablecloth, as Jerzy had done that time when Pani Jawicz came. The silence in the room was suddenly horrible, unending. She couldn't look up, she could feel Teresa watching her, and her throat tightened with fear and embarrassment. She does know what I'm thinking, she thought miserably. How can I look her in the face?

Then the front door of the apartment banged suddenly open, and they both jumped as Jerzy came panting down the corridor and into the kitchen. He saw the cards on the table, and swept them on to the floor.

'What the hell are those?'

'Jerzy!' Thankfully, Anna bent down to pick them up again, praying that her blush would fade before she emerged from beneath the table.

'What's happened?' Teresa was asking him. 'You look dreadful – sit down, I'll make you some tea.'

Jerzy sank into a chair, and Anna scrambled to her feet. 'What is it? What's the matter?'

He had covered his face with his hands; she pulled them away.

'*Tell* me!'

'Well,' he said slowly, 'there's a lot of building going on, across the river.'

Anna looked at him stupidly. 'Building?'

'A wall,' said Jerzy. 'A long wall, I should say a good ten feet high, enclosing what they are calling a Jewish Residential District. That is to say – a ghetto.'

Anna sat down so quickly that she dropped the cards again. By the stove, Teresa was standing absolutely still.

'Go on,' she said quietly. 'Where is it?'

Jerzy drew a long breath. 'I don't know exactly how far it runs,' he said shakily, 'but I don't think it's very long, and it's on the border of the Jewish quarter, anyway. Part of it isn't far from Stare Miasto. Andrzej and I were walking through, and we just found ourselves looking at it . . . Do you know what was really horrible? The point is that the Jews are building it themselves, we saw a whole long line of them, wearing their blue stars, being ordered about by a gang of Nazi pigs – they were standing over them with guns, yelling at them to hurry up . . . Ugh. There were great rolls of barbed wire all along the top, where it was finished, and I should think they must have been another foot high. I've never seen anything so . . . so . . .' He covered his face again.

Teresa came over, and put her arm round him. This time, he did not shrug it off, but Anna could not look at her. If she's a Jew, she thought frantically, her heart pounding, if she is secretly a Jew, masking herself, the Polish wife of a good Polish doctor . . . if she's found out . . . oh God, oh God, what will they do to us all?

'Do you know what else I heard?' Jerzy went on; he ran his hands through his hair, and Teresa sat down beside him. 'Andrzej has an uncle, he's an old boy, but he seems to be in the know, perhaps he's attached to a resistance group, anyway – he told Andrzej that they're just taking people off the streets at random now. Never mind if you're a Jew – they just pick up anyone they don't like the look of.'

Teresa was swallowing. 'Then what?'

'Then they throw you into Pawiak prison – the ghetto wall's going to run near there, too, I think. Or they send you to a camp, some horrible kind of labour camp. Or death camp? He says there are death camps . . .'

'Shut up,' said Anna. 'Stop it. I don't want to hear any more.'

'I can't,' said Jerzy. 'Do you know what else? They're shooting men in broad daylight, out on the street, blindfold, shot in the back. Andrzej's uncle saw it happen, he saw it himself, last week. He says that when there's too many, they just take them out of the city, to the Palmiry Forest, and do it there. He says it's like an execution ground.'

'*Stop it!*' Anna put her hands over her ears. '*Stop it!*'

'Yes,' said Teresa, as white as a sheet. 'That's enough now. I know you're very upset, but . . . that's enough. We must – we must be thankful that we are safe. We have nothing to be afraid of; so long as we are careful, and sensible, we shall be all right.' She was speaking very slowly, deliberately, as if to reassure herself as much as them. 'Now – ' she got up, and took the boiling kettle off the stove. 'Let's have tea, and try to calm down.'

That night, Anna lay rigidly in bed, listening as every creak in the floorboards, every dripping tap or flapping piece of cardboard at the broken windows was magnified and hideously transformed into the sound of SS men creeping into the apartment, kicking open the door, grabbing them, shoving them down the stairs with a gun at their backs, and out into the dark. Jew-hunters. Pole-haters. This was not some terrible revenge, this was something which could happen to anyone, now; you need have done nothing.

But perhaps it could happen particularly to them.

Across the room, Jerzy, too, lay absolutely still. She didn't dare to light the candle, it was too wasteful to light them after you'd gone to bed. But . . . was he asleep?

'Jerzy?' she whispered.

'Yes?'

Oh, thank God. She pushed back the bedclothes, and crept over. 'I'm so frightened.' She reached for his hand.

'You mustn't be. I'm sorry – I just had to tell you.'

'I know.' She sat on the edge of the bed, no longer afraid. 'I'm so glad you're here. You won't ever leave us, will you?'

'Leave you? No, of course not. Why should I?'

'I mean – you'll be careful?'

'Yes.' He squeezed her hand. 'Do you want to come into bed for a bit?'

'Yes.' She slid in beside him. 'Oh, that's better.' She thought of Teresa, alone in the big double bed at the other end of the corridor. It must be awful for her. And if she was afraid, she mustn't show it, must she? Because she was the grown-up, and also because –

'Jerzy?'

'What?'

'Do you . . . do you think . . . suppose Teresa's a Jew?'

There was a long, shocked silence.

'Oh, Christ,' he whispered. 'I never thought of that.'

In early November, Anna went across the river with Jerzy and Teresa for the first time since the occupation began, to visit Wiktoria. Many of the tram lines were still unrepaired, but a line across the bridge was working; when a crowded tram drew up Anna made to get in at the front, but Jerzy and Teresa pulled her back. 'Look – the front is for Germans only.'

'What?' She looked up and saw soldiers and German civilians seated near the driver. Teresa and Jerzy hustled her in the queue along to the doors at the back, and they had to squeeze in among a press of people up against the windows; more forced their way in, and then the doors were closed and the tram began to move. Anna found herself remembering the airless, frightening train journey from Wilno, with Tata. She craned her neck to see beyond the barrier dividing the tram, saw the Germans, with plenty of room to move, smoking and talking as they crossed the Vistula, grey in November light. One soldier was standing with his back to the window, watching the crowd of Poles behind the barrier, his hand resting on the rifle slung across his chest. He was quite young, ordinary-looking beneath his cap; she saw him feel her watching him, and his eyes found hers. He looked at her indifferently, then turned to a soldier next to him, mouthed something, and they both looked at her, and laughed. Anna's face burned, and her knees trembled; she looked away, filled with anger and some kind of humiliation, although she wasn't sure what they meant.

'What's the matter?' asked Jerzy.

'Nothing. Nothing.' If she told him, he'd only get angry, and what could he do?

When they got off, and began the walk to Wiktoria's apartment in Hoża, they found the streets thick with people, although there was little traffic except for the trams and buses and a few improvised rickshaws. No one was permitted to own their own transport any more – not even a bicycle. On a corner of Marszałkowska, Anna noticed that the street sign had been changed to Marschalstrasse, and she felt for a moment so disoriented that she reached for Jerzy's arm.

'Where are we?'

'What do you mean?'

'It isn't – it isn't Warsaw any more.'

'I know.'

It wasn't just that the street names had been changed: there seemed to be hardly any Polish shops now. All the old signs had been taken down or painted over with new, German names. There was a *kawiarnia* on a corner where Tata used to take her and Jerzy sometimes, for a treat – coffee and cream cakes, it was one of her favourite places. Now, she saw the words *Nur für Deutsche* painted across the glass. For Germans Only, and there they were, women in expensive hats and furs, sitting at the little tables inside, lifting their coffee cups, lifting the cakes on silver forks. And now she and Jerzy couldn't go there any more, and anyway, Tata –

'Anna!'

Teresa was a little ahead, turning to wait for her. 'Come on, darling, don't stand and stare.'

'Don't call me that!' Anna snapped, and bit her lip.

Teresa said nothing. She just turned away, and walked slowly on.

Jerzy pulled a face. 'What did you have to do that for?'

Anna's cheeks were burning. 'I hate it. I hate it. Look at it all.'

Swastikas blew in the autumn wind. *Nur für Deutsche* was everywhere – above restaurants, *kawiarnias*, all the good shops. There was a butcher whose windows were hung with strings of fat sausages, and duck; Anna watched two large German women coming out with their baskets piled high, standing complacently beneath the sign, gossiping. Where were the Poles supposed to shop? What were they supposed to buy, with their pitiful ration cards? There seemed to be cafés everywhere, far more than there used to be – it must be a comparatively easy way to earn a living, now, but to stand and serve Them all day long – ugh. They passed a street leading down to a children's playground – that, too, was only for German children, now.

Jerzy was muttering at her, but looking straight ahead. 'I'll show you something in a minute. See the notices?'

'*See* them?'

The walls were plastered with them. Many were headed *Bekanntmachung! Warning!* and followed by lists of 'strictly forbidden' activities. The phrase 'on penalty of death' seemed to be everywhere. It was no longer possible to travel, anywhere in Poland, without German cards to be carried, German offices to report to. It was strictly forbidden to own building materials without declaring it. There was a terse announcement, half-covered by more recent posters, that on 23 October last year Marian Branowski and Wiktor Sikorski, both of Warsaw, had been executed for the possession of hand grenades and explosives. There were notices about which police department ran which district of the city, about the risk of infectious diseases, and especially of typhoid, 'carried by the Jews'.

Anna looked at Teresa, still ahead, and felt tears pricking behind her eyes. Why had she been so horrible? She saw a German patrol, standing on the next corner, armed, watching the movement on the street, and she felt in her pocket for her identity card. Her knees were trembling again.

Jerzy was nudging her, still looking straight ahead.

'Look.'

'What?'

'Sssh! There.' With the slightest gesture he indicated another poster, across the street, another warning: any dealers in weapons whose activities were not known to the police would be regarded as saboteurs, and 'treated with the greatest severity'. At the bottom, scrawled in black paint, she saw the rough outline of two letters, PW, joined to form a kind of anchor: ⚓

'See it?' Jerzy asked under his breath. 'The anchor?'

'Yes,' Anna whispered. Whispering on a crowded street, in broad daylight! 'What – '

'*Polska Walcząca*,' he said, his lips scarcely moving. 'Fighting Poland. Now come on, quick, for God's sake stop looking at it.'

They hurried to catch up with Teresa, trying to ignore the stony faces of the next patrol, as if it were nothing to walk past them, and nothing that they should be there.

Anna slipped her arm through Teresa's. 'I'm sorry.'

Teresa's face was expressionless. 'It's all right.' Two bright spots of colour burned on her cheeks.

'No it isn't. I'm really sorry.'

'Let's just forget about it, we're almost there.'

They turned into Wiktoria's apartment block and climbed the stairs. At the top, they all, as if bidden by a conductor, let out a great sigh of relief, and then they burst out laughing.

'But it's dreadful,' said Anna shakily, wiping her eyes. 'Only to feel safe up here. It's like, it's like . . .'

'It's like living under occupation,' Teresa said simply, and rang the doorbell.

Wiktoria opened the door and fell upon them, hurrying them inside. She took their coats, exclaiming, patting Anna's cheeks.

'Child, how thin you are!'

'You too, Aunt,' said Anna, but although her clothes hung from her, and her face was pinched, Wiktoria's morale had clearly recovered since the first shock of the occupation.

In the kitchen they found the table laid with brown bread, not black, and a pie which smelt deliciously of bacon; dishes of potatoes, carrots and swede were on the stove; there was a bowl of yellow apples.

'Hey!' Jerzy sat down and pulled the breadboard towards him.

'Jerzy . . .' Teresa said mildly, but Wiktoria put a hand on her arm.

'Let him, let him, poor boy – I made it for you all.'

'Your contacts must be good ones,' Teresa said dryly.

Wiktoria smiled. 'I have excellent friends, now – occasionally it's possible to stretch the ration book a little. Or even make a new one . . .'

'What?' Jerzy mumbled through a mouthful. 'Are they forging, now?'

'Help yourselves,' said Wiktoria, putting the hot dishes on the table, 'and don't ask foolish questions.'

'But who are your friends, Aunt?' Anna asked, plunging her fork into the steaming pie.

Wiktoria spread her hands. 'The peasants are smuggling in fruit and vegetables, sometimes even eggs. It's getting more dangerous, but so far our exchanges have not been discovered. And I have friends . . . in one or two shops they can produce a little from under the counter from time to time.'

'Or forge ration books,' said Jerzy. 'Good for you, Aunt, this is the best meal I've eaten for months.'

'I'm glad you're enjoying it. Teresa, my dear, have some more – you've had too many sleepless nights, I can see. You need to eat all you can.'

'I've stopped feeling hungry.'

'Nonsense.'

They stayed the night with Wiktoria, and next morning she and Teresa went out early together, on a shopping expedition.

'Come with me,' said Jerzy, when the door of the apartment had closed.

'Where?' Anna was eating her third slice of toast. With homemade beetroot jam – it wasn't so bad, but the idea of it was extraordinary.

'Just come.'

Outside, Hoża was still misty and grey, the cracked pavements damp. They hurried, shivering a little, down to the last intersection and turned right, walking until they came again to the broad main thoroughfare of Jerozolimskie Avenue, already crowded. It seemed as if the whole of Poland had come to Warsaw, trying to scratch a living. They crossed over, and a few streets later Jerzy said: 'Do you want to walk, or wait for a tram?'

'I don't want to go in a tram, it makes me too angry. Where are we going?'

'I'll show you.'

They walked on and on. After a time, Anna realized that they were approaching the Jewish quarter and, suddenly, that almost everyone in the street, which had become more and more crowded, was moving in the same direction, and that almost all of them were Jews.

In caps and shirtsleeves, or threadbare coats, the men were trundling handcarts, piled with mattresses and chairs. Bearded Hassidic men and rabbis in long gaberdines and dark hats were among the crowd; women in headscarves and cardigans held white-faced children by the hand, and carried bundles. Some of the little boys, each carrying a chair, wore caps and earlocks, many looked simply like some of the Polish children they'd seen in the streets yesterday, but even more undernourished, their clothes patched, holes gaping in their boots and shoes. Everyone wore an armband, white, with a blue star.

They turned into a narrow street. Pressed back on to the pavement, Anna and Jerzy watched the river of Jews move slowly on, through a wooden gate set in a high brick wall mounted with jagged glass and ugly great rolls of barbed wire.

'This is the place?' Anna whispered. 'The ghetto?'

'Yes.'

At the gate stood armed Nazi and Polish police, and they could also see Jewish police, in a different uniform, wearing armbands; their belts bulged with truncheons. At intervals along the wall there were wooden watchtowers: craning her neck up at the nearest, Anna could see two Nazi-uniformed guards inside. Both had machine guns, trained on the slowly moving crowd.

Through the open gate she could see that the great mass of people already inside was simply milling about, still carrying their few possessions, their bundles of clothes or rolls of bedding, their chairs – walking up and down the narrow streets, lined with tenements, looking, it was obvious, for somewhere to stay. But the ghetto was no size at all! And there were hundreds still moving through the gate, hundreds more behind them, there must be thousand upon thousand, hundreds of thousands . . . What were they all going to do in there? How were they going to be fed? Among the crowd pacing up and down, looking into doorways, she could see that some were quite well dressed, carrying suitcases, women in furs and high heels, men in good suits and soft hats. It wasn't just the Hassidic Jews from the old quarter, then, it really was every Jew in Warsaw, it must be, from professors to cleaners, every single one swept up like dirt, and pushed inside the walls.

'Look down there!' Jerzy hissed, and he pointed to a corner of a side street. A uniformed Nazi was crouched behind a movie camera.

'I'm frightened,' said Anna. 'I'm frightened! For God's sake let's go.'

They turned and made their way back, pushing their way through the crowd, past the rattling carts, the silent families.

*

Throughout the spring of the following year, 1941, there was a continuous stream of German traffic across southern Poland, and some through the streets and stations of Warsaw. Tanks, troops, armoured vehicles all moved across the bridges over the Vistula, making their way east, towards the river Bug, the border with Russia agreed under the Nazi-Soviet Pact of 1939. In Praga, from their sitting room windows, Jerzy, Teresa and Anna watched and speculated.

Then, in late summer, every newsboy was suddenly calling out that in June the Germans had crossed the river Bug, and attacked Russia. The Pact was broken; the headlines in the *Nowy Kurier* were triumphant. Now, new posters appeared: anti-Soviet slogans plastered the walls.

'But what's going to happen to all the Polish prisoners?' Anna asked in *komplety*. 'All those officers taken by the Russians? What's going to happen to my father?'

'And mine,' said Natalia, twisting her hands.

'And my husband,' said Pani Sokołowa, whose bedroom now held a cot for baby Adela. She sat at the table with her glass of tea and shook her head. 'We can only keep hoping. No one has heard any more? Not a single card?'

'Nothing,' said Natalia.

'Nothing,' said Anna, remembering *retour – parti* stamped on each of the bundle of letters sent back from Kozielsk. Natalia's mother had had a bundle like that, too. *Parti . . . parti . . .* Where had they all gone?

'I believe there are a quarter of a million missing prisoners,' said Pani Sokołowa. 'That's what Pani Jawicz tells me, from the latest bulletins . . .'

On a darkening afternoon, early in December, Anna and Jerzy were struggling to get the kitchen stove alight with a new firebrick. Teresa had been out since the morning, queueing across the river for cooking oil.

'I think that's it,' Anna said at last, and they both coughed as threads of acrid smoke escaped through a gap in the tiles.

'Damn thing,' Jerzy said irritably, and went to wring out a cloth in the sink. He pressed it over the gap, and there was a hissing from inside the stove.

'If you put it out now,' said Anna, 'I'll scream.'

'Oh, shut up.'

The door of the apartment banged, and Teresa came running down the corridor. 'They're being released! There's an amnesty – they're being released!'

'What?' They swung round, and Teresa danced in to the kitchen.

'The prisoners in Russia! Everyone's been whispering about it in the queue. The Poles are being released to fight the Nazis!'

'Oh, my God,' said Anna. 'Are they coming home? Is Tata coming home?'

'I don't know – no one seems to know yet. But at least we should hear something from him, shouldn't we?'

'If he's home for Christmas . . .' said Jerzy.

'For Christmas!' said Anna. 'Oh, wouldn't that be wonderful?'

They hugged each other, they hugged Teresa, jumping up and down until a loose floorboard cracked. Jerzy spent the whole evening mending it, and then every cracked or broken window frame in the apartment, humming.

By Christmas, hundreds of thousands had been released under Stalin's amnesty. They were formed into an army under the command of General Anders, himself released from solitary confinement. In prison, he had been flogged and half-starved; now he formed his men into the Polish Second Corps, responsible to the Polish Government in London. Since their capture in 1939, these men had been held in freezing labour camps, taken out to work as roadbuilders in the snow. Their fingers and toes dropped off from frostbite; they had seen thousands of their fellow prisoners die in these camps. Now they, the survivors, began the long icy trek out of Russia, towards the Middle East. Thousands more perished on the journey. Those who struggled through eventually formed the Polish forces in Palestine, and later, under British command, took part in Allied Forces fighting in Egypt and Italy.

By Christmas, the Polish underground press had still not a word to report on what had happened to any of the men in the three particular Russian camps where thousands of Reserve Officers and priests had been held: 4,500 in Kozielsk, 3,900 in Starobielsk, almost 6,500 in Ostaszków.

As the new year opened, Anna and Jerzy had still heard nothing from their father. The underground bulletins, so Pani Sokołowa told the girls in December, did report that General Sikorski had flown from London to Moscow, and in a meeting with Stalin had demanded that he explain where the missing men were now held. He was given no answer. Perhaps, Stalin suggested, the fifteen thousand had escaped, and walked the thousands of miles to Manchuria. Why should they do that? He didn't know. How could they do that? He shrugged. Other than that, he had no idea, though inquiries would certainly be made.

The *burka* hung on the back of the surgery door. It was heavy and very warm, a thick, rough brown fabric with a soft woollen lining; Tomasz had had it for years, always wore it to visit his country patients in the winter. Teresa pressed her face against it for a moment, then carefully lifted it from the hanger and went out, closing the door behind her. She did not like to stay in the surgery for long.

In the sitting room she spread the coat over the table, examining the seams, and with difficulty, because of the weight, turned it inside out and examined them again. She had been right: it would make two coats quite adequately, even elegantly, the heavy outer fabric for Jerzy, the beige lining for Anna, who had left for *komplety* shivering in her worn school coat, now much too small.

Could she do it herself? It was really a job for a professional dressmaker, but she had been sewing clothes for the children for years, she should be able to manage. She went into the ice-cold bedroom, where her needlework box stood on the chest of drawers; an oblong of light, caught between two boarded window panes, lay across the bed; she sank down suddenly and put her head in her hands. Was he thinking about her, now? Was he able to think? Had he loved her at all? Was it an act of apostasy not to keep the coat for his return?

It was bitter in here; Teresa shivered, coughing. Then she got up, and took her sewing box into the kitchen. She took out her scissors, made the first cuts in the coat, and ripped the seams apart.

4
Warsaw, 1942–1944

In the spring of 1942, two German officers came to visit the apartment. They were formal, remote, barely looking Teresa in the eye as they asked to be conducted round, and although the family had known for a week that they were coming, and why, it felt quite shocking to have them there. They went without comment from room to room, indifferent eyes glancing at pictures, at bookshelves, into bedrooms. At the end of the corridor one of the men clicked open the door to the surgery. Anna watched him appraise its size, the generous oak desk and the couch, the fresh green leaves of the chestnut tree at the window, and then he nodded to his companion and she knew that they had lost their home.

They were to be moved, like many other families from the better residential areas, to the old Jewish quarter bordering Stare Miasto. The letter of relocation gave an address near Senatorska, one of the main streets, just outside the ghetto wall.

On the day of the move, they carried heavy suitcases along their own street to the tram stop. It was a bright, cold morning; they stood at the stop and waited, not talking. Anna imagined the German officers whose quarters their apartment was to be, choosing rooms, opening the windows on to the courtyard, with plenty of money to do the repairs, and make it all nice again. Except that it wouldn't be nice, because They were living there. When the tram which would take them across the river arrived, she began to cry.

'I don't want to go, I don't want to. How will Tata ever find us now?'

'Sssh,' said Teresa, pushed along by the queue behind her. 'Get on, quickly.'

'He'll go to Wiktoria, won't he?' said Jerzy, taking her bag.

'Oh. Yes, yes, of course he will.' She climbed on, and they swung across the Vistula, the water sparkling in the spring sunshine. They had to take another tram, through Teatralny Square; then they got off, and crossed into Senatorska. Teresa held the letter; they walked slowly along, searching for the address. In cobbled squares off the main street they glimpsed a few trees, just in leaf. Here, towering tenements rose above them; there were endless rows of dark, closed casement windows. Anna remembered the few occasions she had travelled through the quarter, on streets like this one – not on the dreadful day when Jerzy showed her the families pouring into the newly-created ghetto, but before the war. It had been so crowded, then, and everything had looked so foreign: the faces, the clothes, the shops and shop signs. There were a great many people here now, but none of them were Jews, they were just ordinary Polish families like them, weren't they? Forced out of their homes and shunted across the city. The shops were boarded up, the ground-floor windows shuttered; old Yiddish shop signs creaked in the wind above them: there were peeling pictures of umbrellas, of jackets above the tailors', shoes above the shoemakers'. All those shopkeepers and craftsmen were inside the ghetto, now, working in the German slave shops and factories, turning out uniforms, saddlery, mattresses and machinery. People said their ration allowance was two hundred calories a day.

Litter blew along the pavement and across the cobbles. It wasn't hard to imagine rats, scurrying through the gaps and broken shutters of the doorways. Many of the pasted-up notices flapped torn corners; others, put up months ago, were wrinkled from winter snow and rain. A Proclamation in heavy black capitals seemed to appear on every block: Anna slowed still further, seeing the words 'Jewish' and 'Death'. Jerzy and Teresa were ahead; she stood by herself, reading the warning.

PROCLAMATION

Concerning the death penalty for illegally leaving Jewish residential districts.

In recent times Jews who left the residential district assigned to them have in many cases proved to be carriers of typhus. In order to avert the danger that hangs over the population, the Governor General hereby decrees that a Jew who in the future illegally leaves the designated residential district will be punished by death.

He who deliberately offers refuge to such Jews or who aids them in any other manner (i.e. offering a night's lodging, food or by taking them into vehicles of any kind, etc.) will also be subject to the same punishment.

Judgement will be passed by a Special Court in Warsaw.

I draw the attention of the entire population of Warsaw District

to the new statutory decision because it shall be henceforth applied
with pitiless severity.

Warsaw   Dr Fischer
10 November 1941   Governor

'Anna? Anna! We've found it – come on!' Jerzy had left his case
with Teresa and was walking back towards her. 'What are you *doing?*'
   Anna turned to him. 'Are you in such a hurry?'
   He picked up her bag. 'No, but Teresa's tired and jumpy. I just
want to get in there and get it over with. What are you reading?' He
looked up at the notice. 'That. It's months old, it's been everywhere.
You haven't seen it before?'
   'Somehow I haven't. And you didn't tell me.'
   'Anna . . . you knew, anyway. Everyone knows.'
   A gust of the cold April wind sent more rubbish scattering past
them along the cracked, uneven pavement; he turned up the collar
of the *burka* and shivered. Under his cap, his face was very thin.
   'Come on.'
   Anna could see Teresa, a hundred yards or so ahead, waiting for
them. She, too, was so thin now that her coat was hanging off her –
Anna supposed that she must look like that, as well. Had Teresa read
the notice?
   'Jerzy? What's it like, the place?'
   'It looks horrible.' He put his arm round her shoulders. 'Don't
worry,' he said, with a wry smile. 'I'm here.'
   She smiled thinly.
   The entrance to the tenement courtyard where Teresa stood waiting
was tall and narrow. A single iron gate, rusted, was pushed open and
looked as if it could never close again without losing its hinges. Inside,
as they crossed the courtyard, searching for their stairwell, they
passed two lavatories, like sheds, with hanging doors, and they stank.
The windowless flight of stone stairs was worn and dirty and frightening – unlit, with peeling doors to other, unknown apartments.
Theirs was on the third floor, with two more floors above, and had
been shut up since the evacuation of its occupants to the ghetto; it
was dark, and smelt of damp and emptiness. They put down their
cases inside the door and looked into the two small bedrooms, the
kitchen-living room. Furniture from the apartment in Praga would
be coming on a cart, tomorrow. Here, there were bed frames but no

mattresses, a table in the kitchen but no chairs. The plaster on the walls crumbled to the touch, and the floors were thick with dust.

'How many people do you think lived here?' Anna asked, and was chilled by the sound of her own voice.

Teresa shook her head. 'Six? Eight? Too many, anyway.' She crossed the kitchen, and with difficulty pushed open the filthy windows on to a tiny balcony. They stood leaning on the rail, with barely room for the three of them, and looked down on to the courtyard, barred with heavy shadow and motionless slabs of sunlight. Above, the sky had been trapped by the four sides of the block into a square without prospect or horizon.

Jerzy went back inside, and they could hear him move the cases, two into the room he and Anna would share, the heaviest, crammed with everything she could bring, into Teresa's. When they went in they found him in the corridor, holding something.

'This was under one of the beds.'

Teresa and Anna looked at the limbless body of a small cheap doll, its mouth open in a smile, its eyes rolled up into the head. Teresa took it, and gently tilted it upwards, but the eyes wouldn't open any more.

The newspaper boy stood on the corner, waving the *Nowy Kurier* at a passing German patrol. 'Come on, you lot, buy your rag – no one else is going to!' In the bread queue, where he stood each morning, Jerzy heard it with the others, and grinned. It was early, the narrow street thronged with people queueing, or on their way to work; suddenly, crossing it at the far end, a *buda* appeared, a covered German lorry. It stopped, blocking the exit.

There was a ripple, and then heads turned at the sound of another, at the near end, which screeched to a halt, so that the street was sealed. '*Buda! Lapanka!* Round-up!' yelled the newspaper boy, and vanished. There was a surge towards the open shop doors: with a dozen others Jerzy managed to shove through into the baker's just before it slammed shut. Kneeling, he raised his head and peered over the bottom of the window sill.

The street was full of German soldiers, pushing their way through the terrified people who remained, seizing first one man, then another, then another, until they had six, lined up with their faces pressed against the wall on the other side. Forced by rifle butts to stand opposite them, and watch, the crowd fell back, and the officer gave the order to fire. The soldiers raised machine guns; in seconds, the street existed only as a roar of sound: shouts, gunfire, screaming. Six bodies slumped to the ground, and dark pools of blood crept along the pavement.

An utter silence. Then two women ran forward wildly across the cobbles and sank by one of the bodies. What followed happened so fast that for a moment Jerzy didn't know if he could have seen it: the officer gave the order to fire again, and the two women barely had time to raise their heads before they also fell.

Slowly the officer walked over to their sprawled bodies, lifted their heads by the hair, and let them drop with a crack on to the stone. Then he turned to the frozen onlookers.

'A rail transport of supplies vital to the German Reich was sabotaged last night,' he said in broken Polish. 'Let this punishment be a warning to all of you.'

He nodded to his men, and they ran to the waiting lorries and drove off.

Behind him, Jerzy heard someone being sick. He dragged himself up by the window sill as the shopkeeper, his fingers trembling, scraped back the bolts on the door; reaching for hands, sleeves, anything human to touch, and hold on to, they all stumbled out on to the pavement. Already, the bodies were partly hidden by a press of people, bending, lifting, slowly carrying them one by one through a doorway. A woman came out from a shop with a bucket of water. She was about to throw it on the stones, to wash away the blood, but another woman stopped her.

'No, don't,' she said quickly. 'Leave it – let everyone see.'

The woman with the bucket hesitated, then nodded and took the bucket back indoors. Just a little slopped over the sides.

Two days later, when Jerzy went back, as he had to, he saw a bunch of carnations laid on the bloodstained stones, where no one was walking, and a candle, flickering in the open air, but still burning.

Anna had found a job, through a cousin of Natalia's. He ran a chain of dry cleaners, two in Praga, three in the centre of Warsaw, another two in the suburbs. Anna was taken on in the one in Wola, a long tram ride away from their new home. The dry cleaners was in a street near the leafy cemetery in Powązki where Mama was buried – when they first got married, she and Tata had lived not far away. Tata used to bring Anna and Jerzy here, to visit her grave, but that was a long time ago, before Teresa, before the war.

Before the war, the dry-cleaning chain had flourished. Now, with the shortage of chemicals, it was barely possible to keep even two open. Anna took in the coats, suits and dresses from the few people who could still afford such a luxury – she and most of their friends were used, now, to rubbing out stains with tea leaves, mending and remaking everything they owned. It wasn't an enjoyable job, taking in the clothes and sorting them for the central cleaning depot, but it was hardly arduous, and it gave her the document she needed, to prove she was working. To get there, however, she had to take a tram through the ghetto.

When the tram stopped, and stood, humming, at the gate, the passengers travelling through were watched as they got on by armed guards. On her first journey, Anna was issued with a yellow pass; when she was inside she saw that the pass for the Jews was different – yellow, but with a blue diagonal stripe. The tram began to move again. It was early morning, still very cold. Anna had had nothing for breakfast except a slice of the wretched black bread with Wiktoria's beetroot jam – she had come and visited soon after they arrived, and shaken her head. Hungry, still half-asleep, Anna leaned against the grimy glass and peered out. Within moments, hunger and fatigue were forgotten: now she saw things which, when she had first walked along Senatorska, and explored the empty apartment, she had not dared to allow herself to imagine. She gripped the handrail with sweating palms, feeling a wave of nausea.

A woman in rags, her hair matted, her skin blue-grey, was pacing up and down a gutter, holding a baby. She was wailing, but no one on the street took any notice: the pavements were filled with slowly moving skeletons. Grey-faced men and women stood staring from doorways of the tenement buildings, scratching at lice in an endless, abstracted rhythm; just before the tram gathered speed Anna caught a glimpse through an open door of a dark room filled with crouching figures. Down a side street she saw two children picking listlessly through a rubbish heap. There were stalls, if you could call them that – women squatting beside a heap of old shoes, or clothes, or shawls. Later, Anna found out that the shawls were for wrapping bodies for burial. Just beyond the track a man was propped up against the wall, his head lolling forward. Two other men appeared, slowly pushing a handcart piled high with – dear God, with naked bodies. They stopped beside him, and as the tram moved past, Anna, heaving, turned to see them bend down, strip off his clothes and with great difficulty heave the body on to the cart. They trundled it down the street and stopped again.

The tram moved out of the ghetto, and into the quiet streets of Powązki, where it stopped to let off a couple of passengers and take on a few more. Anna stared at the people around her. They were quiet, but they seemed unperturbed, as ordinary as any group of people going to work, some reading the paper, others talking. Then a woman touched her arm.

'Is this your first trip through?' she asked quietly.

Anna nodded, her head swimming. 'Yes.'

The woman patted her. 'It is terrible, I know. But you will get used to it.'

'What?' Anna looked at her incredulously.

The woman shrugged. 'What can we do?'

'But surely – '

'Sssh.' The woman lowered her eyes and Anna, suddenly aware of being watched, turned to see a German officer, at the front of the tram, observing her carefully. She gazed down at the floor, at all the patched and cobbled shoes of the passengers. Then the tram stopped, and she got off quickly, and walked through the streets to the shop without looking back.

Late in the afternoon, before going home, she went to the cemetery; walking along the paths under the trees, she searched for her mother's grave, listening to the intermittent chirruping of the birds as they settled for the evening. It was cold, but as the spring sun sank diffusely into the pale sky she felt able to breathe properly for the first time in months. No one was here, no one was watching; there was only the fading light, and space, and the ordered rows of the graves.

She came at last to her mother's: it took quite a long time to find it again, after those long-ago visits. Now, above the tangled mass of weeds and brambles which had grown, she re-read the brief inscription: To the memory of my beloved wife, Ewa Kurowska, 1898–1932. Like many of the others, the headstone bore a small ceramic oval, with a sepia-printed photograph: as they had done in the picture on Tata's desk, the soft dark eyes she could barely remember looked beyond her, into the dusk. Anna sank down. *I am still here*, she said inside herself. *Shall I tell you what I saw today?*

She made the journey morning and evening for three months. After a time, as the woman on the tram had predicted, she grew accustomed to such sights, or learned not to look. One incident remained with her always.

Returning from Powązki one June evening, she closed her eyes as they entered the ghetto gate, and listened to the numb silence fall on the other passengers, as it usually did: she had probably been wrong to assume, the first time, that they were undisturbed. Everyone knew that some people had made fortunes, early on, by bribing the gate police and then smuggling in food, sold at extortionate prices; many knew, or guessed, that the underground was secretly supplying what they could manage, that some familes were risking or had lost their lives, to hide the few Jews who escaped, or who had been in hiding outside since the wall first went up. Between exploitation and sacrifice most felt impotent and afraid; they shuddered, and concentrated on their own survival.

Anna felt the tram slow down, as it did not infrequently: the track was badly in need of repair. But then she heard a banging, and a shout, and opened her eyes to see people craning towards the doors. There was a mutter from near her: 'Someone's on the side,' and she too craned her neck and saw, clinging to a lever, a young Jew so thin and grey that it seemed impossible he could hold on. There was another shout, in German: 'Stop! Stop the tram!' and as it juddered to a halt the police officer jumped down from the doors right at the front and ran round to the side. Anna cried out involuntarily: 'No! No!' Then she clamped her hand over her mouth and watched as he drew his pistol from his belt. He did not fire. Instead, he cracked the pistol violently across the boy's face – once, twice – and he fell immediately, long thin hands covering his mouth in agony, blood streaming between his fingers, rolling and writhing beside the tram-lines. The officer watched briefly, in disgust, then climbed back on. The doors closed.

'Drive on!' And the tram gathered speed and left him lying there.

In July, Anna began to hear of new rumours going round when she travelled through the ghetto: all Jews living in Warsaw were to be 'transported to the east'.

'What does that mean?' she asked Jerzy. It was a hot, airless evening; they were standing on the balcony after supper, looking down into the well of the courtyard, where no breeze ever came.

He shook his head. 'I don't know. Not exactly. Andrzej seems to think something dreadful is going to happen.'

'What? What sort of thing?'

'Sssh! I've told you, I don't know.'

110

Behind them, in the kitchen, Teresa was washing the dishes. They heard the clatter stop for a moment, and fell silent.

'Are you two all right out there?'

'Fine.'

Somewhere across the courtyard a child who couldn't sleep began to cry; they could hear the mother, snapping irritably: everyone's nerves were on edge. Anna leaned on the balcony rail, and wondered how it could be possible to have kept a suspicion secret for so long, even to have felt it for so long. Surely, in three years of occupation, Teresa would have been discovered by now? She hadn't been, so it must mean they were safe. But Anna didn't feel safe, ever.

A couple of days later, she arrived at the gate of the ghetto to find it closed, the street lined with police.

'What's going on?' she asked a woman hurrying past with a shopping basket.

The woman shrugged. 'Don't ask me.'

Anna took a deep breath, and approached one of the guards.

'Are there no trams any more?'

'All transport through the ghetto has been halted,' he said flatly.

'But – how am I going to get to work?'

'You will have to make other arrangements,' he said, and turned away.

Anna stood for a moment, her heart racing. If she couldn't get to work, she would lose her job, but she had to have a job, she had to have her papers in order . . . The thought of being stopped by a patrol, demanding to see them, was so terrifying that whatever might be going on behind the walls was for the moment forgotten: she stood looking up and down the street, wondering which way to go. Very well – if she couldn't go through, she'd go round. She began to walk quickly, breathing fast. It took her over an hour to get to the dry cleaners. When she told the manager what had happened, he was sympathetic.

'Don't worry, you just come when you can.'

'Thank you.' She began to sort through piles of clothes, packing them in baskets to go to the central depot. Surely there must be something better she could do than this? Perhaps the problem with travelling was a good thing, in its way – it would force her to try to find something else. I am sixteen, she thought bitterly – I should be at the *liceum*, starting my studies for *duża matura*, preparing for medical school! If I can't do that, then perhaps at least I could get a hospital job – I'll talk to Wiktoria, there must be people who knew Tata who could help.

That night, she woke suddenly, shaken as if from a nightmare, but she hadn't been dreaming, she couldn't remember anything . . . Why was she awake?

'Anna?' Across the tiny room Jerzy was sitting bolt upright in bed.

'Yes. What's happened?'

'Listen!'

She listened. There was a distant burst of gunfire. Machine guns? It must be – she remembered it from the seige.

'Oh, my God . . .'

They scrambled out of bed, and ran to the window.

'Where's it coming from?'

'The ghetto,' said Jerzy. 'Where else?'

Silence. Then another burst of firing, and shouts. Anna put her hands over her ears. Behind them, the door was quickly opened, and they swung round. Teresa came in in her nightdress, her face white.

'You *are* awake – I just came to see.'

She came over, and put her arm round Anna.

'It's coming from the ghetto, isn't it?'

'Yes, that's what we thought.' Anna put her own arm round Teresa's thin waist, and felt her trembling. 'Are you – are you all right?'

Teresa nodded. 'Yes, yes.'

The three of them stood, listening. After a time, the shooting and shouting died down, and they went uneasily back to bed.

Within days, Jerzy was coming home full of stories. The shooting had been just a preliminary, something to terrify the Jews into submission. Now, every day they were being herded in groups out of the ghetto, marched to a square near Stawki Street, a few blocks away. The street adjoined a railway siding, and the cobbled square – Umschlag Platz, the Germans had renamed it – was full of *buda*. Sometimes the Jews were driven off in the *buda*, sometimes they were crammed into railway cattle trucks. Everyone was talking about a camp called Treblinka, some sixty miles away.

'Who is everyone?' Teresa asked. 'How do you know all this?'

Jerzy looked away. 'I just do. How do you think?'

The meeting was to be held at seven, two hours before curfew, in an apartment a couple of streets away: Andrzej had told him the number. He didn't tell Teresa or Anna where he was going, although he knew

112

they worried every time he went out in the evening, because he knew that they would worry even more. Anyway, he didn't know himself exactly what was going to happen.

As he came out of the courtyard and into the cold unlit street it began to rain; he pulled down his cap, turned up the collar of the *burka* and began to run, his boots letting in water even before he'd reached the corner. Everything was shuttered and boarded, there was almost no one about; it felt as if he were running through a ghost town, or a film set. The autumn rain was falling fast now; he stopped in a doorway and watched it bounce off the cobbles; in a first-floor apartment, opposite, there was a chink of light in the shutters, and there the rain shone as it fell. He ran on, past the peeling notices on the walls, turning into Plac Żelazna Brama, Iron Gate Square. In the daytime, the square was full of market stalls; now it was empty, the gate leading into the Saxon Gardens closed. Walking over the cobbles, breathing hard, he felt vulnerable and exposed in all this space, and ducked between a row of stalls left standing, and waited, listening to the rain patter on the canvas tops. He could hear voices, but they were Polish voices, just a few people going home across the square; he came out, casually, and walked as slowly as he dared until he was in the right street, and began to search for the address.

The apartment house was almost halfway down; by the time he had reached it he felt as if a dozen German eyes were watching. He entered the open doorway, and leaned back against the wall, sweating. A curving flight of broad stone stairs led inwards, upwards; he peered out from the shadows, quickly, right and left along the wet street. If someone had been following, he must know, now – he thought of leading them to the meeting place, of them creeping silently up the stairs behind him, watching him being let in, then suddenly hammering on the door, bursting inside . . .

He could see no one. No patrol, no watchers. He turned and climbed the dark stairs, lit by a single lamp on each landing, and reached the second floor, the third door along. Knock twice only, Andrzej had said: he rapped softly, waited. The door was opened, just a crack. He saw Andrzej's large fair face, in a grin.

'Well done.'

He led him down the hall into a large cold drawing room, lit by a single desk lamp. Three people were sitting in their overcoats: two boys in their late teens, like him and Andrzej, and an older man, tall and balding, who reminded him a little of Tata. Jerzy took off his cap and held it, awkwardly, waiting to be spoken to.

'*Dobry wieczór* – good evening.' The tall man rose, and shook his hand. 'I am the Captain of this unit.' He gestured to the two boys, who also got up, nodding: he did not introduce them by name. 'This one you know, of course,' he said with a flicker of a smile, indicating Andrzej.

'Yes, sir. We were at *gimnazium* together – and in the same Scout troop.' He cleared his throat, suddenly very nervous.

'Sit down, please.'

The Captain was nodding towards a straight-backed chair, and Jerzy walked over to it, self-conscious, feeling the others watch him closely. Could they tell he was afraid? They wouldn't want a scaredy-cat, would they? He sat down, his cap held on his lap, stiffly, to stop himself twisting it. It was one thing to think about joining, to listen to Andrzej's hints and stories and feel left out and useless. It was one thing to read the *Biuletyn*, scanning it quickly, and passing it on. But to be a proper member, to have to obey orders no matter what, perhaps to have documents in the apartment, and be responsible for distributing them . . . to creep out at night on assignments . . . I'm scared either way, he thought: scared he'll take me, and scared he won't.

'So – you want to join us.'

His hands sweated into the cloth of his cap. 'Yes, sir.'

'Good. Perhaps you could tell me a little about yourself, your family?'

'My father – ' *My father looked like you.* 'Before the occupation, my father was a doctor, in Praga. He was posted east in 1939, then taken prisoner by the Russians. We had a card, once, from a camp called Kozielsk, but we've heard nothing for two years, not even since the amnesty.'

The Captain was nodding. 'There are plenty in the same position. How are you managing? Your mother – '

'My mother died when we were small,' Jerzy said quickly. 'My stepmother and my aunt have . . . have a few contacts on the black market. We were all moved out of Praga in April – I have a sister who is working in a dry cleaners now, but I think she wants to do something else, if possible . . .' He was talking too fast, he was gabbling. 'She has been attending *komplety*, I've been working, odd jobs, mostly with Andrzej . . .' Across the room, Andrzej's head was lowered; he was gazing at the floor, letting him get on with it. He swallowed. 'We've sold coal, paraffin. I tried making some soap, once . . .'

'I see. And do you read our bulletins?'

'Yes, sir.'

'You are very careful about doing so?'

'Yes, sir.' Was that right? Short respectful answers – it sounded military, didn't it?

'You know that we are renamed now. The AK. *Armia Krajowa*. The Home Army – pledged to help the Allies. We are in constant contact with the exiled Government.'

'Sir.'

The Captain was silent for a moment; his fingers drummed on the table. Then he looked Jerzy straight in the eye.

'How old are you?'

'Eighteen, sir.'

'Hmm. You don't look it. And are you absolutely to be trusted?'

Jerzy swallowed again. 'I . . . I hope so, sir.'

'Hoping is not enough. You are aware that every task we undertake, no matter how small, is done in extreme danger? That if you are caught, and betray a single secret, you will put the lives of the whole unit at risk? You could put your family at risk – your stepmother, your sister, your aunt. You understand?'

He wouldn't tell them, not yet. 'Yes, sir. I . . . I understand.'

God, Andrzej hadn't told him he would be put through the hoops like this. But what had he expected – tea and open arms? If he was unnerved by a few straight questions, how would he cope when he actually had to do something?

'You realize that if you are to join this unit, any unit in AK, you are required to take a most solemn oath? Its words were authorized by the Government almost immediately after the occupation, when they were still in France. To break this oath is as serious as to collaborate.'

They shot collaborators.

'Do you still wish to take it?'

'I . . . Yes, sir.'

'Very well. Stand up, please. I shall read it first, you will repeat it, and I shall make a formal reply.'

Jerzy got to his feet, holding his cap before him. The Captain was gesturing to the others: chairs were pushed back, and everyone got up. On the other side of the circle, Andrzej was nodding and frowning at him.

'Your cap,' he mouthed.

Quickly, Jerzy put it down behind him.

The Captain had picked up a card from the table, and a small wooden crucifix. He began to read the words of the oath, and the room was absolutely quiet. He read slowly, but without emotion, as if he were dictating: he's done this so many times, Jerzy thought. I'm just a cog in the wheel.

'. . . that I will keep the secret, whatever the cost may be.' The Captain stopped, and looked up at him. 'You are ready?'

'Yes, sir.'

He was handed the card, the crucifix. The card shook in his hand.

'Before God the Almighty,' Jerzy read huskily, 'before the Holy Virgin, Queen of the Crown of Poland, I put my hand on this Holy Cross, the symbol of martyrdom and salvation, and I swear that I will defend the honour of Poland with all my might, that I will fight with arms in hand to liberate her from slavery, notwithstanding the sacrifice of my own life, that I will be absolutely obedient to my superiors, that I will keep the secret, whatever the cost may be.'

He looked up. The Captain was watching him gravely; he didn't feel like a cog in the wheel.

'I receive thee among the soldiers of freedom,' the Captain said quietly. 'Victory will be thy reward. Treason will be punished by death.' Then he smiled, and came over, taking the crucifix and card, and putting them back on the table. He gripped Jerzy's hand. 'Good. Good.'

There was the lightest knock on the door, three quick taps. Andrzej went to open it, and a small dark woman came in, carrying a tray. She crossed the room quickly, and set it down on the table, nodding and smiling to the Captain. The room was filled with the smell of *ersatz* coffee; there was a plate of cake.

'Thank you, Pani.'

She smiled at the Captain, and went out again, through the door held open by Andrzej. Then he came over, and shook Jerzy's hand, quickly.

'All right?'

'Fine.' Jerzy was passed a glass of coffee; he sipped it too fast, scalding his lip, and winced, spilling some on the floor.

'Excuse me . . .' He put down the glass and bent down, fumbling in his sleeve for a handkerchief to wipe up the spill. When he looked up, they were all laughing at him.

'Relax,' said the Captain. 'Please – sit down, now, we shall all sit down after your ordeal.'

Jerzy sat, scarlet.

'And now,' the Captain said lightly, 'we must find a name for you.'

'Yes, sir.' He knew that the legendary leader of the whole AK was known simply as 'Grot' – a dart, or spike. His deputy was 'Bór', a forest. No one in AK used their real names, ever. What could he be?

'This unit is *lew*, lion,' said the Captain, and I myself am *strzała*, arrow.' He gestured to the others. 'Introduce yourselves to our new man.'

'*Lampat*,' said Andrzej with a shrug, almost as if he were embarrassed to have Jerzy learn something he had hidden from him for so long. 'Leopard.'

'And I am *wilk*, wolf,' said one of the other boys, grinning. He was short and tough-looking, with cropped hair.

'I'm *tygrys*. Tiger.' The other one shrugged, like Andrzej. He looked very young.

'Well?' the Captain asked Jerzy. 'Do you want to choose your own name, or shall we do it for you?'

'Um . . .' He wished he'd thought of one for himself. What other animals were there, for God's sake? 'Um . . . *Antylopa?*' he said quickly.

'Antelope. Yes, I like that,' said the Captain. 'Graceful and fast-running. Welcome, Antylopa. Now – I am going to tell you a little more about our activities.' He finished his coffee, and stretched out his legs.

'You realize, of course, that the whole aim of AK is eventually to coordinate every unit in a total uprising.'

'Yes, sir.'

'There is no doubt whatever that the Germans are going to lose this war. They will never be able to withstand pressure on two fronts, and our most important action is concentrated on the rearguard as they are beaten back in Russia. I need hardly say that although we are cooperating with the Red Army we are making it very clear that it is the Polish Armed Forces, directed by General Sikorski from London, to whom we are ultimately responsible.'

'Sir.'

The Captain smiled. 'I'm making a speech, forgive me. But I have to stress that we have one clear goal before us: to fight with the Allies to win the war and to restore the exiled Government to a liberated Poland. In the meantime, we are doing everything we can to make things as difficult as possible for the enemy. Much of our work is outside Warsaw, of course, in sabotage – derailing trains, blowing up bridges, burning military stores . . . Those of us employed in the munitions factories ensure that as many German arms as possible are sent out in a faulty and dangerous condition. And . . .' His fingers were drumming on the table again. 'We supply papers and passes to those who need them. We have skilled assassins, whose targets are the Gestapo – any of the enemy whose activities are particularly brutal.'

He thought of the street raid he had seen in the summer, of the slumping bodies and the two women, their heads lifted by the hair, the sharp crack on the cobbles.

'Within Warsaw,' the Captain was saying, 'indeed in every city where a ghetto has been built, we are amongst our other activities trying to do something for the Jews. You realize what is happening?'

'That they're being taken away? Oh, yes. It's . . . it's horrible.'

'We've been getting reports from railway workers outside the city which seemed at first, I must say, simply . . . fantastic. Still – ' He shook his head. 'There've been so many that we're forced to believe them. We are in urgent communication with London: the Government is doing all it can to alert the British Government; we have sent a courier to New York, to Roosevelt, to the Jewish organizations there. And here the Jews themselves have formed a Militant Organization within the ghetto, and we're smuggling in what arms we can. As you probably realize, our own supplies are very limited, but we have a good number of people in the munitions factories and warehouses who help us.' He looked at Jerzy closely. 'Have you any contacts of this kind?'

'No, sir. I'm afraid not.'

'Well . . . in any case it's very unlikely that you'll ever become directly involved in any of this.' He looked at his watch. 'It's time we closed the meeting. But first' – another smile – 'first I must brief you on your first assignment.'

'Yes, sir. Thank you.' He listened, his stomach full of butterflies.

Afterwards, he left with Andrzej. They stood for a moment in the doorway of the building, peering out.

'All clear,' Andrzej whispered. 'You all right?'

'Fine. Thanks for getting me in.'

'You got yourself in. See you soon.'

'See you soon.'

They shook hands, and then Andrzej went out quickly, turning left. Jerzy waited for a couple of minutes, to give him time, and then he ducked out, looking up and down again. No one. The rain had stopped, and the moon raced through ragged clouds. He walked quickly home, past the shuttered windows, over the wet, gleaming cobbles.

Before the occupation, the Evangelical Hospital had been one of the best in Warsaw, well equipped, well run – Tata had spoken highly of it, Now, after three years of struggling to maintain its standards, it looked dingy and neglected, the walls peeling, the bedclothes patched and worn, dressings and drugs carefully counted, sparingly used. When the ghetto walls went up, they had enclosed the hospital, and the German authorities wanted it shut down. By sealing up the entrance within the ghetto, and using the old back doors outside it, opening on to a street near Teatralny Square, the Polish administration had managed to keep it open.

Like the patients, and all those working there, Anna had to make her way to the back-door entrance past ruins from the 1939 seige: many fallen buildings in the city had been deliberately left untouched by the German authorities, as a constant reminder to the Poles of their defeat. Her ward, where she had been taken on as a nursing assistant through an old friend of Tata's, was on the first floor, long and narrow, holding some thirty beds. Every window on the ground floor had been bricked in, and the wards and corridors down there were dimly but permanently lit: there was not a single point where a Jew might creep in, and hide. From the tall windows on Anna's ward, however, it was possible to look down into the ghetto. All staff were under the strictest orders from the German medical authorities never to do so, but Anna had looked, once, when the senior nurse was too busy to notice.

It was January 1943 when she began to work in the hospital. The day she looked down was a freezing afternoon, the light beginning to fade, the lights in the wards due to go on soon. Anna peered, cautiously.

The streets of the ghetto below were no longer crowded, as they used to be when she travelled through by tram. Those who remained, and who were out on this bitter afternoon, were like ghosts, their skin a terrible, unforgettable grey. They paced slowly, in rags, as if the cold could no longer touch them, they were already so cold, dying on their feet, crumpling against the walls and slipping down to the gutter. There were a great many bodies in the gutter.

'Nurse . . . nurse . . .' A woman was calling weakly, from a bed across the ward. Anna turned from the tall window and hurried over.

The woman looked very white. White, ill – but not that awful, awful grey. How could living flesh ever be that colour?

'What is it?'

'I feel very sick . . .'

'Poor thing. I'll get you a bowl.' She walked quickly to the sluice, and tried to push away the image of what she had just seen.

Working in the hospital each day, she did feel for the first time since the war began that she had a purpose, and, too, that she was following a little in Tata's footsteps, even if she was only emptying pots, making beds or taking temperatures. The women patients were badly undernourished, as well as ill: they leaned weakly against her as she fed them on broth from the kitchens, or dumplings, potatoes and cabbage.

The spring was bright and cold. Still wearing the warm inner lining of Tata's *burka*, Anna went to the hospital each morning, sometimes by tram, at other times walking, watching the trees in the Saxon Gardens come into bud and leaf. Many of the grass strips down the centre of the wider streets on the outskirts of the city had long since been dug up and turned into allotments: as the weather grew warmer, you often saw old men, housewives and children digging and planting. At least, however hungry they all were, there would always be vegetables. Anna had almost forgotten what meat tasted like.

She hurried through Żelazna Brama, where the market stalls sold cakes and pastries and many used items – old clothes, battered saucepans, chipped plates and serving dishes – anything which could still be used and might fetch a few złotys or be simply exchanged for food. There were no bookstalls, though once Warsaw had been full of them – under the rigid censorship regulations they had all but disappeared. But there were stalls like these ones all through the poorer districts; here, she often saw children in patched or ragged clothes scavenging behind the pastry stalls or in the vegetable baskets. Anna had grown used to these sights, they were everyday, like the call of one of the 'sparrows of Warsaw' – the newsboy on the corner of Teatralny Square, near the hospital, where he sold the *Kurier*. Normally, like most people, she ignored him, but on a morning in April she saw that a crowd of people stood round him, and she stopped.

People were pushing and jostling each other, almost snatching the papers from the boy's hands; Anna heard the word 'murdered' and frowned: who had been murdered? She heard it again – 'murdered!'

120

– as she managed to break through to the front, and then she saw something on the front page which made her snatch at a copy, too.

Polish Officers in mass grave . . .

She pushed her way back out of the throng and stood reading, motionless, no longer hearing the trams, or the people, or the newsboy's call.

Katyń Forest . . . deep in Russia . . . found by party of German troops . . .

But the Germans lied. Every word the *Kurier* ever printed was propaganda, distorted news of the Allies' setbacks, lies, lies. It would so suit them to announce that the Russians were criminals . . .

Some weeks later, new posters were nailed on the noticeboards throughout the city, and Anna, Jerzy and Teresa stood among the press of white-faced families, peering up at them.

Katyń Forest: the names of those so far identified

A long thin column. Another. Another. Another. Badly printed, on coarse paper.

Kurowski, Tomasz.

It was there.

For once, there was no need to rely on the underground press for news: triumphantly pointing the finger at the Soviet Union, the German authorities ensured that the events which followed the discovery of Katyń were kept before the Poles for months. Lists of the dead were published almost every day. Red Cross offices in Warsaw were flooded with letters, asking for documents, pleading to have the bodies brought back to Poland for burial, asking, ever more urgently, about the men who had been held in all three camps: Ostaszków, Starobielsk and Kozielsk. Not for a long time was it learned that only men from Kozielsk had been found in Katyń.

Over the next few weeks, Anna and the family learned that in London General Sikorski had demanded an international Red Cross investigation, and that Stalin had angrily refused, calling the demand an insult: the bullets found in the skulls of the murdered men were German! Within a day, he had severed diplomatic relations with the Polish Government in Exile. Without Stalin's agreement, the Red Cross were forced to abandon their own plans; instead, an international commission with members drawn from twelve German-occupied countries travelled to Katyń in May.

Gradually Anna, Teresa and Jerzy learned that Tata, like the thousands of other prisoners of Kozielsk, must have been murdered in

1940, in April – that was when all the letters and diaries found on the bodies abruptly broke off. They had been deported from Kozielsk in sealed trains, taken off at the tiny forest station of Gniezdovo, near Smoleńsk, and from there driven in covered lorries deep along the road through the trees. When they were taken out, each man's hands were roughly tied behind his back, in many cases using a rope which was then looped up to wind round the throat, so that anyone struggling to get free would only strangle himself. Many of the bodies showed bayonet wounds, many of the jaws were broken, showing the violent resistance put up before the men were bound in this way and gagged. They were then shot, one by one, at point-blank range at the base of the skull, probably as they stood on the edge of the freshly dug mass graves. When the graves were filled in, young pine trees were planted in the light sandy soil, in an attempt at disguise.

It was the freshness of these trees, however, which had alerted forest workers this year, noticing the mounds for the first time, and growing suspicious. And then the German troops arrived, pushing their way through in their retreat from Moscow, and the discovery was made.

No one in Warsaw could talk about anything except Katyń, and the evidence emerging from the grim exhumations. The bullets used were German, as the Russians repeated again and again. But they were of a manufacture which had been widely sold both to Poland and Russia until 1941. Everything else – the make of bayonet, the make of rope, that particular knot in the ropes, the location, and the fact that for two years Stalin had been unable to give Sikorski a convincing answer as to the whereabouts of the missing men – all this pointed to the murders being the work of the Soviet Union.

Gradually, all these facts and findings were published and pinned up on the walls of Warsaw or blared through the loudspeakers. For Anna, for a long time, there was only one fact: that Tata had died in April 1940. That meant that all the time they had been writing to him, until the June or July, when the letters had been returned, he had been dead.

Retour – parti . . .

All the time they had talked about him, or thought about him, and wondered what he was doing, and missed him, and longed for him to come home, all the time they had prayed that with the amnesty of 1941 he would be released, he had been dead.

Retour – parti . . .

She couldn't get that brief, bleak phrase out of her head. And as she walked the distance to and from the hospital each day, she could not rid herself of the image of a dark, unseeing figure, somewhere infinitely far away, waiting to be found.

In the middle of April, Anna arrived on the ward to find patients being helped into the corridors outside, and stretchers bumping down the stairs. Many of the beds were stripped; a nurse, distracted, told her to pile up the linen and help take it down to the basement, where the patients were to be resettled.

'Why? What's happening?'

The nurse bit her lip, shaking her head. 'I don't know.'

'The ghetto . . .' said Anna, her stomach turning. 'Something in the ghetto.'

'I think it must be. Come on – give me a hand.'

Down in the stuffy, half-lit basement, the sister supervised the patients being helped back into beds and on to mattresses, then summoned staff and helpers into a small side room. 'We have received an order,' she said tersely. 'Until further notice, no one is to go to any upper floor or look out of any window for any reason whatsoever. Anyone found up there will be shot.' She paused, very pale. 'I believe that something particularly terrible is about to happen – I need hardly say that our patients will need us to appear calm.'

Within days, the ghetto was surrounded by German troops, and in the small hours of 19 April, Anna and Jerzy were woken once again by bursts of machine-gun fire. But this time there was something else, as well. They ran to the window: between the gunfire and the screams they could hear a dull patter of small explosions.

'They're fighting back!' said Jerzy. 'We knew they were going to – they've got tommy guns and *filipinki*.'

'*Filipinki*? Hand grenades? Do they think they can stop the Germans with hand grenades?'

He was standing on tiptoe, craning to hear more. 'What else can we give them? It's something, isn't it – look!'

The sky was suddenly lit by a billow of flame. Anna grabbed his arm. 'They're burning them out – no! They can't, they can't!'

'Shut up! It might not be that – the Jews might be burning the workshops.'

There was a thunder of shelling, and they clung to each other. Then the door was flung open, and Teresa burst into the room, sobbing.

'I can't bear it, I can't bear it . . .'

Anna ran to her. 'It's all right, it's all right, we're here, we'll look after you . . .'

Teresa held her close. 'Look after me? Darling, I don't need looking after – I came to look after you.' She wiped her eyes. 'I'm sorry . . . But those poor, poor people.'

'But – ' Anna broke off, and buried her face in Teresa's shoulder.

No one went back to sleep that night. Next day, Anna had to make her way to the hospital a long way round, past lines of troops guarding all the streets near the ghetto. No one could get near the walls, and everyone was talking about how at least one German armoured car had been destroyed in the battle last night. Today, it was Hitler's birthday.

On Easter Monday, at six in the evening, whole batteries of German artillery were assembled, and to the stirring blare of a military band they marched inside the gates, and began shelling houses at close range. The walls of the hospital shook: down in the basement next day, Anna and the others could hear windows shattering on the upper floors. For days, the whole quarter reverberated with the sounds of gunfire and explosions: what was the point of being confined below ground in the hospital? All day and all night, the glow of burning houses lit up the sky, and great clouds of black smoke billowed from above the ghetto walls and out across the city. All day and all night, German planes circled the site of the massacre. Jerzy told Anna he'd heard that from the rooftops and windows of the houses still held by the desperate Jews, banners were flying: 'We shall fight till the last.'

The last came on 16 May. Every house had been bombarded, every hide-out discovered. Petrol-brands had been flung down the entrances to the sewers, where the last emaciated survivors were crawling, led through the filth by AK men and women who had themselves crawled in from beyond the walls. A few, perhaps a hundred, escaped like this, and made it to the forests outside the city. For the rest, some sixty thousand – where before the 'transports to the east' there had been four hundred and fifty thousand – men, women and children, it was over, and in the smoking ruins of the ghetto there was only silence.

When Anna's ward, and the others, were finally allowed to return to the upper floors, and she dared to look out through the broken, blackened window panes, she could see only a grey, bleak moonscape of rubble, littering the streets between the gaping buildings.

Soon, this lifeless limb of the city was to be used by the Germans as a more convenient, secret place for the mass execution of Poles, rounded up at random on the streets outside the walls.

In the autumn the terror began a new wave: between October 1943 and August 1944 over eight thousand Poles, men and women, were shot or hanged.

They came out of the safety of the courtyard one at a time. First Andrzej, with the torch up his sleeve and the rolls of paper buttoned inside his jacket; he coughed very softly, and Jerzy came, the old stiff brushes thrust uncomfortably into his trouser pockets. He snapped his fingers and Wilk was behind him, holding two pots of glue and paint. Outside the wrought-iron gateway, on the dark street, they pressed up against the wall, and looked quickly to right and left.

'Okay,' whispered Andrzej, and they crept along to where the posters were thickest, and peered up at them. Carefully, Wilk put the pots down on the pavement, and stood with his back to the others, watching the deserted street. The clock of the nearby church chimed twice.

'Quick!' Andrzej thrust the torch at Wilk and he clicked it on, pointing it downwards so that only a small circle of light rested on the pavement, just enough for Andrzej and Jerzy to see by as they quickly separated the paper into posters and blank sheets. The rustling was louder than he could ever have imagined. They pinned down the posters with the glue pot, and then Andrzej held the blank sheets as Jerzy dipped a brush in the black paint and with a steady hand sketched out a gallows in the torchlight. Hanging from it, he painted the outline of a swastika. Andrzej swiftly slid the paper away, and he did another, then a sketch of a city lamp post, with a little dummy of Hitler, swinging from it on a broken neck.

'Okay, come on,' Andrzej hissed, and bent so that Jerzy could clamber on to his shoulders and paste the sheets up quickly in the torch beam Wilk directed, over the hateful German slogans, *Bekanntmachung!* and lists of punishments. He dropped down and changed places with Wilk, watching the street, his heart thudding until his chest hurt. The other two were breathing heavily as they slapped glue on to the posters and then Wilk was on Andrzej's shoulders and as Jerzy pointed the torch he plastered them up: circles of bayonets, pointing at the swastika imprisoned in their midst.

The church clock chimed the quarter hour. Wilk jumped down. He looked swiftly up and down the street again, and then they each, in the last moments allowed, grabbed a brush and daubed, over and over again, in every blank space or corner on the German posters, the symbol of resistance which everyone knew now: PW, forming an anchor: ⚓ : *Polska Walcząca*: Fighting Poland. Fighting Poland. Fighting Poland.

Then they ran.

A warm golden evening in early July, sun in the leaves of the trees all along the avenues. The meeting tonight was to be held in Wilk's family apartment, in a street running off the broad and beautiful Krakowskie Przedmieście: walking through the market stalls in Żelazna Brama, through the Iron Gate and into the Saxon Gardens, Jerzy might have been out on almost any summer evening. On the long path through the Gardens families pushed prams, lovers held hands: the patrols were not usually much in evidence here, until the approach of curfew.

As soon as he left the Gardens, of course, the brief illusion of freedom and safety disappeared: as always, on the way to any meeting, he felt as though his every step were being watched. And yet, strangely, since they had learned of Tata's death he also felt in some obscure way protected. Before, when they had waited and waited for him to come home, not knowing where he could be, Jerzy had felt alone, adrift, exposed. Now, it was as if his father's spirit were watching over him, standing between him and danger.

The apartment was lit by the evening sun: at last there was no need for candles, or to sit shivering in their coats. Wilk's mother had baked pastries – they stood on the table in the drawing room, where she poured out glasses of weak barley coffee. Pani Wilk, Jerzy found himself thinking of her, not knowing her real name. Pani Wolf. She had taken the oath last year. Her husband, taken prisoner by the Russians in 1939, like Tata, had been released under the amnesty of 1941 – they hoped he was in Palestine now, serving under General Anders with the British troops.

'Antylopa . . .' Pani Wilk was smiling, leading him towards the table. 'No problems getting here? Good, good. The Captain is late this evening, but I'm sure he won't mind if we eat while we're waiting. Help yourself.'

'Thank you, Pani.'

He stood with the others, all a little subdued. Why was the Captain not here? He was almost always the first.

'How's Anna?' Andrzej asked.

Jerzy hesitated. 'Low,' he said. 'Very low.'

126

'Because of your father.'

'Yes. My stepmother, too – well, all of us. I mean, I know it's been a few months, now, but . . .'

Andrzej shuffled his feet. 'I'm very sorry.'

'I know. Thanks. It's the same for Natalia – Anna's friend, d'you remember her? Her father's name was on the list, as well.'

Two quick taps came on the apartment door. 'That's him!' Pani Wilk hurried to open it.

When the Captain came into the drawing room, they all knew at once that something was wrong. He stood for a moment, shaking his head, as Pani Wilk took his jacket, then followed her across the room to the boys. They looked at him awkwardly.

'Something has happened,' said Pani Wilk. 'You were followed here?'

'No, no. I'm afraid that what has happened is to someone far more important.' He looked at the waiting boys. 'You are all aware that the whole AK is under the secret command of "Grot".'

'Yes, sir.'

'Yes, sir.'

'Before I came here tonight,' the Captain said slowly, 'I was contacted with the information that Grot has been arrested.'

'No!' Pani Wilk's hands flew to her mouth. The boys looked at each other in silence. 'It's absolutely certain?' she asked.

The Captain nodded. 'Yes – he was seized four days ago, here in Warsaw. They've been looking for him for years, of course – he was on the way to a meeting, and must have been recognized. Apparently he'd hardly got inside the house when the Gestapo sealed off the street and . . . and got him.'

He looked at the silent boys. 'Sit down, sit down.' He pulled out a chair for himself, and stretched out his long legs. 'Grot has been our inspiration,' he said simply. 'He's a man of immense courage and vision. And of course . . . of course he holds secrets which they will do anything to get out of him. You will remember the words of your oath – "to keep the secret whatever the cost may be". Grot will reveal nothing.'

'But – ' Pani Wilk said hesitantly. 'But . . . imagine what they'll do to him.'

The Captain looked down at his hands. 'Exactly.'

Through the open window came the sound of voices in the street below, the intermittent hum of passing trams, the evening breeze in the chestnut trees. Inside the room, no one spoke.

At last Jerzy said nervously: 'Sir? Excuse me, but . . . who's going to lead us now?'

The Captain raised his head. 'General "Bór",' he said. 'You'll remember that he has been Grot's deputy – I imagine it's fairly certain that London will appoint him Commander-in-Chief.'

'What do you know of him?' asked Pani Wilk.

'I've met him once, here in Warsaw. He's a fine man – very quiet, gentlemanly, but impressive. He's strong. I shouldn't think there could be a better replacement, but – what a sad way to succeed.'

By the next day, the news of Grot's arrest had spread in whispers, bulletins and low voices throughout the city. Within days, crowds were gathering, weeping, by the German loudspeakers, as they crackled and spat with fresh news: returning to London via Gibraltar, from a visit to the Middle East, General Sikorski, Prime Minister and Commander of the Polish Armed Forces, had been killed in an air crash.

Clouds of cigarette smoke wafted from the front of the tram. At the back, Jerzy and Andrzej coughed, with the other passengers, as they swayed along Marszałkowska and slowed down to stop at the intersection with Jerozolimskie Avenue. They were going to visit Wiktoria, but Hoża was another two or three stops away, and it was drizzling, an early autumn morning with the trees just turning and the weather damp. Jerzy watched a trickle of water thread through the dirt on the window, and wondered what Wiktoria might have to eat. He was ravenous.

The tram stopped, and the doors swung open, but then they quickly closed again. He felt Andrzej nudge him sharply.

'What?'

'Trouble,' Andrzej muttered.

There were German voices at the front, he was suddenly aware of a wave of panic rippling through every passenger, and it reached him quickly as he looked from one white face to another, and heard the whispered word: '*Łapanka!* Round-up!' Then the barrier dividing the tram was flung up, and two German soldiers pushed their way through, shouting; 'Papers! Papers!' People were fumbling in pockets and purses, but the soldiers barely glanced at the cards they produced. Instinctively, Jerzy pressed away, towards the centre doors, and at once saw a whole group of soldiers outside on the pavement, and a lorry just in front of the tram. There was a sudden scuffle and he

128

turned back to see a young man in a jacket and peaked cap thrust angrily towards the front.

'Raus! Raus!'

Two more soldiers – he could see now, as the passengers fell back – were waiting up there with rifles.

'And this one,' said one of the Germans, pushing the shoulders of another man. Then he was scanning every face, eyes flicking like a lizard's across the trapped passengers.

Beside him, Andrzej was staring at the floor. Jerzy felt a great pool of fear spread through his stomach, his back and limbs, until the whole of his body was filled with it, and he couldn't move. When the German grabbed him, shouting: 'This one, too,' he knew that the whole of his life had led to this one, pure moment of terror, with nothing to protect him. No father, no God. Then he was stumbling down towards the doors with a rifle pressed into his back, out to where the lorry was waiting.

Anna walked quickly along Senatorska, shivering in the evening chill, her feet already cold. No one had proper new shoes any more: the brown lace-ups had had to last her for two winters, day in and day out, mended and reheeled four or five times until now they were almost beyond repair.

At the opening to the courtyard of their apartment block she stopped for a moment, wondering if she might meet Jerzy on his way home, as she sometimes did. But she couldn't see him, and even in broad daylight people did not stand about in the streets. In the frightening dusk she hurried into the courtyard, and across, and climbed the stone steps, her feet echoing faintly as she went higher and the stairway became enclosed. Still, over eighteen months since they were moved, she found it hard to come back here at the end of each day.

She turned the key in the door and pushed it open.

'Teresa?'

'In here.'

She was in the kitchen, writing at the table; a pan simmered on the stove. Anna went over and lifted the lid. Fat dumplings floated in a broth, nudging slices of carrot and onion. 'Smells good,' she said, and still in her coat and scarf dipped in the wooden ladle and blew on it, taking a burning sip.

'How was today?' Teresa asked, putting away her notebook.

'Very busy – we had four new patients in.' She took another sip, and put down the ladle. 'What were you writing?'

Teresa shrugged. 'Just a journal.'

'Oh? I didn't know you kept a journal.'

'I only really started it in the spring.'

'When we heard about Tata?'

'Yes.'

Anna went across and put her arm across Teresa's shoulders, thin under the green cardigan she'd reknitted from an old jumper last winter.

'Are you all right?'

Teresa reached up and took her hand; she nodded but did not answer.

Anna leaned her head against hers and they stayed like that, heads touching, neither speaking. At last Anna said:

'Where's Jerzy?'

'I don't know,' said Teresa. 'I never know.'

She patted Anna's hand, got up, and began to lay the table. Anna sat on the rickety chair and watched her. Since they'd come here, despite all the shortages, and price rises, despite having to sell piece after piece of china, and utensils, and clothes on the black market; despite all of it, Teresa had managed to make this horrible place a sort of home. Mama's tapestry *kilims* hung on the walls, just as they had in Praga, and in the spring and summer there were always a few flowers – the street flower-sellers hadn't disappeared.

Teresa set out plates, black bread, cracked dishes and the worn cutlery they'd bought in Żelaznej Bramy, after selling the last of the silver plate. Wiktoria had helped them to do that – she knew someone who knew someone. Wiktoria always knew someone.

'Does Jerzy talk to you?' Teresa asked. 'I mean about how he spends his time.'

'Teresa . . .' Anna twiddled a tin fork. 'You know how he spends his time. A lot of it, anyway. Don't you?'

Teresa pulled out her chair and sat down again. 'You mean he's joined.'

'Of course.'

'Through Andrzej.'

'Well, yes. Through the Grey Ranks, that's what they call the underground Scouts, isn't it? That's how they recruit a lot of boys, through the Grey Ranks.' She hesitated. 'I should've kept on going to Guides, too, I wish you hadn't stopped me.'

Teresa looked at her. 'You mean you wish you could join, too.'

'Of course I do.'

'Anna . . .' She looked stricken. 'Do you realize what you're saying? Aren't we all in enough danger already? There are round-ups and executions almost every day – every time you or Jerzy are late home, I worry. It's bad enough knowing that Jerzy is in real danger now. I couldn't bear it if I had to fear for you like that, too.'

'But – ' Anna felt a wave of irritation. 'But there are whole families joining. Other . . . mothers seem to manage.'

Teresa flushed. 'Perhaps it's easier for them, if they are real mothers.'

'Why? Why should it be?' Anna demanded. 'I don't think . . .' She hesitated. 'I don't think my real mother would have stopped us. I think she'd have wanted us to join. To *do* something!'

Teresa was struggling to remain calm. 'I can't possibly know what she would have wanted for you, Anna. I just know that you're only seventeen, and I – I must forbid you to join. I can't bear to think of you taking such a risk for nothing.'

'For *nothing?*'

'I mean – if they shoot you, Anna, it will change nothing. Will it?'

Anna pushed back her chair and stood up. 'How can you *think* like this? Do you think we're ever going to have a life any better than this miserable bloody life if we don't fight back? Don't you know what everyone's saying? "Better to die on our feet than to live on our knees!" Do you want to live on your knees? Do you? Do you think Tata would have wanted us to? I think he would have wanted us to fight!'

'Anna, Anna, please . . .' Teresa's hands on the table were trembling.

'What? Wiktoria's joined, I'm sure she has.'

'She has only herself to think of.'

'And we have to think of you,' Anna said bitterly, before she could stop herself. 'Isn't it enough that we've had to do that all these years?'

'What do you mean?' Teresa stared at her.

'What do you think I mean?' Anna took a deep breath and plunged in, her words tumbling over one another. 'Forgive me, Teresa, but the ghetto is empty now, isn't it? They're all gone. Do you still have to hide away?'

Teresa sat absolutely still, her thin face whiter than white as she looked at Anna with an expression unfathomable. Terror. Fury. Disbelief.

'What are you saying?' she whispered.

'I . . . I . . .' Anna gripped the back of the rickety chair.

What are you saying?

'I . . .' Anna began to cry. 'I'm sorry, I didn't mean it . . .'

'Mean *what?*' Teresa was on her feet now, too, shaking and shaking her. 'Mean *what?*'

'Stop it, stop it!'

'Tell me what you mean. *Tell me!*'

'That you're a Jew!' Anna screamed, and broke away, sobbing.

'*What?* You've . . . you've thought that all these years?'

'Yes! Yes, yes, yes!'

Teresa's hands fell to her sides. As if she were sleepwalking, she made her way back to the table, and sank into her chair. Anna went on crying, leaning against the damp wall by the windows on to the balcony. What will she do to me now? she thought. And suddenly she was as terrified as if the discovery had been made of her, by Teresa.

'Anna, come and sit down.' Teresa spoke dully. 'Please.'

She wiped her eyes on her sleeve, but did not move. Against her hot face, the damp wall felt almost soothing.

'Please.'

She went, sitting in the rickety chair and staring at the scratches and gouges on the table. There was a long silence.

At last Teresa said: 'I – I suppose I must be grateful that you did nothing. You kept your secret. Did Jerzy . . . think the same?'

'He thought it was possible.'

'You thought it was certain. Anna?'

'No. I mean – I didn't know. I just found myself thinking it, and . . . and the thought wouldn't go away.' She still couldn't look at her.

Teresa gave a long, deep sigh. 'Will you believe me if I tell you that it is absolutely untrue? Now you've told me – it explains almost everything about you that I've never been able to understand. And about Jerzy. But I swear to you, on my life – you must believe me, Anna – you have nothing to hide, or to be afraid of because of me. Anna?'

She slowly raised her head. Teresa was looking at her with utter seriousness. 'I am not a Jew,' she said.

'All right.' Anna felt suddenly completely exhausted, drained. And very ashamed. 'All right.'

'Do you believe me?'

'Yes.' Impossible to say no. Impossible to know whether she did or not. After all, if her suspicions were true, Teresa would never admit it now, would she? Did that mean she didn't trust her and Jerzy not to betray it? Did she really think they would betray her? And oh God, oh God, she could talk about fighting, and courage, but would she have been brave enough, if the Gestapo had come, to lie, and risk her own life? I hate myself, she thought miserably, and tears poured down her face again.

'I'm sorry,' she wept. 'I'm sorry, I'm sorry . . .'

And then they both jumped, and grabbed each other's hands across the table, as footsteps came running along the landing to the apartment door, and someone began to pound on it, again and again.

'Oh my God,' Anna whimpered. Someone had heard her screaming – 'You're a Jew!' They must have, how could she have done it? And now what would happen to them? They clung to each other, as the pounding on the door grew louder. Then it stopped, and they heard a voice call hoarsely, urgently:

'Anna! Anna!'

'Oh God, that's Andrzej.' Anna scrambled to her feet, and ran along the corridor. She flung the door open, and saw him, huge and fair in the doorway, panting, the dim light from the landing behind him showing beads of sweat on his face.

He came quickly inside, closed the door, and told her.

'But where is he?' Anna asked. 'Where *is* he?'

'I don't know,' Andrzej said bleakly. He sat at the table looking suddenly much more of a boy than he had ever looked – even before the war, when he and Jerzy were in the same class at the *gimnazium*, he had always appeared older and more adult than any of the others, and particularly than Jerzy. It was partly because he was so tall and large-framed, but more than that – he had always seemed a leader. Now, much thinner, and without Jerzy, whom Anna realized was always with him, he looked younger and awkward, fiddling nervously with a loose button on his jacket.

'I – I have a feeling they didn't shoot them, I don't know why. I've been waiting all day until I could talk to our officer.' Teresa and Anna avoided each other's eyes. 'He's going to do everything he can to find out, but . . . he thinks they'll all be in Pawiak.'

'Have you . . . have you ever heard of anyone escape from Pawkiak?' Anna asked.

Andrzej bit his lip. 'No.'

She watched his miserable face, and couldn't help it: she had to ask. 'Why didn't they take you?'

He shook his head. 'Who knows? Perhaps they only wanted four today. I'm sure they weren't looking for any particular man. Or – well, perhaps they were, and Jerzy looks like him.'

Teresa cleared her throat; she still looked shaken, almost dazed. 'How long have you been in AK?'

He turned to her. 'About eighteen months. I'm sorry, Pani Kurowska – I don't like to upset you.'

She shook her head. 'And when . . . when did Jerzy join?'

'He was sworn in last November. He kept putting it off, he was worried in case anything happened to you two. In the end, I think he decided there was almost as much risk just in going out of his own apartment. Which is true.' He made a move towards the kitchen door. 'I'll go now, but if I hear anything at all, I'll come and tell you. I'm . . . I'm very sorry.'

'Goodbye,' said Teresa. She didn't get up.

Anna followed him down past the peeling walls of the corridor to the front door.

'Thank you for coming.'

'I wish I hadn't had to come for such a reason. Your stepmother . . . she looks very distressed.'

'It's not just because of Jerzy . . . We – we had a sort of quarrel. Just before you came.'

'Oh.' Again, the awkward fiddling with his jacket button, embarrassed. Family things. She didn't think he had much of a family left, just his mother and that uncle. She wanted suddenly to comfort him, to tell him she was sure Jerzy was all right, but she didn't know how to start. Andrzej had been like an aloof older brother all her life – it must be humiliating for him to be seen unnerved.

'I'd better go now,' he said.

'Yes.' She opened the door. 'Goodbye.'

'Goodbye, Anna.' He took her hand and raised it to his lips so swiftly, and kissed it so briefly, that she was barely certain he had done so. Then he stumbled too fast down the unlit stone steps, his feet echoing off the damp walls until he reached the first floor and she could no longer hear him.

She closed the door and leaned against it.

Andrzej, she thought. Andrzej.

'Anna?'

She took a deep breath, and pulled herself away from the door.

'Coming, Teresa.'

Tata was home again, although it wasn't here, in dark Senatorska, nor in Praga, but somewhere by a river, winding away into a distant lake. He was reading, on the bank, and looked up as she walked over to him, and smiled. 'Let me read you some of this,' he said, holding out a hand. 'Where's Jerzy?'

'Oh, we never see him now,' she said. 'He's lost, you know.'

He looked at her, puzzled. 'Lost?'

'I'll have to write it down.' She began to scribble on a piece of paper from her pocket, kneeling, and pressing on the ground: *He has gone to visit Mama's grave in Pawiak*. No, that wasn't right. The pencil slipped, stabbing the paper, and blades of grass poked through.

He has gone to a country called Katyń, she wrote, in a fever. *You know where that is*. She looked up to pass the note to him, but he had turned his head away.

'Tata? Tata? Tata!'

She tore the paper into tiny pieces and threw them into the air, watching them swirl in the breeze across the river, then settle on the water, and float away, towards the distant lake.

She woke, confused, in the small dark room; heard Teresa, in her bed, groan as she turned in her sleep. 'I couldn't explain . . .' she said aloud, and heard her voice break. She saw Jerzy, his head bent, locked in a cell somewhere deep in the grim fortress of Pawiak, and she began to howl.

They were taken out almost every day, to work on clearing the ghetto ruins. In single file, each carrying a pickaxe or spade, they were marched out of the prison and along the dawn-lit streets to the nearby ghetto wall. An armed guard was at the head and tail of the column; two more paced alongside. Inside the gate, they were divided into groups of three or four, and set to work on the heaps of rubble and the twisted pipes of plumbing – mostly it was salvage work. Anything which might be re-used, girders or piping, was piled on to a heap, taken out every few days by lorry.

The overalls they had been issued with were no protection against the cold of the early morning, and they had no gloves. Within a couple of days his fingers were bleeding from cuts and chaps, his palms raw with blisters. They did not speak: in the grey light the only sounds were the metallic scraping of the tools and dull thud of falling brickwork, and the boots of the guards as they paced up and down, stamping to try to keep warm themselves, even though they wore caps and greatcoats. As the day went on, they changed shifts, and the prisoners were allowed a short break and given hunks of dark bread and water from tin mugs. Sometimes, at these moments, it was possible to walk away for a minute, relieving yourself behind the mounds of fallen masonry and taking a quick look around: he had his eye on a high, burned-out voltage point. But you didn't risk staying longer than a few moments.

By the seventh week he was so exhausted and weakened that he could barely hold up his head. As he stumbled along in the column, the pavement began to sway beneath him, and he began to sway with it.

'March!' snapped the guard, suddenly beside him.

He jerked up, felt dizzy, stumbled again and would have fallen except that the guard grabbed him and shook him hard. Behind, in the column, the sound of boots stopped abruptly.

'March!' said the guard again, releasing him, and when he fell bent down and hauled him by the collar of his overalls to his feet and struck him across the mouth. Jerzy yelped, tasting blood on his lips, then forced himself to follow the man in front, his eyes fixed on a patch on the man's overalls. The boots sounded behind him again, and then they were through the gate and once more facing the desolation of the ghetto.

That night, in the airless cell, closing his eyes against naked bulb and spyhole, he listened to the breathing of his three companions and traced in his mind the outline of the high, burned-out voltage point, with its gaping hole and just room enough inside to hide a man.

The next day, as the two guards talked in the change of shift, he moved step by step closer to the edge of the mound of rubble behind which it stood. He was at the corner, they were sharing a cigarette, and then he was past, half-crawling towards it, smelling rust and pushing stubs of wire aside as he squeezed inside. He crouched, listening to the roar of his heartbeat and then to the sudden question in the voices of the guards, the shout, and the click of a rifle. He held his hand over his swollen lip to stop himself crying out, and waited to be found.

The dressmakers' school was in a street not far from Wiktoria's apartment. Very little sewing instruction went on there: the girls might have unravelled sweaters from 1938 and reknitted them, or unpicked dresses and cut them down into skirts, but almost every teacher was in AK; the murmur of conversation above the gentle sounds of scissors and rustling paper patterns was of meetings, bulletins, sabotage, assassination.

Anna was required to attend there soon after Jerzy's arrest. She had a pink attendance card, to be stamped each month, and went every morning, working in the hospital in the afternoons. Natalia was also there, and had already taken the oath.

'Are you going to join?' she asked softly one morning, as they bent over the long table, straightening out a pattern.

Anna shook her head, her mouth full of pins. 'Not yet.'

'Why?'

She took the pins out. 'Teresa is too afraid . . . we've had a dreadful misunderstanding, I don't want to talk about it, but I don't want to upset her any more. Not without some news of Jerzy.'

'You've heard nothing?'

'Nothing. You know I'd tell you if there was.'

'I'm so sorry . . .'

'I know. Thank you.' She slid pins into blue cloth, blindly following the arrows on the paper.

On a wintry Sunday morning some weeks later, she took the tram to visit Wiktoria, deliberately making the same journey Jerzy had made with Andrzej: to relive it felt as if it were the only opportunity she had to be close to him now. She climbed on at the back, felt the vibration as the doors swung to and closed, and looked along at a fixed point above the driver's head. The car was half-empty: only a few old men and women in black travelling to mass because it was too cold for them to walk, and a couple with children. She was not going to be arrested here, but the risk made her feel like a pilgrim of whom a sacrifice might be asked. They approached the intersection with Jerozolimskie Avenue, where the Germans had stopped the tram, and she looked out of the window at the leafless trees, at the few people hurrying along in the winter air, past closed shops with nothing in the windows.

What were they doing to him now?

A thin flurry of snow stung her cheeks as she got off the tram in Hoża and she began to run, slipping once on the uneven pavement. As she reached Wiktoria's building, and climbed the stairs to her door, she thought of the approaching winter, in the dark and bitter cold of Senatorska, without Tata, without Jerzy, with only Teresa and her sadness, and the awful silences between them now, and she thought: I will go mad. She rang the bell once, twice, in a sudden fury of frustration, heard Wiktoria hurrying to the door and hardly cared if she had frightened her.

Then she heard her ask in a steady voice: 'Who is it?' and answered quickly 'Anna,' feeling a little ashamed. When the chain inside slid back, and Wiktoria opened the door, she burst into tears, shivering.

'Anna, Anna . . . sssh. Come and see who's here.'

'Who?' She let herself be led along the passage by the hand, and into the sitting room, lit by the whiteness of the falling snow, where Jerzy sat at the table, very thin, in filthy overalls, with a bruised and swollen mouth, his hands round a glass of tea. She ran to him, and knocked it flying.

He had stayed hidden until it was dark, and the voices had gone away. Perhaps they thought he had fallen in the ruins: there were plenty of places where you might trip and plunge into the crater of a bombed-out building, and no one would ever find you. There was no point in trying to get out while the curfew was on, so he waited all night in the shelter of a half-destroyed house, huddled against a wall in the cold. In the first light, before the working parties returned, he paced the walls until he found a place with a great heap of rubble piled up beside it. He scaled it carefully, managed to heave himself to the top, and leap down on the other side. He'd sprained his ankle when he landed, but at least nothing was broken. Then he limped along the deserted back streets where most people were still asleep and where if he were asked he might – just – be a workman on an early shift. It was too dangerous to go back to Elektoralna, to Teresa and Anna: that was the address on his papers, and the first place they would go to. So he made for Wiktoria's apartment, alarming her with a ring on the door at half-past six in the morning, and stumbled inside, almost blue with cold and exhaustion.

Anna listened, as Wiktoria made more tea and a dish of *pierogi*.

'I missed you so much,' she said. 'I thought I'd never see you again.'

'Perhaps Tata had his eye on me.'

'I dreamt I was trying to tell him where you were, and I couldn't.'

He took her hand. 'I'm sorry – it must have been horrible for you. I missed you, too. But I can't stay here, it's much too dangerous for Wiktoria, and I'd never be able to go out. I'll have to get in touch with Andrzej today, and try to arrange false papers or something.'

She said: 'Andrzej was frantic, I think.' She didn't say: 'He kissed my hand,' or that she had thought about that brief, clumsy touch

quite often since. 'I'll have to go back and tell Teresa, she'll be so
pleased.' She hesitated. 'Jerzy?'

'Yes?'

'I . . . I told her.'

'What? Told her what?'

'About . . . about what we thought.' She lowered her voice as
Wiktoria came down the corridor. 'You know.'

He shook his head, exhausted. 'What are you talking about?'

Had seven weeks in Pawiak made him forget so much?

'About her being a Jew,' she whispered.

'Oh. That. Sorry . . . I'm not feeling too good . . .'

'She says she isn't.'

'What are you two whispering about?' asked Wiktoria, coming in.
'Jerzy, you look terrible, we must get you to bed.'

His head slumped to his chest. Anna and Wiktoria struggled to lift
him; they carried him, deeply asleep, into Wiktoria's bedroom, and
covered him with blankets.

Within two days Jerzy was smuggled out of Warsaw, carrying forged
papers, and went into hiding on a farm, some twenty miles to the
south, which belonged to a contact of the Captain. Dressed like a
peasant labourer, he helped the farmer dig up the last swedes and
potatoes; he learned to milk thin cattle and feed hungry pigs on
mornings when mist hung over the frozen fields like a shroud. Pan
Kruk had taken the oath two years ago: Jerzy was not the first person
to be hidden away here, and in the loft above the kitchen, where he
slept, was a rifle, under the floorboards.

'My father's,' Pan Kruk told Jerzy briefly. 'I hope the next time I
fire it will be to blow a Kraut's head off.'

He talked about the uprising as if it were a certainty; he told Jerzy
that arms had been smuggled out of Warsaw for months, to prepare
the countryside. And he had something else hidden away, too.

When Jerzy had been on the farm for a few weeks, he took him
into the family sitting room, and lifted boxes behind the couch to
reveal an ancient wireless. Jerzy gaped. He told Pan Kruk how
he'd smashed their lovely Telefunken into a thousand pieces before
handing it in to the collecting office, and the farmer laughed.

'Good lad. But I'm glad I kept ours.'

That night, for the first time since the siege of Warsaw, four long
years ago, Jerzy sat listening to a broadcast from London to Poland.

'On every bomb the gallant Poles in the RAF drop on to the cities

139

of Germany, there is written: *oko za oko* – an eye for an eye. Brave men and women of Poland – you are not forgotten!' When the *Polonaise* was played at the end, crackling through the worn transmitter, Jerzy had tears pouring down his face.

He stayed on the farm all winter, and when in the spring of 1944 he returned to Warsaw it was not to Senatorska but to stay with Andrzej, in his uncle's apartment. By then, Teresa and Anna had parted.

On a bright cold morning in March, they left the dark apartment on Senatorska, once more carrying their cases. It's like the day we came here, thought Anna: a beautiful day, and a horrible lump in my throat. The canvas on the market stalls in Żelazna Brama flapped in the wind; ahead, through the Iron Gate, the trees in the Saxon Gardens tossed bare branches. They walked through the gardens to Krakowskie Przedmieście, their faces cold, and at the tram stop by the church they put down their cases. In a place like this, the Champs Elysées of Warsaw, you could see how the *Volksdeutsche* and the better-off Poles were surviving the occupation: well-dressed women hurried along the broad pavements, fur collars turned up round soft faces against the cold. From here, Teresa was going to stay with a cousin, who lived near the embankment. From here, Anna was going to go and live with Wiktoria. They looked at each other, and looked away. Then Teresa put her hand on Anna's shoulder. She had tears in her eyes, but it might have been the bitter wind.

'Goodbye, Anna. Keep in touch.'

'I will. Goodbye. Thank you – for everything you did for us.'

They kissed, suddenly hugging each other. Then Teresa wiped her eyes and bent down to pick up her suitcase. She walked quickly down the avenue, under the trees; within minutes she had reached a side street, and turned on the corner to raise her hand and wave.

Anna waved back, and then she was gone. She paced up and down, waiting for the tram, filled with guilt and relief.

'But it's much more sensible,' said Wiktoria, half an hour later, sitting on the spare room bed and watching her unpack. 'You will be able to be friends, now, without feeling so responsible for each other.'

Anna nodded, but didn't answer. She wanted to confide in Wiktoria, but she was too ashamed. This is what the war has done to me, she thought, and probably to most of us. I couldn't see Teresa for who she really was, I could only look at her through Nazi eyes, and fear for my own skin. If I were religious, if I really believed, instead of wishing I could, I would go to confession now, and ask to be forgiven.

'Anna? What are you thinking about?'

She blushed. 'Nothing.' A book lay on the bedside table; she picked it up and turned it over. 'What's this?'

'*The Forsyte Saga*, dear. We're all lapping it up – I thought you might enjoy it. A nice little bit of escapism for you – I think you could do with it.'

Anna smiled. 'Thank you.'

She shook out the dress with patch pockets she had made in the dressmakers' school, and hung it in the cupboard. And now, she thought – now I have only myself to think of.

In the afternoon, she telephoned Natalia and arranged to meet her.

There were five of them, meeting before curfew in the cellar of a house near Central Park. Natalia and Jadwiga, both recruited through Guides. Henryk, the commander, who worked under cover in a German chemical plant. Wojtek, nineteen, who had been recruited there by him. And Anna, who joined them one evening after leaving work at the hospital, and stood in the middle of the cellar with a cross in one hand and the card with the oath in the other, as they watched her.

'Before God the Almighty, before the Holy Virgin Mary, Queen of Poland,' she read slowly, 'I put my hand on this Holy Cross, the symbol of martyrdom and salvation, and I swear that I will defend the honour of Poland with all my might, that I will fight with arms in hand to deliver her from slavery . . .'

5

Uprising: Warsaw, 1944

The mood of the city was changing. With almost every *kommunikat*, in almost every AK meeting, the news from Europe brought hope: on front after front, the German forces were being beaten back at last.

The third of May was Constitution Day.* Last year, in the Żoliborz district, the underground had celebrated by tapping the wires of the German loudspeakers, and the passers-by had slowed down, suddenly aware that instead of the usual stream of pronouncements and propaganda, someone was fervently delivering a patriotic speech. And they were playing the national anthem! For perhaps ten minutes, people stood listening, cheering, crying. Then the Gestapo swept in, in furious carloads, and the people scattered.

This year, on Constitution Day, people in Stare Miasto crossing Zamkowy Square, before the Royal Palace, found other people nudging them to look up, right up, to the palace roof. Unfurled from the top of the clock tower, the Polish flag was flying, and down below the knots of people became a crowd, gazing up at the white and red, billowing in the early summer sky.

In weeks, the bulletins which Wiktoria and Anna shared were full of the triumph of Monte Cassino. For six months, the Germans had held the Italian monastery, set at the very top of a mountain overlooking the only road between north and south Italy. The monastery was surrounded by the heaviest fortifications; every movement on the road was observed, and so far all attempts by Allied forces either to breach the fortifications or to use the road through the mountain had failed: they were under constant bombardment from German artillery. But on 18 May, led by General Anders under British command, the Polish Second Corps had advanced up the mountain, and in one of the most ferocious battles of the war stormed the beleaguered monastery. By the end, almost four thousand men lay dead or wounded on

---

* The Polish Constitution, the most liberal in its day of any in Europe, was decreed in 1791. Russian intervention prevented it from being enforced, and in 1795 Poland disappeared from the map of Europe. May 3rd is one of the most important dates in the Polish calendar.

the mountainside, but the way was open for the Allied advance on Rome, and in three weeks the capital had fallen.

Warsaw was ecstatic.

'And now I really do believe,' said Wiktoria, putting away her spectacles, and tearing the paper to shreds, 'that we don't have long to wait.'

'For the uprising?' Anna asked, taking the shreds and putting them in a paper bag to burn in the stove.

'For the end of the war,' said Wiktoria. 'For liberation.'

Four weeks later: D-Day, and with the Normandy landings, the Allied invasion of occupied Europe began. Cherbourg was taken by the Americans. Caen fell to the British and Canadians. Now, tanks were able to break through the German defences, and the Allies began to advance on Paris.

Another month. In 'Wolf's Lair', Hitler's headquarters near the town of Rastenburg, East Prussia, a bomb planted by anti-Nazi officers exploded under the table where he sat in conference. Hitler escaped the death intended for him, and well over one hundred and fifty conspirators were executed, but the attempt on his life had been made, and it fuelled the certainty in occupied Europe that a German defeat was now inevitable.

And then –

'The Russians are coming!' Jerzy burst into Wiktoria's apartment. 'Have you heard that? They've crossed the river Bug, they're beating back the Germans – I overheard two officers in a café this morning, they were talking about leaving Warsaw – they're starting to panic.' He grabbed Wiktoria's hands. 'They're starting to panic!'

Wiktoria looked at him. 'And do you really imagine, Jerzy, after everything that has happened, after what happened to your poor father, that we are to feel only gratitude to the Russians?'

He flushed, frowning. 'I know . . . But the Red Army has AK units fighting alongside, doesn't it? It's they and the Russians who will liberate us, after all . . .'

'And I wonder,' said Wiktoria, sitting down, 'if that is what will happen.'

'What do you mean?'

She shrugged. 'I mean I wonder if there will be such . . . cooperation. There are rumours that the Polish cities the AK help to take from the Germans may be retaken by the Russians.' She looked at Jerzy, shaking her head. 'Naturally, I hope that we shall all receive as much help as possible from Russia when the moment comes. But

I should like to think that it is only assistance, to fight against the Nazis, nothing else. I should like to think that with help we shall liberate ourselves, and welcome the Russians as guests in a free Poland.'

'You should be writing speeches, Aunt.'

'Yes,' said Wiktoria. 'I think perhaps I should. And you be careful, Jerzy – what are you thinking of, eavesdropping in cafés? Your escape seems to have gone to your head.'

He grinned. 'Yes. Perhaps it has.'

Soon, the whole of Warsaw was watching a great trail of traffic across the bridges of the Vistula as the defeated German army retreated from the eastern front. Wounded, dirty, exhausted and apathetic, they shuffled through the city streets, and with the news of the attempt on Hitler's life, and the success of the Normandy landings, retreat became flight, and then, as Jerzy had said, it did become panic.

German civilians besieged the railway stations, or paid fortunes for the hire of a horse and cart. All the German offices, including the Post Office, closed down; heavily defended pillboxes, and barricades of barbed wire, surrounded all the major installations and buildings. German newspapers stopped publication. In the headquarters on Szucha Avenue, the Gestapo were burning documents; the mayor and Governor Fischer abruptly departed.

On 26 July, Prime Minister Mikołajczyk, who had succeeded General Sikorski, flew from London to Moscow for urgent talks with Stalin. Mikołajczyk wanted three things: crucially, to establish the voice of the London Government in any new administration in Poland; to reclaim the cities of Wilno and Lwów; to ensure that Soviet aid was guaranteed for a Warsaw insurrection.

On 27 July, Fischer returned. The following day, posters appeared and loudspeakers throughout the city broadcast a call: one hundred thousand men were to report immediately for fortification work – digging trenches, building additional barricades all round the main German strongholds, defences against a Russian attack. Except for a few old men with a sense of humour, who turned up at the recruitment posts in the Old Town next day with rusty spades, the call was ignored.

Within two days, quite different posters appeared, this time signed by the political and military chiefs of the PAL, the Polish People's Army, an underground military organization numbering some two

144

thousand, under Soviet leadership. General Bór and his staff had apparently deserted Warsaw: the people were called on to accept the leadership of the communists in an armed fight against the Germans. This call was also ignored: no one believed that Bór would leave them now.

Gunfire sounded from across the river. Soviet planes flew over the city. The Soviet Army, commanded by Marshal Rokossovsky, drew near to the outskirts of Praga. Marching alongside was the First Polish Army, formed in 1943, when Stalin had broken off diplomatic relations with the Polish Government in London over the Katyń affair. It was led by General Berling, the Polish officer who, unlike General Anders, when captured by the Russians in 1939 had declared himself prepared to serve the communist cause.

Now, every member of every AK unit, some forty thousand men and four thousand women, was tense with the expectation of coming out into the open at last. Office workers, teachers, factory workers, artists, musicians, doctors, nurses, labourers, waitresses, students, clerks and typists – all were waiting for the call to arms.

On the evening of 29 July, the AK monitoring service picked up a transmission in Polish from the Soviet radio station run by the Union of Polish Patriots. The Union had been formed by Polish communists in Soviet Russia in 1943, to act as Stalin's puppet.

'No doubt Warsaw already hears the guns of the battle which is soon to bring liberation. Those who have never bowed their heads to the Hitlerite power will again, as in 1939, join in battle against the Germans, this time for the decisive action. The Polish Army, now entering Polish territory, trained in the USSR, is now joined to the People's Army to form the Corps of the Polish Armed Forces, the armed core of our nation in its struggle for independence. Its ranks will be joined tomorrow by the sons of Warsaw. They will, together with the Allied Army, pursue the enemy westward, drive the Hitlerite vermin from the Polish land, and strike a mortal blow at the last of Prussian imperialism.

'For Warsaw, which did not yield, but fought on, the hour of action has already arrived. The Germans will no doubt try to defend themselves in Warsaw . . . They will expose the city to ruin, and its inhabitants to death. They will try to take away all the most precious possessions and turn into dust all that they have to leave behind. It is therefore a hundred times more necessary than ever to remember that in the flood of Hitlerite destruction all is lost that is not saved by active effort; that by direct, active struggle in the streets of Warsaw, in its houses, factories and shops, we not only hasten the moment of final liberation, but also save the nation's property and the lives of our brethren.'

Next day, similar transmissions were broadcast by this Polish-language radio station, nicely named Kościuszko, after the Polish national hero who had led an uprising against Czarist Russia. It sounded so close and clear that those intently listening assumed it was broadcasting from just across the Vistula, with the Soviet forces in Praga. In fact, it was deep inside Russia, in Tashkent.

Then the Soviet planes dropped leaflets, swirling and fluttering on to the streets. Walking arm in arm down Jerozolimskie Avenue, Anna and Natalia found themselves in a snowstorm of paper. Anna reached out and grabbed one; they stood reading it, as more tumbled out of the sky.

'Poles! The time of liberation is at hand! Poles, to arms! . . . Every Polish homestead must become a stronghold in the struggle against the invader . . . There is not a moment to lose.'

They looked at each other, excited and afraid, and hurried to find Henryk.

On Sunday 30 July, tanks patrolled the streets which were suddenly calm and quiet, and which seemed to have no more than the ordinary amount of traffic, except, perhaps, that there were an unusual number of young people out, heavily dressed in unseasonal anoraks or wind-cheaters. Many carried knapsacks or bags. They ignored the tanks, the police and military patrols as they made their way through the city; some, enjoying the sun in the parks, were openly reading underground newspapers.

Fourteen hundred men and over four hundred women were deported that day from Pawiak, and sent to concentration camps.

On 31 July, in his staff headquarters, General Bór was told by his intelligence units that Russian tanks had been sighted in Praga. Already, the suburbs of Otwock, Falencia, Józefów, Radzymin – all within ten miles of the city – had been taken. Now, in urgent consultation with the Governor Delegate, Jan Jankowski, Bór judged that the time for open insurrection had arrived.

'Very well, then,' said Jankowski. 'Begin.'

Bór turned to General Monter, Commander of the whole Warsaw District of the AK. 'Tomorrow,' he said, 'at five p.m. precisely, you will start operations in Warsaw.'

*

The telephone rang in the empty hall.

'Anna?' Wiktoria was still in her bedroom.

'I'll take it.' She turned down the gas under the kettle, went quickly out of the kitchen, and picked up the receiver.

'*Słucham*. I'm listening.'

'It's me,' said Natalia. 'Are you ready for our outing?'

'Today?'

'Today.' Anna could hear Natalia trying to control the excitement in her voice. 'I'll ring you again later, to confirm the time, but can you have everything ready for the picnic?'

Anna saw herself smile in the shadows of the mirror above the phone. 'Of course. I'll have everything we need. We're . . . we're going to the picnic spot we've talked about?'

'Yes.' Her voice dropped. 'Don't move until you hear more.' The phone clicked.

Anna put down the receiver. 'Wiktoria!' She ran down the corridor to Wiktoria's room, and stood in the door. 'Guess!'

Wiktoria sat up on the pillows, pulling a cardigan round her shoulders.

'It's starting?'

'Yes! Natalia's going to ring back with the time.' She ran across and hugged her. 'I'm going to explode.'

'Perhaps you'd get me some tea first.'

'Of course.' Anna raced back to the kitchen, and while the kettle came to the boil she stood and looked down on to the street. A grey morning suddenly, after the heat of the last days of July. The pavement was beginning to fill with people, although it was still early, and they were hurrying, purposeful, the atmosphere surely already changed: these people did not look as though they were simply going drearily to work in an occupied city.

The kettle sputtered, and she switched it off and poured boiling water into the glasses through the strainer with just a pinch of tea. She carried them through to Wiktoria's room, and found her already out of bed and dressing. 'I'll leave it here,' said Anna, putting the glass on the chest of drawers, and went back to her own small room. She left her glass to cool, and bent to open the drawer at the bottom of the wardrobe. She pulled out the small parcel, and spread the contents carefully on the bed.

Bandages – mostly made from strips of old sheet. A bottle of iodine. Safety pins, two dozen. The nail scissors she'd had since she was twelve. And the small piece of paper she'd been given in the meeting three days ago, heavily printed in small, smudged black letters: AK Courier Pass.

From the wardrobe she took out the canvas shoulder bag hanging inside, and she put all these things into it, fastening and unfastening the stiff buckles and straps until they would open quickly and she didn't need to fumble with them. Then she took her needlecase from the drawer of the little table by her bed, and the two strips of material, one white, one red, which she had hoarded from the dressmakers' school, as they all had. She folded the white one round her arm to check the length, then sat on the bed, sewing them together until she had an armband, in the colours of the Polish flag, and was ready, now, for the next phone call.

It came within the hour. 'Five o'clock. Be there by four.' The number of an apartment house, a coded street, not far from the coded Three Crosses Square. She stood at the window of the sitting room, watching the movement of the people on the street below, as a fine rain began to fall.

That afternoon, 1 August, over ten thousand members of the AK took up their positions in Stare Miasto, the Old Town. In the most overcrowded area of Warsaw, they were preparing to seize and defend key points: Krasiński Square, the Royal Palace, St John's Cathedral; the Polish Bank, the Market Square. In every cobbled street, every winding alleyway in Stare Miasto's few square miles, doors in the tall narrow houses opened quickly, and the people behind them let in men and women from outside without greeting, closing them quickly again.

Inside, the officers and men, the women nurses and cooks and couriers, piled up sandbags at the windows of the first and second floors – rooms where, usually, whole families ate and slept. They ran up the winding stairs to the attics, peering down from gabled windows on to the open squares, and German patrols. They ran down worn stone steps to the sprawling cellars, swiftly assembling and setting out equipment secretly stored there, to turn them into kitchens and field hospitals. They scribbled the names of the streets overhead on the walls, so that you could follow a whole underground route through the district, if necessary, by knocking through from one house cellar to another, and another. Perhaps it wouldn't be necessary – everyone hoped it would be over in days. In every house, the atmosphere was a feverish, heady mixture of nerves and elation.

In a ground-floor room on a street not far from the river bank, the last man in Boar unit had just arrived, panting, furious with himself for missing the deadline by ten minutes.

'Sir. Reporting for duty.' He stood in front of his lieutenant, sweating. 'Sorry I'm late, sir – I was waiting for my mother, to say goodbye, she must have got held up somewhere . . . Sorry, sir.'

The lieutenant looked him up and down, and nodded curtly. 'Uniforms in the next room – go and get dressed, and come back here with the other men for orders.'

'Sir.' Jan Prawicki was seventeen years old, as scrawny as the other boys in Boar, but tough, quick on the uptake, witty. He'd always wanted to join the army – if it hadn't been for the war, he'd have gone to military academy after the *liceum*, and enlisted with the regulars, like his father.

Jan's father was originally from Wilno, a kindly man who in the First World War, in his early twenties, been decorated for bravery. In the golden period of Polish independence which followed, he had commanded a division of the army stationed just outside Warsaw. Like thousands upon thousands of others, Major Prawicki had been captured in September 1939, and taken, the following spring, to the Polish officers' prison camp in the German mountain town of Murnau. Throughout the occupation, Jan and his mother had received brief, lonely, censored letters. Meanwhile, they eked out a living.

Zofia, who had read economics at the university of Kraków, was now a dressmaker. Jan did anything – he had mended burst pipes, sold paraffin, been a porter, mended windows. He had joined the AK very early, recruited by a teacher from the *gimnazium komplet* with his best friend, Paweł Staszewicz.

Paweł was in the room with the uniforms, fighting like the others to grab from the heap of old clothes on the floor. He seized an outsize tin hat and emerged from the scrum, looking up to see Jan come in to the room, panting.

'Hey!' Paweł pulled the tin hat down over his eyes and raised an imaginary rifle. 'You've got here – Poland is not yet lost!'

Jan grinned. 'Idiot.'

The room smelt like a jumble sale. He looked at the heap on the floor, and the other boys frantically trying on khaki trousers and combat jackets which looked like his father's First World War uniforms. They probably were – his mother, and plenty of other women whose men were held prisoners of war, had turned out every wardrobe and chest of drawers for the AK. His mother had taken the oath last year: she was supposed to join up today, too, on the other side of Stare Miasto – why the hell hadn't she come back from work first, as they'd arranged?

'Come on, there's not much left.' Paweł dragged him over, and Jan knelt down, rummaging. He yanked out a pair of cotton trousers and a thick khaki shirt, and stripped fast, pulling them on.

'How do I look?' The trousers were too big; Paweł threw him a belt, and he buckled it to the last hole. Not so bad. 'What about the armbands?'

'Here.' Paweł picked up a little heap of red and white from the window sill. Jan's mother had made all of them, she had made dozens, from an old flag hidden in a chest in their apartment – he'd spent two days last week, distributing them to different units. If he'd been stopped with that lot on him . . . well, he hadn't been. He pulled one on, over the right sleeve, and immediately felt a rush of excitement.

'Yerrrrrrow!' He leapt into the air, making a mock salute. '*Polska Walcząca!* Hitler has only got one ball – *forwarrrrd!*'

The roomful of half-naked, undernourished boys collapsed.

'Men!' Lieutenant Wroński stood at the door, perhaps not more than five years older than any of them. There was instant silence. 'You will all be lined up and dressed and reporting next door within one minute. Kozica – kindly calm down.'

'Sir.' Jan was scarlet. Kozica – chamois – swift and graceful. Humiliating to be reprimanded. But for God's sake – they'd waited four years for this.

'You're a soldier now,' said Paweł, rapidly buttoning his own shirt, grabbing an armband. 'Don't cock it up.'

Behind him, the others pulled up zips and put on caps and armbands, caught each other's eyes and spluttered.

'Hitler's only got one ball,' Piotr sang under his breath.

'Shut up!' Jan snapped. Quickly, he emptied his old pockets and stuffed lighter and cigarettes into the chest pocket of the khaki shirt.

They all filed back into the next room, where the lieutenant was waiting. A wooden box stood on the table beside him. No one could take his eyes off it.

'In this box,' the lieutenant said flatly, 'is the allocation of arms for this unit.' He lifted the lid, and took out a small brown pistol. 'This, and two others. We have twenty rounds of ammunition. Two rifles – fifteen cartridges. Thirty-five *filipinki* – grenades.'

There was an uneasy, incredulous silence. Then Jan said cautiously: 'Between all of us, sir?'

'Between all of us. You must understand that until recently many

150

units outside the city were being supplied with arms from here – it has only been decided in the last two weeks that Warsaw herself should take full part in an armed uprising. After all . . .' He hesitated. 'After all, we suffered a very great deal in the siege. Our leaders have wanted to spare more mutilation to the city itself, and more suffering for the civilians. However – all that has changed. The Russians are approaching, they have encouraged us to seize the moment, and we are expecting reinforcements of arms from them and from Great Britain at any time.' He tapped the little pistol against the palm of his hand. 'In the meantime – this is what we have. The very strictest discipline is to be maintained in the use of ammunition. Weapons will be shared on a rota system.'

The lieutenant looked at them all, subdued scarecrows in caps, tin hats, old patched shirts and trousers, the hastily stitched white and red armbands their only true uniform.

'We are not making a film,' he said quietly. 'We are going into battle. We are going to liberate Warsaw.'

Jan felt for his cigarettes.

At three o'clock Jerzy's unit, Lion, assembled. He, Andrzej, the Captain and the other boys walked one by one to a block on the corner of Krucza and Jerozolimskie Avenue, turning casually in at the entrance, ignoring the German patrol which suddenly appeared across the street, and then pounded up the stairs of the requisitioned apartment, each one let in by Pan Wójcik and his wife, the old couple who had lived there for fifteen years.

When they had all arrived, the Captain gave out the arms which they had smuggled in on Sunday. Two rifles to be shared between the six of them, forty cartridges. A large box by the window was filled with *filipinki*, homemade hand grenades. They had bakelite casings and key rings as detonators.

They stood round, looking at the pile.

'Is . . . is this all, sir?' Andrzej asked.

'At the moment, yes,' said the Captain. 'You are all under the strictest orders not to waste a single bullet: shoot only when you are quite certain you have the enemy within your sights. We expect to be replenished soon.'

'But we'll take the city in a few days, won't we?' said Jerzy.

'We hope to.'

Wilk was at the window. A pale sun had broken through the morning's cloud, and the room was filled with light. 'Things are

151

happening,' he said. They all went over and stood looking down on the crowded trams, on the broad avenue filled with people on both sides, hurrying in all directions. From across the river, which they could not see, came the thunder of the Soviet artillery.

'They'll be here in a day, surely,' said the Captain. He looked at his watch. 'An hour and a half to go. Let me summarize our strategy. At sixteen-fifty hours we take up our positions . . .'

They listened, and grinned at each other, checking their white and red armbands, the letters AK carefully drawn on in ink, slipping cartridges into rifles, arranging a shift system to use them.

'May I try to phone my sister, sir?' asked Jerzy.

'If Pani Wójcik agrees.'

In the kitchen, she nodded, smiling. 'Of course. And I've made some bread – I'll bring it in to you all in a moment.'

'Thank you.' He dialled Wiktoria's number, but there was no answer.

Anna and Natalia did up the buttons on the flannel shirts, printed in tiny grey check. 'They're quite the thing,' said Natalia, and they stood and looked in the mirror, with Jadwiga, just arrived, behind them, her mass of hair brushed out wildly.

'Where did they come from?' asked Anna.

'Some shop on Nowy Świat, I think,' said Jadwiga. 'Everyone's got them round here.' She looked at her watch. 'Half-past four. Where are the boys?'

'In the kitchen,' said Natalia, 'stuffing themselves. The woman upstairs has made a great mountain of sandwiches.'

'Why didn't you say so before?' Jadwiga complained. 'I'm starving.'

In the kitchen, they all stood eating, although Anna was too tense and excited to have more than half a sandwich. Henryk, their leader, was keeping watch with Wojtek at the window, his hand on his pistol.

'Where's Wiktoria?' Jadwiga asked Anna through a mouthful.

'At home. The apartment's been requisitioned for another unit – we heard at lunchtime. I imagine she's looking after them all.'

'And Jerzy?'

'As far as I know he's stationed near Jerozolimskie, but I'm not certain where. He knows where we are, though: I told him three days ago we'd probably be here.' She put down her plate. 'It's no use, I can't eat a thing. I wish I knew if Teresa was all right – I haven't heard from her for weeks.'

'There's two bastards on the corner,' said Wojtek suddenly. 'I'm going to have them. Oh, God, why doesn't it start?'

There was a hammering on the door of the apartment.

'I'll go.' Henryk walked quickly out and down the corridor; they heard him open the door on its chain, the murmured inquiry, then the rattle as he unbolted it, saying, 'Yes, of course.' He reappeared in the kitchen with a small stocky man in shirtsleeves.

'Pan Grabowski, the civilian commander of this block,' Henryk announced, and the man nodded at them all.

'Good afternoon. I should have come to talk to you before, but there has been so much to do . . .' He wiped his face. 'I am on the ground floor, apartment number three. In charge of all matters relating to this block, you understand? If we need to go into the cellars . . . or . . . have any problems with the lighting, or with water . . . I shall direct operations. My mother is with me now, and already baking bread as if for twenty units.' He smiled nervously. 'This is a great day for Warsaw. God bless you all. I must go upstairs now.'

Henryk saw him out, and they turned to each other, eyebrows raised.

'Can't see him directing an outing to the park,' said Jadwiga. 'Oh, God, I can't bear it any longer – it *must* be five.'

'Ten to,' said Henryk, returning. 'Hold on to your hats, everyone. Out of here, now, into the living room. Take up positions.'

They stood at the windows, stomachs churning, looking down on to the rush-hour traffic, at those workers who were not, yet, aware of what was about to happen, and at the leaves of the great trees of Central Park, across Ujazdowskie Avenue, motionless in the cloudy evening air.

Five o'clock. And suddenly, at last, the flash of windows flung open all over the city, a sputtering of gunfire, another, another, an explosion. In street after street, the pounding feet of German troops, the sudden roar of alerted tanks, moving at top speed, scattering civilians. Doors slammed shut. Doors flung open. Screams. The bodies of ambushed German patrols sprawled on the ground.

In street after street taken by the Poles, people were running wildly out of the houses, waving white and red flags, upturning trams and setting them ablaze, staggering under the weight of sandbags, dustbins, slabs of paving, tables, chairs, chests of drawers – anything which might be used for a barricade, even sewing machines, even saucepans. Behind the barricades, pickaxes, spades, forks and shovels were passed along, the road and pavement torn up and dug out, the trenches made under fire from snipers. Many buildings were on fire: lines of fire fighters passed buckets, ancient hoses.

By six-thirty, Anna and the rest of her unit were out in the street, piling up the barricade at the southern end, filthy, laughing, hugging each other. Improvised flags – torn white sheets, scarlet cushion covers – were at the windows, armbands wound round the catches. From a doorway an old man emerged, waving a real flag, threadbare and yellowing. 'I've had this hidden in the cellar for five years!' he called out, and jammed the pole into the mountain of earth and rubble by the trench. A cheer rose, and then, as it died, a familiar tune sounded from an open upper window. Hissing and scratching on a gramophone record from the twenties came the 'Warszawianka' the battle hymn of the 1830 Uprising against the Czar, which had become the anthem of Warsaw; in moments the whole street stood still, listening to the reedy, wavering music, and then singing together, arms locked:

'This is the day of blood and glory,
Let there resurrection be . . . '

Anna saw a young, heavily pregnant woman standing nearby, swaying as if she might be about to faint. She moved quickly across to her, since no one seemed to have noticed, and caught her arm. 'Are you all right?'

The woman slowly turned to look at her, and Anna saw that she was almost in a trance. 'My baby will be born in a free Poland,' she said dreamily, 'I never thought it would happen.'

From Jerozolimskie Avenue, four or five blocks to the north, there came the sound of a raging gun battle. Still holding the young woman's arm, Anna turned towards it, found herself saying aloud: 'Please, please, look after him.'

'Your husband?' asked the girl.

'My brother.'

The whole of the avenue was filling with German tanks and heavily armed patrols at every intersection. From further up, perhaps on the corner of Nowy Świat, they could hear angry crossfire, but down here, for the moment, it was fairly quiet. The trams which had been caught in the sudden explosion of the Uprising, almost three hours ago, stood abandoned on the lines, some pockmarked with bullet holes; Jerzy could see the bodies of two German military policemen sprawled in the middle of the pavement on the far side, and another, much closer, killed by the Captain as he ran for cover. There were other bodies, some with the AK armbands, some without, lying under the trees: to be killed on the very first day of fighting, even in the first hour – Christ! Later, the Captain had said, under the cover of darkness they'd get those bodies back, and bury them.

Crouched beneath the rim of the window sill, he and Andrzej watched the sky begin to redden as fires burned in other parts of the city. Then, just after eight, they heard the Captain behind them draw in his breath. 'I don't believe it!'

'What, sir?'

'The Prudential – quick! Look and tell me what you can see there.'

They craned their necks, and saw to the north-east, on the very top of the Prudential Building skyscraper, the white and red of the Polish flag, fluttering wildly against the clouds.

'We've done it!' Andrzej yelled, and leapt into the air. 'We'll have every bloody swastika in Warsaw shot down by tomorrow.'

Jerzy grinned at him. Wilk and Tygrys – Grzegorz and Ryszard, they all knew each other's names, now – had been on the far side of the room, oiling the rifles. They scrambled to their feet and came over, and they all stood gazing out over the rooftops, where other flags were billowing, as the last of the light faded, and far away, in the Old Town, a bonfire burned like a beacon in the Market Square.

From his new headquarters in a factory in Wola, bordering the ghetto ruins, General Bór issued his first message to the fighting city:

'Soldiers of the capital!

'I have today issued the order which you desire, for open warfare against Poland's age-old enemy, the German invader. After nearly five years of ceaseless and determined struggle, carried on in secret, you stand today openly with arms in hand, to restore freedom to our country and to mete out fitting punishment to the German criminals for the terror and crimes committed by them on Polish soil.'

On the radio station Kościuszko, a repeated broadcast:

'The streets of Praga are being shaken by the roar of Soviet guns. Attacks on the Germans are the duty of every Pole. Your sufferings will be over in a few days. Listen carefully and obediently to our authorities, the Polish National Council, and the Committee for National Liberation.'

At 8.15, General Stahel, Commander of the German Armed Forces in Warsaw, gave an order from his headquarters in the Bruhl Palace:

> 'As of this moment, Warsaw is in a state of siege. Civilians who go out into the street will be shot. Buildings and establishments from which the Germans are shot at will be levelled to the ground.'

He woke with the sound of shooting, felt stiff from sleeping on the floor, thought for a moment he was back in the kitchen in Praga, in the winter after the siege, when they'd all slept by the stove to keep warm and woken each morning with cricks in their necks. But it was Andrzej lying next to him, not Anna, and when he turned to look at the window he didn't see the white light of falling snow but summer rain. The Captain was standing by the heavy curtains, with Grzegorz on the other side.

'Sir?' He struggled to his feet, Andrzej and Ryszard, too, throwing off their blankets. 'What's happening?'

'Something in Napoleon Square – I think it might be the post office.'

They all pressed to the window.

'Keep down!' the Captain snapped, and they flung themselves down and then peered cautiously over the sill. He saw German tanks, overturned trams, uprooted lamp posts, barricades: overnight, the avenue had become a wasteland for battle. From below, in the building, came the sound of heavy banging. Then the door opened and Pan Wójcik came in, saying: 'They're moving down into the cellars – air raids are expected.' When they followed him to the apartment door they saw people spilling out of doors on every landing, carrying bedding, clothes, boxes of food, cans of water. Here and there were AK armbands, but most were civilians, women with children, grandparents. He saw one old man talking to an AK commander, begging to be allowed to join, and the officer shaking his head, explaining that there were barely enough arms to go round as it was.

By the afternoon the rain had stopped, and a hot August sun cast long shadows over the streets. Snipers hid in doorways, behind windows, in attics. The cellars were filling with families, trying to find a space to settle, calling when they found one, offering to share blankets, food, water. Few seemed afraid: a fever-pitch of excited talk rippled under the streets and pavements.

At 5.15, a voice almost breaking with emotion was picked up on the radio in the AK headquarters. 'This is Polish Radio in London. Yesterday, at five o'clock in the afternoon, the Home Army began open fighting in Warsaw.'

That night, Lion unit was repositioned on the ground floor, and it was Jerzy's turn to keep watch, with Andrzej, as more tanks moved into the avenue and the buildings began to shake under mortar fire. In the north, many AK units were making for the Kampinos Forest, hoping for airdrops there, the supplies to be smuggled back into Żoliborz and the Old Town later.

By 3 August, the bridges across the Vistula were still in German hands, but the AK had taken and held the centre of the city, including the post office, the gasworks, the water supply and the Central Railway Station. After a battle lasting nineteen hours they had captured the electricity plant. They held the Old Town, they held the riverside districts of Powiśle and Czerniaków, and Mokotów, where they had stormed the Gestapo Headquarters. They were fighting desperately for Wola district.

In Moscow, Prime Minister Mikołajczyk was appealing for airborne supplies to be sent immediately.

'What sort of an army is this Home Army of yours, without artillery, tanks or air force?' Stalin demanded. 'It has not even enough light arms to fight properly. In terms of modern warfare, it is just nothing. I hear that the Polish Government has ordered these units to drive the Germans out of Warsaw. I do not understand how they can possibly do it.'

On 4 August, the Soviet fighter planes disappeared from the sky over Warsaw. German planes dropped leaflets in broken Polish, supposedly from General Bór: the talks in Moscow had failed, the people were to lay down their arms and go home. They fell on to streets empty of trams, cars, bicycles – of any kind of transport. People ran across the avenues and broad thoroughfares crouched down behind the barricades, stumbling over water and gas pipes in the trenches. From Wola and Ochota in the west, a great flood of refugees was beginning to pour towards the city centre and the Old Town. They were fleeing from German units made up mostly of ex-criminals, the very dregs of the *Wehrmacht*, who were rounding up civilians by the thousands, machine-gunning them in sealed-off side streets, burning them alive in their wooden houses, raping women and children; in the Curie-Skłodowska Radium Institute, they raped the cancer patients in their beds, and the nuns who nursed them.

At two o'clock that afternoon came the first *Luftwaffe* raid since the siege of 1939. Twenty-four Junkers flew over in close formation, dropping a hail of incendiary bombs. They came again at four. Fires raged through the city; fear began to spread in the cellars.

When it was over, Jerzy's unit crept out of the doorway of the apartment block, into the choking, dust-filled air on the avenue, and helped to clear a path through the heaps of fallen masonry.

'Listen,' the Captain said suddenly in the evening, as they tried to settle on the floor for the night, throats parched, skin thick and itching with dust. 'Across the river,' he said, frowning. 'Can you hear anything?'

They listened. Something was missing from the sounds they had quickly grown used to, a background to the sputtering of gunfire, the tearing of falling beams from plaster, groans beneath great heaps of rubble.

From the other side of the Vistula the Soviet artillery no longer thundered. As darkness fell, they strained their ears for it, but only silence came across the water.

Black Friday, 5 August. Daylight raids on Wola sometimes as low as a hundred feet. In some parts of the district the inhabitants were herded street by street into cemeteries, into courtyards, gardens and factory back yards and shot by machine guns. The heaps of corpses were burned, covered by rubble and debris. In headlong flight, the panic-stricken civilians poured out of Wola and into the Old Town, and the next evening General Bór and his staff, under continuous fire in their headquarters, the Kammler Factory, were forced to evacuate, leaving behind vital pieces of damaged signalling equipment, and go to the Old Town too. They moved into a building backing on to Krasiński Square, already named in radio messages to London as a place for airdrops.

So far, the Old Town was untouched by fire or bombing. But fear of the air raids over the city centre had forced people down into the medieval cellars and passageways, and the whole district was now crowded with twice the population of the days before the Uprising. It was difficult to move anywhere: the courtyards and narrow streets were filled with people, looking for somewhere to stay, and where the pavements had been ripped up for barricades a fine sand lay beneath; the streets were ankle-deep in it. Thirty-five people were now crammed into the three-room apartment where Jan Prawicki and his unit were stationed. Already, food supplies were running low.

*

They had knocked through a hole in the cellar wall, into the cellar of the house adjoining, and another through the far wall into the next house, and so on, until it was possible to move along much of the avenue without ever going to the surface. The tunnels and passages through the overcrowded cellars were narrow and airless, filled with an endless two-way traffic of AK courier girls delivering bulletins and messages, older women carefully carrying baskets of bread, or potatoes, or boxes of tinned food, to the soup kitchens and field hospitals set up behind the front lines.

From the news-sheets delivered daily, Jerzy knew that in many parts of the city life was now being lived almost entirely underground. Apartment block commanders controlled the distribution of food, and supervised the digging of wells, for the Germans had regained control of the water supply, and had cut off most of the mains. It had not rained for a week, not since the second day of fighting.

Every night a few people in his building crept out on to the roof and searched the sky for the lights of approaching planes, bearing not the heavy black crosses of the German bombers but the red, white and blue roundel of the RAF, or the white and red check of the Polish insignia. So far, no lights had been sighted, but no one doubted that they were on their way. The avenue was largely controlled by the Germans now, but Lion had finished off a tank crew this morning: from the empty second floor Grzegorz and Jerzy had hurled half a dozen *filipinki* into the ventilation slits, as the tank passed the broken windows, and the Captain and Andrzej, crouching behind sandbags, had picked off the men as they scrambled out in terror. Jerzy hadn't used a rifle yet. Tomorrow night, he and Andrzej were to cross the avenue, to join a depleted unit on the other side. Now, leaning against the sandbags by the window, he listened to Ryszard playing the mouth organ, stopping and starting over the same old tune, 'My Heart's in a Knapsack', until he got it right at last, and everyone cheered. He closed his eyes, suddenly very tired, wondering just before he fell asleep if Anna was all right.

A post box had been put up behind their barricade, a plain wooden box with a slot in the top and a lily painted on the side. Twice a day, two young boys appeared to collect the messages inside – you were allowed twenty-five words, clearly written, with nothing about the actual course of the fighting. Neither of the boys looked more than ten or eleven, and Anna assumed they were Scouts. They wore AK armbands, and grinned from beneath enormous caps at the people who went out each day to rebuild and reinforce the barricade.

The phones in their apartment block had stopped working two days ago. Now, the only hope of contacting Wiktoria or Jerzy was through the field post, and she wasn't even certain exactly where Jerzy was. There was no chance that a note to Teresa would get right across the city.

She sat at the living room table with Jadwiga, writing in pencil on two small pieces of paper. Wiktoria, and her address. *All safe so far. Are you all right?* What else was there to say? *Victory!* And just the letter A, to sign it. On Jerzy's note she could only print Kurowski, J., Lion, Jerozolimskie: she did not know what number, but there was just a chance that another Scout would know where Lion unit was, and be able to find him. *Get in touch with me*, she wrote, with her address. *Be careful. A.* Then she folded over both pieces of paper, and looked at Jadwiga. 'Shall we do it now?'

Jadwiga nodded, folding over the note to her mother. 'Yes. Come on.'

They went out of the apartment and ran down the stairs to the ground floor. From the open cellar door they could hear the families below moving about, coughing, clattering pots and pans. It had been a quiet night; the children might be allowed to come up, soon, and play in the hall.

Outside, it was already very hot, sun on the balconies and barricades; they stood at the entrance looking down the deserted street. 'I think it's all right,' said Jadwiga, and they ran out, slid their notes into the post box and ran back again. The very moment they reached their entrance, they heard a deafening explosion, and clung to each other.

There was the sickening sound of tearing masonry, a building crumbling, then silence. Anna raised her head from Jadwiga's shoulder, and they stared at each other. From the place of the explosion came the noise of bricks falling to the ground from a great height, then more, in ones and twos, sounding almost gentle, and then they heard the screams, and muffled shouts, and they turned and ran out into the street, towards them.

Clouds of dust floated through the air, obscuring the sun, and they coughed and choked, and realized they couldn't move at all until it had begun to settle. They stood pressed against a wall, hands over their mouths, eyes closed again, and listened to the screams and cries for help. When the dust began at last to sink on to the pavement they went out again, and saw doors and gateways opening all along the street, and people hurrying out and down towards a house with a great gaping hole in the front, right down the middle, blasting open the second and third floors and blocking the entrance with a towering heap of rubble.

'You know what that is, don't you?' said Jadwiga, panting.

'The field hospital.'

'Yes.'

They reached the house and stood with a crowd of others, staring at whole apartments exposed above, pieces of beds and tables and sofas hurled like doll's house furniture across the rooms. Then a Red Cross nurse appeared at the ground-floor window to the left of a blocked doorway, her face and hair grey with dust and shock, and called out: 'Hurry!'

From behind the crowd men were pushing through with shovels and pickaxes, shouting to everyone to get out of the way, and they began to tear down the rubble, and clear a path through to the door. Anna and Jadwiga ran towards the window, where daggers of broken glass were sticking all round the frame. Peering through, as the nurse moved back a little, Anna could see nothing but pale shapes in darkness, figures on the floor so thick with plaster dust that they looked like pieces of sculpture. Then something stirred, moaning, and she said to the nurse: 'What do you want us to do?'

'Just help us to move them. I think we can go across the street.'

'We can't get anyone out through here, surely,' said Jadwiga, and the nurse shook her head.

'No, no, but if you can climb through you can help me a little, until they clear the door. We've lost two of our staff . . .' She spoke with such control that Anna wondered if she really knew what she was saying. Then she saw her hands, clenching and unclenching as if in spasm. 'We're coming,' she said, and began to tug at the larger pieces of glass. At once, although she was trying to be careful, blood began to pour down her palm, and she looked at it distantly, feeling nothing.

'Idiot,' said Jadwiga, and bent to tear a strip off the bottom of her dress. 'Tie this round – no, I'll do it.' She quickly tied a knot round Anna's thumb, and said, 'Let's just smash it in.' She picked up a brick, and began to tap all round the frame; the glass fell into the room, and then she pulled herself up on to the sill and said to Anna, 'Come on. Do you need a hand?'

Anna shook her head, scrambled up, and dropped down after her into the room. On the far side, a huge beam had fallen, and from beneath it she could see two or three twisted bodies protrude on split-open mattresses. Beyond was the doorway to the hall, and beyond that the heavy oak door to the cellar, hanging half off its hinges, with a heap of bricks and plaster before it. Groans came up the stairway.

'If one of you can go down . . .' said the nurse. 'I must have someone to help me here.'

From outside the front door the pickaxes sounded louder and closer, and they could hear bricks being hurled aside.

'I'll go,' said Anna, and ran across the room. She began to tear the rubble away from the top of the cellar steps. 'We're coming!' she yelled to the doorway, and scrabbled like a rabbit until she could make her way past the hanging door to the top of the steps and look down.

It was quite dark. Very slowly, she crept down, feeling the wall until she could see a thin strip of light coming through a ventilation slit near the top of a far wall, and made out several figures on the floor. Here, too, a beam had fallen: it lay across the middle, and above it a hole yawned between lath and plaster.

'It's all right,' she said unsteadily to the figures. 'We're going to get you out.' How many were there? Who had been groaning? Who was alive? Something was moving on the other side of the beam. She stepped over it awkwardly, and found a young man half-propped up against the wall. Even in this light she could see that his face was completely colourless.

'My . . . leg . . .' He could barely speak.

She bent down, ran her hands over his legs, saw his left foot twisted inwards as if on a pivot. He must somehow have dragged himself out from under the beam: the edge of a half brick was just supporting it a few inches above the floor.

From upstairs, she heard a sudden shout: 'We're through!' The front door was heaved open, feet ran across the room.

Anna turned back to the young man. 'It's all right . . .' she said again, and he moaned.

'Come on . . .' She put her hands under his armpits and tried to pull him up. He was terribly thin, but tall, perhaps six foot, and as weak as a kitten. 'Come on . . . help me . . . you can do it,' she panted. He pressed his hand to the floor, and his good foot, and somehow they pushed themselves up and she saw that his left foot was hanging half off, like a rag, and as she stepped towards the beam, supporting him, it touched something on the floor and he screamed.

She stood shaking, but still clutching at him. 'I'm sorry, I'm sorry . . . Come on . . .' He leaned on her, and she saw a small gap between the fallen beam and the wall; she led him towards it, and very slowly through to the other side.

He was trying desperately to hop, to help her, as they made their way past the bodies to the foot of the stairs, and then, as she struggled to help him on to the first step he gasped and went suddenly limp. 'Please . . . please . . .' She was sinking under his his weight, turned awkwardly and began frantically to pat at his face, but his eyes were closed. She sank down, half aware of the pounding feet above her, and of more screams as people were lifted. She pressed her fingers to the boy's thin wrist, and felt, beneath the plaster-covered skin, the faintest throb of his pulse. She would have to carry him.

She stood again, bent down and somehow heaved him on to her shoulders, and right over, like a sack, so that his head and arms hung down. Then she turned, put her foot on the first step, and began, clinging to his arms, to climb. He was so heavy that her shoulder burned, but she made it a couple of steps and stood, swaying petrified they were both going to fall. Then she simply looked at the next step, refusing to look at the one beyond, and climbed on to it, and then to the next, and the next, and the next. Her mind was filled only with steps, and the need to reach them, until, with every muscle trembling, she was at the top, and out of the doorway, lowering him to the floor, standing against the wall and gazing almost without vision at the empty room beyond, and the open door across it to the street.

Sweat was pouring down her. She waited until the trembling in her limbs had stopped, then crossed the hall to the main room. They were gone: no nurse, no helpers, no Jadwiga. Through the street door she could see a knot of people staggering across the street with a mattress, a body sprawled across it. She turned and ran back to the boy, lying in the hall, and bent down, feeling for his pulse once more. It was there, the very thinnest thread. She heaved him up, and moved into the room like a crab, stepping over the fallen beam, skirting the mounds of bricks, reaching the front door at last and swaying down the path between the towering heaps of rubble to the street.

Then Jadwiga was suddenly running towards her, with two men, and they stopped, lifted the long thin body from her shoulders and carried him across the street, where the dust still floated up towards the hot blue sky, to the open door of another house, and safety.

★

163

In the morning, Jerzy and Andrzej and the Captain went out into the courtyard, and from behind the cover of sandbags at the wrought-iron gates peered over at the building on the far side of the avenue which was to be their destination. A tunnel had been made from numbers 17 to 22, but that was much further down: here, the only way to cross was above ground, at night. It was perhaps thirty yards they had to cover: the torn-up pavement on this side, with an empty flower trough to crouch behind; then a run across, past the smashed and uprooted tramlines to the central strip of grass and trees, and a last dash to the far pavement, and the gateway. If they made it through there, they were to give the password and ask for the unit commander: he would direct them.

'And you will make it,' said the Captain, crouching down again. 'They've lost four men in that unit: they need you. You will take one rifle, and I imagine you will be under orders to act as snipers in turn, from first light tomorrow. Now – back inside, quickly.'

They crossed the courtyard to the side door, and found the main hall crowding with people coming up for air from the cellars where they'd spent the night. There'd been heavy shelling along much of the avenue, and it had been hard to sleep, but the area round their own block had escaped damage. It could surely be only a night or two before it was hit.

Pani Wójcik met them as they entered the door of her apartment. 'Breakfast is ready, gentlemen.' They could smell fresh bread, and almost kissed her. 'And I have a couple of tins of tongue,' she said, 'by special delivery.'

They followed her into the kitchen, where she spent most of the day, preparing for the unit, on a stove heated by burning wood, whatever food reached them through the tunnel network. Half a sack of flour had been delivered yesterday, and, apparently, tongue. What came through depended entirely on what stores or factories were still in Polish hands, and the supply varied from district to district. The women who carried them often risked their lives as much as those on the front line. Jerzy and Andrzej ate with the others, all grimy and unwashed. Water was rationed now; even though their block so far still had running water, a well was being dug nearby, and there were far too many people here to risk a shortage.

After breakfast, they went to clear their room. The windows had been boarded now with floorboards torn up from under the book-shelves; sunlight came through gaps and chinks, but they had been sleeping here for seven nights, and it smelt stuffy and unpleasant. At night, they used a single candle, set on the table in a saucer belonging to Pani Wójcik. Already, Jerzy felt as if he had been living like this for weeks.

When they had finished shaking and folding their blankets, he and Andrzej made their way out through the main hall again, and up the broad staircase to their observation posts on the second floor, in the apartment where they had first been stationed. They would be relieved at midday, to rest before their sortie at nightfall; now, they crouched behind sandbags at the window, and watched the movement of the German patrols below, and the hulk of a tank far down to the left. From somewhere towards the south of the city came the sound of heavy firing, but when it stopped, and they listened, as usual, for the boom of Soviet artillery in Praga, they still heard nothing.

'Do you think they'll come?' he asked.

Andrzej shrugged. 'They've got to, surely.' He turned to look at Jerzy. 'D'you feel all right about tonight?'

His stomach churned when he thought of it, but it was through excitement, elation even, as much as fear. 'Yes,' he said. 'I want to do it, don't you?'

'I suppose so.' For once, Andrzej didn't sound like the leader Jerzy had always felt him to be.

'What's up?'

Andrzej shrugged again. 'Just a feeling . . .' Then he said abruptly: 'Did Anna ever say anything to you about . . . about anything?'

Jerzy laughed. 'I beg your pardon?' Then he saw that Andrzej was blushing. 'Hey . . . What's been going on?'

Andrzej gazed at the sandbags. 'Nothing,' he mumbled. 'Just that . . . just that I really like your sister, that's all.'

'Oh.' He didn't know what to say. Had Andrzej and Anna . . . 'Have you and Anna . . . ?'

'I kissed her hand, once, that's all. I never said anything. It was the night you were arrested.'

'Oh,' he said again, and thought about the few occasions he had seen Andrzej and Anna together, and how it had never occurred to him that either might be even remotely interested in the other. 'Well . . . good.' He had never had a girlfriend, never even kissed a girl, although he had always thought Anna's friend Natalia, so dark and thin and clever-looking, might be the kind he'd like to have. Somehow, he'd always thought it was something that would happen at the end of the war, not yet. Perhaps he should have spoken to

Natalia months ago; perhaps Andrzej had been an idiot simply to kiss Anna's hand and not tell her how he felt.

The sound of firing faded. From below, Ryszard on the harmonica could be heard once again, the tune drifting up the stairwell, faltering and then more certain, and he found himself humming, the words inside his head:

A loving heart escaped from a young breast
In pain and confusion,
And flew after the army.

A soldier marching along the road
Took pity on the little heart.
He put it in his knapsack,
And went on his way . . .

He put his hand on Andrzej's arm. 'It'll be all right,' he said. 'Don't worry.'

Andrzej looked up. 'I know. Thanks.'

At midday, Grzegorz and Ryszard relieved them, and they went downstairs, to wait until darkness fell.

At 3.15 that afternoon, 8 August, unit commanders with radios picked up another broadcast from Moscow.

'The People's Army has staked its young life, its souls and its hearts, to show the world that it can afford a heroic deed of such magnitude that other nations can only listen.

'The provocateur wireless station Dawn, at the service of the Home Army, pretends that it is the Home Army which has risen to action, and that it is fighting for the freedom of Warsaw and Poland, and that at this moment all operations by the Soviet Army outside Warsaw have ceased – that from the time they started, the Soviet artillery, formerly so closely audible, has become silent.

'Do not believe it, citizens of Warsaw! Do not heed it, heroes! Hundreds of thousands of your friends, the Soviet troops, and with them one hundred and twenty thousand of General Berling's army, are fighting at the gates of Warsaw, and your liberation is only a matter of days away. General Sosnowski and General Bór, the provocateurs, are merely evoking derisive laughter by their pretence that the freedom of Warsaw is being bought with the blood of the Home Army!'

*

166

'Ready?' asked the Captain, and they nodded. 'Good.' They had made a small gap between the two piles of sandbags at the courtyard gates, just wide enough to squeeze through, and tossed a ten-złoty piece to see who should go first. '*Orzeł czy reszka* – eagle or tails?' asked the Captain. Andrzej had chosen the eagle, and on the back of the Captain's hand the eagle came up. Beyond the sandbags the avenue stretched, suddenly far wider than thirty yards. 'You'd better go, then.' He stretched out his hand to each of them. 'Goodbye, men. We'll meet, first thing tomorrow.'

'Yes, sir.'

'Goodbye, sir.'

Andrzej squeezed through the gap, and Jerzy waited a moment, then followed. Andrzej moved slowly, crouched on all fours; he did the same. It was very quiet, past eleven, and the only light came from the summer stars: the sky was cloudless still. Far down to the left, when he dared to raise his head, he saw the great dark shape of the tank they had watched that morning, the cannon raised. As far as they knew, there was nothing else covering this section. He had a scratching tickle at the back of his throat, and swallowed hard, longing to cough. Andrzej was moving faster now, springing up to break into a run; then he was upright, and running like the wind towards the trees. Jerzy stood up, too, ready to run after him, then heard the sudden, out-of-nowhere burst of machine-gun fire, and dropped to the ground, flat on the pavement.

Silence. He raised his head, could see nothing but the pitted surface of the avenue. Where was Andrzej? Very slowly he pulled himself up to a crouching position once more, his blood pounding in his head, and saw him, sprawled on the ground just before the trees. Without even thinking, he ran to him, calling 'Andrzej! Andrzej!', bent down and began to drag him back towards the sandbags, and then the sound of the machine gun came bursting out again, and there wasn't even time to think: not yet!

'Are you coming to the mass?' asked Natalia.

'Yes,' said Anna. 'What time does it start?'

'At ten, I think, but we'd better go soon, it's bound to be very full.'

They were still on the floor in their blankets, but Natalia had got up and fetched glasses of tea from the kitchen – 'Because you're a heroine, now,' she said.

Anna laughed. 'Don't be silly.' But she let Natalia go – she was

167

too stiff to move. She had expected to dream of the endless flight of cellar steps, the crippling weight on her shoulder, but as far as she could remember had dreamt nothing at all. She gingerly pressed the cut on her hand, which throbbed.

'Do you think there'll be a field post today?' she asked, watching the sun stream in between the shutters.

'I imagine so. Have you still not heard from Jerzy?'

'No – I sent a note yesterday, but I don't even know if it'll get to him.' She stretched. 'I expect he's all right – anyone who can escape from Pawiak must have a charmed life, don't you think?'

'Most certainly. Anyway, it's been quiet on Jerozolimskie for a couple of nights now. He might even come to the mass.' Natalia pushed off her blanket. 'I think Jadwiga's *still* in the bathroom – I'm going to dig her out.'

Fifteen minutes later they were hurrying down the stairs and outside, Henryk and Wojtek beside them. It was a perfect morning, the sun not yet too hot, and the trees on the corner rustling. Anna looked down towards the far end of the street, at the ugly torn-off front of the building which had housed the field hospital, and wondered if the boy had survived the night. She would go after the mass to find out. The pavements were filling with people wearing the AK armband, all moving towards a house near the barricade, where a mass was to be held in the courtyard; as they moved inside, and more and more joined them, filling all sides round the makeshift altar in the centre, it felt, still, quite extraordinary to know that they were in an area held by Poles, that despite the shelling yesterday the street was Polish once more, not occupied, not German.

The courtyard was filled with excited voices. Anna kept turning and looking for Jerzy or Wiktoria; after all, there were people here who had come from streets away. She caught a glimpse of the young pregnant girl she had seen on the first day of the Uprising, very pale, arm in arm with an older woman, and she waved, but the girl didn't see her. There was a movement at the gateway and the crowd parted to let through the priest, who wore a white and red armband on the sleeve of his black gown. He moved behind the altar table, where a figure of the Virgin stood next to a vase of roses, and raised his arms.

'My dear friends . . .' It was not usual for a priest to open a mass like this, but there had been no mass like it since before the war. 'Thank you all for coming. It is a miracle to have so many of us here, on a piece of land which we have at last reclaimed for Poland. Let us pray.'

Anna looked down at the cobbles, at the many, many feet in patched shoes or sandals, and closed her eyes. The priest's voice rose above the rustling and shifting in the crowd, and the mass began.

It was an abbreviated service, for no one wanted to linger out of doors. Afterwards, he raised his arms 'Let us join in singing: "Oh God, in your power and glory".'

Anna found herself holding Natalia's hand on one side, Wojtek's on the other, as they all began to sing:

'Oh, God, in your power and glory
For centuries you have watched over Poland.
Before your altar we beg you:
Bless our free homeland!'

The voices rose to a triumphant shout, and fell silent. Anna felt tears pouring down her face, turned and saw that Natalia and Wojtek, and most of the others around her, were crying, too. Never until now had she really felt herself to be in love with Poland, in the way that Tata and Wiktoria had always seemed to be. Now, after five years of fear, and secrecy, after losing Tata, losing any real belief in a future, she felt as those around her must be feeling – liberation, exultation, hope. She was in her own home again. Around her the voices rose in the national anthem:

'Poland is not yet lost
As long as we are alive . . .'

The last time she had used those words was at Christmas, 1939: she had whispered them with Wiktoria, Teresa and Jerzy in a freezing church, wondering miserably where her father was. Now, in the crowded, sunlit courtyard, she wiped her eyes and searched again for Jerzy's thin dark face, but could not find it. This afternoon she would go and look for him, no matter how dangerous it was.

The service was over. People began to file out of the gateway, pausing to shake the priest's hand, or talk to him. He was a burly, middle-aged man; as she got closer she could see deep smudges of purple-black under his eyes, and his skin had the thickened look of extreme fatigue, but he was also, clearly, as moved and excited as anyone else, talking rapidly, gesturing. Anna felt too shy to speak to him, but she saw Wojtek go up and shake his hand. 'Thank you Father.' Then they were all outside, and began to walk with the tide of people back towards their building.

Two figures were standing at the gateway; arm in arm with Jadwiga, Anna only half-registered their presence, two young men with armbands who were obviously waiting for someone, and who looked very grave. As they drew closer, she thought almost idly that they might be waiting for one of her unit, and then perhaps that they were waiting for her. Then she saw one of them step forward, and heard him ask uncertainly: 'Is Anna Kurowska here?'

He was lying in the corridor of the apartment, stretched out on a folded blanket, another one over him, turned back at his chest. They had folded his hands and closed his eyes; someone had washed his face and brushed his dark straight hair. A candle in a saucer burned at his feet. He was a statue, a painting, a romantic image of death.

He was her brother.

Anna knelt down beside him, and heard the others move softly into the main room and close the door. She stretched out a hand, touched his, and found them quite stiff and cold. She put her fingers to his lips, with a touch as light as a brushstroke, then leant across and kissed him.

'I love you,' she whispered. 'Please come back.'

The corridor was very quiet; from outside, intermittently, came the sound of shelling, but it was some way away, and she was scarcely aware of hearing it. She just sat there, looking at him, feeling terribly cold.

After a while she heard the door behind her click open, and footsteps, and felt a touch on her shoulder.

'Pani Anna?'

She turned and saw the Captain, who had received her when the boys brought her to the house, and who looked like Tata. He was looking down at her gravely. 'If you can come with me now,' he said, and helped her to her feet and into the main room, where a thin shaft of sunlight, full of specks of plaster dust, pierced the boarded windows, lighting the anxious faces of the boys, and making the room a church.

Then she saw stretched out beneath the sill another body, also blanketed, also with a candle at his feet.

'Andrzej?' she asked, and the Captain nodded.

'We thought – I thought perhaps you would like a little privacy. That is why we put your brother in the corridor, so that you could be alone with him for a few moments. But we shall bury them together.'

'Yes. Of course.' Slowly she went to the other side of the room, knelt beside Andrzej, and crossed herself. He, too, looked as though he were simply asleep, his thick fair hair brushed away from his face, his features peaceful as she had never seen them. She thought of the soft, almost imperceptible kiss on the hand he had given her once, leaned over and returned it on his mouth.

Then she got up, and went over to the table, and listened to the Captain as he told her of the arrangements for the funeral, which would be held the next day. A black hole yawned open inside her; she felt as though it had been there always, waiting for her to discover that evil could take everything away.

Early in the morning the Captain told her that the street where the boys were to be buried, in the garden of a block of flats, was heavily under fire. Many people now had to be buried without coffins, even under torn-up paving stones, with only a bottle beside them containing a piece of paper bearing their name, and date and place of death. But somehow two plain cheap coffins had been found, and the bodies of Jerzy and Andrzej lay in them side by side in the main hall of the building, waiting to begin their journey. They were to be carried down into the cellar, and along the narrow, choking passages to the apartment block whose garden had, apparently, become a graveyard.

It was just after eight, the cold stone floor of the hall touched by pale light from the half-open door to the courtyard. Anna shivered. Then she went across to the Captain, who was talking to the civilian commander of the block.

'Will you wait for just a few minutes?' she said. 'I passed a flower shop on the corner of the street when I came – it might be open, now, do you think?'

'No,' he said. 'I am sure it won't be. In any case . . . it was dangerous enough for you to come at first light.'

'Please,' she said. 'Please just let me see – it's only a few yards, and this street is ours, isn't it? It's not like . . . not like the crossing they made.' How could he have let them go? When almost the whole of the avenue was held by the Germans – how could he?

She did not voice these thoughts, but she knew he could tell she was thinking them, and he said gently: 'Go on, then. We will wait.'

She slipped out of the door to the courtyard, and across to a back entrance, the one she had used when she came yesterday with the boys, and this morning, at dawn. She ran down the street to the shop on the corner, and saw at once that it was still locked up and dark. She didn't care. She went up and began to pound on the door, louder and louder, calling: 'Please! Please! Open the door!'

From deep inside she heard at last a movement of feet, and voices, and then the bolts on the boarded door were slid back and an old woman said cautiously: 'What do you want?'

'Flowers for my brother's grave,' said Anna.

The door was opened, and she slipped inside. Like everywhere else, the little shop was filled with shadow. She could smell the spicy scent of carnations, and saw bucketfuls on the floor.

'Your brother?' asked the woman.

She nodded. 'He was killed the night before last, on Jerozolimskie.' Surely it could not be true. 'With his friend. We're burying them both this morning.'

The woman shook her head. She wore a black dress with the sleeves rolled up, and an apron. On the stone floor her slippers sounded softly as she moved over to the buckets and bent down. When she straightened up she was holding two dripping bunches of carnations, one white, one red.

'Thank you,' said Anna. 'I have nothing to give you.'

'Have them, have them, my poor girl. Who is buying flowers now?' She saw her out of the shop; Anna blinked in the light, heard the door being bolted behind her, and turned and ran, holding the wet flowers close to her.

They were all waiting when she got back, and she saw that Natalia, Jadwiga and Wojtek were there as well. 'Henryk wanted to come,'said Jadwiga, 'but of course as leader he had to stay on guard.'

'Of course. Thank you all for coming.'

The Captain came over. 'We are ready to go,' he said. 'Will you put the flowers in the coffins for now? I think it might be easier for them to be carried like that.'

'Oh. Yes. All right.' She hadn't thought about how they were to be carried, and handed them to him, watching him carefully lift the coffin lids and slip the bunches inside, red for Jerzy, white for Andrzej. Then he nodded to Wojtek, to Ryszard and Grzegorz, and several other men she did not know, most of whom wore armbands. They lifted the coffins and began to walk slowly through the hall to the cellar entrance, and carry them awkwardly down the steps, bumping and banging. She followed, the girls behind her.

Down in the cellar a path had been cleared between piles of bedding, and ahead she saw the entrance to the tunnel, a small, surely far too small hole blasted into the far wall. She watched the men carry the coffins through, Jerzy first, then Andrzej, saw Wojtek stumble and reach out a hand to the wall to steady himself. The cellar stank of sweat and airlessness, and she thought for a moment she was going to faint, but then Natalia was holding her arm, and pushing her along, and through the hole.

As the column moved slowly along the passage, perhaps five feet across, perhaps less, it felt like less, their feet kicked up dust, and soon they were all coughing and their eyes streamed. Then the passage suddenly became much lower, and there were pipes immediately above them: they had to duck, and move crouching, the coffins banging and banging until the whole tunnel was filled with noise and Anna felt her head begin to throb. Far above, as they moved through another wall, they could hear the sound of gunfire, and the ceiling of the tunnel began to tremble and vibrate. A thin rain of sand and dust abruptly fell, and the whole column stopped. Anna could hear the coffins being carefully lowered to the ground. She no longer thought of Jerzy, or of Andrzej, or the reason they were here. She thought only of the need for air, heard herself gasping and behind her someone retch. The whole tunnel was filled with the sound of people struggling to breathe. Distantly she heard the voice of the Captain: 'Move on.' There was the sound of the coffins being lifted once again and the movement of feet. She stumbled forward.

At last, at last, the blessed lovely sight of a chink of light ahead, and they moved along the last few feet of the tunnel and out into a cellar. The coffins were lowered, and they all sank to the floor, drawing great gulps of stale air. At the top of the cellar steps a door was opened, and sunlight met them as they struggled to their feet and carried the coffins, slipping and sliding on their shoulders, up the stairs to the hall. The door to the courtyard stood ajar, and when the men went out, and set the coffins beside a mound of earth, Anna followed, and stood with Natalia and Jadwiga at the doorway, shaking all over, drinking in light and air. A priest stood at the head of the mound of earth: he beckoned to them, and they began to walk towards him.

The garden was tiny, but already six or seven plain crosses marked the square of grass. The four walls of the block rose high above them. I've been here before, thought Anna suddenly, looking up, and in her mind's eye saw her face pressed to the window of an empty apartment far above, looking down on to the neat patch of green, bordered with late summer roses. They had been here in the siege. This was Żórawia, where she and Teresa and Jerzy had taken refuge, with the keys from Wiktoria. It was here that Jerzy had watched the black hail of bombs fall on to Warsaw and murmured that it was like a film.

The priest was touching her arm. 'You have any other family, Pani? Is anyone else able to come this morning?'

She shook her head. She had been too dazed yesterday to go to Wiktoria's apartment; she would have to try to explain to her later. No, no need to explain: Wiktoria would understand. And Teresa? There was no chance of getting to her now.

The priest looked at the Captain. 'The other boy . . . No family?'

'We sent for his mother and uncle yesterday, but . . . his apartment block has been badly hit . . .'

He shook his head. 'Let us begin, then.'

They stood round the deep pit.

'The flowers,' Anna said suddenly. 'The flowers! They must be taken out.'

'Of course.' The Captain and the boys lifted the coffin lids once more, carefully took out the two bunches, and passed them to her.

'Help me,' Anna said to Jadwiga, standing next to her, and she and Natalia quickly began to separate and mix the flowers so that there was one bunch for each, of white and red. They laid them on the ground, and then the coffins were slowly lowered on ropes the priest had brought with him, into the grave, Andrzej first, then Jerzy, and he said: 'Let us pray.' They bowed their heads.

'Our Father, which art in heaven,' the priest said slowly, 'have mercy on us. Oh, Lord, have mercy on our sons fighting for Poland, and on our brothers dying from bombs and shrapnel. Oh Lord, who has given the smallest bird its nest, and the peace of the sky above its head, save our homes from being destroyed, and our walls from crumbling. Turn thine anger away from us, as we have already suffered so much. We beg thee, oh Lord, to deliver a speedy end to the war, and grant a free and independent Poland.'

There was a long pause. Then he raised his head, opened his eyes, and gestured to Anna.

She bent down, picked up a handful of earth and threw it on to the coffins; it scattered over the lids. Then the boys took the two spades that had been left there, and began to dig at the mound, shovelling the earth back until the pit was filled. They pressed it down, picked up the few pieces of turf which remained, and pressed them down, too, and then Anna set the flowers at the top of the grave, and the priest took two small white crosses from his pocket and dug them into the ground.

Anna stood with the others, looking at the flowers and the crosses, smelling the earth, unable still to believe that Jerzy and Andrzej lay beneath it, and then Natalia was tugging gently at her arm, and she had to turn and leave them.

On 7 August the district of Wola fell entirely into the hands of the Germans. They began then to blast a path across the city, breaking through Polish positions on the way, storming across streets, burning houses, rolling tanks over gardens, over the Monument to the Unknown Soldier, through parks. All along the route, buildings on either side were burned out, and they took up their positions.

The Old Town, housing the headquarters of General Bór and the AK Command, was now quite cut off, the broad avenue of Krakowskie Przedmieście, which linked it to the city centre, covered by German machine guns, and controlled by twenty tanks. They were cut off, too, in the north: the open fields leading to the suburb of Żoliborz were covered by German artillery, machine guns, two armoured trains. Now, the only way to send messages to Żoliborz, or the Kampinos Forest beyond, where a few air drops were being made, would be through the sewers. Pre-war municipal maps of the network were examined; sewage workers summoned to headquarters; manholes were opened up and guarded.

Air raids came every forty-five minutes, then every half hour; more and more people crammed into the cellars. New heavy guns and mortars were installed around the city each day; the exhausted German units who had fled across the bridges from the advancing Russians in the weeks before the Uprising were now being sent back, re-armed. There was a new terror; the 'moo-cow': two mine-throwers joined together, the first sending a hail of phosphorous bombs which set fire to entire blocks of houses, the second blasting whole storeys away. When the low, dreadful mooing sounded, there were perhaps a few seconds before the explosion came. Many of them huddled in the cellars were buried alive. All through the day and night fires raged.

Among the civilians, utterly defenceless, panic was growing, but few people were talking of surrender. Each district, and in places each small group of streets held by the Poles, had its own news-sheet or bulletin delivered from heavy shoulder bags by the Scouts, or the AK courier girls – weekly, twice weekly, some even daily. Anna began to help distribute *Walka*, Fight, whose banner was the Polish eagle perched on a sword; in the Old Town copies of *Warszawianka*

175

disappeared within moments of the couriers' arrival. None of the scores of publications was more than four pages, typed and mimeographed; they were crammed with messages, local details, sometimes house by house, of the fighting, the casualties; they had sketches and cartoons: the Polish eagle rising like a phoenix from the flames of burning buildings; Hitler grimacing in the stocks; Red Cross nurses tending wounded soldiers.

There were posters, too: *In Fighting the Fire, You are Defending Warsaw*. A skull beneath a German helmet – *A German for Every Bullet!* Christ with a lantern, watching over a Red Cross nurse and a wounded AK fighter.

From the headquarters of the AK, the *Information Bulletin* which had been secretly printed and distributed each week of the occupation continued to appear, every day when it was possible; it listed the casualties, the wounded, the gains and losses made on the front line, reported the news from the rest of Europe as it was picked up on the broadcasts from the BBC, from Dawn, the station of the Government in Exile.

Warsaw had its own military radio station now, Lightning, broadcasting from a battered transmitter in the AK headquarters: on 15 August they received acknowledgement at last that they could be heard in London.

Over and over again, as arms and ammunition began to be exhausted, and some unit commanders estimated they had enough for only a few days more, radio signals were sent appealing for supplies to be sent from London, from the bases in Italy, or from the Soviet airfields no more than fifty miles away, to be dropped over the city.

From behind the heap of sandbags piled at the end of the narrow passageway, Jan peered out at the tank, motionless at the far end of the street. It had arrived ten minutes ago, blocking the exit; now it rested, a monster waiting for its prey. Should he go back now, and report its arrival, or wait until he had been relieved?

It was late afternoon, and he had been stationed here since two, after a long and mostly sleepless night in the cellars, listening to the pounding of shells on nearby buildings. Across the street the houses were windowless and black with smoke, the sun indifferently shining on their scars. He closed his eyes for a moment and allowed himself to drift into a blurry haze of thirst and fatigue. He thought of fruit, of running water, saw himself climbing a long ladder up a rustling tree filled with oranges, peeling them, one after another, sucking the juice, licking it off his fingers. His mother was standing below him on the grass, calling up to him: 'Jan! Jan!' His head slumped on to the sandbags.

'Jan!' He was being shaken, and he jerked himself awake in terror. What had he done? Who had been killed?

Paweł was beside him, grinning, his face filthy, his eyes alight. 'They're coming tonight – there's been a signal!'

'What?' Jan rubbed his face. 'Are you sure?'

'Certain – Wroński's just told me – he had a message half an hour ago. The BBC played some tune at the end of *Polish Hour*, it means they're on their way. I knew they'd come, I knew it.'

He felt energy flood into him again. 'What time? What do we do?'

'We don't know what time yet, just – after nightfall. Anyway, Wroński wants us all on standby to be ready to collect containers – we've got to get to them before the Krauts if they fall near their lines. You're relieved now, we can all have a break in the canteen. Come on!'

'Hang on a minute,' said Jan. 'Just have a look out there.'

Paweł peered over the sandbags. 'Christ. Why didn't you come and report it?'

'I didn't want to leave my post. You think it's all right for us both to go now? Shouldn't one of us stay and keep watch?'

'I'll stay, you've done your stint anyway. Go and report it. See you tonight.'

'See you tonight.'

They stood on the rooftop and waited. It was just before midnight, and the sky blue-black and filled with smoke, the outline of streets and avenues all over Warsaw marked by burning houses. At nine, a moo-cow raid had hit a street several blocks away, and from up here they could clearly see how the upper storeys had been ripped open, the timber beams and window frames eaten away by the flames. Down on the street there would be teams of civilian fire fighters, frantically passing buckets, drawing from the well on the block with an ancient hose, but what chance had they? After almost two weeks without rain, the medieval houses, with their wooden frames, were like brushwood.

Jan stood next to Paweł and looked from the burning buildings to the smoky sky, turned to check if he could see a gleam on the water of the Vistula, and found that he could not: it was just too far away.

Were the Soviet guns firing tonight? Did they know the drop was coming? He could hear nothing.

Around them on the rooftop were half a dozen men, and on many of the nearby houses he could see the dark figures of more, ready to catch whatever fell, moving quietly, looking up again and again, checking each possible direction from which the planes might come. This morning, Lieutenant Wroński had announced that they were down to their last two rounds of ammunition. If a container did not fall into their unit's hands tonight, what the hell were they supposed to do?

'Look,' Paweł said suddenly. 'What's that?'

'What?'

'A searchlight . . . Look!'

To the south-west, a beam brushed the sky like a giant finger, then came another, then two more, closer, and suddenly they could hear the throb and roar of low-flying aircraft, swept on and over the heart of the city by the beckoning lights.

'They're here! They're here! They've made it!'

He was hugging Paweł, saw Wroński and the others leaping wildly up and down and then, below them, doors and windows flung open, and the street fill with people pouring out of the cellars and houses, yelling and waving at the sky like children in a playground.

'They're here!'

In streets and squares hurricane lamps were being lit: he'd heard women were lighting them, and lying there, forming the outline of a cross or star, to guide the planes to the dropping places. For a moment he imagined what it must be like, to lie flat on the ground with the roar of an aircraft only a hundred feet above you, knowing that you could die at any moment if the plane was hit, or an engine failed.

From all directions, now, came the sound of anti-aircraft fire.

Jan thought suddenly of the pilots, of how far they had travelled, and how at risk they were, of what they must be thinking as they saw the lights below. Were there Poles among the crew, looking down on Warsaw for the first time since the war began? Then a plane was almost on top of their building, and he forgot to think of anything as it roared overhead towards Krasiński Square and its belly opened.

Bundles spilled out, parachutes swelled open, and the containers swayed and drifted on to roofs, on to the ground. On the housetops they were cheering as the plane flew on, and then there came the deafening sound of anti-aircraft fire, and a burst of flame on the left wing of the plane. It was hit, it was wounded. His fist to his mouth, Jan watched it fly helplessly on, like a great bird trying to escape the pain of a broken wing by flying, until there was a sudden, all-engulfing explosion and it fell.

Jan reached for Paweł and saw him standing white-faced, gazing up at the sky. Then another plane was roaring towards them, followed by two more, and more. An oblong container hit their rooftop, smashing the tiles, and they stumbled towards it, shouting.

12 August: Churchill to Stalin
The Poles request machine guns and ammunition. Could you give some aid, because the distance from Italy is so great?

On 13 August, Prime Minister Mikołajczyk returned to London from Moscow: the talks with Stalin had broken down. That day, Tass issued a statement, broadcast on Moscow radio and on the BBC.

'Information from Polish sources on the rising which began in Warsaw on 1 August by order of the Polish emigrés in London has recently appeared in various newspapers abroad. The Polish Press and wireless of the emigré government in London have asserted that the Warsaw insurgents were in contact with the Soviet High Command, and that this Command had sent them help.

'The Soviet Agency, Tass, is authorized to state that this announcement by the foreign press is either a misunderstanding or a libel against the Soviet High Command. Tass is in possession of information which shows that the Polish circles in London responsible for the Warsaw rising made no attempt to coordinate this action with the Soviet High Command. In these circumstances, the only people responsible for the results of the events in Warsaw are the Polish emigré circles in London.'

They squatted on the dusty floor, counting it all again. Three more revolvers, with twenty rounds of ammunition; a tommy gun with eight rounds; a box of grenades; four tins of corned beef; two tins of dried milk. A picture of Princess Elizabeth – 'I'll have that,' said skinny little Piotr, and pressed it dramatically to his lips. A door opening from the corridor interrupted their laughter.

'Lieutenant Wroński?' A tall fair man in shirtsleeves and armband stood in the doorway. 'You have received your allocation?'

'Yes, sir,' said the Lieutenant, and got up from where he was kneeling between Jan and Paweł. 'Are there any changes?'

'Dried milk is to go at once to the civilian authorities for nursing mothers and children. Now – may I just go over what you have received?' He came across and bent down, his eyes skimming the pile in the centre of the circle. 'I see . . . and you are how many?'

'Six, sir, and myself. Two boys were wounded in the first week of the fighting – they're in the field hospital on the next block.'

'And what arms do you have left?'

Lieutenant Wroński ran his fingers through his hair. 'Two pistols, but they're a different calibre from these rounds, so effectively none. The tommy gun, and two rifles – I haven't checked if they'll fit this lot yet.'

'*Filipinki?*'

'They were all used in the first few days.'

'To what effect?'

'We destroyed an armoured car, sir.'

The Captain shook his head. 'I am under orders to tell you, and all units in this sector, that the very greatest care is to be taken from now on in the use of all arms and ammunition. There may be another drop tonight, but even so, what is arriving is unlikely to sustain us if the Germans mount a concentrated attack on Stare Miasto, and all reports indicate that they are about to.' He looked again at the little heap on the floor, at the subdued faces of the boys. 'I was going to take one of the tommy guns, since the unit in the next house has received even less, but perhaps I'll find one for them elsewhere.'

'Sir.'

He turned and left the room, and they all looked at each other, but not at the Lieutenant.

Then Paweł said lightly: 'Well, the corned beef's a treat. Anyone got a tin opener?'

In a broad semicircle around the perimeter of the Old Town, some forty thousand German troops were assembling, their positions stretching from the Royal Palace in the north, backing on to the Vistula, round to Teatralny Square and Karowa Street in the south. On the western flank, ten infantry battalions were supported by two battalions of engineers, a company of tanks, twenty field guns, and four cannon, one of which was of the same calibre used to shell Dover across the English Channel. There were fifty Goliaths: tiny, deadly, remote-controlled tanks. There was a platoon of mine-throwers, an armoured train.

On 19 August, at 9 a.m., they launched their attack on an area some two miles square, where fewer than five thousand AK defenders were now armed with machine guns, anti-tank missiles, grenades, *filipinki* and bottles of petrol, and the battle for Stare Miasto began.

The afternoon sun still glared, and though the narrow streets were thick with shadow, they were hot, the air oppressive, full of dust. Jan and Paweł followed Lieutenant Wroński, the others behind, as he led them towards their new position. Jan felt sweat and the pressure of the rifle strap on his shoulder beginning to rub it raw, and shifted it to the other without stopping in his steps. They were behind barricades here, the small area still in Polish hands, but nowhere now was far from the German lines, and movement above ground like this was perilous. Everywhere, at the entrance to every alley, every flight of steps, you could see men crouched down, arms at the ready, keeping watch behind hastily assembled piles of tables and chairs, sandbags and dustbins.

One street away were the ruins of the Royal Palace, the outer buildings bombed by the Germans in the siege of 1939, the rooms within held by the Poles since the first days of the Uprising. On the clock tower the white and red flag run up on Constitution Day drooped in the heat. Linked by a small covered bridge to St John's Cathedral, the defended palace now blocked the path of the Germans to the Kierbedzia Bridge across the Vistula: without doubt, it would fall under fierce attack. Wroński that morning had orders from Colonel Wachnowski, Commander of the Old Town, to move his men to reinforce all positions nearby. They were to be prepared, if possible, to move into palace or cathedral, to join the units already there. As they rounded the corner, and saw the apartment block where they were to reposition themselves, they saw, too, that the street was filling fast with men and women running into doorways, into courtyards, pounding up stairs and through passageways.

'First floor!' Wroński shouted over his shoulder, and broke into a run himself, as the sound of shelling burst into the air. They began to run after him, stumbling on the uneven paving, into the open doorway to the stairs, not pausing for breath until they had reached the first floor, and found one room of the apartment already occupied by another unit, sandbags at the broken windows. Jan pushed his way through, moved the rifle off his shoulder, and managed to find a space at the window in the corridor; he stood peering between the shoulders of the two men in front.

'What's happening?'

'It's starting,' said one of the men. 'I don't know if we're going to get out of here.' He looked at the rifle. 'You're lucky.'

Jan nodded. Then Wroński was yelling for him, and he moved quickly back into the main room. 'To the centre window,' Wroński snapped. 'Cover the street as far as you can.'

Jan crossed quickly to the window, and hoisted the gun to his shoulder. From the far end of the street, quite empty of running figures now, came the rumble of a tank, like the one he'd heard the day the airdrop came, and then the sound of shelling, much closer than before. Paweł was suddenly beside him, peering over the heap of sandbags.

'Wroński says we can share this shift. You all right?'

'So far,' said Jan.

By the evening his head throbbed and hammered with the roar of the shelling. Between the bursts of anti-aircraft fire came the sickening tearing rumble of buildings falling apart, thundering to the ground. And everywhere, fires raged.

As dusk fell, Wroński returned from a meeting on the ground floor and announced: 'At first light, we advance: couriers say they need every man.' He nodded to Jan, to Paweł and Piotr and the two others who had each done a shift at the window. 'There's a field kitchen two houses along, access through the cellar. Go and have a break, then get some sleep.'

They put down their arms and went down the stairs, across the hall and down into the sprawling cellar. Lit by candle stubs, every corner, every small storage room or passage was crowded with people huddled on blankets, next to cardboard boxes spilling with clothes, saucepans, tin plates. Children wailed; an old woman was coughing and coughing, bent double. As the boys with their armbands went through, a path was cleared between the families, and one or two people called out: 'God bless you,' but Jan also heard grumbling, and someone mutter: 'You got us into this.'

They bent down to crawl through the hole in the wall leading to the next cellar, also packed full, and lit by a few candles. From the top of the stairs on the far side they could hear loud voices, and plates and saucepans clattering; they could smell soup. They made their way through and climbed the flight in single file. Across the narrow hall a door opened into a noisy, crowded room, a long trestle table under the windows, with a wood-burning stove in the corner. Women in overalls were behind the trestle, ladling hot soup into bowls; a queue of people, AK and civilian, waited. The air was thick with cigarette smoke.

'God, I'm hungry,' said Paweł. They stood in the queue, and Jan saw that the opposite wall was plastered with notes and messages, some scrawled directly on to the plaster, some little scraps of paper tacked up.

'Keep my place a minute,' he said to Paweł, and went over. Was it possible that Mama could have got a message sent here? He searched the wall, his head still throbbing. *Marek: we are in Dobra Street now, number 8. Maria. Tomasz was here, 14.8.44: Krystyna, I love you. Will anyone who knows of my daughter, Hania Kowacz, please try to inform Rybacka Street, number 7. Krysztof: Wojtek was killed 12.8. Please contact. Mama.* There were at least five notes addressed to different Jans but none of them was for him. Where was his mother now? There was no chance of getting back to her; in any case, she would not, could not be at home – he could not even begin to know where to look for her. Despite all this, he fumbled in his pocket, and found a stub of pencil. What could he write on? He went back to Paweł. 'Have you got any paper?'

'No,' said Paweł. 'Of course not.'

A girl in the queue behind said: 'I've got a notebook.'

'Thanks.' He tore off a sheet and smiled at her, then went back to the wall, and pressed on it. *Mama: I was here, 19.8. Thinking of you. We are moving tomorrow. See you when it's all over. Jan.* He folded it and wrote his mother's name, Pani Zofia Prawicka, then took a tack from someone else's note and pinned them up together.

Paweł and the others were almost at the table. He hurried back and stood with them again, winking at the girl behind, who had long brown hair piled up under a cap. She was very pretty.

All night the sound of shelling shook the house, and the sky was filled with the scream of Stuka jets, and the violent light of flares and fires.

'Fire to put out! Fire to put out!'

The shout came every hour; they ran out to stand in a line, passing buckets of precious water from hand to hand. They'd been given a ground-floor room to rest in, but no one rested until just before dawn, when a brief, sudden lull made their ears ring, and they slumped into sleep for perhaps half an hour. Then Wroński was shaking them awake, his own eyes puffy and his face unshaven, and they stumbled after him down into the cellars again.

Early morning light slipped through the cracks and slits of windows, touching the grimy blankets and the grey faces of the sleeping families. Moving between snoring grandmothers, stepping carefully over restless children, all Jan could think of was sleep, of lying down here, beside any one of them, and not having to get up. He fixed his eyes on Wroński's head, and went on, ducking through the holes in the walls of perhaps eight houses, the names of the streets overhead, and arrows to others, scrawled on the walls in chalk, or white paint.

A courier girl, sixteen or so, her face, shirt and trousers covered in dust and dirt, came out of the far tunnel.

'Lieutenant? You are in command of which unit?'

'Of Boar.'

'I have a message for the first officers coming through this morning.' She opened her canvas bag, took out a small sheaf of paper, and passed him a note, roughly duplicated. Wroński took it and read it, expressionless.

'Thank you, my dear.' He turned to the boys, pressed up behind him. 'We are to move as close as possible to the cathedral.' He paused. 'The fighting is very heavy – there have already been a great number of casualties.'

'Sir.' They said it automatically, following him as he bent down and ducked through the hole into the tunnel, where another girl was waiting.

'Maria,' she said, and led them through, and up the steps from the next cellar.

When they came out, they found themselves at a doorway on to an alley littered with rubble: almost opposite stood a small house with shattered windows, the front door riddled with bullet holes.

'There was a skirmish here yesterday,' said Maria rapidly. 'A great many people were taken to the nearest field hospital, and I'm afraid there are bodies in that house we haven't had time to bury yet, it's very distressing. But the house itself – the damage to it is superficial. You are to be stationed here – I think you have already been given written orders.'

'Yes,' said Wroński. 'I have them here . . . We are to defend this house, until ordered otherwise, as a possible place of retreat from the cathedral.'

Maria nodded. 'I'll bring you new bulletins whenever I can.' She looked as if she hadn't slept for days. We all look like that, thought Jan, watching her shake Wroński's hand, and hurry back to the cellar.

They picked their way across the alley, avoiding precariously shifting piles of bricks. Inside the house, in a little room off the hallway, they found the bodies of four boys, laid neatly side by side. They were still covered in plaster dust, but you could see the pools of caked blood beneath. The room stank.

'Check them for arms,' Wroński said flatly, and Jan and Paweł bent down, and fumbled at the leather belts. The boys' eyes had been closed, the dust brushed quickly away from waxy faces; one of the faces had been half shot away, and that side was turned down towards the floor.

Jan felt himself heave. 'One pistol, sir,' he said, getting to his feet, and somehow did not throw up.

Wroński took it and gave it to Piotr, who stood staring.

'Thank you, sir.' His voice was a whisper.

Then they all crossed themselves, quickly, and went out of the room.

They spent the next few minutes making a reconnaissance of the house. There was a tiny kitchen at the back, where a blackened stove stood next to a cracked sink and wooden draining board. On the table was a small cast-iron saucepan, half-filled with water: dust floated on the surface. Who had been going to cook what, before they were ordered out of here, or fled?

A flight of wooden stairs led up from the hall, with a door beneath to a small cellar. Wroński flicked at the switch on the wall, but no light came on.

Jan fumbled for his lighter, and passed it. By its tiny flame, they went cautiously down the stairs, and made out packing cases, firewood, a tin trunk. Though there had been no rain for a least three weeks, it was very damp; somewhere in the walls they could hear a faint trickle of water.

Upstairs there were two small bedrooms. In the one at the front an old iron bedstead had been pushed back against the wall, the mattress lumpy and thick with plaster dust. On it, a book lay open, face down: Jan picked it up, and blew off the dust. *Błysk Gordon* – Flash Gordon: one of the boys downstairs must have been reading that, having a laugh during a lull in the fighting. Was it the one whose face had been shot away? He put it down again, and followed the others on tiptoe and craned his neck – a view of the whole alley from here.

Wroński's boots sounded loud on the bare boards as he moved off the balcony and crossed the room to the one at the back.

The back bedroom had a casement window: they could lean out and crick their necks to see over the red-tiled rooftops to the ruins of the palace, the pink-washed walls blackened, full of ugly holes. Incredibly, the clock tower was still standing, the hands still stuck at half-past twelve, but the flag was filthy, in shreds. The Germans had the outbuildings and perimeter, but the interior, they knew from the bulletins, was still in Polish hands, and battles were raging in there – in the elegant audience chambers, in the ballroom and throne room, places some of them had visited as schoolchildren, before the war. Even from here they could make out the sound of grenades exploding inside, and imagine the black marble pillars crashing down. From the gaping holes in the roof, thick smoke was drifting into a hazy morning sky.

From one of the palace walls, a covered bridge some eight yards long crossed a little street and led directly into the cathedral – a long time ago, kings used to go through there, to mass. The cathedral's steeply pitched roof and massive walls blocked out much of the light and view on the east side of their house: they couldn't see the bridge from here. Jan looked down on to the tiny back yard. Dusty weeds sprouted between the cracks in the flagstones; the wooden door of a privy hung open. From the open windows of other houses in the alley he could make out quiet voices: other units, waiting like them for the action.

'You understand,' Wroński was saying, 'that it may be only the bridge which divides the Polish and German lines?' He looked down on to the yard. 'And now – we bury those poor boys.'

'Yes, sir. Where, sir?'

'Down there. Those flagstones won't take much pulling up.'

They followed him out of the room and down the creaking stairs.

By half-past ten, four rough wooden crosses marked the places in the yard where the unknown boys lay buried. Inside, down in the cellar, Marek and Feliks were hacking at the wall to see if they could break through to the next. Upstairs in the front bedroom, Jan and Paweł stood at the window, sweating behind the sandbags they'd hauled up, listening to the scream of the Stukas diving towards the palace, the cathedral, the whole of Stare Miasto. They had begun just after eight; in the past two hours, four different formations had flown over.

The screams died away; their ears rang.

'We're going to die in this house,' said Paweł.

'Crap. Shut up.' Jan lit a cigarette stub – he was making each one last half a day, three puffs each time. 'Want one?'

'No. I wish to Christ something would happen. I mean here – get it over with.'

'It will.'

Paweł breathed deeply. 'Go on, then, give me a drag.'

Jan had a long drag himself, then passed it over. His hand was shaking with tension and hunger.

'D'you think Wroński's going to let us eat?'

'Piotr says the girls are coming with food later.'

'How does he know?'

'He doesn't. Here.' Paweł passed back the butt, and Jan dropped it, carefully trod on it, just on the edge, then picked it up between wet finger and thumb.

'Mean bastard.'

He grinned, and straightened up; they leaned against the wall. Paweł, with a pistol, was covering the lower half of the alley; Jan, with the rifle, had the cathedral end. His head was swimming with nicotine, hunger, sleeplessness, nerves. The air was full of dust from the shelling – outside, floating and sunlit; and drifting over the balcony, in here, settling lightly on their hair, their hands, their clothes.

Right at the end of the alley, something moved.

'What's that?'

'What?'

'Something moved – come over here.'

Paweł ducked down and crawled along the sandbags. He stood up beside Jan and squinted. 'Can't see a thing.'

'Something *moved!*'

'All right, all right, we'd better report it.'

'You go.'

'You come too, come away from there.'

'I'm keeping watch.'

'Stubborn bastard. Suppose . . .'

'Go on!'

Paweł ran across the room and down the stairs. Jan strained his eyes through the shifting dust. Across the city he could hear the spatter of machine guns, a sound grown almost as familiar as traffic. Here it was still quiet: it felt threatening, unnatural. Why had it all gone quiet? He ran his tongue over dry lips, suddenly afraid. He had a flash of himself five or six years ago, a schoolboy listening to his father's stories on Sunday walks through the Lazienki Park, stories from the 1914–1918 War, of slavering wolves in the snowy forests near Wilno, of artillery drawn across frozen lakes by moonlight, battles where the bodies of men and horses littered the field. His father had never talked about fear, never. Hadn't he ever been afraid? Jan fumbled in his shirt pocket for the cigarette stub, and in the quietness outside heard something scrape. His head jerked up; he leaned out across the sandbags.

'Get back inside!' That was Wroński, but he nearly went through the roof.

'Sir!'

Wroński swiftly crossed the room. 'Paweł says you have something to report?'

'I saw something move at the end of the alley, sir . . . and just now I heard . . . a scraping sound.'

The Lieutenant flattened himself against the wall, and peered.

'Well . . .' He drummed his fingers against his leg. 'If they've covered us at the far end, we'd better check this end. We're nowhere near getting through the cellars that far, it'll have to be above ground.'

If we had a radio, thought Jan. If every unit had a radio . . . But they hadn't, they had a handful of arms.

Wroński was looking at him. 'Do you want to go? You've done a good stint up here – you can both go.'

There was a split-second pause.

'Yes, sir,' said Jan.

'Yes, sir,' said Paweł.

'Very well – check either side of the alley, report back at once.'

'Sir.' They walked quickly towards the door.

'Piotr and Feliks to report up here.'

'Sir.'

They found them playing cards at the kitchen table.

'Wroński wants you upstairs. We've been ordered out.'

'Why? What's up?' Piotr pushed back his chair and frowned.

'We may be covered.'

'Christ.' Piotr went white.

'Oh, for God's sake,' said Paweł. 'Nothing's happened yet, get

188

upstairs.' He and Jan went out into the passage, bumping each other. At the front door, he said: 'After you.'

'Thanks a lot.' Jan reached for the handle, slowly opened the door and they crept out. Dust was everywhere: at once, he began to cough.

'Shut up. Shut up!'

He clapped his hands over his mouth, doubled up, fighting to control himself. Breathing in light, panting, much too shallow gasps, they moved slowly along the wall, knowing Wroński was above them, and had heard the coughing. Who else had heard?

There were five houses on either side of the alley ahead: it ended in a T – two corners which might each conceal waiting Krauts. They crept, keeping low. Second house from the end. Last house. Palms dripping with sweat, slipping on the rifle. Inch by inch, the last few feet. Quick as a flash – look round the corner.

An empty street. Paving stones torn up, hasty wooden crosses marking shallow graves.

Across to the other corner.

No one.

Jan felt sweat pouring everywhere, from his neck, his armpits, the backs of his knees, as he turned, panting, to Paweł, and nodded the all clear.

'Well,' whispered Paweł, grinning. 'Thank Christ for that. Well done.'

They made their way back slowly, slowly, wanting to get there, desperate not to cough, not to run, not to do anything which might be noticed from the far end.

Two doors from their house, one door to go, their own door held open from within – and the sudden, speeding, out-of-nowhere black spider from Hell.

'Goliath!' screamed Paweł.

They fell inside, the door slammed behind them, and then it exploded into a thousand splinters, and they were hurled face down on the floor.

Feet thundered down the stairs above them. Jan felt himself dragged along the passage, realized he was unhurt. In the kitchen, Piotr hauled him on to a chair, Feliks held a cup of water to his lips. Wroński came in with Paweł draped across him, and then went back to fetch Marek, who'd held the door open. White-faced and gasping, they all looked at each other, passing cracked cups.

'Phew.'

'Bloody hell.'

'You all right?'

'I think so. You?'

'Just about.'

The little dark kitchen was no longer dark – dusty sunlight poured in through the gaping doorway at the front: they felt as exposed as if they were out on the street.

'Right,' said Wroński, breathing fast. 'Two to the front room – Marek, Adam. Cover the passage. Piotr – upstairs back bedroom. Paweł and Jan – back to the balcony, fire on anything that moves. Are you up to that? Everyone clear?'

'Sir.'

'Yes, sir.'

Jan pulled himself to his feet, hauled up Paweł. They stumbled out of the kitchen and up the stairs, followed by Piotr, hearing Wroński step cautiously to the front of the house again. Peering back down the stairs they saw him, pistol cocked, creep to the gaping doorway, peer out and duck back inside. There were running footsteps in the alley: Wroński raised his pistol. Then everything happened at once.

A burst of machine-gun fire peppered the front of the house: Wroński leapt back out of the passage, into the front room. For a split second, Jan and Paweł stood frozen.

'He's hit? He's hit!'

'I don't know – come on!'

They ran blindly up the stairs, and the whole house shook with the violent impact of a mortar, fired from God knew where, and with a great, horrible, tearing yawn the front wall above the doorway split open, and came thundering into the hall. Jan and Paweł clung to each other; above them, Piotr began to scream.

Thick, choking plaster dust billowed through the wounded wall; broken beams and brickwork shifted and settled. Upstairs, Piotr was sobbing. Beneath them, a mountain of rubble blocked the passage, the bottom stairs, the entrance to the front room. Beyond was the sunny alleyway, and the sound of German voices. And Polish voices – from other houses, yelling, firing.

'That'll stop them,' croaked Paweł. 'They won't come in now.'

'Of course they bloody will. Come on, for Christ's sake get upstairs.'

They scrambled on all fours, finding Piotr huddled on the landing.

'Get up! We're alive, aren't we? Get up!' Jan hauled him to his feet. 'Go on – back bedroom, that was your order. Move!'

Piotr fled along the landing.

In the front bedroom they found the whole balcony had fallen away, the windows blasted out, a hole where the sandbags had burst and tumbled out. Beyond the edge of the floorboards there was now only a treacherous drop. They stood, confused. Then Jan began to walk slowly across the room.

Paweł grabbed him. 'What the hell . . . don't be a fool! Stay here.'

'I want to see what they're doing.'

'They're waiting to kill us!'

From the direction of the palace came a sudden new shriek from the Stukas, and the house shook violently. They waited, hearing Piotr through the roar of sound: 'I can't stand it! I can't stand it!' He ran back to them. 'Let me stay with you, let me stay . . .'

Jan put his arm round his shoulders. 'Okay, okay, we're here, we're with you, now stop it. Stop it!'

Piotr went on sobbing. 'I'm sorry, I'm sorry . . .'

'*Stop it!*' Jan slapped him, hard across the cheekbone, and pushed him down on to the bed. 'That's enough, you little shit, all right? That's enough.'

Piotr stopped. He sat on the edge of the mattress, his mouth hanging slackly.

Jan dropped to his stomach; he began to slide across the floorboards.

'You fool!' snapped Paweł again. 'Do you want to kill us all? You think you're such a hero.'

'I don't.' Jan didn't think he was anything, he just knew he couldn't do nothing. Beneath him the floorboards were wobbling, creaking; he moved very, very slowly, until he was six inches from the edge, and could raise his head, and look out. Three German soldiers stood across the alley, guns raised. Jan could see two bodies, a white and red armband on one, and he was sure the other was Polish, too. He looked again at the Krauts: they were young, no more than twenty; they had thick belts of ammunition round their waists. He felt a rush of anger and envy. His fear was gone – fear was for babies like Piotr, gibbering on the bed behind him. Now there was only a blinding pinpoint of rage.

The Krauts were very, very close. He reached for the catch on his rifle.

Behind him, Paweł hissed: 'Don't!'

'This is what we're here for!' Jan hissed back. He thought: I'm going to get the one on the right.

He raised the rifle, moved just another inch forward, held the young Kraut in his sights. The boy had deep rings round his eyes, as if he hadn't slept for a long time, either. Jan aimed for the chest, and fired.

The force almost made him cry out, but he didn't, it was the German boy who shrieked, and slumped to the ground. At once, his companions raised their own rifles: Jan sprang up, and as he did so, Paweł ran forward to grab him, and pull him away, and so they were both hit, and both fell to the floor. Jan felt a pain fiercer than anything he could ever have dreamed of plunge into his jawbone, and he threshed and doubled up, and threshed wildly again, rolling over and over on the floor, trying to get away from it, hearing Paweł yelling and screaming: 'Oh Christ, oh Christ, oh Jesus, Jesus, Jesus,' and then a great black wave of sickness and pain swept over him, and dragged him down into nowhere.

He existed now only as a swollen, throbbing, agonizing jaw: the rest of his body had meaning only in relationship to this part of it, where knives of pain twisted through his cheek, his gums, his neck and head, driving deeper and deeper until he could do nothing but lie on the floor and cry for his mother like a child, no longer caring who heard him, who saw him, who wanted him to get up and move, wanting only to die.

'Mama! Mama!' She was coming towards him, smiling, her hair piled up, a blue jug of water in her hands; she moved quickly over the cool stones of a courtyard filled with the sound of fountains.

'Water . . .'

She smiled at him again, then tipped up the jug and let the water splash on to the stones, trickling down into the damp earth between them, a drop falling quite accidentally into his mouth, before she turned and left him, and he began to scream.

Someone else was beside him now, cruelly touching his face, whispering: 'This is the last shot we have left.' He opened his eyes, and saw a girl bent over him: she wore a filthy, bloodstained apron with a red cross; there was a syringe in her hand, and she began to roll up his sleeve. Quickly she slipped the needle into his arm, and pressed the plunger. He stared at her, and at the figures moving behind her in the room. Then she withdrew the needle, and stood up, saying: 'It'll start to work quite soon.' He did not believe her; she was another torturer, there was another lance of pain driving through his jaw, and still no water. Then she was beside him again, with a chipped cup and perhaps two inches of yellowish water at the bottom. 'Here.' She raised his shoulders and he sipped, wanted more, fell back on to her arm and was dragged down once more into nothingness.

When he woke, the pain was still there, but the stabbing knives were not. He lay watching candlelight flicker on the far wall, and listening to the groans of the other men. He wanted water, but he was too sleepy to ask for it, and he closed his eyes again. The next time he woke there were no candles, only a thick grey light at a gap in the wall; he could make out another wall, beyond, and a burned-out doorway. They must be on a ground floor, next to a courtyard. In this hour before the dawn, in this disembodied, placeless place, a refuge where he didn't know anyone, and didn't care about anyone, he began to drift towards the real enemy, the pain coming up to meet him once more, relentlessly. Then he heard a voice cry out, and somehow knew whose it was.

'Paweł?' He struggled on to his elbow, peered at the shapes on the floor. He could barely open his mouth, forced himself to mumble: 'Where are you?' The shape next to him swore. 'Paweł?' A nurse moved across the room towards him.

'Who are you calling?'

'Pa-weł Sta-sze-wicz. My . . . friend . . . I . . . can . . . hear him.' He didn't care what he sounded like.

'Staszewicz? Yes – you came in together, didn't they tell you last night? He's over there.' She pointed to a figure on a mattress a few feet away, and hesitated. 'Can you remember anything of what happened?'

Jan closed his eyes. He was in a room tilted nauseatingly above a crater . . . no, they'd blasted the front of the house away, like that boy's face. Like his face? He raised a hand and felt his jaw, carefully. It felt enormous, disgusting. How had it happened? He remembered he had killed someone, one of the enemy, yes, and when they tried to kill him, Paweł had tried to stop them . . . Jan groaned. Paweł shouldn't have done that. Someone else had been there, too, yelling . . . And all the boys downstairs. And Wroński . . .

'Tell me . . .'

He felt the nurse kneel down beside him. 'You're very lucky to be alive.'

A new knife of pain began to stab between his teeth, and he groaned again. 'Die. Die.'

'No! No – you must see your friend. You two are the only ones from the house who got out – except for the boy who came to tell us. A little fellow – Piotr. He told us he hid under the bed in the room where you were fired on. The ones downstairs were all killed . . .' She took his hand. 'I'm very sorry.'

He managed to whisper: 'Piotr?'

'He's been drafted into another unit.'

'Cathedral?'

'I'm afraid . . . it has fallen to the enemy.' She bent over him. 'Come on, soldier, open your eyes. Come and see your friend, he will be so glad to see you, come on. I'll help you.'

He let her lift him, leaning on her. Every time he moved, the pain shot through him again; upright, leaning on her, it wasn't quite so bad. She led him across to the mattress where Paweł lay, his eyes closed, his hair sticky; under the blanket, Jan could see the stiff straight shape of splints.

'We set his leg last night,' said the nurse, 'but of course we have no anaesthetics now. I'm afraid he suffered very much.' She looked at him. 'You all have.'

He didn't try to answer. He knelt down and touched Paweł's shoulder. 'It's me,' he mumbled. 'Sorry.' Paweł opened his eyes, looked cloudily at him from a long way away and closed them again. Jan sat beside him, holding his hand. After a while, automatically, he felt in his pocket for his cigarettes and lighter. He found them, but he didn't take them out, he felt too sick to smoke. He just sat there, watching the grey light in the gap in the wall grow thinner as dawn broke the sky.

There was a movement at the door, then a sudden excitement in voices outside it; he wanted to go and find out what had happened, but he didn't want to leave Paweł and anyway his jaw was eating away at him again, so he was still on the floor, like all the other wounded, when the voices told them that the day before, on 25 August, Paris had been liberated by the Allies.

For perhaps twenty-four hours they allowed themselves to hope that this was the end for Warsaw, too. In the evening doctors and nurses climbed to the roof of the building where the hospital was housed, and searched the sky for British, American or Soviet planes, but they were soon forced down again, and that night the shelling over the Old Town was fiercer than ever. The palace had fallen. The cathedral had fallen. It was a battle now for every street, every house. Every hour the doors of the hospital were flung open and stretcher after stretcher was brought in, set down, the men and women lifted off and the stretchers taken out to be used again. One room right at the far end of a corridor had become an operating theatre, deliberately placed as far as possible from the wounded and the dying, but the screams of the patients in there could not be muffled. To operate without anaesthetic seemed crueller than leaving the wounded to die, but only the very worst were allowed to do that.

Jan stayed close to Paweł all night, and all the next day, drifting in and out of pain and sleep. Once or twice they were brought cups of the yellow water; once, he thought he heard a nurse talking about dog meat. Some time in the middle of the second night there was a lull in the shelling, and for a while the only sounds were those in the hospital itself: groans, running feet, closing doors. Then, from somewhere outside, perhaps a block or two away, perhaps more, there came cries and shouting, the movement of a great crowd, women pleading.

Jan forced himself to get up, and with a few others move slowly over to the window. As a distant flare lit the sky they could see down a street to another, crossing it, filled with two groups of people, pushing in opposite directions. By the light of another flare it was possible to see that one group wore AK armbands, and that the others were civilians, trying to stop them getting through. Transfixed, Jan leaned against the window frame and watched. At last, it looked as if the AK units had been forced to turn back, and gradually the shouts died away. He made his way back to his place beside Paweł, and lay down.

In the late afternoon of the following day a courier girl came in with bulletins. The previous night, under orders from Colonel Monter, Commander of Warsaw, Colonel Wachnowski, Commander of the Old Town, had agreed that those AK units who still had arms, and men able to continue fighting, should attempt to break through the perimeter to the city centre above ground. What Jan had heard and seen beyond the hospital had been civilians trying desperately to prevent the AK men, already unwilling to obey the order, from leaving them to the Germans. In any case, those units who had reached the front line on the perimeter had been forced to retreat; many had died. There was no hope of breaking through.

In the evening, the door to the room where Jan and Paweł lay with all the others admitted two doctors in grimy, bloodstained white coats.

'We have received an order,' said the shorter man. 'There is to be an evacuation of civilians and wounded, through the sewers to the city centre. We – we cannot hold out here any longer.' He broke off, and his eyes, deep within dark circles, looked over them all. 'I have to tell you that only those whom we feel are capable of making this journey will be allowed to leave.'

Then both doctors came into the room and began to move from mattress to filthy mattress, examining each man, asking questions. Paweł raised himself until he could sit up; when they came to Jan, he was already standing. His jaw felt as though it filled his face entirely; he stared ahead as the doctor who had made the announcement gently ran his hands over it.

'You must be in great pain.'

He shrugged. 'I can bear it.' He could, now.

'No other injuries?'

'No.' His left leg must have been grazed without him noticing it, and until today the pain in his jaw had blotted out everything else; this morning he had realized the surface wound was infected. He said nothing.

'You realize that if you get through you will be called on to continue fighting?'

'Of course.'

'Very well. I think you are fit to make the attempt.'

'Thank you, sir.' Hard to imagine what the attempt might be like; a lifetime ago, before he was wounded, people had said the Krauts were sending flame throwers down the manholes of the sewers. That's what they did in the ghetto. Beside Paweł the other doctor was straightening up. He shook his head, and they moved on to the next mattress.

'I'll carry him,' said Jan.

They were bending over a man who could not lift his head.

'I said I'll carry him.'

His doctor turned, and looked at Paweł. 'He is your friend?'

'Yes, sir.'

'I am very sorry . . .' He looked at him, his eyes clearly willing Jan to understand, to realize how hard the decision was, not to make a fuss.

'Shut up, Jan,' said Paweł. 'I'd never make it. Nor would you.'

'I'm going to carry you!' Jan yelled. 'I'm not going without you.'

'You could risk the lives of many others,' the doctor said, his face pale.

'He saved my fucking life,' said Jan. 'Or tried to, anyway. We're all going to risk our lives to get out of here. For Christ's sake let me try.'

'Very well then,' snapped the doctor. 'Try.'

The manhole was in a square some fifty yards from the hospital. They moved towards it in a shuffling, silent column, led by a doctor and a nurse. The sky was lit, as always, by flares and burning buildings; as they drew near they could see other columns moving slowly towards the square from other streets, and around what must be the manhole a group of armed AK men, facing outwards, covering every approach. There was a barricade at a street on the far side of the square, and that was guarded, too.

Jan had Paweł's arm round his shoulders, and was helping him to hop, slowly enough for him to manage without slipping or crying out or banging his splinted leg, but not so slowly that they held up the column. His own pain had become a permanent, sadistic companion: he thought of it now as something quite separate from him, a being in itself. They drew near to the exit of the street on to the square, and waited.

For several minutes nothing happened. He was near enough to the head of the column to be able to crane his neck and see the men round the manhole talking softly, and he made out the shape of a slender girl, as well. Then the men moved aside, bent down and lifted the heavy cover, laying it on the cobbles, and from the exit of another street a small group of people detached themselves from their column and filed across. He and Paweł, and all the others near them, watched the girl sit on the edge of the manhole, turn, so that she could climb down what must be a ladder inside, and disappear. A man with his head in bandages hesitated, then followed; another man, with his arm in a sling, went after him, then a woman with a little boy, then another wounded man – one by one they dropped into the hole, and vanished.

Jan and Paweł looked at each other. 'The girl is the guide?' Jan whispered.

'Must be.'

'My God.'

All around them, people were shifting uneasily. Jan tried to imagine, as they must be, what it was really like down there. Was there any light at all? Could you breathe? Was it really possible that you could breathe in a sewer? Did you crawl all the way? How high was the sewage level? What if you realized, suddenly, that you couldn't go on, that you must turn back . . . ? What if you fell? He felt his stomach begin to flood with fear. He had been mad to think that he could do it, that he could carry the weight of Paweł for more than a few yards. How far was it they had to go? It must be almost a mile. He shut his eyes. Better to stay here and die.

'Jan?' whispered Paweł.

'Yes?' He opened them quickly. 'What?'

'I don't mind if you say you can't do it.'

'I can do it.'

After a while they grew almost accustomed to watching the little groups slip, at intervals, into the hole and go down. Somehow it was just possible to pretend that they were going, but that you were not going to have to. Then an AK commander came over to them, speaking very quietly.

'The first twenty here will be going down in about half an hour. There is another girl waiting to guide you, and a string is tacked along the wall of the sewer. In places the tunnel ceiling is very low; you are going to have to crawl for most of the way.'

'Is there any light?' asked a woman, sounding unnaturally calm.

'There are candles in a few places, yes.'

Jan felt in his shirt pocket. He had his lighter – thank Christ for that. They could use that, if they needed.

'No one can pretend that you are going to make a pleasant journey,' the man was saying, 'but I can tell you that although people have died in the sewers there are also guides and couriers who have made it several times in the last weeks, and survived. It is your only hope.' He nodded to them, and moved on. They stood and waited again.

At last a girl came up to them, smiling, and quickly counted twenty, under her breath. Jan and Paweł were twelve and thirteen. 'All right,' she whispered. 'It's our turn now. I've done it before, don't worry: the level is quite low, because it's been so dry. Keep hold of the rope, and if you feel two sharp tugs, stop at once, and tug the rope twice yourself, so the people behind you stop too. You understand? I'll only do it if there's an emergency ahead. Three tugs mean we can move on again. We expect the journey to take about four or five hours.'

'Four or five hours . . .' said a man in front. 'And how long is it since you went through?'

She shrugged. 'A week or so. We've got to go now.'

They began to follow her out on to the square. There were gaps between a few of the cobbles, and Jan stumbled once, and with

198

Paweł's arm round his shoulders almost fell. Ahead, the girl stopped, turned, noticed Paweł's leg for the first time and frowned. She came quickly back to them.

'You have been given permission to go through?'

Paweł nodded, very pale. 'Yes, but . . .'

'I am going to carry him,' said Jan.

'How?'

'On my back.'

'It's not possible.'

'Please . . .'

There was a sudden roar of shelling from very near, and the thunder of a house collapsing. Instinctively, they all leapt and clung to each other, the girl too. When the burst of shelling was over, they saw the men round the manhole beckoning urgently.

The girl bit her lip. 'Come on, then. Come on.'

They went after her, to the entrance to the hole, where the guards were parting to let them through. Like the others before her, she sat down on the rim, and turned. Jan waited, as one after another the eleven men ahead went down, drawing closer each time until he and Paweł were almost on top of the curving rim of an iron-rung ladder, clamped to the shaft. He looked down, then back at one of the guards, a bearded man with a rifle.

'Can you help me . . .' Already he needed help. It was just to get down the ladder, that was all, then he'd be able to manage. How deep was it, how many rungs? He couldn't see a thing down there.

The man was looking quickly from him to Paweł. 'You go down first,' he said in a low voice, 'and I will help your friend. You must stand halfway down the ladder and be ready to take his whole weight. Fifteen rungs down, you understand? Then you have a couple of yards to get him on to your back before you bend down. All right?'

Jan nodded, wanting to thank him for not asking questions, or saying that it was impossible. He just muttered, 'Thank you,' then looked at Paweł and said, 'See you at the bottom.' Then he turned, lowered himself on to the top rung of the ladder, and began to climb down, counting the rungs, and staring at the bricks between.

Even before he reached the fifth, the stink below made him retch. He went on down to the sixth, the seventh, the eighth, heard someone coughing down below, and gurgling liquid. Warm, fetid air rose to meet him, and he looked up.

Above, Paweł was being carefully lowered on to the ladder, feeling with his left, useless foot for the next rung, all his weight on his right. Jan moved up a couple of rungs, quickly, realizing he'd come too far down, and touched him. 'All right, I'm here.' He moved up further again, and pressed his head into Paweł's crotch, so that his weight was on his neck. At once, a savage knife of pain shot through his jaw, and he screamed. The sound echoed in the shaft. The weight on his neck eased, and he understood that Paweł was clinging on to an upper rung, which was fine until he needed to get to the one below, and the one below that, and each time, for how many he'd lost count, would need to put the same, terrible pressure on his neck. And there were nine people waiting to come down after him.

'Come on,' he muttered into the bricks a few inches in front of his face. 'For Christ's sake *come on!*'

Slowly, slowly, Paweł began the descent again, his left leg bumping and banging like a dead thing, his right trembling uncontrollably with the pressure. At last Jan was able to call up: 'Wait!' and drop the last few feet to the ground. He stood for a moment, allowing himself the luxury of raising and lowering his head, rubbing the back of his neck until the muscles stopped looking in his mind's eye like burning rope. Then he was able to take Paweł's weight more easily; he came down and leaned, gasping, on the bottom rung.

Jan put Paweł's arm over his shoulders once again, and led him away from the ladder, so that the next man could follow; all around the dark bulk of other figures moved awkwardly in the confined space, coughing. He looked up and saw, far above them through the opening, the night sky and the stars.

'I've found the rope,' Paweł was muttering.

'Good. Can you just lean on me until the others are all down and we have to start crawling?'

'Yes. Are you all right?'

'Yes.'

They stood and waited as the rest of the men came slowly down, moving along inch by inch until they were all crammed up against each other and already feeling sick with the smell which came towards them from the narrow opening ahead.

'Are you all there?' came the voice of the girl. 'Call out your numbers.'

'One . . .'

'Two . . .'

'Three . . .'

The voices of strangers echoed in the chamber.

'Nineteen . . .'

'Twenty.'

'All right,' said the girl. 'Follow me now.'

Jan heaved Paweł on to his back, and bent down.

There were other channels leading into the main one along which they had to crawl, and rats scuttled through them, cats, too. In some places the tunnel was high enough for them to walk, their heads lowered so that they just touched the roof, but mostly they had to bend almost double, or crawl. The sewage was several inches deep; with one hand they had to feel for the rope along the wall, with the other keep upright. Far ahead, the girl had lit a candle, and was waiting for them all to reach it: Jan kept struggling to raise his head to see it flicker – no chance at all of carrying Paweł and holding his own lighter, but at least it was there. He was in such agony it was almost impossible to stretch and look, and the lack of oxygen meant that the candle flame kept going out, so that sometimes he managed it only to find that he was staring into darkness once again. All he could hear was the heavy, rhythmic breathing and gasping of the people in front, the people behind, and the gurgling of the sewage.

He did not know how long they had been travelling, or how far they had come. He barely knew his name, or what it was that lay on his back and crucified him. He simply moved an inch, another inch, another inch, perhaps two inches the next time, then another. In the darkness searing lights began to dance and splinter behind his eyes. Another inch. Then something different happening, another sound. He didn't know any other sound; what was it?

Two sharp tugs on the rope.

The man in front had stopped moving. Jan managed to give two tugs on the rope himself, his hand slipping, and stopped, too. He let Paweł slide down a bit, and waited.

'What's . . . happening?' Paweł asked hoarsely.

'I don't know.'

They crouched, waiting in the blackness. Jan felt panic begin to rise. He fumbled for his lighter. It wasn't there. It must be. It wasn't. The button on the pocket had come off, the pocket was open, empty. Somewhere in the gurgling stream of filth, as he bent down, the lighter had fallen, and drowned. The blackness was all over him, inside his head. Everything was black. He heard himself breathing hard, like an animal.

Someone ahead was muttering. What? What was he saying? They were never going to get out of here, he had been born only to go

201

mad in the arsehole of Warsaw, he was going to die down here, they all were. He began to sob, to shout, to scream.

'Let me out! Let . . . me . . . out . . .'

'Shut up! Stop it, you bastard, stop it, shut up, do you want us all to go mad with you?'

A man was shaking him, then holding him, holding him. 'Look, here's a light. Look. Look. Calm down.'

The man in front had his arms round him, the next one had a stub of candle, and he could see again. Paweł was leaning up against the wall, his chest heaving.

The man who was holding Jan said: 'They passed this back, pass it on, there's another one coming. The girl's sent a message: the sewage level has risen, it's waist high, but she thinks we can get through.'

Jan clung to the candle. Behind him, voices were rising.

'I said pass on the fucking candle!' It was snatched away from him, and went out.

Paweł had his arms round his neck, and they were wading through shit. From somewhere in a channel off to the right he could hear someone laughing dementedly, but it might have been him. He went on, step by step, slipping, staggering, somehow keeping upright, his eyes only on a flickering pinpoint of light far far down the tunnel.

It began to get warmer, warmer still. Sweat was already pouring down him, but as the level of the sewage dropped, and they were able after a long break to move on again, he realized that the tunnel itself was getting hot, and that they must be passing underneath a burning house. They went on, gasping in the heat, and then the man in front was passing back a message: 'A hundred yards to go.'

Impossible to believe they could go further. The level had dropped right down, now, but the tunnel roof was also low again, and they had to go almost on their bellies.

'Paweł?'

There was no answer.

'Paweł . . . get off me, you bastard, let me get down.'

He struggled to lower himself without dropping Paweł, crawled the last, pitiless yards through the passageway with the weight on his back. There were voices ahead, and air. There was air. He went on, sobbing, his head banging the feet of the man in front until he felt him stop and scramble upright, then turn and pull Paweł off his back so that he could stand, too, and stare up at the ladder of the exit shaft, where faces were peering down, and arms ready to help them up, and out into the precious light of dawn.

Anna sat on a broad, leather-topped desk at the open window of an apartment in Three Crosses Square, looking along the length of Ujazdowskie Avenue. She was on observation duty, had been posted here with Natalia and Wojtek early this morning, making their way through the network of trenches and barricades. On their way, they'd seen something which until now she'd only heard people talking about: a little knot of AK soldiers bent down round a lifted manhole cover, hauling out thin, grey-faced, gasping men and women who'd crawled all the way through the sewers from Stare Miasto. They looked terrible, half-dead, and the stench made her heave. But at least they were alive, safe behind Polish lines again.

Here, it was quiet this morning, with little movement along the broad, leafy avenue: she looked through the heavy binoculars which had once belonged to Natalia's father, watching every corner of every street opening into it. At the far end, a tank stood motionless: she was to report any change in its position, any new patrols. The surface of the road and the pavements were pitted with craters; many of the stone balconies and window arches on the five-storey houses shattered. On the whole, however, Ujazdowskie and much of the city centre generally had so far escaped major damage: they knew that at the moment the Germans were concentrating their attack on what had been the stronghold of Stare Miasto.

Anna put down her binoculars to rest. The room they were in must have been someone's study: it made her think of Tata, with the bookshelves, the spacious desk, the sunlight. The door was heavy, thickly padded against noise from the rest of the apartment. Who had sat here before the war, reading and making notes, watching the peaceful rustling of the treetops down the centre of the avenue? Natalia and Wojtek were resting in armchairs pushed back against the far wall: for a moment, it felt as if they were all simply spending an ordinary morning together, on summer vacation from the *liceum:* if the war had not happened, that was what they would be doing now, preparing for university, visiting each other in the summer, going to parties, on holidays. The darkness inside her yawned open once again. If Tata were alive . . . if Jerzy and Andrzej were alive . . .

Wojtek looked up from the chair where he was reading yesterday's edition of *Walka.* 'Anything happening?'

She shook her head, turned back to the window and raised her binoculars again. The tank she'd noted an hour ago, right at the far end, was slowly moving up the avenue. It came past the Botanical Gardens, past the park, on past each intersection, moving a little faster now. She shifted the binoculars, and was dazzled for a moment by the midday sun. The tank came on; as if in a dream of summer heat and haziness, she saw the cannon being raised, higher, then higher still, until it was pointing directly at their building, at the window where her binoculars must be glinting, and she suddenly flung them down and yelled to the others: 'Run! Run for your lives!'

She leapt off the desk, Natalia and Wojtek sprang from their chairs, and they flung open the heavy door and ran into the corridor, slamming it behind them. Within a moment, the study shook with a deafening blast; they were flung flat on the floor and lay there, immobile, listening until the roar at last diminished to the crumbling of bricks, and tinkling glass, and silence. Then came the sound of the tank again, moving closer, stopping, then turning off into another street. They raised their heads, stared at each other, then scrambled up, shaking, and slowly pushed open the door which had saved them.

Inside the study they saw a great hole ripped into the wall where the window had been, the desk, the floor and furniture completely covered with glass and bricks and plaster.

'My God . . .' said Anna, and they stood there staring, watching the dust from the explosion rise into the air and float towards the trees.

They left the building and made their way slowly back to the base in Hoża. Henryk was about to leave to meet them: he looked at their white faces, listened as they told him what had happened. Then he passed them a sheet of paper: an additional communiqué to the usual bulletin. They read it in disbelief at first, and then Natalia began to cry.

Since the second week of August, hardly a single airdrop had been made over Warsaw – the distance from Brindisi, the base in southern Italy, meant that there was barely a hope of making it there and back without refuelling. Now they read that Stalin had refused to allow British and American planes the right to land and refuel on the nearby Soviet-held airfields: his price had been the arrest of the leaders of the Uprising.

The Old Town had fallen. The lovely squares and houses lay in smoking ruins, and now the Germans seized a great mass of women prisoners, and began to herd them towards the barricade which separated the Old Town from the next district to the south, Powiśle, on the riverside, still in Polish hands. Those defending the barricade saw the women approach, and the German infantry behind, and held their fire: how could they shoot at their own people? The Germans pushed on, and as they reached the barricade they shoved the helpless women on to it, and scrambled over them, kicking and punching, into the street behind it. At the sight of Germans in their midst, pounding down the streets and firing indiscriminately, panic spread through Powiśle. Thousands of civilians pressed up to the great barricades transecting Jerozolimskie Avenue and Nowy Świat, the main arteries of the city, partly in German and partly in Polish hands. They stumbled through the deep trenches, and many of those who had managed to reach them were buried by falling earth and sand: as fast as they were repaired, the barricades fell in, under the pressure of the people passing beneath them.

Powiśle was lost, and with it the electricity plant, tenaciously held and defended for over four weeks. Now, at night, the city was plunged into total darkness. The civilians crouching in the cellars of the houses still standing, and in the ruins of those which had been destroyed, were without light, without any but the most pitiful of rations: many of the warehouses had been bombed, and it was becoming more and more difficult to move what little supplies remained from the tunnels connecting one district to another. Babies and children were dying: dysentery swept through the cellars like a medieval plague. On the surface, bodies rotted in the street. The exhausted AK platoons and commanders who moved through the shelters were besieged, now, with pleas for surrender.

On the night of 10 September there came at last the sound the whole of Warsaw had been waiting for: the thunder of Soviet artillery from across the Vistula.

At 8.30 in the evening of 14 September, Moscow radio sent out another broadcast. It was picked up in the AK headquarters: they had been bombed out of the Old Town, bombed out of the cellar of the Polish Savings Bank in the city centre, and were now in hiding in a house to the south of Jerozolimskie Avenue. Here the monitoring staff heard:

'To fighting Warsaw: the hour of liberation for heroic Warsaw is near. Your sufferings and martyrdom will soon be over. The Germans will pay dearly for the ruins and blood of Warsaw. The first Polish Division Kościuszko has entered Praga. It is fighting side by side with the heroic Red Army. Relief is coming. Keep fighting! Whatever may have been the motives of those who started the rising prematurely, without agreement with the High Command of the Red Army, we are with you with all our hearts. The whole Polish nation is with you in your self-sacrificing struggle against the German invaders. A decisive fight is now taking place on the banks of the Vistula. Help is coming. Victory is near. Keep fighting!'

Soviet planes reappeared in the sky, and for the first time since the Uprising began, there were dogfights between them and the *Luftwaffe*. At night, the Russians made their first drops, but they were without parachutes, and containers of arms and sacks of grain smashed and split on the roofs and pavements. Much of the ammunition which fell did not, naturally, fit the British and American arms, or those arms captured from the Germans in the early battles, but the talk of surrender died down: the Russians had shown themselves ready to help at last, and the battle in Praga was raging. By 15 September, the district had been seized from the Germans. Now, each day, everyone waited to hear that the Russian troops had crossed the river: after five weeks without rain, the water-level was so low that in some places whole stretches of sand could be seen: you could almost have walked across.

Then came the news that Stalin had, finally, granted one landing right to American planes.

'Anna! Anna!'

All night she had been helping in the field hospital, where men were being brought in from other districts half dead from hunger and exhaustion, with severed or gangrenous limbs, or with pieces of shrapnel lodged in their heads and faces. There was little she could do, her tiny first-aid stock long since given to the Red Cross nurse she had met the day the hospital was hit, and she had carried the boy with his lifeless foot up the steps from the cellar. He had had it amputated that afternoon, and hobbled now on crutches, his white face grimacing. Last night, Anna had seen him trying to sleep, tossing and heaving under a thin blanket on the floor. She had gone across to hold his hand for a moment, but had quickly been recalled to help with another stretcher.

She came back to the apartment just after dawn, and fell at once into a deep sleep. Now, hearing her name called so urgently, she woke to see Jadwiga looking at her in excitement, saw the shutters flung back so that midday sunshine made her screw up her eyes, and from the street outside heard running feet, and wild cheering. The air was full of a roar of planes.

'They're coming!' said Jadwiga.

'The Russians?' Anna scrambled to her feet.

'The Americans! We're all on the roof – come on!'

She ran after her, up the broad stairs to the ladder leading to the roof. Through the square of the skylight, she could see among the crowd Wojtek and Natalia hugging each other, jumping up and down. Her ears were filled with the noise of the planes, as if the whole sky were taken over by them; she stumbled up the steps and out on to the packed rooftop.

In the cloudless, windswept sky, perhaps a hundred planes with the American white star insignia were approaching from the west. They flew at a great height, too high for the anti-aircraft fire which now burst into the air to reach them. As far into the city as Anna could see, the streets and avenues were packed with people up from the cellars and basements and hiding places in the ruins: the whole of Warsaw seemed to be gazing upwards, at the dark bellies of the planes and then, almost mad with happiness, at the white specks of parachutes, bearing containers which must hold food, and arms, and medicines, opening and descending like a gentle fall of snow.

And then, as if a great satanic hand had swept the sky, the parachutes drifted in the wind beyond the Polish lines. Ten days ago, a week ago even, the places where they were landing were in Polish hands: Powiślé, the Old Town, Napoleon Square. Now, all these places and many more were surrounded by German tanks and armoured cars: the watchers on the rooftops and in the streets stood staring, numb, as container after container tumbled towards enemy territory and disappeared.

'No,' said Anna. 'No, no . . .'

All around her they were weeping; on the streets she could see people moving as if condemned, stricken, silent, back down into the darkness and grimness of their cellar world. How could they have dared to hope that they would be reprieved?

Silence once more from across the river. The Soviet fighters disappeared from the sky as suddenly as they had come, and with their flight the *Luftwaffe* renewed their attack, dive-bombing the last, desperate outposts of the city. Hand grenades were thrown into the long queues waiting at the few remaining wells which still held water.

AK troops guarded other wells, where water for the wounded was sometimes rationed by the glass. The last kilos of barley from stores in the city centre had been ground to make a soup full of husks; dogs, cats and horses had been eaten. From the headquarters of the AK, General Bór radioed London: 'We are starving.'

In the riverside district of Czerniaków they had been without food for four days. For much longer, the Russians had been sending messages promising help with evacuation of wounded and civilians: one hundred boats were to cross the water from Praga, but only a handful came, and in desperation the defenders began to throw make-shift rafts together, and make a frantic attempt to cross by themselves as the *Luftwaffe* bombers screamed down. On 23 September, Czerniaków gave up, and surrendered.

In Mokotów, to the south-west of the city centre, the AK units who had not made their way out to the centre through the sewers were pressed into a few streets. The day after Czerniaków, Mokotów fell.

On 29 September the northern suburb of Żoliborz, beyond the ruins of the Old Town, was attacked, and General Bór ordered its immediate surrender: there was no hope of relieving the defenders now. The only district remaining to the Polish defenders was the city centre: impossible that it, too, would not fall within a matter of days.

At eight o'clock in the evening of 2 October, sixty-two days after the first shots of the Uprising had been fired, the surrender of Warsaw to the Germans was signed.

On 3 October dawn broke over a silent city. No sound of shelling, no scream of bombers, no cries, no falling buildings. As news of the capitulation spread, the doors of the cellars and basements opened, and from each house came wave after wave of thin, grey-faced people, carrying their children and their last possessions, stumbling over the rubble-strewn streets, over the planks across the craters, making their way towards the barricaded exits from where they were to walk to Ożarów and Pruszków, the German transit and prison camps ten miles away.

In a half-bombarded house not far from the street where Anna was stationed, Jan looked down at the place where two weeks ago Paweł had died. He listened blankly to the commander of the unit they had joined when they came out of the sewers, listing the terms of surrender. All those who had fought in the AK were to be protected by the Geneva Convention, treated not as terrorists, or 'bandits' as

Stalin once scornfully described them, but as prisoners of war. In the absence of full uniform, they were to be recognized by their white and red armbands, or by the insignia of the Polish eagle.

The commander was a thick-set, powerful man in his forties. His voice broke as he began to read out General Bór's last order to his troops:

'Soldiers of fighting Warsaw!

'Our two months' struggle in Warsaw, which has been a chain of heroic actions on the part of the Polish soldiers, is fraught with dread, yet it is a solemn proof, above all, of our mighty striving for liberty. The valour of Warsaw is the admiration of the whole world. Our struggle in the capital under the blows of death and destruction, carried on with such tenacity by us, takes first place among the glorious deeds achieved by the Polish soldiers during this war . . .'

Jan saw at his feet the dying body of Paweł, saw him on the first day of the Uprising, laughing and waving an imaginary gun, shouting out: 'Poland is not yet lost!' and he closed his eyes.

The commander cleared his throat and read on:

'Today the technical superiority of the enemy has succeeded in forcing us into the central part of the city, the only district still in our possession. The ruins and rubble are crowded with civilians cooperating valiantly with the soldiers, but already exhausted beyond measure by the ghastly conditions of existence on the field of battle. There is not sufficient food even for bare existence, and there is no prospect of a final conquest of the enemy here in the capital. We are now confronted with the prospect of the complete destruction of the population of Warsaw and the burial of thousands of fighting soldiers and civilians in its ruins.

'I have therefore decided to break off the struggle.'

'I can't bear it,' said Anna. 'All this for nothing – I can't bear it.' She began to cry, helplessly, clinging to Natalia, as they all sat on the floor, hardly hearing the words which Henryk went on reading:

'I thank all soldiers for their magnificent bearing, which did not succumb even when conditions were at their worst. I pay due tribute to the fallen for their agony. I express the admiration and gratitude of the fighting ranks of the army to the population, and declare the army's attachment to them. I ask the people to pardon the soldiers any transgressions committed against the population during the long and protracted struggle . . .

'You soldiers, my dearest comrades in these two months of fighting, one and all of whom have been to the very last moment constant in the will to fight on, I ask now to fulfil obediently such orders as arise from the decision to cease fighting. I call to the population to comply with the evacuation instructions issued by me, the city's Commander, and the civil authorities.'

Henryk broke off. 'Tomorrow,' he said, 'we shall all assemble at the exit barricade. If any of you want to go home, and collect anything before the final evacuation, you'd better go tonight. I think we can all sleep here, though, if necessary.' He looked at them all, and then back at the thin sheet of paper from which he had been reading. 'I suppose we must try to take courage from General Bór's last words: "With faith in ultimate victory of our just cause, with faith in a beloved, great and happy country, we shall all remain soldiers and citizens of an independent Poland, faithful to the standard of the Polish Republic." '

He put down the paper, and they sat in silence, staring at the pattern on the floor made by the sunlight still streaming through the open window, as if it were any autumn afternoon.

She climbed the stairs to the apartment door and knocked.

'Wiktoria? It's Anna.'

There was no answer, and she knocked again, but louder. 'Wiktoria! Wiktoria!'

How could she have hoped that she would still be here? She put her shoulder to the door, and pushed. It gave way quite easily: weeks of vibration from the shelling must have loosened every hinge and lock in the city. Inside, she stood in the corridor and called again, but then she began to be frightened by the image of herself standing alone in an abandoned apartment, and moved quickly from room to empty room.

Dust lay thickly on every chair and bed and table; the windows were shattered. It was like returning to the apartment house in Praga, after the siege, but now she no longer had the hope that her father would be coming home, and now she did not have Jerzy, either.

On the bookshelf in Wiktoria's room was a photograph of Tata and Mama: he stood behind her, his head on her shoulder; two-year-old Jerzy leaned against her lap; Anna, a baby, sat there staring very gravely at the camera. There was another photograph, of Tata with Teresa laughing.

Where was Teresa now?

Anna went out into the corridor, along to her own small room.

From the chest of drawers there she took out a postcard, carefully wrapped, and all her own photographs, some in an album, some still loose in envelopes. Mama. Mama and Tata. Teresa – a print of the photograph she'd had taken for her identity card. Tata and Jerzy on their last holiday together, rowing down the river past the silver birch trees. Wiktoria, holding both their hands when they were tiny, walking in a snowy garden somewhere: that must have been the winter Mama died.

She put all of them into a small, flat, pre-war sweet tin she found in a drawer in the kitchen, and tied it with a piece of string. Then she searched until she found a pencil, and wrote a note to Wiktoria on the back of an envelope:

> Leaving Warsaw tomorrow, like everybody else. To a transit camp, and then God knows. Jerzy was killed 8.8 on Jerozolimskie: he is buried in Żórawia.
>
> Thank you for everything. Will be near Three Crosses Square tonight – same place we've been at through the Uprising. Come if you can.
>
> Anna
3 October 1944

She put the note on the kitchen table, the corner under a cup: it lifted a little in the breeze from the shattered window. Then she picked up the box of photographs, went out of the apartment and closed the door.

Paris was liberated, Warsaw fell. Anna stood in a long, long line of people, each with an AK armband, moving slowly over the torn-up pavements under the eye of the German guards. They went past the skeletons of houses; past the silhouettes of burned-out churches where only a few stone frames of stained-glass windows hung; past court-yards filled with burial mounds and crosses, and courtyards where piles of bodies lay still unburied. All the way through the city the only sounds were the crunch of bricks and rubble under thousands of moving feet, and the voices of the Germans, talking quietly to each other as they watched.

A towering barricade loomed ahead, with a gap cleared away in

211

the middle. They reached it, and Anna looked up. Far above, from a gaping window, a white flag hung limply, like a broken arm. Then the order to march was given, and she followed the people in front, stumbling through the gap in the barricade, and out to the other side.

When all the inhabitants of Warsaw had left, the Germans, on Hitler's orders, razed every last building to the ground. They destroyed it all methodically, street by street, house by house. On 17 January 1945, the Russians crossed the Vistula at last, and liberated a dead city. The following day, down the snow-covered ruins of Jerozolimskie Avenue, they held a Victory Parade.

Part 2

My Country

6
London, 1960

The classroom smelt of powder paint and chalk dust. There were two
posters on the long corridor wall opposite the window: one of British
Birds, perched in stiff profile on twigs – blackbird, thrush, chaffinch
and blue tit, starling and robin, each with its own black silhouette
behind, in flight. The finches rose and dipped – there was a curving
line of dashes, to make it clear. Next to it was Road Safety, where
two small children, a boy and a girl, tightly held their mother's hand
on the edge of a zebra crossing. The mother wore a hat; across the
road a policeman beckoned, smiling. Pinned up by the blackboard
was a map of the world, where all the countries in pink belonged to
Great Britain. A lot of Africa was pink. From where he sat, near the
back of the class and by the window, Poland was almost invisible, a
little splash of purple before the great expanse of green that was
Russia.

The clock above the glass-panelled door showed half-past eleven.
Mrs Thompson, bulging where brown pleated skirt and wine-
coloured cardigan met, was straining up to the blackboard with the
felt-covered wooden wiper, cleaning off the sums from before break.

'No talking, please. And I have eyes in the back of my head,
Joanna Wightman, so please take that gum from under your desk
and put it in the wastepaper basket.'

'Yes, Miss.'

The chalk squeaked as Mrs Thompson wrote in careful print, and
turned back to the class. 'You can all see from the back? Michael,
what does that say?'

'The Romans, Miss.' Michael, the stocky little boy who shared a
double desk with Jerzy, moved his gum into his cheek.

'Good boy. Now – this half-term we shall be learning all about the
Romans, how they sailed here, nearly two thousand years ago, all the
way from Italy, to conquer this country. Who can tell me what "to
conquer" means? Anyone? No? It means to win every battle, until
you can rule completely. The Romans conquered us, and they gave
us new towns, new roads and money and houses – all sorts of things,

even central heating! They were a very civilized people. Now – here is a picture . . .' She picked up a sheet of paper from her desk and taped it to the board. A small cloud of chalk dust drifted to the back of the classroom, and Jerzy coughed. 'No fidgeting, please. There – look at him!'

The children gazed at the profile of a man with a long nose, wearing a helmet. 'A Roman soldier,' said Mrs Thompson triumphantly. 'And here' – she taped up another picture – 'here is what he found.' Wild-looking men with long hair and beards, in ragged clothes, crouched round a fire. The picture was in only two colours, black and inky blue, so that the flames were the same colour as the grass. In the background were blue and black huts, then a forest.

'You can just see from these two pictures how different we were from the Romans, can't you? Now – have any of you ever heard of a Roman soldier called Julius Caesar? No? He was a great leader, and when he came here he said: "I came, I saw, I conquered." ' She wrote his name on the board, and turned back to the class. 'Yes, Jerzy?'

He lowered his hand. 'Poland was conquered, Miss.'

'Well . . . yes. After the war, I suppose.'

'But . . . I mean before that. A long time ago. I don't know if it was when the Romans came here, but it made me think of it. We were . . . partitioned.'

'That's right, dear. Now, shall we concentrate on the Romans? We are all going to make a great big frieze – who can help me pin up all this green paper on the wall?'

'Me, Miss, me!'

'Me, me!'

'Quietly, quietly. Tracy and Steven – here you are, you hold the drawing pins and this roll, the rest of you get out your pencils and crayons. Next week we shall be doing some painting. Each one of you can do a picture to stick up on the background: soldiers, Roman ladies, ships, houses, coins . . .' She had her back to them now, and was stretching out rolls of green sugar paper across the blank wall running from the door to the end of the classroom. Desk lids were banged open, pencil cases unzipped. Jerzy yawned, then coughed again. Beside him, Michael had the lid of his desk propped against his forehead, and with his right hand was turning the first page of *Beano*, while his left fumbled noisily with his pencil case. Jerzy peered sideways at Lord Snooty and His Pals, then nudged him as Mrs Thompson moved heavily from the far wall and down towards the blackboard. Michael's lid closed quietly; books from the school library were passed from the front.

'Turn to the first page, and there you will see the magnificent ships, rowed by slaves, in which the Romans sailed across the Mediterranean Sea . . .'

Jerzy and Michael looked at bright brown and orange and yellow wood, and clothes, and faces. From the prow of the ship a Roman soldier gazed out across sparkling waves at a distant shore, behind him, muscular half-naked slaves strained at the oars, under a cracking whip.

'Cor,' said Michael, and then, as an afterthought: 'My Dad's taking me to see *Gun Fight at Dodge City* tomorrow.'

'So's mine,' said Jerzy automatically. He tried to remember if Tata had been at home at all last weekend, and couldn't. Probably not – he had extra work all the time, now. Anyway, sometimes it wasn't very comfortable when he was at home. He flicked through the pages, glimpsed a map, and turned back until he found it, an outline of Scotland, England and Wales. It was filled in with a creamy wash, dotted with scarlet circles for towns: Londinium, Camulodunum, Calcaria, Longovicium. Sprinkled among the scarlet towns and thin blue rivers were tiny line drawings: castles, villas, vases, necklaces and coins, more ships. A long grey line like a battlement marched across the north of England. Something Wall. Hadrian's Wall – who was Hadrian? Jerzy could imagine that Dziadek would like this map.

'Miss?'

'Yes?'

'Can I make a map? Like this one?' He held it up and she moved down the aisle towards him, and picked up the book. 'Well. You can try. It's a little ambitious, a little difficult for now. I thought perhaps one thing each, but you can see how you get on. It'll take quite a few lessons, I should think. What about you, Michael, what are you going to do?'

'One of them wild men, Miss.'

Giggles from across the aisle.

'That's enough, thank you, Sandra. Now – are you all ready with something?'

Jerzy bent over the map once more, then opened the felt pencil case Babcia had made at the beginning of the term. It was fluffing slightly along the zip. He found the sharpest pencil, and began to draw. The dinner bell rang as he reached the tip of Cornwall.

★

The assembly hall, which served also as the dining room and gym, had a high ceiling and long narrow windows set far above the level of the children's heads. There were double doors, leading out to the playground, but their glass panels were covered with protective mesh, so that you could really see only the outlines of the caretaker's hut, the wall and railings and the council flats beyond. Inside, the scraping of chairs, the clatter of cutlery on Formica-topped tables, the dinner ladies banging stainless steel lids on serving dishes, the children's voices, all rose to and echoed from the vaulted ceiling. There was a permanent smell of chips and beans, with an undernote of cleaning fluid, particularly noticeable now, in the autumn term, when the radiators were on.

Ewa collected her plate of fish, chips and peas, and her bowl of tinned pears and custard, and followed Lizzie Blunden, new this term, across to their class table. They pulled back their chairs and sat down. Lizzie pulled up her sleeves and tucked a mass of curly red hair behind her ears.

'You've got earrings!' said Ewa. 'Let's see.' She leaned over, gently touched a small gold stud. 'When did you have it done?'

'Last night – my Mum's friend does it. I expect she'd do yours, if you wanted.'

Ewa tried to imagine Mama's face. 'I don't think my Mum would let me.'

'Why?' Lizzie took a forkful of chips.

Ewa shrugged. 'She'd say I was too young.'

'Some of the babies on our estate have got them,' said Lizzie. 'And they'd suit you, show up nice with your plaits.' She yawned. 'Thank God it's the weekend. What're you doing tomorrow?'

'School in the morning. I don't know what we'll do in the afternoon. We take our dog out on the common quite often.'

'School?' asked Lizzie. 'What school?'

'Saturday school – Polish school. My grandfather teaches there.'

'I didn't know you was Polish.'

'Well, I am,' said Ewa, feeling glamorous.

'When did you come here, then?'

'I was born here.'

'Then you're English.'

'No. Not really . . .'

'Course you are. If you was born here. Not like the wogs. My Mum's fed up with the wogs – she says there's too many moving in round here, and soon there'll be too many in this place, too.' She dug Ewa in the ribs and nodded towards the two West Indian girls at the next table. 'If you was born here, you're English,' she said again. 'Ain't you glad?'

Ewa didn't know how to answer. She pushed the peas on her plate into a little pile, and took a mouthful.

'What do you do at this school, then?'

'Polish language, and stories. History . . .'

'Blimey,' said Lizzie, finishing her fish. 'Don't you get fed up?'

'No,' said Ewa, flushing. 'We have dancing, too, it's fun.'

'What sort of dancing?'

'Well – folk dancing, I suppose. Country dancing – sometimes we wear costumes.' She suddenly saw herself in her embroidered blouse, and full embroidered skirt and waistcoat, with Lizzie watching, in her earrings, and she felt glamour and specialness evaporate. Across the hall she could see Jerzy's class, stacking up their plates. 'My brother goes,' she said, and pointed. 'That's him, over there by the climbing bars.'

'The skinny one?'

'He's not skinny!'

'Course he is,' said Lizzie. 'Oh, go on, what's the matter with you? Say something in Polish.'

'No.' Ewa pushed away her plate, felt a thick lump forming in her throat and furiously tried to swallow it.

'You're crying! I only said . . .'

'Oh, shut up.'

'Charming.' Lizzie turned exaggeratedly to the girl on the other side, and Ewa stared blindly at the table top. Why was she so upset? What did it matter what Lizzie Blunden thought?

Out in the playground it was cold but free. Ewa and Janet, duffle coat hoods up, friends since the first year, walked round the netball markings, arm in arm.

'What did she say?'

Ewa bit her lip. 'Nothing, really. I just felt she was laughing at me.'

'So what?'

'I know. It's just . . .'

'D'you want to come and have tea after school? You'll never guess.'

'What?'

'I've got the Elvis! Mum brought it home last night. If you come, we can listen to it eight million times.'

'It's now or *never* . . .'

They spun up and down past the caretaker's hut.

'Number One next week.'

'Course it will be. Will you come?'

'Oh, yes. If Mama says . . .'

'She will, won't she?'

'Yes, I'm sure she will.'

'It's now or *never* . . .'

'Look at Jerzy,' Janet said suddenly.

'Where?'

'Over there, by the gate.'

He was standing watching them – or possibly not watching, but daydreaming, holding them merely by chance in his line of vision. His face looked pinched with the cold. Ewa shook her head.

'Mama keeps saying he's got to keep warm, and run about.'

They walked quickly towards him.

'Jerzy?' said Ewa.

He nodded. 'Yes?'

'What are you doing?'

'Nothing.'

'Why not? Mama says you've got to run about, get strong.'

'It makes me cough. I was thinking.'

From the main entrance of the school the afternoon bell rang out. They began to walk back across the playground; Lizzie Blunden ran past them in a group of boys, giggling.

'What do you mean, thinking?' Ewa said irritably. 'Mooning.'

'I wanted to play with you.'

'Well, you can't,' she snapped. 'Haven't you got any friends?'

'No, not really. You two can be my friends.'

They rolled their eyes, groaning, and ran ahead.

Anna stood at the tall school gates, holding Burek's lead. The gates were still closed, the playground empty; other mothers arrived and waited, leaning against the railings, Marks & Spencer coats and raincoats buttoned tight. A bus drove past, splashing up a puddle from the morning's rain, and the mothers moved away.

'Don't care, do they?'

'God, it's cold.'

'Come on, come on, what's the matter with that bell?'

'Your hair looks nice, Jean. Going out?'

'You must be joking – just had it done to cheer myself up.'

'Why, what's he done now, then?'

'Never came home, did he?'

'What, not all night?'

'Not all night.'

'Tch. I don't know how you put up with it. You shouldn't, Jean, it's not right.'

'Yeah, but the kids . . . Come on, bell.' Anna stood looking through the railings across to the lighted classroom windows, set too high up to see inside, and she listened to the voices around her as if to a play on the radio. She could never talk about Jan like that. Her feet were cold; she shifted them up and down, thinking suddenly: my other life was like a play, like a myth, even: the motherless child fighting her stepmother; the father the good man taken prisoner, murdered in an enemy country; the brother dying a hero's death. And I am the exile, arriving on the shores of a new land with only a box of pictures.

Meeting Jan was going to be the happy ending: orphan marries handsome hero. Perhaps it had been too much to hope that he could make up for losing everything else.

Around her the group of mothers grew, and then the caretaker appeared, unlocked the school gates and swung them open. The bell jangled through the sound of the traffic, and the children came pouring out, shouting. Burek whimpered, straining at his lead; he caught sight of Jerzy and his tail beat madly against Anna's legs.

'Wait!' She tugged at him sharply, then stretched out a hand to Jerzy, who bent and buried his face in Burek's coat, laughing.

'*Dzień dobry*, Mama.'

'*Dzień dobry, kochany*. Where is that Ewa? Oh, there she is, let's get home quickly now, it's bitter.'

'Mama!' Ewa came running. 'Can I go home with Janet, for tea?'

'Oh, not today, Ewa – the grandparents have made tea. They're waiting for us.'

She pulled a face. 'They won't mind, just for once. Please.'

'And who will come to fetch you? It's much too cold to come out again.'

'Couldn't Tata come, after work?'

'I don't know what time he'll be back. Another time you can go.' Anna, her ankles painfully nudged by a pushchair, caught sight of Janet's mother, and smiled apologetically. 'Perhaps one day next week . . .'

'No!' Ewa said furiously. 'We want to go *now*.'

'Ewa! Control yourself, please.'

221

'But . . .'

'Why don't I bring her home?' Janet's mother suggested. 'It's no trouble.'

'It's very kind of you,' said Anna, taking Jerzy's hand, 'but Ewa must learn that she cannot always do what she wants, just when she wants it. Now come along.'

She turned away, not looking to see whether or not Ewa was following, and moved through the crush on the pavement to the zebra crossing.

'Ewa won't play with me,' said Jerzy as they stood waiting for her.

'You should be playing with the other boys,' said Anna. She turned to watch Ewa, hugging Janet goodbye, then running to catch up with them, and held out her hand. Ewa did not take it.

'*Why* wouldn't you let me go, Mama? It's not fair.'

'What was so special about today?'

'She's got "It's Now or Never". Her mother bought it for her.' She glared at Anna accusingly.

'Oi!' The taxi driver at the crossing was leaning out into the drizzle. 'You lot standing there all night?'

'Oh, my goodness!' Anna hurried them all over the road, and they walked quickly past the lighted shops.

'I did a map today,' said Jerzy, as they turned into their street. 'Roman Britain. Anyway, I started it. For Dziadek – and you. It's going to have castles on it, and a wall. I wanted to borrow the book but Mrs Thompson said I couldn't. Can we go to the library tomorrow?'

'Yes, I should think so. After Saturday school.' Anna turned to Ewa, to ask what she had done today, and saw that she was crying. 'Ewa! Surely you're not still upset?'

'It isn't *fair*,' Ewa said again. 'You don't understand.'

'Look!' said Jerzy. 'There's Dziadek!' At the third-floor window his comforting square shape in its dark suit was silhouetted against the light from the table lamp; his hand was raised in greeting. Jerzy waved back, grabbed Burek's lead and ran ahead, leaving Ewa and Mama to sort themselves out.

'And what happened then, Mama?'

Rain splashed against the window panes, and above the slate roof-tops the sky was filled with heavy cloud. Lights in the windows across the street shone through the falling rain; below, every now and then, footsteps hurried past, doors banged. Anna and the children were sitting by the gas fire, which sputtered and popped; Burek lay stretched before it, dozing. A pool of light from the lamp on the low shelf beside it fell on to the rug, where Ewa sat, her back to the window, her mug beside her, hugging her knees. The side of her bare leg and her face were burning red from the fire. Jerzy was also on the floor, but leaning against Anna as she sat in the moquette chair, with its scratched wooden arms, and sewed. From down here he could see only the purple-grey sky, the rain hitting and bouncing off the wet black slates, a sluice of water fall from a place where the gutter in the opposite house had broken, and the upper panes of the windows, rectangles of yellow with an occasional figure, moving across, or staring out. Whoever was there would see the light from this room in the same way, of course, but they couldn't see him and Ewa, down here, warm and safe and drinking hot chocolate, listening to Mama tell her stories from the war.

'What happened then?' Ewa asked again.

Anna bit off a piece of thread, and licked it, making a knot. Ewa had borrowed the sewing scissors once too often: she couldn't find them anywhere now. She picked up the grey school skirt again, and went on stitching.

'And then,' she said slowly, 'well . . . then we were prisoners.'

She saw herself standing on a road a few miles outside Warsaw, her feet in the ill-fitting shoes already blistered, stopping to rest just for a moment, and turning to look back. The air was clear and fresh, the sky a sharp, autumnal blue and yellow. Behind them, the city lay like a wounded animal, helpless and abandoned, the column of prisoners stretching endlessly out from it, a Pilgrim's Progress bleakly swung round, leading away from everything known, and loved, and hoped for. The sound of feet, marching, stumbling, slowing down and ordered on again, scrunched and pounded in her head until it was as if the whole world were filled with it, as if life itself had been reduced to a grim, eternal walk along a road, knowing nothing of the destination.

'Poor Mama . . .' said Jerzy, from the floor.

She patted his shoulder. 'Shall I tell you something funny? We were marched to a place called Ożarów, about ten miles away from Warsaw, where there had once been a factory for dyes. There were great empty buildings, taken over by the Germans for use as a transit camp, with thousands of us milling about, trying to find news of friends, or relatives with whom we had lost touch during the Uprising. We were given a little bread, I think, and a few of the taps were

223

working, so we had something to drink, and then we all tried to settle down for the night and get some sleep. The floors were bare concrete, and for some reason there were a number of bales of straw, and some people managed to spread that out and sleep on it, but it was a most uncomfortable night. Anyway, it was dark, naturally, so none of us could really see what we were lying on. And in the morning, when we woke up, we found that our faces, and hands and clothes were stained with deep blue dye! Can you imagine? It must have been all over the floor, and of course it was quite indelible. For weeks afterwards, even longer, it was possible in the prison camps to tell at once who had been in Ożarów.'

'Goodness,' said Jerzy. 'And were *you* blue?'

'Oh, yes. All down one arm and one side of my face.'

'And did you find out what had happened to Teresa?' Ewa asked. 'And Wiktoria?'

Anna shook her head. 'Not then. When I was in prison camp a letter reached me from Wiktoria, through the Red Cross, I think. She told me that poor Teresa had been killed in the first weeks of the Uprising – the house where she was staying was bombed.'

The rain beat against the window. Anna had stopped sewing. 'I was so sad when I read that,' she said.

'Poor Mama,' Jerzy said again.

'No, not poor Mama. I was sad for her, can you understand – for everything she lost . . .' She picked up the grey school skirt again.

'And what about Wiktoria?' Ewa asked accusingly. '*She's* not dead, is she?'

Anna raised an eyebrow at her. 'No. I can't imagine Wiktoria ever dying.'

'She sends us cards at Easter, doesn't she?' Jerzy said. 'From Warsaw. And she sends cards at *Wigilia*.'

'Yes. And you want to know what happened to her? Well, she had AK soldiers stationed in her apartment, and she looked after them all. I can just imagine it – she would have been in her element. But when the news of the capitulation came, she left it at once, and spent the last couple of days before we were evacuated trying to find news of us. If she had left a note for me to find when I went back, we might have been reunited, and left Warsaw together. As it was, we missed each other, and by the time she came back and found my note, I think I must have been already on the way to Ożarów. She was sent to Pruszków, another camp outside the city. I think it was in Pruszków that she heard about Teresa. That was a terrible, filthy place, apparently. Anyway, Wiktoria decided then to do what Babcia – your Babcia – had done, much earlier: she took off her AK armband, and was sent as a civilian to a labour camp. She thought she had no hope of seeing me again, that when the war ended Poland was bound to fall under the Russians, and I would not want to come back. And of course she was right. She felt she was too old to start a new life outside Poland; when her camp was liberated by Russian soldiers she returned to the ruins of Warsaw, like thousands of others. Everyone helped to rebuild it, clearing the rubble, living in bomb sites . . . And she's been there ever since.'

'When I grow up, I shall go and visit her,' said Ewa.

'We'll see.'

'Can't you go back and see her?'

'No. Never.'

'Why?'

Anna sighed. 'Because I am a stateless person now. Like Tata, and the grandparents. We have only travel documents – no passports. If we went back to Poland, we should never be able to come out again. When we came here we had the opportunity of taking British nationality, and of course many people did so, but it was rather frowned upon, by people like Dziadek – he thought it was almost like being a traitor. And the – how shall I put it? – the high-ups, the people who had formed the Federation of Poles in Great Britain, they wanted us to keep our own identity, not be swallowed up and turned into English people. The English, naturally, wanted us to integrate completely.' She thought of the resettlement camp, the kindly welfare ladies, with their orange juice, and coupons, and copies of *Essential English*. And then every Pole in the camp, suddenly, was talking about the Yalta Agreement, and how Poland had been betrayed. 'All that is another story,' she said, and got up to draw the curtains. The street lamps had been turned on, and the pavements were full of puddles: Jan would be soaked, unless he stayed at work.

Ewa and Jerzy stretched. 'Tell us the other story, Mama,' said Jerzy. 'And tell us about Tata.'

'Why doesn't he talk to us about it all?' asked Ewa.

Anna went to the other window to draw the curtains there, then turned to look at them. London in winter. A wet November Sunday afternoon, her children sitting in the lamp and firelight, Burek's ears twitching as he slept, a clean pile of mending on her chair. And an empty chair, on the other side of the fire, where her husband did not sit. Other couples they knew, people they'd spent evenings with in the Polish Club in Balham – in the days when they still went to the Club together – seemed so settled here. Their Polishness, the time they spent at mass, at the Club, sending their children to Scouts, and Guides, and Saturday school: all these things were the centre of their lives, but they had English lives too, didn't they? Anna looked at the box waiting for her across the room, by her sewing machine, a great pile of unsewn garments from the factory. She refused to sit up here doing piecework for the rest of her days! She was going to make an English life for herself! And in the meantime, Jan seemed almost as lost and angry and restless as he had done when they first arrived here. He came home late, he did overtime almost every weekend – what was it doing to the children, to have a father who was never at home? Ewa was climbing up into his chair.

'Ow – my leg.' She rubbed the burning skin.

'I've told you not to sit so close.' Anna crossed the room again, and sat down, putting the grey skirt on the pile of mended clothes. She picked up a white shirt from the shelf by the lamp and rummaged in a coffee tin for buttons. 'What do you *do* with your clothes, Ewa?'

'I don't know. They just seem to come to bits.'

'She dances in the playground,' said Jerzy. 'She dances up and down singing stupid songs.'

Ewa stuck her tongue out at him.

Anna's fingers moved among the buttons. 'I hope you're not getting into silly company.'

'I was with Janet! Don't go on at me, Mama – who came top of the class last term?'

'Being clever isn't everything. Or conceited.' She found a white button, checked it for size against the shirt and re-threaded the needle.

'What other story, Mama?' Jerzy said again.

Anna thought. 'Where were we?'

'Coming to England – and all about Tata.'

'Oh, yes. Well – quite a lot happened before we came here. So – we were in Ożarów. And over the next few days we were taken group by group into Germany, by train.'

Like cattle. Crammed into wooden carriages, the doors slammed shut and bolted, the only light from ventilation slits, high up on the sides, where other women, taller, helped each other up and peered through, trying to work out where we were going. A few hard black loaves thrown to us, before we left, to share, with no knives to cut them; ill-tasting water in canisters. Straw on the wooden floor, where bitter draughts chilled us as the train began to move. We took turns, lying and standing, pressed up against each other; I didn't know any of those women. My periods had stopped, during the Uprising, or perhaps it was before, but I began again, on that journey, with nothing to use as a towel. It took – three days? I think so. Let out every now and then in bare, scrubby countryside, to relieve ourselves under the eyes of the guard. That was so we couldn't escape, of course, but I had no thought of escaping, I just wanted some privacy.

The button on the white school shirt was stiff with thread, sewn and sewn on, over and over again. She tugged at the short piece of thread remaining, and snapped it off.

'And then,' she said, 'after a journey of some two or three days, we were taken off that train, and marched to a prison camp. It was a men's camp, but they had wired off one part of it, one barrack, for women. We spent the winter there. And there I almost lost my last possessions.' She gestured to the photographs in frames on the bookshelves, and hung on the wall. Her father and brother. Her mother. Teresa. Wiktoria. Jerzy and she in a snowy garden somewhere, the winter Mama died. Jerzy and Tata under the silver birch trees, by the river, the morning of the day they heard they were at war. There were more in the heavy album in the cupboard.

'You remember that I brought all those photographs with me, when I left Warsaw? From Wiktoria's flat?'

'In the sweet tin,' said Jerzy.

'That's right. Well, in the prison camp there was a censor – you know what a censor is? Someone who decides what you are allowed to read, or see. There is a censor for the cinema – children are not allowed to see films with a certificate A, or X, are they?'

'But I'd like to see *Gun Fight at Dodge City*,' said Jerzy. 'Do you think Tata would take me? I did ask him, but . . .'

'He might,' Anna said lightly. 'We'll see. So, the censor in the German prison camp was the person who decided what we were allowed to keep. Of course, we had very few possessions, but we had to show him what we had. So I showed him the photographs. And he was going to take them away, and burn them . . .'

She got up, went to the bookshelves, took down the frame containing the photograph of Jerzy and Tata by the river, and began to undo it, slipping aside the little metal tags at the back.

'I begged and pleaded and cried,' she said, 'until in the end he was sick of me, I think, and he threw them across the desk, and said I could keep them. But then, just as I was picking them up, he told me to wait, and from beside him he took a big rubber stamp, and a pad of ink, and made me give them back to him. And so – look . . .' She had removed the cardboard backing, and carefully lifted the photograph. Craning over her arm, Ewa and Jerzy saw heavy black letters, slightly smudged. *Stalag XB.* 'It is on the back of all of them,' said Anna, 'but I didn't care, then. I was only overjoyed to know they weren't going to be destroyed.' She dropped the photograph back on the glass, clipped it into place again, and turned it over. Her brother and her father smiled at her, from a place so far away that she was not always certain, now, that it had ever existed.

Jerzy was leaning against her. She lightly touched the glass. 'Your other Dziadek, and your uncle. Your namesakes – Jerzy Tomasz.'

He nodded. 'Yes, you've told me lots of times.'

'Have I?' She got up again and put the picture back on the shelf. 'Perhaps we've had enough stories now. Would you like to do some drawing? Or tidy your room?'

Ewa shook her head.

For a brief, uncomfortable moment, she thought of Lizzie Blunden's sharp little face. *'If you was born here, you're English. Ain't you glad?'* She looked at Mama, and imagined her begging and pleading with a hard-faced man in uniform to be allowed to keep a handful of photographs. She saw her standing in a long long line of prisoners, being marched through ruins, and she remembered, suddenly, Dziadek telling them at school something about Yalta – the Yalta Agreement, at the end of the war, when Winston Churchill and President Roosevelt had handed Poland to Stalin on a plate. Dziadek, who was usually so kind, had looked stern, even angry when he talked about it.

How could she explain to Lizzie that she would never be anything but Polish? And how could Mama ever understand how much she sometimes wished she had never heard of Poland?

Jerzy was rubbing his forehead. 'Go on, Mama.'

'Well . . .' Anna rummaged in the pile of mending, and withdrew a pair of his socks, with holes in heel and toe. 'You're growing very fast all of a sudden, we shall have to go shopping. Perhaps these will last just for the rest of term. Anyway – where was I?'

'In the prison camp.'

'In the prison camp . . . Yes. We spent the whole winter there, my God it was cold – bitter. So many of us were ill, I had pleurisy, even . . .' She shook her head. 'Never mind. In the spring of 1945 **we were moved, to an all-women camp in a place called Oberlangen,**

228

near the Belgian border. And there, in May, when the war was almost over, we were liberated by Polish soldiers. Can you imagine – we went mad! They had been fighting in Europe with the British, serving under General Maczek. And when they came up in their lorries, we were waving and shouting from behind the wire fences – to see free Polish soldiers! I can't tell you how wonderful that was.'

She looked at her watch. 'Goodness, it's almost five – the grand-parents will be here in a minute. Go and put the kettle on, Ewa, there's a good girl.'

Ewa got up slowly, stretching. 'It's freezing in the kitchen.'

'Oh, go on.'

'And then the soldiers came . . .' said Jerzy, 'And then . . .'

'And then, eventually, there were transports arranged, and I made my way to Italy, to join the Polish forces there – the Polish Second Corps, serving under the famous General Anders. You remember him?'

'Monte Cassino,' said Ewa from the door. 'Dziadek's told us all about it in Saturday school. And that's where you met Tata, isn't it, in Italy?'

'Yes, that's right.'

'And was it love at first sight?'

'Ewa!' Anna tucked Jerzy's darned sock neatly into its pair. 'Run along at once.'

'Is Tata coming back for tea?' Jerzy asked, as Ewa disappeared, giggling.

'Oh, I don't know!' said Anna irritably, and bit her lip. 'Sorry, *maleńki* – I didn't mean to snap. He might come – it depends how much more he has to do.'

Jerzy sighed. Then Ewa was back again.

'Mama?'

'Now what?'

'You and Tata met in Italy . . .'

'Yes . . .'

'And he and Dziadek and Babcia were all reunited then . . .' She frowned, concentrating. 'And then you all came to England . . .'

'Yes.'

'And where did you stay?'

'In camps. Have you put the kettle on?'

'Yes. *More* camps?'

'Resettlement camps. I was in Herefordshire, and Tata in

Hampshire, I think. The grandparents came a little later – I can't remember now where they were sent.'

'But not prison camps,' Jerzy said.

'No, darling, of course not. They were just old British Army camps, turned over to the Poles. Nissen huts, very basic. When we came, it was the winter of 1945–46 – freezing, the worst winter here for decades, I think. It wasn't quite so bad for us, because we were young, and single, but in the family camps they were all crowded together, sometimes they had to walk right out in the snow to the cookhouse. Imagine, with young children. Later on, things were a little better, but at first . . .

'And of course there were Poles from all over the place in those camps, not just from Italy. The ones who'd been taken prisoner by the Russians right at the beginning of the war, like my father, but who had survived, and been released in 1941. They'd served under British command in Africa, the Middle East. And there were those who had been in this country since 1940, who'd served in the RAF and knew their way around. And the ones who'd spent the war as prisoners in Germany. It was a real . . . mish-mash, I think the English would say.

'And there we all were, many of us still trying to find out what had happened to friends, and family, trying to get news from Poland, through the Red Cross, almost everyone bewildered, and unsettled, or grieving for the family they'd lost in the war . . . What a time . . .'

'And did you know you were going to stay here?' Ewa asked.

'Oh, no. I was quite certain when we landed in Liverpool that we'd be going back to Poland in the spring. I think most of us thought that – hoped it, anyway.'

'But then there was Yalta,' said Ewa, frowning again, trying to remember what Dziadek had said. 'Something about the Yalta Agreement?'

'Yes,' said Anna. 'That happened while we were still in Italy, but I didn't hear about it until after our arrival here. Yalta is the place on the Black Sea coast where Churchill, Roosevelt and Stalin all met in February 1945, where Stalin persuaded them to move the Russian/Polish border hundreds of miles to the west, along what was once called the Curzon line, so that a great deal of Poland and two very famous old Polish cities, Wilno and Lwów, were now in Russia.'

'Lwów is where Dziadek was born,' said Ewa. ' "A great walled city." I remember.'

'Yes. Clever girl. And Wilno is where we caught the train back to

Warsaw, after our summer's holiday, when we heard we were at war. Anyway – Poland's western border, with Germany, was to be moved, too, further west, so that we had Silesia, for example, within our frontiers, some little compensation for what Germany had done to us. But Stalin got just what he'd been waiting for – Roosevelt and Churchill agreeing to a Soviet government, a puppet . . . administration. There were supposed to be free elections, as soon as possible, but . . .' She shrugged.

Ewa had her chin cupped in her hands. 'And when did you hear about all that?'

'The following spring, 1946. We heard through the Polish press – they were furious, outraged. The Government in Exile, which had been here all through the war, was told that it was no longer recognized by the British government. Prime Minister Mikołajczyk went back to Warsaw, to have a seat in the new administration – I expect he hoped he could influence things, but it was impossible. The free elections had been a farce – he had no hope of influencing anything. After a couple of years he went to live in America – I think there's a story about how he fled from Poland in the boot of a diplomat's car. Anyway . . .'

From the kitchen, the kettle began to whistle. She got up and went to make the tea. Burek got up, and padded after her, claws clicking on the linoleum in the corridor. The children stretched and yawned, listening to Anna opening his tin, rattling biscuits into his dish. Then she was back.

'Yalta is another reason why many of us did not want to take British nationality,' she said. 'We did feel we had been betrayed. And when we were still in Italy, many people in the Polish Second Corps had a letter, from the British Foreign Secretary, Ernest Bevin – Churchill had fallen from power, there was a Labour government here by then. Never mind. Just that the letter told us we could come here, and start a new life, in recognition of everything the Poles had done to help the Allies. Of course, we were glad that we could come here, but the letter was written in such a way as to make it sound as if really we should all be going back to Poland, to help rebuild our country. That was what we all wanted, naturally – but under Russia? Never!

'Some people did go back in the end – those who had family still living there. If my father or Jerzy had been alive, perhaps I should have done so myself. But as it was – I knew we were simply being occupied all over again. And this time it was worse, in a way. With the Germans, at least we knew we were dealing with the enemy. The Russians have always pretended to be our friends.'

There was a knock at the front door.

'Enough! That's enough. Go and let them in, Jerzy.'

He went to the door, and Dziadek and Babcia came in, smiling.

'What a day! Are we too early?'

'No, no, of course not,' said Anna. 'I didn't realize how late it was.'

'Mama has been telling us stories,' said Jerzy. 'About the war, and . . . everything.'

'I expect I've worn them out,' Anna said. 'But they want to know.'

'Of course,' said Dziadek. Babcia took a seat in Jan's chair, then held out her hand to Ewa.

'Come and sit on my lap, *kochana*.'

Ewa smiled, kindly. 'I'm much too heavy now, Babcia.'

'Just for a few minutes. I've hardly seen you all week.'

'What about mass, this morning?' She sat with her arm round her grandmother's shoulders, foot swinging.

'But you have burnt yourself!'

'She sits too close to the fire,' said Anna, going out to the kitchen. 'Tch, tch.'

Jerzy and Dziadek were leaning comfortably against each other on the moquette sofa.

'Dziadek?'

'Yes?'

'What happened to you in the war? Why were you in prison?'

'In prison camp, *maleńki*. You make me sound like a burglar. We were prisoners of war.'

'Oh. And how did the Germans catch you?'

'Now it sounds like the playground,' said Ewa.

Jerzy flushed. 'Shut up.'

Dziadek patted his knee. 'How can you know all these things? My unit was captured very early on in the war, in the siege of Warsaw, in 1939. Mama has told you both about that time?'

He nodded. 'Yes, I think so.'

'Yes,' said Ewa.

'Very well. We were captured, and taken out of Poland, to a place high in the Alps, called Murnau. A very beautiful place, although of course we were not able to enjoy it. It was a prison camp for Polish officers. I spent the whole war there – I was very angry, to be able to do nothing for Poland. I wrote to Babcia, and to your father when it was possible. And then, when the war was almost over, in the spring of 1945, when the Allies were advancing through Europe, we were liberated by American troops. And eventually transports were arranged, and many of us made our way to Italy, to join the Polish Second Corps, where they had been serving under General Anders, under the command of the British Eighth Army.'

Ewa gave an enormous yawn, and quickly put her hand over her mouth. 'Sorry, Dziadek.' She yawned again, surreptitiously. 'And when you *got* to Italy . . .'

'Then we served in the Second Corps, until the end of the war, and that is where Babcia and I and your father were finally reunited, in a transit camp. Your father had been in prison camp, of course . . .'

'But he escaped,' said Babcia. 'He escaped from two different camps, you know, before liberation.'

'Did he?' said Jerzy. 'Tata escaped from the Germans? He must have been very daring, mustn't he?'

'He was,' said Babcia. 'He was a hero in the Uprising – now you are older, we can begin to talk about it all more.'

'But he doesn't talk about it, only Mama.'

'Well,' said Babcia, shifting under Ewa's weight, 'perhaps he thinks you are still too young.'

'Or perhaps it upsets him,' said Ewa, moving. 'I told you I was too heavy, Babcia.'

'It's all right, stay where you are.'

'And what about you?' Ewa asked her. 'Mama said something about you taking off your armband . . .'

Babcia shrugged. 'I had to,' she said. 'I was separated from Jan – from your father – on the day the Uprising began. I was delayed, I remember I had to deliver a parcel of shirts to a unit several streets away, and there was a scare, we thought the house was being watched, that the Germans somehow had wind of it all . . . Anyway, it was hours before we were given the all-clear, and of course by the time I got home, Jan had gone. I didn't know if I would ever see him or Dziadek again. And the friends with whom I had joined the AK – we were a very small unit, and quickly . . . depleted. I was afraid for my life, and all I wanted was to see my family again. So – I became a civilian, and I was sent to a labour camp.'

Ewa patted her cheek. 'Was it horrible?'

'It wasn't pleasant. We needn't talk about it now – I survived, which was my intention. And as Dziadek says, we all met up again in Italy, thank God.'

233

'And that's where Mama and Tata met, isn't it?' Ewa tried once again to imagine it.

'Yes, that's right. They were stationed in the same town, on the Adriatic coast. A very lovely place.'

Anna was coming back with a tray; she put it down on the table.

'Now – who would like buttered toast?'

'Me!' said Jerzy.

'Me!' Ewa scrambled off Babcia's lap.

'Careful, *kochana* . . .' Babcia rubbed her knees.

'Sorry.'

Anna handed her a pile of plates. 'Pass them round, please, Jerzy – you can hand round the toast.'

'Babcia . . . Dziadek . . .'

Anna lifted the teapot, and began to pour.

'And *was* it love at first sight?' Ewa asked her again. 'When you and Tata met?'

'I beg your pardon?' Anna flushed, and tea spilt into a saucer.

'You and *Tata!*' Ewa settled herself on the floor, her plate of toast on her lap. 'Did you have a wonderful love affair?'

Babcia shook her head. 'What do you know about such things?'

Anna poured cups of tea with care. 'She has been reading too many comics.'

'No I haven't.'

'She listens to the radio,' said Jerzy. 'Pop songs, under the bedclothes. I can hear it.'

'Prig,' said Ewa.

'You must never tell tales,' said Dziadek, reaching to Anna for his cup.

'It is time they had separate rooms,' said Anna, passing it.

'Yes!' said Ewa, and her toast slid to the floor. 'Yes, yes! Can I have the little room, the junk room? Please?'

'I'll think about it,' said Anna, and sipped her tea.

'Oh, thank you, Mama.' She bent to pick up the toast, and took another mouthful. '*Were* you madly in love?'

Babcia sighed, and rolled her eyes. 'What a child . . .'

'I just want to think of them being happy, that's all,' Ewa mumbled. 'After the war, and everything.'

'Thank you,' said Anna, exasperated. 'We were very happy, yes.'

A walk beneath pine trees, on a carpet of needles and warm sandy soil. A dazzling sky. Insects buzzing, a honeyed sun slanting through the trees, nothing to be afraid of, no need even to think. The castle where we were stationed was on the hillside, old and crumbling, with scuttling rats, but even those didn't bother us. We were all at school again, studying for our exams without fear of being discovered, well fed, staying up late to talk and talk and talk, spending the afternoons swimming, rambling over the hills, almost dizzy with the heat and the smell of herbs and wild flowers, or walking in the pine woods, high above the bay. Lots of us fell in love, then.

'*Anna?*'

'*Yes?*'

'*When we go back to Poland . . . if we are separated . . . will we keep in touch?*'

'*Oh, yes. I hope so. I do hope so, Jan.*'

His arm round my shoulders, drawing me close; the heavenly smell of the pines. Our first kiss. My first kiss. Everything else forgotten.

We were happy once, Ewa. We did have a wonderful love affair. And it didn't occur to us, then, that we would never go back to Poland.

A long strip of neon lit this half of the empty office, but beneath it, at his drawing board, Jan was enclosed by the circle of light from an anglepoise, shining on to the thick grey tracing paper and dark ink lines of the plan he was working on. His desk stood next to one of the white-painted metal-framed windows which ran all along the thirties building of the engineering works: in the day, he overlooked the car park, and the road beyond the high brick wall and tall open gates. Now, he could see nothing but the wintry wet blackness of the panes. At the side of the drawing board, among the clutter of pens, an ashtray overflowed; Jan drew deeply on the last of his cigarette and stubbed it out, coughing.

He leaned back in the swivel chair and looked at the board, seeing beyond the lines the shape of the completed machine, oiled, pounding into life, working precisely. At the next desk, some few feet along the wall the plan drawing for a baffle plate was smudged and uncompleted, even though the deadline was for Monday. No chance that Pete would work later than eight, even with overtime, nor come in at a weekend. He was like most of them, did what was adequate, just, and pushed off, never giving another thought to it all until the next day. Jan was the best draughtsman they'd had here in years, he knew he was, better even than the head of section, who'd left to join Ford for a fortune – Jan could have taken his job, no question, but he wouldn't. It was his own work he was interested in, not the others', not having to keep them up to the mark. They thought he was odd and aloof, he knew, but he didn't care. Even Tomek, who'd joined round about the same time, called him an arrogant Pole, but jokingly. Tomek spent most of his spare time in the Balham Club, drinking; he'd been back to Poland, visiting a cousin in Poznań for holidays several times – something Jan would never do. After Yalta, taking British citizenship had been out of the question, and it was impossible to return there with just a travel document. In any case, to go back was to give currency to the communists.

On the desk behind him, the phone began to ring. Jan got up and went to answer it, knowing it would be Anna. His parents had his number, too, but they never bothered him here.

'*Tak?* Yes?'

'Jan . . . have you got very much more to do?'

'Perhaps another hour or two – why?'

He heard a sigh, quickly suppressed. 'Nothing – we'd just like to see you, that's all. Jerzy has been asking for you.' A hesitation. 'He said something about a film? That he'd asked if you could take him one day?'

'Yes, some cowboy thing, I remember. I'll try next weekend, all right?'

'Lovely – I'll tell him.'

'No, don't raise his hopes. I may not be able to.'

A pause. 'I see.'

He could hear the children shrieking in the background. 'What's all the noise?'

'Just bathtime, high spirits. We've been rather cooped up today, with the rain. I've been telling them stories – and your parents came to tea.'

'Not more war stories, Anna – you know I don't like it.'

More shrieks from the bathroom. Anna was calling: 'Quiet, you two! I'm talking to Tata.' Then, to Jan: 'I don't understand why, I really don't.'

'Just – it's gone. You know what I mean.'

'But it's part of their heritage,' she said slowly. 'I like to tell them – so do your parents.' Another hesitation, then: 'Jan?'

'Yes? If you want me to come home, I'd better get on.'

'It's just that . . . Ewa kept asking me about how we met, what it was like. If . . . if we'd had a wonderful love affair.' He could hear her trying to make light of it.

'And what did you say?'

'I told her how happy we were, then. Well, I mean, I didn't say anything, really, but . . . we were, weren't we? When we met, and – and everything . . .' She trailed off.

Impossible to equate this hesitant, even awkward wife, who had seemed for a long time to belong only to her children, with the girl he'd wanted almost as soon as he saw her. She'd been laughing with a group of friends, wandering on a blazing afternoon out of the little town and up towards the flowery hillside above the bay.

Everyone had needed to fall in love, then.

'Jan?'

'Yes,' he said, matter of factly.

'It made me think about it all again – about whether it had to go so wrong. It does seem so sad, such a waste . . .'

Jan picked up the phone and carried it, trying to reach his cigarettes. They were just too far away.

'I'll try and get home earlier,' he said. 'Perhaps we can talk about it.'

'That would be – very nice. Thank you. If – if you could get here before the children are asleep? Just for once.'

He looked at his watch. There was a Sunday evening bus in half an hour. 'I'll try.'

'See you soon, then. You've got your umbrella?'

He smiled. 'Yes, Anna, I've got my umbrella. Goodbye.'

'Goodbye.'

Jan put down the receiver and walked back to his desk. He lit a cigarette, quickly, and looked again at the plan on the drawing board. Outside, it began to rain again, pattering hard against the uncurtained windows. He paced up and down, imagining the children and Anna, talking all afternoon about the war.

In the years since he had come here, the war, and Poland itself, had gradually become sealed away into a part of himself he no longer visited – a distant country, like childhood, to which he could never return. It wasn't just a case of refusing to be like Tomek, and the others in the Club, who went back year after year. Deep down, he did not want to go back, even if it were possible: he didn't want to revisit the streets and squares of Warsaw which he had grown up in, and seen bombarded into ruins, and almost died for.

The rain was slowing down – if he were going to catch the bus, he should leave now. He stubbed out his cigarette, carefully replaced all the caps on his pens, and covered the plan with a sheet of paper. He switched off the anglepoise lamp, and the long cold strip of neon, and pushed through the swing doors. He walked quickly down the stairs, having a sudden, unbidden flash of memory: Anna, her dark head against his shoulder, her arm round his waist, as they walked in the pine forests high above the bay. Falling in love, if that's what it had been, had blotted out everything, then.

They sat at the table in their dressing gowns, having their supper. Outside, behind the curtains, the rain had stopped, but every now and then they could hear wet sounds: a dripping gutter, footsteps in the puddles, a car or bicycle swishing down the road. Burek lay dozing again in front of the fire – Dziadek had taken him out, just for a few minutes, and the room smelt of damp dog, and wet hair: the children always had their hair washed on Sunday nights, to start the school week clean. Ewa would be leaving primary school, and going to the convent next year. Her foot swung under the table, back and forth.

'Mama?'

'Take your elbows off the table, please.'

'Sorry. Mama?'

'And stop swinging your foot.'

She rolled her eyes. 'Mama!'

'Yes.'

'Can we have a record player for Christmas?'

'A record player . . . whatever next?'

'So she can listen to her soppy pop songs,' said Jerzy. 'I don't want one.'

'You don't have to listen, do you? Not if I have a room to myself.' Ewa turned her back on him, exaggeratedly. 'Please, Mama. Please. Everyone's got one – I wouldn't have to go to Janet's all the time, then, would I? Please.'

'Oh, sssh! We'll see. I'd have to ask Tata.' Anna looked at the clock above the fire. 'He should be home any minute, he said he'd try to be home before bedtime.' She smiled at them. 'That's nice, isn't it?'

'You look pretty, Mama,' said Ewa. 'Have you put lipstick on, or something?'

'Just a little. Now – do either of you want any more?'

'No, thanks.'

'No, thank you. Mama?'

'Yes, Jerzy?'

'In the war . . . in the war, what happened to Tata exactly?'

'Oh, Jerzy, I think we've talked enough about all that for one day, don't you?'

'I do,' said Ewa. She stretched, knocking her glass and saving it just in time. 'Can I get down?'

'Yes, go and brush your hair by the fire, make sure it's quite dry.'

'All right.' She slid off her chair.

'But Mama . . .' Jerzy was frowning, flushed.

Anna reached out a hand. 'Have you got a temperature? No, I don't think so, you're just tired. All this talk – it's high time you were in bed.'

'Mama!' He moved away from her hand. 'I just want you to tell me one thing, all right? What happened to Tata's jaw? And what did he get his medal for?'

Anna shook her head. 'That's two things. I expect he'll tell you all about it himself, one day.'

'Tonight?'

'No, darling, not tonight, it's much too late, and – and he doesn't really like talking about it. Don't ask him, will you?'

'You tell me, then.'

'Oh, Jerzy, do shut up,' said Ewa from the fire.

'Shut up yourself! I just want to *know*, that's all.'

'All right, all right, calm down now.' Anna ran her hands through her hair. 'Tata was wounded because the little house in the Old Town which they were defending in the Uprising was attacked by the Germans, and Tata killed one of them. He was fired at, and the bullet hit his face. And his friend, who was next to him, was very badly wounded also, and in fact I think almost all the boys in their unit were killed in that attack. Then, later, when everyone was ordered to leave the Old Town, Tata carried the wounded boy all the way through the sewers – perhaps two miles, in the dark, imagine. He was given his medal for bravery then, and for the part he played in the fighting later. By that time his poor friend had died.'

Jerzy was silent. Then he said slowly: 'How did he kill the German? Did he shoot him?'

'Yes, darling.'

'And – and what do you mean, he carried his friend through the sewers? I thought sewers were . . . were full of . . .'

Anna took a deep breath. 'Yes. They are. But there was no other way of escape.'

'But it must have been *horrible*. Ugh. *Ugh.*'

239

'Do stop talking about it,' said Ewa, her hairbrush in her lap. 'It makes me feel sick.'

'Yes, I think that's quite enough.' Anna pushed back her chair, and began to clear away. Jerzy sat deep in thought. Behind Anna, a key turned in the lock on the front door.

'Tata!'

He came into the room, smiling lightly at them all.

'All right?'

'Fine,' said Anna. 'I'm so glad you're here, they're just off to bed.'

Burek got up from the hearthrug and came over, tail wagging; Jan bent down to pat him. 'Good boy, good boy.' He straightened up. 'Has he been out yet?'

'Only for a few minutes, with your father.'

'I'll take him, then, it's stopped raining.'

'Have something to eat first – I've saved yours in the oven.'

'Thank you.' He pulled out a chair and sat down. 'Well . . .'

There was a silence, as if with an acquaintance just arrived, whom no one knew quite how to treat.

'Off you go then, children,' said Anna. 'Brush your teeth.'

Jan tapped the table top. 'I come home to see them, and you shoo them away.'

'Sorry . . .'

He shrugged, and there was another silence. Across the table, Jerzy was fiddling with a fork.

'Tata? In the war . . .'

Jan frowned.

'Now that's enough!' Anna said sharply. 'We've done far too much talking already. Kiss Tata goodnight, and go to the bathroom – quick!'

Ewa got up and came over, her hair out of the plaits a dark mass spilling over the collar of her dressing gown.

'Goodnight, Tata.' She raised her face and kissed him lightly on the cheek.

'Goodnight, my pretty daughter.'

She blushed. 'Do I look pretty?'

'Very.' He raised her hand, half-mocking, half-serious, and brushed it with his lips. Ewa giggled uncertainly.

'Goodnight, *kochana*.'

'Goodnight, Tata.' She ran out of the room.

'Jerzy?'

'I'll just go and get your supper, Jan,' said Anna, and followed Ewa out.

On the other side of the table, Jerzy pushed back his chair and came round. 'Tata?'

'Yes?'

'How strong are you?'

'Very strong,' Jan said gravely.

Jerzy looked at him. 'You must be. Mama said you carried your friend, the one who was wounded, all the way through the sewers. And Dziadek says you escaped from the Germans twice. How did you kill the German . . .' He stopped, seeing his father's face darken.

'What else has Mama been telling you?'

'Nothing. Nothing . . .'

'You are far too young to hear about such things, and anyway – I don't like it.'

'Why?'

Anna appeared in the doorway, tense, carrying a tray. 'Come on, Jerzy, Tata's tired now.'

'I'm not tired,' Jan said icily. 'I'm angry.'

'Oh, Jan, please . . .'

Jerzy felt his chest begin to tighten, in a dark, uncomfortable way. He coughed, nervously. 'Sorry . . .'

'Go on,' said Jan irritably. 'Go to bed. I don't know what your mother is thinking about, filling your head with all this.' He got up, not looking at Anna. 'Come on, Burek, we're going out.'

Anna set down the tray. 'But your supper . . .'

'I'll have it later!' Jan snapped. Still in his overcoat, he went into the hall, feeling on the hook for Burek's lead. Beside him, the dog thrashed his tail ecstatically. Jan went out with him, banging the door.

'Oh dear . . .' Anna stood at the table, still holding the tray. Steam rose from Jan's plate, filming the glass beside it.

Jerzy coughed, looking at her. 'Mama – please don't cry. I'm sorry . . .'

'I'm not crying,' Anna said unsteadily. 'And you have nothing to be sorry for.'

'I didn't mean to upset him, I didn't mean it.'

Anna pulled him close. 'Of course you didn't, now don't *you* cry. Please don't, darling. Tata's just very . . .'

'Very what?'

'Very . . . very something.' Anna tried to laugh. 'Come on, no

241

more tears now.' She passed him a handkerchief, and he blew his nose. From the bathroom, Ewa was calling: 'What's happened?'

'Nothing!' Anna patted Jerzy's face. 'Teeth! Quick!'

The bathroom was damp, the windows still dripping with steam from the bath, but quite cold now. Jerzy unscrewed the toothpaste cap and brushed, shivering.

'What did he say?' asked Ewa.

Jerzy grimaced, and spat. 'He was cross with Mama.'

'He's always cross with her. Don't worry about it, I expect he's tired; grown-ups are always tired.'

'He said he wasn't . . .'

Ewa took his toothbrush and put it back in the glass on the shelf. 'Leave it, forget it. Race you into bed.'

They pounded down the linoleum corridor.

'Children, children – not so noisy.' Anna followed them from the kitchen. She had combed back her hair, and wiped off her lipstick. Her nose shone. 'My goodness, it's cold in here.'

Ewa leapt into bed, and pulled the blankets up tight. 'Can't we have hot-water bottles?'

'Much too dangerous for children.'

'Fussy Mama.' She pulled a face, and burrowed down.

Jerzy climbed into his bed by the window. Anna bent down, straightening the pillows. 'Goodnight, *maleńki*.' She kissed his forehead. 'Sleep well, and no worries, all right?'

'All right.'

She tucked him in and moved back to Ewa. 'Goodnight, darling. Straight to sleep now.' She felt under the pillow, then went to the door.

Ewa reappeared from beneath the blankets. 'Mama?'

'Yes?'

'Am I really pretty?'

'Yes,' Anna said simply. 'Now, it's school tomorrow, so no chattering.' She flicked off the light.

'Leave it on in the corridor,' said Jerzy quickly.

'Of course. See you in the morning.' She went out, leaving the door ajar.

They lay in the darkness, a long bar of light falling through the gap in the door, across their beds; they listened to her footsteps going slowly down the corridor, and into the kitchen; the taps turned on, the clatter of dishes. Then Ewa turned over, and pulled her pillow down.

'My radio! Mama must have – oh, Jerzy, why did you have to tell her? I can't get to sleep without it.'

'Sorry,' said Jerzy. 'I didn't know she'd take it. Sorry.'

'So you should be!'

There was a silence.

'Do you really want your own room?'

'Yes. You don't mind, do you?'

'I don't know. I think it'd be a bit funny, by myself.'

'You could watch all the trains as much as you wanted.'

'I suppose so. Oh, listen.' He sat up, pulling the curtain back. Ewa groaned. 'Just this one,' Jerzy said, and knelt by the window, the curtain over his head. The sky was very clear now, all the cloud rained away, and a winter moon was rising behind the bare trees and above the factory buildings across the railway line. He turned towards the sound of the train moving down the track, saw the misty plume of steam drift into the night sky, and heard the great animal panting of the engine, as it drew near.

'Who-whooooh!'

It whistled, and thundered past, the windows of the carriages spilling light on to the track, again and again, faster and faster. He craned his neck against the cold glass of the pane, following it until the last carriage, and the guard's van, had disappeared.

Then he lay down, twitching the curtain back into place, and fell asleep.

A dark place. A dark, frightening place, where he didn't know anyone. But it was full of people, moving about, touching each other, asking questions in toneless voices, moving on. Where was Mama? He pushed through the crowd, felt himself almost crushed, and began to panic. From somewhere a long way off there was the sound of a train, rattling and rattling, and he had a feeling Mama might be on it, but he couldn't find the door of the dark place, to get out, and go to meet her. He pushed against the people in front, and they moved, and he stumbled and fell into a slimy pool of something. He struggled to get up, but kept slipping, and the people were stepping over him, their voices asking questions he couldn't properly hear, although he knew that they were lost, too, and couldn't help him.

And then he was on his knees, crawling through the slime, with his limbs dragged by a leaden slowness, so that each move forward was like a film in slow motion, and the people all round were pressing closer and closer. He began to pant, and his chest began to tighten.

'Mama?' He struggled again to get up. 'Mama?' He reached for something to cling on to, and found he was clasping a leg, trying to heave himself up, pulling on the trouser, panting: 'Help me . . .' The person whose leg it was bent down, and pulled him out of the slime, and he found himself looking into his father's angry face. It was streaked with blue. With blue? He looked at the faces of the other people, and saw that they were blue, too, and their hands. 'Mama?' They looked at him blankly.

He could hear the distant train again, and said: 'Let me through. Let me get through!' On the far side of the building an enormous door swung slowly open, and he could see the sky, very black, with a tiny moon, and hear the rattle of the train growing louder. 'Let me through!' But the blue faces only pressed closer, and closer, until he could hardly breathe at all, and was gasping, choking, fighting for breath.

'*Ma-maaaa!*'

Footsteps, running. A door flung open.

'Jerzy, Jerzy . . . it's all right.'

He leaned against her, pyjamas soaked in sweat, hearing the terrifying sound of his own breathing, like a pump, filling the room. Distantly aware of Ewa, bewildered, told to go back to bed. Then another door banged, and there were more footsteps down the corridor, and a dark figure against the light.

'What the hell is going on?'

'Ssssh! Can't you see . . .'

'Is he ill?'

'What do you think? He's had a nightmare . . .'

The rasping, pumping, horrible sound, his lungs filled with knives.

'Call the doctor – tell him it's asthma, it's urgent . . .'

'He'll be all right in a minute.'

'Go on, Tata, quick!'

'It's almost midnight . . .'

'You bloody fool, that's what doctors are for. Call him!'

'I'll go, Mama . . .'

'No, no, Ewa, stay here. Jan, for God's sake – '

A long, tearing, terrible gasp, and a rush of air. He fell back on the pillow, breathing. He could breathe.

'There! And no wonder he has nightmares.'

'Go away, Jan. Go away.'

'I told you . . .'

'Go *away!*'

The footsteps leaving the room, walking down towards the sitting room. The door there closed. He went on breathing, in and out, in and out. Yes, it was all right now.

'Mama?'

'Yes, darling.' Stroking his hair.

'The train was rattling.'

'Outside?'

'In my dream. You were on a train, and I was trying to find you, and it was rattling and *rattling*. Very close. I could really hear it.'

'I know!' said Ewa. 'The sewing machine. Mama's sewing machine. Were you working, Mama?'

'Yes. At the table in the sitting room. Just as usual.' Still stroking. 'Are you all right now?'

'Yes.'

'Tata was horrible,' said Ewa.

Anna shook her head, straightening Jerzy's bedclothes.

'I'll be back in a minute.' They heard her in the bathroom, the kitchen, coming back. 'Here.' She sponged Jerzy's face with a warm flannel, changed his pyjama jacket, gave them both cups of warm milk. She sat on the end of Jerzy's bed, as they drank. 'Tata doesn't understand things, sometimes. He doesn't mean to be like that.'

'Why is he, then?'

'I don't know . . . He was terribly young when all those things happened. In the war.'

'So were you.'

'Well . . . never mind now. Go back to sleep. I'll leave both doors right open.' She bent down, kissed Jerzy's forehead, put the empty cups on the tray. 'No more nightmares, now. Everything's all right.'

'Yes, Mama. Goodnight.'

Over to Ewa's bed. 'Goodnight, darling.'

'Goodnight, Mama.'

She switched off the light again, and went out. They heard her walk down the corridor, and open the sitting room door, just a little. Low, angry voices.

'How *could* you behave like that?'

'What do you mean?'

'Storming out of the flat, storming in again, refusing to call the doctor – how could you just stand there and watch him suffer?'

'Why do you think he had the nightmare in the first place?' Jan was sitting at the table. He had lit a cigarette, and inhaled deeply; as

245

he did so, Anna thought his face looked cruel, even vengeful. She sank into her chair.

'You will say he had a nightmare because we were talking about the war,' she said bitterly. 'But I can tell you that what upset him was your anger. What is the matter with you – do you *want* him to be afraid of you?'

'Of course not.'

'Well, then . . . I just don't understand. Anyone would think I had been telling them dreadful tales, trying to set them against you. Jerzy *asked*, he insisted on knowing something of what happened to you – what is so terrible about my telling him? What are you ashamed of?'

'I'm not ashamed of anything!' Jan shouted, and banged his hand on the table top.

Anna leapt out of her chair. 'Sssh! Stop it – you'll frighten them to death.' She ran to the door, just ajar, and listened. Not a sound. She made her way back to her chair. 'I was hoping for such a lot from this evening. I must have been mad.' She began to cry. 'And don't shout at me for crying, because I can't help it. I have to be strong for them, isn't that enough?'

'Listen,' said Jan. 'Listen. I was thinking, this evening, at work, after you rang. I cannot be who you want me to be, can you understand? I feel half dead, most of the time, can you understand? And I don't like to be made out a hero. What is the point of those two thinking they have some kind of father they don't have at all? So I did a few things in the war. And what did it gain? Nothing! And who am I now? No one! *That's* how I feel, all right, and I can't bear talking about it, or to have my children ask me questions – I'd like to be different, to feel different, but I can't. We gave everything, and everything was taken away, I feel as if – as if my spirit was taken away.' He got up, and made for the door. 'I never want to talk like this again. Now leave me alone – please.'

'I loved you,' Anna said helplessly, no longer crying. 'I loved you so much – please – let me help you, let me try . . .'

'No.'

He lay in the darkness, absolutely still. When he heard Tata's footsteps coming down the corridor, he shrank. Then the door of his parents' bedroom opened and closed, quietly, and he gave a sigh of relief.

Across the room, Ewa was pushing back the bedclothes: she tiptoed over.

'Jerzy?'

'Yes?'

'Are you all right?'

'Yes.'

She got into bed beside him, put her arm across his chest.

'You sounded *terrible*.'

'Were you frightened?'

'It doesn't matter. Let's go to sleep now.'

Silence.

'Ewa?'

'Yes?'

'I'm frightened of Tata.'

'It's all right. I'm here.'

'Don't leave me.'

'No.'

7

England, 1968

He stood inside the engine shed, and waited. Outside the open doors was the siding, and in the bright morning light the main-line track beyond gleamed into the distance, cutting east through the Pennines towards Leeds. Thick white clouds, piled high and lit by the rising sun, moved fast in a fresh wind over the hilltops; sheep were scattered like white stones on the rippling grass. Every now and then, on his walk here from the youth hostel, he'd heard the call of a curlew, spiralling to the sky. The streets of south London, with their litter, the closed-in feeling of school, and the uneasy feeling he often had at home, had all been flung away on the wind, like dark pieces of paper. In the hostel bunk last night he hadn't even thought about asthma.

The engine shed was filled with clanging, echoing noises: spanners and hammers striking iron; hissing sparks flying from a welder; the men shouting to each other, passing tools and crowbars. They didn't mind him there, they were used to train spotters. He was waiting for them to swing round the huge Black Five engine on the turntable in the middle: it must have come in late last night, and to go back to Leeds they'd have to get it facing the track again. The Black Five was rather ordinary, like the Jinty, which made him think of Thomas the Tank Engine, but then most of the beautiful passenger steam trains had given way to diesel now – it wouldn't be long before goods haulers like this went too.

He felt in his anorak pocket for his notebook and wandered over, taking down the number: 47548. He'd check it when he got back against the Allen directory. He never felt he'd completed a weekend journey until he'd neatly underlined each number spotted in the directory, kept beside his bed. There were regional directories, and a national. He had the national, filled with photos of engines, their numbers listed; at the last count he'd underlined four thousand eight hundred and six.

A couple of men were moving across to the turntable now; another came over, quite friendly, as he put the notebook back in his pocket and returned to his watching place.

'Morning, lad.'

'Good morning.'

The man was in his fifties, solidly built with grey hair and a bald patch. He wiped black oil off his hands on to his overall. 'She'll be off in a minute.'

He nodded.

'How many numbers you got now, then?'

'In this notebook? About six hundred.'

'Not bad. Been here before?'

'No – I'm just up for the weekend. From London.'

'Oh aye.' The men at the turntable were bending with their levers, ready to swing. 'What's your name?'

'Jerzy.'

'Eh?'

He cleared his throat. 'Jerzy. It's Polish.'

'Oh aye? there's a lot of Poles up this way, expect you know that. Came over after the war.'

He nodded. 'Yes.'

Then the shed filled with grinding and squeaking, the huge table began to turn, and the engine slowly swung round towards them. He nodded briefly at the man, then escaped, moving with the face of the Black Five as it met the sunlight. The turntable shuddered a little, then ground to a halt, and the engine moved slowly off it on to the track of the siding and down to the main line. He followed, stepping over the rails until he was beneath the embankment, and had a good view as six trucks from beyond the shed were shunted up to the rear and coupled on. They were carrying coal, the trucks chalk-marked on the side as coming from Preston; just a short local journey, then, perhaps to Stockport, or Crewe – he'd done Crewe two months ago.

The Black Five began to puff. It didn't matter how many times he heard those first slow breaths, or where he heard them: always, they filled him with happiness, with a feeling of release, the obliteration of unease. The track shone, waiting. Slowly the engine slid along the rails, and the driver saw him, raised his hand, and pulled the whistle lever. It sounded, two hoarse notes, and he began to run, panting as the train increased its speed and the steam chuffed through the funnel; when he could no longer keep up he stood watching it into the distance, the steam rising and drifting higher and higher with the wind, until it was only a few thin threads, and might have been steam or cloud, and disappeared.

Jerzy climbed the coarse grass slope of the embankment and walked along a little, the Brownie bumping against his chest. The 10.15 from Preston was next; he turned and stood waiting, observing the sharp gabled roof of the engine shed in the siding against the curve of the hills behind. He unbuttoned the canvas case and raised the camera to his left eye, squinting and shifting until he had roof and track and hill in view, and then saw through the shutter the Preston train approach, the steam meeting the wind and puffing thickly. Quick. He waited until it was almost level with the dark entrance to the shed, and snapped. Then he braced himself for its roar past, and snapped again, the whole engine in profile, plume of white steam trailing, black coal shining wetly. He began to cough, and lowered the Brownie, watching the shapes of the passengers through the last coach windows as the mist cleared; another few minutes and they'd be at Burnley station. He never wasted time really noticing or wondering about any of them, not even the ones who got off and on when he was taking numbers on a platform. Nor did he bother much with other train spotters, a bunch of show-offs on the whole, always wanting to compare how many you'd got with how many they'd got. He didn't make these trips to talk, though he didn't mind the railway men – usually they never bothered to find out anything about him, just answered his occasional questions, or volunteered something about one of the engines: neutral, professional talk.

It wasn't just the trains, though, which made him come, it was the travelling. From the windows of second-class carriages – he always got to the stations early, to be sure of a window seat – he was learning the landscape of England, had been as far north as Carlisle, as far south as the Isle of Wight, with Manchester, the Lakes, Plymouth and Southampton in between. At school, he shone at physical geography, was expected to get a Grade 1 at O-level, and intended to take geology in the Sixth. In the word geomorphology he found the beginning of everything: glaciers, and their retreat; the movement of land under the prehistoric pressure of ice and fire; igneous, sedimentary, metamorphic rock; chalk and limestone underground rivers, mysterious places and pools where water dripped in darkness; ridge and hillside, mountain and valley, boulder and clay; the eternal arc of the sky witness to each shift, each heaving alteration, fall and settlement. Cloud and wind and sun and rain – he was pacing along the top of the embankment now, back and forth, waiting for the diesel due in from Bradford, noting the swift change of light and shadow at his feet as the wind blew the clouds across the sun, feeling it against his face, through his hair, lost in his own world, where he could find himself for a while.

He spent most of the day on the embankment, going into the town for chips at about two, browsing in a second-hand bookshop where he bought one book, and late in the afternoon beginning the walk back to the mill town. He watched the sun slide down the sky towards the hilltops and gleam in the river. Not far from the hostel was a millstone grit memorial to the Battle of Waterloo; it stood high above the factory chimneys in the town below; from the dormitory window of the hostel itself you could see right across the valley. He liked it there; he was at home with the usual props – the large reception area smelling of disinfectant, local pictures and posters and pennants on the walls; the noticeboard with bus timetables, duty rota, a map, a list of Places of Interest. The office lift-up counter where you registered with the warden often had the shop there, too: shelves of baked beans, tinned steak and kidney, instant coffee, instant mashed potato, Mars bars and shoelaces, Ordnance Survey maps, John Hillaby books. It was safely familiar, and anonymous: you didn't have to talk much in the kitchen, just wait for your turn at a burner or at the sink, and answer people at the table if they spoke to you. Afterwards, most of them went into the neon-lit table-tennis room or the lounge, but he usually went upstairs and read on his bunk.

This evening, he found the reception hall filled with a party of German students, humping off rucksacks on to the floor, queueing to register, laughing confidently, calling to each other. The girls' hair shone, the boys were tall and fit; they all wore new-looking, light-weight cagoules in yellow or bright blue and expensive walking boots. The asthma had made Jerzy rather thin; his lined anorak was brown, the hood trimmed with nylon-fur fabric; he wore a British Home Stores blue sweater and a drip-dry shirt; beneath his jeans his feet were in greyed gymshoes. At Polish Scout camp, in uniform, he supposed he must look quite smart; now, he saw himself as this lot would see him, if they were to notice him, and felt his chest constrict. He stood reading the bus timetable until he had each stop by heart, breathing lightly because if he took the deep breath he wanted to take it might start an attack, clasping the Ventolin inhaler, his whirligig, as Ewa called it, in his pocket until it was slippery and wet. When the last loud voice from Cologne had registered, and they had all heaved their enormous nylon rucksacks with their aluminium frames on to their shoulders and made their way up the stairs, he took surreptitious puffs of the Ventolin and began to feel a bit better.

He went over to the counter, and looked at the shelves. Last night he'd had a tin of pork sausages in curried beans; he had about eight shillings left, which had to cover the tube fare tomorrow evening. He usually bought Mama something from his trips, but this time he'd have to leave it.

'Can I help you?' The girl behind the counter hadn't been there last night; perhaps she was the warden's daughter, or perhaps she came in from the town to work part time. She had very clean straight brown hair, what he thought of as a country skin, and clear eyes with flecks of green. She wore a green jumper, was small-boned and self-assured. He thought she was about eighteen, like Ewa. She smiled as he hesitated.

'Just, um – a tin of spaghetti. And . . . er . . . do you do single eggs, at all?'

She laughed. 'I can do you a single egg if you want.' She took one from a box and set it carefully on the counter; they watched it slowly roll. He picked it up and asked for a small sliced white. Then the front door opened again and she looked towards it, calling 'Hi!' casually, confidently.

A boy came up to the desk. He was dark and lithe, suntanned above an open cotton shirt, with a sweater slung round his shoulders. He had no rucksack or anything; he looked as if he'd just got out of a bath. He must be local.

'How's it going?'

'Just fine.' She turned back to Jerzy. 'Was there anything else?'

He shook his head. 'No . . . no, thanks.' He paid and quickly left them, taking spaghetti tin and bread through the door to the kitchen at the back. Behind him, he heard the girl say something and the boy laugh, and he didn't know if they were laughing at him, and his egg, or at each other. He didn't care, he just wanted to get his meal over with quickly, before the group came in.

There was no one in the kitchen yet. He found the tin opener and took a blackened saucepan from the shelf. He'd forgotten matches; last night he'd managed to use a flame before the last person put it out, now he looked round and thought he'd have to go back to the desk and buy some. Idiot. The door squeaked open again, and a man came in. He looked like a teacher, somehow: glasses, V-neck sweater

– Jerzy had noticed him last night, but he seemed to be alone, not leading a group or anything.

'Evening.' The man set a plastic carrier bag on the table; it flopped a little, revealing bacon, sausages, a box of eggs, other packets and tins beneath.

'Evening,' Jerzy said. 'Er . . . have you got a match?'

'A match? Of course.' The man brought a box from his pocket, and Jerzy lit the grill, keeping the blown-out match to relight there for the saucepan. He passed the box back. 'Thanks.'

'Oh, keep it,' said the man, smiling at him. 'I've got another.'

'No – it's all right.' He tore open the wrapping on the bread, and put two slices under the grill. No, three, he was starving. Then he shook the spaghetti out of the tin into the saucepan, and relit the match under the grill, almost burning his hand. The man was watching him.

'Little bit stubborn, aren't you?'

'What?' He fumbled for a spoon in the table drawer, moved to stir the spaghetti, already hissing at the edges.

'I expect you know what you want, don't you?'

Outside the window, in the field beyond the hostel garden, sheep bleated thinly. The large, airy kitchen, full of evening sunlight, seemed suddenly very quiet, except for the sound of the sheep; Jerzy wished now that the whole contingent of German students would come in, but no one came. His toast was burning; he pulled out the grill pan and turned the slices over.

'Have you been saved?' asked the man.

'What?' Jerzy felt his breathing going wrong again. He switched off the burner under the pan, and reached for the egg, adrift on the table top. It spun off and fell to the floor and smashed. 'Oh . . . dammit.' Absurdly, he felt tears prick his eyelids, and he blushed.

'Don't cry,' said the man softly. 'Jesus loves each one of us. Here, let me.' He bent down with a cloth from the sink, and began to scoop up the slippery mess as the kitchen filled with black smoke. Jerzy leapt towards the stove and switched off grill and burner just as the door banged open at last and two of the Germans came in, a boy and a girl, smiling cheerfully at them both and waving their hands at the smoke.

'Good evening, good evening!'

Jerzy stumbled past them, and out through the hall to the front door.

*

The walls of the occupational therapy rooms were covered in collages and paintings. A pottery adjoined, and through the open interconnecting doors came the hum of the wheel, the slippery sound of wet hands on clay, the smell of the unmixed clay in polythene sacks on the floor, and of the glazes. It had rained in the night, but the morning was fresh and fine: blackbirds sang, sun shone on the wet lawns, on the roses bordering the gravel paths, and in the pools of water on the terrace. It streamed through the open french windows to the room where Anna moved among her patients. They were seated in small groups at grey Formica-topped tables, where each day a selection of activities was set out: weaving at small handlooms, or in cane; patchwork; woodwork; toy-making; tapestry and embroidery; a long dressmaking table; another for collage; almost always one for watercolours. There was a whole studio for oils in another block.

Anna saved wrapping paper and string, wool, felt and milk-bottle tops, scraps of material, buttons and ribbons; she wrote off to factories for samples of fabric and wallpaper. Quite often, the work begun at each of the tables was incompleted – through frustration, uncertainty, inability to concentrate. But sometimes the materials were transformed; there were collages of landscapes, parks and gardens, faces, machines, primitive animals; there were abstracts, layers of pure colour. Each summer Anna and the other therapists organized an exhibition: this year there was a Noah's ark in painted balsa wood, a *kilim* tapestry wall-hanging using a traditional Polish design, like the one which used to hang in the apartment house in Praga. There were patchwork cushions and babies' quilts; trays and hanging baskets; endless watercolours of the terrace, with blurry geraniums and vague skies.

Broad steps led down the slope from the terrace to wide, well-kept lawns. There, as old as the hospital itself and much taller than the newer extensions, stood the cedar trees. They cast long deep shadows on the grass, shadows filled with a heavy stillness, unrelieved by light or movement in the dense branches so far above. Beyond, in the fields bordering the grounds, oak and ash trees swayed and rustled; cows moved beneath them, swishing flies. But the Victorian imagination which had planned the hospital – an asylum, then – had not, apparently, conceived of the patients needing life and movement close to them. The roses were comparatively recent; once, there must have been only the stillness of the lawns, the paths, the cedars. They were impressive, powerful; perhaps to the Victorians they had conveyed peace, reassurance, eternity. Anna, long ago troubled by eternity, and her place within the world, now thought of the darkness of the trees and their shadows as images of the patients' own retreat from their distress into darkness and silence. Naturally, many of them stayed only a short while; they recovered, they returned to the world outside the hospital, sometimes sending cards – to their psychiatrists, to Anna, who pinned them up on the wall next to the photos of Jerzy and Ewa. Some took longer to recover; some had been here for years. Among them were people who had spent the war in concentration camps, the truly dislocated. Some of those liberated from the camps had been able to make new lives: even with her own, uprooted life, and loss, Anna found it hard to imagine how they did so. Those in the hospital, arriving in England round about the same time that she and Jan had arrived, had tried to rebuild and been unable to. This place, she hoped, was their sanctuary.

'Excuse me . . .'

Anna was tapped on the arm; she turned from the table of patchwork pieces and templates to see one of the patients admitted last week looking at her confusedly. Catherine was about the same age as Anna, but she looked older, although she was rather beautiful, and well dressed. Her hair was greying, and under expensive make-up her eyes were puffy with crying and marked with deep circles. She wore an emerald cotton shirt which perhaps had come from Jaeger, a soft cotton skirt and pretty shoes; if you met her outside here you would hardly think of her as a person who had tried to kill herself.

'I can't seem to settle . . .' Her eyes began to fill with tears, the carefully brushed mascara smudging.

'Of course,' said Anna gently. 'It's still very early for you, isn't it?' She looked round the room for a moment, holding the woman's hand through her arm. 'Let's see . . .' At the moment, most of the other patients did seem to be settling into something, and Sara, the therapist sharing this shift, was talking to a group at the toy-making table. Anna turned back to Catherine.

'Shall we walk outside for a little while?'

Catherine nodded, swallowing.

On the terrace they paced quietly up and down, and Anna listened, as she listened almost every day. After a while, Catherine stopped crying about her husband, who no longer loved her, and her children, who had left home; she went back into the room and let Anna help her find thread and fabric; she sat by the open doors, staring at an embroidery frame.

Anna had no illusions about her work. She did not imagine that to sew or weave or paint was a cure for mental illness, but she knew that it helped a little, that within an atmosphere of safety and acceptance she could encourage her patients to create something outside themselves and perhaps rediscover something within themselves. It was enough.

She had come here four years ago, nervous about her first job since completing her training, a part of her still a little astonished that this was what she had chosen and been able to train for. By the end of the first week she was tired from the commuting from Clapham to Surrey, but she knew that she had found the right place, and would not leave. Of course, if it had not been for the war, if she had been able to stay in Poland, and Tata had been alive, she would have trained to be a doctor, and followed more directly in his footsteps. And yet – it was impossible, now, to imagine herself without the great scar of loss which the war had made, and it simply felt right that she, displaced, should be working with those suffering another kind of displacement. Perhaps, even if the war had never happened, she would eventually have come to this work, or something like it.

'Tata?'

'Yes?' *He was bent over his desk, writing his notes.* 'Sometimes I feel as if there's something missing in me . . . '

What had it been? If the war had not taken everything away, what might she have found?

She moved among the tables in the sunlit room, listening to the murmuring voices.

In the lunch hour, after a salad with Sara in the canteen, Anna took her coffee out into the grounds and sat in a deck chair. From the ground-floor ward next to the occupational therapy rooms, two or three nurses were helping uncertain old men and women to come out and enjoy the sunshine. Some of them wore the hospital-issue striped towelling dressing gowns: Anna observed the muted blue, orange and white against the grey brickwork of the hospital, the mauvey-grey wisteria in bloom, as the figures shuffled unsteadily on sticks or walking frames, or were pushed in wheelchairs on to the terrace. She thought she might paint them one day, the figures, the colours, the bent heads, the timelessness of old age in a last summer.

The sun was warm on her face. Anna closed her eyes. Here, in the calm, ordered grounds of the hospital, in the sweet-smelling lanes nearby, she tried to think of her family with dispassion. Sometimes it was impossible. Jerzy was off on a trip again this weekend, alone as usual, not even taking a Polish friend from Scouts. Such a clever boy, always had been, top of the class or near the top for years, expected to get eight or nine O-levels with good grades. But so withdrawn, so troubled.

'*Tata?*'

'*Mmm?*' *He did not look up.*

'*Sometimes I feel . . .*'

What was it that Jerzy felt so deeply? What was it that he could not tell her?

As for Ewa, she had said she was going to the university library today, which sounded very dutiful, but tonight she was working in the pub, and would probably try to leave dolled up like nothing on earth. She was beautiful, Anna could not help but know that, although she never told her so now: Ewa was becoming too self-assured, too assertive as it was. To lose her innocence, so carefully guarded all these years – to think that she might end up like some of the girls in the street, some of Anna's patients, even, sleeping around, taking drugs . . . Anna shuddered. She had had so much to be afraid of in the war: what might happen to Ewa now seemed almost worse, sometimes, because it would be so pointless, such a waste. Yet somewhere she felt a twinge of jealousy, barely acknowledged, but there, that her daughter should be on the threshold of a freedom she had never known.

The sun had climbed higher; it was very hot now. Anna slept.

In the library of the School of Slavonic and East European Studies, Ewa sat writing at a small plain table. It was one of five or six, set out the length of the room beneath tall windows; they overlooked the plane trees in the garden, the familiar outlines of other London University buildings and rooftops. It was late afternoon, warm and summery in the gardens; behind her, the towering grey metal bookstacks of the Russian and Polish section were cool and dimly lit.

Through the open window came the sound of sparrows and starlings settling in the trees. Ewa stopped writing and stretched, suddenly restless. She sat listening to the birds, to the traffic in Russell Square and the muted, familiar library sounds: the faint squeak of the metal ladder on castors, and footsteps climbing to a high shelf; volumes slipped out and pages turned; the thump of books returned to the wooden trolley at the far end; occasionally a low voice greeting or inquiring; a yawn, a cough, papers being stacked together, a pen rolling off a desk. The narrow spaces between the bookstacks were dim, dark, even, and the whole room smelt of old paper, old bindings. The door at the far end was pushed open as someone went out, and she could hear the hum of the photocopier, and footsteps clicking away towards the lift.

She looked at her watch. Four-fifteen: she should leave before the rush hour. Sometimes, although it was vacation, she stayed late, but tonight she was working in the pub. She snapped her pages of notes into the ring binder, put it into her bag with the books, and pushed back her chair. In the hall, one of her lecturers, looked up from the card index and smiled: Ewa smiled back at him, found herself blushing, and didn't wait for the lift, but ran down the cool stairs to the main hall, and out into the dusty, sunlit street. The traffic swept fast round Russell Square; she ran over the zebra crossing as a taxi drew up, and into the square: she often ate sandwiches or a salad here at lunchtime, on a seat under the trees, unless she was meeting anyone in Dillons' coffee shop.

American tourists were milling round the hotels near the underground; she stopped to point an elderly couple in the right direction for the British Museum. 'Thanks, honey, we'll go first thing tomorrow.' More tourists spilled out of the lift at the station, clutching bags from Carnaby Street. Ewa went down to the platform, full of warm stale air, and waited for the train to rattle in from the tunnel and take her to Clapham. She wondered on the journey who would be dispatched by Mama to fetch her from the pub at the end of the shift this evening. When Tata came he sat at a corner table, watching her, while she tried to ignore him. Usually, it was Dziadek who came, and this she found touching, and embarrassing in a different way, to see him smile at her from the door and simply stand, very correct in his dark suit, waiting until she had quickly washed the last glasses and emptied the ashtrays.

'That your grandad?' Stan the barman had asked on her first evening there, and she nodded. 'Military old bloke, isn't he? Looks like a general.'

'He is,' she said, but did not explain when he gave her a puzzled look. What would Kevin know or care about the Army in Exile? She felt ashamed at Dziadek having to come out of his neat flat and leave Babcia alone after eleven at night, when he preferred to retire at nine, but he and Mama had insisted she must be collected. Ewa knew he disliked her working there even more than Mama did, found it incomprehensible that his clever granddaughter, who thanks to him had passed Polish A-level with a grade A, and was now at university, should be serving strangers, strange men, in a crowded smoky pub, with a deafening juke box.

The train stopped at Clapham with a jerk. Ewa got out and walked among the crush of passengers up the long flight of steps to the barrier; she showed her season ticket to the yawning West Indian woman and hurried through, crossing the main road just as the lights changed.

Then she walked up the long, treeless street, with its heavy green paintwork. Many of the windows were open in the afternoon heat; the light from televisions flickered bluely behind net curtains; dishes clattered; from an upper window a radio blared. She could see, ahead, the third-floor window with the net curtain held aside, and her grandmother waiting. She raised her hand but did not walk faster; almost every day she called in on them, but sometimes, if they hadn't seen her coming, she went very quietly up the uncarpeted stairs, unlocked the front door of the flat where she lived with Mama and Tata and Jerzy and crept guiltily inside. 'We didn't hear you come back.' Babcia or Dziadek would say later, with the lightest brush of reproach in the tone, and she would answer, even more lightly, but inwardly irritated at having always to account for herself: 'Didn't you? Well, here I am.'

Squatters had taken over the ground floor of a house two doors from theirs, and tacked up Indian cotton bedspreads at the window. As she drew near she slowed down a little, and glanced towards it: they had pinned back one of the curtains to let in the air, and she could see through the open window figures sitting on the floor and a candle burning on a low table. The cloying smell of incense drifted into the street, and the smell of something else, too. She stopped, stood for a moment, sure no one inside had seen her, and saw a tall man leaning against the mantelpiece draw deeply on a cigarette and turn towards a girl at the back of the room who was switching on a tape. Music began to throb; the girl turned, took the cigarette, inhaled and saw Ewa, watching.

'Hi. Want to come in?'

She flushed, turned away and walked quickly to her own front door, closing it behind her. Had Babcia been watching her, watching them? The wire-mesh letter box was stuffed full of cards for mini-cab firms; there was a letter from Warsaw for Mama. she took it out and climbed the dusty stairs, hearing above her, Dziadek's and Babcia's door click open; as she rounded the last corner she saw Babcia looking down on her, smiling.

'Hello, *kochana*, I have made you some tea.'

'Thank you, Babcia.' She reached the top, kissed her lightly on both unpowdered cheeks. 'Have you had a good day?'

Babcia shrugged. 'Quiet, quiet. Come in.'

Ewa hung her denim jacket on a peg in the hall, and felt like a granddaughter again. Then she went into the sitting room, hearing Dziadek's paper rustle; as always, he rose, kissed her hand.

'Good evening, darling. Come and sit down.'

Babcia came along the corridor from the kitchen carrying the tray from Peter Jones which Ewa had bought for her Saint's Day, pale green, with roses. She set it on the white cloth covering the varnished table, took three drawn-thread napkins from the drawer, three pale blue tea plates from the tray. A marbled cake in chocolate and vanilla sponge was sliced; tea poured into pale blue cups, where thin slices of lemon floated to the surface. Dziadek unfolded his napkin and spread it neatly on his knee; from his pocket he took a small bone penknife, and carefully sliced the marbled cake on his plate into smaller pieces. Babcia shook her head. The clock on the narrow varnished mantelpiece over the gas fire gave five metallic chimes, a little wavering. It had sounded like that for years.

Ewa sipped her tea.

'No Jerzy today,' Babcia said sadly.

'No. He's on a trip this weekend.'

Babcia sighed. 'Such a strange thing.'

From the far end of the corridor, where the kitchen overlooked the track, came the sound of an overground train increasing speed. The faintest of vibrations shook the teacups.

'You think so?' asked Ewa.

'I think so.' Babcia took another slice of cake. 'Dziadek, also. What does a clever young boy want with trains, trains all the time? Travelling all by himself.'

'It is a stage,' said Dziadek. 'It will pass. And perhaps he is learning something. I worry only for his safety.'

'I shouldn't,' said Ewa. 'I'm sure he can look after himself.'

'But the asthma . . .' said Babcia.

'He says he doesn't have it when he's away.'

Her grandmother shrugged, puzzled.

After tea, Ewa flicked through two or three copies of the *Polish Daily, Dziennik Polski*. Yesterday's front page was full of the news that reservists were being called up from Lithuania, the Ukraine, and elsewhere in the Soviet Union, to carry out manoeuvres along the

Soviet border with Czechoslovakia. 'The undoubted aim is to ensure that the Czech summit meeting proceeds along the lines ordered by the Kremlin . . .'

'Dziadek?'

'Yes?' He was fiddling with the radio, which was old, and buzzed. Tata had offered to buy them a new one, but they said they could manage, he needed his money. Nor did they want a television, though they came in from time to time to watch the one Mama had rented.

'Do you think Czechoslovakia is safe?'

The radio crackled. 'Of course not. It is only a matter of time.' He switched off the radio irritably. Dziadek was not often irritable; she should have known better than to ask that question.

The back pages of *Dziennik* contained, among the personal columns, black-bordered announcements, where the English names of cemeteries in Gunnersbury, Ealing, North Sheen, of the Brompton Oratory, stood out amongst the Polish like signposts in a foreign land. Ewa wondered sometimes about the children and grandchildren of these old people – born in Warsaw, in Poznań, Bydgoszcz, Kraków, Katowcie, Gdańsk, dying in Ealing, in Clapham, in Stafford, Hereford, Edinburgh, Cardiff and Croydon. Sometimes the announcements mentioned mourning relatives not just in England but in Canada, Chicago and New York, South Africa, Argentina: whole families scattered across the world, carrying Poland with them as her parents and grandparents had. Did their grandchildren still believe, as she and Jerzy had been taught to believe at Saturday school, where Dziadek still taught, that one day they or their children or grandchildren might return to a free Poland?

'More tea, *kochana?*'

'No thank you, Babcia.' She put the paper down. 'Can I help you wash up?'

'A few tea things? Of course not.'

'I think I'll go and have a bath, then; I have to be at the pub in half an hour.'

Babcia sighed, and cleared away the teacups.

Dziadek got up as she pushed back her chair. 'Do you not think . . . Would you perhaps like to work at the Club, instead? I'm sure it could be arranged . . .'

'No, no, Dziadek, thank you. It's very kind, but . . .'

She and Jerzy had spent many evenings in the Polish Club on the road to Balham, taken there mostly by Dziadek. They watched films of pre-war Poland, of occupied Poland, of the Warsaw Uprising; they heard talks about the betrayal of Yalta. Last year she had been to a wonderful New Year party, and a few times to discos, where jeans were forbidden; once she had gone to the wedding reception of a girl from a class higher up at Saturday school. She felt at home there, but she did not want to feel too much at home.

'Well, never mind,' Dziadek was saying. 'If you change your mind one day . . .'

'Thank you.' She took his hand. 'Tata should come for me more often – it's a lot for you, isn't it?'

He pulled a face. 'You make me feel a hundred. It is a pleasure to come for you. Tonight, however, I believe your father is coming – your mother mentioned it to Babcia before she left for work.'

'Honestly, I'm sure I'd be all right walking home by myself – it's not far, after all.'

'Never. Go along now.'

She kissed them both, went out and across the uncarpeted brown square of landing, letting herself into the empty flat. Burek came padding out from his basket in the kitchen; he was old and milky-eyed now, his legs trembling as he stood to be patted. She went to open a tin of dog food, then ran a bath.

Mama wouldn't be home from the hospital for a little while. Ewa lay in the bath listening, through the small open window at the top of the swirled glass, to Dziadek and Babcia moving about their kitchen, where they must have a window open, too, on to the tiny balcony overlooking the railway line. She couldn't hear what they were saying: their voices simply sounded reassuring, matter of fact, companionable. She thought about the ordered pattern of their days since Dziadek had retired from the factory. Breakfast at eight, listening to *Today;* a walk on the common with Burek unless it was very wet; a visit to the local library once a week, and to the Polish Library once a month. Lunch prepared by Babcia, whose little English was used only when she went shopping, while he was at the library; if she wanted to shop for herself, to buy clothes, she took Mama, or Ewa went, to quell the bored disdain of the girls in C & A or John Lewis.

After lunch they rested, half an hour each, Babcia on the bed, Dziadek on the less comfortable sofa, reading the paper. Then Babcia wrote letters, or visited her friend in Tooting, or read, while Dziadek spread his books and papers over the table – military histories: of the First World War; of the defeat in 1920 of the Red Army at the gates of Warsaw, where against all the odds Piłsudski had forced the

Russians to turn back, staving off communism for over twenty years. Dziadek was editing a collection of memoirs from his own regiment. Of the Second World War he spoke little: Ewa was aware of the silences between him and her father about those years, which Dziadek had spent interned as a prisoner of war while Tata and Babcia struggled to survive the occupation. Though Tata had been decorated for his part in the Uprising, Dziadek rarely referred to it. He must have felt excluded, impotent.

By four or four-thirty each afternoon he was clearing away, waiting to see Jerzy, after school, or Ewa, back from a lecture or the library. In the evenings he and Babcia read, or listened to concerts on the radio – it didn't buzz quite so much on the Third Programme. Sometimes he went to meetings of the Army in Exile, visited friends or went with Tata to the Club, but on the whole they did not go out much: his pension was tightly budgeted. On Saturdays he still taught in Saturday school; on Sundays they went to mass. Ewa had stopped going; Jerzy still went with them sometimes, but she didn't know if he got anything out of it any more.

The street door banged below, and Ewa heard her mother's footsteps on the stairs. The front door opened and closed, there was the sound of a shopping bag set down.

'Ewa?'

'Yes, Mama?'

They kissed on both cheeks, Ewa's damp hair brushing her mother's face. Her dressing gown was pale blue cotton, old and soft and found in a jumble sale; Anna had repaired it, and thought every time Ewa wore it how innocent she looked, how vulnerable.

'How is my Mama?' Ewa picked up the shopping bag and followed her into the kitchen. 'There's a letter for you – I put it in the living room. From Wiktoria.'

'Oh, good. It seems such a long time since she wrote.' Anna took a jug of orange juice from the fridge and poured a glass. 'I'm tired and hot and worried,' she said wryly, and took a long drink. 'That's better.'

'So everything is as usual,' said Ewa. 'I'd better go and get dressed.'

'Have you seen the grandparents? How are they?'

'Fine. Worrying about Jerzy. I suppose you are, too. I think it's good that he goes off, at least he's doing something.'

'And who says that you do not give me cause for concern, wretched girl? Go on – off you go, or you'll be late. And Ewa . . . try to look nice.'

'Yes, Mama.'

Ewa went to her room, and Anna took her glass of juice into the living room and picked up the letter from the table. The face of Gomułka, stern behind horn-rimmed glasses, looked at her from the stamp. She sat down in the moquette chair and began to read.

Warsaw
July 1968

My dear Anna,

You must forgive me for not writing for so long, I thought that once I retired from the university I'd have so much time, but the last months have been filled with ill-health – my wretched hip; still, I won't bore you with all that again. There have been far more significant events, which I'm sure you must have heard something about already. It's difficult to know how much I should say here . . .

It always is, thought Anna. *You know I'm used to reading between the lines.*

Just before Christmas last year, I went with a friend to the National Theatre, to see the Mickiewicz play *Eve of Our Forefathers.* Did you read it at school? Has Ewa read it at university? Anyway, it's a very powerful play, about the struggle for independence from the Czars at the end of the nineteenth century, and it was presented to coincide with the fiftieth anniversary of the October Revolution.

Of course, we heard about all this over here – a tremendous fuss when the authorities realized that the audience was going mad with every reference to 'rogues from Moscow'.

There was some disagreement about the nature of the play . . .

They banned it. They shut down the theatre and banned it. And on the last night, when everyone had stayed inside, singing the national anthem, there was a great march to the Mickiewicz monument in Krakowskie Przedmieście – the avenue where Teresa and I said our goodbyes – but when they got there the police were waiting. Arrests. Detentions.

. . . and since then, you may have learned that things have not been entirely peaceful.

Within a few weeks, almost every university in the country was in uproar – demonstrations, occupations, marches, police brutality. It was like Paris.

You may remember I told you about my good friends at the university?

264

Which ones does she mean?

They have now left Poland. In April I went to see them off at the station, and the platform was so crowded that we could hardly stand – many, many friends like mine . . .

She means Celia and Jakub. She means the scapegoats they had to find for all the troubles. She means the Jews. Academics, Party members, local bureaucrats – almost any Jew in any influential position: they've lost their jobs, and they've fled from Poland.

. . . It has all been very unpleasant. At the moment, however, the upheavals have died down. It is calm . . .

At least, I imagine, on the surface.

. . . and very hot. What with the heat and my hip, I am only too glad to stay at home. As so often, I think of you, dear Anna, and wonder how you and the family are. It would give me so much pleasure if Jerzy or Ewa were to come here for a visit one day. Perhaps later this year, or next summer? There will always be a bed for them. How I wish that I could see *you* again . . .

Anna looked up as Burek came in, and then Ewa's footsteps were hurrying down the corridor.

'Bye, Mama!'

'Ewa – come here a minute.'

'I'm late . . .'

'Wiktoria wonders if you and Jerzy would like to go and visit her.'

'Oh. Well . . .'

'Have you ever read *Eve of our Forefathers?*'

'Er – I think so. The one all the fuss was about – Mama, I must go!'

The flat door clicked open.

She doesn't want me to see what she's wearing, thought Anna, and got up quckly. 'Just a minute . . .' In the hall, she took one look at Ewa. 'You're *not* going out like that.'

'Oh, yes I am.' Ewa, in thick black eye-liner, chalk-white lips and denim skirt inches above her knees, pulled open the door. Anna pushed it shut.

'Where did you get that skirt?'

'From Bus Stop.'

'From what?'

Ewa rolled her eyes. 'It's a boutique! In South Kensington. If you don't let me go I'll be late.'

'Is this what you spend your money on?'

'Why shouldn't I? It's my money.'

'Ewa . . . can you not see yourself? You look – cheap. To go out looking like that, and work in a pub – you are asking for trouble. Danger, even.'

'Are we going to have this argument every single time I set foot outside the door?' Ewa asked coldly. 'When are you going to let me grow up?'

'It is not a question simply of growing up – it is how you grow.'

'And how am I supposed to grow?' Ewa saw herself, half an hour ago, sitting in the quietness of the grandparents' flat, passing tea plates, looking through *Dziennik*, with its pictures of girls in folk costume, and funeral announcements. She saw herself sitting all evening with Mama, watching television, waiting for Tata to come home, and she grabbed the catch on the door. Anna slapped her hand. Ewa burst into tears.

'How dare you treat me like this?'

'I'm your mother!' Anna said furiously, as angry with herself for that slap as with Ewa for provoking it.

'Do you realize that half the students I know don't even *see* their mothers all term?' Ewa shouted. 'They have their own lives, they have boyfriends, most of them are living with their boyfriends – '

'These are the English students, I presume.'

'Not all of them.'

'There are Polish girls who live like that? Who don't care about their families? Who have lost their self-respect?'

'Oh, Mama! What is so special about Polish girls, for God's sake? Are we all supposed to sit at home like nuns?'

Wearily, Anna shook her head. Across the landing the grand-parents' door was opened; cautious footsteps, then a tap on the door. Ewa, her face streaked with black, flung it open. Babcia, very small, looked up at her in astonishment, then at Anna.

'Is everything all right?'

'No,' said Ewa, 'it is not all right. Now, if you will excuse me, Babcia, I am going out. Goodbye!' She pushed past her grandmother, ran down the stairs and banged the front door so hard that the banisters trembled. A ground-floor door was opened; Pani Kowić could be heard calling out: 'What is going on, with all this noise?'

Anna closed her door and went back to the living room, followed by Babcia. She stood at the window, watching Ewa running down the street: at the corner she stopped, pulled open her shoulder bag and took out a make-up case. Anna saw her look in the little mirror, then fling it into the gutter so that it smashed, and she heard herself gasp. Behind her, Babcia was patting her arm.

'Tch, tch, tch. Poor Anna.'

She took a long breath, watching Ewa stalk off to the corner on endless, shocking legs, and disappear.

'I'm sorry . . .'

'For what?' Babcia was fiddling with the collar of her blouse, rubbing it between finger and thumb. 'It is Ewa who should apologize . . .'

'It will pass,' Anna said carefully, moving away from the window. 'It is only natural.'

Babcia nodded. 'If she could meet a nice Polish boy . . .'

When she had gone, Anna went into the kitchen and unpacked the shopping. She gave Burek his supper, and she leaned against the fridge, watching the trains go past. Do I telephone Jan, she wondered, and tell him what to expect when he goes to collect his daughter?

She went slowly back to the living room, and saw Wiktoria's letter, lying on the floor where she had dropped it. In Poland, she would have been on that march to the Mickiewicz Monument. So would Jan, she was sure of it. What about Ewa? Would she have cared enough to go?

The pub where Ewa worked was in the midst of a network of streets not far from the common, where many of the Victorian red-brick houses were occupied by whole families. Ewa walked past glossy front doors, white paintwork on the windows, roses in the small front gardens and wisteria clambering up to first-floor balconies. If she slowed down and looked into the front rooms she could see pale walls hung with bright abstract prints in aluminium frames, smoked-glass coffee tables piled with magazines; beyond were polished dining room tables, french windows leading into gardens where sprinklers played across the grass. Some of the houses had been converted into flats, and the glossy front doors were unlocked by people in their twenties coming home from work in the City or West End – young men in suits who re-emerged in expensive jeans with sweaters slung round their shoulders, and girls in Laura Ashley skirts and sandals from Russell and Bromley. The streets were lined with Citroëns and Minis: on Friday evenings the flat-sharers piled into them and drove off to restaurants and discos, or out of London for the weekend.

Ewa, nearing the pub, saw a couple turn into the street from a corner just ahead: they were laughing, their arms wrapped round each other, and she felt a sudden lurch of loneliness and envy. She saw herself walking along an endless street, a cheap-looking girl looking into other people's windows. *Do* I look cheap? she thought, and felt herself flush with anger. One day I shall have a house so beautiful that other people will walk past it and want to live there. One day I shall never have to worry about what my mother thinks, or why my parents don't love each other, or feel guilty about my grandparents, or my little brother. She moved from room to quiet room inside the beautiful house, trying to picture a man there, too. She saw a sunlit bedroom with soft crumpled sheets on the bed and herself upon them, naked, stretched out; her naked lover, whose face she could not see, stood beside the bed, whispering her name.

Laughter came from the beer garden of the pub. Ewa, shocked at herself, shook her head and pushed open the door of the saloon bar. There were few customers at the tables, but she could see through the open door at the back that the garden was filling up already.

'Hi, Eve.' Stan was behind the bar, polishing glasses.

'Hello, I shan't be a minute.' She walked quickly between the tables to the Ladies', to repair her make-up in the mirror. Carefully cleaning away the streaks of black, stroking on more eye-liner, she wondered if Mama had seen her from the window, smashing her little mirror in the street, and she bit her lip. How humiliating, to behave like that. Then she went out, across the brown and yellow flowered carpet, and flipped up the bar top.

'You're a bit late, love,' said Stan.

'I know. Sorry.' She took off her jacket and tucked it with her shoulder bag underneath the bar, took another tea towel and straightened up.

'You look bloody gorgeous, though.'

'Oh. Thank you.' Ewa reached for the tin tray of beer mugs, and began to polish. She looked at him, and pulled a face. 'My mother didn't think so.'

'No, well, she wouldn't, not exactly Mummy's style, is it?' Stan reached up and pushed glasses on to the shelves. 'Should've done this sooner. Kevin's rung in sick – very handy, he was fine at lunch-time. So it's just you and me, on a Friday night. Think you can cope?'

'Of course I can.'

'That's my girl. I've rung Barbara and left a message. Otherwise we're lumbered.'

'We'll manage.' Ewa turned to the couple who had just come up to the bar. 'Yes, please?'

'Gin and tonic for the lady, and a pint of Directors for me, please, my love.' The man wore a pink shirt, was small and plump and pleased with himself. His blonde girlfriend – surely she could not be his girlfriend – looked past Ewa into the mirror behind the bar. 'For the lady' – Ewa felt a shiver of contempt, for the man who talked like that and for the girl who let him. When she had served them, she left Stan to look after the bar and went out into the garden with a tray.

Russian vine and honeysuckle spilled over the fence; a string of lights hung from the back of the pub shone above scuffed grass. Ewa moved from table to table, collecting glasses. In the corner a young man with cropped fair hair and very long legs in jeans looked up and smiled as she rested the tray on the edge of the table.

'Hi.'

'Hello.' Ewa remembered him from last week – he'd been inside, then, with a girl wrapped round him on one of the benches. Tonight he was with two friends, a girl with a slightly beaky nose and dark hair cut in a page boy, and a man with a kind, ordinary face, who held her hand. The one with the cropped fair hair, whose face was not kind or ordinary, was still smiling.

'I saw you last week,' he said. 'And before that.'

'Yes?' Ewa reached for empty glasses.

'D'you work here every Friday?'

'Usually, yes.'

'And Saturdays?'

'Yes.'

'I must remember that.'

'Eve!' Stan was bellowing from the doorway. 'Are you staying out there all night? There's people in here getting desperate.'

'Excuse me.' Ewa picked up her tray and hurried back inside. The bar was filling up fast, and Stan had begun to sweat.

'You're supposed to be working, not chatting up the customers.'

Ewa smiled sweetly. 'I thought it was part of a barmaid's job to chat up the customers. Anyway, I wasn't.'

'Come off it, Goody Twoshoes. You don't doll yourself up like that for nothing. Now move!'

Ewa moved, thinking briefly as she filled and set down glass after glass, and rang up the till, that there was no one she knew who talked to her in the way Stan did. He was like a comfortable father, a father who flirted, and bossed her about, but somehow did not patronize or upset her. She felt safe with him, even though he knew almost nothing about her. 'That's what you think,' she could hear him saying, and giggled.

'What's so funny?' Stan was reaching past her for the ice bucket.

'You.'

He snorted.

By nine the whole pub was packed, the juke box so loud they could hardly hear the orders. One or two regulars who hadn't moved from their bar seats since opening time had begun to glaze over; Ewa dealt with a forest of hands and pound notes.

'*I* can't get no-oh satisfaction . . .'

Ewa, turning to measure two tots of gin, for a moment imagined the young man with the cropped fair hair moving through a crowded disco towards her, reaching out to pull her on to the floor. She put down the glasses, bent for two tonics, and saw him in the mirror when she stood up again, watching her. Her knees felt suddenly full of water; she tried to smile lightly, as if at any customer, but blushed. She turned back to the counter, putting gin and tonics carefully in front of the man who had ordered them; she took a pound and gave him his change, avoiding the eyes of the young man until he had moved right up to her and was the next customer, waiting.

'Yes, please?'

'Can I have two pints of bitter, and a lager and lime?' He asked as if hoping she would give them as a particular favour. I should say No, certainly not, thought Ewa. That is how you flirt. Instead, she pulled the pints without speaking, and did not look at him in the mirror when she added the lime.

'Six shillings and ten pence, please.'

He felt in the pocket of his jeans. 'Here . . . thank you.' He had given her the right money; she put it in the till, turned back and found he was still there.

'Is your name really Eve?'

'Yes.' She straightened the brewery mat on the bar, hating herself for being unable to look up at him. Then she did, and saw that he was half a head or more taller than anyone else there. His eyes were blue, with pale flecks, and his face tanned, as if he'd spent the afternoon lying in the sun. He looked, too, as if he might not have shaved today.

'My name's Leo.'

Ewa nodded politely.

'We're going for a meal later. Would you like to come?'

She would, she would, even though the thought made her nervous. But if Tata came and found she had gone, or if she had to explain to him that he needn't have come, or had to introduce them all . . .

'It's very kind of you, but . . .'

'Not kind. Please come.'

'I'm afraid I can't. My father will be picking me up.'

He raised an eyebrow. 'We can see you home.'

'No,' said Ewa quickly. 'It's all right.'

He put his hand on the bar, a long-fingered, suntanned hand, with bitten nails, and patted it, as if soothing a highly-strung horse. 'Don't be so jumpy.'

'I'm not.' Ewa felt his soothing pats insulting, over-intimate. And yet – wasn't she being rude and gauche? Wasn't he just trying to reassure her? She straightened the bar mat again, very carefully away from his long, stroking fingers, and then looked up at him again, because she had to, or look a fool, when he was still standing there. He smiled at her with such unexpected sweetness that her stomach did a nosedive, and she couldn't think of anything at all, certainly nothing to say.

'Two pints of bitter and a barley wine, please, love. If it's not too much trouble.' A large red-faced regular was tapping the bar impatiently.

'Excuse me . . .' said Ewa, both to the regular for not looking after him and to Leo, who was picking up his glasses.

'I'll talk to you later,' he said, still smiling, and moved through the tables towards the garden door. Ewa, pulling the bitter, watched him go: he walked gracefully, confidently, and the image of him coming towards her across the crowded disco floor flashed into her mind again. She was moving towards him – no, she was waiting for him to come and reach out to her, take her by both hands and pull her close . . .

'Watch it,' said Stan, behind her.

Ewa flicked back the beer-pump handle and carefully lifted the glasses on to the bar.

'There – that'll be . . .'

'And the barley wine,' the regular reminded her.

'Oh, yes . . .'

When he had paid her, and taken the drinks, Ewa turned to Stan, stacking bottles in the floor crate. 'Did you say something?'

'I said something,' said Stan, straightening up. 'And you know very well why.'

Ewa attended to her customers.

Behind Jan the unlit length of the office stretched twenty shadowy feet into darkness, shrouding the empty chairs, and the great pale squares of the plans on the drawing boards. Into the silence, the telephone began to ring; he lit a cigarette and moved to answer it.

'Yes?'

'You're still there,' said Anna. 'You know you're collecting Ewa tonight?'

He had forgotten. 'Yes, of course. I was just about to leave.'

'Jan – it's well after ten.'

'I said, I'm just leaving.'

'Well . . . it's just that we had a disagreement before she left.'

'Oh?'

'About her appearance.'

'Oh.'

Anna gave an exasperated sigh. 'Oh, oh. Is that all you can say?'

He took a deep puff of his cigarette. 'You haven't told me what's happened.'

'It wouldn't matter if I did.'

'Then why have you phoned me?'

'Oh, never mind! I'd better not keep you. Go on – go and fetch her and see for yourself. I'll see you later.'

The telephone clicked, and buzzed. Jan replaced the receiver, took another puff, walked back to his drawing board and put the cap on his pen. He would come in and finish off tomorrow. Sunday, too, if necessary. He switched off the anglepoise, and at the door turned out the overhead neon strip, too. Then he walked along the passage to the shallow flight of stairs, and ran down.

In the hall, the night watchman was sitting in his cubbyhole, reading the *Evening News*.

'I was just coming up there,' he said. 'Did you switch off?'

'Yes,' said Jan. 'Goodnight. See you tomorrow.'

The watchman shook his head. 'Why don't you move in?'

Jan hurried out, across the empty car park and on to the main road. He walked quickly, looking back every now and then to see if the bus was coming; when he saw it, he ran ahead to the stop, feeling his chest burn and his heart pound. He got on, climbed to the top deck and lit another cigarette. Impossible now for him and Anna to have the briefest exchange without the tension rising. What was he supposed to have said?

The bus stopped before the Clapham clock tower and he got off. It was warm, and the air smelt of beer and the chip papers littering the pavement. Pubs emptied noisily; he sidestepped giggling girls in mini-skirts, and the boys who followed them, and walked across the dusty city grass of the common, past the bordering trees, orange from the street lamps, the black gleam of the pond. He cut through side streets, passing drawn curtains and the dark shapes of cats on small front garden walls.

I have failed my family, he thought, and at once refused to think of it further, crossing into the network of quiet, expensive houses where Ewa's pub stood on a corner, lights shining between the leaves of the creeper at the front, and in a string across the garden. At the saloon door he hesitated, preparing for Ewa's cool nod in his direction, and the wait, while she finished her work and ignored him. The door swung open, and two young men came out, laughing; they brushed past him as he stood on the pavement.

'Closing time, mate, what're you waiting for?'

Jan went up to the door and pushed it open, blinking in the light and seeing behind the bar a girl who must be Ewa but who did not look as if she could be anything to do with him. She was slender and dark, hair falling to her shoulders instead of coiled up as she often wore it, her face and lips very pale, her eyes enormous. Leaning on the bar was a tall boy in denims, his fair hair cropped short, his eyes following every quick deft move that Ewa made, as she rinsed and wiped glasses and mugs, stretched up to replace them on the shelves. He was asking her something, and she shook her head, turning to straighten the bottles at the back, her reflection splintered in the mirror all along the wall. From where he stood, Jan thought he had caught her eye there, just for a moment, but then she looked down and methodically tidied the small bottles of Bols, Worcestershire sauce, cherries. She turned, flipped up the bar top and walked out towards the garden, carrying a tray. Her skirt was shorter than any he had seen on the giggling girls out in the street: how could Anna have let her come out like that? The tall boy in the denims went out after her – she was leading him away, so that he need not meet her father? Jan sat down at a corner table, and waited.

'Come along now, *please!*' Stan was moving among the tables, wiping them down, emptying the ashtrays into a bucket. He nodded to Jan. 'Won't be long now.'

'Busy night?' Jan asked politely.

'Very. The usual boy off sick, and my other girl out. Eve's been great, of course.'

Eve? Did he usually call her that?

'Ewa,' said Jan.

'Sorry?' Stan banged a metal ashtray into the bucket and wiped under the beer mats.

'Her name is Ewa.'

'Course it is. Ay-vah – I get muddled, all these girls.' He winked at Jan, who did not wink back. 'They come and they go. Not many like her, though. You must be proud.'

'You have a daughter?' Jan asked stiffly, and felt the shape of his own father settle over him as he asked. I sound a generation older than this man, he thought: I am as ill at ease as you might expect a grandfather to be in here. It is absurd.

'Son in the army,' said Stan. 'Next time he's on leave I'll introduce them. Don't worry, I'm only joking.' He picked up the bucket and walked back to the bar, where he switched off the wall lights. Now there were only the small lights over the mirror, and the glow of the juke box, which hummed.

'Time now, *please!*'

The last few customers straggled out, banging the swing door, and Stan went into the garden. 'Come on, you lot!'

Ewa is part of the 'lot', thought Jan. She has worked here for less than six months, and this barman is more at ease with her than I have ever been. Laughter came through the garden door, and he got up, and walked past the humming juke box and the bar, down the little linoleum passage leading outside.

'She knows a big bad wolf when she sees one, that's why,' Stan was saying.

'Who, me?' The tall fair boy was standing with his hand on Ewa's shoulder: she looked happy, excited, embarrassed. Very young. No younger than Anna had been, but Anna had been in army uniform, without a trace of make-up. Perhaps she had been as shy.

'You can come too, if you want,' the boy said to Stan. 'Just to keep an eye.'

'She's got someone inside who'll do that,' Stan said. 'Dad's here, darling.'

'What?' Ewa moved quickly away from the suntanned hand on her shoulder. 'I'd better go . . .' She moved towards the doorway, saw Jan standing there, and froze. 'Tata?'

274

He stepped forward. 'I was just coming to fetch you . . .'

'I'm coming. I'm *coming*.' She said it quietly, angrily, turned to the others. 'Goodnight.'

'Night, Eve. Sorry – Ayvah. See you tomorrow.'

'Yes.' She did not look at the boy, but brushed past Jan and stalked along the passage to the bar. He nodded to the two men in the garden, and then followed her inside, where she was taking her money from the till. She pushed the drawer shut hard, and bent to pick up her bag from the floor. When she stood up he saw that the thick black make-up round her eyes was smudged and streaky.

'What is wrong?'

She didn't answer, just reached for her jacket and pulled it on, then came out and walked to the door without looking at him or looking to see if he were behind as it swung to. He hurried after her, touched her elbow. She shook him off, and her bag banged against him.

'Ewa . . .'

'You were *spying* on me.' Her voice broke.

'Of course I wasn't.'

'You *were*. Hovering in the dark, checking up on me. Why couldn't you have waited? Why the hell do you have to come at all?'

'Ewa! Do you speak to your grandfather like this when he fetches you?'

She didn't answer, striding ahead until they were out of the quiet streets with their creeper-covered houses, and on the main road. Chairs were being stacked on tables in the fish and chip shop; lights went off behind the plate glass of the furniture stores, over the three-piece suites, the double beds with plastic headboards, the fun-fur animals whose heads you took off to put in your dirty clothes. Jan saw a car slow down beside his daughter, still ahead; he saw the dark shape of a man turning inside to get a better look, and ran to catch up with her. The car drove on, and he saw that Ewa was still crying.

If he spoke she would bite his head off. If he touched her again she would shake him off. They reached the bottom of their own long street, where voices shouted, car doors banged. Ewa fumbled in her bag; Jan reached into his pocket and passed her a handkerchief. She blew her nose and passed it back to him.

'Keep it,' said Jan.

'I don't *want* it.'

'That's enough!' He stopped, and caught hold of her wrist. 'That is enough, do you understand? You are being rude and ridiculous.'

Ewa wrenched her hand away. 'Don't touch me!'

'What is the matter with you? You liked that boy? Why couldn't you introduce him to me? You want to think that I was spying on you because it pleases your sense of melodrama, that's all.'

'That's not true. You don't understand.'

'No, I don't. I don't understand why you are dressed and made up like a . . . like a street girl. Or why you change your name there. Your boss seems to think you're called Eve.'

'So what? That's the English.'

'But why not keep the Polish?'

'Why should I?'

'Because it is a beautiful name. And because you're Polish.'

'Oh, Polish, Polish, Polish! I am eighteen, Tata. I'm not living in Warsaw thirty years ago, I'm living *here*. If you and Mama and the grandparents want to shut yourselves off from this country, that's your problem. You've shut yourself off from all of us, too, haven't you? You're never at home, Jerzy is scared to death of you, none of us know who you are. And as far as I'm concerned, it can stay like that.'

She was off again, paces ahead of him, and as he followed, no longer hurrying, he looked up to see Anna, waiting at their window, the curtain drawn back. She dropped it, and he knew she would be going to open the flat door, realizing from the distance between them that he and Ewa had quarrelled. There would be another scene.

Ewa had reached the front door, and was pressing the intercom. He heard the answering buzz and saw her push open the door and disappear inside, leaving it to close again. He reached it too late, and pressed the button.

'Yes? What is going on?'

'Ewa will tell you,' said Jan, and heard Anna sigh. The buzzer sounded again, and he let himself in, Ewa's footsteps loud on the stairs above him, and Anna's voice, asking again: 'What's happened?'

'*Nothing!*' Ewa shouted. 'Nothing, nothing, nothing!' He heard her hurrying along the corridor to her room, and banging the door. She would wake his parents. He reached the landing, pushed open the flat door and saw Anna standing in the corridor, pale.

'What on earth – '

He shrugged, not knowing how to begin, and knew at once that she would misinterpret him.

'You can *shrug?*'

'Oh, for God's sake – ask her yourself.' He moved past her into

276

the living room, where Burek rose shakily, his tail wagging. Jan bent to pat him, reached into his pocket and pulled out his cigarettes. He lit one quickly, switched on the television and stood staring at it blindly, some old film, while behind him, Anna sharply closed the door and hurried along to Ewa. Let them sort it out.

'When I married you . . .' Anna said, and stopped.

'Go on.' Jan, beside her, lay stiffly, inches away, as if the bed had been divided by a wall. It was very late, the darkness undisturbed by passing trains or the crack of light from Ewa's room across the corridor, switched off now. Jan had come in here over an hour ago, and lain, unable to get to sleep, listening to the rise and fall of Ewa's and Anna's voices, then to Anna, moving quietly about the flat, switching off lights, going to the bathroom. She had undressed there, and slipped in beside him almost holding her breath. Then found he was awake.

'Go on,' he said again. 'When you married me? Would it not be kinder, Anna, to say "When we married"?'

There was a pause. 'It hasn't felt for a long time as if *we* did anything,' Anna said slowly. 'Sometimes I feel as if I *did* even get married by myself.'

'Don't be so melodramatic.'

Anna shifted angrily in the bedclothes. 'That's what you said to Ewa – she told me. No one's feelings matter except yours, do they?'

Jan didn't answer. Then he said: 'You told me that you and Ewa had quarrelled this evening, in any case. I imagine you tried to stop her leaving the house looking like a prostitute, which is what some man thought she was, on our way back here.' He described the slowing car, the dark shape of the driver, turning to get a better look.

'She didn't tell me about that.'

'She didn't see him. She was crying – over nothing, as far as I'm concerned.'

Anna shook her head. 'And to think she wants to be allowed to come home by herself.'

'Doesn't she think that you, too, ride roughshod over her precious feelings?'

'Don't *talk* like that. Of course she does, but – '

'But you are both women, so you can understand each other. I might like to think that my son and I could share the same kind of . . . comradeship, but of course that is impossible, because he, too, finds me an ogre.'

'You sound so *bitter*. How have you become like this?'

'It's true, isn't it? Ewa said so. He's scared to death of me. That's your fault, Anna.'

'Don't be ridiculous!' Anna flung back the bedclothes, and made to get out of bed. Across the corridor, the thin crack of light under Ewa's door flicked on, and she stopped. Slowly, Ewa came out of her room, and they heard her stand, as if listening.

'All right, darling?' Anna called lightly.

'Just going to the bathroom.'

Anna slid back into the bed, and they waited until she had come out.

'Come and say goodnight,' Anna called.

'Goodnight,' said Ewa, and closed her door again. After a few moments, her light went out.

Anna sighed. 'What did you mean?' she asked. 'About Jerzy?'

'A boy like that needs challenges,' said Jan. 'You have fussed over him and his asthma and his nightmares until he thinks he cannot move an inch without Mama. He needs to be told to stand on his own two feet, to grow up.'

'You cannot stand on your own two feet on shaky ground,' said Anna. 'Probably the biggest challenge in Jerzy's life is having you as a father.'

'That is something he cannot change.'

'But you can change. Can't you?' She moved a little closer, took his hand. 'Couldn't you try? When he comes back this weekend . . . make some kind of move towards him?'

'Such as?'

'Oh, God! I don't know. Ask him about his trip? Have a game of chess? It doesn't matter what it is – just make him feel you're interested.'

'Jerzy must learn to accept me as I am.'

'Why? Why must he? When you can't accept him as he is?'

'Because that is life,' Jan said coldly. 'He is still growing, and he has hope. Or he should have hope.'

'And you do not.'

A long silence.

'No.'

Another silence fell between them. At last Anna said: 'I don't know whether to think of you as the most self-pitying man I have ever met, or to feel pity for you, that you should be so . . . desperate.'

'I don't want your pity.'

'But perhaps,' said Anna, and swallowed, 'perhaps I can still . . . give you something?' She put her head on his chest, and they lay without speaking. After a while, Anna began to stroke his hair, his lips, moving closer to him, gently beginning to undo the buttons on his pyjama jacket. 'It has been such a long time . . .'

Very deliberately, Jan took her hand away.

'I'm sorry, Anna. I can't.'

'Having problems, love?'

'What? No, not really.'

'Course you are.' Stan straightened the chairs at the last table, and walked back to the bar. The door to the garden, where Kevin was checking for lunchtime litter, stood open, letting in early evening light and the sound of the birds. It was five minutes before opening time, the pub empty and quiet; Ewa stood behind the polished bar, fiddling with the corner of a towelling brewery mat.

Stan leaned on the bar and took it away from her. 'Twitch, twitch, twitch. How come you're still living at home?'

'I wanted to stay there for my first year at university,' said Ewa. 'I didn't know anyone to share with at first, anyway. Perhaps next term I'll move out.'

'Good idea. Only natural you clash with Mum and Dad, isn't it? Your dad thinks a lot of you, though, I can see that. And Grandad – he's a nice old chap, isn't he?'

'Yes,' said Ewa, 'very nice. Stop taking the mickey.'

'Who, me? I wasn't, honest.'

'All right.' She looked at her watch, and felt her stomach tighten. Two minutes before opening time: would Leo come in tonight?

'And that's a very nice get-up you're got up in,' said Stan, eyeing the pale mauve T-shirt tucked into the mini. 'I'd go easy on the make-up myself, but . . .'

'Yes, well, it wouldn't really suit you, would it?'

'That's my girl. First smile I've seen out of you since you got here. Right then, better open up.' He walked to the double doors, and bent to slip the bolts, straightened up and pulled them open. 'There we are, then. Ready for anything.'

From behind the bar Ewa looked out at the sunny street, the parked cars and the windows of the houses opposite. Where did Leo live? What had he thought of her last night, disappearing with Tata without even saying goodbye? He must have thought she was rude.

279

Or peculiar. If he did come in, she wouldn't be able to think of anything to say.

'Now don't you worry about a thing,' said Stan, coming back. 'It'll all be all right on the night.'

Ewa smiled weakly. 'Which night is that?'

'The one that matters.' Stan went out into the garden, whistling. 'Come on, Kev, what you doing out here, planting grass seed?'

The evening began quietly. Ewa, serving, chatting politely to regulars, waited impatiently for it to get busy, so that she would not have time to wonder about each sound of footsteps approaching the pub, each figure appearing at the doorway. It got busy, but she still found herself looking over the heads of the crowd to check for a very fair one, taller than any of them. By ten she had given up. I'm glad he hasn't come, she thought, snapping the tops off two bottles of tonic; I couldn't handle it. Now I don't have to worry about what to say, or how to say it, or what he thinks of me, or what Mama will say if I go out with him. I hope he never comes in here again, then I can just be myself. And who is that? she wondered wryly, turning to set two glasses and two bottles before her customer.

'Hi.'

'Oh. Hello.'

He was right at the front of the crush, and she hadn't even seen him.

'That'll be five shillings, please,' she said to the gin-and-tonic man, and tucked the note into the till.

'What can I get you?' she asked Leo.

'A pint, please.' He was looking at her quizzically. 'Get home all right? Last night?'

'What? Yes, thank you, I mean I'm sorry if I was rude . . .'

'You weren't. Your pumpkin coach just came too early, that's all. I looked for the glass slipper this morning, but no luck.'

She smiled, blushing, carefully setting down his pint. 'One and ten, please.'

He reached into his pocket, and passed her half a crown. 'How about tonight? Or is it the same story?'

'My grandfather is collecting me,' said Ewa, giving him his change, and had to laugh at his expression.

'Your grandfather. And who comes tomorrow, Granny?'

'I'm not working tomorrow.'

'Aha. May I have the pleasure of your company, or should I ask your father's permission first?'

'If you only knew . . .'

'I think I get the picture.' He picked up his glass. 'Okay – meet you . . . where's a good place? Or should I come to fetch you?'

'No,' she said quickly, and he raised an eyebrow. 'Bad as all that?'

'Just – no. I mean no, don't come. Sorry.'

'Stop saying sorry. Why don't you come to my place, and we'll take it from there.'

'Oh. All right.' Ewa felt a sudden shiver. Wouldn't it be better to meet somewhere neutral? I'm nervous enough now, she thought. How will I cope if we're in his house? And I won't be able to tell Mama where I'm going.

'I'm not going to eat you,' said Leo, with the same incredible smile. 'Not yet.'

Her stomach did another nosedive.

'Here . . .' He reached into his inside pocket, and pulled out a Biro and a scrap of paper. He scribbled down his address, and gave her the paper. Ewa looked at it – just round the corner from here. 'Middle bell,' said Leo. 'Come about seven, okay?'

'Fine. Thank you.' She folded the paper quickly.

'When you two have quite finished,' said Stan, behind her, and she jumped.

'Evening, Stan.' Leo picked up his glass and made his way across the crowded room with his lazy, graceful walk. Watching him, Ewa was suddenly struck by the difference between the way he and Jerzy moved. Jerzy walked as if he felt awkward; even when he got up from a chair, or went to answer the phone, he was stiff, self-conscious. For a moment she felt a pang of love and pity for him, and then there were three people waiting to be served, and she forgot all about him.

Sunday afternoon, and the platform for the London train from Manchester was almost empty. Jerzy walked slowly past the waiting carriages, old canvas rucksack on his shoulders, camera slung round his neck. Above him, on the girders of the vaulted roof, pigeons murmured sleepily; on other platforms, train doors slammed. Ahead, beyond the roof, a forest of overhead electric wires stretched above the track. He looked at his watch: still a good ten minutes, but he might as well choose a seat. Near the front of the train, he climbed into an empty non-smoker, pushed his rucksack up on to the luggage rack and sat down, suddenly very tired. Hungry, too, but there was nothing he could do about it until he got home. He leaned back, waiting for the train to fill up a little, and the whistle to blow, feeling nothing of the usual disappointment that the trip was almost over, but a great wave of relief that he was safe, and going home.

'Anyone sitting here, love?' A large middle-aged woman with two children and a bulging suitcase was clambering into the carriage.

'No. no.' He got up and helped her heave the suitcase on to the rack, sat down again and watched her unwrap an enormous packet of sandwiches.

'Want one?'

'No, no thanks.'

The children munched, unblinking.

As the train began to move, sliding slowly past the rows of small brick houses by the track, the old mill buildings and modern office blocks beyond, Jerzy gazed out of the window, thought about the previous evening, and couldn't decide what had been the most unpleasant.

There was the feeling of awkwardness and exclusion – from the group of students, from the flirtation at the desk, but he was so used to dealing with this on the trips that once away from such situations and enjoying his solitude again, he barely thought of it. Still, he wished he didn't feel like that. There was the sickening, frightening fact of being approached by a man, and wondering why he had been. Had he been covertly watched on the Friday night? Would the man have been like that with any boy on his own, or was it something peculiar to Jerzy which had attracted him? The worst thing, he thought, was the way the man talked about being saved, and the love of Jesus, smearing it all with creepy disgusting intimacy. He was a nutter, that was all; he should be able to forget the whole thing and count himself lucky that nothing else had happened, that he'd had a top bunk, and the man obviously wasn't going to try anything on in a crowded dormitory. Should he have reported it all to the girl at the desk? No, unthinkable.

Have-you-been-saved? Have-you-been-saved? The train kept asking it: why should he find it so disturbing that a sick man was hooked on sex and religion? *Have-you-been-saved?* As long as you were baptized, the question didn't exactly apply if you were a Catholic, although you could fall from grace, of course. He had fallen from grace. He could think about baptism, even communion, with detachment now: that must be a sin in itself. He could not think detachedly about confession, in which he lied through omission; above all, he could make none of the sacraments – ceremonies, as he was beginning to think of them now – reconcile with his deepest feeling, which he felt too ashamed of to discuss with anyone, certainly with none of the priests at school: that he was losing his faith: worse, that he would prefer God not to exist.

The train flashed past fields and willow trees. It was starting to rain, a sudden summer downpour. He closed his eyes, and tried to recapture the image of creation he'd had when he was eight or nine: a grey-green sea under an empty sky, and silence. That was all. It seemed to him now to be more an image of the end than of the beginning of life, yet it also felt subtly perfect: the first form, awaiting the first breath. Now, he felt caught in pincers: if God had moved across the face of the waters, if he really existed, then Jerzy felt as he had been taught to feel: accountable. And afraid, although that was his secret; he didn't know himself why he should feel that God had marked him out for especial punishment. If God did not exist, then Jerzy was safe from his anger, but the world seemed a meaningless, arbitrary, chaotic place, and human beings no more than ants. And he was afraid of these feelings, also.

Two years ago, Jerzy had stood with his Scout troop amongst thousands of Polish children and their families, filling the White City stadium, confidently singing hymns from his childhood, celebrating the Millenium: 1966, the thousandth year of Christianity in Poland. White and red flags fluttered on the stadium roof; banners with the crowned Polish eagle were held high; as well as the troops of Scouts and Guides, there were hundreds and hundreds of children in folk costume, embroidered dresses and trousers and waistcoats – some made here, as Mama had made Ewa's dress for Saturday school when she was younger – but some sent all the way from Poland.

'Oh God, in your power and glory,
For centuries you have watched over Poland.
Before your altar we beg you:
Return a free homeland to us . . .'

He had sung the words so fervently, remembering that once in the war Mama had been able to sing not 'Return a free homeland' but 'Bless our free homeland'. Among all the exiles and children of exiles in White City that day, he had felt part of a great circle of Polishness, certain that somehow, despite centuries of suffering and oppression, his country had a particular place in God's plan: wasn't the Virgin Mary traditionally Queen of Poland?

Later, they heard that in Poland itself, the government had tried to suppress the Millenium events by another celebration: one thousand years of nationhood. Military parades had blared next to open-air masses; a pilgrimage had been broken up by the police. The procession, carrying flowers, singing hymns, had been moving towards Warsaw from Częstochowa, bearing from the monastery Poland's most cherished, most sacred image: the Black Madonna, traditionally said to have been painted by St Luke. The painting was seized by the police, and taken back to the monastery, the pilgrims were scattered; a few days later a demonstration in protest outside the Party headquarters in Warsaw was dispersed by riot police. On the orders of Gomułka, the border was closed to foreigners for over a month.

Jerzy had listened to Dziadek and Babcia discuss all this one Sunday. Later, going into their bedroom to fetch Babcia's cardigan, he looked again at the familiar postcard reproduction of the Black Madonna on the wall, and standing amongst the utility furniture and candlewick bedspreads had tried to imagine the long procession winding through the countryside, singing the hymns they'd sung in White City; then the sudden arrival of the police, and the painting wrenched away.

Had his doubts and fears begun then? He wasn't sure, but even if they had, he knew that they were more to do with something already lacking in himself than with anything outside. His grandparents, after all, had lost everything they knew without losing their faith – in fact it seemed to be all the stronger. Why couldn't he be like them, going to mass every Sunday, praying every night, unafraid of death and what lay beyond it, even as exiles sure of their place in the world?

He opened his eyes. Rain dashed the carriage windows; he watched the hypnotic trickling across the glass of long thin snakes of water, each with a rounded head, pushing through the brownish dirt towards the corner. Beginning as a single drop, each gathered more into itself on its journey, and grew thicker and faster, the movement jerky, almost comical, until it reached the corner, and splashed into nothingness. At once, another followed.

Jerzy fumbled in his anorak pocket for the Ventolin, took it out and had a few quick puffs, cupping it in his hand. The little girl across the carriage looked at him curiously, still munching. He put the Ventolin down, felt in the other pocket, and pulled out the book he'd bought from the second-hand shop yesterday. It was called *Of the Imitation of Christ*, and had an inscription on the flyleaf in thin brown ink: To Lawrence, from Mother, 1889. He held it to his face

284

and sniffed the pages: they smelt musty, like the dark interior of an empty church, or an old damp cellar. He opened at the first page.

'He that followeth me walketh not in darkness, saith the Lord. These are the words of Christ, by which we are admonished how far we must imitate his life and manners if we would be truly enlightened and delivered from all blindness of heart . . .'

Outside the window the rainswept landscape blurred. He shifted in his corner, and tried to concentrate.

A low wall before an unkempt privet hedge stood in front of the house where Leo lived, and a green-painted gate leaned awkwardly open, missing a hinge. Ewa walked up the short concrete path to the front door, which was scruffy white; it stood beneath a small tiled porch, between two bay windows. Net curtains hung there, almost the only ones in the street, and she had the feeling that someone very old lived behind them. The house proclaimed itself as rented, jointly uncared for, quite unlike the owner-occupied sleekness of most of the others. She hesitated in the porch, looking at the Biroed labels to the flats, the fingermarked bells beside them.

Over Sunday lunch with the grandparents, Ewa had slipped in lightly to Mama that they were short-staffed, and needed her to work an extra night this weekend – 'but it's only for a couple of hours or so, I expect, so there's no need for anyone to meet me. I'll be home long before it gets dark. If there's any problem, I'll phone.' At the time, convincing her, and actually getting out of the house without being told to go and change seemed such a triumph – and so easy, really, Mama quiet and preoccupied today, clearly wanting no more quarrels – that nothing else had mattered. Now, it seemed less triumphant than foolish – though wasn't it absurd that she felt like this? After all, as she'd yelled at Mama on Friday, most girls of her age weren't even living at home, and they went out by themselves all the time.

Perhaps they told their flatmates where they were going.

Ewa cautiously bent down and pushed open the aluminium letter box. She couldn't see a thing, was just aware that the hall was very large, and windowless. From far above she could hear music, and then she thought a door was being opened somewhere, and quickly snapped the letter box shut. For a moment she wanted simply to run away; she thought briefly of going into the pub, only a street or so round the corner, to tell Stan what was happening, he would understand; and then she remembered that it was his night off, Kevin and Barbara did Sunday nights.

She took a deep breath. If I don't like it, I can always go, she told herself, and pressed the middle bell. Her hands felt clammy; she wiped them quickly on her skirt – washed and hung on the balcony to dry last night, carefully pressed this morning – and waited, hearing the swish of a bicycle go past the broken gate, and then the thump of footsteps running down the stairs inside. The door was pulled open, and Leo stood there, smiling.

'Hi. You made it.'

What had she been afraid of?

She smiled back, feeling slightly at a disadvantage with him already so tall, standing on the doorstep looking calm and ordinary, while she had been standing here all nervous. His tan had deepened, and his eyes were very blue.

'Come on in.'

She followed him into the hall, which was high-ceilinged, carpeted in chocolate brown and needed a Hoovering. There was a faint smell of damp. Leo led her to the curving staircase, past a painted shelf where uncollected bills and letters lay; a time switch on the light hummed as they went up the curving stairs.

'Right – go ahead.'

He held open a door left on the latch, and she walked into a narrow hall with a long cheap mirror almost opposite the door, so that she couldn't take in what the rest of the flat might be like at all, seeing only the reflection of a startled girl in a black T-shirt and denim mini, and Leo behind her, closing the door.

'Go on, sweetie, the living room's to the left.'

She turned down the narrow passage, carpeted in the same brown as the hall and stairs, and saw an open door, with a small flight of steps leading down from it.

'That's it,' said Leo, behind her, and Ewa felt a little as if she were being pushed. Then she had reached the steps through the doorway, and went down them into a large, airy room with tall windows on the far wall overlooking the street. A sofa stood in the middle of the room at right angles to the windows, and a coffee table was piled high with old newspapers and music magazines. Bookshelves were planks on metal supports; they were crammed with LPs.

'It's – very nice.' Ewa stood uncertainly.

'That's the kitchen, through there,' said Leo, indicating another door. 'I'll get you a drink. What would you like?'

'Oh – well, just a glass of wine? White wine?'

'Sure. Nice to be able to get it for you, for a change.' He came up beside her, and lightly touched her shoulder. 'Please don't look so nervous. Sit down. Relax.'

Ewa sat on the sofa and pulled her bag off her shoulder. 'I'm not nervous.'

'Yes you are.' He disappeared into the kitchen, and she looked round the room, thin coats of white emulsion not quite concealing the floral wallpaper, posters of Greek islands pinned up next to Dylan and Lennon.

'Here we are.' He came back with a bottle and two smeared glasses, already filled, and gave her one. 'Cheers.'

'Cheers,' said Ewa, and drank quickly.

'So,' said Leo, still standing above her, 'no problems.'

'What?'

'With the family. They let you out.'

'Yes,' said Ewa, 'they let me out.' She wanted to make a joke of it, but was still too ill at ease. And she felt a thin thread of irritation, or defensiveness. Was Leo laughing at her? At her family? She took another quick sip of the wine, and looked round the room again, avoiding his eye. Through the open door to the kitchen she could see milk bottles, unwashed dishes on the table.

Leonard Cohen murmured soulfully in the corner. Leo sat down beside her. Ewa stared at the doorway.

'Have you lived here for a long time?'

'Just a few months,' said Leo. 'I share it with these two friends, Mike and Sara – they were in the pub on Friday, remember?'

'Yes.'

'But they're out now.'

'Oh.'

Leo moved closer, took another drink and put down his glass. 'Poor little Evie, does that worry you?'

'I am not poor little Evie,' Ewa said sharply.

'Ouch.' Leo shook his hand as if he'd burned it.

'Sorry,' said Ewa, 'I didn't mean to snap.' But she had meant to, and she wasn't sorry. She felt confused and slightly drunk, having eaten almost nothing at Sunday lunch. Who was the girl Leo had been with in the pub last week? How could she ask? Was poor little Evie a quick one on the side? If only she could think of something to say. She finished her drink at a gulp.

Leo leaned forward and refilled her glass. He put his arm round her, tried to turn her face to his.

'Come on, baby, what's the problem?'

What's the problem? That did make her feel as if she were making a fuss about nothing. She was, she supposed, but it didn't stop her feeling like this. She'd wanted to be so cool and – and to enjoy herself, for heaven's sake, and if she didn't pull herself together he would never want to see her again, and anyway why should she care so much about seeing him again, when he just made her feel small?

'I'm sorry . . .'

'No more sorrys. No need.' He was stroking her hair; with every gentle stroke a shiver of excitement ran through her, and she closed her eyes.

'May I kiss you?' he asked softly. 'Am I rushing you?'

'I don't know,' Ewa said shakily. 'I don't think so.'

'Please don't tell me it's your first kiss.'

She didn't answer and he drew her very close. 'Is it?' he whispered, and his lips brushed hers. His hand moved down from her hair to her shoulder, still stroking, to her breast, still stroking, gently, gently. Then his hard mouth was covering her mouth, his tongue meeting hers, and she clung to him, forgetting even her name.

The street had the quietness of a summer Sunday evening: empty and dusty, a few windows open to catch the last of the sun before it slid behind the rooftops. Jerzy turned into his front doorway, rang the grandparents' bell, and waited. At the far end of the street a couple of West Indian kids were kicking a ball about; he yawned, closing his eyes, and heard its thumping and scraping on the pavement magnified through tiredness: a ball bouncing on brick and concrete shutting out the memory of openness, and space, cool air and rippling grass.

'*Słucham?*'

Always, Dziadek answered doorbell and telephone with the Polish: 'I am listening.' If English people rang, there would follow a silence, an uncertain 'Hello?' Then he would rescue them: 'Yes, please?'

'*Słucham?*'

'*To ja*, Dziadek. It's me.'

The buzzer sounded, and he pushed open the door and slowly climbed the stairs. Dziadek was waiting for him at the top, smiling: almost always, after a weekend trip, Jerzy rang his door first.

'So – how is the traveller?'

'Fine, fine.' He put down his rucksack on the little square of landing, and called through his own letter box: 'Mama? I'm back.' Then he followed Dziadek into the flat, where Babcia was in the kitchen, chopping tomatoes.

'Jerzy . . .' She put down the knife and waited for him to come up and kiss her.

'How are you, Babcia? Have you had a nice weekend?'

'Without you? How would that be possible?' She patted his cheek, and passed him an open biscuit tin, full of *katażynki*. 'Have you been all right?'

'Of course.' He took one and ate it hungrily.

'Many trains?' asked Dziadek. 'Anything special?'

'A Black Five, a couple of Britannias, a Jinty. Ordinary, really.'

'And did you meet anyone nice?' asked Babcia. 'Go on – have another *katażynka*, have two, I saved them for you specially. Was there anyone in the hostel? Other boys?'

'Oh – a few students, that's all.' No point in saying they were German. 'I must go and see Mama – I just wanted to say hello.'

'Thank you, darling.'

Across the landing outside they could hear the other door open, and Anna calling.

'Coming, Mama.' He patted Babcia's shoulder. 'See you later, perhaps.'

'If you have time. Mama will be so glad to have you home, we all missed you at lunch. And your father is there.'

Jerzy stopped at the kitchen door. 'Tata? Why?'

Babcia looked at him, amused, a little puzzled. 'Why shouldn't he be there? Aren't you pleased?'

'Yes . . . yes,' he said uneasily. 'It's just that he isn't usually . . .'

'Then you have a nice surprise. You'd better go along now.'

'Yes.' He stood in the doorway and looked at them, Babcia with her apron over her Sunday dress, wiping a strand of grey hair from her forehead with the back of her hand; Dziadek beside her, arranging the sliced tomato in a dish. So secure they probably didn't even need to think about each other.

'Ewa's there, isn't she?' he asked.

'No, she's working again.' Babcia sighed. 'She and Mama had a little upset.'

'What do you mean?' Ewa never worked on Sundays. When was she coming back?

'Let Mama tell you, darling, or perhaps you'd better just let her forget all about it.'

Jerzy looked at Dziadek, who winked. 'Women . . .'

He winked back. 'Bye, then.'

'Goodbye, Jerzy. Thank you for coming.'

On the landing, he found Mama had taken in his rucksack, leaving the door on the latch. He pushed it open, almost cautiously, suddenly filled with resentment, as well as anxiety, that his father should be there.

'Mama?'

'In the kitchen, darling.'

He went in, sniffing. A large casserole dish stood on the stove, gently reheating. 'I'm *starving*.'

'It won't be a minute.' She reached up to touch his cheek. 'You've caught the sun. Have you grown, too?'

'I don't know. Where's Tata?'

'In the sitting room. He thought you might like a game of chess after supper.'

Jerzy helped himself to a slice of bread and butter from the worktop. 'Why?'

'Oh, Jerzy, come on,' Anna said lightly. 'Wouldn't that be nice? It would please him so much.'

He shrugged. 'I'm filthy, can I have a bath?'

'Of course. Are you all right? Was it a good trip?'

'So-so.' He took the bread out of the kitchen, along towards the bathroom.

'Jerzy?' Tata was calling from the sitting room, and he stopped. 'Yes?'

A silence; Tata was waiting for him to go back. More questions: how was it, who did you see, who did you talk to. But with Tata it was like a trial, an inquisition.

The living room door swung open. 'I called you.'

Jerzy drew a breath, turned round. 'Sorry, Tata, I was just coming.'

'No, you weren't.'

He bit his lip, and looked down. 'I'm going to have a bath.'

'You can say hello to your father first, can't you?'

Between them, Anna's clattering in the kitchen stopped abruptly.

'Of course. Hello, Tata. How are you?'

'I am well. Must I talk to you across ten feet of carpet?'

Miserably, Jerzy walked towards him.

'Look at me!'

He jerked his head up, ashamed of the tears stinging his eyes, unable to stop them. Through the blur he could see his father in the sitting room doorway, looking at him with contempt.

'Excuse me, Tata . . .' He turned and walked unseeingly along the corridor to his room, longing to slam the door, not daring to do anything more than close it with the utmost care. Then he flung himself on the bed and cried, muffling the sound in his pillow until he began to have a fight for breath, and sat up. Where was the Ventolin? Not in his pocket – Christ, was he going to have to go outside to get his rucksack? No, Mama had put it in here already, thank God; he got up and wrenched the flaps open, panting, fumbled inside but couldn't find it. It must be in his pocket then: he felt again, beginning to panic, gasping, but it wasn't there, it must have fallen when he got off the train, or else he'd left it on the bloody seat. There was a spare one in the bathroom – but if he went out there he'd have to face Tata again. Sweat was pouring down his face, he'd have to go. He made for the door, pulled it open, heaving. At the far end of the corridor, thousands of miles away, he heard his parents' voices, very loud. He made his way slowly down, towards the bathroom, hearing Mama say suddenly: 'Jerzy!' and run towards him.

'Ventolin . . .'

She ran to the bathroom, came back, thrust it into his hands and he puffed and puffed it, standing gasping, until he could breathe again. It felt a very long time before he was able to lean weakly against the wall.

'Better now?'

He nodded, his head swimming. 'I'll lie down.'

She helped him back to his room, pulled off his anorak and gymshoes as he sat on the side of the bed. 'There . . . Poor Jerzy.'

He drew a long breath, feeling the pain in his chest begin to fade. 'Mama? Where's Ewa?'

'At the pub. She's covering for someone off sick, that's all.'

'Oh.' He leaned back on to the pillows. 'Babcia said you'd had a row – a "little upset".'

They both smiled. 'A row,' said Anna. 'Never mind – it's all blown over.' She got up. 'I'll bring you some supper, all right?'

'Thanks.'

At the door, she paused, hesitating. 'Would you like Tata to come and see you?'

He turned away to the wall. 'He hates me.'

'Of course he doesn't.'

'He does. You know he does.'

'Well . . . I'll talk to him.'

He didn't answer, and she went out quietly, leaving the door open.

Jerzy lay for a few minutes, exhausted. There was a slow, unsteady sound from the corridor, and then Burek came in, and put his nose on the edge of the bed.

'Hello, boy.' He reached down and patted him. Burek sat, his tail moving slowly from side to side. 'Dear old boy.' Jerzy swung his legs carefully off the bed and went over to his rucksack again. He took out *The Imitation of Christ* and put it on a high shelf. The evening sun slanted through dusty window panes – impossible to keep them clean for long, even though no steam trains puffed by now.

The sun touched the photographs of engines cut out from the *Railway Magazine* and taped all over the wardrobe doors, and the wall beside his bed. It touched the photographs on the chest of drawers which Mama had put in a large frame for his Saint's Day last year: he and Ewa on the common when they were little, playing with Burek; both of them in national costume for a Christmas concert at Saturday school; Dziadek and Babcia in their sitting room, he reading, she doing her tapestry – he had taken that one himself, it was one of his best. He took his camera out of his rucksack and put it on the chest of drawers. Tomorrow he'd take the film to be developed.

With the photographs here, of family and places he knew, were others: the family he had never known, the country he had never visited. His other Dziadek, Mama's father, who had been murdered by the Russians at Katyń; his uncle, his namesake, who had been shot down in a Warsaw street by the Germans. They were sitting together under a silver birch tree by a river, laughing at Mama, who was taking the picture. The photograph was small and cracked and faded, like the one of Mama and Uncle Jerzy taken by their father on the same holiday, just before the war, smiling at the camera from a boat on a glinting river. Mama had her hair in plaits, and wore shorts; Jerzy, in cotton shirt, had his arm round her. In the studio picture of him on Mama's chest of drawers he looked very intense, dark and clever; here he was carefree and ordinary, the kind of person Jerzy himself would like to be. But his uncle had been a hero, had been killed running under gunfire to try to save his friend's life.

Also in the frame was a picture of Tata, wearing his white and red AK armband, standing smoking behind a heap of sandbags in the early days of the Warsaw Uprising. He looked young and tough; he had been tough, noble, even, carrying and dragging his best friend for hours through a sewer, when he himself was wounded. No wonder he hates me, Jerzy thought: I can hardly run down the road. He went over to the window, looked out on to warehouses and trees across the track. Beneath the window a tube train rattled past, and he saw in his mind's eye the Black Five, puffing faster and faster along the gleaming track through the hills, the steam rising towards the fresh blue sky,

Behind him, his father coughed. Jerzy jumped, and turned round. 'Tata?'

'Are you feeling better?'

'Yes, thanks.'

They stood awkwardly, as the sound of the train faded. Jerzy, conscious of sweat-stained shirt and jeans grimy from the train, shifted in his socks on the lino, and almost fell over his feet, knocking the narrow bed frame.

'Your mother thinks I am too hard on you,' said Jan, watching him.

'It's all right,' Jerzy mumbled.

'What do you mean, it's all right? I am too hard on you, or not?'

'No. I mean . . . it doesn't matter.' He couldn't think straight, wanting only for his father to go, and leave him alone.

'Perhaps when you've eaten – and had your bath, of course – we could have a game of chess.'

He'd have to sit opposite him, perhaps for an hour, trying to concentrate, nervous of making a mistake.

'Okay.'

'Good. Well . . . I'll leave you to have your meal in peace.'

They could hear Anna coming along the corridor with a tray, the clink of knife and fork. She came in smiling at a space somewhere between them, as Jan brushed past and went out. Jerzy settled himself on the pillows again and she put the tray on his lap.

'There . . . all right?'

'Fine. Thanks.' He took a mouthful, broke off a piece of bread and dipped it in the gravy. 'Delicious. God, I was hungry. Mama – I'm sorry, I couldn't bring you a present this time.'

'Darling, it doesn't matter.' She sat down on the bed. 'Did Tata talk to you?'

'Sort of. He wants me to have this chess game . . .'

'But you're too tired now? I'll tell him.'

'No. Don't. It'll only make it worse. I'll do it.'

She shook her head. 'I thought it would be something to share. Not an endurance test.'

Jerzy went on eating. From the other end of the flat they could hear the television murmur, and Jan's cough. 'Don't Mama,' he said. 'Don't try to throw us together, it won't work.'

'Such a sad thing . . .'

'You sound like Babcia.' He finished his plate, put down the knife and fork. 'I'm going to have a bath now, all right? Then I'll tell him.'

Anna picked up the tray. 'I'll run it for you as I go past.'

'Thanks.' He looked at his watch. Well after nine – Ewa might be back by ten? He heard the water running, yawned and got up, taking his spongebag from the rucksack, a clean pair of pyjamas from the drawer. In the bathroom, almost all the natural light had gone; he did not turn on the switch but stood looking in the mirror, clouding with steam, seeing his features blur and disappear. Then he undressed quickly, and lay in the bath, already almost asleep. He could just hear Mama and Tata talking, their voices no longer raised. Like an ordinary family, he thought sleepily. After a while, he got out and got dry, and into his pyjamas, and then he crept out and back to his room, slipping guiltily into bed. By the time he woke up tomorrow, Tata would have gone to work: they might not have to see each other all week.

It was almost dark. A train went past, the light from the windows flickering along the ceiling. Then it was very quiet.

He woke with the sound of running water and blinked, wondering for a moment where he was, half-expecting to see rows of bunks around him and sense beyond them the silence of the countryside at night. Then he recognised the bluish fluorescence of the lights from the railway line, and turned over, hearing Ewa, in bare feet, going quietly down the corridor, back to bed.

'Ewa?' He propped himself up on his side. 'Ewa!'

'Sssh!' She came into the room, looking for a moment quite ghostly in the bluish light, wearing her long cotton nightdress, her hair tumbled over her shoulders.

'Are you all right?' she whispered. 'Mama said you'd had an attack.'

'I'm fine now. Come and talk to me.'

'It's the middle of the night.' She came over, and sat on the edge of the bed. 'How was your weekend?'

'It was a beautiful place,' he said, yawning. 'But . . . something happened.'

She rolled her eyes. 'It would. Go on, what was it?' She moved on to the bed so that she could hunch up her knees with her arms round them, leaning against the wall, and the pictures of the trains, and gave an exaggerated sigh. 'You look awful, Jerzy. Why can't you be normal?'

They both giggled. Then he said slowly: 'There was a man. He was sort of . . . after me. I think.' Already it seemed as if the whole thing might have happened to someone else, or been imagined. He told her, remembering the quiet, sunny airiness of the kitchen, the bleating sheep in the field beyond the window, and the sudden sense of menace in the man's approach.

Ewa listened. 'He didn't touch you, or anything.'

'No. I think he would have.'

'Saved by the Germans. Tata would like that.'

'Yes.' They giggled again, helplessly.

'Sssh!'

'Oh, Ewa, I'm so glad you're back.' He thought of the train journey home, his thoughts eating away at him, gnawed at by doubt: it wasn't just that the man might have . . . touched him, it was the fact that he and the man had something horrible in common, some sort of twisted thing about God, where faith had become obsession. Suddenly none of that seemed to matter now – he reached across to Ewa and hugged her. 'What about you? Where were you tonight?'

'Working. Your feet are poking me – move up.'

He moved, rustling the sheets. 'You never work on a Sunday.'

'Well, I did this Sunday.' There was a pause. 'If I tell you what I did, you won't tell them?'

'Of course not.'

'I've got a boyfriend.' She buried her head in her knees.

'Oh.' He felt a sudden, sharp pang of disappointment. Ewa with a boyfriend. 'Oh.'

She looked up at him and he noticed suddenly that her eyes were very swollen. 'He's called Leo,' she said dreamily. 'Isn't that a beautiful name?'

'No, I think it's awful. Like a pop singer, or something.'

'What's wrong with that, you little swot? Anyway, he works in music, that's his job, he works in a recording studio.'

'Does he?' He tried to imagine Ewa with someone like that, and couldn't.

'He's really lovely,' she said, in the same dreamy voice. 'I never thought I'd ever meet anyone like him.'

'Why've you been crying, then?'

'I haven't.'

'Yes you have.'

'Oh, well, perhaps I cried a bit.'

'Why?'

'Oh, shut up, Jerzy, I just did, that's all.'

He shook his head, not knowing what to make of it. 'When are you seeing him again?'

'Oh, soon, I expect. He lives quite near the pub.'

'Is that where you met him?'

'Yes.' There was another long pause, and then she said hesitatingly: 'I . . . something's happened to me, too.'

'What?'

'You promise you won't tell?'

'Of course not.'

Silence.

'Go on, Ewa, please, you can trust me. Something with – Leo?'

'Yes.' She moved suddenly off the bed. 'It's no good, I can't. It just doesn't feel right, not yet.' She went across to the window, pulling back the thin curtain. A summer moon hung above the trees across the track, vast and pale. She shivered.

'Anyway,' she said slowly, 'I don't suppose I'll ever love anyone the way I love you.'

'No,' said Jerzy. 'Nor me.'

Leo did not come into the pub when Ewa went to work the next Friday. On Saturday she recognized the friends he lived with, but she didn't like to ask after him. The following week he didn't come in either. After that the summer became, in her later recollection, a hot, dusty, long-drawn-out day where London shimmered under a burning sky and she walked through it, looking for Leo. She saw his face half turned away from her in café windows, saw him walking gracefully, unhurriedly, just ahead of her among the crowds of tourists milling round Dillons', the British Museum, Oxford Street. Endlessly, she saw his silhouette appear at the open doors of the pub, and his smile, and endlessly she realized it wasn't him, and looked blankly at the people who were there, waiting for her to serve them.

'It's no good, darling,' said Stan one evening, seeing her jump as the door banged to with the last customer's departure. 'He's found another pub.'

'What do you mean?'

'Come off it.'

She looked down at the glass in her hand, turning it slowly, over and over again, in the blue-checked tea towel.

'Want to tell Uncle Stan all about it?'

'No.'

'Yes you do.'

She smiled thinly. 'There's nothing to tell.' Then the street door swung open again, and she looked up to see Dziadek, gravely raising his hand as he came in, taking off his hat and placing it neatly on a corner table. He sat down, and waited.

It was *summer*, for God's sake. The evenings were light. Surely they would let her go home by herself now. I'll have to move out, she thought, quickly wiping the sink beneath the bar. I'll put up a notice next term. Then Leo's light, cruel words, which played in her head repeatedly, slid into it once again.

A bit intense, aren't you, sweetheart? Not sure I can handle this.

And he hadn't, he'd dropped her like a stone.

Perhaps she was too intense for anyone to be with for long? Ewa trembled between anger and self-doubt. How could she have allowed this to happen? A one-night stand – not even a night, a few hours before she had known she must go home quickly or have to fight with Mama every time she wanted to leave the house. And now it looked as if Mama might have been right all the time: she had made herself look cheap, she had acted cheaply, and – she could hardly bring herself to go on to the next bit of the story.

At her desk in the university library, Ewa stared blankly at pages of notes and pulled out her diary, counting days. She was often irregular, sometimes a week late, once this year it had been ten days. And if you were tense it could throw you out anyway. She closed the diary and sat with her head in her hands. Should she go to his house? And stand on the doorstep like a little girl: 'Hello, Leo, why haven't you been to see me? Hello, Leo, guess what's happened . . .' Never. She bit her lip, then pushed back her chair and for the third time that morning went out to the lavatory. Perhaps it was all right.

It wasn't. She stood in the empty washroom, smelling institutional soap and floor cleaner, and her hands felt cold and clammy. Another week, she thought bleakly. I'll give it another week before I tell Mama. She pictured her face, and hurried back to her desk.

That night, as they were doing the till, she told Stan she wasn't coming to work there any more.

'What?' He looked up from the pile of notes beside the open drawer, and put his hand on his heart. 'How can you do this to me? You're my best girl ever.'

'I'm sorry. But term starts again in a few weeks, and I want to get down to my work. You'll easily find someone else.'

'Oh, yeah, easily. Don't give me any notice, will you?'

'I'm sorry,' she said again.

Stan wrote down a total on a pad, and came over to her. 'Taken it hard, haven't you, darling? I should've warned you off properly, kept you away from him.'

'Don't be silly. I can take care of myself.'

'Oh, I can see that.' He put his arm round her and she stood stiffly, not looking at him. 'Eve? You are okay, aren't you? I mean . . .'

'I am okay,' she said, and carefully moved away. She bent down to the shelf under the bar where she kept her bag, and straightened up. If there were anyone she could tell, it would probably be Stan. But not yet.

'If you need me,' he said, 'you know where I am.'

'Yes. Thanks. Thanks for everything.'

He was beside the pile of notes again, counting out her money for the week. 'I ought to deduct half of it for giving me no notice,' he said, 'but I'm giving you an extra fiver as a bonus. Here we are.'

'Oh, Stan, thank you.' She leaned forward and brushed his cheek with her lips. 'Goodbye.'

He touched his cheek. 'Wish I'd made it a tenner now. Bye, darling. All the best.' He lifted the bar top for her just as the door swung open and Jan came in, nodding to them both.

'I'm ready, Tata,' Ewa said quickly. 'Let's go.' She hurried past him to the door, without looking back.

'You won't need to come and pick me up any more,' she said as they walked down the street.

'Oh? May I ask why?'

'Too much work. I want to concentrate on my studies.'

'I'm glad to hear it.'

They walked on in silence. As they approached the main road he said awkwardly: 'That boy . . . the one you liked . . . did you ever see him again?'

'No,' said Ewa. 'Never.'

*

The second week of August slid into the third. Unable to focus on essay or translation, Ewa gave up going to the library and took to walking over the common with Jerzy and Burek. Lovers lay kissing beneath the trees, transistor radios blared, mothers took their children to watch the toy boats sail across the pond. Babies with bare feet kicked under canopies in their prams, or fretted in pushchairs. There seemed to be babies everywhere.

'What happened to Leo?' asked Jerzy.

She shook her head, not answering. Beside them, Burek panted. They stood by the pond, watching the pretty white sails of the boats; some of them had motors, and boys stood on the edge with remote control panels and aerials. The buzzing cut through the hot afternoon air like a power saw.

'Not like when we were little,' said Jerzy.

'No,' said Ewa. 'Everything's different now.'

Out on the road, from cars with their windows wide open or sun roofs back, rock music pulsed through the traffic. They walked on, into the shade of the chestnut trees, and then to the children's playground, where an ice cream van stood waiting.

'Want one?' Jerzy asked.

Ewa nodded. 'I'll pay.'

'I'll get them. You sit down for a bit.'

She sat on a bench and watched him walk over to the queue, perhaps less stiff and ungainly than she'd thought, or he was changing. He'd grown taller, and with their walks and his trips away had got brown and fitter-looking. He hadn't had an asthma attack for at least a couple of weeks. He moved up in the queue and she turned to watch the children on the swings and the slide, the toddlers digging absorbedly in the sandpit. If I told him, she thought, would he know how to help me? Oh God, oh God, what am I going to do?

'Here – a choc ice, is that all right?'

He sat down beside her, and she took it from him. 'Fine. Thank you.' Burek flopped at their feet, and they sat licking the ices, brushing off flies.

'Ewa . . . tell me what's wrong.'

'What do you mean?'

'You know what I mean.'

She closed her eyes. 'I'll tell you soon. Just not quite yet.'

After a while, they got up and began to walk home. 'We'll get supper for Mama, shall we?' said Jerzy, as they approached the shops.

'All right – just some salad or something. I can't even think about food.' That was a sign, wasn't it? 'Have you got enough money?'

'Yes, she gave me some this morning.'

They stopped at the greengrocers they often used, open on to the street, cool and dark inside. As they went in, Ewa felt suddenly very weak; she stood beside Jerzy, distantly hearing him buy cucumber, watercress, lettuce. Her head swam, and then she felt a warm, unmistakable trickle between her legs, and she reached out to hold on to an orange box, unbelieving.

'Ewa? You okay?'

'I'm fine. I'm fine.' She drew a deep breath – it was unmistakable, wasn't it? Outside the shop, she began to walk quickly towards the turning to their own street, feeling the familiar dull ache in her stomach, the first twinges of cramp.

'Slow down a bit,' said Jerzy. 'Poor old Burek can't take the pace.'

'I'm going ahead, all right? I need to go to the loo, I'll leave the door . . .'

She broke into a run, along the burning pavement to their front door, inside and up the stairs. At the flat door she paused, hearing the television: Mama was home early. She quickly unlocked the door, leaving it on the latch, and went straight away to the bathroom, sensing somehow that there was something odd about the television being on so early, and Mama not calling out at once, but she had to be sure, before she went in to her.

In the bathroom she pulled down her pants and saw the bright, reassuring bloodstain. She had been spared. For a brief moment, as she felt for the box of tampons in her bag, she saw Leo's sunburnt face, his beautiful smile, and was pierced by a stab of hurt and disappointment. Then she thought: I hate you. I hate you. When she had finished, she went out and down the corridor to the sitting room, where Mama and Jerzy were motionless before the television, as an enormous tank crawled across the screen, past tall, beautiful buildings.

'What on earth . . .' said Ewa, and then knew. 'Czechoslovakia. That's Prague. They've invaded.'

'Yes. This morning.' Mama was sitting as if transfixed, her face white. Another tank moved along the street, then another, pushing through a furiously shouting crowd. Young men and boys in helmets, carrying guns, looked down on them from the tanks, bemusedly. Then Dubček's face was flashed on to the screen, a photograph taken

300

a little while ago: at the sight of his smile, unassuming, almost vague, his eyes avoiding the camera, Ewa began to cry, and then to howl.

'Ewa . . . *kochana* . . .' Mama was out of her chair. 'It's terrible, but please . . . don't cry like that . . . what is it? Something has happened to you? Stop it, stop it . . .'

'I thought I was pregnant,' Ewa sobbed. 'I thought I was pregnant, and I'm not, I'm not . . .'

'Oh, my poor darling. My poor, poor darling.'

Years later, when Ewa looked back on that summer, she could remember nothing, really, after that day, when she had seemed to cry for everything, all at once: when history lessons at Saturday school, Mama's stories, all the feelings for Poland she had dismissed or buried filled her with a sudden and overwhelming sense of loss and anger, as painful and acute as her own, furious frustration: with Leo, with her father, for whom she felt the first glimmer of understanding; with herself. She let her mother rock her like a baby, while Jerzy went to fetch a handkerchief, a glass of water. Then she dried her eyes and sat down, feeling very cold, still watching the television screen, as the tanks rolled into Prague.

8

London, 1970s

1976

'I should like to order a wreath,' said Anna.

'A wreath. Yes, dear, just let me find my book . . . And what name is it?'

'Prawicka,' said Anna. 'Mrs Prawicka. Shall I spell it?'

'If you would, dear.'

She spelt it, gave her address.

'Right,' said the woman. 'And what flowers would you like?'

Anna looked round. It was a Saturday morning, early still, and she was the only customer, although out on the main road the pavements were filling with shoppers. The florists' was full of chrysanthemums, of tight yellow roses without scent; in the window, beneath the leaping god on the Interflora sign, were white china hands, and christening baskets trimmed in blue or pink nylon lace.

'Take your time, dear,' said the woman at the counter. She began sorting out a sheaf of invoices, tidying away spools of shiny lick-and-stick ribbon.

Many of the flowers were arranged on shelves and stands, but there were also bucketfuls on the floor. Anna looked at the masses of carnations, pink and white and crimson. Why was she deliberating?

'Carnations,' she said. 'I should like white and red carnations.'

'White and red . . .' The woman retrieved her book and wrote it down. 'Just the carnations, was it? Or anything else? A little touch of green?'

'No, no, thank you. The flowers on their own will be quite sufficient.'

She bent down for a moment and breathed in their sharp, spicy smell. Beyond the plate-glass window the hum of Saturday morning traffic in Clapham faded: she was in another shop, boarded and shuttered, where an old woman in an apron and flattened slippers shuffled across the floor and lifted dripping bunches from bucketfuls of black water, thrusting them into her arms. From a distant part of the city they could hear gunfire; she ran through the early morning

302

street holding the wet flowers close to her, to the house where her brother's body lay waiting.

There was another grave, a mass, terrible grave, beneath freshly planted pine trees.

'And when is it for, dear?'

Anna stood up slowly. 'For September 18th,' she said.

'September 18th . . .' the woman wrote it down.

'That'll be six pounds, then. Do you want it delivered, or . . . is there a funeral parlour looking after it all for you?'

'It's not for a funeral,' said Anna.

'Pardon, dear?'

'It's for a memorial – well, a monument. My father – my father died a very long time ago.'

'What a shame,' said the woman. 'In the war, was it?'

'Yes,' said Anna. 'It was in the war.'

Cars and coaches lined the roads round the cemetery. At the entrance, on a main road roaring with traffic, a throng of people moved slowly through the tall iron gates between brick pillars: whole families in black, many men in uniform, small children carrying bunches of flowers. They made their way down the broad gravel path between the graves, between ranks of Polish Scouts and Guides bearing standards, between row upon row of Polish Ex-Combatants in uniform, wearing their medals. At the far end of the path, on either side of shallow white steps, stood more standard bearers, their flags a sea of white and red and gold. From the centre of the steps rose a tall obelisk, shrouded in Polish and British flags.

'Mama?' asked Jerzy. 'Are you all right?'

Anna nodded. She was holding the wreath, collected this morning and carried on the tube, and on the main-line train to Gunnersbury station, from where they'd all walked amidst the crush. The flowers still looked fresh; the card was in her handbag. It was growing warm, although the day had begun cloudy and drizzly; she hoped that Dziadek and Babcia were going to stand up to all this – the crowd at the end of the path was enormous. When they could move no further, they stopped, and stood together. Ewa holding Babcia's arm, Jan and Dziadek next to each other. Anna would have liked to slip her arm through Jerzy's, but she needed both hands for the wreath. He stood beside her, very tall, his camera round his neck; every now and again he brushed his flopping straight hair off his forehead, in a nervous gesture.

The sun rose higher, drying the pools of water on the steps; the crowd grew. A commemorative brochure was being given out; there was the rustle of pages, feet shifting on the damp gravel, hundreds of voices talking subduedly; everywhere the scent of flowers. On the left of the steps stood tall red rose bushes; white roses flanked the other side. Behind the obelisk stood two chestnut trees. Anna stood looking at them, at the heavy chestnuts among leaves touched with the first dry gold of autumn.

The apartment house in Praga had a chestnut tree in the courtyard. Such a short time before the war began, she had stood at the window there, listening to the rustling leaves, hearing the occasional drop of a spiky case on to the cobbles. Now, this monument was to be unveiled almost exactly thirty-seven years to the day that Poland, already invaded from the west by Germans, had been invaded by Russia from the east. On 17 September 1939 she and Jerzy and Teresa had been holed up in the empty apartment in Żórawia . . . As the Russians advanced, they captured thousands upon thousands of Poles, among them the cream of the Polish intelligentsia, all the reserve officers called up from their civilian professions – teachers, lawyers, priests, civil servants, doctors. After April 1940 not a word was heard from any of the three camps in which they were held: Kozielsk, Starobielsk, Ostaszków.

'They're being released! Everyone's been whispering about it – the Poles are being released to fight the Nazis!' Teresa came dancing into the kitchen . . .

That was a dull December afternoon in 1941; perhaps, Anna and Jerzy had thought, Tata would be home with them for Christmas.

A spring morning in 1943; walking to work in the hospital alongside the ghetto; hearing the newsboy calling on a corner of the Square. *Mass grave found by the Germans in Katyń Forest . . . thousands of Polish officers murdered by the Russians . . .* Later, among the long long lists of the dead, her father's name.

To this day, the Russians insisted that the murders were the work of the Germans, committed when they advanced into Russia in 1941, but all the evidence – the diaries of the murdered men, stopping abruptly, the pathologists' reports, the freshly planted young pines above the graves – pointed to the Russians: deliberately, in April 1940, removing over four thousand intellectuals who might have resisted the imposition of a communist puppet government after the war. Tata, who had been held in the camp at Kozielsk, from where he had sent his only postcard, was found at Katyń; the other ten thousand, from Starobielsk and Ostaszków camps, had never been found, but there was every reason to suppose that they too, for the same reason, had died at the hands of the Russians, and the monument was to their memory, also.

In the last few months, *Dziennik Polski* and the British press had contained stories of the furious protests from the Russian and Polish Soviet embassies against the erection of the memorial; there had been problems over finding a site; not a single representative from the British Government was here to attend the ceremony.

Anna touched Jerzy's arm; he looked down at her.

'Mmm? All right?'

'Yes. Can you hold the wreath for a moment . . .'

He took it and she opened her handbag, feeling for the plain white card, and the pin. Then Jerzy held the wreath steady as she carefully fixed it on. So much she could have written, and wanted to write, but in the end she had last night put only two words: *Dla Ojca* – For my father.

Eleven o'clock. From beyond the gates came the steady drone of cars and lorries travelling west; an aeroplane climbed the sky. There was a ripple through the crowd, then a small party, including the President of the Government in exile, slowly mounted the shallow white steps, and Anna and Jerzy, Ewa and Jan, Dziadek and Babcia joined with the hundreds of voices singing: *'Jeszcze Polska nie zgineła . . .'*

'Poland is not yet lost

As long as we are alive . . .'

As the last words died away, the Chairman of the Katyń Memorial Fund, Lord Barnby, stepped up to the microphone.

'This ceremony we are assisting at today will become historic,' he said slowly. 'First because it records a victory for truth . . . Secondly, because it establishes a shrine which will offer comfort to the remaining relatives of the victims. But even more than that, a shrine to which future generations of Polish sympathizers may resort, from wherever they may come . . .'

At the end of Lord Barnby's speech, President Ostrowski stepped up to take the microphone. He was a short, white-haired man in glasses; like most of the others on the steps, and like Dziadek and many of the men in the crowd, he wore a heavy dark winter coat.

'As President of the Polish Republic,' he announced, 'I solemnly accept in the name of the Polish people the ownership and custody of this monument, commemorating an inhuman crime committed against the Polish nation during the Second World War.

'I express my profound thanks first and foremost to Lord Barnby, Chairman of the Katyń Memorial Fund, to the members of his committee and to all those who, moved by a sense of justice and humanity, have made it their business to remind the world that the crime of Katyń still awaits judgement . . .'

When the applause had died away, the last speech was made, by Lord St Oswald.

'Let it be known that from this hour forward, this hallowed plot of British soil, once it has been consecrated by Bishop Rubin, Delegate of the Cardinal Primate of Poland, will be for all time one of the most sacred, one of the most honoured and one of the most significant points in the whole land heritage of the British Isles . . . This monument is a beacon . . . very specifically a Polish beacon, pointing upward, to the better, aspiring future for which Poles have fought and striven so heroically through the centuries . . . The barbed wire encircling the Polish Eagle, wrought into the design, symbolizes only the present status, behind the Iron Curtain, of this nation, from whose intrepid example we have so much of value to learn. One day that cruel, criminal wire will be dismantled . . .

'This simple obelisk commemorates, at face value, the brutal extermination of thousands of brave, irreplaceable human lives, of men who were the leaven of leadership of their nation, and who were killed deliberately on that single premise. We stand in poignant awareness that among us today are some who loved and venerated individual victims of that crime. They have been granted no other accurate or fitting cenotaph, until today.'

Anna felt Jerzy's arm slip lightly round her shoulders; then he at once removed it, as if embarrassed, or perhaps simply because he did not wish to intrude. She listened as the speech continued, a powerful piece of rhetoric which somehow both dignified the terrible way in which her father had died and made her own connection with him seem very small and far away.

'There are some English words, perhaps too commonly quoted for so imcomparable an occasion. They were written by a young English poet, shortly before he was killed in battle in the First World War. "If I should die, think only this of me, there is some corner of a foreign field that is for ever England." By proxy, across many thousands of miles from the place of violent death, but soon to be enshrined by Bishop Rubin, the corner to which we have all been drawn today will be for ever Poland . . .

'We are not here only to mourn those Poles who died, defenceless and still defiant. We are here to celebrate the invincibility of that spirit of Poland for whom they died. This is not simply a memorial to the dead past. It is a pledge to the living future.'

But do we really have a living future, wondered Anna, as he stepped aside, to wave after wave of applause. Where is the spirit of Poland now?

Three people were mounting the steps: two other members of the Memorial Fund Committee, and a woman, widow of one of the men who had died at Katyń. There was a roll on a drum, played by a Polish Boy Scout, and then the whole crowd was silent, and Anna forgot to think or question as the shroud of flags fell away and the black granite obelisk was revealed. In the centre was engraved the Polish white eagle, encircled by barbed wire. Beneath, in gold, was the single word: Katyń, and the date: 1940. There was an inscription in gold on the plinth, but from where she stood Anna could not read it.

The memorial was blessed and consecrated; the hundreds of voices rose again:

'Oh God who for centuries has watched over Poland

Before your altar we beg you:

Return a free homeland to us!'

In the press of people all around her, Anna felt herself begin to sway. Beyond the tall black column she could see a sunlit courtyard, hear another open-air congregation singing the same hymn but with a different ending; she was standing in a Warsaw street reclaimed from the enemy, in a free Poland! And outside the courtyard gate, two young boys were waiting for her, white-faced and ill-at-ease:

'*Is Anna Kurowska here?*'

'Jerzy . . . Jerzy!'

'Mama . . . Mama . . . Don't cry . . .' His arm was round her; she leaned against him, then blew her nose, and looked up – at Jerzy, then at the rest of the family; Ewa, watching her anxiously, streaks of mascara all down her face; Jan, nodding to her as if to a stranger, but trying, she supposed, to convey that he understood; Dziadek and Babcia very grave and still. A long procession of dignitaries was climbing the steps to set their wreaths at the base of the black plinth: flowers on behalf of the Polish Armed Forces abroad; of all former prisoners of the USSR; of Polish youth; of the World Federation of Polish Ex-Combatants; of the Anglo-Polish Society . . .

'Look,' said Jerzy suddenly. 'Isn't that Churchill's grandson?'

Anna peered. The column moved on: wreaths from the Czechs, the Ukranians, Lithuanians, Hungarians; from the Russian Human Rights Movement . . . When the last of the official flowers had been laid, two Highland pipers walked slowly round, playing a lament, and Anna moved forward, joining a long, silent line of people waiting to lay their own tributes.

At the top of the steps she stopped to read the inscription, half covered now by the heaps of flowers:

Sumienie Świata Woła o Świadectwo Prawdzie
Calling on the Conscience of the World for the Truth
In Remembrance
Of 14,500 Polish prisoners of war who disappeared in 1940 from camps at Kozielsk, Starobielsk and Ostaszków, of whom 4,500 were later identified in mass graves at Katyń near Smoleńsk

Anna set down her circle of white and red carnations with the card: *Dla Ojca*, For my father, and stood for a moment, her head bowed. A flash of memory. Not of the grey morning when he said goodbye, and she and Jerzy had seen him for the last time, but of the three of them, camped in a riverside wood of birch trees, enclosed within their tent; the paraffin lamp glowed yellow, making the moths and insects bump against the canvas, as he read to them the story of the old, exiled Pole, standing on the balcony of the lighthouse where he had come to rest, watching the cone of light flung out across the blackness of the sea.

Then she came down the steps and was on the damp gravel path again; a few moments later, as she rejoined her family, two trumpeters sounded the Last Post, and the Reveille.

Ewa and Jerzy walked along the paths at the side of the cemetery. The grass on the verges grew higher here; daisies and dandelion clocks stood between the tombstones. From this perspective, the tower block on the road behind the chestnut trees dominated the sky: during the ceremony they had barely noticed it. A flyover soared between the other trees bordering the ground; invisible cars flew past.

They were looking for the grave of Bór-Komorowski, leader of the Warsaw Uprising. Their feet sounded lightly on the scattered stones along the path.

'Poor Mama,' said Ewa. 'My God, I cried. I didn't think I was going to.'

'No,' said Jerzy. 'Nor did I.' He wandered over to a group of gravestones, raised his camera then lowered it again. 'It must be here somewhere.'

It was mid-afternoon, the cemetery almost deserted except for a man in overalls raking the grass on the far side, and an old couple in black, walking arm in arm past the graves beyond the memorial. After the ceremony, the family had all gone out to lunch; then Anna and Jan went home on the train from Gunnersbury, with the grandparents.

'Come with us,' Anna said, but Jerzy wanted to go back and take more photographs of the cemetery when everyone had left, and Ewa said she'd go with him, since she didn't see much of him these days. Perhaps they would both go home tomorrow.

'Here it is,' said Jerzy suddenly, and they stopped, by a flat dark square of granite, lying on the ground at the edge of the path, surrounded by a nest of Polish graves. The granite was bordered by four short lengths of grey stone, and the whole grave was slightly slanted, tipping over towards the left where the earth must have sunk a little beneath its weight.

Gen. Dywizji Tadeusz Bór-Komorowski
1.6.1895 – 24.8.1966
Dowódca Armii Krajowej Naczelny Polskich Sił Zbrojnych
Leader of the Home Army, Commander-in-Chief of the Polish Armed Forces

Ewa stood by the ragged grass bordering the path, and looked down at the inscription. Ten years ago, she and Jerzy had come to the cemetery with their Guide and Scout troops to attend Komorowski's funeral: a hot, late-summer day of which she could recall little except the fact of their presence, the crowds, the sombre faces and the flags. Now she thought of what she had since learned about the Uprising, directed from beleaguered outposts of the city by this man: of the books she had read, the stories her mother had told her. Bór's widow must have been at the funeral – Ewa thought she remembered her, but perhaps it was imagination which placed her at the graveside, a figure in black supported by her sons. Two years later she was buried beside her husband.

Irene Lamezar-Salins Tadeuszowa Komorowska

309

14.5.1905 – 22.10.1968
Żołnierz Armii Krajowej
Soldier of the Home Army

Soldier of the Home Army – Irene had been separated from her husband during the sixty-three days of the Uprising; their first son, Adam, was still a toddler, and she eight months pregnant on the night when she and her maid were given ten minutes to get out of their house before it was set on fire. They ran through the burning streets of Warsaw, taking it in turns to carry the child, ordered on by SS men over fallen barricades and dead bodies. 'I was afraid that it would probably end with the firing squad. I cannot say I felt any fear for myself. I thought of you, that when you were told of the plight of the civilians it might break your heart. However, I kept faith in your inflexibility . . .'

It had not ended with the firing squad. She had written that letter to him after the war, and in the autumn of 1945 they were reunited in London. Now they lay here together, and in a corner of the granite was a small raised circle of glass, engraved with the symbol of the Rising: PW, forming an anchor: ⚓ : *Polska Walcząca*. Fighting Poland.

'What's underneath?' Ewa asked, and they bent down. Sealed beneath was a brown leather pouch, and a scroll of paper. On the mildewed metal encircling the glass was another inscription:

Ziemia Polska z Terenów Walk Armii Krajowej – Polish earth from the battlefields of the Home Army.

Traffic roared on the arc of the flyover beyond the trees. Ewa and Jerzy knelt by the gravestones, lightly touching the circle of letters.

'I'd forgotten about this,' said Ewa.

'Perhaps we didn't see it on the day,' said Jerzy. 'Or perhaps it wasn't here then. I can't remember much.'

'Nor me. Too many people.'

'Yes.' Jerzy straightened up, walked a few steps across the path and raised his camera. 'Stay there. No, don't look at me.'

She looked at the pouch of Polish earth, and heard the camera click. Then she got up, and they walked together along the path, and round the circle at the end until they were standing once more at the foot of the white steps of the memorial. Scores of wreaths lay against the plinth; the afternoon air was full of the scent of roses and carnations. Birds sang from the chestnut trees and then a lawnmower started up, somewhere in the grassy stretch on the far side of the cemetery, where no graves had yet been dug.

Jerzy slowly climbed the steps and took one more photograph: the white and crimson flowers reflected with the sky in the last pools of water. Then he came down, and Ewa slipped her arm through his.

'You don't come home any more,' she said.

'Yes I do.'

'Not often.'

They paced beneath the trees.

'Babcia and Dziadek miss you terribly,' she said. 'All the time you were away at university they looked forward to the holidays, and now you're back in London and they still hardly see you.'

'It used to be you,' said Jerzy. 'Avoiding them.'

'I know. I suppose I don't want to any more.'

'You don't need to avoid them – you're at home with yourself.'

Am I? thought Ewa. Aloud she said: 'Not really.'

'But you're established, settled – look at you: you have a career, your own flat, you have English friends . . .'

Ewa laughed. 'If I have English friends, I must be all right.' She thought of her desk by the window in the translation agency behind Oxford Street, the desk at the window of her beautiful Blackheath flat, and of the journey made each day between the piles of papers, books and dictionaries, leaving alone and coming alone.

'You have a life that has nothing to do with the family,' Jerzy was saying. 'You can go home to them as your own person.'

The lawnmower went back and forth, back and forth; they could smell faint petrol fumes and grass.

'And what about you?' she asked. 'Don't you have a life?'

He smiled down at her, and she said: 'You're very good-looking now, you know. And clever. Your photographs are wonderful. I wish you were happy.'

'I'm all right. The photographs are my life – I never thought they would be; they just slid into the centre and stayed there.'

'I once thought perhaps you'd be a priest.'

Jerzy was silent. Then he said: 'I don't believe any more.'

'Is that why you're unhappy?'

'I don't know.'

It was growing cold, the air no longer filled with the scent of flowers or grass but the dampness of an early autumn evening. The lawnmower stopped; above the trees the sky was streaked with darkness. They walked up the long path to the gates.

Afterwards, they went their separate ways, parting when the main-line train from Gunnersbury stopped at Hammersmith. Ewa went to catch the tube to Charing Cross, and then the train to Blackheath, and her attic flat; Jerzy stayed on the train, watching the surburban gardens alongside the track grow dark, and fill with squares of light from back kitchens, upper windows. At Hampstead Heath he got off and walked slowly up the hill, a busy road, with Saturday night traffic speeding past him, and the pubs full of people. He moved off the pavement, and up the slope of the grass a little way, then did the rest of the walk on the heath itself, past the trees. Near the top, he crossed the road, feeling in his pocket for the keys to the front door of a large shabby house divided into many flats; inside, he climbed the stone stairs to the last door at the top, and let himself in.

Inside, he could hear his landlady's television, and her children playing; Jerzy did not know how long they had lived there, or even if the flat was theirs, but she and her husband let off rooms in the attic. The stairs were carpeted in worn yellow and mauve flowers; he went up, past the family's living room, and the other tenant's room, past the shared bathroom, up the last flight to the top landing. There was a kitchen here, six by six with sink and gas stove, which overlooked half London; as he filled the kettle and put it on the stove, he could see the Post Office Tower, winking in the distance.

Across the landing was the little room he used as a darkroom; at the end was his bedroom. He let himself in, switched on the light, and put his camera down on the bed. It lay beneath the sloping eave; on the other side of the room was a desk, set into a corner, with a lamp; the floor was bare boards, with a rug Ewa had bought him from Heal's; the window at the far end overlooked the heath, and his armchair was there, with low bookshelves along the wall. When the kettle boiled, he made a cup of coffee, then came back; it began to rain, and he opened the window at the bottom and sat in the armchair listening to it fall, pattering, on to the roof, on to the trees on the heath across the road; a car swished down the hill, parting the slanting fall with the headlamps' beams. Jerzy lay back against the armchair and closed his eyes. He found himself thinking of lines from an English poet he'd read at university – not Rupert Brooke, quoted this morning, but another who had died in the First World War:

Rain, midnight rain, nothing but the wild rain
On this bleak hut, and solitude, and me
Remembering again that I shall die

And neither hear the rain nor give it thanks
For washing me cleaner than I have been
Since I was born into this solitude.
Blessed are the dead that the rain rains upon . . .

Dziadez, not the Dziadek he knew, but the one he would never
know, had been rained upon in a mass grave; somewhere in Warsaw
was the grave of Jerzy's namesake, unvisited.

> . . . here I pray that none whom once I loved
> Is dying tonight or lying still awake
> Solitary, listening to the rain,
> Either in pain or thus in sympathy
> Helpless among the living and the dead,
> Like a cold water among broken reeds,
> Myriads of broken reeds all still and stiff,
> Like me who have no love which this wild rain
> Has not dissolved except the love of death,
> If love it be for what is perfect and
> Cannot, the tempest tells me, disappoint.

Was he in love with death? Or with the image of those in his family
who had had something to die for? From the switch on the skirting
board, Jerzy turned off the lamp. He sat in the darkness, listening.

1977

The people in the house changed from time to time. Jerzy had come
here three years ago, by chance: a summer walk across the heath,
with university behind him, and bewilderment as to what he might
do once his results came through; a coffee afterwards on South End
Green, and a browse through advertisements in a shop window.
Rooms to let, a call from a phone box, an Irish voice answering, and
he was up the hill again to view them, just vacated by a visiting
American writer. He had taken them at once.

He moved in, put his books in the low bookshelves; he pinned
black and white photographs on the walls: steam engines puffing
through sunlit valleys, the shadows of clouds drifting over the hills;
the railway line behind the house in Clapham empty at night, the
light of a distant train approaching. Mama sewing at the table, Tata
with his back to her, looking out on to wet slate rooftops; Ewa
reading, watched by Dziadek; Babcia gardening on the balcony above
the track, Burek panting beside her – that was the last picture before

he died. Next to them Jerzy pinned the photographs he had inherited: from the war, from before the war, all the pictures which had watched over his childhood, and it came to him then, with the simplicity of a gift, that he was meant to go on doing this.

When his results came, he found he had a very good degree in geography and geology, but by then it did not matter. He had found a part-time job in a commercial photographer's studio off the Finchley Road, two stops away on the overground train. Three days a week he retouched transparencies of magazine cover girls, sold to *Honey*, or *Cosmopolitan;* he helped to light still-lifes of Christmas trees and candles, and chocolate-box photographs of kittens and baskets of flowers. The rest of the time he spent behind his own camera, or in the darkroom: the American writer had kept her clothes in here, but he put up shelves for developing fluid and trays, and for boxes of negatives, and bought a third-hand enlarger through an advertisement in the *Ham and High*. He stayed up late into the night, watching the day's prints sharpen into focus from the blur beneath the water. Halfway down the stairs, he could hear the other tenant cough, and the chink of bottles.

The other tenant was a nameless man in his fifties, who did not work and rarely spoke. Occasionally he left his door half open, when he went to the bathroom, or to see if his giro had come; Jerzy glimpsed row upon row of washed milk bottles, half filled with water, all round the room. He had speculated on this, but found no answer. Sometimes a woman came to stay, younger, but with puffy eyes, and they quarrelled violently; when she and Jerzy met on the stairs she smiled as if nothing had happened.

It was a house of people passing each other in doorways, or on the flight of stone steps that ran all the way down it. The walls on the stairway were cold plaster, divided by a dado into dark green at the bottom and dingy cream at the top, like school walls, where fingerprints were not allowed to show. There were at least three other flats before you reached the bottom, and the opening and closing doors, and the feet on the steps echoed up and down all through the house. Outside, there was an area of cracked paving, and then another short flight of steps, descending behind a low wall to a rambling basement: it was here that the tenants changed most often, in and out of the single rooms. Since Jerzy's arrival he had nodded to an assortment of Irishmen living alone, to students and summer tourists, to couples looking for somewhere permanent. They came for a while and went when they had found something better: it was damp down there.

At the back of the house was a large untended garden. Neglected apple trees bore tiny wrinkled fruit which dropped into the long grass; the beds were full of stones and a tangle of self-seeded wallflowers, forget-me-nots, hollyhocks and foxgloves, half-choked by a convolvulus which crept all over the broken fence, by dandelions and groundsel. At the back of the garden was a row of garages; they were rented by people who did not live here, who crunched along the flint path to take out their cars. Amidst all the money in Hampstead, the boutiques and restaurants, the film stars' and rich writers' homes, the shabby tenanted house was an anachronism, a reminder.

It was late September. The leaves of the trees along the Vale of Health, and all across the heath, were turning to yellow and russet; in the misty morning air a few swirled gently on to the grass. Jerzy's landlady took the children to school and swept up the piles which had begun to drift over the road, and up round the doorway. On a day when Jerzy did not have to go to the studio he walked into the village for milk and the paper, and when he came back he stopped to watch her.

'Nice morning.' She poked the broom into a corner by the drainpipe, and brushed out summer dust. A long line of commuters' cars moved slowly down the hill.

'Very,' he said, and felt the sun on the back of his neck. 'I think it's going to turn out hot again.'

'Do you now? After this summer we'll all be glad of a drop more rain. Wouldn't you say so?'

'Mmm.' He scanned the headlines, then looked up as the door of the basement banged shut and a girl he hadn't seen down there before came up the steps. She nodded to the landlady, and glanced at Jerzy, in his jeans and T-shirt, leaning against the wall with the paper and carton of milk.

'Good morning. Lovely day.'

'Isn't it now?' The landlady swept leaves and dust and cobwebs into a heap. 'That's it. Better get the dustpan.' She pushed open the front door and went inside.

Jerzy put down his paper. 'Have you just moved in?'

The girl nodded. 'Two days ago. Do you live . . .'

'In the attic.'

'Oh.' She looked at her watch. 'I must go. I expect I'll see you . . .'

'Yes.' He stepped back a little, although she was already on the pavement and there was no need for him to move. He watched her walk up the hill towards the main road leading into the village: she was slender and fair; she wore faded jeans, and a loose shirt, with a sweater across her shoulders, and espadrilles. She carried some kind of home-made cotton shoulder bag and her walk was graceful.

The landlady came out with her dustpan and brush; she bent down to sweep up the pile. 'There now, that's one job done for the day.' She straightened up, and looked at Jerzy, looking at the girl. 'And what might you be thinking about?'

He laughed, and followed her into the house.

He saw the girl again, several times over the next couple of weeks. She came up the basement steps as he left for work, and they said hello, or remarked on the weather, before she went up the hill and he went down, to catch the main-line train to Finchley Road. Once he saw her ahead of him, going down, and wanted to catch up with her, but felt it too important a conversation to get wrong, and was sure that he would. He thought he might see her again on the station platform, but he got there just as a northbound train pulled out, and didn't know whether or not she was on it. He crossed the bridge to the southbound platform, and walked irritably up and down amongst the other commuters.

On a Friday he came back from the studio tired. The evenings were drawing in; when he reached the house he saw the light from her window glow behind drawn curtains. He stood at the top of the steps, hesitating, then went down; he was about to ring the doorbell when he heard voices from inside. He climbed the steps again, and went up to the attic. He telephoned Ewa on the landlady's phone, but she was out.

On Saturday he went to an exhibition at the Serpentine, and then rang Ewa again, and met her for a drink. He wanted to tell her about the girl downstairs, but he didn't. When he came back to the house again it was dark; he walked from the tube station in the village through the quiet expensive side streets, hearing the church clock strike nine. He came out on the main road and looked to see if there was a light in her window, but there wasn't. Later, reading in his armchair at the window, he found himself listening to the footsteps on the pavement below, waiting to hear someone stop, go down the basement steps, and open the door. It grew late, and the only sounds were the landlady's television, the traffic on the hill, and the voices of strangers in the street. He went to bed, and turned the light off. Just as he drifted into sleep he thought he heard a door bang to, but it could have been anywhere.

On Sunday morning when he woke he lay for a while in the whiteness of the room, enjoying the quiet of early morning, pale sunshine washing the walls and the bare floorboards, the misty tops of the trees just visible from where he lay, beyond the uncurtained window. There were no cars, no television, no voices, only the birds. He turned over. From below came the sound of the basement door, opening and being closed. Light footsteps came up the steps, and went over the road to the heath.

Jerzy got out of bed and crossed the room. Naked, he crouched at the window and looked out. The girl was walking over the wet grass; she wore jeans and a greeny-grey cardigan over a cotton shirt; her shoulder bag bumped against her as she broke into a run. There were one or two people out walking their dogs, but apart from them the heath was empty. Jerzy watched until the girl had disappeared down the slope of the Vale of Health, then he pulled on Dziadek's old dressing gown, put the kettle on in the kitchen and went down the creaking stairs to run a bath.

Afterwards, he dressed and had a cup of coffee, and wrote a note. He went down the stone stairs and slipped it through the door to the basement; he walked down the hill for the Sunday papers and bought croissants as well, from the café just opening. He walked up the hill again, as the sun rose and the mist cleared, pausing every now and then to look at the headlines, trying to ignore the churning mixture of excitement and nervousness in his stomach.

When he was near the top he saw the girl sitting on the low wall before the house, waiting for him.

In the years that followed, Jerzy returned many times to this moment; even now, as he slowed, and drew closer, he knew that his life had already changed, in a way it had always been meant to change, so that excitement and nervousness, even desire, all fell away, and it felt simply and uncomplicatedly right that he should stop, and look down at her without speaking, and that she should smile, as if they were greeting each other after only the briefest absence.

They sat on a rug in the tangled garden, under the apple trees.

'Elizabeth,' said Jerzy. 'Elżbieta . . .'

'Jerzy,' she said. 'Yer-jeh – does that sound right?'

'Very nearly.'

'And in English it's what?'

'George.' He pulled a face.

'I prefer Jerzy.'

'And I Elizabeth.'

They looked at each other, and then away. From above, the curtains of a window at the back of the house were pulled aside, and the bottom half raised a little. They saw a figure, looking down on them, and then it moved away into the room, and they could hear a drawer pulled open, a cat meow, the rattle of cutlery.

'Who's that?' asked Elizabeth.

'I don't know.' He leaned back on his elbows, looking up and trying to work it out. Perhaps there were two flats on the second floor. 'I think it's the old woman and her husband who were here when I moved in. I don't know everyone.' He told her about the man who lived in the attic, sharing the kitchen and bathroom, about the milk bottles, and the woman who came to stay.

'Have you been down to the basement?'

He shook his head. 'Just to let the gasman in once, when the landlady was ill. Not into any of the rooms. I see people coming in and out, that's all.'

He had waited at the top of the steps while she went down to fetch the rug, a worn red tartan. Sunlight flickered on to it through the apple trees, and a fragile garden spider crawled across the corner, towards her feet. He broke off a dandelion leaf and placed it on the rug, so that the spider moved on to it; then he stretched out, and put leaf and spider among the long grass.

Elizabeth watched him. 'The action of a Buddhist.'

'Lapsed Catholic,' said Jerzy. He turned to look at her again. She had a clear skin and wore no make-up; silky hair brushed the soft white cotton of her shirt collar, above the greys and greens of the Fair Isle cardigan. He wanted to stroke her face, her hair, her mouth.

'Is that important?' she asked.

'What?'

'Being lapsed.'

'Possibly.' He gestured to the brown paper bag of croissants, lightly patched with grease marks. 'I asked you to have breakfast with me – shall I bring a tray down here?'

'Isn't that a bother?'

'No, I want to. Perhaps you'd like to read the papers.'

'All right, perhaps I would.' She smiled at him as he got up.

He went round to the front of the house on the flint path, and out on to the pavement, looking down at her half-open casement window. The curtains were drawn back, and moved a little in the breeze, but the interior was too dark for him to see anything.

318 ·

'Jerzy! You forgot the croissants . . .' She held out the paper bag. 'Sorry – but were you going to warm them?'

'Warm them. Yes. Yes – thank you.' He took the bag and went up to the front door; when he reached his attic kitchen he was not aware of having climbed the stairs, and he stood for a moment, looking out on to a view which was somehow completely different. Then he filled the kettle, lit the gas and from the floor beside the cupboard took the tray Babcia had given him when he came here: plain wood she had hand-painted in the pattern of one of her *kilims*. It must have taken days. One corner had been spoilt the first week he moved in and put a saucepan on it, straight off the stove, leaving a charred circle. He put a plate over it now, lit the oven, put the croissants inside and laid the tray with cups and saucers, a dish of butter, knives, marmalade. Down the stairs he heard the landlady's children thumping about in their room, and her husband shout; there was no sound from the man with the bottles of water.

Jerzy warmed a pan of milk and made coffee in the blue enamel pot; he went into his room and stood in the coolness, looking at the photographs on the white walls, framed and unframed, and the empty armchair. He thought of her sitting in it, curled up in the light from the lamp on the floor, listening to music; he tried to see it all as she might see it, if she came up here. Then he went back to the kitchen, put the croissants on the tray, covered with a tea towel, and carefully carried it downstairs. As he reached the door to the flat he saw his landlady, eyeing him speculatively from her kitchen doorway; he smiled at her, not caring what she thought, and almost tripped, sending the whole lot flying.

Outside, Elizabeth was lying on her stomach on the rug, the papers spread out, her feet in the air. She looked up and watched him come crunching along the path; he moved on to the grass, and set down the tray beside her.

'All right?' He took off the tea towel.

'Fine.' She sat up and moved the papers aside, bent over the tray and sniffed. 'Thank you.'

He poured out coffee, passed her a plate, and they ate in silence, feeling the sun grow warmer, listening to people in other flats above them, and in the neighbouring houses, open windows, turn on radios, run baths. After a while, the church bells began to ring.

'More coffee?'

'Please.'

He poured it, then asked: 'What are you doing here?'

319

'I thought it was time I lived by myself – I never have.'

'And I have never lived with anyone,' said Jerzy. 'Except my family.'

'Where are they?'

'South London. Clapham.'

He tried to imagine her there, and could not.

'Where are you from?'

'Northamptonshire,' said Elizabeth. 'Do you know it?'

'I've been through, on train journeys . . .' He pictured a large house, cool and quiet, rain dripping from tall trees on to lawns and bushes. Elizabeth, in a pale dress, was moving about inside; he watched her from the garden, but did not open the door.

'And . . . are you working?'

'I'm a painter.'

'Are you?' he said. 'You don't paint in the basement . . .'

'No. I rent a studio in a house in Gospel Oak – very convenient, I can walk, or catch the bus from South End Green. I don't like working and living in the same place. Anyway, I can't afford to go there every day – half the week I'm a secretary. That's when I go up the hill – to catch the tube to work.'

'Oh. And what do you paint?'

'People. Interiors. Ordinary things.' She finished her coffee. 'Come and see them one day, if you like.'

'I would like to. My mother paints. Well – a little.' He told her about the hospital, and Anna's work there.

'She and your father came here after the war?'

'Yes. And my grandparents.' He stacked the plates on the tray. 'My grandmother painted this.'

'Did she? I was thinking how unusual it was. And what do you do?'

'I take photographs. I have a part-time job, like you.'

'What sort of photographs?'

'People – I used to take my family, mostly. And trains . . .'

He stood up, lifting the tray, feeling some kind of curtain move slowly across, separating her from him, and the sense of ease evaporated. He tried to imagine her paintings, saw lightness and colour. How could he ever explain himself, his childhood?

Abruptly, he said: 'I'm not very good with people, I'm afraid.'

For a moment Elizabeth looked disconcerted. Then she said: 'People at ease in the world don't much interest me.'

*

And believed she meant it. They went for a long walk over the heath: past the ponds, where a few people swam among the ducks, and feathers nudged the reeds; down the long avenue carpeted with yellow leaves to the hill where families flew kites. They stood for a while, watching. It was warm, lazy weather, the very last of summer, but with enough wind to keep the kites aloft; they sailed past distant thick white clouds, and the children bobbed up and down.

Elizabeth looked at Jerzy, watching them. He had a rather thin face, with a high, clear forehead; the wind lifted his hair. His eyes were a greeny-grey, and deep-set; his features had a cast which she supposed was Slavic: she was trained to look at faces intently – the first time she had seen him, talking to the landlady, outside the house, she had thought he might not be English. What was he thinking about?

He turned and saw her looking at him. 'Shall we go?'

'All right.'

She had brought a plastic box for blackberries, and they moved down on to a sheltered grassy path banked with dense bushes and brambles. They picked for a while without talking. Clouds of midges drifted across the path in the afternoon sunlight; occasionally someone went past with a dog, or children ran by, shouting. The shadows on the path began to lengthen; beyond the bushes they could hear parents calling: 'Time to go home!' Their fingers were scratched and stained purple.

Elizabeth stopped picking and carefully eased herself down from the bank, holding the box. She stood watching Jerzy again, reaching up towards a thorny tendril; his expression was as full of concentration as if he were reading, and she wasn't even sure if he'd noticed she was no longer near him. She did not try to explain to herself why to look at him felt so satisfying: she felt simply as if for a long time she had been waiting for a space within herself to be occupied, and now it was. There was a sense of knowing him and of not yet knowing: a strange, exciting sense, too, that she would not fully know herself until he began to do so.

'Jerzy?'

He looked at her, and jumped down.

'Here.' He dropped a handful of blackberries into the box, reached out and brushed a strand of hair from her face. She closed her eyes, felt him run a finger over her lips.

'Are you all right?' he asked.

'Yes.'

321

'Shall we go home?'

'Yes.'

They walked back over the heath, their arms around each other. At the house, they stopped before the stretch of cracked paving leading to the front door, by the low wall and the steps, leading down to the basement. Jerzy looked down at her and raised an eyebrow.

'Your place or mine?'

They smiled at each other. 'I think my place is a winter place,' said Elizabeth. 'It's dark, and there's a fireplace.'

'Come upstairs, then,' said Jerzy.

'And see your photographs?'

'And see my photographs.'

She followed him up the cold stone stairs past different doorways. At the last one, painted white, he took a key from his pocket and let them in. They climbed the stairs, carpeted in mauve and yellow flowers, and up past more doors – 'That's where the bottles are,' Jerzy hissed – to the very top, where a landing held a tiny kitchen. At the end was another door. He unlocked it, and held it open: Elizabeth saw whiteness, and early evening sun pouring on to bare boards from an uncurtained window.

'It's beautiful . . .'

'I know.' Jerzy came in behind her, and she heard him close the door and follow her as she went to the window and looked out, over the road towards the trees and the heath, where other people were making their way home. There was a large armchair by the window, with a bedspread flung over it as a cover. She moved to sit down in it, but Jerzy took her hand and turned her towards him. They stood, face to face but suddenly hardly able to look at each other. Somewhere in the house a door banged shut; voices sounded from beyond the trees.

He drew her a little into the room, and then they did look at each other, and this time could not look away. Jerzy put his hand behind her head, and stroked her hair; with his other hand he slowly traced the outline of her lips. Elizabeth put her arms round his waist; they stood motionless, hardly breathing; then they undressed each other, very slowly, and stood naked, running their hands everywhere, until Jerzy picked her up and carried her, over to the bed beneath the eave.

She sat in the armchair at the window, wearing his dressing gown, looking at the photographs. Jerzy was kneeling on the bare boards by the lamp, passing black and white prints to her one by one; those she had seen were piled in the lid of the cardboard box on the floor. There was a series of the landlady's children, sprawled on a leatherette sofa watching television; doing their homework at the table while their mother ironed. There was another, of the North London railway line: the station at Hampstead Heath on a late summer evening, a single passenger waiting for a train, walking away from the camera towards the end of the platform, the track stretching ahead between tall banks of ferns and weeds and lupins; the architecture of wires and pylons beyond Camden Road; a black ticket collector at Willesden Junction sitting in his box at night, lit by the ticket office beyond; Hampstead Heath again, but in winter, the banks covered in snow, and early morning passengers pacing, their breath hanging on the air in clouds.

And now there was something else. Elizabeth sat looking at a photograph of crowds of people in a cemetery, at a woman in black standing at the foot of a tall black column, whose steps were piled with wreaths. Her head was bent, her eyes closed; above her on the column was a single word and a date: Katyń, 1940.

'Who's that?'

'My mother.'

'And Katyń?'

'You don't know about Katyń?'

'I don't think so,' said Elizabeth. 'Something in the war?'

'Yes,' said Jerzy. 'It was something in the war.'

1978

The first snow had fallen on the heath, and it was very cold. Jerzy and Elizabeth spent winter weekends walking under the bare trees, watching the wind whip the surface of the ponds and a scattering of yellow leaves swirl in the water. Canada geese swept honking across a grey sky; ducks huddled beneath the bushes at the water's edge.

'Tell me about your family,' said Elizabeth.

'Tell me about yours.'

'It's ordinary.'

'So is mine.'

'Tell me anyway.'

'You'll meet them one day.'

'When?'

'One day.'

The ponds iced over, and warning notices went up; people threw

323

bread on the ice and the ducks waddled awkwardly over, sliding and squabbling.

'I have a sister,' said Elizabeth, 'older than me, married, with a little girl. They live in Northamptonshire, near my parents, who are retired. Our childhood was calm and happy. My father was a bank manager and my mother a teacher. My sister teaches too, and her husband is a surveyor. I have a feeling she is restless.'

Jerzy laughed, 'I have an older sister, also. She lives in Blackheath, and works for a translation agency. She is not married, but – she is rather beautiful, and clever.'

'Like you,' said Elizabeth, kissing his jacket. 'And how many lovers have you had?'

'Hundreds.'

'How many?'

'A few, at university. Enough to know that none of them were right. The right one is here, beside me.'

'Thank you. Me too.'

Lights in the houses on the heath went on early; they went home for tea in her room, lit the fire and made toast. The room was quite a good size, with wooden cupboards and shelves on either side of the fireplace; there was an armchair, a table at the window, beneath the passing feet, a lumpy single bed. They grew used to sleeping without enough space, curled round each other, down here or up in the attic. Elizabeth kept her clothes on a rail; they grew damp, and she put them in plastic bags in a drawer under the bed. They did not talk about moving, so that some of these inconveniences could be solved, and they had spent Christmas separately, with their own families.

It snowed again, thickly, and the paths over the heath were criss-crossed with footprints and bird tracks. Children shrieked down the hills on toboggans, hungry rooks cawed from bare white branches. Jerzy and Elizabeth walked through the woods to a stone bridge across a stream, where few other people came, and scattered bread and bacon fat for starlings and robins and blackbirds. Jerzy took photographs: Elizabeth with the hood of her jacket up, feeding the birds, walking towards him, away from him, smiling, serious, reaching up to bend and release a low branch and send a spray of snow flying over them both. She borrowed the camera and took pictures of him, leaning over the bridge, walking under the trees with his hands in his pockets, laughing as she pulled a face behind the camera. There were none of them together.

'Tell me,' Elizabeth said again. 'What are you so afraid of?'

'I'm not afraid.'

'You are. You think I won't understand anything.'

'Why should you have to?'

'Because I love you,' said Elizabeth. There was a silence. 'Do you love me?'

'You know I do.'

'Why don't you say so?'

He shook his head. 'I've never said it to anyone.'

'Why should that stop you saying it to me?'

'I'm sorry. I will one day.'

'When?'

'One day.'

They walked on, through the white silent woods. Every now and then there was a sudden fall of snow, from a branch or a rhododendron bush; pigeons clattered over the treetops; a crow called, throaty and hoarse.

Jerzy said: 'I've met other Poles, born here, who find it difficult to talk about their families to English people. It sounds . . . precious, to say that, as if we think of ourselves as special, or superior, but it isn't that, or at least I don't think it is. It's more a fear of embarrassing, or something. I mean, there's hardly a Polish family which wasn't amputated, or imprisoned, or suffered in the war in a way the British can't understand – because you weren't occupied.'

He took his arm away from her, and paced up and down.

'When my family came here, with thousands and thousands of others, most of them had histories which they all had to bury, while they got on with starting a new life. But of course they couldn't bury them, and they told their children. My mother and grandparents – my father's parents – told Ewa and me. We grew up in another country. Perhaps for others it was less so, or more so – I can remember plenty of children at Saturday school whose mothers wouldn't let them speak English at home at all. It wasn't like that for us, exactly, but neither were we like the families who became extremely successful here. We didn't quite manage that: my grandparents simply buried themselves, like lots of their generation, in the exile community – the *emigracja*. My father was young, he was supposed to make a go of it, but . . .' He paused. 'But he was scarred by the war, I think, in a way which cut him off from everyone, even us. Especially us. He and I . . . I was very afraid of him when I was young.'

'But not now.'

He didn't answer.

'Jerzy? Tell me about it. About him.'

They had walked in a circle, and were back at the bridge again: they stood, looking down into the cold brown water, frozen hard. Jerzy brushed snow from the parapet and leaned on it, a little away from her. Their breath streamed on the air.

Elizabeth reached out and touched his arm, but he didn't turn. She felt a faint, guilty flicker of irritation.

'You do realize,' she said lightly, 'that we suffered too, in the war? My father was in a Japanese prison camp.'

'Was he?' Jerzy scratched the surface of the parapet. 'But then – forgive me – but in the end your country had its freedom. And Poland began another occupation.'

'Is that how you think of it?'

'Of course. How else are we to think of it?'

Elizabeth shook her head, and fell silent. The snow that remained on the bridge was delicately marked with the prints of birds' feet; from below, a blackbird cautiously looked up at them, head on one side, hungry.

After a while, Jerzy said: 'I told you when we met that I wasn't very good with people, didn't I? You can give up now, if you want.'

'I don't want. Don't be so defeatist.'

He stood up, and moved away from the bridge. 'Am I defeatist? You sound like my father. Incredibly, that's who you sound like.' He began to walk quickly away through the snowy trees, and she ran to catch up with him.

'Jerzy . . . I didn't mean to hurt you. Please . . .'

'Leave it,' he said. 'Just forget it, all right?'

They walked home in silence, across the white, empty heath.

A few weeks later, Elizabeth took Jerzy to her studio, small and plain, at the top of a house full of people renting rooms. The studio had two windows overlooking roads and rooftops; a slope of the heath was just visible, with the last of the snow in patches.

'You just . . . look around,' she said, and took the kettle, plugged into the wall outside, to the landing bathroom.

Jerzy walked over to the easel, and stood looking at the canvas there. He was standing at a glass door, opened on to a long narrow garden, full of trees. Greenness and yellowness clustered round the door; shrubbery and sky were blurrily reflected in the glass. A path led down the garden, and a small girl was sitting in the middle, her back to him, bent over a doll whose legs flopped from her lap. The foreground of the painting was as he had imagined, full of light and colour, but something else was there, too, in the long bars of shade which fell from the trees at the end of the garden, across the path, and across the little girl.

The studio door opened.

'Who is she?' he asked.

'My niece,' said Elizabeth, behind him, and switched on the kettle.

He moved round the room, looking at the paintings on the walls, stopping in front of canvases propped against the wall, tilting them forward, lifting smaller ones to the window. Among the portraits were several of the same woman, with a broad-planed face and dark eyes, her hair drawn right back, head and shoulders almost filling the canvas, as if she entirely occupied the space between herself and Elizabeth.

'And she?'

'A sitter at art school. She died last year, of cancer. Everyone wanted to paint her.'

He went on looking. There were interiors of her parents' house, corners of kitchen or study or bedroom, illuminated by lamps or sun or falling snow. There were several landscapes, different parts of the heath. There was, finally, a canvas propped against the wall between the two windows which at first he hadn't noticed, because he was looking at the easel. He bent down, looked closer, and Elizabeth took the painting of the little girl off the easel and said: 'Put it up here, if you want.'

He picked it up, put it on the pegs and stood back. It was large, almost monochrome – greys, muddy white, dull browns – and painted without detail, so that the figures were featureless. Two children were sleeping in beds next to each other, the tops of their heads just visible above the blankets. Behind them the door was ajar, and the figure of a man stood watching, lit from a hall or landing beyond. The man's shadow fell on to the floor, between the beds, and was darker than the figure itself.

'When did you do that?'

'A week or so ago.' Elizabeth switched off the kettle and came up beside him.

He went on looking at it, without touching her or speaking. Then he said: 'That is my family. It is my mother's childhood, and in quite another way it is Ewa's and mine, as well.' He put his arm round her. 'How did you know all that?'

'I didn't know, exactly, but it came to me.'

'After we'd been talking.'

'Yes.' She reached up and kissed him lightly on the mouth.

Jerzy drew her close. 'I do love you,' he said slowly. 'I do, do love you.'

'I love you too,' said Elizabeth. 'You are difficult and moody, but I never thought I could feel so much for anyone.'

After a while they went out of the studio, closing the door on the little girl in the garden, on the eyes of the dead woman, which had once looked into Elizabeth's, and on the figure beyond the sleeping children, and the dark shadow cast.

They sat round the table over Sunday lunch. Anna passed plates and dishes to Dziadek and Babcia, and to Ewa, who had arrived late. Jan was still not back, but they couldn't wait for him any longer. She put a covered plate in the oven, then returned and sat down.

'There. Have you all got everything?'

'It is very good, Anna.' Dziadek lifted a small piece of *pierogi* on his fork, with a hand that shook a little. At his side, Babcia watched him covertly.

'How are you, Dziadek?' Ewa asked.

'I am well, darling. You look pretty.'

'Thank you.' Ewa was wearing a black mohair sweater threaded through with scarlet and emerald which had cost half a month's salary.

'Too thin,' said Babcia.

'Nonsense.' Ewa helped herself to potato and beetroot. 'Look how I eat.'

'Only here,' said Anna. 'I'm sure you starve yourself during the week. How much was that sweater, if I may ask?'

'A sale bargain. This is delicious, Mama.' She looked round the table. Dziadek and Babcia were thawing out after the walk back from mass – it was a long walk, and very cold, going past the common, where the last wet snow had only just gone, but they had to do it, they'd taken their exercise walking back from mass almost every Sunday for twenty years. She looked at Anna, who never went, and at Tata's empty chair, opposite her. To go to work even on a Sunday morning, to have, always, a reason not to be with them, or to arrive late . . . did he really dislike being here so much? Or did he think they didn't want him, now?

She took a sip of water. The other empty chair was Jerzy's, but that had been pushed back against the wall for a long time. There was another, on the other side of the dresser: the visitor's chair. Ewa, enjoying the easy familiarity of Sunday lunch, viewed the prospect of a visitor with irritation. Or perhaps it was this particular one.

She put down her glass and said casually: 'Has Jerzy phoned this week?'

Anna shook her head. 'You know what he's like.'

'He did say he was going to.'

'Well, he hasn't. Why, was there something particular?'

'Sort of.' Ewa reached for the vegetable dishes. 'He has a girlfriend. He wants to bring her home to meet us.'

'Really?' Anna put down her knife and fork. 'Has he really? Well – that's very . . .'

'Surprising? Why? Why shouldn't he have? Did you think he was gay, or something?'

Anna flushed. 'For heaven's sake . . . Of course not. Have you met her? What's she like? Is she Polish?'

'Mama . . . do calm down.'

Anna looked at her sharply. 'I am perfectly calm, thank you, Ewa. It seems to be you who has something biting you – what is the matter with you?'

It was Ewa's turn to flush. 'Nothing.' She put the lid back on the beetroot dish very deliberately.

'Children, children . . .' Dziadek said mildly.

There was a pause; Ewa smiled, shamefaced. 'Sorry.'

'You're tired,' said Babcia. 'You work too hard, darling.'

'Well, anyway,' Anna said. 'Shall we begin again? Who is this girl?'

'She's called Elizabeth, and she's a painter, apparently. I haven't met her. Jerzy says she's very pretty. She's English, and . . . that's all I know. Except that they live in the same house.'

'What?'

Ewa explained. Babcia dabbed at the corners of her mouth with her napkin.

'And he wants to bring her here to meet all of us at once?' asked Anna.

Ewa shrugged. 'Perhaps he wants to get it over with.' She put down her knife and fork. 'What's for pudding?'

'*Szarlotka*.' The front door downstairs banged. 'That must be Tata, I'll get his first course.' She went out to the kitchen.

'Well,' said Dziadek. 'We have something to look forward to.'

'*Szarlotka*?' Ewa asked innocently.

'The pretty girlfriend.' He pushed away his plate, barely touched.

329

'And what about you, darling?' Babcia asked Ewa. 'It's time you found a nice husband and settled down.'

'Nonsense.'

A key turned in the lock.

'Jan . . .' said Babcia, and her face lit up as he came into the doorway of the room and stood, surveying them. It's the same every Sunday, thought Ewa, stacking plates: even after years of doing everything without him, it's as if we're not a proper family until he's come home. Especially for the grandparents, especially since Jerzy left.

He moved into the room; Babcia waited for him to kiss her hand.

'*Dzień dobry*, Mama . . .'

'*Kochany* Jan . . .'

Then he and Dziadek shook hands, and he pulled out a chair and sat down, nodding to Ewa. Waiting to be served, she thought, and picked up the plates.

'*Dzień dobry*, Tata. We have an excitement.'

He raised an eyebrow.

'Jerzy has a new girlfriend. An English girl, called Elizabeth.'

'Elizabeth,' said Dziadek. 'Elżbieta. Very pretty.'

Jan grunted. God, thought Ewa, he's worse than me – what will it be like for Jerzy bringing someone here? She pushed back her chair as Anna came in, carrying Jan's plate.

'I've kept it warm for you . . .'

Jan adjusted the positions of his knife and fork as she put the plate in front of him. 'Thank you.'

'Has Ewa told you about Jerzy?' Anna asked. 'He's bringing a girlfriend home to meet us, next Sunday.'

'He didn't say next Sunday, Mama,' Ewa murmured, and carried the pile of plates into the kitchen. She ran the tap in the sink and put them in, and then she went to look out of the window, across the empty railway line. Not many trains on a Sunday. For a moment the daylight ordinariness of it disappeared: she was in her bed, in the room she and Jerzy had shared as children, lying awake and watching him kneel up at the moonlit window, the curtain over his head, as a train thundered past, and he held his breath.

'*I don't suppose I'll ever love anyone the way I love you.*'

'*No. Nor me.*'

They hadn't been children, then.

'Ewa? What are you doing?' Mama was calling from the table.

'Coming. Shall I bring the *szarlotka?*'

'Please.'

Ewa picked up the apple tart, and the pudding bowls. I don't want to meet this girl, she thought. I don't want to be patronized by some stuck-up English painter.

The telephone rang in the living room and she heard Mama get up and hurry to answer it.

'*Słucham?* Jerzy? How are you, darling? Ewa says you're bringing someone to meet us . . .'

A bright March morning, windy and cold; on the heath, dogs off their leads had raced, barking wildly, down towards the ponds. In Clapham, many of the curtains were still drawn. Elizabeth hurried along beside Jerzy, trying to keep up, no longer trying to talk to him. There were dogs here, too, their faces at the windows, waiting to be taken to the common. A man was washing his car; three boys were kicking a ball about, up against the dustbin bunkers; a front door banged, and a man came out and went past them towards the tube.

Jerzy slowed, and raised his hand. Elizabeth looked up to see a grey-haired woman at a third-floor window drop a net curtain held aside, and disappear.

'My grandmother,' he said. 'We'll go and see them first.'

'All right.'

They stopped outside one of the green front doors, and Jerzy pressed a button on the intercom. There was a pause, and then Elizabeth heard an old man's voice say something she couldn't understand.

'Jerzy, Dziadek.'

The intercom buzzed, and Jerzy pushed open the door. She followed him inside, and up the stairs, past the closed doors to different flats, hearing *The World At One*, and foreign voices. At the top, she could see light from a door held open, but it was quiet, as if there were no one there. Then they had reached the landing, and beyond Jerzy she saw a shrunken man with white hair, in a dark suit, nodding and smiling. He held the door open wider: a small grave woman in a grey dress and amber necklace stood beside him.

Jerzy seemed not to introduce, but rather present her, as if at court.

'Elizabeth. My grandparents.'

She smiled at them, and they shook hands in perfect silence, all crowded into the doorway. Then the grandfather gestured to them

331

to go in, and she followed Jerzy down a corridor and into a sitting room where a clock ticked above a gas fire.

'Please . . .' said the grandfather. 'Sit down.'

Elizabeth sat, on a brown sofa beneath a wall hanging. The grandmother sat in a chair with wooden arms, by the fire. Again they smiled at each other, hesitantly.

Jerzy's grandfather was asking him something.

'Dziadek says would you like a drink?'

She looked up at him, towering over them all.

'Are you going to have one?'

'Yes. Sherry – all right?'

'Fine.'

On the mantelpiece above the fire was a photograph of a young man in uniform, wearing an officer's cap.

'My . . . husband,' said Jerzy's grandmother, seeing her look at it. She shook her head. 'I am sorry . . . little English . . .'

There was a chink of glass from the table.

'I don't speak Polish,' said Elizabeth. 'I must learn.'

Jerzy's grandfather stood before her, offering a round metal tray with four small coloured glasses on it.

'Please . . .'

She took one. 'Thank you.'

'*Na zdrowie*. Cheers.'

They all raised their glasses, and sipped.

'So . . .' said Dziadek. 'How are you, Jerzy?'

'I am very well, Dziadek. And you?'

'He . . . is . . . not . . . well,' said Babcia, pronouncing each word as if for the first time.

'Please,' said Elizabeth. 'Please speak Polish. I don't mind at all.'

They began to talk, and she sipped her sherry and looked round the room. The titles behind the glass bookcase doors were unpronounceable, impenetrable, full of endings like -cz and -sz and -ość. More photographs stood on top of the bookcase: children, who must be Jerzy and his sister, in Scout and Guide uniform, or folk costume, or running with a large black dog on the common. There was one of the grandparents themselves, which looked like something Jerzy would have taken: on either side of the gas fire, his grandmother doing a piece of tapestry, his grandfather reading. There were military photographs on a shelf: another of a young, faraway Dziadek in uniform, but on horseback, and two of a regiment, or part of a regiment, taken outside a barracks. Many of the officers had thick moustaches; they held canes, and looked formidable.

'Well . . .' said Jerzy, after a while. 'Perhaps we should go and see my parents now . . . Dziadek and Babcia are joining us for lunch.'

'Fine.' Elizabeth finished her glass and set it down on the low table before the sofa. They all got up; Jerzy moved towards his grandmother, bent down and kissed her on both cheeks.

'*Dziękuję*, Babcia.'

'Jerzy . . .'

She gave her hand to Elizabeth, who found herself kissing both cheeks also. They smiled at each other again, more confidently, but still as if from a great distance.

Dziadek took her hand, and kissed it.

'I am so glad to have met you,' she said.

'Please. Come again.'

'We will,' said Jerzy. He led her out of the room, along the narrow corridor. 'See you in a few minutes, then.' He opened the front door, went across to the one opposite, and knocked.

'Mama? It's me.'

They stood on the square of landing and waited. Behind them, the grandparents' door discreetly closed. Elizabeth reached for Jerzy's hand and he smiled down at her.

'All right so far?' The palm of his hand was damp; he released it, quickly wiping it on his jeans, and took a deep breath.

'It's all right,' she said. 'I knew it would be all right.'

Then the door was swung open, and a slim, dark-haired woman said: 'Well . . . hello, darling. Come in.'

'This is Elizabeth, Mama,' said Jerzy, and then quickly, as if despite himself: 'Is Tata here yet?'

His mother smiled, shaking her head, and led them into the living room, larger and lighter than the grandparents', with daffodils on the table. 'My husband will be here in a little while,' she said to Elizabeth. 'In the meantime I am delighted to meet you.' Her hair was coiled in a knot at her neck in a style which did not belong to 1978 but which suited her perfectly. Her gaze was warm, but not quite uncritical, and shaking hands Elizabeth felt herself assessed. And found wanting?

'And this is my daughter . . .' said Anna, and Elizabeth turned to see an unquestionably beautiful girl in the doorway, holding a tray. She had dark hair cut to the jawbone, and wore a black mohair sweater threaded through with a dazzle of colour; she came into the room and observed them all coolly, setting down the tray of cutlery on the table.

'Hello, brother.' She crossed over, stood almost on tiptoe and kissed him quickly, on both cheeks.

'Hello, Ewa. You look very nice. This is Elizabeth.'

'How do you do?' Ewa shook her hand with formality, and gave a formal smile. 'Jerzy has been telling me about you.'

'Oh?' For a moment Elizabeth was about to play the game: 'Nothing too dreadful, I hope?' She realized at once that it would be quite out of place. Ewa didn't look as if she played games of any kind, and Elizabeth was aware of being at once made to think not: Do I like you? but: Please will you like me? She saw herself in her Fair Isle cardigan and wished she had worn something very dark, and bold.

'Well . . .' Anna said again. 'Do let's sit down. Did the grandparents give you anything to drink?'

'Sweet sherry, I expect,' said Ewa, and went back to the tray. 'I'll lay the table while you all . . . socialize.'

Elizabeth saw Jerzy frown, flickeringly, as Ewa carefully counted out knives and forks. Then they were sitting by the fire, which popped quietly into the silence.

'Jerzy says you are a painter,' said Anna. Behind her, on a bookcase and the wall, were photographs: Elizabeth saw one, cracked and faded, of a boy and girl in a boat, on a sunlit river. Another, sepia-tinted, of a boy – the same boy? – with dark cropped hair and cheekbones like Anna's, eyes burning into the camera.

'Yes,' she said, looking back at Anna. 'I'm a painter – I do portraits, mostly, and interiors, still-lifes. Rather ordinary.'

'That is not what Jerzy says.'

She thought of the picture of the family she had done for him. 'Perhaps I'm beginning to move in a different direction, I'm not sure. Jerzy says you paint, too.'

'It sounds like a new game,' said Ewa, from the table. 'Jerzy says. He'll say something now, you know, if you press the right button.'

'Shut up, Ewa,' said Jerzy, in a tone that wasn't quite joking.

'There, you see?'

Far below, the street door banged. 'There's Tata,' said everyone at once. Elizabeth felt suddenly very nervous, though she was also fleetingly aware that the situation had its comic side: The Ogre Climbs the Stairs. Then, seeing Jerzy get to his feet, brushing back his hair in a quick tense gesture she had never seen before, she felt ashamed

334

of even considering mockery, and stood up beside him, taking his hand.

A key turned in the lock, and the front door was opened.

'We're in here, Jan,' Anna called, with a lightness Elizabeth sensed was unaccustomed, artificial.

The front door closed, and a man who looked quite unlike Jerzy came into the room, nodding to them all rather as Ewa had.

'*Dzień dobry* – good afternoon. I am sorry to be late.'

Jerzy was tall, and slender to the point of thinness; his lips and nose were finely drawn, his colouring fair – grey-green eyes, light brown hair. His father was a good head shorter, but much more muscular, thick-set, and despite the grey in his hair and deep lines in his forehead he looked far stronger than Jerzy, whose hand in Elizabeth's was soaking wet. He ushered her forward.

'Tata – this is Elizabeth. My father . . .'

'How do you do?' said Elizabeth.

'How do you do?' The hand which took hers was cool and hard. He seemed to look at her only briefly, with the same polite, empty smile Ewa had given her, and then he released her hand and felt in his jacket pocket.

'Excuse me if I smoke.' It was not a request.

'We are just about to eat,' said Anna, gesturing at the table. 'Ewa – perhaps you could call the grandparents?'

Jan lit a cigarette, and coughed. 'I'll put it out when they come.' He moved aside as Ewa went past him to tap on the grandparents' door, and he nodded to Jerzy, who smiled at him, awkwardly.

'How are you, Tata?'

'I am well. And you? Still taking photographs?'

'Well . . . yes.' Jerzy ran his hand through his hair again.

'May I ask what you do?' Elizabeth said to Jan, deliberately.

He took another puff of his cigarette, and shrugged. 'I'm a technical draughtsman. Very dull, I'm afraid.' He turned as the door opened. 'My parents – or perhaps you have met them already?'

Elizabeth nodded, and smiled as they came in, following Ewa, and stood like guests who came infrequently: very correct, waiting to be shown to the table. Anna, who had been in and out, carrying dishes, was indicating places.

'Babcia . . . Dziadek . . . Elizabeth – perhaps you could sit between Dziadek and Jerzy. Jan, please . . .'

He stubbed out his cigarette in an ashtray on the table by the fire, and came to sit down.

'So,' said Ewa, pulling out the chair beside him. 'Here we all are.'
She sat down and smiled at Elizabeth with more warmth, obviously
making an effort. 'That's a pretty cardigan.'

'Thank you.'

Anna was passing plates, indicating dishes.

'This is *bigos*,' she said to Elizabeth, lifting a lid. 'A kind of
sauerkraut, with sausage.' Steam rose from the dish; it smelt of
vinegar and spices. 'And there is *kasha* – buckwheat – in here, and
cucumber with dill . . . I thought you might like to try Polish food.
Please help yourself.'

'Thank you – it looks delicious.'

Babcia and Dziadek were carefully unfolding napkins. Babcia asked
Anna something in Polish, and Anna said in English: 'No, I made it
this morning.'

'Please,' Elizabeth said again. 'Please speak Polish. I don't mind
at all.'

'It's all right,' said Anna. 'The grandparents understand enough.'

But as the meal began, and remarks were exchanged in English,
Elizabeth felt ill at ease: they might understand but they did not
speak. If she and Jerzy stayed together, perhaps there would always
be someone excluded in family gatherings: the grandparents, too
polite to insist on Polish being spoken, or herself, the newcomer, the
outsider.

Dziadek said something in Polish. Ewa answered in Polish. It
started to rain. Drops splashed the window panes and bounced off
Anna's window boxes; they bounced off the slate roofs of the houses
opposite whose windows were hung with net curtains, like Dziadek's
and Babcia's. A door banged down in the street. In the middle of
Clapham Elizabeth felt as if she were in a foreign country: up here,
enclosed by the falling rain, listening to a language she did not
understand, with a family whose history was locked within the room
in books she could not read, in photographs of the dead.

There was another silence, disturbed only by the pattering rain.
She heard herself saying to Ewa: 'Do you ever think of yourself as
English?'

'No,' said Ewa flatly. 'I don't.'

Jerzy looked at her. 'You used to. Part of you used to.'

'But not any more.' She turned to Elizabeth. 'Has Jerzy taught
you any Polish yet?'

'A few words, that's all. I was thinking that I might go to classes one day. Or perhaps . . .' Would this be tactful? 'You're a translator, aren't you?'

'Yes,' said Ewa, 'but not a teacher.'

Beside her, Elizabeth felt Jerzy stiffen.

I shall be conciliatory now, she thought, because I have no choice, in our first meeting, on your territory. Perhaps not another time.

'No,' she said calmly. 'Of course not.'

'Classes would be a good idea,' said Anna, and gestured at the table. 'Please – do have some more.'

'Or perhaps you are going to anglicize him,' said Ewa. 'Do you think that's what will happen? I believe that in many Anglo–Polish marriages, Poland almost disappears.'

'Ewa . . .' said Jerzy, 'what is the matter with you?'

'Nothing, I don't think.'

'No one,' said Elizabeth, 'is talking of marriage. And even if we were, I don't think that would happen.' She turned to Jerzy. 'I haven't tried to . . .'

'On the contrary.'

'Good,' said Ewa coldly, and set down her knife and fork. 'Because the British betrayed us, you know, in 1945.'

'Ewa!' Anna put down the lid of a dish with a clatter.

Ewa ignored her. 'Did you know that?' she asked Elizabeth.

'I . . . No, I don't think I did.'

'Then perhaps Jerzy should tell you. I'm talking about Yalta, where Churchill and Roosevelt handed us to Stalin on a plate.'

'Ewa,' said Jerzy, 'I really don't think this is necessary.'

Ewa ignored him too. 'The Allies did almost nothing to help us,' she went on, 'when we – when my parents' generation – fought in the Warsaw Uprising, and then, after signing Poland away, the British tried to repatriate us. The government said to all the people like my parents, and grandparents, who had endured the occupation, and fought in the resistance, and been forced to leave their country, to all the Poles who had fought – in this country, in Africa, the Middle East, in Italy – under British command. "Of course, you are heroes. Of course, you can come and live here if you really want to – but actually, if you really want to go on serving your country, we advise you to return there." Knowing that we would have to live under Stalinist rule!'

Ewa's hands on the table were trembling, her face pale. Elizabeth saw the grandparents exchanging horrified glances. 'And look at Poland now,' Ewa said, her words falling over each other. 'It's a downtrodden, crippled, corrupted country, that's all. Do you know that I can just remember hearing about the workers shot dead in Poznań in 1956, when I was a little girl? And I can remember it happening again, in Gdańsk, in 1970, but I don't suppose you noticed it in the papers. Where's Poland, after all? Shot dead by the militia, for protesting about prices!' She drew a long breath, as everyone began to talk at once. 'Yalta,' she said loudly, 'is one of the reasons why I do not feel English, or British, or whatever this country is supposed to be now.'

'*Ewa!*' Anna was looking at her in horror. 'You have been quite unforgivably rude.'

'Have I? It used to be the other way round, didn't it? Didn't it, Tata? I used to be too English. Now I am too Polish?'

Jan was reaching into his pocket; he lit a cigarette, and Jerzy coughed. 'You have surprised me, Ewa,' said Jan. The only one, thought Elizabeth, shaking, who does not look shocked, appalled.

'May I have one?' Ewa asked him, and he lit one for her, and said something quietly, in Polish.

Ewa inhaled deeply, and turned back to Elizabeth.

'My father says that he admires my patriotism, but that I owe our guest an apology. Forgive me. I wasn't aware myself that I felt so strongly.' She tried to smile.

Elizabeth did not know how to answer.

There was a silence, eyes avoided. Under the table, Jerzy took her hand.

Elizabeth found herself thinking of another table, her parents at breakfast, reading the *Telegraph* and *Express*, trees rustling soothingly beyond the window, the gate at the end of the path going click, as the gardener arrived. At the edge of this world, where you canvassed for the Conservatives, who needed no canvassing here, where you went to fêtes for the church, lurked the fairy-tale evils of post-war Britain: socialism, communism, blacks. I've spent years of my life trying to get out of that garden gate, she thought. Ever since I left home and came to London, nationalism has been something to laugh at, to apologize for; something, at worst, to equate with the National Front. But if you are Polish . . . if you are Polish, apparently, the world is a bitter place. The West has abandoned you, the East has overrun you. You stand alone. It is that kind of thinking which has made the Poles so proud, so passionately interested in themselves. This room is full of nationalists – patriots, they would say. There should be a difference.

Smoke drifted across the table, and Jerzy coughed again.

'For goodness' sake, Ewa, take that cigarette somewhere else, or put it out,' said Anna, and got up to clear the table.

There was a general movement of chairs pushed back, hands reaching for the neutral zone of cutlery and plates. Ewa took herself to the ashtray on the table by the fire, and sat down.

'Sorry, sorry, everyone.' She took another deep puff. 'Sorry, Jerzy. I was going to be quite different.'

The rain stopped, and sun shone in the puddles down in the street. Dziadek and Babcia had cups of tea with floating slices of lemon, and returned to their own flat, seen across the landing by the whole family.

Dziadek bowed over Elizabeth's hand. 'My granddaughter . . .'

'It doesn't matter,' said Elizabeth. 'Please don't worry.' What else could she say?

He shook his head.

When they had gone, Jerzy said: 'Come and see my old room.'

She followed him down the corridor. 'That was Ewa's,' he said, as they passed a very small one, next to the bathroom. 'When we got older. Dziadek comes in and uses it as his study now.' At the far end of the corridor were two doors. 'That's my parents' room.' He indicated one to the side. 'And this is where Ewa and I used to be.'

He pushed open the door and she saw a small square room with a narrow bed, table and chair, a shiny utility furniture wardrobe. Jerzy closed the door behind him, and they went to stand at the window. Beyond were factory buildings, or warehouses, and trees; below was the railway line. They stood at the window with their arms round each other, looking out. A Sunday underground train rattled past, almost empty.

'It used to be steam,' said Jerzy, 'when I was very small. It was wonderful – I can't tell you how . . . magical, otherworldly. Especially at night.'

Elizabeth put her head on his shoulder.

'And what did Ewa think of it?'

He looked down at her. 'Has she upset you very much?'

'Hasn't she upset you?'

He hesitated. 'Actually she really shocked me. I never realized she felt so . . .'

'So bitter.'

'Well . . . I suppose it did sound bitter. I was going to say – so passionate.'

'About Poland.'

Jerzy frowned. 'Of course about Poland. What do you mean?'

'You don't think she's jealous.'

'Jealous. Of me?'

'Of me.'

'Because you're English?'

'No!' She drew away. 'Why should she be jealous of that? The English are to be despised, aren't we? Aren't we? After all, we only went to war for Poland, didn't we? And swam through it all unscathed while Poland was martyred. And betrayed her.'

Jerzy was scarlet. 'She has upset you.'

'Of course she has! Does it surprise you?'

'No . . . no.' He looked stricken, pacing up and down. 'I'm so sorry . . . I knew it wouldn't work, bringing you here. I told you.'

'It would work, except that she doesn't want it to.'

'Because she's jealous . . . because I have you, now, and she has no one?'

'I don't know about that. I mean because I have you.'

'What? Oh, don't be absurd.'

Elizabeth said nothing.

'You don't understand,' he said. 'At least, I thought you did, with your painting, but . . .' He shook his head. 'I mean – I suppose you understand that the shadow was there, but . . . not what it felt like. For us. Especially for me, I think. Not Ewa. If anything, I should be afraid of losing her.' He was pacing again. 'Never mind. I'm just very sorry.'

Elizabeth moved towards him again. 'So am I. It's all right, Jerzy, it's all right. Perhaps if you'd just warned me she was so . . . fierce.'

'I didn't realize she was, still. She used to be very fierce. She used to fight like hell with my parents – I just had asthma.'

'Poor Jerzy.' She moved into his arms. 'And then what happened?'

'Then she had a sort of . . . crisis. Years ago. Never mind about that. But afterwards she seemed to reconcile everything – she's seemed very settled, to me, for years. In the meantime – I've moved away. And met you.'

'And tried to come home, and now it's all gone wrong.' She shook her head.

'It doesn't matter,' he said. 'Now . . . you're my home.' He was stroking her hair. 'Are you?'

'Perhaps. In a way.' She gestured at the room. 'You'll always carry . . . all this with you.'

'Don't you carry your past?'

'Not in the same way, no.' She shook her head slowly. 'I don't think so.'

There was a tap at the door.

'Jerzy?'

He released Elizabeth, and went to open it. Ewa came in, smoking.

'Am I still in disgrace?'

Jerzy looked at her. 'You've upset Elizabeth.'

'Have I?' Ewa blushed. 'I am sorry. I've already apologized, but let me do so again. My mother has been lecturing me.'

'Is that why you're sorry?' Elizabeth asked, and immediately wished she hadn't. God, I've had enough of this, she thought. Let's just forget it.

Ewa was holding out her hand. 'No,' she said. 'I'm ashamed of myself.'

'Well . . .' Elizabeth took her hand, trying to imagine shaking hands with a single one of her own friends. 'Let's just . . . let it go.'

Their eyes met briefly, then Ewa dropped her hand, and sighed. She stood beside them, looking out on to the track, where the wind blew spring clouds across the sky, behind the warehouses, and the bare trees swayed.

'Mama also sent me to ask if you'd like some more tea,' she said. 'Or coffee. She's in the sitting room.'

'Not for me,' said Jerzy.

'I think I will,' said Elizabeth.

'I think you're the one she wants,' said Ewa.

Elizabeth turned from the window, and stood looking round the room. On shelves above the small table were piles of folders, and magazines. She a stood on tiptoe and saw one at the top: the *Railway Gazette*, covered with a thin film of dust. Pressed right against the shelf was an old book, brown with a gold-leaf title. She peered.

'*The Imitation of Christ* . . .'

'I bought that years ago,' Jerzy said, sounding embarrassed, awkward.

Elizabeth stopped peering. Under the table were cardboard boxes, labelled in Polish with black felt-tip pen.

'Our toys,' Ewa said, watching her. 'Is there anything else you'd like to see? I expect your mother has kept yours, too.'

'Yes,' said Elizabeth, 'I expect she has.'

She left them standing at the window, and went out along the corridor to the sitting room.

'Mrs Prawicka?'

Anna was in the armchair by the fire, a tray of tea things on the table beside her.

'Please – come and sit down.'

Elizabeth sat, taking the chair opposite. They looked at each other, cautiously.

'Ewa has apologized . . .'

'Yes. Yes, she has. It's all right.'

'You would like some tea?'

'Please.'

'Is Jerzy coming?'

'No. He's talking to Ewa.'

'Ah.' Anna poured tea; the thin slices of lemon gently swam. 'Or perhaps you would prefer milk?'

'No, no, this is fine. Thank you.'

They sipped in silence. The flat felt very quiet.

'May I ask – where is your husband?'

'He has gone back to work,' said Anna.

Elizabeth could not stop herself. 'Already?' And then: 'Excuse me . . . It's none of my business.'

Anna shrugged, and Elizabeth sensed her embarrassment. 'Or perhaps he has gone for a walk on the common.' There was another pause. 'Perhaps my husband seems a little eccentric, but he is a very . . . private person.'

'Please . . . you don't have to explain anything. I'm sorry I . . .'

'But I want to explain. It must seem extraordinary that Ewa can have such an – outburst, and if I tell you that my husband has never really recovered from the war, or settled here . . .' She smiled, quizzically. 'Are you wondering what you have walked into?'

Elizabeth smiled back, liking her. 'A bit. But perhaps it's a good thing Ewa had her outburst – I suppose I do understand a little how she feels. Do you know that when I met Jerzy, and he was showing me his photographs, there was one of you at the Katyń Memorial? I'm afraid I hadn't even heard of Katyń.'

'It doesn't matter. Poor Elizabeth. It really doesn't matter.' She hesitated. 'I wonder . . . have you had enough for one day, or may I show you something?'

'Please . . .'

342

'Just a few things I brought with me, when we had to leave Warsaw.'

'When the Allies had abandoned you.'

'Well . . .'

'I'd like to see them.'

'Good.' Anna got up. 'I'll just go and fetch them . . . help yourself to more tea, if you want.'

'Thank you.' Elizabeth watched her go quickly out of the room. She could hear another train clicking along the track at the back of the house, where Jerzy and Ewa were still talking. The gas fire was very hot; she yawned, suddenly feeling at home.

Then Anna was back, carying a small flat tin box. She put it on the table, removing Ewa's ashtray, and carefully lifted the lid. The box looked as if it had held sweets or toffees once.

'When I left Warsaw, for the prison camp, I carried in this little box all the photographs from my family that I could find. Most of them are in albums, now, or here – ' She indicated those on the wall, the bookcase. 'Now I use the box for the other things I managed to bring with me.' She put the lid on the table: Elizabeth saw small objects wrapped in greying tissue paper. Anna took them out one by one, and said: 'In fact I haven't looked in here for many years, you know. Perhaps Ewa and Jerzy hardly remember it.'

The tissue paper was so old that it did not rustle; it looked very fragile as she unwrapped the first small parcel. A circle of gauzy cotton, hand-stitched into two bands, one red and one a yellowed white, fell limply.

'This was my brother's armband . . . We all wore them in AK – the Home Army – in the Uprising. Jerzy's told you a little about it all?'

'Oh, yes.' Elizabeth carefully picked it up, feeling the frail cloth.

Another circle of white and red slid on to the table. 'And this was mine – I made it the day the Uprising began. I don't know who made Jerzy's. He was stationed some way away. Now – what else is there?' She unwrapped something flat, somewhere between the size of a cigarette card and a postcard. 'Ah . . .'

Behind them the door was opened, and Jerzy and Ewa came in.

'We are having a history lesson,' said Anna. They came over and looked at the card, coarse grey-green, stamped in Russian, with a handwritten address in flowing black.

'Oh, yes,' said Ewa. 'Dziadek's letter.'

'Dziadek?' Elizabeth asked.

'The other one,' said Jerzy. 'Mama's father.'

'The only letter we ever had from him,' said Anna, and turned it over. Two or three lines were written there, in a strong hand.

'May I?' asked Jerzy, and took it from her, slowly translating:

'My darlings: I am in good health. Are the children going to school? I hug and kiss you with all my heart. Write to me. Tomasz.'

There was a silence. Then Anna reached into the box. 'The last things now . . .'

A small piece of white paper, with the heavy black print of a handpress, in small letters, dropped on to the table.

'My AK courier pass. And this – oh, I remember the day I was given this.' She shook her head and put another card on the table, but this one was folded like a membership card, stamped on the outside in German. Beneath the words was a black eagle: his talons held a circle, and within it a swastika.

'My identity card,' she said drily, and opened it. The thin face of a dark-haired girl stared out at them. 'We had to carry these with us all the time.'

Elizabeth picked it up, and looked at the face which looked beyond the camera. Anna had been years younger then than she herself was now: she tried to imagine living in an occupied city, in constant fear, having to carry such a card, terrified of losing it. Nazi soldiers stood on the corners of London streets, or ran up stairways in the dead of night, dragging people out from their beds. She remembered the films they had shown at school of London in the Blitz, silent black and white figures scurrying to shelters as the air-raid siren blared, lining the platforms of the underground. She tried to imagine also an armed insurrection, with whole districts barricaded from one another, some in German and some in English hands: Camberwell cut off from Peckham, Chelsea from Fulham, Hampstead from Highgate, Stockwell from Clapham, the pavements torn up, bodies unburied, houses blazing.

There came to her at once the names of other cities: Belfast. Beirut.

Ewa took the card from her, and looked at it, her face burning.

'It makes me want to kill.'

They stood in the doorway and kissed each other goodbye. Anna and Jerzy, Anna and Elizabeth; Elizabeth and Ewa, diffidently, Ewa and Jerzy, in conciliation.

Then they clattered down the uncarpeted stairs and out on to the street. It was quite dark now; they walked a few paces, then turned to see the windows up on the third floor, lit, and Anna and Ewa waving. From the corner of a window in the grandparents' flat a curtain was pulled aside, and they saw them both there, Dziadek raising his hand.

They waved back, then walked away, quickly, towards the tube. It was very cold.

Before they reached the station, Jerzy stopped, took Elizabeth's hand and kissed it. 'And now I'm going to take you out to dinner.'

'Oh? Where?'

'To another part of Poland.'

They caught the tube to South Kensington, and walked past bookshops and cake shops to turn up towards Cromwell Road. Jerzy pointed to a little restaurant on the corner, lit behind leaded windows. 'That's the Daquise,' he said. 'It's Polish, and they do wonderful cakes. We'll go there one day, but now . . .'

Their arms wrapped round each other, they walked up to the traffic lights at the end of the side street and stood waiting to cross. Taxis swept past; they hurried over, and into Exhibition Road, past the unlit museums and along porticoed terraces up towards Hyde Park. There were few people out, and the wind was biting. Halfway up the road, Jerzy stopped.

'This is it.'

They were standing before one of the porticoed houses: on the black front door a metal plaque was nailed, announcing *Ogniske Polskie*.

'The Polish Hearth,' said Jerzy, and they climbed the steps and pushed open the door.

Elizabeth stepped into a high-ceilinged hall, brightly lit and spacious. On their right was a lobby, where a woman waited to take their coats; beyond a glass-fronted bookcase, mounted on the wall, rose a wide, curving staircase. From the left came the chink of glasses and murmured laughter: they walked through the doorway into a large and beautiful room, running the depth of the house. There was a bar at the end where the windows overlooked the street, and at the other end a restaurant, lit by a chandelier. The tall french windows were hung with heavy, faded curtains, the tables covered in snowy linen. Many of the diners were white-haired: Elizabeth had an impression of correctness, uprightness, dark suits and elegant dresses; nods and smiles and expensive make-up; neat black evening bags snapped open, hands kissed; assurance, courtliness.

A waitress was approaching them.

'*Dobry wieczór, panu* – good evening. You have reserved a table?'

Jerzy nodded. '*Prawicki.*'

'*Proszę.*' She led them to a small table for two by the far wall. A menu and wine list lay on the snowy cloth.

'Hungry?' asked Jerzy, as they sat down.

'Er . . . no,' said Elizabeth. 'But this is a lovely surprise.'

'The place, or my bringing you?'

'Both. Thank you.'

'What we really need, after today, is a drink. Yes?'

'How right you are.'

The waitress smiled at them expectantly. Jerzy ordered white wine. 'And I should ask you what you want to eat,' he said, 'but I'd like to choose for you.' He scanned the menu. 'How about *śledzie* to start with, followed by *gołąbki*? With a salad.'

Elizabeth laughed. 'Go on – tell me.'

'Herrings in sour cream, followed by stuffed pigeons.'

She groaned.

'And *naleśniki* for pudding. Stuffed pancakes.'

'Stuffed . . . I tell you what, Jerzy, would you be very hurt, after going to all this trouble, if I said I couldn't touch any of it?'

'Not even the salad?'

'Not even the salad.'

He pulled a face. 'We could just go and sit in the bar. Not so – ' he gestured – 'not so *fin de siècle*, but . . . they have comfortable seats.' He took her hand across the table, and raised it to his lips. 'Come on.'

The bar was softly lit; they sank into plastic-covered chairs.

'*Proszę, panu . . .*'

Their waitress had followed them, questioning, bearing a small round tin tray, with their wine.

Jerzy explained; she nodded, not quite mollified, and poured out their wine into glasses from the bar.

'*Dziękuję . . .*'

'*Na zdrowie, panu.*' She took away the small tin tray.

Their glasses brimmed and shone.

'*Na zdrowie*, darling.'

'*Na zdrowie*, Jerzy. And thank you.' Elizabeth sipped and leaned back, watching the to and fro of dinner guests, so dignified, and so at ease. 'My God, I'm tired.'

'We've all worn you out.'

'You have. Never mind. Tell me what else goes on here.'

'There are discos – Ewa and I came to one once, years ago, but I was so shy I could barely get myself inside the room.'

'Not like now.'

He smiled. 'Of course not. And what else? There are conference rooms, and upstairs they play bridge. All afternoon, elegant old Polish ladies in hats sit at green baize tables and play. There's another painting for you.'

Elizabeth moved closer, and took his hand. 'It sounds like it,' she said. 'And when you say that, I remember why I love you.'

'And why is that?' He put down his glass and gently separated her fingers, running his thumb up and down each one.

Elizabeth closed her eyes.

'Tell me why you love me.'

'Because of the way you . . . do that. And because – ' she opened her eyes, and looked at him. 'Because I know you'll make me a better painter – you know already what I want to see, or should see. And I know you'll know. We're very close, Aren't we?'

'In spite of the yawning chasm of history which divides us?' he said, raising an eyebrow.

'In spite of it.' She put his hand against her cheek. 'Your mother asked me if I wondered what I'd walked in to.'

'Is it too much?'

'I don't think so – only time, as they say, will tell. And after all – I might be too much for you, and you haven't met my family yet.'

'I don't want to.'

'Thank you.'

Jerzy took her other hand, and put it against his own cheek, so that they were facing each other, and very close. A discreet cough came from near the bar, but they ignored it.

'Shall we for the moment forget our families entirely?'

'Please,' she said.

'Well, then . . . You said to Ewa that no one was talking about marriage.' He hesitated. 'Is anyone . . . thinking of it?'

Elizabeth felt a sudden, unexpected chill run through her.

'I . . . I . . . oh, Jerzy. Not yet. Forgive me . . . No.'

He dropped his eyes, flushing. 'I'm sorry . . .'

'Please don't be. Please. I'm surprised myself, at feeling so . . . wary.'

He took his hand away and leaned back against the plastic seat.

'It is too much for you. I knew it was.'

Elizabeth thought: I don't like this. I want it to be just us, as we

347

were. Melancholy was settling over Jerzy's features like a mask. And that's one reason I'm wary, she thought: he shuts me out when he's like this. Utterly. He's too vulnerable, and I'm too afraid of it. It isn't anything to do with our families, or the yawning chasm of history – he was so dry and charming when he said that: how is it possible for someone to be so light and so unhappy within moments?

'Jerzy, please . . .'

He shook his head. 'I shouldn't have asked.'

'For heaven's *sake*. Have I said no for ever? Have I said I don't love you? I love you, I love you, I've only just told you . . .'

The bar was filling up; two more couples were sitting near them now. Jerzy shifted uneasily, and finished his drink. Then he took her hand again.

'I'm sorry. May I ask one other thing?'

'Please.'

'Would you like us to live together? For now?'

'We do live together.'

'You know what I mean. Should we find a proper flat together? I mean – you would still have your studio . . .'

'What about your darkroom?'

'If there's just a cubbyhole I can use, like now . . . I just want to be with you. In a double bed. Our bed.'

'Ah. Well . . . yes. That would be . . .' She made a rueful face. 'Our lovely shabby house.'

'I know. But we could look. Shall we?'

'Yes. Yes. Let's look.' She leaned across and kissed him lightly. From the next table came another cough.

'Come on.'

They fetched their coats and went out into the street, where a cold rain had begun to fall, and people were hurrying from the Albert Hall, hailing taxis. They ran through the rain to the station, and caught the train home.

Hampstead village was brightly lit; they walked up the hill past the restaurants and boutiques and through the side streets to the house behind the church. Bare trees tossed in the wind on the heath.

'Come upstairs,' said Jerzy, and they went up to his room, and and switched on the electric fire, shivering.

'How have we survived a whole winter like this?' asked Elizabeth.

'I survived three others before you arrived,' said Jerzy. 'I can't imagine how. Come here. Come here.'

They switched off the lamp and kissed, clinging to each other, then undressing quickly in the burning light of the fire. Jerzy lit a candle, and put it on the floor by the bed; they huddled under the bedclothes, kissing and stroking each other until they were warm.

'I love you.'

'I love you.'

They made love at last with aching slowness.

An evening in mid-October, cold and wet. Anna hurried up the street under her umbrella, stepping aside to avoid being splashed by a passing car. She was tired; she could feel the beginning of a cold. She was supposed to be going to supper tomorrow with Jerzy and Elizabeth, who had rented a flat in Gospel Oak, near Elizabeth's studio. She thought she might have to put it off: it was too much on a weekday, though she enjoyed seeing them.

'Anna! Anna!'

She looked up and saw Babcia waving from their window, open despite the rain. Unheard of for Babcia to lean out and call like that into the street: had something happened to Dziadek? She began to run, stopped outside their house and called up: 'What is it? Are you all right?'

'The Pope!' Babcia called down, but a car drove past, and Anna couldn't hear what she said next and wasn't even sure she'd heard correctly. She unlocked the front door, shook and furled her umbrella and hurried up the stairs. Above, she heard the door open, and Babcia call down again: 'The Pope! He is Polish!'

'What?'

As she climbed the last flight she could hear the grandparents' radio and the six o'clock news. Then she had reached the top, and saw Babcia and Dziadek standing in their doorway, with tears in their eyes.

'He is from Kraków,' Dziadek said. 'A Polish Pope . . .'

'I don't believe it,' said Anna, but she felt a great wave of happiness and excitement rush through her. 'Come in,' she said quickly, and unlocked her own door and ran to the sitting room. She switched on the television, and a light, and they stood watching film from Kraków and Warsaw, and the picture of a man with a strong, quiet, smiling face flash on to the screen. Babcia burst into tears, and then the telephone rang. Anna went to answer it, as the television abruptly switched to the next item.

'Hello? Ewa? . . . yes, yes, we've just heard. Isn't it

349

wonderful? . . . Yes, do come over. And will you ring Jerzy? All right . . . see you in a little while . . .'

She hung up, and went back to the sitting room, just as the phone in the grandparents' flat began to ring.

'The whole world is on the telephone,' said Dziadek, and he went out to answer it, smiling, moving like a man of forty.

9
Poland, 1979

Jerzy and Elizabeth were sharing the couchette compartment from
Hook of Holland to Warsaw with four Poles: a middle-aged husband
and wife, who looked like farmers; a thin single man in his sixties
with a bulbous nose and red, sweating face; and a grandmother who
sat surrounded by a heap of bulging plastic bags. Elizabeth watched
Jerzy helping to heave their companions' suitcases on to the luggage
rack, and gestured to the old woman.

'Shall we . . . your bags . . .'

She shook her head. 'Thank you . . . I keep them.'

'What about this?' Jerzy asked in Polish, indicating a worn cardboard suitcase by her feet.

'Yes, yes, that, please . . .'

He swung it up to the rack, and looked around. 'Anything else,
anyone?'

The man on his own said something Elizabeth couldn't understand,
and Jerzy laughed. He sat down, opposite her; she shifted on the
plastic seat and looked at her watch.

'We'll be moving in a minute.'

'How about something to eat?'

She opened her shoulder bag, brought out sandwiches and
Thermos. The single man watched, got up again and reached to the
luggage rack, snapping open a plastic suitcase. Looking up, Elizabeth
saw he had a hole in his throat, a clean, round, unmistakable hole.
A tracheotomy? A bullet wound? She kicked Jerzy gently across the
narrow space between the seats, but as he raised an eyebrow the man
turned round, and she felt embarrassed, and shook her head. 'Never
mind.'

The man waved a bottle of vodka at them, and a glass.

'Aha,' said Jerzy. 'That's more like it.'

He poured a shot and raised the glass, grinning.

'Na zdrowie.'

'Na zdrowie, said everyone.

There was a shunting and clanging and the carriage jerked. Then the door to the corridor was slid open with a bang and their courier beamed at them from behind Edna Everage spectacles.

'You all have everything? Tickets, passports, your badges? We are about to leave. Ah – I see the celebrations have begun already.' They all laughed. Pani Maria was enormous, kindly, had marshalled them all at Victoria Station, Dover, disembarking. She cast a glance at the old lady, then at Jerzy and Elizabeth. 'You will take care of little Babcia?'

'Oh, yes.'

'Very good. If there is anything you need, I am in carriage D.' She banged the door across again, and moved heavily along the corridor. The train began to move.

There was a general shifting and settling in the carriage.

'Happy?' Jerzy asked Elizabeth.

'Very. And you?'

He nodded, and she thought: he looks more relaxed than he has for months – perhaps than I've ever seen him.

The train gathered speed, and she sat looking out of the window, as they moved through towns and villages, past trees just turning yellow, through a flat landscape under a grey late afternoon sky. It was five o'clock; they had left Victoria at nine, oversleeping and almost missing the train after having supper with the family the night before and staying up late to finish packing. In Jerzy's case was an empty jam jar.

'What *are* you taking that for?' Elizabeth asked, as he brought it back from the kitchen, washed and dried, and slipped it in between two pairs of jeans.

'Polish earth,' he said, putting a sweater on top. 'Dziadek asked me to bring him some. He was half-joking, but . . .'

Through the window, Elizabeth saw two white swans, slowly moving across a dyke covered in thick green algae. It was growing dusky, lights appearing in the towns. Ahead the factory chimneys of Rotterdam sent thick smoke drifting into the sky and she could see the darkening outlines of cranes and ships. Then the lights in the carriage flicked on, and it became difficult to see anything outside. She turned to watch Jerzy, talking animatedly in Polish. She had been to evening classes last winter, but still found it very difficult, could understand more than she could speak, but understood only the basics. What was he talking about now? She made out *passport*, and *border*, and there were roars of laughter. In her corner, the Babcia was falling asleep, still in her headscarf, her Tesco's and Arnotts' Food Store bags beginning to slide a little towards the floor.

'She's going to visit her son in Poznań,' said Jerzy. 'Are you all right?'

'Tired. How are we all going to sleep?'

'With enormous difficulty, I should think. Shall we have something to eat now?'

The farmer and his wife, who she discovered lived in Bradford, were unwrapping mounds of sandwiches, and a long sausage. The man on his own eyed them, and took another swig of vodka.

'Hasn't he brought any food?' Elizabeth asked under her breath.

Jerzy shrugged. 'We could give him something . . .'

'Go on, then.'

But the man shook his head. '*Nie, nie, dziękuję* . . .' He got up, slid back the door and went out, swaying down the corridor.

'And where does he live?' asked Elizabeth, munching a cheese sandwich.

'In a hostel in Ealing. He comes back quite often – this is his seventh or eighth trip.'

'Oh.'

Two weeks before they left, Ewa had had a birthday party, a small gathering in her flat for family and friends. Among the friends was a girl with a Polish mother and English father, born and brought up in north London. Hanna used to work in the same translation agency as Ewa, and was married to an Englishman. She and Elizabeth had spent some time talking; her attitude towards many of the older-generation Poles was brisk.

'Absurd, this business of not going back. They could have got British passports and be going every year, if they wanted – why not? And the way some of the grandparents have never learned English, closeting themselves away . . .' She frowned. 'My grandmother still wants me to go to mass – I try not to think about all that, now.'

She couldn't have been more different from Ewa. Elizabeth had wondered if Ewa minded that she was going to Poland: it did feel somehow inappropriate, that Jerzy's first visit should be with her, and not his sister.

'No, I don't mind,' Ewa had said last night, at supper. 'I don't think I'll ever go, I don't think I want to.'

'Why?'

'You know why – because it would be supporting the regime.'

'Do you think that's what we're doing?' Jerzy asked. 'Shouldn't we be going?'

Ewa shrugged. 'You go. Of course you must go if you want to. I just wish I could see Wiktoria.'

'So do I,' said Anna. 'I hope you can manage all the parcels, Jerzy. They won't weigh you down too much?'

'No, Mama. Anyway, it's only until we get to Warsaw.'

Elizabeth looked up at the luggage rack. They'd hardly been able to shut his suitcase this morning – it was filled with the things Wiktoria had written to ask for: chocolate, shampoo, writing paper, toilet rolls, soap powder. They would stay with her for a little while, then hire a car and travel as much as they could, taking a tent. It had taken them almost a year to save for the trip, helped at the last minute by Elizabeth selling a painting and Jerzy four photographs, in his first exhibition, small but well received, in a new gallery.

'*Passeporte!*' The door slammed open; a German border guard inspected them, their documents. '*Bitte . . . danke schön.*'

The carriage windows were black, now, the countryside invisible except for occasional lights. They drank coffee from the Thermos, and stretched. The farmer and his wife were standing up, prising open their suitcases again, passing spongebags. In her corner, the Babcia was snoring lightly, headscarf askew.

'Is she going to share a couchette with Bullet Hole?' asked Elizabeth.

'I hope not. I'm going to the loo – coming?'

They went out together, found the corridor crowded, and pushed through to the toilet, queuing for almost twenty minutes before they could each get in, pee, and have a wash. It smelt, and was running out of toilet paper. Swaying, Elizabeth remembered the rolls in Jerzy's case – oh well. Tomorrow morning.

When they got back to their carriage they found the couchettes already down, thin sheets and coarse grey blankets folded at the ends. The Babcia, awake now, was sitting bolt upright on hers at the bottom, the farmer and his wife on the second and third bunks. Jerzy and Elizabeth clambered up, on the opposite side, he to the third, she to the middle, and held hands for a moment, whispering.

'I love you.'

'I love you. Goodnight.'

Elizabeth dropped her hand, turned over, listened to everyone trying to settle, to pretend the others weren't there.

The carriage lights dimmed, the train moved faster and faster. Just as they were drifting into sleep, the door slid open and Bullet Hole stumbled in, muttering. Elizabeth raised her head, and saw him stand for a moment, blinking at them all; then he felt his way to the bunk beneath hers, sat down and pulled off his shoes and was almost instantly asleep, snoring loudly.

She pulled her pillow over her head, and after a while fell asleep too, the sound and movement of the train deep within her.

'*Passeporte! Passeporte, bitte!*'

It felt only moments before they were shouted awake again, the door of the carriage banged back as loudly as if it were broad daylight, and they crossed into East Germany. Then, in the small hours, into West Berlin, and the door banged open again. Then again: East Berlin. Peering through a grey half-light, Elizabeth saw two Russian soldiers, in guardboxes, silhouetted. Then the train jerked forwards and they were moving on; she drifted back into an uncomfortable doze, her head throbbing. And then again, one last demand for passports, and by early morning they had crossed the border into Poland.

Sunflowers nodded from cottage gardens, from the wild borders of fields where rounded haystacks rested like cows in the sun. There were silver birches all along the track; grey wooden carts moved slowly through the hayfields, the horse driven by a man or boy; women and children in kerchiefs gathered the hay into stooks. White geese flapped along winding roads; stacks of sawn wood stood in yards. The train passed through a forest, then endless maize fields.

'There's a stork!'

At Poznań station, Babcia and Bullet Hole got off. He was going to visit his sick brother; they watched him weave his way towards the exit. The little Babcia stood on the platform, waiting for her son. She looked up and down. People came and went.

'Where *is* he?' asked Elizabeth.

'Drunk in a bar on the other side of Poznań, I expect.'

The train began to move again; they craned their necks. As they pulled out of the station, she was still standing there, suitcase and Arnotts' Food Store bags at her feet, quite alone on the platform.

Jerzy began translating the names of the stations they passed through, as they sat drinking milkless tea from glasses fetched earlier from the end of the corridor: in a cubbyhole with a kettle, a man in cap and shirtsleeves was supplying the whole carriage, perhaps the whole train.

'Stumps . . . This is Rome . . . These are the Seasons . . . In the Manner of a Wolf . . . Hawks' Nest . . . Scalders.'

'*Scalders?*'

'I think that's what it means.'

'And what does that mean?' asked Elizabeth. 'Look.'

They gazed at enormous red lettering on the white walls outside the next station:

UMACNIAMY SOCJALISTYCZNĄ PRAWOŻĄDNOŚĆ!

'Let us Strengthen Socialist Justice!' said Jerzy.

The farmer roared.

There were similar appeals on a number of other walls. Inside the carriage, the main topic of conversation was currency exchange. Two hours from Warsaw the sky darkened; by mid-afternoon, as the train pulled into the station, it was drizzling and chilly. Pani Maria stumped along the platform in a transparent plastic mac, glasses steaming, seeing off her passengers.

'*Do widzenia, do widzenia* . . . Enjoy yourselves.' She looked at Jerzy and Elizabeth.

'You have somewhere to stay?'

'Yes, thanks,' said Jerzy, 'We're just having a breather.'

'Ah. You want a lift?'

They looked at each other.

'All right – thank you.'

She led them into the station car park, where a man in very military uniform stood waiting by a Polish Fiat. There seemed to be no other make of car there.

'My colleague,' said Pani Maria, and they realized that although he looked like a major, or perhaps a police officer, he was another travel agent. 'Please – get in. Where are you going?'

Jerzy gave them Wiktoria's address, and they drove out through the damp streets. Trams moved down the centre; tower blocks and skyscrapers rose above shop façades; Fiat taxis hooted. There were people queuing at kiosks, coming in and out of the shops, but Elizabeth's first impression was of space, and few people.

They stopped in a quiet, tree-lined street some way from the centre. From the front seat, Pani Maria turned round, and asked Jerzy something in Polish. He nodded, and withdrew his wallet. The military man snapped open a black plastic briefcase; they saw wads of złoty notes. More words were exchanged, in low voices, and then Jerzy passed over a small sheaf of dollars and was given what looked like

356

a million złotys. The black plastic briefcase snapped shut; they drove on. The whole transaction had taken less than a minute.

Elizabeth envisaged military police, waiting for them as the train to London stopped abruptly, on the track outside Warsaw. She saw herself, weeping, as Jerzy, despite his British passport, was taken away; imagined pleading in consulates, embassies, returning to England without him, telling the family. Worse: even now they were about to be arrested, the driver not a travel agent at all, but a member of the military police, and Pani Maria a decoy, paid to trap Western tourists. In a few moments the car would stop. they would slowly turn from the front seat, look at them coldly. '*Passports, please.*'

The car drew to a halt. Elizabeth's stomach lurched.

'This must be it,' said Jerzy.

'What?' She grabbed his hand.

'Wiktoria's . . . are you all right?'

She nodded, feeling sick.

'Is it his driving?'

'No, nothing, tell you later.'

They clambered out, pulling their luggage, and shook hands with Pani Maria, who beamed.

'Very good – I shall see you in three weeks, yes? On the platform. Enjoy yourselves.' She slammed the door, and the car sped away. Elizabeth clutched at Jerzy's hand.

'Hey – what's the matter?'

'I thought . . . I thought . . .' She explained, feeling ridiculous.

'*Honestly.*' He hugged her. 'People do it every day, all the time. We'll probably be stopped in the street tomorrow.'

'But are you sure it's safe?'

'Not if you do it outside a police station, I suppose, but otherwise.'

'How do you know?'

'People have told me.'

'And what if you're caught?'

'A fine? I shouldn't think anything very terrible. Everyone's doing it, they're desperate for dollars. Are you all right now?'

She pulled herself together. 'Yes. What a way to arrive. I wouldn't be much use in a war, would I?'

'I shouldn't think either of us would be much use. Come on.'

They were outside a low apartment block, some five or six storeys, with concrete balconies, one of a half dozen along the street.

'Number four,' said Jerzy, and they went up to the main entrance and inside climbed the concrete stairs. At a plain white door, like a fire door, they rang the bell, and waited. After a few moments it was opened, and a tall, stooping, white-haired woman in glasses looked at them, looked again at Jerzy, and burst into tears.

'Jerzy . . . Jerzy . . .' She held out her arms, kissed him on both cheeks, over and over again.

'This is Elizabeth . . .' Jerzy said at last.

Wiktoria nodded to her, kissed him again. 'Come in. Come in.'

They followed her inside, into a small white-painted corridor hung with a mirror and flower prints.

'Please – you can put your bags in the bedroom – and there is the bathroom – and then come and have something to eat.'

She indicated a room off to the right, and wiped her eyes. 'Forgive me.' She smiled at Jerzy, their eyes on a level. It was the first time Elizabeth had seen him with a member of the family who was not dwarfed by him: Anna's father must have been tall, too. They went into the bedroom, put down their bags. A fifties light-fitting hung from the ceiling; when they went out into the sitting room the square couch and armchairs, the lamps, the spindle-leg tables and plastic-seated chairs all looked as if they'd been made twenty-five years ago. They noticed this later in many public places, too – hotel lounges, restaurants, office reception areas.

Wiktoria came from the kitchen, moving stiffly, carrying a tray.

'Sit down, sit down.'

'Have we taken your bedroom, Aunt?' asked Jerzy.

'It doesn't matter. I can sleep on the couch quite well.' She was laying the table, slowly setting out flowered plates, small cotton napkins. A wooden carving in relief hung on the wall, the Virgin Mary in a shrine. On another wall, above a shiny sideboard, hung framed photographs.

'So – perhaps you would like to wash, before we eat?'

'Please.' Elizabeth got up again, and went out to the bathroom. It was very small, and smelled, though much more faintly, like the toilet on the train. She washed her hands with soap quite unlike any soap she had ever seen in England: green, slimy, flecked with gritty specks of something. When she went back to the sitting room, Jerzy and Wiktoria were talking rapidly in Polish.

'Excuse us – ' Wiktoria broke off as she came in.

'No, no – I'm quite used to it. I can understand a little, anyway.'

Wiktoria smiled. Elizabeth gathered that they were talking about the family. They all got up to look at the photographs above the sideboard.

'My niece,' Wiktoria said to her, leaning on Jerzy's arm, and pointed to a picture of a family picnic. 'This was taken in . . . 1937, 1938. There is Anna . . . and Jerzy and their father next to each other . . . this is me . . . and that is Teresa.'

The family sat or stood under a clump of sun-dappled trees, a rug spread on the ground, a wicker basket open. Anna looked sunburnt and happy, wearing a cotton dress, her hair in plaits. Jerzy and Tomasz leaned against each other, smiling; Teresa was a little apart from them, her face shadowed by a straw hat, and Wiktoria, tall and plain and big-boned, wearing horn-rimmed spectacles, sat leaning back on her hands, at the edge of the rug.

'We have this at home,' said Jerzy. 'In Mama's album. Who took it?'

'My mother,' said Wiktoria. 'Your great-great aunt. She died the next year. I was very glad, later, that she had not lived to see the invasion, and the war,' She shook her head. 'And then there is this one . . .' She pointed to a much smaller print of the photograph of Anna's mother, her hair cut short in a twenties bob, her eyes very dark. 'Poor Ewa,' she said. 'Such a terrible thing, to die so young. I don't believe Tomasz ever really recovered, although he and Teresa were happy, I think. And this is the children, the same winter Ewa died, when I was looking after them.' There were the two small figures, in fur gloves, walking in the snowy park. 'And this last one – Anna just a few days before the Uprising, after she had come to live with me.'

'We haven't got this one,' said Jerzy.

'No? No – you wouldn't have. I didn't have the film developed until after the war.'

They saw Anna sitting at a kitchen table, drinking from a cracked cup and saucer. The print was pale, over-exposed. 'I was trying to be clever, to take an indoor photograph. We knew we were going to be called to our units in a matter of days – I wanted a photograph of Anna, just in case . . . And as it happened, of course, it was Jerzy who was killed.' She sighed. 'And poor Teresa. Sometimes afterwards I used to think it had been madness, you know, ever to think we could have overcome the Germans. All those lives lost, Warsaw destroyed . . . And yet – we had to do it. There was no question.' She patted Jerzy's arm. 'And now, poor children, nothing to eat. Come and sit down.'

They ate a coarse bread, margarine, a rubbery cheese like Edam, sliced tomatoes, a kind of spam, and some very old Jaffa cakes. There was also a dish of something like a cross between cream and yoghurt, tasting of vanilla, and delicious. They drank tea from heavy cups.

'He is a good man, your father?' Wiktoria asked Jerzy.'He has taken care of your mother?'

He flushed. 'Yes. Yes, I think so.'

'Good.'

'He also . . . suffered in the war.'

'Naturally.' She poured more tea. 'You realize it is the thirty-fifth anniversary of the Uprising?'

'Oh. Yes, I suppose it must be.'

'And shall I tell you something? We are being . . . exhorted? I think that is the word. We are being exhorted on the television, almost every day, to remember those times. There is a shortage of coal, or there are problems with rail transport, so that it does not arrive; there are food shortages, and in another month or two it will be winter, and the temperature will fall. And what do they tell us? To be as selfless and patriotic as they were – we were – during the Uprising! To endure as we did then. Do you know there are posters up, official posters, showing the anchor of the AK – the symbol of Fighting Poland? We are to fight now, apparently, by putting up with shortages and queues and freezing apartments. They have been showing films from the Uprising all through the summer, to encourage us. Yet do you know that it is almost impossible to place an obituary in any newspaper, and say that the person mourned was a member of the AK? Or announce any kind of AK meeting or reunion?'

'Incredible,' said Jerzy.

'No. Not really. Have you had enough to eat? I have asked you nothing of yourself. Anna says you are a photographer?'

'Yes. And Elizabeth is a painter.'

'Ah.' She turned to Elizabeth. 'And what do you paint? Portraits? Landscapes? Anna used to draw and paint a little, you know; perhaps she still does?'

'Yes,' said Jerzy. 'But mostly in her work. With the patients.'

'She is working in that psychiatric hospital still?'

'Yes.'

'Hmm.' Wiktoria began to clear the plates. 'The whole of Poland is a psychiatric hospital. Or rather, that is where Mr Gierek and his friends should be residing, if it were not too good for them. Now – do you want to rest, or go out, or go on talking to an old woman?'

Elizabeth's head was beginning to pound.

'Perhaps . . .'

'Perhaps we should just go for a stroll,' said Jerzy. 'Stretch our legs after the train.'

'Of course. And if you decide to stay out late – well, I can give you a key.' She smiled at them; Elizabeth felt her unbend towards her. Just a little.

'The presents!' she said to Jerzy suddenly. 'We must give your aunt the presents first.'

'Great-aunt,' said Wiktoria. 'What presents?'

'Just what you wrote and asked for. And a few other things . . .' Jerzy disappeared into the bedroom, Elizabeth helped Wiktoria clear the table. He came back carrying the parcels, and laid them all out on the table. Wiktoria picked up soap, soap powder, shampoo, chocolate, tissues and toilet paper, writing paper, talcum powder, tins of fruit and ham, boxes of biscuits.

'But you have brought a shop!' She put down a tin and kissed him again. 'It must have been so heavy.'

'Not really. And here is a letter from Mama.'

'Ah. Thank you. I shall read it while you are out.' She snapped open a plastic handbag. 'A spare key . . . I will see you later. Or in the morning. Off you go now.'

They were approaching the shopping centre, open and spacious, the tall buildings predominantly grey. There were a number of department stores, but there was almost nothing in the windows, although they were well lit, and the stores open, at nearly seven o'clock. Women carried plastic string bags of potatoes or apples; they walked past a number of hot dog stalls, but saw few cafés or restaurants. They walked on, along quiet, unlit streets, until they narrowed, and they found themselves in winding alleyways, a cobbled square ahead of them.

'This must be Stare Miasto,' Jerzy said. 'The Old Town.'

The houses in the narrow streets were painted in dilapidating pastels, dark green, cream; ornate wrought-iron lamp fittings hung from them at street corners; the roofs were red-tiled. As they came into the square they saw empty tables and chairs in a corner, with folded parasols. Jerzy pulled out their paperback guidebook, unfolded the map. 'This is the Market Square,' he said eventually.

'Where is everyone?'

He shrugged. 'I don't know.'

Further on, they came to another square, before the Royal Palace, graceful, pink-washed. Here, too, there was only a scattering of people. The sky was darkening; Elizabeth shivered. Their arms round each other, they stood looking up at the palace, and the long column in the square bearing the statue of King Zygmunt III, holding a cross.

'Do you realize,' said Jerzy, 'that every single thing we're looking at is a complete reconstruction? The palace was only finished two or three years ago. All these medieval houses, the monuments, the streets – they were just ruins in 1945. They've been rebuilt brick by brick.'

'And this is where your father was, in the Uprising?'

'Yes. There were hand-to-hand battles here, while the bombs fell. And under here, I suppose . . . or somewhere not far away, Tata crawled through the sewers. All the way through to the city centre, where we've walked from.'

'Jerzy?'

'Mmm?'

'You're a bit pale.'

'I'm all right.' He looked at the map again. 'Somewhere near here must be Krasiński Square, where the RAF dropped supplies, early on. And further away was the ghetto, and Pawiak prison. That's where my uncle escaped from.' He folded it up. 'We'll visit all that another day. Shall we try and find somewhere to have a drink?'

'Yes – I'm frozen.'

'I suppose people simply don't come out in the evenings,' Jerzy said, and they walked on. 'Groups of people out in the streets are discouraged – it's only a few years since the last food riots. And anyway – there's nowhere to go, is there?' They passed a few bars, a couple of cafés. And plaques, in almost every street, on walls, on corners, set into the brickwork with candles burning beneath them: *On this spot 30 Poles died at the hands of the Nazis, 8 November 1943; On this spot 50 Poles . . . On this spot 100 Poles . . .*

'Shall we go in here?' Jerzy said at last.

They looked into the window of a restaurant advertising Polish specialities, and saw small candlelit tables, a bar at the far end. When they pushed open the door they could hear Muzak with a fifties flavour, and saw wooden speakers on shelves: the waitresses wore flowered pinafore dresses. They sat down, and examined a long menu in Polish and English.

'*Proszę?*'

One of the waitresses, in heavy eye-liner, was standing beside them.

She smiled thinly. Jerzy asked if they were serving *bigos*. She shook her head.

'Chicken, veal . . .'

'I don't think so,' said Elizabeth, suddenly too tired to think of food.

They had lemon tea and nutcake, the cake sandy and tasteless. At a nearby table a group of people were talking animatedly.

'I think they're from the university,' said Jerzy. 'They're talking about films.'

There was a very drunk man in a grey check jacket at the bar; the waitress not serving stood a little way from him, expressionless. Elizabeth felt suddenly exhausted, a very long way from home.

'Shall we go?'

They paid, and walked slowly through the streets to Wiktoria's. On the corner of her street an old woman was feeding six or seven stray cats from tin dishes, calling to them softly. The moon rose above the trees and low blocks of flats. When they unlocked her front door and went inside, Wiktoria was just coming out of the bathroom in her dressing gown.

'Hello, children. Have you enjoyed yourselves?'

They nodded, yawning.

'Go on now, straight to bed. Sleep as long as you like in the morning.'

They went, half expecting her to come and tuck them up.

They sat at a table in the Market Square, which this morning was livelier: other tourists sat beneath the cotton parasols, although it was still cloudy, or took jingling pony and trap rides. From an open upper window, rock music throbbed; a hurdy-gurdy played on the far side. Jerzy was reading a guidebook, his camera round his neck, Elizabeth was sketching; their cups of coffee, undrinkable, stood between them, sour whipped-cream topping floating on the surface.

'There's a museum of photographs from the Uprising,' Jerzy said. 'Would you like to go?'

She nodded. 'In a bit. What else?'

'There's Pawiak: the prison reconstructed, with a museum. And there's the cemetery where Jerzy is buried – reburied. Where all the Uprising graves are.' His fingers drummed lightly on the metal table. 'Does that sound like too much? Too grim? I don't want to inflict death on you on our first day.'

'But you want to make your pilgrimages.'

'Yes.' He reached across the table and she put down her pencil and gave him her hand. They looked at each other, thinking of the night before, naked between Wiktoria's cool sheets.

A little later, they wandered across the square, and through the narrow streets as the sun began to filter through the cloud, and it grew warm. At breakfast, they had asked Wiktoria if she wanted to come out with them this morning, but she shook her head. 'You can see how stiff and creaky I am – it is no pleasure for me to walk. Besides, I'm sure you want to be by yourselves.'

'But we must take you out somewhere before we leave Warsaw,' Jerzy said. 'For a meal . . .'

They all laughed.

'We'll see. You make the most of the time you have.'

'I think this is it,' Jerzy was saying now; they were standing at an open doorway to a gallery, small white-painted rooms leading off each other. A woman in a paisley-patterned dress sat at a table inside, knitting; the sun shone through the windows on to the wooden floor. She took their money and they walked through, stopping at each framed photograph hung on the walls, or on screens dividing the rooms.

In bomb-shattered streets, women moved awkwardly behind barricades, carrying buckets of water over the rubble. Little knots of people stood watching hasty burials; a boy no more than twelve, in makeshift uniform, bit his lip in a nervous smile; a young soldier in his teens sat on an upturned bucket amidst torn-up paving behind a barricade, laughing over a Flash Gordon novel – *Błysk Gordon*. An old woman picked her way over a heap of rubble through a hole in the wall of a ruined house: below, in the exposed foundations, her son reached up to help her. A man in a hat and black suit stood motionless, in a street piled with bodies. A bunch of carnations rested on a shallow grave, a soldier's tin helmet hung on the plain wooden cross; in the background were ruins, beneath a lowering sky.

They looked at them all in silence, then left, thanking the attendant; she nodded, barely looking up from her knitting. Out in the street, they passed more plaques, more shrines with candles burning. *On this spot 42 Poles were executed by the Nazis . . . On this spot 12 . . . Here were 19 . . .*

Some had small bunches of flowers laid in the niche in the wall, or white and red ribbons, and some had postcards of the Pope, smiling, his hand raised.

'We must ask Wiktoria about the Pope,' said Elizabeth. 'Do you want to go to mass while we're here?'

'Perhaps.'

'Only perhaps? I thought that would be one of the first things you'd want to do here.'

'Why? We never go in London.'

'I know, but – '

'But what?' Jerzy said irritably.

'But nothing,' she said. 'I'm sorry I mentioned it.'

They came to a small park, and sat on a bench, beneath the trees. There were trees and parks everywhere in the city; the impression, still, was of space, and cleanliness – not a shred of litter anywhere. In the main roads and streets away from the nest of the Old Town, traffic squealed. Pedestrians had right of way: if you put a foot off the pavement, cars were meant to let you cross. It felt absurdly dangerous.

Elizabeth turned to look at Jerzy, who was scuffing at the earth beneath the bench with his heel. He looked withdrawn and troubled. Well – you could call it troubled if you were feeling sympathetic and understanding. Otherwise you might say sulky.

'Jerzy?'

'What?'

'What's the matter?'

'Nothing. I'm just thinking.'

'Are you all right?'

'Yes.'

Not: yes, thank you for asking, and sorry I've suddenly cut off without warning or explanation. Just: yes.

Elizabeth gave up. A squirrel danced across the path; Jerzy scuffed again, and it scampered away and up a tree on the far side. She sat watching it, feeling Jerzy's silence descending like a cloud between them. I hope this isn't going to happen all through the holiday, she thought, remembering days in London when he left home in the morning perfectly equable and came home dark-faced, not speaking. It didn't happen often, but it happened, and at first she'd been reduced to tears of frustration. The last couple of times she'd fled to the studio. I really didn't think it would be like that here, she thought, and realized she had been hoping, all the time they planned this trip, that Jerzy would come to Poland and feel somehow cleansed, purified, made whole. What a very Christian image. People didn't have road-to-Damascus changes in themselves like that – unless they were on the road to Damascus.

'Jerzy?' she asked again, and put out a hand towards him. He went on scuffing. 'Shall we go and find somewhere for lunch?'

'I'm not hungry.'

'I am – come on, let's go and look.'

'You can go if you want.'

She moved away and stood up. 'I thought we were on holiday together.'

'So? Can't you be independent for five minutes?'

'Jerzy! What is the matter with you?'

'I just feel low, that's all.'

'I know you do. You don't have to take it out on me.'

He didn't answer. Elizabeth began to walk rapidly away, down the path towards the iron railings. No studio to escape to now: where was she supposed to go? Across the road, further up, there was a large café, with tables and chairs set out on the pavement; she stepped off the kerb, and a Fiat braked sharply, horn blaring. She jumped and stepped back again, waiting until at last a driver slowed and waved her across. Then she ran down the road to the café; she suddenly heard Jerzy call her, but she didn't stop. She pulled out a metal chair and sat down at a metal table, and waited.

'Elizabeth – I'm sorry.' He was standing beside her, panting; he pulled out a chair and sat down, shaking his head. 'Sorry,' he said again.

'Are you going to tell me what's wrong?'

He waved at the air. 'Forget it, forget it, I'm just being neurotic. For God's sake let's have something to eat – where's the waitress?'

The waitress, in cotton dress and flowered apron, looked tired and took their order indifferently. There was, in any case, almost nothing to order, certainly nothing you could call lunch, and they waited twenty-five minutes for two glasses of tea and two slices of cake with a topping which tasted of nail-polish remover.

'Listen,' said Jerzy, when they'd paid. 'Do you mind going to Pawiak this afternoon? We don't have to. I suppose one of the things I'm worried about is that I'm going to burden you with my family, and all its history here, and you'll just get bored, or find it oppressive, and then I'll feel guilty, but frustrated, because I really need to see it all.'

'I know you do,' Elizabeth said. 'What do you think I am? I know you do. If I didn't want to see, and be with you when you saw, I wouldn't have come, would I? Frankly, just at the moment I hardly care what we see as long as you talk to me.'

'Sometimes talking is the last thing I want to do.'

'Well – at least acknowledge that it's difficult when you cut off. Can't you do that?'

'Yes,' he said, 'I can.' He reached across the table, and brushed a strand of hair away from her cheek. 'You look so earnest when you lecture me.'

'I look earnest? You should see yourself sometimes.'

'I'm glad I can't. Come on, let's go.'

They got up and he took her hand. Elizabeth gave it to him feeling more or less reconciled, still a little wary; then he bent to kiss her and for a moment they clung to each other, eyes closed. A passerby coughed in disapproval, and they drew quickly apart.

'Not the done thing here,' said Jerzy.

'Quite right too.' Elizabeth felt the tension between them slip away as they walked on, following the folded map from the guidebook, through the Krasiński Gardens, which were very beautiful, and were near to the place where the ghetto had stood, high walls sealing off four hundred thousand Jews. Now, it was as if it had never been.

'There's a Monument to the Jewish Heroes a few streets away,' said Jerzy, looking at the map again.

'Is there?' Elizabeth found herself remembering something: not long after they'd met, she'd told a Jewish friend, a woman she'd known since art school, that she'd fallen in love with a Pole. Hannah had not been pleased. 'They're anti-Semitic,' she said. 'Hitler didn't choose Poland for the camps for nothing, you know.'

This seemed such a terrible thing to say that Elizabeth had never told Jerzy. And she wasn't going to tell him now, either.

They walked on, down Dzielna Street, until they saw a deep paved and cobbled space across the road, with a leafy tree set into it, the trunk covered with metal plaques. Beyond the tree was a long low wall, with a dark, semicircular entrance at the foot of a flight of steps; a pillar of original brickwork, concrete and plaster stood before the steps, and from it projected an iron girder, surmounted with rolls of barbed wire, all that remained of the original entrance. On the wall above the gaping black semicircle, in relief, was a single word: PAWIAK. Trees and tower blocks rose beyond it. Jerzy and Elizabeth crossed the road, and went slowly down the steps.

Off to the left ran a long corridor, with reconstructed cells, and straight ahead of them was what looked like another cell, but which they quickly saw was where the attendant made her tea, and sold postcards. She was tiny, old, wearing an apron; they saw a mug and kettle on a shelf behind her. She nodded at them, unsmiling, and they heard her follow them, as they made their way down a further flight of steps into a windowless area, half underground. On the left an open space held glass cases, all along the wall; they looked at papers documenting labour camps, street round-ups, executions. Photographs of members of the AK resistance hung on the walls; they could not tell if they had been taken by Poles or the Gestapo. There were other photographs: endless rows of hangings – bodies swinging or hanging limply from gallows, from balconies. Elizabeth saw Jerzy wander into another room, and glimpsed what looked like iron and metal objects – instruments of torture? She did not follow him, but went over to another low case, resting her hands lightly on the glass as she looked at the list of names on a yellowing sheet of paper. Behind her there was a hiss: she turned to see the tiny old woman shaking her head at her, gesturing to her to take her hands off the glass. She jerked them away and stood, uncertainly.

Jerzy was still in the far room; she couldn't face going in there, but neither did she want to stay here, being watched with disapproval, even animosity. What was the matter with this old woman? She went out, into another long dark corridor. There seemed to be no other visitors; she walked slowly along, past cell after cell, each with a small spyhole set into the door. Anna's brother must have been in a cell like one of these. She stood on tiptoe, and lifted the spyhole flap aside, peering in. It was very dim, and shadowy inside; for a horrible moment she imagined herself hearing the screams of other prisoners as the door was slammed shut on her and bolted.

Footsteps came towards her, very quietly, from the other end of the passage. She thought: I don't belong here, I don't even belong with Jerzy, I want to go home. The footsteps came closer, and she suddenly heard herself giggle, like a nervous child who doesn't dare to cry but is about to. At once, there was a spitting, cackling torrent of Polish, and she swung round to see the old woman advancing on her, furiously waving her hands, shouting. Elizabeth turned and ran.

'Jerzy! Jerzy!'

She bumped against him at the corner. 'What's she saying? What have I done? I giggled – it was only because I was so frightened – '

Behind them, the tiny, wrinkled woman was still shouting. Jerzy held Elizabeth, and listened.

'She thinks we're German,' he said. 'She thinks we're German, that we've come to mock . . .' He let her go, and walked over to the old woman. *'Proszę, Pani . . .'* Elizabeth, still shaking, saw him towering over her, explaining in a low voice. The old woman shook her head, and did not apologize.

'Let's go,' said Elizabeth. 'Please, let's go . . .'

They made their way back to the entrance, past the cubbyhole where the old woman spent her days, up the steps to the sunlit cobblestones. Elizabeth drew a deep breath.

'Are you all right?' Jerzy asked.

'Yes, I think so. My God . . . she must be half-mad, working down there all the time.'

'But that's how people here must feel, still.'

They walked across to the tree, and stood looking at the white metal plaques, shaped like shields or scrolls. Each bore a name, in capitals, dates and an inscription, and the outline of a cross, lying on a strip of weeping willow.

'What does S.P. mean?'

'Świętej Pamięce – In Holy Memory.'

There were dozens of plaques: to Stanisław Kajak, Bartłomiej Urban, Jerzy Bielski, Piotr Kwiatkowski, Wladysław Bloch – all round and up the trunk, beneath the leaves.

'And your uncle escaped,' said Elizabeth, still shaking, as they walked away.

'Hard to believe, isn't it?' said Jerzy. 'It must have been like a fortress – but he escaped from the ruins of the ghetto, on a working party, not from here.' He told her the story, as they walked on down Dzielna Street. 'I will understand if you don't want to go to the cemetery now,' he said. 'We can go another day.'

'No – let's go today. After that, a cemetery might even be quite soothing. And we can do something quite different tomorrow. But can we take the tram?'

The tram cost 1 złoty, for any distance. They stood near the front, on the slatted wooden floor, as it swung humming down the street past buildings which, Elizabeth distantly noticed now, reminded her a little of Oxford Street. It was late afternoon, the tram filling with people leaving work. They looked tired and grey, but so did people on London Transport. It was their clothes which made them look different: everything was in Western styles of five, ten years ago – there were flares and bell-bottoms, platform shoes. And shiny, synthetic fabrics: many of the men wore cheap grey suits and open-

369

necked shirts; dresses and skirts looked like Crimplene or polyester, cardigans acrylic.

'We're here,' said Jerzy, and the tram swayed to a halt, and the doors hissed open. They got off, and walked the hundred yards or so to the cemetery. It was very large, bordered with trees, criss-crossed with gravel paths. There were row upon row upon row of identical large grey headstones, each carved with long columns of names: dozens, hundreds, thousands of names, soldiers and civilians killed in the Uprising, an endless roll call of the dead. At the foot of almost every stone were bunches of flowers – marigolds, michaelmas daisies – and all through the cemetery scores of candles in low dishes burned. The sky was grey, now, the air cool; they bought a candle in a dish from a woman selling them at the gate, and carried it along the paths. There were other visitors, mostly Poles, mostly older, talking quietly in twos and threes, or walking alone, bending to lay flowers, or light candles, one from another.

It took them almost an hour to find the headstone, and the name: the stone was almost at the end, and the name on it in the third column, amidst dozens of others: Jerzy Tomasz Kurowski. They stood looking at it, and Elizabeth remembered the photograph of the laughing boy in shorts, on the sunlit river. Jerzy bent down and lit their small red candle from one of the others, and put it beside them; then he stood up and slowly crossed himself. For a moment Elizabeth felt taken completely by surprise, as if she had expected to see Jerzy beside her, and found a stranger there instead. Almost at once, she realized that the gesture in fact suited him perfectly, as if he did it all the time.

He reached towards the stone and lightly touched the name below his uncle's: Andrzej Maciejowski.

'His friend.'

'The one he tried to save?'

'Yes.' He stood looking out across the cemetery, the sea of stones, and said something quietly, under his breath.

'What did you say?'

'*Myriads of broken reeds,*' Jerzy repeated. '*Myriads of broken reeds, all still and stiff . . .*'

She frowned, trying to remember. 'Edward Thomas,' she said at last. 'You read it to me once.' She put her arm through his, leaned her head on his shoulder. After a while, he disengaged himself, and took a photograph of the headstone, for Anna. Then they turned away, and walked along the paths until they were at the gate, and out in the street again. Afterwards, Elizabeth could remember only colours: grey stones, mauve and gold flowers, the pale flickering flames and the sharp autumnal coolness of the air, as if it were like that always.

Night. A dark wet street with alleyways leading off it, the only light from the moon, moving behind ragged clouds. Someone was following him. He had to make his way to the other side of the city, in secret, but there were footsteps behind him. He stopped. They stopped. He turned, his heart pounding, but there was no one there. He went on, ashamed of feeling so afraid. There was a patrol on the corner, three or four Germans in uniform, rifles raised; they were talking very quietly – he could make out a few words, hear them shifting from foot to foot on the wet pavement. He ducked into an alleyway, and leaned against the wall, hearing the sound of his own breathing. How was he to get past?

He shifted, and his foot struck something which rang, something metallic. A manhole cover. Very slowly he bent down and tried to lift it, scraping his fingertips until they were raw, managing at last to heave it off, and aside, and he knelt at the rim and looked down. The rungs of a ladder clung to the side of the shaft; below was nothing but yawning darkness, and the sound of water. He couldn't go down there. He could not. But if he didn't reach them, on the other side of the city, if he didn't warn them . . . Then he would be safe. Shame and fear flooded him. He could not bring himself to go down, but he must go on through the streets. he crept to the entrance of the alleyway again, and looked out.

The patrol had gone. Quickly, he ran, and at once the sound of the footsteps behind him came again, and someone panting. He did not dare to stop; he ran on, stumbled, found his legs suddenly heavy and slow, and ahead of him heard the click of a gun. He stopped, and the footsteps stopped. He turned, and saw a thin dark figure, a boy in a jacket, and his own face, very white, staring at him.

'Jerzy?'

The boy did not answer, but went on staring.

He moved towards him, held out his hand; the boy turned, and now it was he who was following, with sudden loud German voices behind them, pounding feet. The boy ducked into the alleyway, and disappeared. He ran after him, tripped on the manhole cover laid aside, reached out to darkness, and slipped, with a lurch of terror, over the rim of the shaft, and fell, and fell and fell.

Someone was sobbing. He was sobbing, uncontrollably, his whole body shaking, hearing Elizabeth from a long way off, saying his name, feeling her hold him. He stopped, at last, and sat hunched in the bedclothes, shaking his head. Dawn light filtered through the curtains. He drew deep breaths, wiping his eyes on the sheet, and turned to see her anxious face, silky fair hair tangled, cotton nightdress slipping off her shoulders. He put his arm round her, and drew her close; she was very warm.

'Tell me,' she whispered. 'What was it?'

'In the morning. I don't want to think about it now. Come here.'

Her mouth like a flower, opening to his.

'The Pope's visit?' said Wiktoria. 'It was remarkable, of course. Even before he came it was remarkable.' She sat at the top of the table, passing plates. 'You two still look very tired this morning. Did you sleep well?'

'Not very,' said Elizabeth. 'Jerzy had a nightmare.'

'A nightmare?'

'But I'm fine now,' said Jerzy. He kicked her under the table, gently, and Wiktoria looked away.

'Well,' she said. 'The Pope. Help yourselves, please. When we heard the announcement from the Vatican on the news it was as if . . . as if a miracle had happened. Like a sign, that God had not forgotten us. I expect that sounds absurd to you young people, but that is how we felt. Were Anna and your family in London pleased?'

Jerzy nodded, spreading stale bread with jam. 'Particularly my grandparents.'

'Naturally. Anyway, people in the streets were stopping complete strangers to talk about it – that in itself is a little unusual now – and of course a lot of us were crying – ' She looked at Elizabeth. 'We are rather emotional, you know, the Poles. I expect you are finding that.'

'Yes.'

'Exuberant and hospitable,' said Wiktoria. 'Also depressive. I imagine Jerzy is not easy to live with?'

He laughed. 'We're managing,' said Elizabeth. 'Just about.' She felt completely at ease with Wiktoria now. No wonder Anna and her brother had leaned on her during the war.

'Good. So – everyone was in a flurry, and when we knew he was coming here, in June, the city was suddenly full of people, going to visit the places he would be visiting, walking and talking. It was summer, of course, so the evenings were long . . . I went with a friend, and we felt as if we were in Warsaw before the war, you know, free to come and go as we pleased; just seeing so many people was extraordinary. Many of them had travelled long distances to come here, from all parts of Poland, and there had been stories of how the city would be overrun with peasants, or crowds of people out of control. It wasn't like that at all. It was just . . . a kind of calm excitement. There was an enormous cross in Victory Square, draped with a red banner; it was opposite the Tomb of the Unknown Soldier, and it towered over us . . .'

'That was where he celebrated mass?' Jerzy asked. 'We saw it on television.'

'Did you? Yes, it was there. You could hardly move; people were holding up crosses, pressing forward to get a closer look, children on their parents' shoulders. And when he began to speak . . . "Dear fellow countrymen! Dear brothers and sisters! Fellow sharers in the Eucharistic Sacrifice that is being offered today in Warsaw's Victory Square!" I shall never forget it.' She shook her head. 'We felt as if we were worth something again – more than that. We were the people we knew ourselves to be, not what we were told we were, or should be. Simply – ourselves.'

Jerzy and Elizabeth had stopped eating. They sat, listening.

'Everyone says that old age romanticizes,' Wiktoria said slowly. 'That you see the past in a warm nostalgia that has nothing to do with how it really was. And of course the Poles are experts at that. Naturally the time we had between the wars, our brief independence, was not perfect, but now – the whole economy is collapsing. We are in debt everywhere, and already you can see the shortages, not just food, but flats – you have to wait for ever. Furniture, cars, clothes – everything. And perhaps none of these things would matter so much – after all, I'm sure the West is not paved with gold the way the young people here think it is – if only we were not all the time told that the past was worse, that everything wrong now is the fault of the past, that if only we will work and work and work, and never raise our heads, it will all be better. How do you work when you have no spirit left, when you are fed lies all the time about what is really happening?'

She tapped the table impatiently. 'You saw the Victory Square mass on television? Do you know what we saw, when we got home, and switched on the television? The Pope against the sky, as if he had dropped out of the clouds, and was almost alone. I think the cameramen were told to shoot only from below, that's what everyone was saying, because if they did that, then you couldn't see the crowds! Can you imagine? And when there were shots of the crowd, wherever he went in Poland, it was almost always of old peasant women, or nuns, or priests – we hardly ever saw a young face, or a family, but we knew they had been there because we were standing amongst them! Well . . . That's enough, now. Forgive me. What are you going to do today?'

'I thought we might try to visit Chopin's house,' said Jerzy. 'But you don't have to change the subject, Aunt. We want to hear.'

'No – it makes me too angry if I talk like that too much. Chopin's house – in Żelazowa Wola. Yes, that would be a very pleasant day for you.'

'Would you like to come with us?' Elizabeth asked. 'We thought we might hire a car today.'

'So the streets of the West *are* paved with gold, after all,' said Wiktoria. 'It's all right, I am teasing. Yes – yes, I should like to come in that case. Perhaps you could pick me up?'

The road out of the city was flat and lined with willow trees. There were no proper borders, and Elizabeth, driving an unfamiliar Fiat, her nerves scratched by driving through Warsaw on the right-hand side and stalling twice at traffic lights, drove slowly. They were overtaken by cars roaring down the centre of the road, twice sending them nearly into the ditch. When this was not happening they found themselves stopping to let horse-drawn waggons move slowly on to the road from a side lane, and then they travelled behind them, looking up at an enormous, swaying mountain of hay. Sometimes children were perched on the top, eating apples; the waggons turned after a couple of kilometres into another lane, followed by honking lines of white geese. There were sunflowers everywhere, and the fields full of hayricks.

They passed women scything in the fields; a little girl in a kerchief sucked her thumb and watched them drive by; behind her a bare-chested man in a beret guided a horse-drawn cutter through the stubble. They came to a wooden church, and stopped again.

The church was locked. They walked round to the side, to a graveyard full of trees. Early afternoon sunlight dappled the paths; ahead, in the middle of the main one, rose a plain wooden cross, perhaps twenty feet high. Birds sang; tiny red and black beetles scuttled; a rich tangle of weeds and bushes grew between the crowded graves. Here they had no one to look for, they simply walked hand in hand along the warm sandy paths, where insects buzzed in the flickering light beneath the trees. Many of the graves were large and raised, with stone borders, railings and stone crosses set high above them, and many of the headstones bore small ceramic ovals with sepia photographs of those buried there. Elizabeth stopped before one of a young girl, perhaps sixteen, with dark hair, dark eyes – she looked a little like Anne Frank. There were older men and women, sombre in spectacles, or smiling broadly; on every single grave there seemed to be fresh flowers. They stopped before a stone with a verse inscribed beneath the name of a man who had died at Auschwitz.

Łatwo jest mówić o Polsce
Trudno dla niej pracować
Jescze trudniej umierać
A najtrudniej cierpieć.

'What does it mean?'

'That is a verse you will see everywhere in Poland,' said Wiktoria, who had been walking stiffly behind them. She leaned on her stick, and brushed away a fly.

'And on Polish graves in England too,' said Jerzy, and slowly translated:

It is easy to speak of Poland
Hard to work
Harder to die
Harder still to suffer.

They stood for a moment in silence, then went on, stopping by a low wooden railing, beyond which lay untilled ground, no graves, and the graveyard wall. Before the railing was a small stone cross, with a white shield bordered in red nailed to the centre, an inscription: *Żołnierz W.P.* – Soldier of the Polish Forces – and a name, Kazimierz Słoma. At the foot of the cross there was no plinth, and the grave was without a border, but a helmet lay there, pockmarked with six bullet holes. Lilies grew round it.

Jerzy photographed that, too, and then they went slowly back to the car, and on to Żelazowa Wola – 'Or it will be closed before we get there,' said Wiktoria.

As they drove, Elizabeth remembered Jerzy asking yesterday morning about 'inflicting too much death'. It was impossible to go anywhere without touching on it, even in a tiny shrine in a city street.

Memories and melancholy were everywhere; she could feel it all becoming a part of her, too.

What had Jerzy dreamt about last night?

'That's it,' said Wiktoria, and Elizabeth turned left and down a gravel drive between tall trees, and stopped before a small whitewashed cottage, covered in creeper, with a red-tiled roof. Chopin's house. They climbed out of the car, and saw a handful of other tourists walking into the gardens. Inside the cottage, they smelt fresh paint, and the polished tables shone. There were flowers in vases; net curtains at the windows moved gently in the breeze; the whitewashed walls were hung with prints and portraits. They moved from room to quiet room, stopping by the small piano. Elizabeth felt like an American at Stratford, but with a real sense of awe, too, as she looked quickly round, then stroked the yellowed keys.

'Tch, tch, tch,' said Wiktoria, raising an eyebrow.

Elizabeth smiled at her, went across to Jerzy and took the guidebook out of his jacket pocket. She turned the pages. *Żelazowa Wola* . . . Chopin had lived here only in his youth, had spent most of his life in exile in Paris. She looked out of the window, saw a small boy playing in the gardens, a hundred and fifty years ago, humming.

'They give concerts here,' Wiktoria was saying. 'On the Steinway grand in the sitting room. I came to one, once, before the war.'

Jerzy had moved towards the front door. They followed him out into the gardens, helping Wiktoria down stone steps to a sunken lawn and a lake covered with algae and waterlily pads. Frogs and small toads hopped in the long grass at the water's edge. It was very warm, now; their shadows fell across the still green lake, and then, from speakers in the trees, came the music, exuberant waltzes and mazurkas, and the slow, aching nocturnes, drifting out across the water.

They found a wooden bench and sat listening, as the sunlight grew richer and more golden, and the shadows lengthened. Every now and then, in the breeze, a few yellowing leaves fell, spinning gently, to the ground.

Wiktoria had closed her eyes. Her hands rested on the handle of her walking stick, held before her; after a while, it began to sway a little, and they realized she was asleep. They left her sitting there, and walked slowly round the lake.

'What were you dreaming about?' Elizabeth asked.

Jerzy bit his lip. 'I can't remember it properly, but . . . I suppose it was my life, and everything I am afraid of. Not having courage.

Not . . . living up to the kind of people my father was, my uncle was. Or as I think they must have been. Jerzy was following me – when I turned and saw him, his face was my face . . .'

The last notes of a nocturne hung on the air. Across the lake Wiktoria had woken, and was waving.

'Do listen to this,' said Jerzy. They were sitting in an open-air café in the Centrum, in a side street off Jerozolimskie Avenue; they had spent the morning in the State Museum of Art, and browsing in bookshops. Elizabeth was turning the pages of a book of photographs of Warsaw as it was when the Russians entered, in 1945, showing how it had been reconstructed. Jerzy was reading the text of a large glossy paperback full of colour photographs, called *Poland Today*.

' "Whoever does not understand the nineteenth century will not understand today's Poland," ' he read aloud. ' "The constant insurrections then have created the cult of armed heroics and, at the same time, a dislike for slow, patient work whose effects will be visible after many years. The foreign authority caused a certain distrust which has now disappeared in the basic issues but is still there in matters of secondary importance." ' He raised an eyebrow. 'What do they want us to understand by that, I wonder?' He read on: ' "The years of captivity have invested Polish patriotism with suffering and sacrifice; someone has maliciously but not without reason remarked that 'it is easier for Poles to die for their country than to live for it'." '

He grimaced. 'This isn't a tourist book, it's a lecture to the Poles, it's published in Polish as well. Listen: "Who knows but perhaps this excessive looking back has an adverse effect on our prospects, perhaps it would be better not to constantly hark back to war memories . . . Poland was left alone in the face of Hitler's blackmail because her sympathies lay where no help was forthcoming. It was only the change in the political system and the acceptance of socialist orientation that bound us to the Soviet Union and other countries of Eastern Europe with the same political and social system. Now Poland is safe." '

He flicked back to the introduction. ' "Compared with Poland's modern history the present exceptionally long period of peace has created a mood of sunny and stable optimism, unknown to previous generations." ' He banged the book down on the metal table. 'Riots in Poznań, 1956. Riots in Gdańsk and Gdynia, 1970, with shipyard workers shot by the police. There were food riots and strikes here in Warsaw only four years ago, and workers were shot in Radom, then.'

'Someone is watching us,' said Elizabeth.

Jerzy stopped. 'What?'

'Over there, two tables away. No, don't turn round, wait. He's reading a newspaper.'

'And he's wearing a raincoat with a turned-up collar and a hat pulled down over his eyes.'

Elizabeth shrugged. 'All right, don't believe me. But he's been listening to you.'

Cautiously Jerzy turned. A waitress went past him, carrying a metal tray; he waited until she had gone. 'The one in the grey suit?'

'Yes.'

Jerzy shook his head. 'I don't think . . . I really don't think he is.'

'I do. Can we go?'

'No. Let's outsit him.'

After the incident with the currency exchange on their first day, Elizabeth did not like to argue. She sat, nervous, sipping a fizzy and synthetic orange juice. The man turned the pages of the newspaper; they had bought a newspaper this morning, and read column after column of stories from factories and workplaces where production was increasing; photographs of local party officials sprinkled the pages.

'He's gone,' said Jerzy.

She turned to look at him, and saw the empty table beyond. 'Where did he go?'

'He's just walking away down the street – look.' She followed his eyes, and saw the man in the grey suit, among many other men in grey suits, walking away until he came to the intersection with the avenue, and disappeared round the corner.

'I'm sure he was watching us,' she said.

'Well – even if he was. I think we're all right. What would you like to do now?'

Elizabeth stretched. 'Let's have a lazy afternoon.'

'What about going to Łazienki Park? The palace is closed, but the gardens are open – we could wander.'

They walked back into Jerozolimskie, and caught a tram down the last few blocks of Nowy Świat, and through Three Crosses Square. 'Where Mama was stationed,' Jerzy said. 'This is where she looked through her binoculars, and saw the tank, moving towards them up Ujazdowskie Avenue. Has she told you that story?'

Elizabeth nodded. 'Yes, I think so.' She looked out of the window as they swung down the avenue, bordered with tall, beautiful trees, just turning yellow and gold. Beneath them, a few people walked along broad paths. The tram moved past parks and gardens. Jerzy glanced down at the map.

'Here we are – we can get off and walk through.'

The park was large, with a network of paths beneath the trees and a long, meandering lake, fed by the Vistula. They stood beneath Chopin's monument; a great stone cloak billowed round his head. 'They give Sunday concerts here, too, it says in the guidebook,' said Jerzy. Swans glided slowly over the lake; it was hot, now, the yellow leaves very still. Squirrels scampered across the paths, and from the distance they could hear peacocks. When they reached the eighteenth-century palace they found the terrace before it full of tourists; families threw bread and ice cream cones to fat carp, breaking the surface of the lake. Jerzy and Elizabeth watched for a while, then walked on, passing an open-air theatre with broken columns.

'Shall we stop and rest?' Elizabeth asked.

They lay on the grass beneath the trees; after a while, Elizabeth, her head on Jerzy's shoulder, heard him breathing deeply. She raised her head, saw he was asleep, and lay, looking up at the branches stretched out above them.

Jerzy seemed calmer since his nightmare – if you discounted his outburst in the café this morning, and she did discount it: better to shout about hypocrisy than brood over – over what, exactly?

I told you I wasn't very good with people . . .

Nothing could have prepared her for the deep sense of isolation Jerzy felt, and she still didn't know how much of it sprang from the way he had absorbed the proud Polish sense of loss and exile within the world, and how much came simply from the family and his place in it. She closed her eyes. The early flash of intuition, illumination, which had enabled her to paint the picture of the figure at the door, beyond the sleeping children, seemed extraordinary: even now, she was only just beginning to understand.

Did she want to spend a lifetime trying to understand?

'*Proszę, Państwa . . .*'

Elizabeth opened her eyes to see a woman standing over them, telling them something. She nudged Jerzy awake.

'What?' He sat up, yawning, saw the woman, and listened. Then he pulled Elizabeth to her feet. '*Dziękuję, Pani . . .*' He led Elizabeth away, half laughing, half irritated.

'What was all that about?'

'If you lie on the grass you're fined three hundred złotys.'

'Seriously?'

'Seriously.'

They had tea in a café in the park, then walked through the maze of paths towards the embankment. They stood, watching the sun sink beneath the broad calm waters of the Vistula, and then they went back to Wiktoria's, to pack. Tomorrow they were leaving Warsaw, and driving south.

'Would you like liver, liver or liver?' Jerzy asked. He put down the typewritten menu on the plastic tablecloth, and they looked at each other.

'Liver . . .' said Elizabeth. 'Any vegetables?'

'It doesn't say so.'

'Oh well, you'd better order it.'

Jerzy got up and walked across the campsite dining room to the counter at the far end; Elizabeth watched him, yawning. It was eight o'clock, and they'd been driving for most of the day, through an endlessly repeated scene of families harvesting with scythes and horse-drawn haycarts under a burning sky; all the way along, plaster shrines stood on corners and grassy verges adorned with flowers and picture postcards of the Pope. Every now and then, outside small towns or villages, they passed a drunk, sprawled in the grass, oblivious to the traffic. Now, they had pitched their tent on the bank of the river Pilica; from a couple of tents away a transistor radio blared, and there was much laughter and shouting. Jerzy listened. 'They're Russians,' he said after a while. There was another burst of laughter.

Most people seemed either to have brought their own food or to have eaten already – the vast dining room was nearly empty. Bright blue shiny curtains separated it from the kitchen; the walls were painted in orange, much scuffed and covered in fingermarks; unhemmed net curtains hung at the windows, which needed cleaning. Jerzy came back from the counter.

'There's soup as well, apparently, so I've ordered some.'

After a while, a waitress appeared from the kitchen, and put two dishes before them. From two battered, steaming tin mugs came a rich, meaty smell; they peered into them.

'Liver soup!'

The waitress upturned the mugs and departed. They tasted, warily. It was delicious, very rich, very substantial. A slice of stale white bread accompanied each mug.

'Well,' said Elizabeth, when they had finished, 'I feel much better now. I thought there was a meat shortage.'

'But not of liver, clearly.'

They went out, past log tables and benches set on scuffed earth beneath pine trees, past their first sight of Polish litter, and past the camp disco, now in full swing. They stopped to go to the lavatories. In the women's, which stank, an old woman sat on a metal chair with a few sheets of paper draped over the back. She nodded to Elizabeth, and gestured to the paper. Elizabeth took a sheet, and gave her five złotys. The paper was brown and rough; she thought perhaps the shortage was something peculiar to the campsite, but found it later in public lavatories in many places, restaurants and museums.

Afterwards, she and Jerzy walked down past their tent, along the river bank. Flocks of snow-white geese were settling in the bushes for the night; across the broad river the sun had almost disappeared behind trees, behind the tiled rooftops of the town and the cupolas of a medieval monastery. From the campsite, the disco throbbed. They made their way back to the tent, and switched on the battery lamp they'd bought with the tent from a camping shop in the Strand. It hung from a loop in the middle, and cast a bright, cold light; Jerzy bumped his head on it as he undressed, and they could see the dark shapes of moths outside begin to gather round it. Their funds had not run to a double sleeping bag: he had brought the one he used to take to Polish Scouts, circa 1966, and Elizabeth one she'd found in the cupboard under the stairs at her parents' house. They unzipped them and scrambled in; it was already quite cold. They lay in the bright light from the lamp, listening to the disco.

'Perhaps we should have gone,' said Elizabeth.

'I couldn't face it,' said Jerzy. 'We'll try to find somewhere more secluded after this.'

'You are the most deeply antisocial person I have ever known.'

'I did warn you.'

'I know,' she said. 'I was thinking about it yesterday, in the park.'

'Oh?' He rolled over on to his elbow, and leaned over. 'And what were you thinking?'

The light above them was cold and flat, casting no shadows. 'Why don't we turn that thing off?' she asked. 'Or put it down in a corner. Hang on, I'll do it.' She reached up and untied it, then stretched to tuck it towards the front, near the flaps, half under the ends of the sleeping bags. The tent was transformed: a warmly lit nest, enclosing them from the noise outside, and the night sky. She moved back towards Jerzy, and they lay with their arms round each other, watching the moths which had beat against the sides begin to flutter away and then bump against the flaps, still struggling to reach the light.

'My mother and her brother used to go camping,' Jerzy said suddenly. 'I can remember her telling us – they were camping by a river near Wilno with their father when the war broke out. And he'd been reading them a story about exile – isn't that strange? And now . . . here we are.' He moved closer, and turned to look at her, their faces almost touching. 'What were you thinking about, yesterday?'

'Just – how lonely you still seem to be. I was trying to work out why.'

He frowned. 'I don't feel lonely.'

'Don't you? Apart, then. Perhaps that's what I meant.'

'Am I really so difficult to live with?'

'Sometimes. You know you are. I can't stand it when you're so – unreachable.'

He rested his cheek against hers. 'You shouldn't take any notice.'

'That's impossible. Anyway – let's not talk about it any more.' She rubbed her face against his, and he began to stroke her hair, her eyes.

'I do love you,' she whispered. 'You only have to touch me, and I know that.'

His tongue slid hard between her lips; they clung to each other in their separate sleeping bags, rolling against the sides of the tent. Elizabeth broke away, laughing. 'Unzip me now.' Jerzy unzipped her, pulled down his own sleeping bag and rolled on top of her, very warm.

'Scouts was never like this.'

They woke late, and heard laughter and shouting from the river. When they had dressed and walked down there, they found children swimming in the shallows, boys canoeing past, splashing them. The snow-white geese had come out of the bushes, and were sailing along on the far side, and gathering on a sandbank further upstream. Stocky men in berets fished and smoked; Jerzy took photographs. As they turned to walk back there was a shout from near the tents and they saw a peasant woman in a black headscarf standing up in a large rickety cart, and shaking the reins of her horse. Beside her sat her husband, also wearing a beret; they stopped near a stretch of mown hay, got out and began to rake it into a heap.

'*Dzień dobry*,' said Jerzy as they passed.

The couple nodded, without raising their heads.

They washed in the communal washhouse, divided into men and women by a wall. In the cafeteria, the breakfast menu offered a piece of pig, boiled in water.

'Or tea,' said Jerzy.

'No bread?'

'It doesn't say so.'

They ordered tea, and waited. At a nearby table, two teenage boys were eating pig.

'It's just boiled bacon,' said Elizabeth. 'It looks all right – let's have some.'

When it arrived, however, it resembled not bacon, but a leg of boiled pork: like the liver, it was delicious. Afterwards, outside, they went to the camp shop, a long dark cabin lined with shelves. A couple of dozen tins of peas and *bigos* stood on the shelves, and loaves of bread. There was almost nothing else except a choice of mint or honey sweets in boxes on the counter, where the woman was serving wrapped bread in coarse sheets of brown or green paper. They bought a packet of honey sweets and went to pack up the tent. When everything was ready they found that the boot of the hired Fiat, which had closed without difficulty the day before, now had a broken hinge. They tied it with a piece of string, and drove slowly out of the site and on to the road to Częstochowa. The monastery there housed the painting of the Black Madonna, the focus of pilgrimages for centuries. The Pope had celebrated mass here.

It was sunny and growing warm. They passed more wayside shrines, and after a while saw a long procession ahead: covered waggons and people on foot. They slowed, and carefully overtook, stopping a few hundred yards further on to get out and watch it from the front. There were perhaps a hundred people singing, men, women and children, the waggons rumbling behind them; many of the men wore sashes or neck scarves, of red and white over working clothes, and one or two had swords tucked into their sashes; the women were in anoraks or cardigans. Someone was playing a pipe: thin music wove itself between the footsteps, the singing and the slow clip-clop of the horses. Jerzy raised his camera as the first people drew near; they eyed him, some with suspicion, others indifferently, and went on singing.

'Do you really think we should keep taking photographs?' Elizabeth asked. 'It does feel – intrusive.'

'I know.' Jerzy clicked again. 'But after all . . . this is who we are, now – tourists.'

They stood and watched the procession go by, then got back in the car and slowly overtook again.

'Is it a particular pilgrimage time?'

'I don't think so. Just Sunday. I thought we might try to stay in the convent at Częstochowa – I think they let rooms.'

But when they arrived in the town they found it so crowded with people and traffic that they knew at once they would never find a room here. They parked in a side street and walked through the packed streets towards the monastery and cathedral. At the far end of the road leading away from them stood a monolithic Monument of Gratitude to the Soviet Army.

A long procession was moving slowly between throngs of people in the Cathedral courtyard: children carried small shrines with plastic Virgins, or dolls dressed as angels, with feather wings. A brass band loudly brought up the rear. It was early afternoon, and very hot. Elizabeth and Jerzy followed the crowds.

'You do want to go in?' she asked him, as they reached the doors, remembering what had started their quarrel in Warsaw.

'What? Oh, yes. Of course.'

The cathedral was packed. A vast baroque birthday cake, full of sunbursts, pink and white cherubs, painted plaster angels, every available patch of floorspace taken up by peasants and workers, standing and kneeling. The whole interior was lit by the streaming afternoon sun and by thousands of flickering candles; mass was being celebrated, and the chanted responses reverberated round the walls. Airlessness and incense and the smell of burning wax hung like a thick cloak; Elizabeth stood watching a peasant woman in black, a black headscarf knotted under her chin, kneeling and crossing herself, her lips moving in an endless mutter, her eyes closed, and found her own eyes filling with tears. It was vulgar, it was sentimental; it was impossible not to be moved by it. But after a while, the airlessness began to close in on her; she began to feel faint. I don't want another Pawiak panic, she thought nervously, and reached for Jerzy's hand. He was standing still, gazing over the heads of the crowd towards the altar and the priest, whom Elizabeth could hardly see.

'Jerzy . . . I don't feel well . . .'

'What?' He turned to look down at her, irritated, distracted.

'I'm sorry . . . Can we go outside?'

They pushed their way out through another door, into the corridors adjoining the cathedral. She leaned against a wall; nuns and tourists walked past. It was cooler here, the walls whitewashed and doors at the far end wide open on to what looked like a market. Jerzy put his arm round her; it felt impatient, more than reassuring.

'Better now?'

'Yes, I think so. I wouldn't mind a drink.'

'There might be something outside.'

The walls of the corridor were lined with blown-up black and white photographs of the Pope's visit: blessing the crowds, blessing small children and cripples, kneeling to pray. Elizabeth, recovering, noticed one in particular, and tapped Jerzy's shoulder.

'Look.'

The Pope held a priest in his arms: the man, perhaps in his forties, leaned against him, his eyes closed, his face filled with exhausted and complete relief. No photograph Jerzy had ever taken, no photograph Elizabeth had ever seen had so moved her. The image of exhaustion said clearly: I have come home. They stood looking at it for several minutes, hearing footsteps and voices in the stone corridor go past them, the swish of the robes of nuns and other priests.

'I shall never feel like that,' said Jerzy.

Elizabeth looked up at him. 'What do you mean?'

'You know what I mean.' His foot tapped the floor. 'I'm lost. Not just "apart" as you call it. Lost, God help me.' He turned away from the photograph and walked quickly down the corridor towards the open doors. Elizabeth followed, pale spots dancing in front of her eyes.

Outside, the sun was dazzling. The path all along the cathedral was lined with stalls: brightly varnished, violently coloured postcard pictures in ornate plastic frames – Christ crucified; the Madonna and Child; Our Lady of Częstochowa; the Black Madonna. There were plastic rosaries, plastic bunches and garlands of flowers – emerald, vermillion, orange and yellow, shocking pink; toy trumpets, shrines, angels; ice cream stalls. Elizabeth saw Jerzy striding past it all and away from her, not stopping to notice if she were following, and she felt a wave of anger.

'Jerzy?'

She ran after him, feeling the sun beat down. There were ice cream sellers, but nothing, it seemed, to drink.

'Jerzy!' She caught up with him, took his arm. He shook her off.

'Leave me alone.'

'Don't be ridiculous. How can I?'

'Leave me *alone!*'

He broke away, almost running down the slope towards the town, leaving her crying with fury and frustration. She thought, as she walked blindly past the stallholders, of how less than twenty-four hours ago she had said she found it hard when Jerzy was unreachable, the gentleness with which he had told her to take no notice. She thought of them making love in the tent, passionate, sure of each other, and of the irritation in his face a few minutes ago, when she'd told him she felt unwell. And she thought, reaching the town, and seeing him ahead of her under the trees, striding past parked cars: if we were married, it would always be like this.

'You don't understand.'

'How can I understand if you don't talk to me?'

'How can I talk to you, when I know you can't possibly understand? How can you? You're English, you're nice and safe – '

'You sound just like Ewa.'

'So? Perhaps I am just like Ewa.'

'I hate you when you're like this.'

'Go on, then, hate me – I can't help it.'

After that, Elizabeth stared out of the car window at the darkening countryside; distant factory chimneys rose into the sky. *Please don't let him make us camp out here.*

In Częstochowa, they had found their car and in the main street found a café where they sat in angry silence, sipping something called Cola, very sweet and neither still nor fizzy. It took them quite a long time to get out of the town, and they had driven off without discussion about where they were going to stay the night.

Jerzy tapped the guidebook above the dashboard. 'Have a look.'

Elizabeth reached for it, flicked through the pages. There was nothing about a campsite anywhere near. 'There's a hotel in a town called Zawierce,' she said. 'About forty kilometres from Częstochowa. It says it's a tourist hotel. What do you think?'

He shrugged. 'We can have a look.'

The landscape grew darker; here, too, geese were settling for the night. Elizabeth felt empty, as well as unhappy, and realized they had had nothing to eat since breakfast.

'I'm hungry.'

'You're always hungry. You ate half a pig at breakfast.'

I'm going to leave him, she thought. The minute we get back to England.

Half an hour later they arrived in Zawierce. There were almost no street lights, so it took them some time to find the tourist hotel, a large plain building of two or three storeys which looked like part of a school, or a sports centre.

The reception area was lit by uncertain neon; behind a much varnished tongue-and-groove plywood counter a woman who looked like a gym teacher flicked through a large black register.

'*Proszę?*'

Jerzy put down their case, and asked for a double room. While they waited for the key, Elizabeth looked at a long strip of mirror hung on the wall beside the counter. There was something not quite right about it; she moved closer, and saw that it was made not of silvered glass but some kind of plastic. Faint wavy lines ran all across, and her reflection was blurry and indistinct, as if she were in front of a fairground mirror.

'Coming?' asked Jerzy beside her.

'Yes – look.'

He looked, saw his own distorted reflection, and shrugged. 'What do you expect?'

She followed him up stone stairs smelling of disinfectant. On the second floor Jerzy unlocked the door to a small square room and switched on the light. That, too, was neon. Two single beds with shiny blue covers stood on either side of a varnished table with a plastic glass and a tin ashtray; on the opposite wall was a large, varnished wardrobe. There was more yellow-varnished tongue-and-groove plywood along the wall behind the beds, and a low plastic chair at the window, which was hung with shiny blue curtains.

Elizabeth sat down on one of the beds and felt her heart sink. To be in this drab, shoddy room with a man who would not talk . . .

He had put down the case and was by the wardrobe, reading a typed list.

'An inventory of the contents of this room,' he read aloud. 'It includes a *smok*. Do you know what a *smok* is?'

'No.'

'A dragon.'

They looked at each other, and very cautiously smiled.

'I haven't seen him yet,' said Elizabeth.

'Nor me.' He came over and sat next to her. 'Do you forgive me?'

'No. Not unless you talk to me. I can't just switch on and off like a light bulb.'

Jerzy sighed. 'Are you still hungry?'

'Very.'

'Let's go and find something to eat, then, and talk there.'

They walked back into the main street over cracked pavements, past a lit-up window filled with identical lamps with red plastic lampshades. The chimneys of several factories loomed above the rooftops; an enormous painted slogan on a wall was just readable in the light from the restaurant.

'Translation?'

'The Programme of the Party is the Programme of the People.'

They went into the restaurant. An empty glass-fronted counter stood at the far end; one or two men on their own sat smoking at small tables. The waiter shook his head at them; he and Jerzy exchanged a few words.

'Closed?' asked Elizabeth.

'Yes – there's nothing left.'

'It's not even nine . . .'

'I know. He says there's a place near the station.'

They walked through almost empty streets to the station. A café advertising 'Rarities' had its door open; inside, through a haze of cigarette smoke, they saw men in dusty blue overalls queuing at a counter. They went inside, made their way through crowded metal tables to the counter and waited in the queue. At the head, a stony-faced waitress in a brown apron was slapping ladles of stew on to thick white plates; she looked as though she had been doing it for ever. When they reached her, Jerzy turned to Elizabeth.

'*Bigos* or goulash.'

'I'm past caring. Goulash.'

The waitress banged the ladle twice, pushed the plates at them, turned and banged two open bottles of Cola on to the counter, and a plate with two hard-looking rolls.

They paid, and found a table. Elizabeth looked at her plate: five or six gobbets of meat sat in a thick, yellowish sauce. She dabbed at the sauce with a weightless fork and tasted. It was stone cold. Hunger and the day's accumulation of misery welled up in her: she put down the fork and burst into tears.

'Hey – please – not here.' Jerzy was flushed with embarrassment. 'Calm down . . .'

'Oh, shut up!' Elizabeth shouted, and got up, scraping back her chair. Around them, the workmen at the tables sat and smoked; one or two turned round to look at them, without much interest.

'Elizabeth – please . . .'

'Please what? Please bloody *what?* It's all right for you to moan and groan in cathedrals and walk out on me when I'm almost fainting, but it's not all right for me to show you up in some dreary awful café where no one's even *looking* at us? You want me to leave you alone? All right – I'm going to, and you just see how you like it.'

She turned, pushed her way through the tables, tears pouring down her face, and banged into an enormous blue-overalled workman coming in at the door.

'*Proszę, proszę . . .*' he said mildly, stepping aside.

She pushed past him, and out into the half-lit street. Now where did she go? Could she remember the way back to the hotel? She stood looking wildly up and down the street, still crying. Which way had they come? She stumbled towards a lamp post and leaned against it. I don't care if I never stop crying, she thought, and I don't care who hears me. As for Jerzy – I wish I'd never met him.

'Elizabeth? Darling, darling, come here . . .'

He was standing beside her, trying to pull her into his arms, and she pushed him violently away.

'You self-centred bastard – don't you dare start saying sorry. You'll only do it all over again, I know you will. You don't care about anything, except your precious psyche and your precious Poland. You want to know what I thought about in the park yesterday? I'll tell you. I thought it would take me for ever to try to understand you, and I wondered if it was really worth it. If I loved you enough to make it worth it. Well, I don't. You know why? Because you don't love me. You keep saying you do, but you couldn't really give a fuck – '

'Stop it! Stop it, that isn't true.' Jerzy was crying, now; they stood under the street lamp like orphans who had lost everything, and now each other.

'I can't bear it,' Elizabeth sobbed. 'I've tried so hard, and all you do is push me away. I'm leaving you when we get home.'

'No!'

'Yes! Yes, bloody yes, yes, yes. Now go away!' She began to run down the road, following the intermittent lights ahead until she was back on the main street, and could work out where the hotel was from there. She slowed, wiping her eyes. Behind her, she could hear Jerzy, keeping his distance – at least, she supposed it was him. She walked on, feeling completely drained.

At the door to the hotel, he came up right behind her, and took her hand. 'Please. Let's just go to sleep now. We'll talk tomorrow – I'll make it better, I promise.'

She was too tired to argue. Inside, they climbed the stairs in silence; in their room they undressed without looking at each other, and fell into separate beds, exhausted.

They woke to a dull grey sky, and when they went out in search of breakfast saw that the factory chimneys were belching clouds of black smoke over the town. A short queue stretched from a green-grocery shop, and no women they had ever seen in any London street had looked so tired. They were grimy with tiredness, standing in cheap coats and headscarves, holding plastic shopping bags, not speaking. Boxes inside the shop held wrinkled carrots, onions, tomatoes, jars of gherkins. A single red cabbage stood on the counter, there was a small box of lemons, weighed on purchase. They could see nothing else. On the way to the empty restaurant they'd visited last night they saw more slogans in giant red and white: HARDER WORK MEANS A BETTER LIFE FOR OUR FAMILIES. WE WORK FOR THE GOOD OF THE PEOPLE. Above the blown-up painted faces of local party officials hung a single word: SOCIALISM!

The restaurant offered tea with lemon, hard white bread and a mixed fruit jam, very red. They fell upon it. Outside the window, a man in an open-necked shirt, very drunk, staggered past. It was just after nine.

They walked back over the cracked pavements to the car, found a filling station and drove out of the town. The black factory smoke drifted after them into the outskirts, where half-completed breeze-block housing estates stood on a wasteland of mud and scrubby grass. A peasant with his horse and cart stood waiting near one of the blocks, a few yards from an idle Ursus tractor.

'This is Poland,' said Jerzy bitterly, pointing to the book of photographs they'd bought in Warsaw, which was poking out of the glove compartment. 'This is Poland.'

'I know it is,' said Elizabeth. 'And where are we going now?'

'Kraków. Anywhere that isn't here.'

'But we'll stop and camp on the way?'

'Yes – we'll find somewhere to make up for this. And for last night.'

'And then you'll talk to me?'

'Then I'll try to talk to you.'

A meadow of tall grass, of scarlet, blue, white and gold wild flowers nodded beneath a hot, cloudless sky. It stretched from the untended border of a thin road, winding upwards, to distant clumps of trees; beyond rose forested limestone cliffs. Butterflies danced, birds sang, among the nodding flowers they could hear the busy scrape of grasshoppers. Elizabeth sat on the rug with her watercolours and paper; beside her, Jerzy was stretched out, watching.

'You should have painted Zawiercie, too.'

'I know. I probably would have done if things hadn't been so bad between us.'

From behind them, on the other side of the road, they could hear water: the stream at the top of the hill, where they had put up the tent, ran down here through rocks, and there was a spring. They were near a little town called Ojców, about twenty-five kilometres north of Kraków.

Elizabeth's eyes flicked up and down from the paper to the warm stillness of the meadow; her hand moved quickly, in washes and sprinkled dots of colour. Beside her, Jerzy yawned. 'This is heaven.'

'I take it you're feeling better,' she said drily. 'I suppose this is really not the moment to ask you to account for yourself.'

'Too hot. Much too hot.' He fell asleep.

Elizabeth unclipped the paper and set it to dry on the grass beside her. She clipped in another sheet, and moved away a little, so that Jerzy was not so much on top of her, and then she began to sketch him, lying outstretched on his stomach, his head on one side, thin features partly obscured by flopping hair, long legs reaching out beyond the edge of the rug. The sun rose still higher; an occasional car drove past them, down the hill; from somewhere in the woods beyond the water she could hear a bleating goat. A butterfly settled on the rug, then fluttered off as Elizabeth moved her hand. Jerzy's chest rose and fell. After a while, it began to grow so hot that she could see trickles of sweat running down his cheek. She put away her materials and gently shook him awake.

'Mmm? What . . .'

'You'll get sunstroke if you stay there.'

He reached up an arm and tried to pull her down beside him. 'Lie down with me.'

'No. Come on.'

He groaned, and got to his feet, yawning.

They crossed the road to the spring and drank and drank, splashing their faces. Then they walked slowly through the cool woods, crossing the stream by a wooden footbridge, passing two boarded-up, dilapidated wooden houses, and a thatched cottage with peeling blue paint and sunflowers in the garden. The bleating goat sounded from the back; bees buzzed in and out of a hive. A hutchful of rabbits stared at them from behind rusty netting.

Footsteps came along the path, snapping twigs. An old peasant man in a beret carried a stick, and a polythene bag with something dark inside. He nodded to them as they drew near each other, and held up the bag: they saw four or five large flat field mushrooms, with thick stalks.

'*Dzień dobry.*'

'*Dzień dobry.*' He assumed immediately that they were not Polish, and simply raised the bag again inquiringly, and rubbed his fingers.

'We've nothing to cook them with,' said Elizabeth, and Jerzy explained. The man nodded again, and walked on.

'What a pity. Will he sell them in the town?'

'I expect so. Let's stop, now, and have our picnic.'

In Ojców they had bought some supplies: bread, apples, curd and gouda cheese, a tin of pilchards, and a tin of fresh orange juice, which fizzed. They spread the rug under the trees, and leaned against each other, tearing off hunks of bread.

'This is where we should dig Dziadek's Polish earth,' said Jerzy suddenly. 'Remind me to bring the jar.'

'All right. You really think this is the place?'

'I think it's perfect. I read in the guidebook while you were in the shop that there's a cave somewhere in these woods. Seventy families lived down there with all their animals for a month, some time in the First World War. Dziadek would like that.'

'Yes, I'm sure he would.' Elizabeth reached for an apple. 'Now – explain yourself.' The dizzying heat of the flowery meadow below them, and the coolness here, had already pushed the memory of Zawiercie into the distance. The idea of leaving Jerzy now seemed like a horrible dark thing best forgotten quickly. Which perhaps was foolish.

Jerzy was shaking his head; he spread his hands. 'What can I say that I haven't said already? Perhaps all the feelings are more acute here, that's all.'

'Because you expected so much.'

'I must have done. I suppose I thought that I'd feel I belonged here, that at last I'd be in the right place . . . But it hasn't happened. I don't.' His foot scraped the dark earth and leaf mould.

'You keep on saying that I don't understand,' said Elizabeth, 'but

I do. I realized almost as soon as we got here that I was waiting for you to – find yourself here.'

'And did you imagine that things would be easier between us then?'

'I suppose I did, yes.'

'Well, I'm sorry.'

'So you keep saying.'

'Don't.'

Insects rose and fell on the bars of sunlight pouring through the trees. From below, behind the cottages, the little goat still bleated.

'The picture of the Pope,' said Elizabeth. 'When you talk about your – lostness – are you talking about not being wholly Polish? Or about God?'

'Both, I suppose.' His foot was wearing a runnel in the earth.

'Doesn't God trouble you?'

'No. Not in the way you are troubled, I don't think.'

'Before I met you,' Jerzy said, 'after the Katyń Memorial Service, I remember telling Ewa I didn't believe any more. It wasn't true, not exactly. I don't believe – and then everything seems meaningless and empty. And if I take a step towards believing I find the very idea of a God quite . . . terrifying. Either way, I can't let it go. It gnaws at me, like a rat.'

'All the time?'

'A lot of the time.' He ran his hands through his hair. 'I've rational-ized it by thinking it was tied up with Polishness, and the grand-parents, and going to mass when I was little. But Ewa has all these things as a part of her, too, she even went to a convent, and I don't think she feels like this at all. Anyway – now you see why I got so uptight about the idea of going to mass as soon as we got here.'

'But perhaps . . . perhaps you really should talk to a priest. Or a psychiatrist?'

'No! I wouldn't trust either of them.'

'Then you're condemning yourself.'

'I know.' He was breaking small twigs, dropping them one by one into the furrow of earth.

'And perhaps you're condemning us, too. Supposing I can't cope with all this?'

Jerzy brushed the earth over the twigs and turned to look at her. 'What can I say? Truly, truly, I'm sorry for hurting you so much yesterday. Do you still want to leave me?'

'No. But perhaps it's just the sun.'

He bit his lip and she put her arm round him and kissed his cheek.

'Perhaps you should leave me – perhaps I'm simply not the right person to help you.'

'You are. You do. I thought when I met you that everything was going to fall into place then. And now I'm just afraid I'll drive you away.'

'So am I. But not at the moment.'

In the nearby undergrowth a bird was hopping, pausing every now and then, scratching among the twigs. From somewhere near the cottages came the peaceful inquiring voices of hens.

Elizabeth ran her hand down Jerzy's chest, his stomach. 'Make love to me.'

'Here?'

'Here.'

'What about the old man?'

'I'm sure he won't come back.'

'But someone else might . . .'

She gave a long sigh. 'Puritan. Faint heart.'

'What have I been telling you?' He stood up, and pulled her to her feet, then bent to pick up their bags. 'You bring the rug – we'll go deeper into the forest.'

They stayed in Ojców for three days, resting and walking. On the third day, they packed the car again, and set off towards Kraków. The landscape was hillier, now, the fields on either side of the road sloping gently towards distant mountains, and full of endless rows of stooks. Steam trains puffed along winding tracks across the valleys. In many of the villages the cottages were painted a mauvey-blue; there were window boxes full of geraniums; everywhere they stopped to let lines of ducks and geese waddle across the road. In one village the children were just coming out of school, running home for lunch, the little girls in scarlet stockings.

'I should think this must be the best sort of place to grow up in in Poland,' said Elizabeth, watching them.

'Yes. I'd love to live here.'

A few miles from Kraków, they passed three waggons loaded with straw, stopped by an enormous rusting threshing machine, which wasn't working. The horses stood tossing their heads, flicking flies.

'Stop a minute,' said Jerzy. 'I'd like some photographs.'

Elizabeth drew in and reversed. She followed him towards the waggons, and the men standing with their arms folded, talking. From the doorway of a cottage a woman and child were watching; behind the cottage were square brick houses, with flat roofs. A pylon soared above the apple trees. Jerzy walked over to the men, and began talking. He photographed them, waiting for the machine to start, and then it did, without warning, and they jumped, ran towards it and began loading the straw into the chute. Hens picked their way amongst the dusty piles of chaff. Jerzy and Elizabeth stood watching for a while, then went back to the car.

'They said the machine had stopped working at midday,' said Jerzy, as they drove off. 'It's now after six? Six hours, waiting . . . the machine is collectively owned, and apparently there are power cuts without warning almost every day. Three hundred hectares of land was taken by the Party last year, and the wheat in their fields is just rotting, unharvested. To think that Poland used to be a great agricultural country. One of the men said: "They show us on the television how much there is of everything – where is it? There's no beer or orangeade to drink when we come in from the fields, sometimes there's not even anything for the evening meal." '

Half an hour later, they were on the outskirts of Kraków. They followed the guidebook directions for the campsite: it was very large, and stood high above the city, dominated bizarrely by an enormous cross. Litter scattered the scuffed grass between the tents; there was not a single pitch to be had. They drove off again, down into the city centre; the tourist office was still open, and two smiling girls with long shining hair recommended a tourist hotel some ten minutes' drive away, and booked them a room.

By now it was quite dark. There was not a single working street light; they drove very slowly, across intersections without working traffic lights. In the intermittent glow from a café or shop window, they could see that many of the pavements were badly cracked, or had slabs or half-slabs missing; as in Warsaw, there were few people about.

The hotel was at the top of another hill, reached by a twisting road. They thought of Zawierce, and prepared themselves. This hotel was different. On the forecourt of what might once have been very good officers' barracks stood a number of foreign cars; the women who came out of the front doors were so expensively dressed that Elizabeth felt like an unwashed scruff in her jeans and tee-shirt. They carried their bags inside, and were eyed by a brisk waiter in a cream jacket. The receptionist was a blonde, very pretty girl, who gave them their key and pointed out the restaurant. Elizabeth thought suddenly that they might not be able to afford it.

Their room was on the ground floor, spacious, with two soft beds and tall windows overlooking a garden at the back. But even here, the furnishings had a look of making do about them, and the lights were very dim.

'I must have a shower,' said Jerzy.

'Me too.'

The shower was a little way along the corridor. They padded past expensively suited foreign businessmen, clutching their spongebags. Naked, they stood in the chipped bath, and turned on the shower-head. There was a gush of scalding water.

'Ouch!'

Quickly they turned the tap towards cold; a few lukewarm drops were spat out, then stopped. They turned again, and waited, standing back. Nothing. Ten minutes' irritated twiddling of taps and knobs yielded only drips and spluttering in the pipes. They gave up, washed in the basin, dressed again, and went out.

At the door to the restaurant they skimmed through the menu. It was indeed very expensive, and they were fairly sure, by now, that few of the dishes would actually exist.

'Let's go and see some night life. There must be something.'

There was a large open-air café near the main square, where musicians in folk costume played violins all round the candlelit tables. They ordered a bottle of red wine, and sat drinking; every now and then, one of the violinists came over and played especially for them, before playing for the middle-aged Americans at the next table. Most of the other tables seemed to be taken by tourists; the waitresses wore checked aprons and a lot of make-up; they moved swiftly, taking orders indifferently. Later, Jerzy and Elizabeth walked through the streets looking for their car. They passed large nineteenth-century apartment blocks, tenements, where dimly lit flights of stone stairs curved upwards and inwards past peeling plaster walls.

Elizabeth yawned, and almost tripped over a broken paving stone.

'Are you safe to drive?' asked Jerzy.

'I don't think so. Are you?'

'I'll try.'

They wove their way up the hill to the hotel. In their room, as they undressed, Jerzy said: 'I think we've got enough money for two nights here. We can explore Kraków quite well, before we go down to the mountains.'

'Good.' Elizabeth stood at the basin, brushing her teeth.

'Also we're not very far from Auschwitz.'

Elizabeth stopped brushing.

Auschwitz in German. In Polish: Oswięcim, which was what the signpost indicated. The car park in front of a long low building selling books and postcards was packed with coaches, many from Holland and Germany. There were foreign cars, as well, queuing for a place. Groups were assembling with guides; Elizabeth and Jerzy found a parking space and walked by themselves round past the bookshop to the main entrance.

They stood before the gate famous from dozens of history-book photographs, looking up at the rusting wrought-iron words hung in an arc across it: *Arbeit macht frei* – Work brings freedom. Ahead, on grass, on either side of a long path, stood rows of red-brick two- or three-storey buildings, with narrow black-boarded windows. They looked very ordinary, like barracks, or perhaps some kind of farm building, to store grain. A group of men in shirtsleeves and women in light cardigans and summer dresses stood round a Dutch guide, listening. Jerzy and Elizabeth walked on.

Some distance from the rows of brick buildings was the museum. They followed a long, slow-moving queue down an entrance corridor hung with line upon line of black and white photographs: men and women, not easily distinguished because all their heads were shaved, and almost all were dressed in identical striped shirts, like pyjama jackets. The faces were gaunt, the eyes beneath the stubble of hair stared at the camera from great hollow sockets, as the visitors moved past.

At the end of the corridor the queue moved into a series of large rooms. The walls were hung with charcoal drawings and more photographs: skeletal figures lay in bunks, limbs flung outwards, eyes closed, mouths gaping; some were huddled up, arms round their knees, heads bent. At one end of one room, behind glass, was a pile of possessions, reaching almost to the ceiling: battered brown suitcases with labels from towns all over Europe; heaps of scuffed thirties shoes; children's shoes, with small buttons at the side; watches, clothing, broken toys, purses; thousands of pairs of horn-rimmed spectacles; yellowing dentures. Behind another glass-covered recess was a mountain of hair.

The queue moved on; people were talking in low voices. There were more photographs: of workshops where skeletons sat sewing; reproductions of secret sketches of the dying; of Commandant Hess, whose children had played in a well-kept garden on the borders of the camp, and been very happy here. At the end were the pictures taken on liberation: shaven-headed men, women and children crowding behind a wire fence, staring.

'It wasn't just the Jews,' said Jerzy, as they walked out into the sun. 'That is something you have to know. Millions of Poles died in the camps. Russians, too.'

They walked on, to the shell of the crematorium: here, when the bodies had been dragged from the gas chambers, they had been burned, the smoke drifting over the town nearby.

At the end of the camp stood a monument, an ugly towering heap of black blocks of stone, erected from all nations of the world. At its base were plaques in nineteen languages, each bearing the same inscription: 'Four million suffered and died here at the hands of the Nazis, 1940–1942.' In June, three months ago, the Pope had knelt here. Then he drove on to Brezinka-Birkenau, a part of the camp two or three miles away, where the prisoners had arrived by train. There, before a crowd of a million, he had celebrated mass, and in his homily called upon the crowd to remember Maximilian Kolbë, the saint of Auschwitz, who had gone into the starvation cell to save another man, still alive in Poland.

It was mostly women who were kept at Birkenau. The road to reach it ran past hayfields. Elizabeth and Jerzy parked the car, and walked past a wooden watchtower through the gateway. From behind the netting and barbed-wire fence a man with a scythe stood watching them. There seemed to be no other visitors. Here, the buildings were single-storey, like long cattle-sheds, with tiled roofs, eight dark windows on each side, two at each end, usually just a single door. At the end of the long main path stood another watchtower, made of brick, high enough to observe the whole camp. Jerzy and Elizabeth moved off the path, and walked across the scythed grass. There was no museum here, no photographs or remains or belongings: just a few notices, and the rows of empty buildings.

They stopped at one, at random, and went inside.

On broken stone-flag floors two-tiered wooden bunks ran along each wall. Each bunk was about five foot by five; on each, at the end of the day's work, up to eight women had groaned, and tried to settle, gnawed at by hunger, and lice and typhus. Terrible fevers had raged through the camp; the women vomited in here, or staggered outside. They tried to sleep on these wooden shelves, and tried to die.

Elizabeth walked slowly past them. She heard Jerzy's footsteps at the far end of the building, and then he went outside again. When she reached the end, she turned, and stood in the silence. Shafts of sunlight came through the cracks in the boarded windows, and through the open door. The tall unspeaking figure of a naked faceless woman seemed to be in here, not a ghost, not a spirit, simply a presence, which Elizabeth knew she would try to paint one day, somehow there in the pale yellow light, between the grey wooden stalls.

The warm scent of hay drifted through the doorway. She went outside and found Jerzy, waiting for her. Poppies and tall daisies grew in the long grass which had not yet been cut; outside one of the rows of buildings, quite close to them, a little group of people was having a picnic.

There were two plump women in sleeveless cotton dresses, and three men. From where Jerzy and Elizabeth stood watching them, it looked as if they were eating hard-boiled eggs.

'Do they work here?'

Jerzy was photographing them. 'They must do. They can't be first-time visitors. They can't be.'

They walked back towards the square gateway; the man with the scythe stood watching them again, as they went out, got into the car and drove away. Elizabeth, in the passenger seat, closed her eyes and saw faces staring at her, thousands of faces with dark defeated eyes, and a little group of people, with a picnic on the grass.

'Is it true that the Poles are anti-Semitic?'

Jerzy flushed. 'No.'

'People say they are. I read somewhere that Begin had said he'd never set foot on Polish soil again.'

'In the Middle Ages,' said Jerzy coldly, 'under a liberal king, Poland was the refuge for every Jew in Europe. It was the one safe country.'

'Why do you sound so angry?'

He flushed again. 'I don't feel angry. Not exactly. I just can hardly talk about it without churning inside.'

They were driving south, heading for the Tatra Mountains running along the border with Czechoslovakia. There were three more days left before they had to return to Warsaw.

'I want to talk about it,' said Elizabeth. 'We never have. When I told a Jewish friend from art school that I was having an affair with you, she didn't like it. She said a lot of Poles were anti-Semitic, that there were stories about how the peasants near the camps had turned in Jews to the Nazis, had actively cooperated.'

Jerzy slammed on the brakes, and the car screeched into the roadside.

'Listen,' he said, 'you tell Mama that! Or any of my family, any Pole. And they will tell you that the penalty for hiding a Jew in occupied Poland was death. The whole family was shot, or sent to the camps, no questions asked. And despite that, for every story about a peasant turning in a Jew there are stories about people who risked their lives to hide them. There was a resistance movement in Auschwitz, did you know that? No. Well, there was, of course there was, people were smuggled out, and hidden by Poles. The AK helped the Jews in the Ghetto Rising in Warsaw. There were bastards before then who exploited them, who made fortunes by smuggling in food at sky-high prices – but to blanket Poland with "anti-Semitic" is just not *right!*' His hands on the wheel were trembling.

'For heaven's sake,' she said. 'We're not even talking about anything which touches you personally.'

'None of my neuroses, you mean. It "touches me personally" just as much, to think of you thinking things like that.'

'I didn't say I thought like anything, I just *asked*. Surely I'm allowed to ask?'

There was a long pause. Then Jerzy restarted the car and swung it out on to the road again.

'We're talking about something which neither of us has any experience of, aren't we?' he said. 'There was a witch-hunt in the sixties, here – a persecution of the Jews in the Party after all the university troubles in 1968, but that was whipped up by the Russians, by Khrushchev, because there had to be a scapegoat. Thousands left then – I think some good friends of Wiktoria's did. She's not anti-Semitic, for God's sake. Anyway – there's that. There is the war. And in the eighteenth and nineteenth centuries there were pogroms – but then Poland was under Russian rule. There may be Jewish blood on Polish hands, but there is also Polish blood lost for them. I can't bear it if you think anything else.'

You can't bear it, Elizabeth thought, if Polishness is not perfection. They drove on in silence.

Months later, on a rainy afternoon in London, in a Polish book-shop, they bought a book containing hundreds of verbatim accounts of how, all over Poland in the war, Jews had been hidden and saved from the camps and ghettos. Among them was the story of a woman in the Warsaw ghetto, who had managed to creep into one of the German workshop offices at night, and use the telephone. She had dialled the number of a Polish woman she'd known through their children before the war, and very softly spoken her own name. There was a long, stunned silence. She spoke it again, and whispered: 'May I come to you?' Another silence. Then a single word: 'Yes,' and the click of the receiver.

Of all the stories they read, that was the one which addressed Elizabeth. She lay awake that night thinking of the voice which came from behind the ghetto wall, after a year or more in which the woman's friend must have assumed her dead. She thought of the silence, then the single word which had saved her, and she imagined, with sudden terror, a time when a ghetto might be built in London. For Jews in Stamford Hill? For blacks in Finsbury Park or Brixton? For Asians in Southall?

She thought of herself receiving a phone call from someone behind the wall, perhaps from Hannah, begging for shelter, and knowing that if she said yes she put at risk her own life, and Jerzy's, and perhaps, if they had children, their lives, too. She tossed on the pillow, and lay looking into the darkness, unable to decide if the knowledge that she might hesitate, might even refuse, made her more or less human.

The days in the mountains were cool and fresh. They camped for two nights, and for one night treated themselves to a room in the hotel in Zakopane which felt like the Polish equivalent of the Hilton, though even here the shower didn't work. Zakopane was where Anna had come skiing as a tiny girl, before her mother died. Ponies and traps with jingling bells trotted down the main street, taking tourists up into the lower slopes of the forested mountains. Everywhere they drove they passed new houses being built, large, opulent, clearly costing a fortune. 'For Party members,' said Jerzy. 'No doubt about that.'

They climbed to Morskie Oko, the Eye of the Sea, a large, beautiful lake where the cloud-topped peaks of the mountains were reflected with the sky. They drank tea in a wooden café on the lakeside, and then climbed still higher, to a smaller, deeper lake, where few other people had come.

'Almost our last day in Poland,' said Elizabeth, feeling the mountain air wash her skin like the purest water.

'Are you glad we came?' asked Jerzy. 'Even with all our – upsets?'

'Oh yes. And you?'

'Of course.'

'Even though you didn't find your home?'

'Even though.'

They went slowly down the mountain path again, and began the long drive back to Warsaw.

Wiktoria was waiting for them, late at night, a meal laid ready. She had a letter written for them to give to Anna.

'And I do hope that you two are going to come again.'

'So do we,' said Jerzy. 'I wish we could take you back with us.'

She shook her head. 'I'm much too old to travel now, though I should dearly love to see Anna again before I die.'

In the morning they kissed her goodbye, but she did not come to the station. 'Too many goodbyes . . .' she said. 'I don't want any more.' She closed the door of her apartment, and they heard her slow, stiff footsteps, walking down the corridor.

They took back the car, and spent the time before the train left in the Cepelia tourist shops, buying wooden carvings for presents. And then they went to the station, where Pani Maria was plodding along the platform, greeting her charges. She smiled at them broadly.

'You have enjoyed yourselves? Good, good. I will talk to you later.'

They found their compartment, settled in, and sat looking out of the window as other passengers got on. There was a young couple on the platform, kissing. She was small and very blonde, with white flowers in her hair. He was lanky, with glasses. A few minutes before the train was due to leave, he climbed in with them and thrust a bulging zipped suitcase on to the luggage rack. The girl with white flowers pressed her face to the window, smiling. They kissed through the glass, very quickly, and then the train began to move, and they waved to each other until the girl was out of sight.

The lanky young man leaned back against his seat, and shook his head. Jerzy and Elizabeth eyed him sympathetically.

'My wife,' he said. 'We met in Croydon last year, when she came to visit her aunt. We came here last month to have a Polish wedding, and they took her passport away. I don't know when they're going to give it back. She's been a student here for three years – she says she might have to work for three years to pay back her fees before they let her leave the country.'

The train gathered speed; the suburbs of Warsaw were behind them. Pani Maria slid back the door to the corridor, beaming. 'The gentlemen from Customs are on the train.' She shut it again, and went to the next compartment.

Elizabeth remembered their black-market currency exchange. There was something about declaring how much money you had brought into the country, and how much you were taking out? What were the Customs men going to ask about? When they arrived, they asked only about valuables being taken out of Poland without an export licence. They had no valuables, nothing to declare. The men went out again. Much later in the journey, Jerzy and Elizabeth discovered that Pani Maria had cheerfully paid a fine of thousands of złotys for smuggling crystal.

They sat on deck on the ferry from the Hook of Holland, and the crossing was calm. Jerzy was reading a book of poems by the Pope, translated into English, which he'd found in the library before they left, and hardly looked at until now. A light breeze lifted the pages. He passed the book to Elizabeth, open.

'Read that one.'

Elizabeth took the book. The poem was called 'Refrain', and was very short.

When I think, my Country, I look for a road running upwards, like a high voltage current cutting through slopes. This road is in each of us, steep and upward, not allowing us to stop.

The road follows the same slopes, returns to the same places, becomes a great silence, visiting the tired lungs of my land evening after evening.

They put down the book and stood leaning on the deck rail, their arms round each other, feeling the wind from the sea on their faces, as the ship cut through the water, leaving a foaming wake of white behind them.

Part 3

Winter is Yours

10

Warsaw and London, 1980–1981

Warsaw, July 1980
The queue outside the butcher's where Danuta had waited since
seven o'clock this morning now stretched out behind her to the next
block and beyond. It was half-past ten; she had already left twice,
once to run to the toilet across the road and once to phone the School
of Planning and Statistics, to make sure that her tutor was still there.
It was vacation, but she still went in from time to time – next spring
she would have completed her finals, and in the meantime she had
her thesis to write, and be supervised.

'When you sit your exams, you stop,' Mama said yesterday. 'It's
too much for you to study and waste time in a queue.'

'I can read while I'm waiting, it's all right.'

'But all that standing – it's not good for you.'

'Or for you. And you go to work afterwards.'

'Never mind. I'll live.'

The secretary of her department in the school was clipped but
reassuring – her tutor would wait for her. Danuta put down the
phone and ran back to the queue. On both occasions her place had
been held for her by a little old lady in black; the woman behind was
now complaining loudly. She was large and puffy-faced, in her fifties;
her plastic holdall bulged with toilet rolls, and Danuta thought she
was probably a professional, paid by two or three families.

'I've had this place since seven o'clock this morning; why should
I let you get in front and then dart in and out? If you go again, I'll
move up.'

'I shan't go again,' Danuta said wearily. 'I also had my place
booked.'

'No you didn't.'

'Yes I did.'

'Don't you argue with me, young woman.'

Danuta turned away, looking over the head of the little old lady
to the distant door of the shop, still firmly closed. There were jokes
about butchers. That before the war you'd see a sign saying Butcher,

and go inside and find meat. Now, you saw a sign saying Meat, and went inside and found a butcher. Or there was plenty of meat, so long as you didn't mind eagle. Danuta didn't find them funny any more. She and her mother spent half the week in queues: for meat, sugar, butter; for almost unobtainable soap, washing powder, toilet rolls, sanitary towels, shampoo. There were days when you queued for four hours without even knowing what might be in the shop when you got there. Or found that all the toilet rolls, which were what you really needed, had gone, but there was still flour, so you bought flour, pounds and pounds of it, even if you had plenty at home, just in case next time you needed it, there was none.

Of course, there was always the black market. But the prices were so high you couldn't possibly use it for basics, not unless you got desperate. She felt desperate quite often for shampoo: last month she'd used washing-up liquid, and her scalp had itched for days. There were people at the school who thought that the authorities deliberately kept things back from the open market, so that the factories could be sure of a higher price on the black, and she thought they were probably right – how else was it that Tata's Sport cigarettes last year had been almost impossible to find, and yet they knew people selling any number of packets you wanted, for ten or eleven times the kiosk price?

If you had the money, of course. Who had the money? They didn't. Even with Tata's job in the car factory and Mama's afternoon job in the café, they could barely get through the week. Yet everyone knew about the waste, and borrowing, bad management and bribes. Danuta didn't hear about all this on her course, not officially, anyway. On the course they studied foreign exchange and the balance of payments, trade within the Community for Mutual Economic Assistance, principles of socialist economics. They were taught that Poland was fortunate in having agreements with the Soviet Union which assured her a permanent export market. No one mentioned the transfer ruble, the worthless coin, like a token, in which Poland was often paid. No one really addressed the fact that First Secretary Gierek had plunged Poland into such debt to the West that she might never recover. No one openly compared their life in the queues with the life that Warsaw Radio and the television described, or raised the question of Party-member managers enjoying country villas and trips to the West. Danuta had never been to the West, though she hoped her job might take her there one day, but she had a number of friends who had, spending their summer holidays working in cafés and hotels in

London, Oslo, Vienna. They came back with dollars to spend on the black market, and suitcases bulging with clothes. Danuta wanted to work in one of the foreign trade enterprises, checking contracts and agreements. If she did that – and why shouldn't she, with no unemployment in Poland? – she might one day be able to travel. It helped if you had a relative in the West to stay with, of course. She had Aunt Halina, who lived in London and was not really an aunt, except by marriage. Tata's brother, Henryk, was dead, and no one had ever met Aunt Halina, though they always exchanged Christmas cards.

Was the queue beginning to move? There was a side street leading to the side entrance of the butcher's: Danuta could see heads turning towards it, and she heard the delivery lorry drawing up and the rattle of the doors at the back being opened. Thank God for that. Maybe only another hour? She was hoping for chicken – *another* chicken? To wish for beef was impossible. She yawned, and looked at her watch. If she got home by twelve, she'd have an hour and a half before she need leave for the school.

The front door of the shop had opened; people stopped talking and began to move along the pavement. The first three women were going inside; she opened her purse and checked again how much Mama had given her – it should be just enough. She lifted first one foot and then another from her shoes: plastic made your feet sweat, it was terrible for standing. Of course, if one had the money, leather was obtainable, but one hadn't. She wiggled her toes, slipped each foot back, and began to feel better. Not long now.

Loud voices came suddenly from the head of the queue. She craned her neck. It didn't seem to be the usual pushing and shoving, or quarrelling about a place. What was going on? A ripple of anger ran down the line, someone was shouting: 'They've put the prices up!'

'What?'

'They can't have.'

'They have, the bastards, he's just told us – and there's almost nothing there.'

'What is there?' Danuta called out.

'Beef. At three hundred złotys a kilo!'

Three hundred złotys. She had stood here almost four hours, and now she could buy barely enough to feed a cat. In front of her, the little old lady in black was trembling; behind her, number 84 was pushing and swearing. Up at the front the women were shouting, banging on the windows of the shop: 'We won't stand for it any longer!' and Danuta began shouting too.

London, 12 August 1980

'*Wave of Strikes Challenging Authority of Polish Leaders.*

Poland's six-week-old wave of strikes is developing into a challenge to the authority of the Polish leadership. Poland has become a minefield, not only for the Polish Communist Party, but for the Kremlin, and therefore for the whole communist bloc . . . An increase in meat prices in July triggered off a series of strikes which have now reached a total of 150 stoppages . . .'

The hall of the house in Gospel Oak where Jerzy and Elizabeth rented their flat was long and narrow, the carpet Hoovered infrequently, newspapers and letters for all the tenants picked up by whoever came down first, and left in a pile on a shelf by the door. Jerzy stood reading the *Guardian* in his dressing gown, a bill and a letter for Elizabeth in his pocket. The front door of Flat 1 opened behind him.

'Anything for me?'

Miss Falmer, who lived with her sister, and worked as a clerk at the Royal Free Hospital, was ready for work. She smiled at Jerzy, who looked at her absently.

'Sorry?'

Miss Falmer picked up the *Daily Mail* and a postcard, and opened the front door. Mothers and children hurried past on their way to school. Miss Falmer looked at her watch.

'I must be off. Goodbye.'

'Goodbye,' said Jerzy, stepping aside. The lock on the front door was awkward sometimes; he closed it behind her, and slowly climbed the stairs, still reading.

'*In almost every case, the official trade union bodies have been supplanted by unofficial strikers' committees. They are using a group of dissidents, the Workers' Defence Committee – KOR – led by Jacek Kuroń, to publicize their strikes in the foreign press. But there has been no attempt to organize nationwide action, nor, as yet, a systematic attempt to voice economic and political grievances . . .*'

Radio One blared from behind the door of Flat 2, the smallest in the house, where the tenants changed frequently. A black plastic bag of rubbish had been left on the landing overnight. Jerzy bumped into it, pushed it into the corner and went on up the dusty staircase, past Flat 3, where Mr and Mrs Austin had lived for twenty years. They found the stairs a problem now.

'*With every government concession the problems grow . . . There are people in the liberal wing of the Communist Party who are increasingly convinced of the need for genuine political reform, including, for example, the transformation of the present strike committee into an independent, democratically elected trade-union movement . . .'*

Jerzy pushed open the front door of Flat 4, and smelled burning toast. Threads of black smoke wafted from the kitchen; Elizabeth flung open the bathroom door and rushed along the passage with wet hair. He dropped the paper and followed.

'Sorry, sorry . . .'

'What on earth were you doing?' Elizabeth switched off the grill just as a lick of flame lit the top of the stove. Jerzy pushed open the window above the sink.

'It's all right, isn't it? Nothing's caught.'

They retreated, coughing. Elizabeth's hair was dripping. 'I must get a towel. Can you make some more?'

'Okay. Another cup of tea?'

'Please.' She went back to the bathroom. Jerzy could just hear John Timpson on *Today*, but nothing about Poland. He went to draw back the sitting room curtains.

The flat had been a find: the whole top floor, with two small bedrooms so that one could be his darkroom, and a sitting room just large enough to put an easel in the window without feeling too cramped, if Elizabeth wanted to work here at times. Sometimes they thought she might have to work here all the time anyway; two rents were a lot, and Delia had put up the studio rent in the spring.

'We should be saving for somewhere to buy,' Jerzy said then. 'Ewa can't be paying any more on her mortgage, and she's made an investment in that flat.'

'Do I hear the voice of early middle age?' Elizabeth asked. 'A mortgage sounds a bit permanent to me.'

'You mean marriage does,' said Jerzy, and then let it go.

He went out into the passage, picked up the *Guardian* and returned to the kitchen. With two more slices of bread under the grill, he read on.

'Inflation is becoming more acute as a result of the strike settlements. Food will be even scarcer after the poor harvest. Loan repayments, amounting this year to a staggering $7.6 billion, absorb almost all of Poland's exports.

'Imports of much-needed consumer goods have had to be slashed drastically, further reducing the government's ability to satisfy demands for a better standard of living . . . Now the Polish Government is seeking still

*more foreign credits to finance essential grain imports, technology, and even
debt servicing . . .'*

'Where's my tea, then?' Elizabeth was turning over the bread, her
hair wrapped in a towel. 'You've almost done it again, you'd better
have an early night.'

Jerzy put down the paper. 'Things are happening.'

'Oh?'

He pointed to the headline. Elizabeth leaned against him, reading.
He bent to kiss her bare neck, above the cotton nightdress.

'Stop it, how can I concentrate . . . What do you think's going to
happen?' She turned to kiss his shoulder, as a thin curl of smoke rose
from the grill. 'Oh my God, the toast . . .'

London, 15 August 1980
Shipyard Walk-out Rattles Warsaw

'*Labour unrest in Poland took on a new and more explosive dimension
yesterday, when thousands of shipyard workers went on strike in Gdańsk.
Stoppages there ten years ago led to the downfall of Gomułka, and his
replacement by Mr Edward Gierek, the present Communist Party Chief.*

'*The symbolic significance of a strike in Gdańsk was emphasized by the
workers yesterday when they won the government approval for the erection
of a monument to the workers killed by the militia in 1970.*'

A late summer morning, warm and clear; in the street outside the
house where Ewa lived commuters were hurrying towards Blackheath
station, to the train to Cannon Street, London Bridge, Charing Cross.
Ewa, in cotton shirt and trousers, sat at her table, toast and marmalade unfinished, coffee cooling, rapidly reading the *Guardian* front
page.

'*Polish radio and TV last night admitted that strikes were taking place,
and confirmed that there were stoppages in Gdańsk, Łódź and Warsaw.
The unprecedented announcement at the beginning of national news broadcasts was made as officials negotiated with the 16,000 shipyard
workers . . . also reported to be making demands that went far beyond
improved pay and pensions, and had far-reaching political
implications . . .*'

Ewa read all this, and felt her stomach tighten with a mixture of
nervousness and excitement. It was as if she had for a long time been
sitting in an obscure corner of a crowded assembly hall, half hoping
not to be noticed, half wishing she were important enough to be, and
suddenly heard her name called out, and been asked to stand, and
receive a prize. She put down the paper, and looked at her watch.

Half-past eight – she took another bite of toast, and swallowed the cooling coffee. Then she put everything on a tray and carried it out to the kitchen.

Ewa's flat consisted of one large magnificent room, impossible to heat, with a tiny kitchen and bathroom across the corridor. The main room was the attic of the house, and stretched almost its whole width, with a ceiling where beams and rafters were exposed; at one end was a fireplace, with a rug on the floor and an old sofa, low table, and reading lamp in front of it. At the other end of the room was a huge leaded window, with a stained-glass border. Ewa had seen the rafters, the window and the space, bought it immediately, and spent every winter since crouched over the fire. Her bed was in an alcove beneath the window, covered in a bedspread made from two old brown velvet curtains found in a jumble sale. The table, where she ate and often worked on her translations in the evenings, was set against the wall, between two smaller, plainer windows.

The rest of the house was occupied by the family who owned it, and who had sold the attic to Ewa. She supposed this was a rather unusual step, but they had bought the house fifteen years ago, when houses were just affordable, and since then neither had really gone in for money: Stuart was an administrator with a charity, Jane a fabric printer – very Blackheath, Ewa had since realized. Selling the attic must have saved their lives. They had two sons with Blackheath names, Toby and Ben, who watched television a lot, played rock music a lot and shouted at each other. It was a warm, untidy, comfortable house: there were times when Ewa, in her beautiful top floor, felt like going downstairs for a coffee and chat, as if she were part of the family, but she was too shy. Occasionally, she had a coffee with Jane when she came in from work but she always disappeared as soon as Stuart or the boys arrived.

Stuart was in the hall this morning when she went downstairs, taking his jacket off the peg; from the kitchen at the end of the passage beyond the stairs, Ewa could hear Jane washing up, and the radio.

'Morning,' said Stuart, putting on the jacket. 'Going to the station?'

'Yes,' said Ewa, and opened the front door. She liked him, she liked them all, but she didn't enjoy spending the walk to the station and the crowded train journey in polite conversation.

'Goodbye, you two,' Jane called from the kitchen.

'Bye, darling.' Stuart picked up his briefcase and closed the front

413

door. Late-blooming roses clambered over the fence in the small front garden.

'I see Poland's in the news,' he said.

'Yes,' said Ewa, and felt again that strange, exciting sense of having the spotlight suddenly turned on her. Who had cared about Poland until now?

'I can't remember,' said Stuart, swinging his briefcase as they walked, 'if you said you'd ever been there.'

'No. No, I haven't. On principle.'

He turned to look at her quizzically. He was a handsome man, tall, with grey hair and a loose-limbed, easy walk; with a slightly undarned air about him, like the house, as if there were more important things to do than keep up appearances.

'You strike me as a very principled person,' he said. 'Very . . . correct.'

'Do I?' said Ewa, and blushed.

'In the nicest possible way,' said Stuart, and she blushed still deeper.

'I'm sorry,' he said kindly. 'Bit early for this kind of conversation. What sort of day are you going to have?'

'Much as usual, I imagine,' said Ewa, hoping she sounded flippant and knowing she sounded abrupt, and wishing, as always, that she didn't care what she sounded like.

Stuart laughed. 'Sorry I spoke. You're not a morning person.'

'No,' said Ewa, wondering what kind of person she was at all. 'I'm afraid not.'

They walked through Blackheath village, and caught the train to Charing Cross, travelling, he to the offices of his charity, and she to her translation agency, in what she hoped was a companionable silence.

Warsaw, 18 August 1980

Gierek was on the television. He was always on the television – there were jokes about it. 'I've stopped buying tinned food.' 'Why?' 'When I open a newspaper there is Gierek. When I switch on the TV: Gierek. I don't want to open a tin and have Gierek jump out of it!' Now, he was appealing for a return to work. From the corner of Stefan's and Krystyna's living room his long, horsey face, with its cropped hair and bushy eyebrows, flickered slightly on the screen – it was a very old set – as he tried for over an hour to find the right, reasonable note, the balance between understanding the problems and remaining in control.

'I would like to say as frankly as I can that we are aware that, quite apart from many objective factors, mistakes in economic policy have played an important part . . . We understand the working people's tiredness and impatience with the troubles of everyday life, the shortages, the queues, the rise in the cost of living . . . But strikes do not change anything for the better . . . Together we must find another way.'

Sitting at the table where the plates from the evening meal had not yet been cleared away, Stefan picked up an imaginary violin, and began to play. Beside him, Krystyna laughed, then quickly removed Olek's exploring fingers from the breadknife. He squirmed on her lap, struggling to reach it again.

'No. Now keep still.' She turned him away from the table, towards the television; he reached for Stefan's sleeve and tried to tug. Stefan patted him, still watching Gierek, who was promising to freeze the price of meat until the autumn of next year, and increase child benefits. Olek twisted and wriggled.

'Oh, stop it!' said Krystyna.

'He should be in bed.'

'Do you want to put him to bed?'

'In a little while . . .'

'Well, then. I want to watch, too.'

'You can watch Gierek almost any night of the week,' said Stefan.

'But this is different, isn't it? Stop it!' Olek was standing up against her, tangling wet fingers in her hair.

'Come on, come on, I'll have him.' Stefan turned and lifted him on to his lap. 'Come to Tata. See that big bad man over there?' He pointed to the screen. 'Worse than Tata.' He reached out for Krystyna's hand. 'All right? Now don't be cross any more.'

She shook her head. 'You think you can . . .'

'Sssh!'

'Attempts by irresponsible individuals and anarchic, anti-socialist groups to use stoppages for political ends, and to incite tension, are a dangerous aspect of recent events at plants on the Gdańsk coast. Any actions which strike at the foundations of the political and social order in Poland cannot and will not be tolerated . . . Our country's socialist system has a significant international importance and is one of the most essential features of the European order created after the

Second World War . . . There are limits that no one is allowed to cross.'

Stefan gestured rudely at the screen; Olek grabbed his hand, and they all burst out laughing.

'We are giving your demands our full attention,' said Gierek, drawing at last to a close, 'but we cannot promise to meet them all, for that would be a promise we could not keep.'

'All right,' said Krystyna, getting up. 'I'll put him to bed. You make me some tea. Yes?'

'I am giving your demand my full attention,' said Stefan, and tweaked Olek's ear. 'Goodnight, boss.'

Music sounded from the television; the announcer who followed Gierek looked grave, as if the weight of government were on his shoulders, too. They all looked like that, arselickers. Stefan went over and switched it off, then he began to clear the table, listening to Krystyna and Olek, protesting, in their bedroom. His cot was right next to their bed – when he grew out of the cot, he'd have to sleep in here. Or start off in their bed and be brought in here when they wanted to go to bed. They'd been on the waiting list for a flat for two years before they were married; for two years afterwards, while Stefan finished his engineering degree at the Politechnika and got started as a supervisor at the factory, they had lived with Krystyna's parents. Then Olek came along, just as they'd been allotted this place, in a suburb quite a tram ride out of the city: they had little hope of getting two bedrooms now. Anyway – who cared? The way things were going, anything could have happened by the time Olek was out of his cot.

Stefan took the plates and dishes into the kitchen and put on the kettle. It could take for ever to come to the boil, when the gas pressure was low. He reached up for their glasses on the shelf, and the tin of tea. They were almost out, and no lemon, of course, they hadn't seen lemons for months. It's as if we were in the war, he thought, remembering stories his parents had told him – living on flour and water for days after the siege of Warsaw in 1939, people eating dog meat in the Warsaw Uprising – they'd told him so much he sometimes felt he'd lived through it with them. Their album was full of photographs of relatives killed then – an uncle at Katyń, another in Pawiak prison, two aunts in the Uprising.

Even a month ago, he'd thought about trying to take the family to the West, at least for a while. No more queues, no more slogans, no more empty shelves. And now . . . And now? He paced up and down the tiny kitchen.

'Stefan? Come and give him a kiss.'

'Coming.' He went out through the living room again, into the small square bedroom, where the curtains were drawn but a chink of the summer evening light slipped through. Olek was drowsy in his cot, one hand holding Krystyna's through the bars, the other jammed into his mouth. Stefan bent down and gently removed it; Olek whimpered, and put it back.

'You're too big to suck your thumb,' he whispered.

'He's still a baby!'

'Look at him – he's enormous.'

'But still a baby.'

'All right.' He kissed his son's hot damp head. 'Has he got a fever?'

'I don't think so.' Krystyna frowned. 'I think he's fine – it's just a hot night.'

'Yes. Tea's almost ready – come out now.'

'I'll just stay till he falls asleep.'

'You spoil him – he should be able to go to sleep by himself.'

'I know.'

But she stayed, sitting on the bed, one foot swinging, her finger through the cot bars clasped by Olek's little fist. Stefan kissed her bent head: she looked as if she should be asleep already, too – it was a lot, looking after the baby and working, and queuing, but everybody did it. Someone in the factory today said they were demanding three years' paid maternity leave in Gdańsk. And free Saturdays – he and most of the workers went into the factory almost every Saturday, not for overtime, but simply 'to meet production requirements'.

Back in the living room, he stood for a moment looking at the photograph on the bookshelf of the three of them, taken when Olek was just a few months old. Motherhood suited Krystyna, there was no doubt about it: she was twenty-four when he was born, but she looked much younger, smiling at the camera with the baby on her knee, dark shining hair in a band, her eyes shining too – broken nights hadn't quite caught up with her, then. He had his arm round her, oh yes, very much the husband and father, incredible to think that that was him, he'd never thought he'd be a family man. There was a picture of the Pope on the wall in the background, supposedly smiling down on them, the photographer must have thought his customers would like all that. Of course, it was a crappy, sentimental photo, really, but still . . . Olek might like to have it one day.

He lit a cigarette and wandered over to the window. There was a little park not far from the apartment block: he could see people strolling out there as they did every summer evening. It wasn't his imagination, was it? They were talking more. It was like the Pope's visit, last year, everyone out in the streets as they hadn't been for years, smiling at strangers, excited. At the factory in the last couple of weeks no one ever stopped talking. It used to be quiet, everyone doing their job mechanically, or skiving if they could. 'Stand up or lie down, you're worth 3,000 złotys' – that was the motto. Now you went in in the morning to an excited buzz, copies of KOR bulletins passed round almost openly, everyone reading the demands: for the reinstatement of Anna Walentynowicz, crane driver, sacked from the Lenin Shipyards for distributing dissident material – that was what had started the strike four days ago; demand for the reinstatement of Lech Wałęsa, electrician, sacked for 'agitation' in February; demand for a memorial to the martyrs of Gdańsk, the workers shot dead by the militia in the food riots of 1970. He'd still been at school, then, but he could remember his parents' shocked faces; that was how Gomułka had fallen, and Gierek come to power. And Gomułka had returned from Stalinist exile with the Poznań riots of 1956. There was a joke, in 1970, there was always a joke. 'What's the difference between Gomułka and Gierek?' 'None, but Gierek doesn't know it yet.'

And now? His heart was racing, as he stood at the window watching the people in the park. *There are limits that no one is allowed to cross.* But everyone was crossing them, and what was going to happen when Gierek, like Gomułka, fell?

London, 23 August 1980

Beneath an enormous scarlet banner, the grey iron gates of the Lenin Shipyard in Gdańsk were hung with flowers. Scarlet gladioli, scarlet and white carnations, pink and yellow roses – bunches and hastily made posies were tied all along the top, brushing the heads of the people pressed up against the railings. When the camera drew back for a long shot, you could see that the crowds stretched back for hundreds of yards, uncountable heads of men in jackets and open-necked shirts, women in summer dresses, standing in the shade of the few clumps of trees or out in the sun, beneath the concrete tower blocks and medieval-style houses. Flags fluttered above the flowers; among the leaves and petals the face of the Pope smiled from postcards.

The camera was moving in again; the gates swung slowly open, and a priest walked through alone. Inside, flanking the main path, hundreds of shipyard workers, men and women in heavy blue cotton jackets and trousers, stood waiting, their hands clasped, as he walked slowly towards a makeshift altar. Photographers clambered up on to window sills, cameras flashed, journalists pushed through the crowd, thrusting microphones.

In her quiet attic room, Ewa sat watching her rented colour television. There were no shots tonight inside the main hall of the shipyard; when there were, you could see that the air was thick with cigarette smoke, the faces all along the negotiating tables tense, exhausted, excited. Ministers had been flown in from Warsaw, sent back again, returned. Party leaflets were being dropped on the yards from helicopters; today the first issue of a daily bulletin had been circulated among the strikers. It was headed *Solidarność*. Impossible to believe all this was happening:

'Poland is not yet lost

As long as we are alive . . .'

The voices of the crowd rose into the air as the priest approached the altar and climbed the steps behind it; they faded on a close-up of his face, and then there was a cut, and Ewa was back in the studio again. She lit a cigarette and watched the rest of the news, hardly listening. When it was over, she switched off the set and walked up and down the room, smoking. Through the open stained-glass window came the summer evening sounds of suburban gardens: a distant lawnmower, the click of a ball on a plastic cricket bat, glasses chinking, the snip of shears on privet. Someone was calling her children in to bed. Ewa went to the window and looked down. Rows of walled, tangled gardens stretched out on either side of the one below, belonging to this house, where Jane, in sleeveless cotton shirt and old, pocketed Laura Ashley skirt, was clearing away the supper from the table on the terrace. The kitchen backed on to the garden, the french windows of the sitting room, too, and through them Ewa could hear the television, still on, and Ben and Toby laughing. Jane put the last of the dishes on to the tray, and then looked up as Stuart came out, yawning. He put his hand on her shoulder, and instead of picking up the tray she leaned against him, and then they walked slowly round the garden, as they did almost every evening, stopping now and then to tug off a dead rose, or push back the honeysuckle. They walked in what seemed to Ewa to be the rarest companionship;

only with Dziadek and Babcia did she ever have the same sense of a marriage of contentment, order, a silence shared.

I shall never have that, she thought, no longer questioning a feeling which seemed always to have been with her, and she turned back to her room, where the blank television screen and a pile of papers waited.

London, 30 August 1980

Her head on Jerzy's shoulder, Elizabeth lay sleepily in bed, listening to the birds. The curtains at the open casement window were heavy and old; morning sun ran in a scalloped strip all along the top, and fell between the gap where they did not quite meet, on to the wardrobe and the foot of the bed. Elizabeth yawned, turned towards Jerzy and kissed his neck. He didn't stir. It was Saturday, it didn't matter. In the week they were disciplined: he went to the Finchley Road photographer's, and she to the office, and on 'their' days they kept to the same hours, Jerzy taking photographs or working in the darkroom, Elizabeth in her studio. Often they worked at weekends as well – impossible to be freelance and not work at weekends, but they could start when they wanted, and they shopped together, walked over the heath, went to the cinema in South End Green, had people to supper. Tonight they were having Delia, who rented out the studio; last weekend it was Ewa and Anna. Jan never came. No, not true. He had been once, soon after they moved here, dragged by Ewa: perhaps even enjoying himself; but he hadn't come again.

The sun was growing brighter; Elizabeth turned over and looked at the clock. Almost quarter to ten; she kissed Jerzy again, slid out of bed and went to run a bath, then to put the kettle on. Waiting for it to boil, she went into the sitting room, drew back the curtains and pottered about, picking up fallen petals from the vase of flowers on the table, newspapers from the floor. Jerzy had marked an article in the *Guardian* from a couple of days ago with a large ink cross: he was starting to keep cuttings on Poland, there were columns of newsprint all over the desk. Was it a coincidence that he hadn't been low or dispirited for weeks? She picked up the paper with the others, and read:

'*As the Polish journalist surveyed the committee hall at the Lenin Shipyard, crammed with strikers' delegates from over 300 factories, he kept repeating; "I never thought I would live to see such a scene in Poland."* '

There was a picture of a small, wiry man with a moustache.

420

'*Two weeks ago, Lech Wałęsa was an unemployed electrician harassed by the police because of his dissident activities, and struggling to maintain his wife and six children . . . Today he is the effective leader of hundreds of thousands of strikers along Poland's northern Baltic coast . . . So organized have the strikers become that they have set up their own secretarial unit, refreshment service, information office and "free printing press of the Gdańsk Shipyard". A well-produced four-page bulletin of strike news called Solidarity appears daily . . .*'

The kettle was boiling. Elizabeth went to switch it off, made the tea and finished the article, leaning against the cupboard. There was a nice touch at the end, an item from *Solidarity*:

'*Polish recipes: Take some ingredients in short supply, add a little salt, and mix well with something temporarily not on the market. Add what we cannot afford. The mixture can be fried or baked. We have all been eating this meal here. There is always enough for everybody. It is what the Polish miracle consists of.*'

'Elizabeth? Any chance of tea?' Jerzy sounded croaky.

'I've just made it.' She put down the paper, stirred the pot and poured out two cups, carrying them along to the bedroom. Jerzy was lying under the duvet right across the bed, arms flung back, eyes closed. 'Thank you. I'll do it tomorrow.'

'So you keep saying.' She put the cups on the low table by the bed. 'Shall I draw the curtains?'

He opened an eye and squinted at the sunlight. 'Absolutely not. Turn off that bath and come back to bed.'

'Please.'

'Please.'

She went to turn off the taps, and climbed in beside him. He was naked and very warm; he drew her close, running his hands through her hair, pulling up her nightdress, sliding his fingers hard between her legs. 'I love you. I love you.'

'Mmm. Especially in the mornings.'

'Especially. But always.'

'Darling.'

On the bedside table the cups of tea grew cold. Beyond the soft, heavy curtains at the window, the birds sang, garden doors opened, people called. Jerzy and Elizabeth hardly heard them.

Afterwards, they lay in the bath, Jerzy at the taps end, his shoulder on the worn bit, where years of hard water had left a long, interesting green mark, like a map.

'It's almost our anniversary,' said Elizabeth.

'Anniversary of what?' Jerzy swished his feet.

'Meeting. The blackberry walk, I mean. Falling in love.'

'Having it off. Did you really fall in love with me just like that?'

'You know I did. You didn't, of course.'

'I did. The moment I saw you, sitting on that wall in the sunshine, remember? It was just like today, you're right, the end of the summer.' He reached for the sponge.

'What shall we have for supper?' Elizabeth asked, yawning.

Jerzy sighed. 'Salad? Chicken? Strawberries and cream? The last of the summer wine.'

'Very English.'

'That's what you've done to me.'

'No chance.' Elizabeth stood up, and reached for a towel. 'I'm hungry. I'll get breakfast, you make the bed.'

'Yes, dear.'

They had breakfast, cleared up a bit, then walked up to the shops on South End Green. The sun was bright and warm, the pavements full of pushchairs and wicker baskets bumping into each other, and the café on the corner of Pond Street had the door wide open.

'Let's have a coffee,' said Jerzy.

Inside, as always, old men with East European features sat in silence over chess boards, cigarette smoke drifting across to the counter, where an espresso machine hissed. Sometimes Elizabeth came and sketched them.

'It's such a pity your father hasn't found a community like this,' she said now, stirring her coffee.

Jerzy shrugged. 'He's not like these people. He wouldn't have anything to say to them.'

'They're not talking.'

'You know what I mean.' He stretched, long legs bumping against her feet. 'Shall we go for a walk this afternoon?'

'And pick blackberries?'

'If there are any – it might be a bit early.'

They took a box anyway, and set out on the path to the heath which led up from behind Gospel Oak station, past the athletics track, climbing the hill where the kite flyers came. The summer wind blew through their hair; they stood on the top with their arms round each other, looking down across the rippled grass towards the ponds, where little sailing boats skimmed the water.

'My image of childhood,' said Jerzy. 'One of them, anyway. Ewa and I seemed to spend every weekend going to watch the toy boats on the ponds on Clapham Common.' A dog went bounding past them, after a ball, and he stood watching it go. 'I remember one summer, much later, taking poor old Burek for a walk, not very long before he died. We heard the new motor boats buzzing across the water and hated them. It was as if our childhood had been taken away, or at least was over for ever.' He paused. 'Which it was. Ewa's especially.'

'Why?'

'Oh – I think I told you, didn't I? The first time we went home. She had a sort of crisis.'

Elizabeth looked at him, brushing away the hair which blew across his forehead. 'You'd never tell a secret, would you?'

'No,' he said. 'Never.' He took her hand and lifted it to his lips. Nearby, a little girl was clinging to the end of a kite string. 'Look at it! Look!' The kite tugged and bobbed, its long tail streaming. Elizabeth turned away from Jerzy and watched her.

'Do you want us to have children?' she asked after a while.

'Yes, I think so. If you do. One day.'

'You never talk about it.'

'Nor do you. Why are you talking about it now?'

'Just that little girl.' She pointed to her. 'And wondering about Ewa.'

'Well, don't. It wasn't anything so dramatic, really.'

'But it was for her.'

'Yes.'

They walked on down the hillside, along the broad, shady path running past the pond with the sailing boats, past the reed-fringed duck pond, and up into the woods. They found, after a while, a bramble bush full of blackberries, and they picked for a long time, without talking.

'Falling in love seemed so simple,' Elizabeth said at last.

'It feels simple now,' said Jerzy, straightening up. 'Easier for me now, to love you, than it was then. Easier to tell you.'

'I wonder why.'

'I feel safer, I suppose. I do feel loved.' He sat on the grass, and looked up at her. 'You do still love me? What do you mean, it *seemed* so simple? Why isn't it now? What's happened?'

She laughed. 'Nothing. Nothing.' She sat quickly down beside him, put her arm round his shoulders. 'You look like a worried little boy.'

'I feel it.'

'Don't. I only meant it was simple because nothing was known. There was just the feeling, the certainty that I loved you, without having to try, or do anything.'

'Then you found out what I was really like.'

She leaned against him.

'Yes. Perhaps I love you even more, now, after our dramas. I remember having this strange feeling when we met, that I'd never really know myself, until you began to know me.'

'And has that been true?'

'Yes, in a way. I don't think I'd be painting with such – concentration now, if you weren't there to see it.' She turned to kiss his cheek.

They walked home hand in hand, carrying the blackberry box in a string bag. The sun was beginning to sink behind the line of the hill, where a few kites still soared, and the light across the grass and through the trees was golden, casting rich deep shadows. They stood for a while watching it sink still lower.

'The light leaving the world,' said Jerzy. 'Our lord deserting us.'

Elizabeth took her hand away. 'How *can* you say that? I was thinking quite the opposite: that it's like a benediction.'

'It is,' he said, taking her hand again. 'I was joking.'

'No you weren't.'

'Half joking.'

She shook her head.

Inside the house, they climbed the dusty stairs to their front door; when they unlocked it, they saw the sun still at the windows of the sitting room, making the flowers in the vase translucent. The room felt stiflingly hot; Elizabeth crossed the room and pushed the windows open.

'I don't know why we shut them. It's not as if any burglars could get up here.'

'Mmm.' Jerzy was by the television. 'I just want to watch the news, to get the headlines. Do you mind?'

He had already pressed the button, and was turning up the volume. The theme tune sounded; the voice-over announced:

'The Six o'Clock News from the BBC: Poland's striking shipyard workers sign an agreement to return to work as the Polish Government appears to give way to their demands.'

'My God, they've done it,' he said. 'They've done it!'

'The agreement, signed in the Baltic ports of Szczecin and Gdańsk, is subject to government ratification in Warsaw. If approved, it gives the strikers the right to free trade unions and strike pay . . . Tim Sebastian reports.'

Tim Sebastian and his brown moustache seemed to have been living with them for weeks. As he appeared on the screen again they could hear a constant clapping in the background. Then the camera flashed to Wałęsa, flanked by endless men in suits, flourishing an outsize ballpoint pen in the smoke-filled hall of the Lenin Shipyard.

'The signing of an historic agreement between workers and government . . . the end, it appeared, to a strike that brought economic and political chaos to Poland. The workers here say they'll be back at the shipyard on Monday . . . If the assurances over the trade unions are implemented, they'll be the first of their kind in the communist bloc. The men, at least, seem to feel they've won a victory.'

They were back in the studio.

'Fantastic,' said Jerzy. 'Amazing. I can't believe it.'

'The people of China have heard for the first time that their Prime Minister, Chairman Hua, is to step down.'

He moved over and turned down the sound. 'I must ring Ewa.' He went quickly to the phone, and began to dial. His fingers were trembling slightly; they slipped, and he banged down the receiver and tried again; Elizabeth watched his thin, excited face. 'Engaged,' he said. 'Probably talking to my mother.'

'Or trying to phone you.'

'Might be. I'll just try the grandparents.' He dialled again, and was answered almost at once. '*Dobry wieczór, jak Dziadek się ma? Tak! Tak . . . telewizja . . .*'

Elizabeth got up and went out to the kitchen. There was half a bottle of wine in the fridge, left over from a couple of nights ago. She uncorked it and found two glasses in the rack above the sink. As she poured, she could hear the murmur of the television, and Jerzy talking rapidly in Polish, fluent and assured. When she went back he was laughing; as soon as he had said goodbye and put down the phone it rang again.

'*Słucham?* Ewa!'

Elizabeth put the glasses down on the table beside him. She scribbled on a piece of paper: 'Can I talk to her?' and pushed it towards him. When he didn't turn to look at it, she scrunched it up, and threw it into the wastepaper basket by the fireplace. Then she picked up her glass again, and sat in front of the television, watching the news from the rest of the world, turned down.

425

Warsaw, 30 August 1980

'They've done it! They've done it!' In the courtyards of the School of Planning and Statistics where the students had spent all morning listening to the radio, they were shouting and jumping up and down, hugging each other, waving newspapers. Danuta found herself kissed by her thesis supervisor. He was a thin, balding man in his fifties, who wore spectacles and usually looked hurried and tense. Now, he was jubilant, crazy, ten years younger overnight, grabbing her hands and whirling her up from the low wall round the courtyard.

'They've done it!' A kiss right on the lips.

She burst out laughing, hugging him back.

Someone was talking about a party – Piotr, he was always ready for a party, and now he was inviting everyone – Basia, Hania, Jan, Staszek, Danuta, all of them chanting: 'So-li-dar-ność! So-li-dar-ność!', spilling out of the building, on to the hot, dusty pavement, running under the trees, past the sunlit Vistula, past the flower-sellers and the newspaper kiosks where people were snatching up the papers.

'They've done it!' On the housing estate outside the city, Stefan was racing up the stairs of his block, bursting into his own apartment, where Krystyna and her parents, and his parents, and the family from down the corridor were all crammed into the living room, chinking glasses, as the television in the corner showed, almost despite itself, Lech Wałęsa, carried through the shipyard shoulder high.

Stefan pounced on Krystyna, hugged her, took her off her feet. 'Isn't it fantastic?' He put her down, took a glass and a bottle of vodka from the table, and suddenly remembered. 'Where's Olek?' Everyone laughed. And Krystyna said:

'He's asleep. Can you imagine?'

'He can't be. Wake him up!'

'You're joking.'

'Can't a nation share its triumph with her sons?'

'You're drunk already. Was everyone getting drunk at work?'

'What do you think? Where'd you get the vodka?'

'Tata brought it.'

'Well, good for Tata.' Stefan raised his glass to his father-in-law, standing across the room in his shirtsleeves, broad peasant face grinning from ear to ear.

'*Na zdrowie!*'

'*Na zdrowie!*'

'*Za Solidarność!*'

And everyone raised their glasses. '*Za Solidarność! Za Solidarność!*'

Warsaw, 3 October 1980

At midday the factory sirens had sounded: all over Warsaw, all over Poland. Under a mild, cloudy sky, Stefan stood at the gates of his factory, wearing a white and red armband, holding the Polish flag. They were on strike again, just for one hour. A warning.

On 1 September, the Baltic coast shipyards went back to work. 'We all know what that date reminds us of,' said Wałęsa – it was the eve of the German invasion of Poland, in 1939. Within days, Gierek had collapsed with what was announced as a 'malfunction of the heart' and been rushed to a Warsaw hospital. There were rumours that he was wandering the grounds in his hospital gown, a pale drawn figure, telling anyone who would listen that his hands were innocent of the blood of Polish workers. He was replaced by Stanisław Kania, jowly and corpulent, an ex-police chief, once in charge of relations between church and state, approved of by Moscow. He and his Prime Minister, Józef Pińkowski, both made speeches promising major reforms.

'Our most important task is to restore public confidence,' Kania declared in his opening address to the parliament, the *sejm*. There was also a warning: 'Our anti-socialist adversary wants to exploit the conflicts that have arisen . . . We shall act decisively against cases of disruption of order.'

In the third week of September, rooms in the Hotel Morski, a run-down seamen's place, became the Gdańsk headquarters of a national union: Solidarity represented thirty-five unions, members drawn from workplaces all over the country. Now, in the squalid little rooms grudgingly allotted to them by the provincial authorities, the newly formed branches were fighting to establish themselves, without cars, telex machines, telephones or money, with battered old duplicators and typewriters and, as always, insufficient paper. They had registered three million members. Three million! Everywhere you saw the armbands, the badges: each region had its own, but the centre was always the same, the Solidarity logo which the whole world now seemed to know, the flag flying from it defiantly. Krystyna said she'd seen an old man yesterday wearing a badge with the Polish eagle re-crowned.

The Warsaw branch had quickly become one of the most active and most radical. It was called after the historic name for the central flatlands of Poland: Mazowsze. Chaired by Zbigniew Bujak, a worker in the Ursus tractor factory, the Mazowsze region had its headquarters in rooms at the top of a narrow flight of stairs in a house in Szpitalna

Street. It was near where the walls of the Jewish ghetto had been, and, ironically, almost opposite the old Trade Union Council building. There was a good coffee house round the corner.

Stefan had already climbed the narrow stairs quite often, flattening himself against the wall to let others come down, the buckles of his canvas shoulder bag pressing into his back. Boots tramped up and down all day. At the top, the yellow-painted rooms were a hubbub: foreign journalists came and went, two ancient Roneo machines were on the go all day, the air smelt of cigarettes and printer's ink. Stefan stuffed the canvas bag with flysheets, bulletins. They were talking about producing a weekly paper, *Niezależność* – Independence: in Gdańsk, *Solidarność* was sold out in minutes. There was a time when he had used his bag to smuggle copies of KOR bulletins into the factory; now, there was no need to smuggle: he could distribute information sheets openly – at work, on the estate. Their living room was full of paper – posters on the walls, bulletins on the table, a banner Krystyna had painted at the window. Just occasionally, when Stefan carried the shoulder bag down the concrete paths or echoing corridors of the apartment blocks, or turned at the top of a stairway, he looked over his shoulder. Occasionally, he wondered if everyone who took a copy was what they seemed, an ordinary worker, or housewife, or pensioner. Then he stopped himself, angrily – he shouldn't be thinking like that any more: since August, everyone was out in the open, talking in shops, at work, in cafés and clubs, in the food queues, in queues outside cinemas. Last month, while his mother babysat, he and Krystyna had stood in a queue outside the Relaks, in Marszałkowska. They were showing Woody Allen, in *Manhattan*, but that was not why everyone was queueing. There was a black and white sequence in the middle of a news film about the August strikes: for the first time, the beating and killing of the workers on the Baltic Coast in the 1970 food riots were shown to the people. To think that you could go to a cinema and see that! Something suppressed for over a decade.

And yet – and yet. In the midst of all this, the union itself, while registering hundreds of thousands of new members each day, had still not yet received the authorities' official recognition. Last week Stefan had stood among the crowds lining the pavement outside the Provincial Court, cheering with everyone else as Wałęsa and his colleagues arrived in a bus – almost a triumphal chariot, covered in flags and an enormous Solidarity banner. 'Leszek! Leszek! Leszek!' Little Lech, our Lech – it was like a football chant, as he climbed out, grinning, waving the papers in his hand, the statutes of the union, and climbed the steps to the court, giving the victory sign before he disappeared.

They were all still waiting for the formal registration.

They were waiting for a lot. The strikers on the Baltic coast had made twenty-one demands, supposedly answered in the August Agreement. He had torn out the page from the Bulletin of 23 August in which they were published, and pinned it up on the wall of the living room. Demand for free trade unions, independent of the Party; demand for the right to strike; for freedom of speech, publication and the press – ha! Elimination of privileges of the police, the security services, the Party apparatus – ha! Many of the responding clauses in the Agreement were cautious: they spoke of discussion, of outlines of principles to be presented to the provincial authorities by the end of the year. But Clause 8 dealt with wage rises: 2000 złotys a month, as compensation for the recent price rises. 'These increases will be introduced gradually,' the Agreement read, 'worked out through agreements in individual factories and branches . . . put into effect between now and the end of September.' By the end of September, in many places, negotiations had not even begun.

And so – a one-hour warning strike. Muscle-flexing: preparing for another confrontation? For a long hard winter?

Behind him, the siren sounded once again: the hour was over. Stefan picked up the flagpole and carried it from the factory gates down the concrete path to the main entrance; from inside he could hear cheers, and he saw the workers walking back to their places at the machines. An orderly demonstration completed – as Wałęsa said later: 'We showed we knew how to call a strike, and how to call it off.' Stefan felt a sudden rush of happiness, and quickened his pace towards the doors. If the flagpole had been a baton, he might have twirled it.

Warsaw, Autumn 1980

It grew colder, the leaves swirling from the trees on to the broad paths of the avenues, on to the parks, the lakes. The mornings were darker: it was dark when Krystyna took Olek to her mother's, and only beginning to grow light when she caught the tram to work; Stefan left long before then. The afternoons were sometimes hazy, sometimes lit by a clear, golden sun, pouring through the branches, through the windows of the library, where she took in books and reshelved them, thumbing through yellowing card indexes. The queues outside the shops where she waited afterwards were no shorter, and what you could buy when you reached the top was no more than before, but she didn't mind them quite so much. The atmosphere had changed: people were expectant, recharged, on the alert.

They had to be: they were jolting from crisis to crisis. Three weeks after Stefan had stood outside his factory gate in the one-hour warning strike, the Provincial Court had refused to register the statutes of Solidarity. The clause relating to the leading role of the Party, fore-most in the Gdańsk Agreement, was not in the statutes, and the court, without notice, inserted it. Wałęsa refused to accept it, he argued that since Solidarity was an independent, apolitical union, there was no need for it. First Secretary Kania insisted that there was. The debate on the radio, the wrangling between lawyers, lasted well into November.

Winter was coming. The golden afternoon light faded to grey skies, threatening snow. Like a beacon, the news came that the exiled writer Czesław Miłosz, living in New York, had been awarded the Nobel Prize for Literature. The head of Krystyna's library was a reserved man; he spent his lunch hour in his tiny office eating sandwiches and listening to the radio. When he came into the main room to tell them about Miłosz he was smiling as if he himself had been awarded the prize. Hurrying to her tram stop at the end of the day, Krystyna saw many of the people in the queues at the newspaper kiosks talking as excitedly as they'd done when they heard about the Pope two years ago. On the window of her tram, someone had stuck a placard: 'We demand the registration of Solidarity! No modification of the statutes!'

'Our star is on the ascendant,' she said to Stefan that night, putting a wriggling Olek into his pyjamas. 'John Paul, Solidarity, Miłosz . . .'

' . . . Olek,' said Stefan, looking up from the paper, and she smiled.

'Olek, of course. To think that this baby is almost fifteen months.'

'Time to start another,' said Stefan, turning the page.

'You're joking.'

'Stop saying that all the time – was I joking when I asked you to marry me?'

'Probably.' She did up the last button at the back, and plonked Olek on his knee. 'Hold him while I get the bottle.'

'Tata. Say Tata,' Stefan commanded.

'He's not a budgie.' Krystyna disappeared into the kitchen.

'Tata,' said Olek, banging his fist in Stefan's face.

'There! You see?' Stefan took the fist and punched it gently against the baby's own cheek; he began to giggle. 'Just like Mama,' said Stefan. 'Nice to think I can make my family laugh. Do you want a little brother? A sister?' He punched the fat cheek again. 'Of course you do.'

'Not now,' said Krystyna, returning. 'No, not now.'

He pulled a long face. 'Poor little lonely only . . .'

'You have one then,' she said, giving him the bottle. 'I'm too tired. And anyway, who knows what's going to happen? It's hard enough to feed and clothe this one.'

'You just said our star was rising.' Stefan rocked the baby, who was sucking like a vacuum cleaner.

'You know what I mean. You know perfectly well.'

'We have seven million members now,' said Stefan. 'Seven million and one since your father joined. That's well over half the working population.'

'And we haven't even been registered.'

'We're going on strike if we're not.'

'Are we?' Krystyna went to switch on the television. Last week, Mr Kania had flown to Moscow, just for the day. The communiqué he brought back with him had been read on the news by the usual po-faced announcer:

'Comrade Brezhnev expressed the confidence . . . that the communists and working people of fraternal Poland will be able to resolve the acute problems of political and economic development facing them.'

'Oh, good,' said Stefan.

However, there was a warning.

'The participants in the meeting resolutely denounced the attempts by certain imperialist circles to mount subversive activities in socialist Poland, and to interfere in its affairs.'

'Hear hear,' Stefan said solemnly. 'Absolutely right,' and as usual he'd made them laugh.

On 10 November the Supreme Court of Warsaw overruled the Provincial. Solidarity was registered, and a compromise agreed: the leading role of the Party was to be included in an Appendix. Wałęsa came out of the court shaking his arms above his head. 'We have got everything we wanted!' he shouted to the crowd through a mega-phone, from the side window of the coach, which drove him and his colleagues away and off to the Primate's Palace, where Cardinal

Wyszyński was waiting to receive them, with greetings from the Pope. That night, there was a celebration, a gala performance in the Teatr Wielki, the largest theatre in Warsaw. The stage was hung with an enormous Solidarity banner. There were readings from Miłosz, from Mickiewicz; there were cabaret acts, and satirical sketches of the television news. Stefan and Krystyna didn't go to the performance, they couldn't possibly afford it, but next day everyone was singing the refrain of the song sung there by Jan Pietrzak, star of Warsaw's most famous political cabaret.

Żeby Polska była Polską – 'So that Poland shall be Poland.' The tune was gentle, the words sung at a pace which was almost melancholy, but no one could get it out of their heads.

'So that Poland shall be Poland . . .' You heard it in queues, in coffee houses, restaurants and bars; people hummed it on the way to work; Stefan sang it in the bath so often that Krystyna had to ask him to stop.

Winter was coming; an icy wind blew through the city. But the next night, Stefan did go out – he stood among a crowd ten thousand strong before the Tomb of the Unknown Soldier, in Victory Square, in celebration of Independence Day – 11 November 1918. The dark sky was lit by firebrands, wreaths were laid on the tomb, whose unknown soldier, everyone knew, had died defending Warsaw against the Red Army in 1920. Speeches were made – about Katyń, about the Nazi–Soviet Pact: the most recent, most terrible stains on the history of Poland since her brief independence was lost again in 1939. And then they sang the national anthem. Even as a child, Stefan sometimes found himself having to blink back tears with the national anthem – that was partly, then, because the family made such a big thing of it, telling him over and over again of the times in occupied Poland when it had been sung so bravely, so defiantly. Now, with all the emotion of the past few days behind them, the precious, longed-for feeling that with Solidarity there was real hope for change, there were tears freezing on almost everyone's cheeks as they sang it over and over again:

'Poland is not yet lost
As long as we are alive . . .
What the foreign power has seized from us,
We will recapture with the sabre . . .'

The trams and buses afterwards were packed. Stefan didn't even bother to wait for one, he was too charged up. He walked all the way home, crossing the bridge over the Vistula where the lights of the riverboats danced in the water, his breath streaming out in front of him, and thought about his little son, and what he might one day inherit.

Within ten days, the next crisis came. Among the volunteers in and out of the crowded rooms at the top of the stairs at 5 Szpitalna Street was a young mathematician, Jan Narożniak, a lanky, sweet-looking fellow who worked as a duplicator. Someone passed Narożniak a secret document. The someone was a clerk in the Chief Prosecutor's Office; the document was clumsily entitled 'On the present methods of prosecution of illegal anti-socialist activity'. It consisted of a cobbled history of dissident groups since the fifties, including KOR, the Workers' Defence Committee, and although it did not mention Solidarity by name, Solidarity was clearly implicated. The 'methods of prosecution' listed searches, confiscation of material, arrests, fines, imprisonment.

Late in the afternoon of 20 November, the boots of the militia tramped up the stairs of Szpitalna Street; they were led by a woman, the Deputy Prosecutor, and they turned the rooms over until they found the document. Next day Narożniak was arrested. So was Piotr Sapieło, the clerk who had passed it to him.

At once, Zbigniew Bujak, the Mazowsze Chairman, issued a statement. It called for the immediate release of Narożniak and Sapieło, and threatened a strike. He added that he had not known that the document was on the premises, but if he had he would at once have ordered it to be duplicated 'in a number of copies sufficient to distribute to every branch of our union'. The men were not released.

On Monday, the Prosecutor's office announced that Narożniak was being held under a ninety-day detention order, charged with disseminating state secrets. The maximum sentence was five years. By Tuesday, Stefan's canvas bag was stuffed with hastily duplicated flysheets: 'Today Narożniak – tomorrow Wałęsa – the day after tomorrow – you.' He helped to plaster *Free Narożniak* posters on buses, trams and buildings all over the centre of Warsaw.

Next day, Bujak held a press conference. To the demands for the release of the two men, he added five more, including an investigation into the role of the police and the Chief Prosecutor himself in brutally harassing the workers of Ursus and Radom after the strikes of 1976 – had they, themselves, been acting beyond the limits of the law? He wanted actions against those who had produced the document, an end to harassment of Solidarity members, cuts in the police budget . . .

'He wants the moon,' said Krystyna that evening, reading out all this. 'He's going too far.'

'No he's not, he's right, you know he's right.'

'All right, all right, he's right. And when are you going out on strike?'

'Tomorrow.' Stefan let out a whoop.

By Wednesday there were twenty factories on strike, including Stefan's. In the afternoon there was a passionate meeting in the Ursus works.

'Better to die on our feet than live on our knees!' shouted one of the speakers, and with that ancient battle cry the whole audience burst into applause. The deadline for a general strike in the Mazowsze region was set for midday on Thursday; the workers of the giant Huta Warszawa steelworks began an occupation. A head-on collision with the authorities, perhaps more dramatic even than in August, seemed inevitable: for the first time, it was Warsaw leading events, with Gdańsk, Wałęsa and the national leaders following in the wake of the capital. There were urgent phone calls, desperate attempts being made for compromise by the older members of the union, including, surprisingly, Jacek Kuroń himself, founder of KOR, in and out of prison for years, arrested and released in a game of cat and mouse throughout the strikes in Gdańsk.

In the small hours of Thursday, exactly a week after their arrest, Narożniak and Sapieło were released. They were driven to the Ursus works by Stefan Bratkowski, the radical Chairman of the Polish Journalists' Association. Up all night, listening in the factory, Stefan and the workers in his section heard Warsaw Radio announce at 2 a.m. that Bratkowski had personally guaranteed to the authorities that with their release the strike would be called off. There were cheers – but also a detectable sense of anti-climax: they had been all geared up for days of this, and now the deadline had been lifted and there was nothing to do but go home.

In the steelworks, no one was going home. They were ready for a fight, and they were determined to have it. So Narożniak and Sapieło had been released – but what about Bujak's other demands? Who had answered them? They weren't ending the strike until someone did.

'We showed we knew how to call a strike, and how to call it off,' Wałęsa had said in October. Now, it looked as if neither he, nor Bujak, nor anyone else in the Solidarity leadership could call off what was happening in the Huta steelworks. It took Kania himself, in a small-hours phone call to Gdańsk, promising that Deputy Prime Minister Jagielski would come and talk to the men next morning, to quieten things down for the night. Next morning, however, Jagielski refused to go. If the men wanted to talk to him, they could wait until after the next Party plenum, due in a few days.

The steelworkers went into a fury. Within hours, the strike was threatening to start again in the factories where overnight it had been abandoned.

Jacek Kuroń came down to plead with them. Stefan Bratkowski collapsed. In a plane seat paid for by the government, Wałęsa flew in from Gdańsk. In the end, the government announced on television that the talks on the powers of the police which Bujak had demanded would begin. Even that was not enough. The television announcer was dragged out of his bed by workers demanding to see the actual text of the broadcast announcement. Only then did the steelmen vote, at last, at 4 a.m. on the Friday, to go back to work.

Exhausted and unshaven, Stefan left his own factory and crawled into bed at dawn. Krystyna was asleep, but Olek, hearing his father creep past the cot, was awake at once, heaving himself up and rattling the bars. 'Tata!'

'Sssh!' said Stefan. 'Go back to sleep.' He fell on to the pillow. Beside him, Krystyna murmured crossly, then asked: 'Are you all right?'

'Fine,' said Stefan. 'Fine.'

'Compatriots! The fate of our country and our people is at stake! The continuing disturbances are bringing our fatherland to the brink of economic and moral destruction.'

On 4 December, Kania's appeal to the nation was published in every newspaper. Just as people were recovering from November, longing for a breathing space, the alarms which had been sounded in the Western press about a possible Soviet invasion began to appear, as strongly worded hints, in Poland. Next day, it was announced that a Warsaw Pact summit meeting had been held in Moscow: once again, confidence was expressed in the working people of fraternal Poland, but no one doubted why the meeting had been called. That weekend, a number of Soviet army divisions moved west, camping in the bitter cold along the Polish border.

'Remember Czechoslovakia!' There were few people who had not thought about Czechoslovakia ever since the first wave of strikes spread to the Baltic coast in August. But not once had those words been officially spoken in the last months, either by the Solidarity leaders or by the government: no one wanted to press the panic button. Now, the fear of invasion began to surface openly, in rumours, warnings.

'It's not like Czechoslovakia, though,' said Stefan, looking up from Kania's appeal in *Życie Warszawy*. 'The Czechs were all on Dubček's side, weren't they? Who loves Kania? Or any of them? They'd call in the tanks if they had to.'

Krystyna shuddered, spooning mashed potato into Olek's open mouth.

'Don't.'

He spread his hands. 'What do you mean, don't? Can't we talk about it?'

'I read about it all day.'

The reading room in the library was always stocked with foreign papers, and they had never been so busy – people queued for their turn to read them. 'They're hysterical,' she said. ' "Poland On The Brink", "Poland Faces Collapse". It's almost as if they *want* an invasion, to wring their hands and wail over, something horrible they can watch from a safe distance.'

'You don't think,' said Stefan, 'that they're doing it to show the Russians that they won't take it quietly if they invade? That they'll face a real fury from the West, perhaps even another cold war?'

Krystyna put down the spoon of mashed potato and looked at him. 'And what,' she said, 'did the West do for us in 1939?'

'They went to war,' said Stefan mildly. 'They did go to war.'

'You know what I mean. You know perfectly well what I mean. Where were the British planes in the siege of Warsaw? Where were the French? Haven't your parents told you about going to sing "God Save the King" and the "Marseillaise" outside the embassies, the day after the Nazis marched into Danzig?'

'Yes,' said Stefan, 'of course they have.' Olek was banging on the table, trying to reach the spoon. 'Go on, feed the poor child, or shall I?' He took the spoon from her, and dipped it into the bowl. 'Talk about stars on the ascendant, or the course of the planets – to think that Danzig is now Gdańsk.'

'Yes,' said Krystyna, 'and to think that after all that, after the war, the West who care so much for us abandoned us at Yalta! Do you really think that if the Russians invade us now they will do anything to prevent it?'

'You are becoming more strident than me,' said Stefan. 'It's almost

Christmas, please don't let's quarrel. There you are, Olek, all gone, *nie ma* – no more.'

'*Nie ma*,' said Krystyna, getting up. 'That's all we ever hear in the queues, even now. No more sugar, no more ham, no more eggs, or butter – what kind of Christmas are we going to have?' She took Olek's bowl and spoon to the kitchen, almost in tears.

Stefan picked up the baby and went over to the window. Condensation trickled down the panes; he rubbed one, and looked out towards the little park. It was freezing, the first snow on the ground, and no one was out there now. The walls of the apartment block across the path from theirs were scrawled with old grafitti: *Solidarity! We demand registration . . . Strike! Demand the release of Narożniak . . . Strike! The TV lies . . . We demand access to the media . . . Brezhnev: Stay Home!* It seemed only days since he had stood here after Gierek's last address, wondering what was going to happen to them all.

And yet – before it ended, the year did contain another triumph.

London, 16 December 1980

Factory sirens faded, and the screen was filled with floodlit figures, standing in the rain outside the gate of the Lenin Shipyard, beneath an enormous monument: three giant crosses whose arms, metres above the upturned faces of the crowd, were each hung with an anchor.

'In Poland,' Kenneth Baker announced, 'hundreds of thousands of people attended this evening's rally in Gdańsk, commemorating the riots there in 1970 in which forty-five Poles were killed. This was also the scene of this summer's strikes, which led to the country's first independent trade unions.' Among the crowd, the yellow helmets of the shipyard workers gleamed. From a cord tied around the crosses, the Polish flag blew in the wind; a choir began to sing the opening bars of a *Lachrymose*.

'Why the anchor?' asked Elizabeth.

'I'll tell you in a minute,' said Jerzy.

'Struggle and redemption,' said Ewa from the floor, without taking her eyes off the screen.

'*Polska Walcząca*,' said Anna, leaning out of her chair.

'Fighting Poland,' said Jan, from the other side of the room.

Elizabeth turned to look at him, standing in the doorway with his arms folded, neither quite in the room nor out of it. He has changed, she thought – not completely, or he would be in here, next to his wife. But since August he is different – he is calmer, more open, more alive.

'In 1970, shipyard strikers clashed with the police and army. But this evening the ceremony united the three most powerful elements in Polish society – with representatives from the independent unions, the Government, and the Catholic Church all attending.'

The camera moved along a line of seated dignitaries: cardinals in black cloaks, scarlet cassocks, scarlet hats; men in winter coats and glasses; Wałęsa in a brown anorak, getting up, stepping forward.

'Lech Wałęsa, leader of the Solidarity Trade Union, lit the flame beneath the monument to the dead.'

In the falling rain it took him three attempts to light the oxyacetylene torch passed to him by two helmeted workers. On the third, the torch sparked into life; he thrust it forward and an enormous flame sprang up at his feet. He watched it, waved the torch to the crowd, and stepped aside as wreath after wreath, one for each shipyard worker shot dead by the militia, was carried up and laid upon the plinth. There were lines from Miłosz engraved at the base of the monument, from his translation of the Psalms:

The Lord giveth His people strength
The Lord giveth His people the blessing of peace.

Ewa was sitting on the floor at her grandparents' feet, smoking. As Kenneth Baker and the camera moved away from Gdańsk, Babcia leaned down and gently took her hand. 'Stop it, *kochana*. You smoke far too much.'

Ewa shook her hand. 'I can't help it.'

'Of course you can.'

'Oh, Babcia! Here we are watching one of the most moving things that's happened in Poland since August, and all you can do is go on about smoking.'

'That's enough.' Anna was blowing her nose. 'To think that we should be sitting here watching all this – I never, never thought it would happen.' She got up and went over to the table. 'Does anyone want more?'

'No thanks, Mama.' Jerzy rose and put his arm round her. 'All right? Are you all right?'

'She is reliving her memories,' said Jan lightly from the doorway.

Jerzy looked at him – and that's another thing that's changed, thought Elizabeth. Jerzy's not so ill at ease with him, they have something to talk about now. 'Aren't you reliving yours?'

Jan shrugged. 'Of course.'

Dziadek was holding out his cup; it trembled slightly in the saucer. 'Perhaps just another cup? If there is one?'

'I'll make some more,' said Ewa, leaving her cigarette smouldering in the ashtray, getting to her feet. She took it from him, kissing him on the cheek. '*Kochany* Dziadek – what do you want for Christmas?'

He gestured at the screen, not answering. Babcia patted him.

'He's got his present,' said Jerzy.

'Yes, I know.' Ewa took the cup out to the kitchen. 'Excuse me, Tata.' She lit the gas under the kettle and washed the cup, cut another slice of lemon. Then, waiting for the kettle to boil, she wandered out, and down the corridor to the empty room she once had shared with Jerzy. It was dark; she switched on the light and stood looking at the narrow bed, with its neat candlewick quilt, at the shiny wardrobe, where there were, even now, marks of Sellotape from where the pictures of trains had once been stuck. Someone else should be living here, using this room, she thought. What do Mama and Tata do with themselves, rattling about in all this extra space?

She switched off the light again, and went across to the window, where the curtains were not drawn. Fluorescent lights ran all along the track, and it was raining here, too, a thin sheet of silver, shining as it fell. She pressed her face against the glass, hearing laughter from the other room.

Warsaw, January 1981

The courtyard of the school was inches deep in snow. Sitting at the window of the library, two floors up, Danuta watched the caretaker digging and clearing it, his spade scraping on the ground, the piles he heaped in the corners glistening as the morning sun rose behind the rooftops.

It was cold in the library, colder than at home, where the old tiled stove heated the apartment like a friend. But she couldn't spend every day huddled up at home, it was lonely once her parents had left for work, and anyway in her last term she didn't want to miss what was going on here. The caretaker stopped for a rest, leaning on his spade, his breath rising in a cloud. As he shifted, feeling in his blue overalls for his cigarettes, the sun caught the shining red and white of a little badge pinned on his top pocket: Solidarność. Danuta leaned forward and tapped the window, wanting to give him the thumbs up, but he couldn't hear her. Her badge was on the lapel of her winter coat, hanging behind her on the chair – in the first weeks after the August strikes, something like two thousand students had queued downstairs to join.

Since then, her course had been turned upside down. There were students having to rewrite whole theses in the light of the mismanagement revealed in the last few months. In the Ursus factory Solidarity had compiled a fifty-page dossier on the huge piles of equipment rusting away in the snow, the new spare parts dumped on scrap heaps. There were stories like that, apparently, in Solidarity bulletins all over the country – about the five-year plans which could last not a month less, the towns where factories were so overmanned it was impossible to get a job – even though officially there was no unemployment. The trainloads of Polish goods speeding towards Moscow. There was the story about the fish which couldn't be canned because suddenly there was a shortage of linings for the cans. Sweden offered to purchase the surplus – but 'our people need fish', and so the whole uncanned, unmarketable lot went to waste. There were stories of Swiss bank accounts, of silver grouting in the bathrooms of private villas, of sheepskin coats for the winter which went not to workers but directors; of the economists' report commissioned by Gierek which was stuffed at the back of a drawer. Danuta found watching television was quite a bit more interesting now; journalists gave ministers a grilling and exposed almost laughable depths of ignorance about the departments they were supposed to be running. Almost the only person to come out of it all unblemished was Tadeusz Fiszbach, the Party Secretary in Gdańsk who had helped to negotiate the August Agreements, and openly respected the shipyard workers. He had no villas or secret bank accounts, he was straight, a true communist if you like.

For the rest, it was as if a dark, heavy stone had been turned over, revealing a crawling mass of nasties: negligence, incompetence, indifference, lies and deceptions. But revealing it all had not in itself changed anything – there were still the shortages, there was talk of rationing. People began queuing at five in the morning. Naturally, the authorities were blaming Solidarity – it was the strikes which caused economic chaos, as if it hadn't been chaos for decades. In reply, Solidarity was demanding access to information on a national scale. It was one thing to know that in a textile factory in Łódź no one could do any work because there weren't any bobbins. If the authorities wanted Solidarity to cooperate in lifting Poland out of the quagmire by denying themselves some of the 21 Demands, then the authorities would have to come clean: to announce exactly how much coal was produced, where it was exported; how exactly food was distributed, who decided it. There was hardly a person in any queue Danuta had stood in since last autumn who did not believe that there were food mountains rotting in warehouses, deliberately held back from the open market so that Solidarity could be blamed for the shortages.

In the meantime, there were the farmers, over three million of them, the last privately run cog in the machine, neglected for years, demanding registration of their own union, Solidarność Wiejska – Rural Solidarity. They were backed by Wałęsa and the Solidarity leadership, but in October the Warsaw Provincial Court had ruled that self-employed workers could not form a trade union. Two weeks before Christmas, in heavy boots and sheepskin coats, the farmers had marched into Warsaw from all over the country, again demanding registration; since the second day of the New Year, they had occupied the headquarters of an old trade-union council in Rzeszów, a provincial town right down in the south-east, where many of the roads must be almost blocked by snow.

The caretaker had cleared half the courtyard. Watching his square, blue-overalled shape bending and lifting spadesful of snow Danuta thought that he or his father had probably come from the country. The image of the peasant farmer, tilling the earth with medieval tools, exploited both by the old estate owners and by the communists, was as old as Poland itself – she had tried, once, to write in an essay about how the rapid, forced industrial expansion under Gierek missed the whole point: that Poland was above all an agricultural country; she could grow rich just through investing in the land. When the essay was returned, her comments were ignored. Now the peasant farmers, who had always refused collectivization, were marching together under their own banner – which, it was noticeable, drew a much quicker and more sympathetic response from the Church than industrial Solidarity had done. The simple son of the soil – a gentle, Christian image. But the simple sons of the soil might refuse to send their produce to the towns this winter. Piotr, the boy who'd held the party on the night of the August Agreements, had been down to Rzeszów, where the double doors of the occupied building were padlocked and guarded by enormous men in heavy coats and felt boots, wearing red and white armbands.

Amongst the graffiti on the walls inside was a nice little piece:

We don't care about life

The pig also lives

441

We want a life of dignity.

I want a life of dignity, too, Danuta thought. She looked at the empty sheets of paper in front of her, and realized that she'd been sitting here chewing the top of her pen until it was almost off, and had written nothing. 'Principles of Trade within the Community for Mutual Economic Assistance . . .' She had two more months of this. Everything might have been turned upside down, but she still had to finish her revision, sit the exams. After that – providing she passed – she would be qualified. And then what?

To work in Warsaw you had to have a Warsaw Identity Card – naturally, she had that, but actually to get a job in a foreign trade enterprise now – well, it was not going to be as easy as she used to think. She used to think all she had to do was qualify – Solidarity had revealed that was only the first step. There was unemployment in Poland just as there was everywhere else. To get the kind of job she wanted she would have to pull strings, and she knew no one with strings.

If there's nothing for me here, she thought, watching the sun rise still higher, and the piles of snow begin, just for a few hours, to melt a little, I'll go to the West anyway, I'll do any old job there for a while. After all, I know a little English, I have Aunt Halina to go to. Suppose she won't have me? I won't tell her I'm coming, then, I'll just surprise her. I'll get out of this country before something happens so that I never can.

Warsaw, 12 February 1981

'I am a soldier, so every job, every duty entrusted to me I regard as a service, a service to the nation and to socialist Poland.'

A dark winter evening. Stefan walked away from the queue at the newspaper kiosk, reading as he went. So there was a new voice in the *sejm*, the voice of a man whose eyes were hidden behind dark glasses. The photograph in *Życie Warszawy* showed him in full military uniform, medals on his chest. General Wojciech Jaruzelski, Defence Minister, had been a quiet background figure in the last six months. Now, he had been made Prime Minister, replacing Pińkowski, who had once been accused of favouring Solidarity. Jaruzelski declared that there had been 'many positive changes' since the signing of the Agreements; there were also 'serious anxieties'. Here we go, thought Stefan. He bumped into someone, looked up and apologized. *'Proszę, proszę.'* The man he had bumped into was also reading the paper; they grinned and walked past each other.

Stefan was making for Krystyna's library; he was going to surprise her and pick her up after work, something he couldn't often do because of working overtime, and especially since the dispute about free Saturdays last month, which after warning strikes had only just been settled. They still had to work one a month, and in return for the others off they had to work extra time anyway to make a forty-two-hour week. But today he had skived – to hell with it, for once, Krysia needed a surprise, or something, anyway, to cheer her up: this winter had been a pig.

The library was in a quiet network of streets off Jerozolimskie Avenue. Heaps of cleared snow lined the pavements; under the lamps, people were leaving offices and hurrying towards the avenue to catch trams and buses home. They were huddled up in cheap coats against the cold, their faces pinched; a lot of them had probably been up queueing since dawn. He and Krysia took it in turns now. Sugar had been rationed – to think that even last summer he had thought it was like living in a war. It was a hell of a lot worse now. He reached the library, climbed the steps and pushed open the heavy front door. Inside, it wasn't much warmer than out; he sat on a bench in the hall and waited for Krysia to come downstairs. On the noticeboard someone had pinned up one of the Rural Solidarity flysheets he'd been distributing. Hang on – the someone was probably Krysia, wasn't it? He'd given her a handful. It felt suddenly rather strange to think of her doing something like that by herself, so that a stranger could come in here and perhaps wonder who'd pinned it up. It was his wife, for God's sake! For a brief, uncharacteristic moment, Stefan had a small, chilling vision, like a snapshot, of Krysia, without him, in trouble. He felt in his jacket pocket for his cigarettes, remembered he couldn't smoke in here, swore, and went back to the paper, to the report of the speech Jaruzelski had made yesterday.

'*The expected stabilization has not materialized . . . Evil, hostile political forces are pursuing activities aimed against socialism, our alliances, our economic stability . . . striving to turn back the wheel of history and achieve a counter-revolution . . . To resist this process is not just the business of the authorities, it is also the patriotic duty of all forces of prudence and responsibility, including the millions of members and activists of Solidarność, who support the constitution and believe in the precepts of the socialist system.*'

Well, of course, thought Stefan, there is always patriotism. No one can ever resist that – especially from a soldier. Shades of Piłsudski, Sikorski. Hands up those of you in Solidarity who are not patriots.

Well, then – you will resist the evil, hostile political forces! Even if those forces are in fact yourselves. If there wasn't a joke about that yet, there soon would be. Coming next, perhaps, as in 1968: It's All the Fault of the Jews.

Jaruzelski concluded by calling for a strike moratorium. 'I appeal for three months of hard work, for ninety peaceful days.'

Three months of hard work – that sounded like more of the same. But ninety peaceful days . . . that sounded all right. Like a holiday. There were a lot of people who'd buy that.

Footsteps came running down the stairs. 'Hey, what are you doing here?'

He shot the newspaper up in front of his face, croaking like a robot. 'I-am-invisible.'

'No you're not.' Krystyna pulled it away, and quickly kissed him on both cheeks. 'I'd know those feet anywhere.'

'And I'd know those tits.'

'Stefan! Sssh!'

He got up, grinning, and folded the paper. 'You've seen all this, presumably.'

'About Jaruzelski? Yes.'

They went to the door and he held it open, bowing low.

'What has got into you?'

'I don't know, really. It must be love.'

'What nonsense.'

They hurried down the steps and along the pavement, arm in arm.

'So what do you think?' he asked.

'About Jaruzelski? Well . . . he's clean, isn't he? No one can pin anything on him, anyway.'

'I thought you'd be frightened. That he's just paving the way for the tanks.'

'Don't! When I first heard about it, I was. Now – I'm not so sure. He seems . . . sincere.'

'They all seem that, my darling.' He stopped under a street lamp, and kissed her. Her face was freezing. 'Poor baby. Shall we go for a drink?'

'What about Olek?'

'I've phoned your mother – she's going to take him home and put him to bed.'

'Wonderful. What about money?'

'I've borrowed some. Come on, let's go!'

Their arms round each other's waists, they walked on to the coffee house near the avenue where they used to meet a long time ago, before they were married. It was small and crowded and warm. Jazz came through the speakers, candles burned in saucers, cigarette smoke wafted to the ceiling. There were Solidarity posters pinned up everywhere. They pushed their way through to the back.

'It's taken,' said Krystyna, looking at their old table.

'Never mind, we'll wait. Two coffees coming up.'

When he came back, they stood drinking and listening to the music, a slow, melodic sax that seemed to go on for ever. After a while, the people at their old table got up to go, and they moved quickly across before anyone else could take it.

'I feel better,' said Krystyna. She slipped off her coat, and they sat with their hands clasped across the table. The candle was quite low; with his free hand Stefan picked up a match from the saucer and began to catch the drips of wax, feeding them back into the centre. The flame spluttered and fizzed.

'If you do that too much, it'll go out,' said Krystyna, watching. She reached out to try to take the match away. 'Stop it.'

Stefan shook his head. 'Sorry. I'm thinking.'

'What about?'

'I have an idea. I'm not sure if you'll like it.' He dropped the blackened match into the saucer and looked at her. 'How do you feel about travelling?'

'Travelling,' said Krystyna. 'Travelling where? You mean in the summer? Anything could have happened by then.'

'Exactly. I mean going to the West for a bit. Perhaps to England. All of us.'

She looked at him in astonishment. '*Now?* You want to leave Poland *now?* When there's everything left to fight for? I can't believe it.'

Stefan took his hand away and lit a cigarette from the candle. He puffed at it quickly. 'I knew it – you *are* more radical than I am. I thought you'd jump at the chance – for God's sake, everyone does it! Go over for a few months, have a break, earn some real money – '

'Doing what?'

He shrugged. 'Waitressing?'

'And who'd look after Olek?'

'We could do shifts. I could work on a – I don't know, a building site or something. Or be a waiter. Decent food, decent clothes, no more queuing. We could do a lot for the parents, with that kind of money.'

445

'We'd do a lot for the parents if there was – God forbid – an invasion, and we were swanning about in London.'

'You said you thought Jaruzelski was all right.'

'No I didn't. I said he seemed all right, but – ' She reached over and stroked his arm. 'I thought you were so excited about everything. Still. What's happened?'

He ran his fingers through his hair. 'I don't know. Perhaps I'm just tired. I thought you were, too. I felt sorry for you. And I don't know – every now and then I think: Have we really got a chance?'

'Well you mustn't think that. Come on, Stefan!'

'And to think I was bringing you here to cheer you up.'

'You have, you have. It's lovely being back.'

He took her hand. 'All those years ago, my Krysia. How long have we known each other?'

She held his hand against her cheek. 'Always. It feels like always, anyway.'

Warsaw, 20 March 1981

'They've beaten up men in Rural Solidarity!' Stefan banged open the door of the apartment, and kicked it shut behind him. Olek, staggering across the floor towards him, sat down with a bump and began to scream.

'Hey!' said Krystyna sharply. 'Mind what you're doing, Stefan. It's all right, Olek – come on, come on, that's enough.' She bent to pick him up. 'What are you talking about?'

'There's three men in hospital,' said Stefan. 'In Bydgoszcz. Olek, Tata didn't mean to frighten you. Bad Tata, go on, beat him up, go on.' He took Olek's hand and punched it on his arm. Olek went on screaming.

'Oh, for God's sake just leave him alone,' Krystyna snapped. 'It's your free Saturday, isn't it? We've been waiting and waiting for you to come back so we can go to the park. You've been hours.'

'I know, I'm sorry, but everyone in Szpitalna Street was talking about it, I couldn't leave. Let's go now, come on, let's just take him out, he'll be fine as soon as we're in the fresh air.'

They bundled Olek into his clothes and clattered down the concrete stairs to the ground floor, his yells echoing on the landings, then diminishing. Outside, Stefan lifted him from Krystyna's arms and they crossed the road to the little park, where he put him down. 'There you are, old chap, off you go now.'

It was late afternoon, the sun sinking fast behind the trees, lighting the patches of snow on the grass. At the far end of the park stood a few old swings, a see-saw. Olek toddled off along the path towards them, a small square teddy bear in his boots and snowsuit, chatting away to himself.

'He knows seven words,' said Krystyna. 'And he understands almost everything I say.'

'Does he? I hope he knows the right ones, that's all; one day he's going to need them. Do you want to know what's happened or not? You're supposed to be the fighter.'

'Just tell me, all right?'

'Okay.' Stefan began to walk fast. 'There's a meeting yesterday in the Provincial People's Council in Bydgoszcz. Local Rural Solidarity reps invited to attend, including the leader, that Rulewski guy. They want to press for full registration, and so on. They wait. Meeting suddenly adjourned in the early afternoon before they've had a chance to speak. They stay, anyway. They're asked to leave. They refuse. At eight o'clock – presto! The riot police. Get out or we'll get you. They stay firm, and start singing the national anthem, and then the militia move in with truncheons and just grab them, one by one, and drag them out of the building, shouting: "Get Rulewski!" Twenty-seven people beaten up, three very badly, including Rulewski and one old guy they suspect of being brain-damaged.'

Krystyna whistled. 'Bastards.'

'Yes, you teach Olek that.' He drew a deep breath. 'Anyway, I think Wałęsa's calling a strike. And so he bloody well should.'

They had reached the swings; Olek was pulling one of them back, and calling: 'Mama!' He let it go and it swung forward: as it came back, it would hit him straight in the eyes. They both ran towards him. 'Olek!' Stefan grabbed him, and Krystyna the swing.

'Phew.'

'Naughty Olek. You mustn't touch the swings till Mama gets here, all right?'

She brushed melted snow off the seat and lifted him on, pushing him gently towards Stefan, back and forth. The chains were very cold, and needed oiling at the top: with every swing they creaked and squeaked. Olek clung on, smiling.

When it got too cold to stay out any longer, they went back to the apartment, and made tea. The news on TV played down the incident at Bydgoszcz.

Next day, the whole family went into Szpitalna Street. The walls of the three rooms at the top of the stairs were plastered with photo-

447

graphs of Rulewski and the two others, bruised and bleeding: in red and white across the top was lettered *Prówokacja!* – Provocation! Warsaw radio and the television could no longer play anything down, but their coverage was exclusively biased against Solidarity.

'Wałęsa's called a four-hour strike for the 27th,' said one of the printers. 'And a general strike for the 31st if the authorities don't meet our demands.' As they left, they caught a glimpse of Bujak, arriving, waving his arms.

Solidarity's demands included the immediate sacking and punishment of those responsible for the beatings; recognition of Rural Solidarity; guarantees of freedom from harassment of all Solidarity members and closure of all cases pending against people arrested for opposition in 1976 – when KOR was founded – and 1980. On the 25th, Wałęsa and the new Deputy Prime Minister, Rakowski, met for talks which became almost a shouting match. On the 26th, Cardinal Wyszyński, on his deathbed, summoned Wałęsa for a last meeting.

Everyone, now, was talking about the possibility of an invasion. As the day of the four-hour strike approached, the whole of Warsaw was covered in flags: on buildings, fluttering from windows, painted across posters. There were instructions being telexed from Gdańsk to all the regional offices of Solidarity: No. 1 – in case of a General Strike; No. 2 – in case of a State of Emergency; No. 3 – in case of a Foreign Intervention . . . In case of No. 3, street names were to be painted out, signposts turned round. That was what they'd done in Czechoslovakia, in 1968. The mood was united, defiant. Everyone seemed to be wearing an armband, a badge. 'It's like this all over the country,' said Stefan, the night before the strike. 'Did you see that poster on Marszałkowska about the building site?'

'Yes.' Krystyna was stitching up her armband. The poster proclaimed: *No Entry! Building in progress.* Beneath it was an outline map of Poland. 'I suppose,' she said slowly, slipping the armband on, 'that it must have been a bit like this getting ready for the Uprising. In 1944.'

Stefan lit a cigarette. 'Yes. Yes, I suppose it must have been.'

'Except they were at war.'

'We are, almost.'

'But not quite,' said Krystyna. She held out her arm. 'How do I look?'

'Wonderful,' said Stefan. 'My militant librarian.'

They got up early next morning, and Krystyna took Olek with her to the library. 'After all, if I'm not going to do any work . . .'

448

'What about this afternoon?'

'Oh, he can stay for once, for a treat. Why not?'

They took the same bus, hoping to get into the centre before the strike began. At five to eight they got off; five minutes later, they stood listening to the factory sirens, hearing every bus, every tram, come to a halt and sound the horn. It was a bright, sharp morning: hard to know whether they were shivering from cold or from the sense of drama, listening to the strange music of horn and siren, blaring across the city as the morning wind lifted the flags.

Afterwards, they kissed goodbye and hurried off, Krystyna to the library, pushing Olek, Stefan to the factory. Not until midday was the strike ended. 'You realize,' said one of Stefan's workmates, 'that there's never been anything like this in the whole history of the communist bloc. Not even last August.'

'I do,' said Stefan. 'I can't wait for the 31st. A general strike!' He punched the air. 'Bloody hell.' He suddenly remembered saying to Krysia the night in the candlelit bar, that perhaps, really, they didn't stand a chance. How could he have said that? The whole country was speaking with one voice, nine and a half million members. Nine and a half million!

On the 30th, negotiations between Wałęsa and Rakowski were still going on. That night Stefan and Krystyna sat waiting for the 7.30 news. 'Pass me a cigarette.'

'What? You don't smoke. You've never smoked.'

'I'm smoking now,' said Krystyna. 'Just for tonight. I can't bear it any longer.'

He passed her one, lit it; she began to cough. 'Ugh.' But she didn't put it out; she sat with it between her fingers, then got up and began to pace up and down the room. Stefan watched her. In a corner, his packed bag was waiting – two changes of clothes, a torch, notebook and pen, flask waiting to be filled with tea tomorrow morning. He saw Krystyna look at it and look away. She hadn't packed a bag – general strike or not, how could she stay night after night in the library with Olek? Should he be taking him in to the factory? What would it be like to be barricaded in there, perhaps only able to talk to Krysia and Olek through the gates, as the shipyard workers had done?

'All right, Krysia?'

'Very jumpy. Aren't you?'

'Yes. A fantastic feeling, I've never felt like this before.' There was a new poster on the wall in Szpitalna Street, a quotation from Brecht:

When things remain as they are
you are lost.
Give up what you have and take
what is denied you.

'It's starting,' said Krystyna. 'Look!'

She grabbed his hand and they sat waiting for the grim-faced announcer to tell them in solemn, regretful tones that from tomorrow all Poland was on strike. Instead –

'Wait a minute. *What?*' Wałęsa was flashed on to the screen; he looked nervous. Beside him stood his deputy, Andrzej Gwiazda, holding a piece of paper.

'It has been decided, after long talks with the authorities, in particular with Deputy Prime Minister Mr Rakowski, to suspend the call for a general strike from tomorrow. We have here an agreement . . .'

'They can't have! They *can't* have.' Stefan was out of his chair, banging his fist on the wall beside the television. 'Idiots! Cowards!'

'Sssh! You'll wake Olek.' Krystyna was looking shaken.

'I don't care if I wake him! The whole bloody country ready, our real chance to show them . . .' He glared at the television.

'Shut up!' said Krystyna. 'Just listen for a minute, can't you?'

The agreement was being read out: punishment of those responsible for the beatings at Bydgoszcz; Rural Solidarity recognized, pending full registration . . .

'Well, that's not so bad, is it?' she demanded. 'We've won, without a strike.'

Stefan looked at her. 'One minute you tell me I'm running away when there's everything to fight for – the next you can accept *this!* Remember what you said about it being like preparing for the Warsaw Uprising? How do you think our parents would have felt if it had suddenly been called off? Just as they thought they were about to get their revenge? Do you think we'll ever be able to get to this point again? With everyone behind us, everyone ready to go?'

From the bedroom, Olek was wailing.

'I told you . . .' Krystyna was crying. She made for the bedroom, and Stefan caught her wrist.

'Okay, go and get him, but what does it matter, now? What does anything matter? I told you, didn't I, that I sometimes thought we didn't really stand a chance? You were the one who spurred me on. But I was right – I don't think this precious agreement means a thing,

450

I think it'll all come tumbling back down on top of us, I think we should get out now, and if you won't come, I'll go by myself.'

'Stop it, stop it!' Krystyna wrenched her wrist away and ran to the bedroom. 'Go on, then, go. You're completely wrong-headed, but go.'

Stefan grabbed his cigarettes and his jacket and banged out of the apartment. He ran down the stairs and stood at the bottom, panting. It was cold and dark and beginning to rain. He lit a cigarette, and walked round to the front of the block; he crossed the street and paced up and down for a few minutes, trying to get calm, looking up at the small lighted square, three floors up, which was their living room window. He waited for Krysia to come there, with Olek, to draw back the curtains and look out for him, but she didn't. After a while, he began to walk, not caring where he was going. There was a man coming towards him, walking his dog. He nodded to Stefan as he drew near, and he recognized him, he lived in the next block.

'You've heard they've called the strike off?'

'Yes,' said Stefan bitterly. 'I've heard.'

11
London, 1981

The sky above Heathrow Airport was full of small, racing clouds; as they crossed the tarmac from the plane Danuta felt a cold wind on her face, and would have stopped, and turned up the collar of her raincoat, but her shoulderbag was very heavy, and there were people behind her, all of them wanting to get on, and into the arrivals hall ahead. Warsaw this morning had been cold, with a stinging rain; had she thought that the spring sky over London would be filled with warmth and sunshine? She realised now that she had, always.

An airport bus was passing them. Still hurrying after the passengers in front of her, Danuta registered Arab faces beneath white head-dresses, all along the windows. Then they had reached the arrivals building, where huge glass doors slid back to admit them, and she felt her mouth go dry.

I have a return ticket. I am staying with my aunt in Islington. How many times had she practised that? Inside the building, ahead, were two signs, one for British subjects, one for foreign visitors. Bored, confident English voices from different flights receded; Danuta stood in the foreign queue, among the Poles. They were mostly young people, like her, students who'd just finished their exams; she noticed a tall, pale guy in a thin grey sweater, he was turning to look out at the waiting planes. He's left someone behind, she thought, a wife, or a girlfriend, and she thought of herself, just a few hours ago, kissing her parents goodbye at Warsaw airport, hurrying across the departure lounge so that it looked as if she hadn't noticed her mother crying, and so that they couldn't see that she wasn't.

It was very hot in here. At the end of the queue the men behind the counters stood expressionless, opening passports, asking questions. Danuta bit her lip, and took her passport out of her enormous shoulder bag. Some of the presents from the Cepelia shop for her aunt were in here: painted pottery bowls, a crystal vase. The *kilim* was in her suitcase. Her parents had helped her to buy it all – she couldn't arrive empty handed. Particularly as Aunt Halina had no idea she was coming at all.

I have a return ticket. Everyone knew they didn't want to let you in, were suspicious that you were coming to work, trying to stay on. She flicked open her passport so that the ticket was ready to show, and saw that it wasn't there. It must be. It wasn't. She stood stock still, and felt a sudden chilling sweat, and then she wrenched open the buckles on her bag again. The ticket was there, tucked carefully between her make-up bag and the English phrase book with a penguin on the spine. She pulled it out, fastened the bag, and felt her knees trembling. She took a deep breath, shocked by the recognition of being an alien, someone whose identity and proof of existence depended solely on pieces of paper, who could be dispossessed by the loss of a single one of them. For a moment she felt really scared, as if she were about to face the worst interrogation, for the worst of crimes; then she pulled herself together, thinking: I have only to get through this one, little barrier. That is all.

'Yes, please?'

She was at the top of the queue; the uniformed man at the desk was holding out his hand, and she gave him her small blue passport, with the uncrowned eagle stamped on the front. He flicked through the pages without speaking, looking from the photograph to her face, skimming her date of birth, address, profession. She had no profession yet.

'Have you completed your studies?'

'*Proszę?* Excuse me?'

'Have you finished studying?' he said slowly. 'At university.'

'Oh. Yes. Yes.'

'And what do you intend to do in this country?'

'Excuse me?'

He repeated, slowly.

'I have return ticket,' she said, and produced it.

He looked at it impassively. 'And what do you intend to do here? Where are you staying?'

'With my aunt. She lives in London – in Islington.' She spoke the syllables carefully.

'Is she expecting you?'

'Excuse me?'

The man repeated, impassively: 'Is she expecting you?'

'Yes.'

'Have you anything to prove that? A letter?'

Oh my God. 'Excuse me?'

'Have you got a letter from her? Inviting you to stay?'

'I left it in Warsaw. I'm sorry.'

He looked at her. 'I see. And how much money do you have?'

'I have one hundred dollars,' said Danuta. 'My aunt . . . helps me.'

'What family do you have in Poland?'

'My parents. They are living in Warsaw.'

He picked up a stamp and thumped it on the first page of the passport. 'Four weeks tourist visa. No working.' He passed it across the desk, and looked at the man behind her in the queue as if she had never existed. Danuta put the passport and the ticket in her bag, and walked through the barrier into the baggage hall. She'd done it! Suddenly filled with excitement, she stood waiting with everyone else for the bags to be unloaded and reclaimed from the revolving daise; when hers came into view, brown and bulky, she carried it through to customs.

'Excuse me, miss.' One of the officers was beckoning to her. 'Could I see your bags a moment, please?'

She took them over to the counter, snapping open the light lock on the suitcase, undoing the buckles on the shoulderbag. He lifted the piles of cheap clean clothes, turned over the presents from Cepelia, shaking out the *kilim*. What did they expect people from Poland to be smuggling?

'Thank you,' he said at last, and carefully replaced it all. 'I hope you enjoy your visit.'

'Thank you,' said Danuta, and smiled at him, feeling a rush of excitement. 'I will.' She snapped shut the suitcase and hurried out of the hall. She had to find the underground station; she had to change her money, find a map. Where was Islington? She followed a crowd of passengers from different flights out into the arrivals area, where a sea of faces waited, waving or holding up placards. Seeing them, she wished after all that she had told Halina she was coming, and had someone there to meet her. But if Halina had written no, she couldn't come and stay, then what would she have done? She had to have somewhere to start, even if it was only for a few nights, just until she found a job.

Bureau de Change. . . . Her precious dollars, saved and borrowed from Mama, changed for ten-pound notes and fives. She tucked them into her purse. 'Please . . . underground?'

The girl behind the counter nodded indifferently towards an overhead sign out in the concourse. Danuta looked at it, unable to understand a word. She moved into the crowd.

'Please . . . underground?'

'Over there, dear,' said a woman. 'Follow that sign, see?'

A red circle with a line across. 'Thank you.' She followed the sign along corridors, down stairs, escalators, along a moving floor, her case bumping against her. She was beginning to feel hungry; on the plane this morning they'd had sausage and ham for breakfast, the best breakfast she'd eaten for months, but she could have done with a coffee and something now. Better not: even a coffee was bound to be very expensive here. Down in the station she looked on the wall for a street map, couldn't find one, looked for a map of the stations and stood in front of it, bewildered. It was like a diagram for a radio circuit, incomprehensible. Warsaw's underground was just a single line. She pulled out her notebook, looked again at Halina's address. No station on the map seemed to match it – wait, Highbury & Islington. That must be it. She queued for a ticket, got on a silver train and sat in a side seat gazing out of windows that needed washing as it rattled past leafy roads and neat little houses. After a few stops, it went suddenly into a tunnel, and from then on grew more crowded with each station. She had to change at Piccadilly Circus – she had seen pictures of Piccadilly, dwarfed by a giant Coca-Cola sign, with young people squatting on the steps of a statue, wearing jeans and smoking.

When they reached the station, she got off the train, pushing her way through a throng of people on the platform, which smelt of stale air. Should she go up, now, and have a look at it? Her case banged against her calves. Someone was shoving their way through the crowd to get on to the train as the doors closed, a young black boy, sweating, holding something close to his chest. A handbag. A woman was shouting: 'Stop him, quick!' and there was a sudden rush, but then the doors closed, and the train gathered speed and rattled off through the tunnel.

'Bastard!' said the woman. 'Black fucking bastard.' Danuta stared at her, clutching her own shoulder bag, no longer thinking of going up to look at Piccadilly. The woman stood looking helplessly after the train, then turned and ran down the platform. 'Where the hell's a policeman? Aren't there any police down here any more?' Shaken, Danuta looked up at the overhead signs, trying to find the way to a train to Highbury & Islington. She went to the map on the wall and looked at it again, frowning, and realized she didn't need to change here at all. She should be changing at somewhere called Green Park. Just for a flicker, she felt very lost, right down here on a crowded platform where pickpockets roamed. Then she pulled herself together, and followed the sign to the Victoria Line.

Someone was playing the guitar, and singing: she followed the arrows and the sound, and found herself walking down an endless tiled corridor. The boy who was singing was standing by the wall, his open guitar case filled with a scattering of coins; she wanted to give him something, because he made her feel better, but she couldn't, not yet. A little further on, a dark shape lay huddled against the wall; as she drew near she smelt a repulsive mixture of alcohol and sweat and urine, saw an empty wine bottle beside the shape's matted hair, and hurried on, like everyone else. There were plenty of drunks in Warsaw, too.

She had to go up an escalator to get to the Victoria Line; holding the handrail, her case in her other hand, she moved slowly past endless advertisements: for whisky, for swimsuits, chocolates, underwear, hi-fi. It was easier to understand the written words than people speaking: on one she recognized Lonely? On another: Pregnant? Then she was at the top of the escalator, and finding the way to the right platform, which wasn't too crowded. More advertisements, plastered on the wall across the track: for coffee, tights, more underwear. Women with their breasts almost falling out of tiny bras talked seductively on the telephone, half-naked, or looked directly at you, at the men on the platform.

'Spare anything, love?' A low monotone beside her.

'*Proszę* – excuse me?' Danuta turned to see a girl holding out a grimy hand. She was small, dressed in black trousers, black cotton jacket and black tee-shirt, a black headband pulled over short, unwashed dark hair, her face pale and pasty. Her eyes were small, with circles underneath; she looked half dead.

'Excuse me?' Danuta said again.

'To score,' said the girl in the same flat voice. 'Spare anything?'

Danuta shook her head, not understanding, feeling sorry for her.

'Fucking cow,' said the girl indifferently, and walked past her, very slowly, to the next woman waiting, who looked kind, and ordinary, with shopping bags, and who also shook her head. Danuta stood watching the small girl, moving in scuffed espadrilles at the same slow pace from passenger to passenger, with no one helping her. For a moment she almost opened her bag, then she remembered the black, sweating boy, and kept it shut, and then the train came rushing in, and she moved towards it, quickly. When the doors had closed, and they were moving towards the next tunnel, she turned in her seat to see if the girl was still there, but she had gone.

At Green Park she found the northbound Victoria Line quite easily. After Piccadilly, Green Park sounded soothing and cool, and she wanted to go and walk through it, but then she thought of Aunt Halina, and an uncertain reception. Better to get it over with: she caught the next train.

Highbury & Islington had a very long escalator, and a mirror all along the right-hand wall at the top. Danuta caught sight of a reflection as she got off and for a moment didn't recognize it, a stranger among strangers hurrying past, with her suitcase, belted raincoat and dark hair cut short especially for the trip. She should be standing in a queue, or sitting in the library. No, she shouldn't. She walked away from the mirror, up to a black ticket collector, and out towards the street. There was a little fat man in glasses, selling flowers, with buckets ranged all along the wall outside a pub. She stopped, and lifted out two bunches of carnations, one white, one red: that would be a nice gesture, wouldn't it? Eighty pence each: my God. Perhaps one bunch? No, do it, it was worth it. The man wrapped the flowers in mauve and grey paper, which killed the red, and stapled it hard.

'Right you are, love. One pound sixty – there we go.' He handed her the change. Beyond the stall she could see a zebra crossing, trees, a roundabout where huge container lorries and double-decker buses locked ordinary cars into an endless circular traffic jam.

'Please . . .' She showed the man her notebook, with her aunt's address. He shook his head, then called out to the man on the newspaper stand.

'Off the Essex Road, innit?' He pulled a worn book out from somewhere in the booth and beckoned her over. 'Have a look in there.'

Danuta took the book: A-Z was printed on the front; she found the index at the back and ran through the list of unpronounceable streets and roads. Was Halina in a street or a road? A road. She found the name, and the reference, but even when she had peered at the maze in the grid, and found the right one, she still had no idea how to get there. Where was she now? She looked across the zebra crossing to the name on the wall of a bank. Holloway Road. She looked back at the map, and couldn't find it. All she really wanted to do was walk across the road to where the trees began; she could see grass, and what looked like a little café. No. If she bought the flowers she couldn't have a coffee as well. When she'd got settled, perhaps she'd come here at weekends, read the paper, and write her letters home. She turned to the newspaper man and gave back the book with a shrug. 'Thank you.'

'Find it all right?'

'Excuse me?'

'I said: find it all right?'

She shook her head.

'Here . . . let's have a look. What was the name again?' He peered at her address book, and at the map. 'Here we are, told you it was off the Essex Road, didn't I? Bit of a walk. You go down that road straight ahead, take a bus if you like, right down to the second lights, get off, turn right, that's the Essex Road, got a good long walk right up there, about halfway, I think, innit?'

Danuta looked at him and laughed.

'Didn't understand a word of that, did you? Where you from, then?'

'From Poland. From Warsaw.'

'*Warsaw*.' He whistled. 'Look, I'll tell you again . . .' He told her, pointing out the main road she was to take.

'Thank you. Thank you.'

'That's all right, love.' He turned to a waiting customer. Danuta walked over the zebra crossing, and turned past the trees, and the stretch of green beyond, and the terrace of houses running alongside. She began to walk, past a little supermarket, where a tired-looking Indian woman sat at the till near the door; the shop was poorly lit, but even from outside she could see that the shelves were crammed. There was a dry cleaners, another little shop with a man inside who might be Greek, or Turkish, and a window stuffed with enormous loaves of white bread, piles of tins – pet food, peas, beans, carrots, tomatoes, jars of fruity jam, then a double-fronted chemist's with windows of suntan creams, scent sprays, sponges, lotions, tampons, nappies, bright-coloured plastic hair slides.

And there was a butcher's . . . Danuta stopped, put down her case and stared at joints and chops and mince and chicken, whole lambs hanging at the back, an enormous ham waiting to be sliced. She remembered standing in the queue less than a year ago, when the news of the price rises came, and thought of everything that had happened since then – a revolution! She picked up her case and walked on. When the row of shops ended, she walked past porticoed houses where the paint was peeling and the windows thick with dirt from the traffic. She looked at the people, and thought most of them

458

looked scruffy; she felt as if she were in quite a run-down part of London, and yet they could buy anything!

It was growing warmer, or perhaps it was the walking. She felt her skin beginning to tighten, and her eyes sting. The case felt very heavy, but she wouldn't take a bus: even if she wanted to spend the money, she wouldn't trust herself to get off at the right place. One set of traffic lights. An endless walk to the next, past the same peeling houses, with glimpses of others, beautifully done up, in side streets behind them. Across the road at the lights, a factory on one corner and a huge grimy church on the other. Up the Essex Road, yawning, her feet aching, checking the names of the side streets as she went. Many of the streets had tall, elegant houses, clearly restored quite recently; others were full of skips, and cement mixers. At a junction, Danuta saw another station: Essex Road. This was where she should have come in the first place? And surely she should have found Halina's street by now?

A little further on, she came to a small market, just a few fruit and vegetable stalls, and she stood still, almost as shocked as she had been by the butcher's. The fruit! Mountains of glistening lemons and oranges, polished apples, ripe bananas hanging all along the top, boxes of grapes, yellow melons the size of footballs. Danuta thought of herself and her mother, and the hours they had spent each day in the queues, the evenings when they came home with nothing, or almost nothing, and what Mama's face would be like if she could show her all this, now. She realized she was almost crying, standing there watching the line of perhaps five or six women at each stall, waiting to buy, and she blew her nose and noticed a flower stall where carnations were only sixty-five pence a bunch. Where on earth was Aunt Halina's road?

Danuta walked on one more block, then stopped again, and asked three different people the way, each time showing the little notebook, with the address in black ink in a handwriting she realized they found hard to read. The third person was a man in overalls; he knew where it was.

'You've come too far, love.'

'What?'

He threw a cigarette stub into the road.

'Back down there, third or fourth on the right.'

How could she have missed it? 'Thank you.' She turned back, walking slowly once she saw the name on the corner: she was very tired, but it wasn't just that, she was suddenly frightened. How could she have thought it was all right just to land on a doorstep? Months ago, in Warsaw, to have an address, the address of a relative, seemed enough, to make it all so simple, coming here. But why on earth hadn't she written, to check it was all right? Wasn't it really a dreadful nerve? Then she thought again of what she would have done if Halina had written to say she couldn't come, and knew she'd had to do it. She turned into the street, where a few of the houses were done up and many looked untouched. Halina's, when she found it, looked untouched. She pushed open the garden gate and walked up the path. The door was painted brown, with heavy net curtains at the windows. The doorbells had a row of names beside them: English, Irish perhaps, and at the bottom a single Polish name. Danuta pressed the bottom one, and waited, hearing footsteps down an uncarpeted hall inside.

The door was opened; a small, fat woman in a flowered overall and slippers looked at her from a wrinkled, very Slavic face. She wore a cotton headscarf, tied at the back; wisps of grey hair escaped from it, above sharp brown eyes.

'Yes?'

'*Dzień dobry*,' said Danuta, hesitantly, holding out the flowers, and the woman smiled. Then saw the suitcase. 'I . . . I have come from Warsaw,' Danuta said in Polish. 'You are my Aunt Halina. I am Danuta – Maria's and Tadek's daughter. They send you their very warmest wishes. I . . . I arrived in London this morning.'

Halina shook her head. 'This is quite a surprise. Come in.' She took the carnations. 'Very nice. But I have nowhere for you to stay.' She gestured at the row of names beside the doorbell. 'All my rooms are let.'

I knew it, thought Danuta. I knew it. But just for one night? A couple of nights? She followed Halina inside, past dark-painted doors which, she knew instinctively, had remained the same colour for over twenty years. There was a smell of *bigos;* Halina led her down a small flight of green-carpeted steps at the back of the hall to a kitchen, where a large black and white cat sat on the table, half on, half off a pile of newspapers.

'This is Henryk,' said Halina. 'I named him after my husband.'

'Oh. Hello, Henryk.'

The door was open to the garden: a long stretch of grass, bordered by concrete paths and flowerbeds full of polyanthus. Washing flapped on a line. Danuta put down her case, and reached out to stroke the cat, seeing the names of the newspapers, poking out: *Dziennik Polski*.

460

The *Islington Gazette*. A large, brightly coloured picture of the Pope was pinned to the wall above a shiny sideboard.

'Sit down,' said Halina, gesturing to a green-painted chair. She put the flowers on the table. 'You would like some tea?'

Danuta sat. 'Thank you.' She leaned down and began to unlock the suitcase. 'I have brought you some presents.'

'Very kind,' said Halina again, lighting the gas under the kettle. She turned to watch Danuta unwrapping from coarse paper the pottery bowls and folded *kilim*, the crystal vase. It sat on the table, next to the newspapers and the cat. Halina picked it up, turning it in the light from the open garden door. 'Very pretty. Thank you.' Outside it began suddenly to rain, and she put down the vase and hurried to the washing line. Danuta watched her rapidly unpegging aprons, sheets and tea towels, enormous women's vests, dropping them into a plastic basket. Beside her the cat stretched, fat white paws patting the vase. Danuta moved it.

'Careful, Henryk.'

'Well . . .' Halina was inside again, dumping the basket of washing in a corner. She closed the door to the garden, and the rain pattered invisibly on to the panels of starred glass. 'You like your tea with milk or lemon?'

'Lemon, please,' said Danuta, still stroking the cat. 'Until just now, do you know how long it has been since I saw a lemon?' She wanted to be light, bantering, somehow to make Halina like her.

Halina grunted, taking teabags from a tin. 'And now I suppose you think you can make your fortune in the West?' She dropped a teabag into a mug, as the lid of the kettle began to rattle, turned off the gas and poured on boiling water. 'All you young people, coming over here, expecting everything to be done for you. What do you think we had, when we came here after the war? We had our few pounds from the Resettlement Corps, and we had to get on with it.' She cut off a slice of lemon, angrily, and dropped it into the mug. 'What are you going to do in London? Study? You look like a student.'

'I . . . I'm not sure, yet, what I'm going to do,' said Danuta, taking the mug from Halina. How was she to answer all this? Perhaps it was better to deflect? 'What . . . what happened to you in the war, Aunt? Before you came here?'

'I was in Siberia, my girl.' Halina made tea for herself, and came to sit down at the table. Henryk jumped on to her lap, then to the floor, meowing by a dish. 'Always he wants more food, this cat. Wait

461

a moment, Henryk, I am talking.' She looked at Danuta, sipping her tea. 'I suppose you are hungry, too.' She reached across to the side-board, and pulled off a tin. 'Help yourself.'

Prince Charles and Princess Diana smiled up at her. Danuta lifted the lid, and took out a packet of *katażynki*. She smiled at Halina: 'It's a very long time since we had these in Poland, either.'

'Hmm. There is a nice little Polish shop not far from here, below the Polish church. You go to church at home?'

'Well . . .'

'Of course not. Everything has changed. You ask me about the war? I was in Siberia, from 1939 to 1941 – the whole of our village was taken prisoner by the Russians. In 1941, when we were all released – those of us who survived, my sister died' – she waved her hand, impatiently – 'I was sent by train to Palestine. I spent the rest of the war there, I came here in 1945 – I met Henryk here, in a camp. I could do nothing for Poland, during the war. Nothing. So we come here. Henryk and I save for years to buy our own home; we work in Lyons Corner House – you won't know what I'm talking about, never mind. We find this house, we buy it, letting off rooms. We have no children. Henryk dies. I stay here, letting off rooms. I watch the television, and I see all you young hot-heads, with your slogans, and your demands. You are crazy! Don't you know what they will do to you all?'

'But – we have to do something, Aunt. It has been so – dramatic, exciting. A liberation.'

'Then why are you here? Why haven't you stayed with your drama and excitement?'

'I have a return ticket!' Danuta said hotly. 'I have only just arrived! I came because in spite of everything Solidarity is trying to do, things are still appalling, I seem to have *no* future there . . .' She broke off quickly. Where was her self-control? 'Perhaps I don't have a future here, either,' she said, more quietly, watching the slice of lemon float slowly across the surface of her tea. 'But I have to find out. I hope you will forgive me for knocking on your door, for not warning you. I was hoping perhaps to stay for a night or two. That's all.'

'Tch tch tch.' Halina shook her head. 'And where am I to put you? You will have to sleep in the front room, there is a couch.' Footsteps came running down the stairs to the hall, and the front door banged. She pushed back her chair from the table, and got up, sighing. 'So noisy, all my lodgers. Come on, I'll show you where you can sleep.'

'Thank you. Thank you.' Danuta picked up her case and followed her out of the kitchen and up the little flight of steps. Halina puffed. 'And what sort of job do you think you are going to get?'

'I thought perhaps something in a hotel.'

'You have a work permit?'

'Um . . .'

'Of course not.'

'Got a work permit?'

The demolition site foreman was a large man with an enormous stomach. From beneath his orange safety helmet a small trickle of sweat crept down his cheek; he rubbed it away as Stefan shook his head. Behind them the bulldozer roared; clouds of brick dust hung in the air.

'Not yet.' They were almost the only two phrases he knew properly. *Got a work permit? Not yet.* He'd been using them all morning.

The foreman scratched the back of his neck.

'Nothing at the moment. You can try next week, I might have a lad going Friday, but it's half pay, right? Because of the risk.' He looked Stefan up and down. 'Think you're strong enough?'

'Excuse me?' He'd understood only a few words, enough to know he hadn't got a job.

'Where you from?'

'From Poland. I am factory supervisor.'

'Hmm. Well, like I say, come back next week.' He turned away and climbed the steps into the prefab hut. Stefan walked back across the site towards the wire mesh gates and out on to the street. He was somewhere off Oxford Street, getting further and further from it and not sure he could find his way back. Last night he'd lain on his bed in the hostel and written to Krystyna.

'I've been here only two days and already you seem a long way away and I miss you and Olek all the time. As soon as I find a job it'll be better: I'll be doing something for all of us, able to bring something home.' He hadn't posted the letter this morning because he wanted by the end of today to be able to write and say: 'I have a job.' There were other Poles in the hostel, all young like him, here for what was left of spring, and the summer; he wasn't sure if any of them were married. One guy, Bogdan, had told him building site jobs were there for the asking, but he hadn't told him where he worked.

There was nothing to do except keep going from site to site; it was only midday, and he'd only asked at about half a dozen. He crossed the street and stood listening: was the drilling he could hear from another site or just a roadmender's? He turned the corner and followed the sound: perhaps he'd have to be a roadmender for a bit. He walked quickly along the pavement; behind the plate-glass windows very thin unsmiling models wore summer skirts, and sleeveless tops in soft cottons, cool trousers and light jackets which made him feel uncomfortable, in his old check shirt and thin trousers. What the hell did it matter, he was going for a job on a building site, not on a reception desk, but still – he was Polish, he didn't want passers-by thinking he looked cheap. Not that any of them seemed to be looking.

The buildings were tall; they cast deep shadows on the pavement, and he found himself thinking of streets in the centre of Warsaw, especially Marszałkowska – they weren't so unlike. It didn't lessen his sense of utter apartness, a strange sense of adrenalin-charged bewilderment. For the first time in his life, he didn't know where he was going, what he would be doing tomorrow, how much he would earn this week, where he would be this time next week. He felt in some ways diminished, no longer absolutely certain, as he had always been, of who he was, but he also felt lighter, more free than he had ever done, a different feeling from the charged-up frustrated energy which he'd put into Solidarity: it seemed there was nothing here to stop him doing anything he wanted.

The noise of the drilling was very close now; he turned the corner, and saw both some roadmenders and, fifty metres or so beyond, a site. Right, well he'd try there. They were knocking down a narrow building between a pub and what were probably offices; there were hoardings set almost to the edge of the pavement, plastered with pictures of snarling guard dogs, and at first he couldn't work out how to get in. After the last eight months, the guard dogs looked almost surreal – he expected them to be transformed into the faces of the militia, at the very least to have slogans scrawled over them. It had felt strange ever since he got here to see posters and know that they had not been slapped up by him, or by anyone he knew, that no risks had been run in putting them up – and to realize that most of them probably weren't about anything more subversive than a rock group. He had seen something yesterday, which must be for a meeting, and recognized the words Socialist Worker. That did feel strange, as if everything had been turned upside down, or looked at from the wrong end of a telescope.

He came to the end of the hoardings, and found a narrow padlocked door set into them, with a flysheet showing a safety helmet. That at least looked familiar. He banged on the door and realized at once he'd never be heard. He looked up, saw men tramping along scaffolding, whistled and yelled: 'Excuse me!' It took four or five yells before one of them looked down, and when Stefan beckoned, and pointed to the door, a good five minutes before it was opened.

'Excuse me – I look for a job.'

'Right, mate, through here. Mind you, I think we're full.' The man in overalls picked his way over a long path of rubble, and pointed to a short, stocky man on the far side of the site in shirtsleeves and safety helmet. He had a clipboard in his hand and was waving a stub of pencil at the driver of an earth mover. Piles of bricks, girders and breeze blocks stood in the corners.

'That's him.'

Stefan flattened the air, unable to remember the English for short. '*Mały* – little man?'

The man in overalls grinned. 'That's the one. Where you from?'

'From Poland.'

'That's funny – so's the boss.'

'Yes?' Stefan made his way over to the man, and waited for him to stop waving the pencil. He cleared his throat. '*Proszę – dzień dobry.*'

'*Tak?*' The stocky man turned, saw Stefan and nodded. '*Dzień dobry.*' They shook hands. 'Can I help you?'

'I came over a couple of days ago,' said Stefan. 'I'm looking for work – I wondered . . .' He shrugged.

The man had silvery hair, cut very short; something in his face, Stefan realized now, was pure Pole: there were features like his all over Warsaw. He nodded again. 'You have a work permit?'

Stefan shook his head. 'Not yet.'

The man looked at him. 'I see. Where are you from?'

'From Warsaw. That is where my family – my wife and child – are living.'

'Yes? We've been following events in Poland with much interest – you can imagine. Very dramatic. At present a little alarming. You have been a member of Solidarity?'

'Yes. Yes – I have been quite involved.' Stefan wondered suddenly if there was any need for caution. No – for God's sake, he was just bringing all the old feelings with him. 'May I ask how long you have been here?'

'In this country? I came here in 1940, from France. I was in the RAF. Now – ' He made a gesture to include the site, the men, the machines. Above them a steel ball went crashing from a crane into the last remaining brickwork on the third storey and it crumpled and sank in a cloud of plaster dust. Stefan coughed and covered his mouth, stepping back. The man patted his shoulder. 'And now I have my own business,' he said, smiling. 'I have a vacancy at present for one man, but you don't look like a builder.'

'I work in a factory,' said Stefan, recovering. 'I have an engineering degree from the Polytechnika in Warsaw. But for now – I'm pretty strong.'

'Yes?' The man smiled again. 'Well – you can start tomorrow, you'll simply be doing what's needed. You drive?'

Stefan shook his head.

'Of course – no one in Poland has a car. Never mind – there is plenty for you to do. Eight a.m. start, please be on time.' He held out his hand.

Stefan shook it again. 'Thank you.' He hesitated. 'May I ask – the wages?'

'One pound an hour,' said the man, and raised his clipboard again. 'Your name?'

One pound an hour. Stefan thought fast. That was, say, forty pounds a week. He had his hostel fees, his fares – he'd have to walk. He had food, which he'd discovered already was terrifyingly expensive: a cup of coffee at ten this morning had been forty pence. A sandwich yesterday was sixty. He had, above all, to save, to be able to send money home and take some with him. One pound an hour – it was nothing!

He cleared his throat again. 'Excuse me – is it possible to raise that a little?'

'I beg your pardon?' The smile disappeared.

'To raise the money . . . Forgive me, but are the wages usually so low?'

'You think one pound an hour is *low*?' The man looked at him unpleasantly. 'Do you know what I did here at the end of the war? I washed up. For a year. For shillings! I was discharged from the RAF and like everyone else I had my civvy suit and my £5. I had my family to support, my mother over from Poland at last, after surviving the occupation, my sister, my wife. We lived in rented rooms, in Earl's Court – it was known as the Polish Corridor. Have you heard of it? Of course not. We worked! We saved – even though

466

we were earning almost nothing – we had to be patient, to wait for years for a home of our own, to build up a business.' He banged on the clipboard. 'Do you think you should be able to come over here, walk into a job, when there are over a million British people unemployed? Do you not realize that? And fuss about how much you are paid?'

'I – excuse me – but . . .' Stefan felt as if he'd just been punched.

'There is no but. You are of a generation which has known nothing of the true Poland, the true spirit of Poland, and you will destroy our good name here if you think you can come here simply to grab. You are the children of communists! Opportunists!'

Stefan stared at him.

'Mr Kubiak – could you come over here a minute?' A man in plaster-grey jeans, stripped to the waist, was pointing to an area of the site still uncleared. 'There's a lot of gas pipes there – can you come and check?'

Kubiak nodded, and looked up at Stefan. 'If one pound an hour is not enough,' he said coldly, 'I suggest you go elsewhere.'

'You have no need to tell me that!' Stefan snapped.

He turned and walked furiously across the site towards the hoardings, stumbling over the line of rubble so fast that he almost sprained his ankle, and banged open the door. He almost slammed it behind him, but stopped himself from looking a fool in the middle of the street and instead pulled out his cigarettes and lit one, flicking the match into the gutter. The cigarettes were Marlborough, bought duty free on the plane, his first Western cigarettes – you could get Marlborough in Warsaw, but they were much more expensive than Sport. He inhaled deeply – what a greedy bloody communist he was!

He strode along the pavement, almost talking aloud, until he found himself on a six-lane main road, and stopped, confused. Now where was he? He looked up and down, pulled the tourist map someone had left on the underground from the airport out of his pocket, and folded it back. Oxford Street was a long way behind him, so . . . there was an enormous park on the map, with a lake. Regent's Park – was that the trees, right across the road? Okay, he'd go to Regent's Park, and job hunting could go to hell. He crossed what must be Marylebone Road at a traffic light – yesterday he'd almost got killed stepping out into the traffic and expecting it to stop. On the other side, he walked along cream-painted porticoed terraces towards the trees, finding himself at last inside the park, where he walked and walked, under the chestnuts full of blossom, following the path until he reached a boating lake, and stood watching the sun sparkle on the water, and a few little boats rowed out by tourists. He wanted to be taking Krysia and Olek out in a boat, he wanted to ring up Krysia and tell her about Pan Kubiak – he'd certainly never expected that one. Had he been naive? He lit another cigarette and walked on, feeling a little calmer. They couldn't all be like him. It grew very warm; he took off his jacket and lay down under one of the chestnut trees, yawning. They reminded him of home, too.

He woke feeling hungry and uncomfortable, and for a few moments couldn't work out what on earth he was doing sleeping in a park in the middle of the day. He should be at the factory, or was there a strike? Then he remembered, and remembered Kubiak, and sat up quickly, rubbing his face. He had to find something to eat, that was the first thing. There was a little café near the lake, bound to be a tourist trap, but even a packet of crisps would help. He made his way back there, found a toilet and had a pee and a wash and felt a bit more civilized.

In the café he stood in a queue among middle-aged women in pleated cotton dresses and linen jackets, and bra-less girls in sleeveless tee-shirts. He couldn't take his eyes off them – he couldn't in Warsaw, either: Krysia was always complaining about his roving eye. There were one or two families, a sprinkling of older men, but as a young man on his own he felt completely out of place. The food on glass shelves on the counter was out of this world: bulging sandwiches, cakes and pastries piled with real cream, chocolate biscuits, baskets of fruit. There was a strong, delicious smell of coffee – he bought a cup to pull himself together, and a ham and salad sandwich and found he'd spent almost two pounds. He'd brought forty dollars with him, złotys borrowed from his father and changed on the black market, changed again into pounds at Heathrow. Already, in two days, it was melting away. He sat at a table by the lake, refusing to panic. '*Kochana Krysiu – I am coming home much sooner than I expected.*' No. He'd find something today, and he'd better take anything, low wages or not, though he certainly wasn't going back to Kubiak.

When he'd finished, he walked back through the park, and this time crossed the main road a little further up, near the Planetarium. He walked down Baker Street; the map showed side streets where he might find something, and he did. There was a skip and a cement mixer outside a tall, shabby house in a long, elegant street. The door to the house was open, and when, on an impulse, he climbed the steps and looked inside he could see right through to the back, to an open door to a garden, and empty rooms. The stairs were uncarpeted, and from upstairs he could hear banging and shouting; clearly the whole house was being renovated. Well – perhaps this was more like it: he'd done up their apartment completely when they moved in – new wiring, plastering, painting, shelves in the kitchen. He should have thought of this in the first place.

'Hello? Excuse me!' He shouted up the stairs, and the banging stopped.

'You what?' Footsteps came running down; a young guy in vest and jeans and very dusty hair came down with a bucket. 'Yeah?'

'I – I look for job,' said Stefan, and then, more firmly: 'I am good worker – a good worker.' He always forgot the 'a'.

'Oh yeah?' The guy carried the bucket out to the mixer. A long hose wound its way all through the house, and down the steps and into the mixer. He looked inside it, and said: 'Want to turn off the water, then?' He nodded towards the back of the house. 'Kitchen's through there.'

'Yes – yes.' Stefan climbed back up the steps, found his way to the kitchen, which was empty except for a very old sink, and turned off the tap. Outside the window the grass was knee-high; petals and dust were drifting over it. He went back outside, past a room with a high, moulded ceiling, and tall dirty windows.

'Right,' said the guy, wiping his hands on his jeans. 'Where you from?'

For the seventh time that morning Stefan told a stranger he was from Poland, from Warsaw, and had no work permit yet.

'Oh, yeah? Well, I'm not too bothered about that. I've got a chap off sick, very sudden; you can fill in for him till the end of the week, if you like.'

The end of the week – well, it was a start, it was something.

'Thank you. Yes.'

'Fifty quid,' said the guy. 'What's your name?'

Fifty! 'Stefan. Your name?'

'Tony.' He looked Stefan up and down. 'You can start now if you want, this is a big job and I'm running over time.'

'Okay.' Stefan followed him up the steps again, and into the house. *Okay, Krysia, I have found a job . . .*

The hotel in Lancaster Gate had a basement which ran the length of the building, and had a number of rooms, each divided once, sometimes twice, to make bedrooms for the staff. The staff were foreign. Danuta's room had space just sufficient for a bed, cheap built-in cupboard, bedside locker and washbasin. There was no bedside lamp, only light from the ceiling, without a shade. Opposite the door the window was hung with a thick net curtain pockmarked with cigarette burns; the panes did not look as if they had been cleaned for a very long time, and beyond, in any case, was only a narrow strip of concrete, and the low wall above set with railings. When the window was closed the room was unbearably stuffy; at night, when it was open, the noise from the street would have made it difficult to get to sleep except that Danuta worked so hard during the day that when she crawled into bed she was asleep at once.

She had been a chambermaid here for three weeks, responsible for fifteen bedrooms, with bathrooms en suite. Each morning she got up at six-thirty, washed, dressed and put on her overall and went upstairs to have breakfast with the other staff in a room off the kitchens. The other staff were all without work permits also: there were many Poles, including Basia, a pale blonde girl from Kraków, who had been studying pharmacy, and a woman from Łódź, where the food shortages had been particularly bad. She was separated, had two children, left with her sister while she came over here. The other workers – chambermaids, washers-up – were mainly from Portugal, Colombia, the Philippines, a sprinkling of students but mostly men and women trying to support families here or back home. There was a washer-up called Enrico, who was very small, and swore elaborately; there was a chef called Franco, tall and beautiful. The main language spoken was Spanish.

The domestic supervisor was English, a woman in her thirties called Lisa. Lisa had an over-tanned face and frizzy blonde hair. You were not allowed to leave your floor until she had checked each room.

After breakfast, Danuta and the other chambermaids went upstairs. In each of 'her' rooms on the fourth floor Danuta stripped and remade the double bed with fresh linen: four pillow cases, one bottom sheet, one enormous duvet to manhandle into a new cover. She vacuumed the carpets with a huge, heavy Hoover, cleaned the bath and basin and lavatory, put out fresh towels, mopped the bathroom floor, dusted the bedside cabinets and dressing table, cleaned the ashtrays, wiped clean the window sills, washed the aluminium trays of aluminium tea things, and the cups and saucers.

At the end of her first morning, when she had finished the fifteenth room, she was soaked in sweat, her arms and legs trembling. She leaned against the wall of the landing, carpeted in red, and waited with her eyes closed for Lisa to come and inspect. New arrivals came out of the lift at the far end; through the smell of floor cleaner, toilet cleaner and scouring powder which clung to her, Danuta realized she could smell scent, and she heard American voices laughing and talking. Many of the guests were American, there were also Arabs, and a few French and Germans. At least, she thought, exhausted, the tips should be good. Everyone said the Arabs were fantastic. There had been nothing on the dressing tables this morning, when Lisa had shown her which were her rooms, but that must be unusual.

'You asleep or something?'

She opened her eyes, almost jumping away from the wall. Lisa was frowning.

'Excuse me – I am sorry . . .'

'Well come on, let's have a look.'

Danuta followed her from room to room, nervously watching her straighten duvets, look under each bed, run a finger along the window sills, check the toilets.

'There's dust behind here!'

'Where?' Danuta hurried to look. There was a thin film of dust on the wastepipe leading from the toilet in Room 206. 'I'm sorry, I didn't see . . .'

'Well you'd better look. Go on, don't just stand there – where's your cloth?'

Danuta bent to wipe the wastepipe clean. The soft net curtain at the window blew a little in the breeze from the open bathroom window; outside it was hot and sunny and she could see the trees of Hyde Park. Perhaps she could sunbathe there at the weekend. She went out of the bathroom just in time to see Lisa slip something from the dressing table into her pocket. A tip? It must be – how had she missed *that?* She followed her out, and along to the next room. At the end, Lisa said only: 'Right, you can take the linen along to the lift. The laundry's down in the basement.'

There were six Filipino women in the laundry, chattering in high-pitched voices. They smiled at Danuta and she put down the basket of bedclothes and smiled back.

'Lisa . . .' she said cautiously.

'Lisa is a cow,' one of them said cheerfully. 'On Fridays you check your money.'

'I will.'

Next morning, Danuta was so stiff she could hardly get out of bed.

By the end of the week, some of the stiffness had gone, but still, when she straightened up from each bath her back ached so much she had to lie on the floor before she went on to the next room. She had managed to get to most of her tips before Lisa and that was the money she was saving to send home: her wages were going to pay for her fees at a language school in Oxford Street. Basia, the pharmacist from Kraków, had told her about it. After lunch that Friday she went to Lisa's office on the ground floor, to collect her wages.

'Right, then.' From a pile of small brown envelopes on her desk, Lisa took the one with her name and gave it to her.

'Thank you.' She took it along the passage and opened it quickly. There should be thirty-five pounds. There were two ten-pound notes, and three ones. She hurried back to the office.

'Excuse me – I think there is a mistake?'

Lisa looked up from her desk. 'What do you mean?'

Danuta held out the envelope. 'There are twenty-three pounds. It should be thirty-five?'

'But there's your deductions, isn't there? See your paper inside.'

She looked inside the envelope, pulled out a folded piece of lined paper written in smudgy ballpoint capitals. National Insurance. Tax. 'But . . .'

'But what?'

But if she was working illegally, how could they be deducting these things? Who was the money going to? She opened her mouth to speak, but felt an enormous lump in her throat. Anyway, to argue that in English was beyond her.

'If you don't like it,' said Lisa, 'you can always leave.'

Danuta couldn't look at her. She walked out of the office with her envelope and ran down the stairs to her room. Twenty-three pounds! How was she supposed to live on that? What about her school fees?

She sat on the edge of the bed with her head in her hands.

If she didn't like it, she could always leave. But she couldn't, could she? Not after just one week, when it had taken her a week to find this job. She couldn't go back to Halina and her lectures and the couch which smelt of Henryk, and where she was in the way. In any case, it might be the same in any hotel, and she couldn't look for a restaurant job without somewhere to live. Danuta got up and went out of her room, along the corridor to Basia's. She knocked on the door, asking in Polish: 'May I come in?'

After a few moments the door was opened; Basia looked pale and sleepy.

'You were resting,' said Danuta. 'I'm so sorry.'

Basia yawned. 'It's all right. I have to go to school in a little while anyway. Are you coming with me?'

'Yes – but the money!' Danuta held out the pay packet.

Basia nodded. 'I know. What can we do?' Danuta followed her into her room. There were pictures of her family on her bedside cabinet, just as there were on hers, and a young man, a snapshot taken in the mountains.

'Is that your boyfriend?'

'Yes. I miss him, but he has another year to study. What about you? Have you got someone at home?'

Danuta shook her head. 'No. Perhaps I should try to find a rich Englishman.'

They both smiled wryly.

'How much did you say the fees were?'

'Fifty pounds a month,' said Basia. 'That's to do the Cambridge Proficiency – it's really difficult, but they say it's the one with status.'

'Oh. Well, I suppose that's all right. Just.' Danuta looked down at her heavy skirt and nylon blouse. 'I was dying to buy some clothes, you know.'

'I work in the evenings as well,' said Basia.

'Do you? I wondered why I never saw you. Where?'

'In a restaurant in Knightsbridge.'

'Where's that?'

'It's right across the other side of the park. It's very expensive, rather glamorous. You might find your rich Englishman there.' She yawned again. 'Come on, we'd better go. You can enrol today, but I suppose you won't start classes till Monday.'

'Do you think it's all right if I just put down a deposit?'

'Oh, I expect so.'

They left the hotel together, walking along to the Bayswater Road. 'Should we get a bus?' asked Danuta.

Basia shrugged. 'Actually I always walk, to save money.'

'And in the evenings?'

'I get a cab back from Knightsbridge, I have to, it would be madness to walk back alone, don't you think? I don't leave till after midnight. But I walk there.'

'And you're up again at six? My God, no wonder you're tired.'

Buses thundered down from Marble Arch, past the park railings, hung with violently coloured paintings. It was very hot suddenly, and there seemed to be tourists everywhere, licking ice creams and

473

wandering slowly under the trees. In Oxford Street, Danuta looked in window after window of summer dresses, cotton trousers and jackets, cool cotton tops, pretty coloured sandals. She could feel sweat trickling down the back of her neck, and her feet in last year's plastic shoes were killing her. Music pounded out of the boutiques, girls five years younger than she were swinging carrier bags full of new clothes.

'Does it make you upset?' she asked Basia, as they stopped at a doorway. She gestured at the shops, the sunny street, the throngs of people buying things.

Basia nodded. 'My first week was such a shock. I don't think I'm going back to Poland.'

'What about your boyfriend?'

'He'll come over next year. He's a pharmacist also – perhaps by the time he comes I'll have a proper job, I hope so.'

'Were you in Solidarity?'

'I was still studying, I couldn't – I wore a badge, of course, but – ' She smiled. 'I'm not really political.'

'How can you be Polish and not be political?' Danuta asked, half serious.

Basia laughed. 'I don't know, but that's me.' She nodded at the doorway. 'This is the school, come on, I'll show you where the office is.'

That was three weeks ago. Now, Danuta's days had a routine of work, school, study, fall asleep and work, school, study. Tiredness had become a part of her; she couldn't remember not feeling tired, and she knew that once her English was better she would try for an evening restaurant job, like Basia. What was the point of coming over here if she was almost as poor and twice as tired as she'd been in Warsaw? What was the point of missing her parents, and them missing her, if she couldn't even send them anything to make it all worthwhile? So far she had sent one parcel, a cardboard box packed with tins of ham, tins of fruit, soap, soap powder, shampoo, Marks & Spencer tights for Mama and Marks & Spencer socks for her father. Still, every time she bought anything at all, she thought, automatically, that she should be buying more – dozens of bottles of shampoo, or packets of sanitary towels – luxury! – just in case, next time she came, there was nothing. On her days off, she sometimes went sightseeing. She had been to the National Gallery and the National Portrait Gallery. On her days off, she could sleep in, but she discovered they were all expected to work up to nine days without a break. She wrote long letters home. Once she had telephoned, using five pounds of ten-pence coins to talk to Mama.

'I miss you so much, *kochana*, are you all right?'

'I'm fine, Mama. I'm making lots of money, and I have a nice friend in the hotel, another Polish girl.'

'Are you sure? Are you really all right?'

'I'm *sure!*'

What was the point of saying anything else? Mama would only worry more. The queues in Warsaw were even longer, but otherwise, apparently, things were calm. For the moment, Mama said, Solidarity was out of the limelight: it was shake-ups in the Party which had taken the headlines.

On a humid afternoon, Danuta and Basia set out for school, testing each other on verbs as they walked up the Bayswater Road.

'The past tense of *Think?*' Basia asked.

'Thought, I thought, You thought, He, She or It thought . . .' The grammar wasn't so bad, easier than Polish in fact, but the pronunciation was a nightmare. How were you supposed to tell between *thought, cough, bough, through, rough?* 'We thought, You thought, They thought.'

'Very good. *To speak?*'

'Spoke. I spoke, You spoke . . .' They crossed the Edgware Road, where taxis swept past, and Danuta suddenly grabbed Basia's arm. 'What does that say?' She pointed to a newspaper placard.

'What?' Basia followed her arm, frowning. 'Oh, my God.'

'Something about the Pope, isn't it? What's happened?'

'He's been assassinated! Quick!'

They ran towards the *Evening Standard* seller. 'Thank you . . . oh, he's not dead, he's not, but someone's tried to kill him in Rome, look.'

Danuta and Basia stood reading the paper until they were knocked into twice, and moved out of the crush, standing against a shop window.

'A *Turk?* Why should a Turk want to kill John Paul?'

Danuta bit her lip. 'He was paid to do it, he must have been.'

'By whom?'

'Who do you think?'

Basia looked at her.

'He's our most powerful ally in the West, isn't he?' said Danuta, and realized she was shaking all over.

They walked on arm in arm to the school, where few people seemed to have noticed, and not particularly to care, that the Pope was in a Roman hospital, fighting for his life. Within a week or so, when it was clear he was recovering, Danuta had almost forgotten the shocking, dizzying impact of that afternoon. It was only months later that she remembered how she had felt, and realized that perhaps it really had been the beginning of the end.

The translation agency where Ewa worked was in a second-floor office in a small street behind Oxford Circus. It was an old building, with a creaking lift; once you were above the carpeted ground floor, the corridors were covered in linoleum and rambled through the building past endless brown doors with nameplates. There were solicitors, travel agents, insurance brokers and accountants, a theatrical agent. Some of the doors opened on to offices where walls had been knocked down and low partitions put up: there were carpets, potted palms and yucca plants, word processors, coffee machines and canvas chairs, gleaming photocopiers, posters and prints from Athena. In others, little had been touched; ancient, even wartime filing cabinets were heaped with battered cardboard ring-binders, and dusty files; there were kettles and trays of cups in corners. Ewa's agency belonged more to the second category, and she liked it. The only thing she didn't like was the journey from Blackheath, but it was manageable, and she had been working here for years and wanted to change neither her job nor her home. Was the Blackheath flat home? It was where she lived, she didn't want to live anywhere else, and she had made it hers. On Sundays, often, she went to have lunch with her family. That was home. So, in a way, was her desk in the agency.

Ewa sat in a corner by the window, a privilege she had earned through being here for so long. When she first came, she was by the door. There were four desks, and many translators had sat at them over the years. The unchanging element was the woman who ran it, a tall, spare, unmarried Englishwoman in her sixties. She was called Patricia, and Ewa had never met anyone quite like her. Patricia had worked in the War Office, then the Foreign Office. She had travelled. She had come home – no question where that was. She was very, very English, but she was also fluent in three languages and understood more. She had inherited the agency in the late fifties when the Hungarian founder died, and she had left it much as he had liked it. There were word processors; there were also box files dating back to the fifties, theatre posters curling at the edges, a library of dictionaries and old reference books, constantly updated. The agency's clients ranged from publishers to export companies; there were plenty of opportunities for freelance work, and Ewa often had a book or a series of articles in her briefcase.

It was June, a warm summery morning with a breeze. In spring and summer Ewa often walked to work from Charing Cross, across the Strand, and up St Martin's Lane and Charing Cross Road. She did it partly for the exercise, partly so that she could look in the bookshops. Sometimes she scanned the windows, sometimes, if she had time, she went in and browsed. This morning, she had woken early, was out of the house by eight and had time to spare. She wandered into one of the shops, just opened, a smell of dust as if the floorboards had just been swept, and a smell of coffee from the back. She browsed for a while among the new novels, then in the East European section. She wandered across to the magazines on the rack in front of the counter. A red and white title caught her eye: she pulled out something called *PSC News*. The Polish Solidarity Campaign newsletter: at the bottom, the scarlet Solidarity logo was printed on either side of a slogan: Solidarity with Polish Workers. The front page was headlined 'The Bydgoszcz Crisis and After.' Ewa looked at it, frowning. The issue was No. 2 – how had she missed No. 1? She had been following events in Poland ever since last August – no, devouring them. Was she really so out of touch with her own community here that she didn't know about a whole campaign?

The newsletter cost twenty pence. She bought it, tucked it into her bag to read properly in the lunch hour, and hurried off to work.

'Morning, Ewa.' From her desk beneath the bookshelves, Patricia looked at her over her glasses.

'Good morning.' Ewa smiled at her, and hung up her jacket. Her Solidarność badge was pinned on the lapel – Wiktoria had sent that at Christmas, one each for all of them. 'Would you like a coffee?'

'I have one, thank you. Help yourself.'

There was no one else in yet; Ewa helped herself and carried the mug over to her desk. The window was open at the top and she could hear the buses and taxis from Oxford Circus; on the sill, a window box of lobelia and petunias stirred in the breeze. Patricia had already watered them. Ewa sat down, and pulled her papers towards her.

In the lunch hour she went, as she often did, to Regent's Park. Sometimes she had lunch with one of the other people in the agency – she was fond of Marika, the Dutch girl who had come a couple of years ago, and was married to an English doctor. Occasionally she had lunch with Patricia, occasionally with François, who made her blush. Today, everyone had their own arrangements, and she went to the park by herself, buying fruit from a stall on the way. The park smelt of cut grass, drying. Everywhere, office workers in deck chairs had lifted their faces to the sun and fallen asleep. On the boating lake children were laughing and shouting, and the summer wind rippled the water, beneath a cloudless sky.

Ewa found a deck chair and sat down. She hung her jacket on the back, pulled an apple from the paper bag and the *PSC News* from her jacket pocket, and began to read, munching. The paper had been launched, it appeared, by English people. A brief statement of aims announced that *PSC News* was 'issued in order to acquaint trade unionists and other sympathizers of the Solidarity movement in Poland . . . We hope the newsletters will also serve to coordinate activity and information about contacts and support for Solidarity within the British Labour movement.' The story of the militia's brutality in Bydgoszcz, and its aftermath, took up three pages. There was a long list of other, violent acts against Solidarity members: assaults, the windows of offices broken, the barn belonging to the son of the old peasant beaten up in Bydgoszcz burned to the ground while he visited his father in hospital. Inside, there was an eye-witness account of the four-hour strike in the Ursus factory in Warsaw, and an exchange of open letters between Wałęsa and Gwiazda, his deputy, clearly revealing the growing rift between them over the decision to call off the general strike. And there was the text of a moving appeal made on Polish television by Jan Kulaj, a leader of the newly registered Rural Solidarity.

'*Dear Countrymen, Brother Peasants,*

'*A great thing has happened to Polish agriculture . . . we have signed an agreement at Bydgoszcz that says that by 10 May we will have a peasants' trade union in Poland.*

'*Our country is in a critical situation. It is important to know who was responsible for it, but it is also even more important to be aware who will lift us out of this grave situation. It will be the peasants, of course. Until recently they were the most neglected of all. In our fatherland, we peasants in company with the combined might of the workers and of the whole nation must play the key role . . . We . . . have the bread in our hands, and must feed the nation . . .*

'*The union must organize the grass roots, take control of everything that is happening in the villages, the parish authorities, rural cooperatives, banks, local councils, agricultural circles, dairies. We cannot allow the countryside to witness any more falsehood, cheating, lying or denunciations.*

478

'We must concern ourselves above all with village children; next winter they should not stand waiting at the bus stop in the frost and cold, like the condemned awaiting their sentence . . .'

'Proszę Pani . . . Excuse me?'

Ewa jumped, and put down the magazine. A young fellow in overalls was standing in front of her, blocking the sun. His hair was grey with dust, but he had a nice face, a kind and intelligent face. Also, a heavy Polish accent.

'Excuse me,' he said again, and nodded towards the magazine, and the Solidarność logo on the front page. 'You read about Poland?'

'Yes,' said Ewa. She looked up at him, feeling rather awkward down here in the deck chair, but not feeling able to get up, and stand beside him. The sun was very bright, and when he moved she had to screw up her eyes. 'Are you from Poland?'

He nodded. 'From Warszawa – from Warsaw.' He squatted down beside her. 'Forgive me – you speak Polish?'

'Yes,' said Ewa. 'I am Polish.'

He raised an eyebrow. 'Your voice . . .' He meant her accent.

'I was born in this country.'

'Ah.'

There was a pause. He pulled out a packet of Marlborough cigarettes from the top pocket of his overalls and held it out.

'You smoke?' he asked in Polish.

'Too much,' said Ewa, in Polish, and took one. He leaned towards her, and lit it with a lighter which flickered a little, and smelt of butane. Ewa coughed. He lit one for himself, and closed the packet, tapping the lid. 'American cigarettes, Polish lighter,' he said, and grinned, wryly.

Ewa smiled back. 'How long have you been over here?'

'A few weeks, only.' He looked down at his overalls, and grinned again. 'I am helping to rebuild this magnificent country.'

'Legally?' asked Ewa before she could stop herself, and he frowned.

'It's all right,' she said quickly. 'I was joking. You can trust me.' And felt the hated blush creep into her face again.

He drew on his cigarette. 'I think it's the oldest trick in the world, isn't it, to be trapped by a pretty girl?'

Ewa shrugged, and studied the magazine, her cheeks burning. Was this fellow trying to pick her up? She supposed he was. And was she just going to sit here blushing? She should get rid of him, or hold a proper conversation. Surely, at thirty years old, she was capable of that?

'I'm sorry,' he said, 'I am disturbing you.'

He made to get up, and she said, 'No. No, it's all right.' She raised her head and he looked at her quizzically, then at the magazine.

'It's about Solidarity, about Bydgoszcz? What is this paper, exactly?'

Ewa read him the brief editorial, translating as she went. He nodded. 'It's good. I didn't know there was such a paper.'

'No,' said Ewa, 'neither did I. I bought it just this morning.'

'Did you?' He smiled at her. 'How strange. May I?' He took it from her, leafed through the pages. He pointed to the photographs of Wałęsa and Gwiazda. 'Last time I saw these guys was on television, telling us the general strike was off. You heard about that?'

'Of course. Everyone here was on tenterhooks. You would have been on strike?'

'Of course. Of course.'

'Weren't you all afraid of what might happen?'

He spread his hands, still squatting, then sat down on the grass. 'We were too angry to be afraid. There's an expression, rather melodramatic – you know it? "Better to die on our feet than live on our knees." That's rather how we felt.'

'I know it,' said Ewa. 'It was used in the war, wasn't it? My mother told me.'

'She was in Poland during the war?'

'In Warsaw, yes.'

'And your father? Were they in the Uprising?'

'Yes. I don't think my father's ever got over it.' She told him that lightly, as if, she realized, she didn't have to worry about whether he'd understand.

He nodded slowly. 'My parents, too. But they went back, of course. I was born there.'

The sun was high in the sky, and it was very hot. On the path between the stretches of dry grass people were strolling slowly towards the lake. At the same moment, Stefan said: 'May I ask your name?' and Ewa looked at her watch, and said: 'I must be getting back to work.' They smiled at each other.

'Ewa,' she said. 'And . . . yours?'

He stubbed out his cigarette on the grass and got up. 'Stefan.' He hesitated. 'You work near here?'

'Not far.' Ewa bent down and put out her own cigarette. She put the magazine in her bag, and got up, taking her jacket off the back

480

of the deck chair. He saw the Solidarność badge, and shook his head, laughing.

'What?' asked Ewa, then saw what he was looking at.

'It just makes me feel good,' he said simply, and made, as if automatically, to help her on with the jacket, then hesitated again.

'Thank you,' said Ewa, 'but it's too hot, don't you think?'

'Of course.'

They began to walk down the long path towards the gates. 'What about you?' she asked. 'Where are you working?'

'In a little road off Baker Street. We are renovating a house, four of us. There is another Pole there now. The guy who employs us is English, he's okay. Not like the Pole I met on my first day.'

'Oh?'

He told her about Kubiak, the pound an hour and the children of communists. Ewa shook her head. 'I wonder how many of my parents' generation think like that.'

They had reached the gates, and came out on to the Edgware Road. 'I came here after that interview,' said Stefan. 'But I didn't have such pleasant company, then.' He stopped, and looked at her. Ewa blushed, and looked away.

'Well – I have to go now.'

'Of course. Me, too. I don't want to get the sack in my first job.'

'No, no, you mustn't. Well – goodbye.'

'Goodbye.' He held out his hand, she gave him hers, and he lifted it very quickly and brushed it with his lips. Then grinned. 'Even the sons of communists have the traditional Polish manners.' He released her hand. 'Perhaps you find such things rather old-fashioned?'

'No – I – ' Ewa couldn't think. 'I must go now, excuse me.' She turned away, stood waiting for the traffic lights to change, and hurried across the road, walking fast in the shade as she approached her street. Footsteps came running up behind her.

'Ewa!'

She turned round quickly, saw him running up towards her. And felt suddenly happy. 'Yes?'

'Forgive me – ' He stood in front of her, suddenly awkward, and rubbed his face. 'I – is it perhaps possible to see you again?'

'Yes,' she said. 'Yes, I should like to.'

'Good, good.' He rubbed his face again, streaking the builder's dirt with sweat. 'Well – what shall we . . .'

'Perhaps we could meet again after work?' Ewa realized that she wasn't blushing. 'What about . . .' She pointed to a pub just ahead of them, on the other side of the road. Hanging baskets of geraniums, lobelia and mignonette swung gently above the door. 'In there? What time do you finish work?'

'I can be there at six.'

'Fine. I'll see you at six, then.'

'Yes.' He looked down at her again, and said: 'You are not a builder.'

She laughed. 'No.'

'I don't know what work you do. Let me guess. You are – a teacher?'

'Do you see any schools round here? No, I'm not.' She pulled a face. 'Do I look like a teacher?'

'No, but – you have a clever face.'

'Do I?' The blush was returning.

'You are a journalist?'

'No, never. I'm a translator.'

'A translator. Ah.' He raised an eyebrow. 'That could be useful.'

Ewa felt suddenly apprehensive, a feeling much more familiar than happiness. 'I must go,' she said.

'Of course. Until six, then.'

'Until six.' She did not give him her hand again, but walked quickly away, bumping into a man in a suit and blushing again, not looking back to see if Stefan were watching, but almost running until she was in her own street again, and by the safety of the open double doors leading into her office building. Inside, it was cool; there was a Ladies' on the ground floor, and she went in and splashed her face with water. She dried it on the towel, and brushed her hair, looking in the mirror beneath the strip of neon, and seeing her face as a stranger might see it: pale, dark-eyed, possibly an interesting face, she would grant herself that, but in no way revealing anything of who, ashamed, she felt herself to be: uncertain, uneasy, somehow set apart.

This is how Jerzy used to feel, she thought: that he didn't belong anywhere, with anyone. She went out and waited for a moment by the lift, then felt too impatient, and climbed the stairs. At her desk, she sat looking out through the open window at the street below. The breeze stirred the papers on her desk, held down by a paper-weight Jerzy and Elizabeth had brought back with them from Poland two years ago. She remembered, suddenly, something Jerzy had said to her long before then, when they were walking through the cemetery after the Katyń memorial service. *'You have your own life, you can go home as your own person.*' It had been she trying to comfort him, then, laughing off what seemed to be the success she had made of her life after that terrible, long-ago summer. And now? He had Elizabeth.

'Ewa? Are you all right?'

She turned quickly from the window, and saw Patricia watching her. 'You're rather pale – have you got a headache?'

'No, no, I'm fine. Sorry. It must have been the sun in the park.'

She bent her head to the paper on the import of Polish bottled fruit, not seeing it. The sun in the park – a nice phrase, it sounded like the title of a love story. She thought: But I have no place in a real love story, and then, angrily: This is stupid self-pity, this is the twentieth century. What happened to me was something that happens to hundreds of girls. You think for a little while that your heart is broken, then you recover, and rejoin the human race; you don't let it scar you for the rest of your life. But she thought of meeting Stefan in a few hours' time, and felt stinging tears of humiliation at the awkward, diffident woman she still was. She brushed them away, covertly. I can't help it, she thought. I can't help it if people aren't supposed to be scarred. That seems to have been what happened to me.

He was waiting at a table in a corner of the pub, and as soon as she saw him she felt better. The doors were open on to the street, so that the bar was filled with early evening sunlight, and the glasses and polished table tops gleamed. Stefan had a pint glass beside him; he was bent over the evening paper, frowning and smoking, still in his overalls but he'd obviously washed, and run a comb through the dusty hair. For a moment, as she stepped inside, Ewa recalled that other pub, where she had waited for Leo with such pitiful longing; then she pushed the memory away and walked over to Stefan, who was waiting for her, and who somehow looked already familiar, a friend.

'*Dzień dobry.*'

He almost jumped, putting down the paper quickly, and getting to his feet. '*Dzień dobry.* I'm sorry – I didn't see you come in.'

'It's all right.'

They stood there, not quite knowing what to say next. Stefan gestured to the table. 'Please – sit down. May I get you a drink?'

'I should be buying one for you,' said Ewa.

'No, no. What would you like?'

'I'll just have a white wine and Perrier, please.' She laughed at his

483

puzzled expression. 'It's a mineral water! I don't drink very much. And I'll buy you the next.' Was that a bit presumptuous? They might have run out of conversation after one drink. She sat down, putting her briefcase under the table, and watched him go up to the bar and ask, in awkward English, for her drink.

'White wine and – and – ' He turned round and raised an eyebrow, asking quickly in Polish: 'And what?'

'Perrier,' she said, and he pulled an enormously exaggerated face, a foreigner at sea amidst outlandish local customs, and she laughed, feeling again the rush of happiness.

He came back, put her glass down in front of her, and pulled back his chair.

'Thank you. Sorry if it was a problem.' She raised the glass. '*Na zdrowie.*'

'*Na zdrowie.*'

She saw a couple at the next table look at them for a moment, curious, clearly wondering what language they were speaking. Ewa used Polish at work all the time, but hardly ever in public, only if she were out with one of the family, and she realized that perhaps she had always, without questioning, thought of it as a private, even secret language, used to keep others out.

Stefan was offering her a cigarette.

'No, you have one of mine this time.' She felt in her jacket pocket, and took out a packet of Camel.

'Aha! The Camel. He is everywhere in Warsaw.'

'Is he? Here.' She held out the pack.

'But very expensive. Thank you.' He took one, but did not light it, waiting until she had hers, and offering the lighter again. 'Is the Camel your favourite?'

Ewa inhaled, and shrugged. 'Cigarettes are disgusting. I wish I could give it up.'

'I don't. It's been my only pleasure here – well, so far.' He looked at her with an unmistakable twinkle, and she went scarlet.

'I – have you smoked long?' she asked, idiotically.

'All my life,' he said gravely. 'And you?'

'No. I mean, I don't know. About ten years, I think.'

'Ah.'

They fell into what seemed to Ewa, looking at the table, to be a silence full of floundering embarrassment. When she felt the blush fade, and looked up, she saw Stefan studying the paper again.

'I can hardly understand a word,' he said, as if there had been no awkwardness at all. 'I must go to classes, I suppose. Or perhaps you could help me a little?'

'Um – yes, perhaps.'

'I speak Polish at work, too,' he said, 'now this guy Wojtek has come. I should speak nothing but English.'

'My grandparents speak nothing but Polish,' said Ewa.

'Still?'

'Still. After thirty-five years. My grandmother can barely do the shopping.'

He shook his head. 'Fantastic. And who else is there in your family?'

'My parents and my brother. He's called Jerzy, and he lives with an English woman.'

'They are not married?'

'No. I don't know why, I'm sure they'll stay together.'

'And you?'

'I'm not married, no.' She looked away, taking another sip of her drink. 'I'm – not really interested in all that.'

'All what? You're not interested in marriage?'

'Or – any of it.' Her cheeks were burning; the thought of her quiet attic flat, and solitude, was like a long cool swimming pool, there to step into, and recover, and drown if she wanted to.

'That is rather unusual,' Stefan said lightly. 'Ewa?'

'Yes?' She looked at him, cheeks still burning, daring him to ask another question.

'Forgive me,' he said slowly. 'I have upset you. It wasn't my intention.'

'Of course it wasn't.' She had embarrassed him, made him feel he had blundered, and he was so nice, so funny. Was she going to spend the rest of her life in this dreadful, intense, neurotic way, barely able to hold a conversation with a man without making a fool of herself? Did she have to pay like this for one, ridiculous mistake? She shook her head again, blindly. 'I'm sorry. I'm afraid I'm a rather peculiar person.' And tried to laugh, as if people who had just met had conversations like this all the time.

He drew on his cigarette, watching her. 'I think perhaps you were once very badly hurt?'

It must be written all over her. 'Please – can we not talk like this any more?'

'Of course. May I get you another drink?'

'No. No thanks.' She stubbed out her cigarette clumsily. 'What about you?'

'I'm fine,' said Stefan. 'I'm fine. Now – can you translate some of this for me? Please?' He pointed to the columns beneath a photograph of a man being hustled into a car with a blanket over his head. 'If I were in Poland, I should say he was being guarded by Solidarity from the militia.'

'Would you?' Ewa glanced at the caption. 'He's a murderer.'

'Oh.'

They both laughed, weakly. 'It's not funny,' said Stefan.

'I know.'

'Then why are you laughing?'

'I feel a bit better,' said Ewa, and went on laughing, slightly hysterically, feeling herself about to cry.

'Oh my God,' said Stefan, seeing it also. 'You are a nervous wreck. I can see I shall have to look after you while I'm here.' He pulled out a handkerchief from his pocket and passed it across to her. 'Do you need something to eat?' he asked kindly. 'Would that help?'

'Possibly.' Ewa took the handkerchief and blew her nose. 'What sort of food do you like?'

'I have been living in a hostel on steak and kidney pies,' said Stefan. 'Made by Walls? Before that, as I expect you know, we had some little problems with food in Poland.'

They laughed again, helplessly. 'There's a place near Goodge Street,' said Ewa, 'a sort of trattoria place. We could go there, I'll treat you.'

Stefan bowed. 'That would be extremely kind, but unacceptable. But let's go there. What exactly is a trattoria place?'

Ewa pulled her briefcase out from under the table. 'Just a little Italian restaurant. But very good. Delicious in fact.'

'Lead on,' said Stefan, and they walked out of the pub as at ease as if they had known each other for years.

'You realize we are very near the Embassy?' said Ewa, as they turned into Cavendish Square. Pigeons and starlings were settling for the night in the trees and on window ledges; every now and then, in a lull in the traffic, they could hear faint twitterings, or the sudden flutter of wings.

'I do,' said Stefan. 'At the moment, as you guessed, I'm more concerned about the Home Office.'

'Is it all very difficult?'

'It's okay. I'm not supposed to work, but – ' He lightly took her

486

arm as they tried to cross Portland Place and a taxi raced towards them. 'But everyone is doing it. It's not for long, after all. I've applied to have my visa extended; I expect they know very well what's going on.'

'Suppose they don't renew it again? Look, it's all right to cross now.' They ran, and on the other side walked slowly along Mortimer Street, which was clogged with traffic.

'If they don't renew it,' said Stefan, 'I might have to go back, but that's another reason to go to classes. If I become a student, they may let me stay a little longer. In any case, I don't intend to stay more than six months or so.'

'No, of course not,' said Ewa. 'Look, that's our place, over there.' She pointed to a restaurant covered in creeper, where the windows were bordered with small lights, just switched on with the summer dusk.

Stefan stopped. 'But – my clothes. Will this – trattoria? – will it allow in builders?'

'Oh, I'm sure. It's not so grand.'

'It looks very nice. I'd better take them off.' He grinned. 'I do have something on underneath, it's just that I'm wearing very old clothes these days because of course they're more suitable – ' He stepped into the doorway of a shop and began swiftly to unbutton his overalls. 'Stand guard, okay?'

'I thought you said you had on something underneath,' said Ewa, giggling.

'Did I?' He pulled out the front and peered inside. 'Oh yes, I think I can see something. Okay, here we go.' He pulled down first one sleeve and then the other, lightly humming 'The Stripper'. 'You think we are unsophisticated in Poland? I tell you, we are up there with the best of them.' He slipped down the overalls over his hips, and struggled with the legs. 'Is that the expression? Anyway, usually I put my boots on afterwards. Oh God, I'll have to take them off.' He slid down the wall and sat on the step, the overalls round his ankles as he unlaced each boot, waving each foot, still humming. Ewa laughed until it hurt.

'*Et voila!*' He leapt to his feet and bowed, a ludicrous figure in check shirt, flared trousers, and socks, his overalls and boots beside him. 'Unfortunately, my suit is in the dry cleaners; otherwise, naturally, I should be escorting you in more appropriate style.'

'Naturally.' Ewa was wiping her eyes. And a nice change to be

487

doing that because I'm laughing, she thought. You silly, silly girl, what have you been afraid of, all this time?

'Do I look so odd?' he demanded, bending to tie up his bootlaces again.

'No, no. It's a pity about the flares, but – ' She took a deep breath, and pulled herself together.

Stefan picked up his overalls. 'And what do I do with these, I wonder? Wear them round my neck?'

'I'll put them in my briefcase,' said Ewa, and unclicked it, took them and folded them up. She stuffed them between a book of poems and the Polish Solidarity Campaign newsletter. Stefan watched her, shaking his head.

'Do you often put strange men's clothes into your briefcase?'

'Only from time to time.' Ewa felt as if someone had slipped a thick, heavy black cloak from round her, and thrown it away, leaving her light, almost airborne. '*Et voila*,' she said, and raised an eyebrow. 'Shall we go?'

They walked towards the open doors of the restaurant.

'Are the flares really dreadful?' Stefan asked.

'Yes, but rather – endearing, with the boots. Anyway, what does it matter? I'm surprised at you, caring.'

'I've had a lot of very serious things to think about for a long time,' he said, and sounded serious. 'Just for once, it's pleasant to think about things that don't matter.'

Ewa looked at him. 'Of course. I'm sorry . . .'

'Don't be. Let's just enjoy ourselves.'

They had reached the open doors, and went inside. A waiter approached, smoothly, taking in at a glance Ewa's cream jacket and well-cut cotton trousers, and Stefan's dusty hair, the crumpled shirt, the flares, the boots.

'Yes, please?'

'A table for two,' said Ewa firmly, and he led them through to the back, well away from the other diners.

He pulled out chairs, lit the candle in the centre of the table, gave them each an enormous menu and departed, smiling. Stefan leant forward and lit a cigarette from the candle.

'I'm sorry – you want one?'

'No, not yet, thanks.' Ewa was looking at the menu. 'How hungry are you?'

'Very. Ravenous.' His eyes travelled quickly down the prices. 'But also on a budget.'

'I've told you, I'll treat you. Anyway, it's not very expensive.'

'Isn't it?' He shook his head. 'It looks it to me, and it doesn't feel right.'

'Oh, for heaven's sake!' She blushed. 'If it makes you feel better, you can always do the same for me one day, when you've made your fortune.' And would have been astonished at her own temerity, except that she knew, without having to think about it, that they would see each other again.

'Well, certainly,' said Stefan. 'There is always that possibility.'

'Good. Shall I translate?'

'Please.' He looked at the menu again. 'I think the choice is pasta or pasta?'

'More or less.'

The waiter returned; she ordered red wine, cannelloni, salad.

'*Na zdrowie,*' said Stefan again, when the wine had appeared, and they raised their glasses. He took a long sip. 'My God, that's better.' He looked around at what they could see of the restaurant, at the candles, the flowers, the tanned, relaxed faces of the people at other tables reflected in the mirrored walls. He caught sight of his own reflection, and shook his head. 'The first thing I do when I make my fortune is to buy clothes,' he said, and turned back to her. 'Have you visited Poland?'

'No,' said Ewa. 'Jerzy and Elizabeth have.'

'Did they tell you that a lot of us are walking around wearing crap? Perhaps not so much in Warsaw, but in the provinces – my God!' He drew on his cigarette, angrily. 'Excuse me. It makes me feel ill at ease being here. I know I shouldn't let it, but – '

'Do you want to go?'

'No, no. Of course not.'

Ewa felt awkward and embarrassed. How could she have been so thoughtless? They should have just gone somewhere cheap and cheerful, but there weren't many places round Oxford Street, only Macdonald's, and – well, perhaps they should have gone to Macdonald's.

The waiter was beside them again, smiling at Ewa, putting down plates and flourishing an enormous pepper mill. 'My God,' Stefan said again, recovering, 'what's *that?*'

Ewa laughed. The waiter retired, and they began to eat.

'That's better, too,' said Stefan. 'I really was hungry, it always makes me irritable, I'm sorry.'

'It's all right, I understand.'

'But do you know,' he said, 'that in some of the so-called fashion magazines, they've been known to print photographs of people in the West wearing what you wore five or six years before? To try to make us think that the styles our factories are still churning out are what you are all rushing to buy?'

'They haven't.'

'They have. Our daily life consists of that kind of stuff all the time.' He took another mouthful. 'I should say, of course, that that is what it was like before. Solidarity is changing all that, it has been – fantastic.' He put down his fork and refilled their glasses. 'Thank you for all this. Now tell me why you've never been to visit us.'

'It's just always been a point of principle. My parents have never gone back, they don't have passports because they refused to take British citizenship.' She took another sip of wine. 'They are stateless persons, lost souls,' she said lightly. 'We are a very principled community, the *Polonia*. I can remember when I was little, at Saturday school, where my grandfather taught, the teachers used to receive parcels of books from the embassy, to use with us. They were all sent back, unopened.'

'And they were probably the books we were using in school,' said Stefan. 'I expect we both learned, though, how the British and French let us down, at the beginning of the war.'

'Oh, yes. But I imagine your version of what happened at the end was rather different.'

'We were liberated by the magnificent generosity of the Red Army,' he said, and reached for the salad bowl. He helped her to a pile of watercress, apples, orange, walnuts. 'This looks very nice.' He put down the spoon and fork. 'I am trying to imagine you as a little girl, going to – Saturday school? You must have been extremely pretty. Did you blush all the time then, too?'

'I can't remember.' Ewa put her hands to her cheeks. 'I hate it.'

'You shouldn't. As you kindly said about the flares, it's – endearing. You're not eating, I'll change the subject. Tell me about your brother. Did he go to Saturday school? Is he older or younger? I guess older.'

'Younger. He's a photographer, a dreamer, really. He was the one who really was a lost soul – I mean, it was worse because there was no reason for him to be, he hadn't lost anything, he should have been all right . . .' She stopped, feeling she was gabbling. 'Anyway, I think he is all right now. I think. What about you? Do you have brothers or sisters?'

'No,' said Stefan, 'I'm an only child.'

'What was that like?'

He shrugged. 'Okay. I had my friends, my parents were very good about that, they were always in and out.'

'And do you live with them now?'

'With my parents? No.' He looked at her carefully. 'I live with my wife.'

Ewa put down her fork.

'She is called Krystyna,' he said slowly. 'We have a little boy.' He reached for the cigarettes. 'I'm sorry – even though we have only just met, I feel I should have told you earlier.' He leaned forward, lit a cigarette from the candle, and made to give it to her. Their eyes met, and she saw in his an expression of apologetic tenderness. Then she looked down, ignoring the cigarette, and stared at her plate.

There was a long, humiliating silence.

'Ewa?'

She couldn't speak.

'Look at me.'

She shook her head, knowing that she was making it all infinitely worse, but she couldn't look at him. The murmur of voices from other tables was broken every now and then by laughter.

'Please.'

She raised her head, addressing the mirror behind him, seeing the dusty back of his head, and her own face, which was not blushing, but very pale, as if she were cold, or shocked. 'You should have told me,' she said. 'I know we have only just met, and that it is nothing to do with me, but even so – '

'I know.' He reached across the table and took her hand. 'We have only just met, and I – ' He drew a deep breath. 'And I am married, but even so. There is something between us, isn't there?'

She bit her lip. His hand was warm, and roughened; he held hers as if it were only natural that he should, because he wanted to comfort her, and more than that, because, after all, there was something between them. 'I – I don't know.' She looked at him, and blushed. He gently took his hand away and reached out to touch her cheek, and as he did so he knocked the candle, and a burning drop of wax fell on his hand.

'Ouch!'

'Are you all right?'

'Yes, yes.' He shook his hand in the air, and knocked the candle again. Wax flew. 'Oh, my God, what is the matter with me?'

Ewa began to laugh. Stefan rubbed his hand against his lips, and

491

then carefully picked the wax off and dropped it into the ashtray, where it caught the lighted end of his cigarette and spat.

'Is everything all right?' The waiter was beside them, smiling but a little reproving.

Stefan grunted. 'Fine.' He looked at Ewa. 'Shall we have a coffee?'

'Would you like to?'

'Yes.'

'Two coffees, please,' Ewa said to the waiter. 'And perhaps we could have another ashtray?'

'Of course.' He picked up the one with bits of wax in it, and the plates, and took them away.

'You don't seem in the least neurotic when dealing with waiters,' said Stefan.

'I beg your pardon?' Ewa ran her hands through her hair. 'You talk to me as if you were my brother. Correction. Not my brother, but as a brother might talk.'

'You think so?' There was a brief, unbrotherly pause. Then the waiter was rattling cups, and pouring coffee.

'You like it black or white?'

'Black, please,' said Ewa.

'Black,' said Stefan, and when the waiter had gone, leaving a clean ashtray, he said, 'I've hardly had a good cup of coffee for months without paying a fortune for it. We were living on weak tea, without lemon.'

'Were you?' said Ewa, wondering if by 'we' he meant his family, or the whole of Poland. She thought how impoverished English pronouns were, that there was only 'you', with no indication as to whether it meant one person, or two. In Polish, she had not used *ty*, meaning Stefan, but *wy*, meaning Stefan and Krystyna. Or the whole of Poland. 'Don't you miss your wife?' she asked abruptly.

'Of course. Of course I do. And Olek, very much.'

'That's your little boy?'

'Yes. Well, he's still a baby really, not even two.' He hesitated. 'Would you like to see a photograph?'

'No, thank you.'

'No.' He lit another cigarette, from the candle, carefully. 'But – ' He drew on it, and coughed. 'But I have to say that they seem very far away. I mean in my mind. It's not how I imagined – you mind if I talk like this?'

'No.'

'You live with someone for years, you know, every day, and you don't even need to think what it might be like to live alone, and you have a child, and it is impossible to imagine how you lived without him, or how you could ever live without him now, and then – puff. You are away, and sometimes it seems as if you never had a child at all. Sometimes I miss him so much I think I'll have to take the next plane home, and sometimes I forget all about him.' He shook his head. 'I can't believe it is me saying these things. Or even being here.'

Ewa watched him, thinking that he talked more like a woman than a man, and perhaps that was one reason why she had felt so safe with him, so soon. Also, that despite that, he was very male. She reached for her cup, spilling coffee in the saucer, and taking all her courage to ask as lightly as she could: 'And what about your wife? Do you forget all about her, too?'

He looked at her. 'It's not the same. I do, but – I am here because of her and Olek, because I want to take money home to them, to make things easier for her. She didn't want me to come, but . . . there is nothing there at the moment, I am not needed by Solidarity, or let's say I am a little disillusioned at present. So – I'm here, and that is why I'm working, and not buying clothes, and so on. Even when I forget all about her, there's a part of me that knows she is always there. With Olek, because he is so small, I suppose, it is as if I can blink and he might have disappeared for ever. I am ashamed to realize that, but it's true.'

She shook her head, not really understanding, not knowing if that was her question answered.

'So – I come here to make the family fortune. And then – then I meet Ewa,' he said slowly, and reached across the table for her hand again. 'And she seems very important, very quickly.'

His hand was so warm, with the touch of a lover and a friend who you knew you could trust. She wanted to take her own hand away, to stop the trembling inside her, and she wanted to leave it there, to feel him begin to stroke her fingers, gently, tenderly.

At last she said: 'You are a long way from home in a strange country. It's not that I am important; you – need someone. It's natural, I suppose. But it could be anyone.'

'I don't think so,' said Stefan. 'I really don't think so. Do you?'

They sat in silence, looking into each other's eyes, no longer laughing.

'Was I right?' he asked at last. 'Did someone hurt you once?'

'Yes,' said Ewa, 'but I shouldn't have let him. I shouldn't have let

493

it affect me so much. Almost my whole life. It wasn't – it wasn't as if I loved him.'

'You didn't love him?'

'No. To tell you the truth, I hardly knew him.' She shivered suddenly and took her hand away. 'I hardly know you, either.'

'Yes, you do, in the way it matters. You know you do.'

She shook her head, and pushed back her chair. 'I think we should go. I think I should go home. I think you should go back to your hostel and write to your wife.'

'And you think I will hurt you, also, but I won't. I would never hurt you.'

'But you will,' said Ewa, and clicked open her bag, looking blindly for her purse. 'Or I will hurt you. Or your wife will suffer. If we – if we go on seeing each other, how can it be otherwise?'

He drew a long, deep breath, and did not answer. Ewa beckoned to the waiter, paid the bill, and picked up her briefcase. Then they both got up, and walked to the doors of the restaurant.

Out in the street the air had the acrid smell of a city on a summer night. It was warm, and the sky was almost dark. Couples were strolling, hand in hand. Ahead, buses revved up along Tottenham Court Road, brightly lit. Ewa turned to Stefan, and held out her hand without speaking. He took it, and raised it to his mouth, and this time did not simply brush it with his lips, but kissed it, once, and gave it back to her, gravely.

'Do you have far to go?'

'To Blackheath – it's the other side of London. I have to catch a train.'

'Would you let me take you to the station?'

'It's Charing Cross, it's quite a way, I mean, it's not far, but – '

'Let me walk with you,' he said. 'Please.'

'Where is your hostel? Don't they close those sort of places early?'

'It doesn't matter where it is, and it doesn't matter if they close the doors, I can climb in through the window. I should like to see you safely on to your train.' He put his arm round her, and she leaned against him; they stood for a moment, very close, and then she put her own arm round his waist, and they walked slowly past the neon-lit hi-fi shops and across Oxford Street, where lonely drunks were swaying by the tube, and on down Charing Cross Road, past the bookshops.

'That's where I bought the magazine,' said Ewa, and nodded towards it. 'Just this morning. It feels like last year.'

They walked past Leicester Square, hearing disco music throb, and seeing the lights of cinema hoardings and crowds of people coming out.

'Do you go to the cinema often?' asked Stefan.

'A bit. Do you?'

'A bit.' He smiled down at her, and did not suggest that they went together one day. When they reached Charing Cross Station, and walked across the concourse, he let go of her for a minute, and she saw him stop, and look at a dark shape, huddled at the top of the steps leading down to Villiers Street. 'Is he sleeping?'

'I expect so.' Ewa opened her bag and took out her season ticket. 'You should see them down on the Embankment. There are hundreds.'

'Even in the winter?'

'Oh yes.'

He shook his head, and she said: 'It's not all so easy in the West.'

'No. No, it isn't.'

The station stank of cigarettes and chips. A whistle blew, and Ewa looked up at the board above the platforms. 'My train goes in a couple of minutes,' she said. 'Thank you for coming with me.'

'Which is your platform?'

'Number three. Here . . .' She walked quickly towards it, and flashed her ticket at the black ticket collector.

'Okay, darling, hurry now.' He made to wave her through, and she turned to Stefan.

'Well – goodbye.'

'Goodbye, Ewa. You won't give me your phone number? Just so we could meet once or twice? We are friends, after all, aren't we?'

'Yes,' she said, 'we are friends. But I don't think I should give you my number.' Another whistle blew, and she said: 'Quick! That's my train, I must go.' And rushed past the ticket collector without looking back. On the platform she ran, searching, as always, for a carriage with several people in it: it was much too unsafe to get in one which was empty. She found one, wrenched open the door and got in, hearing the whistle blow once more, and slamming the door behind her. As the train began to move, she allowed herself one look out of the open window, and saw Stefan, running frantically along the platform towards the moving train, and shouting: 'My overalls!'

'Your overalls – oh, my God.' She grabbed her briefcase from the seat, but the train was swaying too much for her to get them out in

495

time. She leaned out of the window, and he yelled: 'Now will you give me your number?'

Ewa began to laugh again. 'Prawicka!' she shouted. 'It's in the book.'

'I'll call you!'

The train gathered speed, and she sank back on to the seat, seeing the other passengers look at her with curiosity, then look away. She leaned back, still laughing, as they crossed the river, full of reflected lights, the carriages creaking over Hungerford Bridge towards the South Bank concert halls, Waterloo, and the unsung stations of south London.

Danuta was working in the evenings in a large, busy eating house off Leicester Square. Now her routine was extended: work in the hotel from eight until two, go to the language school from half-past two to half-past four, and then it wasn't worth walking all the way back to the hotel, because she'd only have to set out again in half an hour, so she went to a café she'd found on the edge of the maze of streets which became Chinatown. Here she had her only peace of the day. She sat at a table in the corner, and made one coffee and a roll last for forty-five minutes, while she read, wrote letters, sometimes almost fell asleep. At half-past five, just as it was closing, she got up, paid, and walked to the eating house, where she worked from six until eleven. Then, unlike Basia, who spent money on a taxi home, she walked back up to Tottenham Court Road tube station, where she could get a bus all the way down to Lancaster Gate. It was only a few minutes' walk from the stop to the hotel, which was, after all, on a brightly lit street, and in any case, Basia left work much later. Basia often looked as if she were sleepwalking: she sat in the class at school with her head nodding over her translations, and Danuta, too, spent most of the time yawning. She made herself go, though: she had paid the fees and her English was improving.

The Home Office had extended her visa for three months, that took her up to almost the end of August, still officially a tourist. It was now the middle of July. At the end of August, what could she do? There were other Polish girls in the hotel now, and one of them, from Wrocław, had been to England before, and said you could sometimes find a sponsor, an English person who would write to the Home Office explaining that you were living with them, and that they were financially responsible for you. Danuta thought her chances of finding someone like that were extremely unlikely. Another girl had said that of course, you could always try to find someone to marry. Then you were set up fine. Danuta didn't want to do that. She sat in her corner in the café near Chinatown, and wrote her letters home.

'Dear Mama and Tata,

'The weather here is fine, and my English is improving fast. Work at the hotel isn't too bad, and now I have an evening job! The money is good. I hope you're getting the food parcels all right, I sent one last week, with some chocolate in it for Babcia, and also a shirt from Marks & Spencer for Tata – I hope the chocolate doesn't melt. Some of the girls in the hotel say their parcels aren't getting through, that perhaps they're stolen at the border. Is it true there have been hunger marches?'

The papers here had reported that. While Solidarity was holding a three-day conference in Gdańsk, hundreds of people have marched through the city of Kutno, carrying banners and empty saucepans. 'We are tired of being hungry.' 'We are tired of queueing.' 'We demand life on the level of a civilized country.' Adam Michnik, co-founder of KOR, and one of the most respected intellectuals in Solidarity, had announced: 'Poland faces hunger uprisings.' Was it as bad as that in Warsaw?

Mama wrote that it wasn't quite as bad as that, but the shortages were still dreadful, even with the ration cards.

'The black market has become impossible now, the exchange rate has rocketed. Every day there seems to be a new story in the queues. Lorryloads of cigarettes have been found on a rubbish dump – you can imagine how Tata reacted to that! He has had to queue for two hours, sometimes, at the kiosks. Everyone talks about Gierek's luxury private villa, and everyone, still, is convinced that the government is deliberately holding back food supplies. I remember you used to say you thought that was a bit far-fetched, but really I am not so sure. Thank you for the parcels, darling, and please, please look after yourself, and don't spend all your money on us. Use it to go out and enjoy yourself, buy some nice clothes . . .'

Danuta kept the letters in a folder from the language school. She had bought some new clothes, spending hours on her days off in Benneton and C & A, and the cheap end of Covent Garden, trying on everything, looking in the mirrors over and over again with different trousers, sandals, shirts, cotton dresses. She had lost six kilos since she came here, everything fitted, but she knew she also looked wan, even grey. Out of the hours spent trying on, she had bought a pair of trousers, two cheap Indian cotton shirts, one thin, expensive sweater from Benneton and a pair of sandals. She took pleasure in consigning last year's plastic shoes to the dustbin. She also bought a bottle of Body Shop shampoo. Occasionally, when she had slept in on a day off, washed her hair in the basement bathroom shared with a dozen other hotel workers, and dressed, slinging the sweater round her shoulders, she thought, ironically, that she looked as she should have looked if she'd got a good job in Warsaw: slender, well dressed, hair gleaming – ready to meet any foreign trade representative. Instead, she was cleaning baths and toilets, half asleep, and changing bedclothes; at night she was serving egg and fries, burger and fries, chicken and fries, scurrying from table to table, the only waitress there, the manager had told her, who they could be absolutely sure would not muddle up the order tickets, or give the wrong bill at the end. The manager told her she could train to work on the till if she stayed another three months: that wasn't nearly so tiring, but you had to be sharp, and he thought she was sharp. Danuta hedged about the training, and hedged when he asked her out. She didn't want to be there in another three months, but she didn't want to lose the chance of getting off her feet.

She worked six nights out of seven, trying to make evenings off coincide with the following day off, but that wasn't always possible. On an evening towards the end of July she was free, but had to work in the hotel next morning. She wanted an early night; after supper in the kitchen she waited for forty-five minutes until the bathroom at the end of the basement corridor was empty, and went in to have a bath and wash her hair.

The bathroom had cracked white tiles and a cork bath mat with a corner broken off. A small window was set high in the wall; there was a large tin of scouring powder and a cloth, and notices. On the door: Please Leave This Bathroom As You Would Wish To Find It. Above the basin: Now Wash Your Hands. A long piece of string was tied above the bath, so that if you were desperate you could hang your tights and underwear to dry, but it was risky. Danuta supposed people dried them on the radiators in the bedrooms in winters; at the moment, they drooped outside the windows, below the basement railings. They all spent fortunes in the launderette.

She turned on the taps, which were large and stiff, and sat on the edge, waiting for the bath to fill. Upstairs, every bath had a shower unit. Down here, there was one, but it didn't work properly, you were either scalded or chilled, so Danuta and Basia, like several of the girls, had bought a rubber hose, which just fitted the taps. The bathroom began to fill with steam. Danuta stood on the edge of the lavatory and tried to reach up to the little window in the wall, to open it further, but it was just too far. She climbed down again, and ran the cold tap. It was half-past eight; she wanted to be in bed and asleep by half-past nine. She took off her pyjamas and climbed in, lay back and shut her eyes. Three days before her next day off, ten before her next evening and day together . . . she seemed to spend hours in calculations like this, it was like being at school, and waiting for the end of term. But then there was something to look forward to. She sat up, and reached for the shampoo. From the passage outside the door she could hear footsteps, voices, doors opening and closing, the radio, sounds that went on all the time, but there was a man's voice she didn't recognize, as well. Most of the men in the hotel didn't sleep here; those who did were Colombian, or Spanish, and this voice was English. And someone was banging on a door. She sat listening for a moment, hearing the English voice again; then it all went quiet.

She tipped the bottle of shampoo into her hand, and the bathroom began to smell pleasantly of jojoba oil, whatever that was; she turned on the shower and began to rinse; shampooed again, rinsed again, and ran her hair between her fingers until it squeaked. She turned off the taps, reached for her towel and wound it round her head. She had forgotten about the English voice; she washed, got out, dried herself, put on her pyjamas, cleaned the bath. Then she opened the door and went out, carrying her spongebag. There were doors open all along the corridor, and no radios on now. She knew at once that something was wrong, but couldn't work it out – was her door open, too? Then two men appeared suddenly from the room where the girl from Wrocław slept, and Danuta jumped as they came towards her. They were both in suits, one had a gingery moustache: he flicked open a little plastic wallet and waved it towards her.

'Home Office. May I see your passport, please?'

Danuta's stomach lurched, and turned over.

'You speak English?' the man asked brusquely. 'You understand?'

'I – yes.'

At the far end of the corridor, behind the two men, a door was opened quietly, and Danuta saw Enrico, the little washer-up who swore, creep out. He looked up towards them, and immediately backed into his room.

'Your passport, please,' the man with the ginger moustache repeated. 'Which is your room?'

'I – this one.' Danuta moved on bare feet towards it, so frightened she thought her knees were going to give way. She tugged open the zip on her spongebag, feeling for her key, then fumbled trying to get it into the lock. The men stood watching, impassive. She got the key in, turned it and pushed the door open. It was a heavy door, and swung to unless you held it open. The ginger moustache followed her inside; his colleague, who was younger, and very thin inside his suit, waited, one foot against it, watching.

Danuta bent down and opened the bedside cabinet. What were they going to do to her? Would she be deported? Sent to prison? There was a silence, as they watched her, naked under thin summer pyjamas, feeling for her passport. She stood up, and handed it over without looking at them. The man with the moustache flicked through it, quickly, turned and nodded towards his colleague to come and look too. As the younger man moved a little towards him, Danuta heard a click, at the far end of the corridor, and knew, straight away, that Enrico was making for the stairs. He could have got out of his window, but the wall and the railings were probably too high, and anyway, Enrico wasn't very bright. The stairs began halfway along, he might just have time.

The moustached man held open her passport.

'What are you doing here?'

'Excuse me?' Danuta looked at him, not knowing how to answer.

'I said what are you doing here? In this hotel.'

'I – I am staying here.' Trickles of water from her wet hair were escaping beneath the towel on to her neck.

The man shook his head. 'Don't try and be clever.'

'Hey!' His colleague darted suddenly out of the room, and ran down the corridor. 'Just a minute, you!'

Danuta put her hand to her mouth. Moustache moved swiftly towards the door. 'Stay here, please.' The door swung to, and she heard scuffles, Enrico swearing and shouting in Spanish. He had been here illegally for over a year, he was supposed to be supporting two families: his sister's, at home in Colombia, and his own here. What was going to happen to him now? She crept to the door and pulled it open a crack. She could see the two men hustling him up the stairs; they must have a car outside. Moustache still had her passport. She ran to Basia's room and knocked on the door. No answer – of course, she was in the restaurant, she'd escaped. Would they come back to check her room later? Were they going to bring back her passport? They must, surely they must.

She turned away, hearing a voice behind her on the stairs say suddenly: 'Where do you think you're going?' and she jumped and screamed. Moustache ran down the stairs, and came up behind her. 'I asked you to stay in your room. Go in, please.'

He pushed open the door, and she went in, shaking.

'There's no need to scream like that,' he said coldly. 'You understand what is going on?'

She nodded, feeling the little room horribly airless and crowded with them both in there. He was a big man, and she thought suddenly: My God, he could rape me and I wouldn't stand a chance.

The man leafed through her passport again, and looked her up and down, at the outline of her breasts beneath the cotton pyjamas.

'Your visa has not expired,' he said.

'No.'

'But you are specifically forbidden to work. Aren't you?'

'Yes.'

'So I will ask you again: what are you doing here?'

What could she say? She said nothing, looking down at the worn carpet beneath her feet, thinking only: Let me be safe, and I don't care about anything else. Let me be safe. Please.

He tapped the passport. 'What were you doing in Poland?'

'I – I finish my studies in March. I have a degree in economics and statistics.'

'Do you really? And now you're working here as a skivvy. Is that right?'

She didn't answer or look up.

'No jobs in Poland? Nothing you could do there?' He held out the passport. 'If I were you, I'd go back to Poland the minute that visa runs out,' he said. 'You understand?'

'Yes.' She took the passport and watched him go to the door. He didn't turn round or look at her again, simply opened it and walked out, closing it behind him. Danuta sank on to the bed, and burst into tears. She felt her damp towel begin to slip until it fell on to her shoulders, and she picked it up and hurled it across the narrow, shabby room. It hit the wardrobe door and fell to the floor. She ran her hands through her wet hair, still crying. What was she going to do? She'd have to leave the hotel, and look for somewhere else. Was she really going to have to go back to Poland? She thought of her parents, of being safely with them at home, of her mother bringing her tea in bed, hearing her father calling goodbye as he left for work, and she couldn't even remember why she'd left. Then she thought of cold dark winter mornings, of she or her mother getting up at six to go and queue, for bread, for flour, for meat, for everything.

If I go back, she thought, there will be a job perhaps as a filing clerk, with nothing to hope for. If I stay here, I have the thin hope that perhaps, once my English is fluent, I can get a work permit, a good job, a proper job, with proper money to send home, I can visit Mama and Tata, even bring them over here to visit me. God, I never imagined all this! I thought it would be so easy – a fortune saved in a few months, and then I'd go home, I suppose, and try again. I'm *not* going back with nothing! But supposing I don't get a proper job here? Well, then I'll *have* to go home.

She reached for the tissues on the bedside locker, and blew her nose. Then she got up, picked up the towel and shook it, and began angrily to rub her hair. She thought: I am twenty-three years old, I am educated, with a good degree, I should be at the start of my career. Instead, I have the choice between certain poverty and possible poverty, while my parents, who have worked every day of their lives, live on rationed food in a cramped apartment and look forward to a retirement spent in queues, counting every złoty.

She finished rubbing her hair, and looked round for her spongebag, with her washed hairbrush in it. It was on the bed, where she had dropped it when she came in with the men from the Home Office, and beside it was her passport. I was lucky, she thought, running the brush through her hair, or he was kind. Then she remembered Enrico, struggling and shouting as they hauled him up the stairs, who by now must be sitting in a police cell, waiting to be deported. Enrico didn't have a degree, he could barely write. She drew a deep breath, and finished brushing her hair. There was an urgent knocking on her door.

'Yes?' She hurried across and opened it. The girl from Wrocław stood outside, and clearly had been crying, too.

'Are you all right?'

'Yes,' said Danuta. 'I was lucky. Are you?'

'Yes. It was the Colombians they were looking for. Did you hear Enrico?'

'Yes. I was just thinking about him.'

'I've been up to the kitchens, they're making tea. Apparently one of the cooks, Franco, you know that one? He jumped out of the window when they went in. He's sprained his ankle, but he's okay.'

She put her arm round Danuta. 'Do you want to come up and have some tea? We're all right – not our turn yet.' She grinned wryly. 'Come on.'

Danuta went upstairs with her. She stayed up late, drinking tea in the neon-lit kitchen and talking. She wanted to wait up for Basia, but by half-past eleven she couldn't stay awake any longer. She crawled into bed and switched off the light. Out in the street, a group of boys went by, laughing and shouting. She could hear guests coming up the steps to the hotel front door, back from the West End. There was a coachload of Scandinavians arriving tomorrow, she remembered Lisa telling them. Twenty rooms, not fifteen, to do in the morning. She turned over, and fell asleep.

In the morning, over breakfast, she told Basia about the raid.

Basia shook her head. 'I'm leaving.'

'Where will you go?'

She hesitated. 'I've been going out with one of my customers from the restaurant. A French guy – he's very sweet. He's offered to let me stay with him, he has a lovely apartment near Sloane Square, I think he's extremely rich.'

'Oh.' Danuta looked at her. Basia was so pale and thin these days that in another age you might have thought she had consumption. 'But – what about your boyfriend?'

Basia pushed back her soft blonde hair. 'I don't know – I haven't written to him for a few weeks. Perhaps he's forgotten me.' She looked at the clock on the wall. 'Come on, we'd better go up.'

It felt strange to collect their plates and not see Enrico, cursing at the sink as they passed them to him. They climbed the stairs, and prepared for the Scandinavians.

As she finished the last room, Danuta thought: But there must be someone here who can help us, some organization for Polish people. After lunch, before leaving for school, she went into the foyer of the hotel where, next to the glass case of plastic dolls holding union jacks, and plastic models of Big Ben, there were two phone booths, and directories. Even now, it felt strange to be up here, among all the tourists, looking, once she had changed out of her overalls, like a tourist herself, but feeling so different. The coachload had arrived: the foyer was filled with enormous blonde people heaving suitcases. She pushed her way through to the phone booths, and pulled out the L-R directory. She rifled the pages until she came to P and Polish, and ran her finger down the column. Polish Air Force, Polish Airlines, Bookshop, Catholic Centre . . . There was a committee for refugees.

She wasn't a refugee, at least, thank God, so far she wasn't that, but the address was in the West End, she could go there after school, perhaps, and they might be able to advise her about how best to stay here, her chances of getting a work permit. She wrote down the number and address, and put back the directory. Then she looked at her watch and thought: I'll try them now. But when she dialled the number, it was engaged. She waited a few minutes, dialled again. Still engaged. Behind her, a Scandinavian was waiting.

'You have finished, miss?'

She put down the receiver. 'Yes.' She hurried across the foyer and down the steps. Basia wasn't coming to the school, perhaps she wasn't going to come again at all, now she had her Frenchman.

Danuta walked along the street towards the Bayswater Road, and crossed over so that she could walk alongside the park, beneath the trees. The sky was overcast, it was humid, debilitating; she felt suddenly so tired that the thought of going to sit in a class for two hours was almost unendurable. Also, she had a sudden vision of going back to the hotel tonight to find that there had been another raid. She had been given a chance, last night – next time, if it came, might be very different. I'll go to this refugee place now, she thought, and stopped and pulled out her A-Z.

The office was in a long street running parallel to Oxford Street. In the oppressive closeness of the afternoon, it took her about half a hour to walk there, and find the brass plate outside the door. There was a Polish clinic here, too – that might be useful.

The clinic was on the first floor. Through an open door, she had a glimpse of a very old, beautifully dressed woman talking softly in Polish to a girl in dark blue behind a typewriter. Then an old man in a tweed jacket and glasses came out of a door further along the landing; he closed it quietly behind him, and came past her.

'*Proszę . . .*' He said it to the air, rather than to her, and went in to the office. He was one of the doctors? Danuta tapped on the open door.

'*Tak?*'

'Excuse me,' she said in Polish, and explained who she was looking for.

'On the top floor.' The woman smiled at her, vaguely.

'Thank you. And – may I use the bathroom?'

'Well . . . yes. It is through here.'

'Thank you.'

She walked through the little office, up a couple of steps and pushed open a door with a brass handle. The bathroom which lay beyond it was cool and spacious; set among the plain white tiles were some which were hand-painted, oriental-looking, figures in crimson and prussian-blue robes. The bath and basin were enormous, with brass taps; soft net curtains hung at the open window. Danuta went to the lavatory, and washed her hands, and thought: I wouldn't mind living in here for a few days. Then she went out, and up the stairs, which as they approached the top floor became narrow and were no longer carpeted. There was a closed door on the top landing. She knocked, and waited. There was no answer. She knocked again. When there was still no answer, she tried the handle. The door was not locked; it opened, and she walked into a square room with a window at the far end. There were three desks, an unlit gas fire beneath a mantelpiece, and large, very old-looking filing cabinets. On the walls were two large posters: Danuta stepped a little further into the room, and stood looking at them.

On one an emaciated man was crawling across a pile of rubble, or perhaps emerging from a sewer hole. The man was exhausted, probably wounded, an arm upraised as he struggled forward, gasping. Behind him lay the ruins of defeated Warsaw. There was a date on the poster: 1944. And an inscription: *Their struggle is your struggle, their fight your fight*. The other poster was on the wall near the door. Again, the piles of rubble, and skeletal, devastated buildings, very dark. There were no words here, just the full-length shadowy silhouette of Christ, in the crown of thorns, walking silently through the ruined city.

Danuta looked at them for a long time. There were no other posters, nothing to suggest Solidarity even existed. She waited in the empty office for someone to return, and offer to help her, but no one came. After a while, she felt like an intruder, and went out and closed the door. She went slowly down the stairs to the clinic.

'Excuse me – there is no one upstairs.'

'No?' The woman shrugged, not indifferently, but not quite knowing what to suggest. 'They must be out – I think they have an old people's home somewhere in the country. Perhaps they are visiting . . . You can always come back.'

'Yes,' said Danuta. 'I can always come back. Thank you.'

She went out, and down the wide clean stairs and out into the street. Then she walked slowly through the street behind Oxford Street, towards her café on the edge of Chinatown, and her evening job.

*

Pip-pip-pip-pip-pip-pip. Then a coin, pushed into the slot quickly. Then a voice.

'Ewa?'

At once, the rush of happiness, hearing his voice.

'Yes,' she said, having known from the first pip who it was. She had waited for five days for him to call, jumping each time the phone rang. No one else needed to ring her from a phone box.

'It's Stefan.'

'Yes.'

'How are you?'

'I'm fine,' she said. 'What have you been wearing to work?'

'I borrowed a pair of overalls from my boss,' he said, and she could tell he was smiling.

'Oh. Good.'

There was a pause. She had thought he would phone her the next evening – for the overalls, but also . . . He had borrowed a pair from his boss. So there had been no problem. And no need for him to phone.

'Ewa? Are you angry with me for not calling earlier?'

'Don't be silly,' she said, because of course she had to say that, it was absurd that she should have been angry, or worried, or hurt. Or to be feeling terribly nervous, now.

'I didn't phone you because I was thinking.'

'Oh.'

'That you were right not to give me your number.'

'Oh.'

'For both our sakes.'

'Oh. Yes.'

Pip-pip-pip-pip-pip-pip. Another coin.

'Hello? I'm sorry. I can't get used to these things.'

'Shall I call you back? Where are you?'

'I'm in the hostel,' and she could hear, now, voices behind him, echoing, as if in a foyer or hall with a very high ceiling. 'They don't take incoming calls.'

So his wife couldn't call him from Warsaw, either. That must be strange. That must be horrible.

'Ewa?'

Ewa? Always, on that tender, inquiring note, as if it were a name that really mattered. Fool! How could she think such things?

'You understand what I'm saying? That you were right, that it's better we don't see each other again?'

Outside the window overlooking the long, tangled garden behind the house, it was raining, a light, summer evening fall. Ewa, at her desk, held the receiver in one hand, and put her head in the other, and shut her eyes.

'Yes,' she said. 'Yes.'

'But I won't forget you,' he said. 'Even though it was only one meeting. We won't forget each other, will we?'

Stop it, stop it. 'I don't know,' she said flatly. 'Anyway – thank you for phoning. I hope everything goes well for you.'

'And you, Ewa. And you.' A pause. 'Be happy.'

Pip-pip-pip-pip-pip-pip. Always, there were a few seconds after the pips in which you could say a quick goodbye. But he wouldn't know about those, and anyway – anyway. She put down the receiver, and sat with her head in her hands. Ridiculous, absurd, shaming, to be so . . . stricken.

And yet. And yet. To find someone she liked so much . . . She pushed the thought away, and got up quickly. Her cigarettes were on the desk, and she lit one, remembering his voice. *Ah, the Camel. He is everywhere in Warsaw.* She went out to the kitchen to make a cup of coffee, hearing Toby and Ben come into the house, banging the front door and calling: 'Mum? Mum!' She put on the kettle, and the phone rang. She ran to answer it, stubbing her foot on the door.

'Hello?'

No pips.

'Hello, Ewa.'

'Oh. Jerzy.'

'Are you all right?'

'Fine, I just banged my toe . . . Hang on.' She put down the receiver, and the cigarette in the ashtray, and rubbed her foot. *There was something, wasn't there? Stop it, stop it!* She picked up the receiver again.

'Sorry. Sorry, how are you?'

'I'm fine. Is your toe all right?'

'Yes, my toe is fine, it's just the rest of me. Never mind. What do you want?'

'Would you like me to ring back later?'

'I'm sorry. I've had a bad day. How are you? How's Elizabeth?'

'We're both perfectly all right. I just thought we hadn't heard from you for a little while, and Mama said last time she spoke to you, you sounded a bit . . . odd.'

That was yesterday, when she'd thought it was Stefan phoning.

'Well, I'm all right, it's just been a bit hectic at work. Would you and Elizabeth like to come to supper? This weekend? You haven't been for ages. Come on Saturday.'

'Okay, thanks. I'd better just check.' She heard him cover the receiver with his hand, and muffled voices. I don't mind if Elizabeth says no, she thought, or if I hear her saying no. She's not going to say anything else, is she? That I shouldn't hear?

'Hello,' said Jerzy. 'Yes, that's fine. Actually . . .' He hesitated. 'Actually, there was another reason for phoning, to tell you something . . . but perhaps we'll tell you on Saturday.'

'Tell me now,' she said, knowing at once what it was, for what else could it be, with those two? 'But you don't need to, I know what it is.'

'What?'

'You're getting married.'

'Yes. Ewa? Are you pleased?'

'Of course,' she said. 'Of course I am. It's lovely.'

'Are you sure?'

'Oh, for God's sake,' she snapped. 'What does it matter what I think about it? So long as you're happy, I don't care what you do.'

'Hey! What's the matter with you?'

'Nothing! I told you, I've had a bad day, do I have to explain every blessed thing to my family? I'm delighted you're getting married, and please give my love to Elizabeth. I'll look forward to seeing you on Saturday. Goodbye.'

'I'll phone you in the week,' said Jerzy slowly. 'I hope you're okay. Bye.'

He put down the phone, and Ewa banged down hers, and picked up her cigarette again. It was raining harder, and it was growing dark; she leaned across the table and snapped on the little lamp. It made a gentle pool of light, on the books and papers, the magazine of the Polish Solidarity Campaign, and she reached up and drew the curtains, hearing the kettle come to the boil, and thinking: it looks like a home. Then she went and switched off the kettle, and ran a bath, and lay in it for a long time, with the water very hot and the radio on very loud.

Afterwards, she lay on the sofa in her dressing gown and had her supper on a tray. There was a concert on Radio Three from the Festival Hall: two of the Brandenburgs, they always had them in the summer, for the tourists. When they had finished, in a thunder of applause, she turned off the radio, and lay listening to the rain, falling through the trees on the garden, and against the window panes. When the telephone rang, she was almost asleep.

She jumped, and sat up, scrambling over the back of the sofa to reach the receiver.

'Hello?'

Pip-pip-pip-pip-pip-pip. A coin pushed in, and then two more.

'Ewa?'

'Yes?'

'It's Stefan.'

'I know.'

'I'm sorry.' She could hear him take a breath. 'Do you mind me phoning?'

'It depends what you're going to say.'

Another pause. Then: 'Something that I shouldn't say.'

Ewa thought: If I let this man think he can pick me up and put me down again as he chooses, and I say nothing, I will never, never have any respect for myself again. I'm afraid to tell him, because I'm afraid of men, that's how it is, but – I have to say it. And she said carefully:

'Will you please stop playing cat and mouse with me?'

There was a silence. Ewa could hear again the echoing voices behind him in the hall; she imagined a blue neon light, a smell of disinfectant, a book on a counter where you signed yourself in and out. Was that how Stefan was living? Away from his home and his family? Was that why he was phoning her, late at night?

At last he said slowly: 'You're right to say that, but wrong to think that that is what I'm doing. Or rather what I intended to do. I'm sorry if it seems like that.'

And at once she felt full of remorse, and embarrassment at perhaps embarrassing him because, after all, she had known, hadn't she, that he did care; and the wretched, wretched feeling of awkwardness and uncertainty came back, and she didn't know what to say.

'It's all right,' he said quietly. 'It's all right. Don't be afraid.'

'I'm not.'

'You are.' A pause. 'And so am I. What were you doing when I rang?'

'Listening to a concert. What were you doing before you rang?'

'I have been lying in the dormitory here, and thinking for a long time,' he said, 'and all I could tell myself was what I think is true: that if Krysia – if my wife – were to find herself in a similar situation, I hope I should be generous.'

'Oh.' She shook her head. 'I don't know how to answer that. I really don't know how to answer.'

'Well . . . Don't. But may I see you? Just once, at least?'

She closed her eyes. 'Yes.'

'Thank you. Well then . . . when?'

Again, she could tell that he was smiling, and the awkwardness slipped away, and she began to feel at ease.

'Do you know what happened after you rang?' she said, curling up on the sofa. 'My brother phoned, to tell me he was getting married. I wasn't very nice to him. But he and Elizabeth are coming to supper on Saturday. Would you like to come too?'

He hesitated. 'You think that's a good idea?'

'Yes, I think it's a very good idea. Then we have someone to keep an eye on us. Shall I give you my address?'

'Please.'

She gave it to him, and he said: 'I'm trying to imagine what it looks like. What kind of place you would live in.'

'And what do you imagine?'

'I think . . . an attic. I don't know why.'

She laughed. 'Well, it is an attic. And I've been imagining where you are, all bare floors, and neon and disinfectant.'

'Yes,' he said. 'And that is what it's like.'

Pip-pip-pip-pip-pip-pip-pip.

She waited.

'Goodbye, Ewa. See you on Saturday . . .'

'Goodbye.'

And the dialling tone buzzed. Ewa leaned across the sofa and put down the receiver. Then she hugged herself, and laughed. There was a small clock on the desk; it was after eleven. Was it too late to phone Jerzy and apologize? Yes, she'd ring him tomorrow. I'll have one more cigarette before I go to bed, she thought, and lit it, and walked up and down because she couldn't keep still.

The door to the narrow hall, once a landing, was open, and below the front door of her flat she could hear Jane, coming upstairs, leaning over the banisters on the floor beneath and calling down: 'Stuart? Bring up my book, will you, darling? It's on the kitchen table.' She heard him call: 'Okay. I'll be up in a minute,' and imagined him going round the house, putting out the lights, and the cat, locking the front door and making the house secure. How long had they been married? Twenty years? Had either of them ever had cause to be 'generous'? What a strange way for Stefan to look at it. Or was it so strange? Perhaps she was simply so inexperienced in affairs of the heart that she didn't know what people did.

She put out her cigarette, went to brush her teeth, and then switched out her own lights and went to bed. She lay there awake for a long time.

'The train standing at platform two is the 7.21 to Greenwich, calling at New Cross, Lewisham, Deptford, Blackheath . . .'

The woman announcer on this line was well spoken, and sounded as though she were speaking into a glass jar. In their carriage, a non-smoker whose windows were nonetheless almost opaque with grime, Jerzy and Elizabeth sat opposite each other, swaying as the carriage swung out of Waterloo and rattled past skyscrapers and back-to-backs.

'It makes me think of going to Poland,' said Elizabeth.

'Why? We've been on lots of trains since then.'

'I know. Perhaps it's because it's almost the same time of year.'

'We should have gone there last year,' said Jerzy. 'We should be in Warsaw now. Much more exciting.'

'Yes.' There were pictures in the paper of a motorcade protest blocking the whole of Marszałkowska; it had been like that for two days, a furious protest against food shortages and ration cuts, as talks between Solidarity and the government broke down. 'Still,' she said, 'we didn't go there for excitement, did we? We went so that you could discover your heritage. Didn't we, dear?'

Jerzy nodded. 'Yes, dear.' And then, more serious: 'But don't mock it too much. I had to.'

'I know. You know I do.'

He patted the seat beside him. 'Come and sit next to me.'

She shook her head. 'I like to face the way we're going. You come and sit next to me. And can you open the window?'

He sighed, rolling his eyes, but got up and pulled down the window, then came over. 'Am I going to spend the rest of my life doing what you want?'

'I hope so.' Elizabeth slid her arm in his, and put her head on his shoulder. 'Not really.'

He leaned across her, and took her other hand. 'Why won't you let me buy you a ring?'

'Because engagement rings are absurd. At least for couples like us they are.'

'Are you intending to wear a wedding ring?'

511

'I might, I'm not sure. I'm intending to marry you, that's the main thing, isn't it?'

'Yes.' He put his arm round her, and they sat looking out at lupins, weeds and long grass growing alongside the track. The train stopped, carriage doors opened and slammed shut and they went on again, the sun sinking slowly behind more skyscrapers, bordering empty school playgrounds.

'What do you think this Polish guy's going to be like?'

Jerzy shrugged. 'I don't know.'

Elizabeth raised her head from his shoulder. 'You don't want to meet him, do you?'

'What do you mean?'

'You know what I mean.'

'No, I don't.'

'Yes, you do.'

'Oh, for God's sake!' He drew away, irritably. 'We could go on like this all night. Say what you mean!'

'Forget it,' she said. 'Forget it.'

'No. What do you mean, I don't want to meet him? Why the hell shouldn't I?'

'Why are you being so defensive?'

'I'm not!'

'Yes you are.'

The train drew into Lewisham. Jerzy moved away as two other passengers got in, and went back to his old seat, opposite. The new passengers sat across the aisle, and pulled out paperbacks. The train started up again, and Elizabeth reached across and touched Jerzy's knee.

'Please . . .'

'What?'

'I'm sorry,' she said. 'That was my fault.'

'Yes, it was. I don't know what you're on about, but if you're on about something, for God's sake just come out with it.'

The paperbacks across the aisle were lowered.

'Okay, okay,' she said. 'Let's just forget it.'

They travelled the rest of the way in silence. At Blackheath, several people got off, and as they walked along the platform towards the barrier Elizabeth found herself looking, covertly, for someone who might be Ewa's – Ewa's what? Anyway, she couldn't see anyone on their own except a tall, loose-limbed man with greying hair, striding ahead of them. He looked familiar. She touched Jerzy's arm.

512

'Is that Stuart? You know, the chap who owns Ewa's house?'

'What? Who?' He looked along the platform. 'Yes, I think so. But I don't feel like idle chat on the way, if you don't mind.'

Elizabeth bit her lip. 'Are you still angry with me? Please don't let's spend the whole evening like this. We're supposed to be celebrating, aren't we?'

'All right. Don't go on about it.'

The train creaked past them, out of the station; the leaves on the still, dusty trees on the other side of the track moved a little in the disturbed air.

'Listen,' said Elizabeth, as the last carriage disappeared, 'if you don't make it up with me now, I'm not coming. I've said I'm sorry, and it wasn't so terrible, anyway.'

Jerzy kicked a stone on to the railway line. 'Just tell me what you meant, that's all I ask.'

'I don't think I'd better, now. It'll only make it worse. All right, all right, don't get angry again. I just meant that you didn't want to meet this guy because – I suppose because he's Polish in a way you and Ewa will never be. He's what your grandparents call a Pole from Poland, isn't he? I know they say that disparagingly, meaning from the new Poland, but even so – he's the real thing, isn't he?'

'No,' said Jerzy. 'No, he's not.' He saw another stone, bent down and picked it up, and spun it across the track. Then he turned round and held out his hand to her. 'But is that all you meant?'

'Yes. What did you think I meant?'

'Nothing, nothing.'

'Don't you start.'

They looked at each other. Jerzy held out his arms, and Elizabeth moved into them; they kissed, drew apart, and walked towards the barrier with their arms round each other, so that it was difficult to get their tickets out and show them.

Outside, they walked slowly up the hill from the station, and into the village, turning into the street leading to the street where Ewa lived. They walked up the path to the grey front door, their faces brushed by roses. Jerzy rang the top bell.

'Lovely house,' said Elizabeth, as they waited. 'I've always loved it here.' They could hear Ewa, running down the stairs. 'Perhaps she thinks we're him.'

'Perhaps he's here already.'

The door was opened, and Ewa stood there, smiling, beautiful in black cotton dress and amber necklace, tense.

'Hi. I'm so glad you've come.' She kissed them swiftly, on both cheeks, and then they followed her inside. At the end of the hall, hung with watercolours, Elizabeth could see the soft evening sunlight on the garden, beyond the open kitchen window; there was the sound of cutlery being taken out of a drawer, and Mozart was being played in the sitting room. This is my kind of house, she thought. I'm the one who should be living here, and painting. How strange that I've never realized that before. She followed Jerzy up the stairs. A door on the landing – cream paint, pale green carpet – opened, and Stuart came out, humming. Yes, it had been him on the platform.

'Evening, Ewa,' he said, and nodded to Jerzy and Elizabeth, smiling.

'Good evening,' said Ewa, quickly, and held open the door at the foot of the attic stairs. They followed her up, and into her enormous room. At the far end, the brown velvet covers on the bed reflected a pattern of pink, green, yellow, blue, from the stained-glass window high above. There were roses in a blue jug on the mantelpiece, the table was laid with a cloth, and blue china, and no one else had arrived.

'I must come here and paint this room,' said Elizabeth. 'I really had forgotten how beautiful it is.' She looked at Ewa, passing a bottle of wine to Jerzy. 'I'd like to paint you, here,' she said. 'I've never done a portrait of you.'

'No,' said Ewa. 'I know. Well, perhaps one day . . . Open that, please, Jerzy.'

'We've brought a bottle,' said Elizabeth, and pulled it out of her shoulder bag. 'Here.'

'Thank you, you needn't, but thanks.' She took it, and put it on the desk. Jerzy drew the cork on the other, and she took it, and poured out three glasses.

'*Na zdrowie*. And congratulations, I'm so pleased. Really.' She raised her glass. 'Mama is over the moon, of course. When's the day?'

'We haven't decided,' said Jerzy. 'Have we?' He looked at Elizabeth, and she shook her head, feeling Ewa at once excluded by that 'Have we?'

'No, not yet.'

'But this year?' asked Ewa.

'Oh, yes.'

'Good.'

There was a silence, and they all sat down, and waited.

'What are the family like?' Elizabeth asked Ewa.

'The family? You mean the family here?'

'Yes.'

'They're all right. They're nice. Why?'

'I just wondered. You seemed rather abrupt with Stuart just now.'

'Did I?' Ewa shrugged. 'Oh, well. You know what I'm like.' She looked at her watch.

'What time's he coming?' asked Jerzy, and she kicked him, half serious. 'Shut up.'

'What do you mean? I only asked. I'm hungry.'

'Oh, Jerzy . . . Actually, I've realized I didn't say a time.'

'So we could wait here all night.'

'No, of course not.' Ewa got up and went to switch on the stereo. It was tuned to the radio, and she fiddled with the knobs. 'Did you hear the news? About the motorcade in Warsaw?'

'Yes,' said Jerzy. 'Is this guy from Warsaw?'

'Yes, he is.' She put on a record, a quartet, and straightened up. 'His name is Stefan,' she said, 'I thought I'd told you.'

'You did,' said Elizabeth, watching her pick up her packet of cigarettes. No one else in the world she knew smoked Camel. 'And . . .' How should she put it? 'Has he been here before?'

'No,' said Ewa. 'We've only just met.' She looked as if she might be going to add something, but then she quickly lit a cigarette, and then the doorbell rang, and she visibly jumped.

'I'll be back in a minute.' She put down the cigarette and went to the door. Jerzy and Elizabeth looked at each other.

'It makes me feel as if we've been married a hundred years,' he said.

'I know,' said Elizabeth. 'But anything could happen to us, even now, couldn't it? Complacency is death.'

He frowned. '*Now* what do you mean?'

'Don't let's start that one again. I just mean – anything can happen to anyone, can't it? In affairs of the heart.'

Jerzy stood up, and went to the window. 'I've had enough of this kind of talk for one evening. I hope this guy talks politics.'

'He probably talks nothing else. That's probably why Ewa liked him.'

'I'm quite sure you're wrong about that.' Jerzy leaned across the table, and opened the window wide. 'God, it's hot. I wish it would rain again.'

'Do you?' said Ewa from the doorway. 'Jerzy – this is Stefan. My brother. And Elizabeth – I think I told you they are getting married.'

515

She spoke in English, but slowly, clearly. She was holding a small tissue-wrapped bunch of flowers, and blushing.

Stefan smiled at them, and held out his hand. 'Hello. How – how do you do?' His accent was heavy, and he had obviously been practising.

'How do you do?' said Elizabeth, and he took her hand and lifted it to his lips, a gesture only, returning it unkissed.

'*Dobry wieczor*,' said Jerzy, and they shook hands. 'Can I get you a drink?'

'A drink? Oh yes!'

Something in the way he said it made them all laugh. I like you, thought Elizabeth, watching him turn to Ewa, and smile, and seeing her blush. You look like the kind of person one could trust. He was saying something to Ewa in Polish, something about the room; he looked round, whistling at the size of it, the stained-glass window. He wore jeans, which looked new, boots, which were scuffed and looked old, and a shirt and thin grey sweater which needed ironing. He was quite a bit shorter than Jerzy, but then most people were; he had short hair, no particular shade of brown, and slightly irregular features. If you passed him in the street you wouldn't notice him, but she knew that you could quickly become a friend, he just had that look, and gave that feeling: direct, open, warm.

Ewa was still holding the tissue-wrapped flowers. She said to Elizabeth in English, 'I must put these in water.'

'Of course. And – Ewa, I don't mind if you all speak Polish.'

'Don't you?' Ewa looked at her. 'I'd have thought you would feel very left out.'

'No. It's my fault for not learning more. Anyway, I like watching.'

'And then we never know what you're thinking.'

'Does that matter?' Elizabeth nodded towards Jerzy and Stefan, talking rapidly in Polish. *Solidarność* . . . *Jaruzelski* . . . *Bydgoszcz* . . . *Warszawa* . . . 'I haven't seen Jerzy look so animated for months,' she said. 'Do you want any help with supper?'

'No, no, it's all ready, thanks. We can eat in a few minutes, if Jerzy's so hungry.' She went out to the kitchen, and Elizabeth went to sit on the sofa, and watched Stefan and Jerzy, one smoking, one coughing. She understood Stefan apologizing, and he moved away, Jerzy indicating that it was all right, he had to get used to it again whenever he saw Ewa. Then she was back in the room, carrying a tray, with a small glass vase of anemones among the dishes, and Stefan moved over and took it, and put it on the table.

They ate by the open window, hearing the family of the house entertaining in the garden below. Once, Elizabeth leaned out and watched them; she saw Stuart, pouring wine for their guests, then letting his hand rest on his wife's shoulder as he said something which made them laugh, before he sat down again, and she wondered: Will Jerzy and I be like that in twenty years' time? Thirty years? My parents try to be like that, but they're not, not inside; I don't know if they really love each other still. Dusk was falling: she saw Stuart's wife get up and go into the house, and return carrying candles. She lit them, and insects hovered above the wooden table. Elizabeth turned back to their own table, seeing how dark the room had become.

'They've lit candles down there,' she said.

'Have they?' said Ewa. 'I don't think I've got any. But we can have the lamp on.' She leaned across and pressed the switch: at once, they were enclosed in a soft circle of light, which shone on their faces and the flowers, and Stefan turned to her as she sat down, and said in English: 'Very nice. This is all' – and he gestured at the table, and at all of them – 'very nice.' They laughed, and he put his arm lightly round Ewa's shoulder, and Ewa, just for a moment, leaned her cheek against his, smiling, then drew away. Elizabeth watched Stefan, watching Ewa, and Ewa, reaching for her cigarettes, and thought: they look right together.

She said to Stefan in slow English: 'How long have you been over here?'

'Just a short time.' He took a cigarette from Ewa's packet, and lit hers for her, and then his own, and looked at Elizabeth. 'I only stay for a few months, I think.'

'Oh.'

'Shall we have coffee?' said Ewa, rather quickly. 'Would anyone like coffee?'

'Why don't you let one of us make it?' said Elizabeth.

'No, no.' She got up and began to clear the table.

'At least let me do that.'

'Well – all right. Thank you. I'll put the kettle on.' She carried the salad bowl out of the room, and Elizabeth put plates and dishes on the tray, as Stefan and Jerzy began to talk again. As if they've known each other for a long time, she thought, and carried the tray to the kitchen. The kettle was on; Ewa was standing looking out of the window, at the attic lights of other houses.

'That was delicious,' said Elizabeth, putting the tray on the little table.

'I'm glad you enjoyed it.' Ewa didn't turn round.

'Ewa? Are you all right?'

'Fine.'

Elizabeth realized she was trying not to cry. 'Ewa . . . what is it?' She went across and put her arm round her; Ewa put her hands over her eyes, and pressed them, hard, fighting to control herself.

'Something about Stefan?' Elizabeth asked gently. 'He – he seems to care for you a lot.'

Ewa wiped her eyes, in a single, angry gesture. Then she moved away, and reached for a roll of kitchen towel on the wall. She wiped her eyes again, and said shakily: 'We've only just met.'

'I know,' said Elizabeth. 'But look at Jerzy and me. We fell in love at first sight, or almost.' It seems a very long time ago, she thought, but said aloud: 'I didn't really believe it could happen until then.'

'It seems to have taken you for ever to decide to get married.'

'I know. It all seemed very easy at first, and then . . .' She laughed. 'And then it didn't. But somehow you and Stefan . . .'

'Stefan and I know what our difficulties are already,' said Ewa flatly. 'He's married.'

'Oh.' Elizabeth floundered, filled with pity, also feeling a fool. 'Why – why didn't you tell us that?'

Ewa shrugged. 'Why didn't he tell me as soon as we met? Perhaps I wanted to try and pretend it wasn't true, just for this evening. but – you heard him say he's going back soon, to Poland. What's the point of – of caring about someone in those circumstances?' The kettle came to the boil, and she switched off the gas, looking helplessly round the kitchen. 'Where the hell have I put the cups?'

'I'll find them.' Elizabeth began to open cupboard doors. She found the cups, and saucers, and began to put them on another little tray, seeing Ewa pour boiling water into the coffee pot, looking pale.

'I am so, so sorry,' she said. 'I was looking at you both earlier, and thinking you really did look as if you belonged together.'

'Don't!' Ewa snapped. 'I don't need you to tell me that now!' She slammed the kettle down on to the stove.

'Are you two all right, out there?' Jerzy was calling from the sitting room. 'Do you want any help?'

'No,' said Elizabeth quickly, loudly. 'We're fine, we'll be out in a minute, we're just talking.' She looked at Ewa, and said: 'You've never liked me, have you?'

'No,' said Ewa, looking at the floor. 'Never. I want to, but I can't.'

'Because I've taken Jerzy away from you.'

Ewa didn't answer.

Elizabeth moved to pick up the tray of coffee cups, and leave.

Ewa said: 'Why do you suppose it is that you have Jerzy, and are happy, and I have no one?'

'I don't know,' said Elizabeth. 'I don't know anything – there seems to be no reason at all, in the scheme of things, why one person should have more than another. Perhaps I'm more like Jerzy than I thought. Life is cruel.'

'Not to you.'

'Not so far,' said Elizabeth, and picked up the tray and went out of the room.

When Jerzy and Elizabeth had gone, Ewa and Stefan sat finishing the wine, Stefan on the sofa, Ewa in the old armchair by the fireplace. The curtains were drawn; the lamps on the table, the mantelpiece, and by the low, brown velvet bed at the other end of the room, made three yellow pools of light, on the rugs, on the floor, the books, the papers. On the mantelpiece a small clock, moved from the table, ticked silently, showing long past eleven, and long past the last train back into London. Chamber music had been playing all evening; now the last record clicked off, and Stefan got up and went over to the stereo, running his fingers along the LPs on the shelf above it. He took one out, and looked across at Ewa.

'You think it would be . . . too much, to listen to a little Chopin?'

She shrugged. 'I don't know.' She was looking straight ahead, towards the door, her legs stretched out, bare beneath the black cotton dress, feet in black espadrilles crossed at the ankles. Stefan bent down and put on the record; he moved the needle across, the first melancholy bars of a nocturne began, and Ewa closed her eyes. Stefan went back to the sofa; they sat listening, not talking. After a while, the nocturnes ended, and a waltz began.

'They play all these in the Łazienki Park, in Warsaw,' Stefan said. 'My parents used to take me sometimes, when I was little, on Sundays.'

'Did they?' said Ewa. 'And when I was little, we used to dance to this, in Saturday school, I can remember Pani Dąbrowska, she was like a fat old hen, thumping away.' She smiled, opening her eyes, and Stefan said:

'That's better.'

'Have I been such bad company?'

'You haven't smiled for an hour. What happened this evening? Something went wrong?'

Ewa shrugged. 'Elizabeth and I had a sort of quarrel. I told her I'd never liked her.'

He looked at her, astonished. 'You told Elizabeth that? Tonight? When?'

She laughed, because she couldn't help it, though it wasn't funny, just the way he said it. 'In the kitchen. When we were making coffee.'

'Why? Why did you tell her that?'

'It doesn't matter.'

Chopin had ended; the record switched itself off, and the stereo hummed, softly. Stefan said: 'You are even stranger than I thought.'

'I'm not strange at all,' said Ewa. 'I was upset.'

'What about?'

'Nothing.'

'Oh, my God. What am I going to do with you?'

'Nothing,' said Ewa angrily. 'Nothing, nothing. Why are you still here? You should have gone with them, and caught the train. And had a nice chat. What did you think of them, you haven't said – '

Stefan got up, and came across, and pulled her to her feet, and took her into his arms. She leaned against him, her head on his shoulder. He pressed his cheek against it, ran his hand through her hair, put up her face towards him, and kissed her eyes. He pulled her closer, stroking her neck, her cheeks, her lips, closing his mouth at last over hers, warm and loving.

Ewa opened her mouth, feeling his tongue probe hers, gentle and insistent, warm, warm. She felt his hands run down her back. pressing her hard against him, and she felt desire flood through her, wanting him to touch her everywhere, to come into her and never, never, never leave her, and she broke away, panting.

'Stop it. Stop it.' She sank down into the armchair, covering her face.

He knelt down in front of her, and put his head in her lap. They stayed like that for a long time. At last he raised his head, and gently took her hands away from her face, and kissed them.

'You are so, so beautiful.'

'Don't.'

Stefan held both of her hands in one of his; with the other, he began to unlace his boots, and pulled them off. 'I have to do that,' he said, 'because they are killing me. I was at work all day today, and you see I have bought these jeans, to seduce you in, but I couldn't afford new shoes as well.'

Ewa looked at him uncertainly, not knowing whether to laugh, and feel safe, or to be afraid.

'How can I be afraid of you?' she said slowly. 'When you are everything I have ever wanted. It's just . . .'

'I know.' He covered both her hands with both of his. 'And now I am going to ask you one question, although I think I know the answer, and please don't be angry with me. You are on the pill?' His expression was both affectionate and comically unsure.

'No,' said Ewa, and leaned forward and kissed him on the forehead. 'No, of course not. As you guessed.'

'Yes,' said Stefan. 'And so – there will be no seduction, if that is all right with you? Just . . . what I think in the good old days they used to call heavy petting?'

They both began to laugh, rocking back and forth in each other's arms, kissing shoulders and necks and hands and mouths, like lovers and like friends. Then Stefan drew away, no longer laughing. He knelt by her feet, and gently pulled off her espadrilles, and put them beside his boots. He looked at her, his face filled with desire, and carefully parted her knees, and pushed up the black cotton skirt, and lifted her so that he could pull down her pants. His fingers brushed her, and she shivered, and his eyes never left hers, as he drew her pants down and over her bare legs, and her feet, and put them softly on the floor.

'We could do this on the bed,' he whispered, 'but I want to do it to you here.'

'So do I,' Ewa whispered.

'And I want to take off all your clothes, and mine, and . . . and be with you properly. But now, I just want this. Just this. Yes?'

'Yes.'

He leaned over, and kissed her, parting her lips with his tongue, and she closed her eyes, and lay back in the old armchair, with her legs far apart, waiting for the sweet, exquisitely sweet, lingering and delicious moment when his hands moved up them, stroking, stroking, and his fingers slid hard at last inside her, and inside her, and out, and inside her again, over and over again, slowly, slowly, slowly, over and over again, his mouth leaving her mouth, and his face travelling down her, over her breasts, her stomach, over the rucked-up black cotton dress, on to her, his lips and his tongue on the deepest, most intimate, most thrilling and terrifying part of her, his fingers beneath sliding in and out, in and out, his tongue flicking back and forth, rubbing, rubbing, his hands spread all over her, everywhere, until she felt herself begin to come at last, and came and came, and came, as she had never ever thought would happen, and she began to cry, helplessly, hopelessly.

'*Kochana, kochana, kochana*. Darling, darling, darling.' Stefan was holding her, rocking her, he moved and lifted her so that she was cradled in on his lap now, and stroked her hair, softly, lovingly, until she stopped.

'I'm sorry, I'm sorry . . .'

'For what? It is I who should be sorry.' He went on stroking her hair, and he pulled down her dress, and smoothed it.

Ewa sat up, and looked at him. 'How can you be so generous?'

Then she remembered the last time she had heard that word, and bit her lip.

'You just make me feel like that,' he said, and drew a deep breath. 'Shall we go to sleep now?'

'Yes.'

He carried her over to the bed, and gently lowered her. 'You have a nightdress?'

'Under the pillow. I feel like a baby.'

'Good.' He felt underneath the brown velvet bedspread, and pulled out the nightdress. He shook it out, a pale pink lawn, and said: 'Everything you have is so lovely. The room, your clothes.'

Ewa reached up and put her arms round her neck, trying to undo her zip. 'It's what I always wanted,' she said, 'to have beautiful things. Now I've met you, I couldn't care if I lived in a cowshed.'

'I could. Let me do that.' He sat beside her on the bed, slid down the zip and slipped her dress off her shoulders. She lifted herself so that he could draw it down, right off her, wearing now only a white lace bra and amber necklace, and he carefully unfastened the bra, and looked at her, and said: 'And now I want to do that to you all over again. Lie down.'

She lay, and watched him pull off his sweater, his shirt and jeans and socks, and then she sat up and said: 'Wait,' and got off the bed and stood in front of him, and pulled down his underpants and ran her hands all over him. They sank on to the bed, and she lowered her mouth on to his, and he slipped his fingers into her again, and it seemed as if they spent all night like that, crawling between the sheets at last, and falling asleep.

Sometime in the small hours, Ewa woke, and saw that the lights were still on. She crept out of bed, and went to the bathroom, and then she came back and switched them off, one by one, and slid into bed beside Stefan, and put her head on his chest. He wore a cheap medallion, in its centre the Black Madonna of Częstochowa. She kissed it, and kissed his sleeping face, and lay very close to him, unable to stop herself thinking, before she fell asleep, that it had not, in the end, been an act of adultery, not in the letter of the law; but it had, unquestionably, been a betrayal. She closed her eyes, trying not to think that thought again. After all, Poland was, really, a very long way away.

Early September. The first leaves yellowing in the trees in the gardens of Blackheath, in the garden behind the house where Ewa and Stefan had breakfast at the open window, watching Jane rake the grass below, feeling the chill of autumn. The first leaves yellowing in the parks all over London, drifting on to the grass in Regent's Park, where they had met, and in Hyde Park, where Danuta hurried past the railings to the language school, leaving her new hotel. Chestnuts dropped on to the paths across Clapham Common, where Anna and the grandparents, and occasionally Jan, took their walks on Sundays. Leaves spun on to the paths and lakes on Hampstead Heath, where Jerzy and Elizabeth walked, and discussed Ewa and Stefan, and made plans for a quiet wedding.

In Gdańsk, in a sports hall, Solidarity was holding its First National Congress. A statement was issued, a Message to the Working People of Eastern Europe.

'We greet the workers of Albania, Bulgaria, Czechoslovakia, the German Democratic Republic, Romania, Hungary, and all the nations of the Soviet Union.

'As the first independent self-governing trades union in our post-war history, we are profoundly aware of the community of our fates. We assure you that, contrary to the lies spread in your countries, we are an authentic, ten-million-strong organization of workers, created as a result of workers' strikes. Our goal is to improve the condition of all working people. We support those among you who have decided on the difficult road of struggle for free trades unions . . .'

The delegates to the congress also approved another message, a Letter to Poles in the whole world. It began: 'Here, on the Vistula, a new Poland is being born . . .'

These messages were reported in the London papers. The headlines, the comment, were shocked, appalled. For Solidarity to speak so daringly, so brazenly, of the 'nations of the Soviet Union'! To declare that a new Poland was being born! Danuta scanned the papers on the bookstall in the foyer of her new hotel. The bookstall carried foreign papers, too: understanding Solidarność in English, French, German, Italian, seeing the exclamation marks, understanding the headlines in the *New York Times*, the *Washington Post*, she swallowed, and felt afraid. The whole of the West was waiting – one more foot wrong, one more strike, march, outrageous and audacious statement, and – and what? Was the press really on the side of Solidarity? Hadn't there, always, been the suggestion that the union was asking for too much, too soon? It had never felt like that when she was there – perhaps, now, all these Western papers were exaggerating, and the danger was not so great. Looking at the stall again, she had a sudden unpleasant image: lips being licked. She moved quickly across the foyer, and out into the street. It had rained last night, and the sunny air smelt damp. She would ring Mama tonight – no, tomorrow, tonight she was working.

Danuta had changed both her hotel and her evening job, the hotel to get away from the Home Office, and the eating house to get away from the Manager. Her visa had expired, her passport was in the Home Office: she had sent it in with a letter, asking for another extension. She was hoping to re-train, perhaps in computers, her English was improving fast, she had saved sixty-seven pounds in tips, opening her first bank account. But if the Home Office demanded to know how, all this time, she had been living, or how she intended to live now, with no work permit . . . Sixty-seven pounds wouldn't impress them. They must, in any case, already have notes on her from the raid. Walking fast along Oxford Street, moving through the shoppers, Danuta went through the vocabulary for this afternoon's test, and tried not to think about any of it. She was hoping to sit the Cambridge Proficiency next spring: it was, as Basia had told her, a very stiff paper, but her tutor seemed to think she'd be all right. She reached the doors of the school, and climbed the narrow stairs. If she saved enough from the new evening job, she might take an afternoon off from here each week and learn to type. There were typing schools advertised everywhere.

After the class, she went to her café near Chinatown. She sat over her coffee, and wrote to her mother – silly to phone, much too expensive, especially now, when she was saving every penny.

'The papers here are sounding alarms over the Solidarity Congress. Every now and then I do feel afraid – '

She stopped, and crossed the second sentence out, heavily.

'However, all is well with me! I'm working as a waitress in a new hotel, and I have a new evening job, much better than the last, it's in a restaurant in Covent Garden, a very pretty, touristy part of the West End, still very busy, but the tips are good, I was lucky to get it. There are two other Polish girls there, they seem all right, one is from Warsaw. My friend Basia, from Kraków, who was in the last hotel, has dropped out of circulation, I think she is going to marry her rich Frenchman. I'm glad you liked the last parcel, I'm hoping to send another next week, and please *tell me* if there are things you particularly want! I had a treat last week – a visit to the dentist – they have injections here, automatically, even for fillings.' Not like at home: a visit to the dentist in Poland could be terrifying.

She finished the letter and got up, paying for the coffee. No need to buy a roll these days – they gave her a good meal at the restaurant, down in the kitchen with the other evening staff. She walked back through the little street on to the Charing Cross Road, where she used to work, passing the eating house near the tube, and crossed into the network of streets leading to Covent Garden, full of tourists window-shopping, drinking at the tables in the piazza, listening to the evening street musicians, wandering arm in arm, well dressed, secure.

The manager of Danuta's new restaurant was English, the chef was Spanish. Many of the staff, working on morning, afternoon and evening shifts, were Australian or New Zealanders, passing through, nearing the end of the summer vacation and talking about the journey home through Europe. There were also the Poles, a Czech woman who had lived here since 1968, a sprinkling of French students, Scandinavian students. When Danuta arrived, it was still early and quiet, a lull before the evening rush began. She hung up her jacket, and went to eat with the other girls. 'Did you see the papers?' she asked Maria, as they sat down.

Maria was the girl from Warsaw. She was large and fair, and had been studying history. 'Oh, yes.' She reached for the mayonnaise, and piled spoonfuls on to a mountain of tuna fish salad.

'And do you think they're right? Do you think there's going to be an invasion?'

'It's possible, isn't it? We've always known it was.'

'But I mean now, soon.'

'I'm trying not to think about it,' said Maria. 'I work, I send my parcels home, I write to my family and tell them not to worry.'

Danuta laughed. 'So do I.'

'Of course, we all do. Can you pass the bread?'

They finished their meal. The restaurant upstairs began to fill. Danuta and Maria and the rest of the evening shift gulped down cups of coffee, and hurried up there. It began, very soon, to get busy; Danuta grew hot and tired, moving between the tables in the smoke, carrying trays from the hatch which led down to the kitchen, going through the menu with the customers in English. A couple in the corner beckoned her over. The woman was fair, wearing a bleached cotton shirt; the man was tall, with flopping brown hair; he had a camera on the table beside him. He smiled at Danuta, almost with diffidence. 'We should like to order . . .'

'Of course.' She pulled out her notebook and pen, smiling back at him. 'What would you like?'

'Trout and green beans.' He nodded towards the fair-haired woman. 'That's right?'

'Yes. Fine.'

'And I'll have the kidneys.'

Danuta looked quickly over his shoulder at the menu. He had an old one, last week's. 'I'm not sure if we have kidneys now . . . Can you wait a moment, please?' She turned away, saw Maria going past with a trayful of starters, and asked quickly in Polish: 'Maria? Are we serving kidneys this week?'

Maria nodded. 'Yes. I've just taken an order.'

'This customer has last week's menu . . .'

'Give him this week's then. But the kidneys are on anyway. Revolting, how can anyone eat such things?'

Danuta turned back to her table, and saw that the man was laughing.

'You're Polish. And your colleague.' He nodded towards Maria.

Danuta flushed. 'I'm sorry – you speak Polish? She didn't mean to be rude.'

'It's all right, it's quite funny. May I ask how long you've been over here?'

'Just a few months, I came at the end of April. And – and you?'

'Oh, I was born here. Well . . . I'll have the revolting kidneys, if your friend doesn't mind too much. And we'd like to order wine.'

'Of course.'

'We're celebrating,' said his girlfriend, smiling – or was she his wife? – and spread her hands as if in deprecation.

'Oh.' Danuta didn't know quite what to say. 'Very nice.'

She took the order for wine, and went to send the food order down the hatch. She could hear the chef shouting, he reminded her of poor Enrico. Was he back in Colombia now? She went into the little lobby at the far end of the restaurant, where the wine racks were, found the Médoc, very expensive, and thought: they must be celebrating. But they seem rather nice, those two.

During the evening, when she had time, she watched them. They talked a lot, at one point it seemed almost as if they might quarrel, but next time she looked they were holding hands. When she went to give them their bill, she said in Polish: 'I hope you have enjoyed your celebration.'

'We have,' said the man, in Polish, and then translated for his companion, who smiled again.

'May we ask your name?'

'Danuta,' she said. 'I'm from Warsaw.'

'Really? We visited Poland in 1979, we spent some time in Warsaw.' He pulled out a wallet, and put notes under the bill, on the saucer. 'My name is Jerzy Prawicki,' he said. 'This is Elizabeth – today is the anniversary of our meeting. Hence the celebration.'

'Oh. Congratulations.'

'Thank you. We wondered – would you like to come and have supper with us one evening?'

Danuta was astonished. 'Yes. Yes – I would. Thank you.'

'Where are you living?' asked Elizabeth.

'Oh – in a hotel in Bayswater. I work there.'

'As well as working here?'

'Oh, yes.'

'You must get very tired.'

She shrugged.

'Well . . .' Jerzy had written down their address on the back of the bill, and their phone number. 'Do phone us.'

'Yes, I will.'

They got up, and she went with them to the door. Some of the lights in the shop windows had been switched off now, but there were still plenty of people about. It felt cold, after the warmth of the restaurant; she saw Elizabeth shiver, and Jerzy put his arm round her.

'Come on.' He smiled briefly at Danuta. 'Goodbye.'

'Goodbye, and thank you.' She hurried back inside.

Londyn
28 September, 1981

'Kochana Krysiu,

'Forgive me for not writing for so long. I have something to tell you, and I don't know how to tell you.'

No. He couldn't do it straight away, just like that at the beginning of the letter. He lit a cigarette, and crossed out the last sentence, going over each word so that there was only a thick black line. He drew on his cigarette, and sat staring out of the café window. He was in a little sandwich bar, not far from the Embassy, not far from the BBC; there were a few tables, with sauce bottles and metal ashtrays. Outside, people in suits, in their lunch hour, walked quickly past, hailing taxis. The light was autumnal, golden, it reminded him of this time last year in Warsaw, when Krysia had been full of the news about Miłosz, and the Nobel Prize. He remembered seeing a bus driver in a Solidarność armband being hustled and pushed by the police as he climbed up into the driver's seat. He remembered a lot of things, and none of them had anything to do with Ewa, or what he was trying to say now.

Forgive me for not writing for so long. Forgive me for what I am about to tell you. No.

'Since I last wrote, the papers have been full of horror stories about Solidarność, the Congress, the reaction of our neighbours on the border. There is an organization here, a campaign supporting Solidarność, they have a magazine.'

And through it I met . . . No.

'I haven't joined it yet – it is all run in English, and anyway, I'm afraid that if anything should happen, it wouldn't be a very good idea for me to have my name linked with it.'

Were they censoring letters, yet? Would this reach Krysia unopened? If it was opened, would she think all the lines crossed out were crossed out by the censor?

'Anyway, I hope nothing is going to happen, and that I'll soon be home. My passport is in the Home Office, I am waiting for an extension. I think of you and Olek, and wonder how you are, and I miss you both very much.'

He did, he did miss them, though he couldn't tell Ewa that. And there were, still, times when he forgot them utterly, and he couldn't tell Krysia that.

'I have been working pretty hard. The house is almost finished, and we expect to be paid a bonus. Did you get the parcel? Since I last wrote, I have moved. I'm not in the hostel any more, it was rather unpleasant there, I'm staying with friends.'

I am staying with a woman called Ewa. In a way she reminds me a little of you: she is dark, like you, and beautiful, like you, though I know you never believed I really think that about you, Krysia. She is very emotional, and lonely, not like you, and I think I love her. No. No, no, no.

'If you want to write to me, I think it's best if you go on writing to the *poste restante* in William IV Street. There are a lot of people in this new place, it's almost as bad as the hostel, and letters go missing.'

Liar. Shit.

But perhaps he was giving her the chance to read behind that lie, if she thought about it, and realize for herself, without him having to tell her.

Coward. It wasn't just cowardice – absurd, he wanted to be with her, when she read it.

'I'll write again soon. My love to the parents, both sets. And I hold you and Olek, and kiss you both with all my heart.

Stefan'

He stubbed out the cigarette, sealed the envelope, got up quickly and paid at the counter, and walked back to work, fast, dropping the letter in the pillarbox on the way, and trying, after that, not to think about it.

A few weeks later, Danuta went to supper with Jerzy and Elizabeth. She sat on the edge of their sofa, feeling shy, and looking through Jerzy's photographs, while Elizabeth was in the kitchen. Over supper, they asked her questions. She told them, mostly in hesitant English, occasionally appealing to Jerzy and speaking Polish, for him to translate, about what it had been like in Poland, before she left. She told them about the first hotel, and the Home Office raid; about Enrico being arrested and Franco jumping out of the window. She told them about the eating house and the persistent manager; about her new hotel, where she served breakfast and lunch; she told them about the restaurant, and Maria, and all the Polish girls she'd met since she came here – Basia, who she'd seen again last week, and who was going to marry her Frenchman, though she didn't think she loved him, and the girl from Wrocław, who had also been questioned in the raid. She didn't say anything about the possibility of finding an English sponsor. She found that once she'd started to talk, she couldn't stop: no one else had listened to her since she came – she had abandoned Halina and her cat Henryk, named after her dead husband: Halina didn't want to know about her difficulties. She told them about the visit to the Polish refugee place, and the posters on the wall, Christ walking through the ruins of wartime Warsaw, and she realized they hadn't spoken for a long time, and fell silent, embarrassed at talking so much, realizing she knew nothing about them, at all.

'Excuse me – I talk too much.'

'No you don't,' said Elizabeth. 'You have had a difficult time, of course you must talk about it.' She pushed back her chair. 'Would you like coffee? Jerzy? Would you?'

'What?' He was sitting with his elbows on the table, his head in his hands.

'Are you all right? I asked if you wanted coffee.'

'Oh. Yes, please.' He pushed his hair off his forehead. 'You know what I'm thinking about?'

'The poster.'

'Yes.'

'I knew you would be.'

Danuta watched them, not really understanding.

Jerzy spread his hands again, in that deprecating gesture. He said to Danuta: 'I know what that poster must have looked like to you – an anachronism, yes?'

'Excuse me?'

He translated.

'Oh. Yes. It was very moving, of course, but – '

'I understand. But to me – ' He turned and looked at Elizabeth. 'It speaks to me in the same way as your painting did. Even without seeing it.'

She nodded, and took his hand.

Danuta looked at them, and looked away, taking in the paintings, the one on the easel at the far end of the room, a half-finished portrait of an old man with a very Polish face, and the ones on the walls, more portraits, still-lifes, summer landscapes, landscapes full of snow, a watercolour of a street in Warsaw, in the Old Town. She and Mama had coffee in that street sometimes.

'However,' Jerzy was saying to her, 'all this does not help you,

530

now.' He and Elizabeth dropped their hands, and Elizabeth said: 'Sorry. Couples can be rather stifling.'

Danuta shook her head. 'It is very nice to see people who are happy.'

Elizabeth laughed. 'We have our moments.'

'When are you getting married?'

'At Christmas. We've only just decided that – it's just going to be a register office affair, nothing grand. Now – *do* you want some coffee?'

'Yes, please. Can I help you?'

'No, no – you do quite enough waitressing as it is.'

Danuta yawned. 'And I must go soon, I have to work in the morning.'

'Poor you. We must think of something.' She took the tray out to the kitchen, saying to Jerzy: 'I take it you want one.'

'Yes. Thanks.' He looked at Danuta, sitting at their table with her hands in her lap. She had short, shining dark hair, a pale face with circles under her eyes; she wore a sweater which was much too thin for this time of year.

'How do you think we could help you?' he asked in Polish.

She shook her head. 'It's kind of you – I'm all right.'

'Have you made many friends since you came here?'

'Just the hotel girls, the ones I told you about.'

'And how long do you think you'll stay here? Do you have anything to go back to in Poland – anyone?'

'My parents, that's all, really. My friends, of course, but – I want to stay here if I can. There is nothing there, and I can help my parents more by being here. I hope perhaps they'll come over here next year.'

'If nothing happens.'

'Well – ' She swallowed, thinking of last month's headlines. 'Perhaps . . . things are quietening down for the winter. Perhaps next year things will be easier.'

'I hope so. Anyway – in the meantime, if there is anything we can do for you, you must say.'

'Thank you. There's just one thing – ' Wasn't it too much to ask that, on a first meeting?

'What's that?'

'Well – it's just that some of the girls have talked about finding a sponsor. Especially if they don't extend my visa, or if – if anything happened. I would need someone who could act as a sort of inter-

531

mediary, with the Home Office, reassure them that – I'm sorry, this seems rather dreadful, to ask, but reassure them that financially I'm all right. That I have somewhere to live, a permanent address.'

Elizabeth was coming back, with a tray of coffee. Jerzy explained to her, in English. Danuta thought: It feels rather odd, that he and I speak the same language, and she doesn't. We could keep something from her, if we wanted to.

Jerzy turned back to her. 'I don't think that would be a problem for us at all,' he said. 'You can use this address if you need to. If they want a letter from me, from either of us – that's all right. The only thing is, I don't think we can actually afford to support you – '

'No. No, of course not. I didn't mean that – '

'No. So – there we are, anyway. No problems.'

'Thank you. Thank you.'

Elizabeth was passing coffee cups. 'You know,' she said, 'when we were in Poland, apart from Jerzy's aunt, we spoke to no one. I mean no one like you, who might need us one day. Now, suddenly, we have two Poles from Poland in the family – you and a fellow called Stefan, who's living with – staying with – Jerzy's sister. He was very involved in Solidarity, he must have come over about the same time as you, I think.'

'After Bydgoszcz.'

'Yes. And Jerzy likes him, too, don't you? He hardly used to like anyone.'

Jerzy frowned. 'For heaven's sake . . .'

'Sorry. I'm only teasing.'

'I shouldn't think it's very interesting for Danuta.'

Danuta thought: There's something about these two. They're not so happy. Or they move to extremes too quickly. Or something. I don't know. She said: 'I don't mind. Anyway, I must be going.' She swallowed the last of her coffee. 'Thank you again, so much. It has been lovely meeting you.'

'And you,' said Jerzy.

'Come again,' said Elizabeth.

'Thank you, I will. I like your paintings.'

'Good.'

They saw her downstairs, to the dusty hall. Jerzy pulled open the front door, and a gust of cold wind blew in. Elizabeth looked at Danuta's thin sweater, and cotton trousers. 'You can't go home like that, I'll lend you a sweater. Hang on – '

She turned, and ran up the stairs. Jerzy shut the door again, and they waited. The hall was rather bleak, it reminded Danuta of the atmosphere in the first hotel, in the basement. She looked up at Jerzy, and said: 'Do you think of yourself as Polish?'

He laughed. 'I've been trying to answer that all my life. I don't know how to answer it now.'

Elizabeth came running down, holding out a thick blue jumper.

'Are you sure – '

'Of course.'

Danuta pulled it on. 'Thank you.'

Jerzy said: 'I'll walk you to the station.'

'No, please don't bother.'

'Let him,' said Elizabeth. 'It's late, he's right, you shouldn't be out alone.'

'Well – goodbye.'

'Goodbye.' They kissed, lightly, on both cheeks. Then Elizabeth held open the door, and the wind blew in again, and Jerzy and Danuta hurried out, into the lamplit street.

'I shan't be long,' said Jerzy.

'Don't worry.'

She climbed the stairs again, more slowly. When she was in their flat again, she went to the sitting room window overlooking the street, to wave, as Anna and the grandparents always did, when they visited. She pulled back the curtain, and looked down, but Jerzy and Danuta had already rounded the corner, and there was no one else about.

Warszawa
30 October 1981

'Kochany Stefanie,

'Thank you for your letter. I was worried at not hearing from you for so many weeks, and especially without a phone call. We miss you, too. Olek is talking quite a lot, now, not sentences yet, but a lot of words, and he has *grown*. I have to tell you that he does not use the word Tata so often, now. I show him the photograph of us, most days, and tell him that the funny-looking guy underneath the Pope is Tata, but of course he doesn't understand. Mama says she has not had a letter for weeks, and she worries more than I do. I know you must be very tired after work, but even so . . .

'Do you follow all the news from Poland? I'm sure you do. You know what they have started showing on the television? The countryside swarming with army personnel. They show us officers in the villages, talking to the peasants as if they were old friends, helping to mend tractors, checking the stocks of grain. They are "earning the confidence of the people". I can imagine your face, if they were to visit your factory, with their comradely smiles.

'Another thing: people from Szpitalna Street drop flysheets and bulletins in here from time to time, for me to put up in the library, and pass round. You remember that the Solidarity News Agency has always had that heading "Against Solidarity" in its regular statements? A couple of weeks ago there was an item which we all found a little sinister: Jaruzelski has formed a Committee of National Salvation. Six men. What does that mean, exactly?

'Oh, Stefan.'

Here there was something heavily crossed out.

'I know how much you want to stay for a little longer, and of course it has been wonderful to have the parcels. Olek looks sweet in the pyjamas, and what he really needs is something warm for the winter, a new, thick snowsuit, size 2–3, all right, because he's so enormous. Cigarettes *doubled* the price at the beginning of the month. Can you imagine? So Tata was very pleased with the Marlborough. And all the tins . . . I cooked a meal for all the parents when the last parcel came, and your father and Tata were drinking your health, and all we women were looking at each other and thinking we'd rather have you home again.

'Please – couldn't you just get your passport from the Home Office and come home in time for Christmas? I can't bear the thought of Christmas without you.

'Who is the friend you're staying with? Aren't you on the phone? It was bad enough not being able to phone you when you were in that hostel, but now . . . Is it a woman – no, I don't even want to ask. I know you, Stefan, but I know you wouldn't want to do anything to hurt us, so I won't ask.

'I'll let Olek give this letter a kiss – there, he's done it, you can see the mashed potato. And I kiss it too, with all my heart. I wish we hadn't quarrelled, before you left. Write again soon.

Your Krysia'

The post office in William IV Street was always crowded, the floor littered with cigarette butts, bits of string, scrunched-up bits of paper. Also, there were often drunks in here – there was a hostel for the homeless round the corner, and another at the far end of Covent Garden. Stefan stood reading the letter in a corner, by the long counter running the length of the plate-glass window. He lit a cigarette and read it again. Then he looked at the clock on the wall. Six-thirty. Ewa would be already ahead of him, on the train from Charing Cross by now: sometimes they met after work, but usually he worked overtime, and she went on ahead to be there, in the attic flat, when he got home. He rubbed his face, thinking. An hour behind in Warsaw, so Krysia would be just leaving the library, she would be at her mother's to pick up Olek in half an hour? An hour? There was the chance, just, that she hadn't gone to work, or that she had left early, and was already home.

He felt in the pocket of his overalls, pulled out a five-pound note, and went to queue for change. They didn't like it when you asked for change for the phone, but to hell with that. He stood in the queue, watching the office workers weigh their parcels. When he got his change, he went out to the phone booths, and dialled the number of their apartment in Warsaw. It took three attempts to get a ringing tone. When he got it, he stood, listening, for a long time. He imagined the living room, all tidied up before Krysia went to bed last night, Olek's toys in a cardboard box; their photograph on the mantelpiece, the Solidarność posters on the wall. Outside the window was the park, with the swings and silver birch trees; the graffiti on the wall of the nearby apartment block. What were they writing now? He imagined the tiny kitchen, and the bathroom where the water pressure was low, and their bedroom, Krysia asleep in the double bed alone, Olek sucking his thumb in the cot beside her. Or perhaps she took him into bed with her, now?

The phone rang and rang.

'Excuse me, mate, you going to hang on all night?'

'What?' He turned round, saw another guy in overalls, looking impatient.

'No. Sure – go ahead.'

He put down the receiver and came out. He lit another cigarette and read the letter again. Quarter to six. He could phone Ewa, and tell her he was working late, have a drink, and read the paper, and come back here to phone. Then he thought: I'm already deceiving one person. That's enough. He put the letter in his pocket, and buttoned it, and went out, and across the Strand to Charing Cross.

November, and very cold. Grey skies. Occasionally, the clouds were diffusely lit by a pale and watery sun. At the weekend, at the end of the garden behind the Blackheath house, Stuart made bonfires of the leaves from the bare trees, and the smoke drifted over the grass, the straggling michaelmas daisies, the tight-petalled dahlias, over the wall into other gardens, and into the wintry sky. He came in for an early tea by the fire, and television, bolting the french windows.

At the Academy cinema in Oxford Street, they were showing *Man of Iron*. Ewa and Stefan stood in the queue after work one evening, arm in arm. It had rained this afternoon, and the puddles on the pavements and in the gutters gleamed in the lights from the shop windows. Taxis swished past, and buses, with the lights on. The queue was long: it was a Friday night, and Wajda was talked about a lot, these days. Outside the cinema was a large blow-up of the leading actor, in his overalls and cap, smiling up at the sun. In the papers, in the reviews, there were photographs showing scenes from Gdańsk. A bus went past, very close to the kerb, and splashed up water. Ewa jumped, and moved away. Stefan looked down at her wet feet.

'Okay? Are you okay?'

'Yes. It wasn't very much.' She leaned against him, the collar of her coat turned up, brushing his cheek with her hair. 'Does it feel strange, to be going in to watch this here?'

'A little.' He turned to brush her hair with his lips.

There was a movement at the head of the queue, and a voice, and they looked up and saw a tall man with a beard, wearing a T-shirt over his sweater stamped with the Solidarność logo. He was calling out and waving copies of a magazine, moving slowly down the queue.

'Would you like to help us help the struggle for freedom in Poland? Profits from *Polish Solidarity Campaign News* go to Solidarność in Poland.'

'That's our magazine,' said Ewa.

'Yes.'

'We should have taken out a subscription. Or joined. Or something.'

'We can buy it now.'

The man was taking money, giving out copies. He drew near to them and Stefan felt in his pocket.

'How much?'

'Twenty pence,' said the man, and gave them their copy, and moved on. 'Would you like to help us help the struggle . . .'

They looked at it, quickly, as the queue began to move towards the box office. The front page was headed: Solidarity's First Year. There was a picture of a street blocked by buses and cars decked with the Polish flag, watched by thousands of people. The caption read: *Hunger marches block Warsaw city centre.*

Ewa watched Stefan flick quickly through the pages. Anna Walentynowicz had visited London, just a little while ago. He moved along the pavement, scanning the headlines, not looking up. At the box office, Ewa said: 'Stefan? Where do you want to sit?'

'What? Oh – sorry.' He lowered the magazine. 'I don't mind – somewhere not too close to the front, that's all.'

She bought the tickets, and they went inside. When they had found their seats, and sat down, she asked carefully: 'Stefan? If anything happens – I mean in Poland . . . could you go back? What would happen to you if you went back?'

He rubbed his hand across his lips. 'I don't know. I don't imagine I would be very popular. None of us who did anything active would be.'

Ewa was silent. Then she said, not wanting to know, but suddenly feeling she had to: 'When does your return ticket expire?'

'At the end of the year.' He put down the magazine, and turned towards her, putting his arm round her shoulders. 'There is perhaps a possibility . . . that I should go back by the end of the year. At least for a visit. You understand?'

Ewa looked at him, and saw in his eyes an expression she had seen before: tender apology. She turned away, feeling her own eyes fill with tears, and then the lights went down, the curtains drew back, and the film from Poland began.

12

London, December 1981

Sunday 13 December

Jerzy woke early, from a dream he couldn't remember. He lay next
to Elizabeth, feeling his heart racing, knowing only that the dream
had been something about his father, not wanting to know more than
that. He opened his eyes. It was still dark, and cold outside the bed,
but he had to go for a pee. He waited until his heart had slowed down,
pushed back the bedclothes and stumbled out to the bathrooom. God,
it was cold. The house was absolutely soundless, deep in sleep; when
he came out, he could just hear the milk float whining along the
street at the far end. He was thirsty; he went into the kitchen, and
opened the fridge. It began to hum, spilling a patch of light on to
the floor, and he had a drink of juice, still half asleep. In the light
from the fridge he saw the radio on the table, yawned, and switched
it on, to get the news before he went back to bed. And stood there,
rigid, still holding his glass, the fridge door still swung open.

'Good morning, this is Pauline Bushnell.

'Poland is in the grip of a major crisis. The country's leader,
General Jaruzelski, has declared a state of emergency, the
government's been taken over by a military council, there've been
arrests. The move follows a crackdown by riot police on the
Warsaw headquarters of the union Solidarity.'

'Oh, Christ. Oh, my Christ.'

'Britain faces another day of icy weather – after a night of
record low temperatures.

'And the American authorities are having second thoughts
about a visa for the Reverend Ian Paisley.'

Jerzy kicked the fridge door shut and sat down at the kitchen table.
He turned up the sound.

' . . . About two hours ago, the Polish Prime Minister and
Party Leader, General Jaruzelski, went on the radio to announce
that a state of emergency was being declared, and that the country
was being taken over by what he called "a military council of
national salvation". As he spoke, police were occupying

538

Solidarity's main offices in Warsaw after a raid there at around midnight in which there were arrests and documents were seized . . .'

The bulletin was a long one. There was a report from Kevin Ruane: 'Solidarity extremists' had been interned, with dozens of others, including ex-First Secretary Gierek. Phones and telexes were cut off – Tim Sebastian had managed to telex a message describing security men in steel helmets with visors, armed with truncheons, on guard outside the Solidarity offices in Warsaw. When the bulletin had finished, Jerzy realized he was shivering violently. He got up, and carried the radio out and down the corridor to the sitting room, and dialled Ewa's number. He stood shivering in the dark, hearing her phone ring, and voices on the radio, turned down, discussing the British weather.

'Hello?' Her voice sounded cracked with sleep.

'It's me. Something – something's happened. Poland's under martial law. It's just been on the news.'

A long, shocked silence.

'You'd better listen – the bulletin's over, I had to listen to it all before I rang you, sorry. There've been masses of arrests, it all happened in the middle of the night.' His teeth were chattering. 'Is Stefan asleep?'

'Of course.' Her voice dropped. 'I'll . . . I'll wake him up. Oh God. He was supposed to be going home for Christmas.'

'You didn't tell us.'

'No. I . . . I couldn't.'

'I'm freezing,' said Jerzy. 'I've got to go back to bed. Ring me later, okay?'

'Okay.'

'Tell Stefan they said all the phones were cut off.'

'What, from outside, you mean?'

'Everywhere, I think. I might have got that wrong. Talk to you later.'

'Will you ring Mama?'

'Yes, in a bit. Goodbye.'

He put the phone down and went shivering out and into the bedroom, still carrying the quiet voices on the radio, and fell into bed. He huddled next to Elizabeth and she woke up, and turned over, saying sleepily: 'You're frozen.'

'Hold me, hold me.' He buried his face in her neck, her hair.

'What's happened? Are you ill?'

'Poland's in a state of emergency – martial law. It's on the news.'

'Oh, my God.'

'Hold me. I'm so cold.'

She rubbed his back, his arms and chest, until he was warm again. There was nothing more on the radio about Poland, and after a while she leaned over and switched it off.

'I'll hear it all later, okay? Have you rung Ewa?'

'Yes.' He was drowsy again, longing to go back to sleep, he couldn't help it. They lay very close, under the rugs and the duvet, hearing the first few winter-morning birds begin to call as darkness faded, and then they fell asleep. When Jerzy woke again, he thought perhaps he had dreamed about Poland, too. Then he heard Elizabeth in the kitchen, listening to the news, and the bulletins repeated, and he thought of Warsaw, snowbound, cut off, patrolled by tanks, and felt a great weight begin to crush him: a sense of shame which he knew was absurd, and misplaced, but which nonetheless overwhelmed him – that in Poland the iron curtain had slammed down, and he was outside it, safe, cosseted, free.

She stood by the low bed, looking down at his sleeping face turned towards where she had been lying before the phone call: inside, next to the wall beneath the uncurtained stained-glass window. The medallion was buried in the pillow, but in the light from the desk lamp she'd left on she could see the chain round his neck, beneath rough brown hair. His skin was rather coarse, open-pored, unremarkable features thick and blurred with sleep – such an ordinary face, but she felt as if it had always been beside her on the pillow, that that was where it belonged; impossible that he should ever be somewhere else, somewhere without her. The dressing gown she had bought him lay sprawled across the foot of the bed, soft dark blue wool, incredibly expensive.

'Ewa! You shouldn't buy me something like this. You know I can't do the same for you.'

'But do you like it?'

'Of course I like it, it's the most beautiful thing I've ever had, but you know I won't be able to – ' He didn't finish the sentence. He wouldn't be able to take it with him. Then she would keep it, for when he came back. She had refused to think he might not come back.

And now he might never be able to leave her.

She crept into bed beside him. He murmured – *'Kochana?'* – and

540

put out an arm and pulled her close. 'Who was that?' She shut her eyes, thinking: I needn't tell him, not yet. Let me have just one more hour, just that, before I tell him, and see what it does to him. Let me protect him, and be protected. She kissed his lips, his cheeks, put her arms round him and held him, and he began to kiss her, opening her lips with his tongue, moving to lie on top of her, naked, pulling up her nightdress, covering her face with his warm hands, his eyes still closed, still half asleep. She felt him begin to push his way into her, and all she wanted was to open herself to him, to be his woman, and she found the strength to say to herself: This is the ultimate deception, and to push him away and sit up, clasping her knees, shaking.

'Hey..' He lay on his back, rubbing a hand across his eyes. 'What did I do?'

She buried her face in her knees.

'Ewa?' He sat up beside her, put an arm round her. 'What's the matter? Something about the phone call? Was there a phone call?'

'Yes, there was. It was Jerzy.' She couldn't raise her head.

'Someone is ill? Your mother?'

'No.' She took a deep breath and looked up, into his kind, concerned, sleepy face, and said flatly: 'Poland's under martial law.'

Stefan stared at her.

'What?'

'He said Poland's under martial law. It was on the seven o'clock news. I'm so sorry, I'm so sorry . . .' She reached out towards him, but he didn't take her hand.

'Is the news on now?'

'No, it'll be on again at eight.'

'What did he say? What's happened? Quick!'

'Just . . . that there've been arrests, it must have all happened in the middle of the night. He . . . he said all the phones are cut off.'

Stefan flung back the bedclothes. 'Excuse me – I have to try . . .' He went quickly to the phone, not bothering with the dressing gown, and picked up the receiver. She saw him begin to dial, then he put down the receiver, and turned to look at her. 'You want to make some tea?'

'What? Oh, yes, of course.' She got out of bed, shivering, and picked up the warm wool dressing gown. She tried to give it to him as she passed, but he was already dialling again, and didn't look up. She left it hanging on the chair behind him.

Out in the kitchen, she switched on the gas under the kettle and stood leaning against the stove, trying to get warm, and listening. She heard Stefan dial, and wait, and put down the receiver and dial again, and again, and again. He slammed down the phone and called out: 'International operator – what's the number? Where do I find the number?'

She hurried back and searched for the code book, among the papers, then on the bookshelves, all the time hearing him dial and dial, and finding it at last tucked between the directories on the floor. She flicked through the pages.

'You just dial 100 and ask for Freefone BTI.' She wrote it down. 'Thanks.'

He dialled it, and she went back to the kitchen, thinking: If Stefan were mortally wounded, he would still be polite to his friends. She waited to hear him get through, but the kettle came to the boil and she heard the receiver slam down again. She made tea, suddenly remembering Elizabeth in this kitchen, in the summer, saying so lightly: 'Life is cruel', and then Stefan was in the room, wearing the dressing gown, looking rumpled and pale.

'I can't get through. I mean not to the operator, either. Every bloody Pole in the country must be trying.' He put his hand over his eyes.

Ewa went over and put her arms round him. 'I'm so sorry,' she said again.

He shook his head. 'We must listen to the next bulletin, okay?'

'Of course. Tea's made.' She felt like a wife, comforting. 'Shall we take it back to bed?'

'Sure, sure.'

She put the things on a tray, and they went back into the large, cold room. 'Here.' Ewa gave him the tray and went to light the gas fire. She heard the cups rattle violently, and got up to see Stefan just standing there, about to drop the tray. She ran.

'Come on, come back to bed, you're shocked, come on, darling, I'll look after you . . .'

She took the tray, and put it on the desk, and led him across the room. She helped him into bed, and arranged the pillows, and drew up the bedclothes, and then poured him tea, and helped him to drink it. After a while, the colour came back into his face, and she climbed in beside him.

Dawn was breaking. They sat propped up on the pillows, drinking tea, and waiting for the eight o'clock news.

*

The hotel dining room was open for breakfast from seven every morning. It was a large, hideous room, acres of patterned carpet beneath pale brown tables with rounded corners and spindly legs, and chairs with plastic seats. It was lit, first thing in the morning, by dull blocks of neon; in the evenings, there were wall lamps, clinging to embossed and patterned paper. Danuta had twelve tables to look after; even in winter there were tourists, especially now, in the lead-up to Christmas, and businessmen, and couples. Beyond the swing glass doors was the foyer, brightly lit; beyond the swing fire doors at one end of the room were the kitchens. Danuta came out of the kitchens, carrying a tray of bacon, eggs and tomato for four, and set them down on the table at the side, by the coffee machine. She filled coffee cups for four, and carried them, and then the breakfasts over to the table where four men in suits, from somewhere outside London, sat trying to make jokes and conversation. They brightened as she approached.

'That's more like it. Oooh, I needed that. That's a good girl.'

Danuta smiled, setting out cups and plates. The tips could be good from the men, though no one really bothered to tip much at breakfast. The work was far easier than being a chambermaid, but she wasn't making much. The restaurant in Covent Garden was doing wonderful business at the moment, though, even if it did mean staying very late, and getting a taxi home. She smothered a yawn, putting down the last cup of coffee.

'You would all like toast?'

'We would, my dear. If that's all right with you.'

She smiled again, wondering how they talked to their wives. 'Of course.' She took the empty tray back to the kitchen. Amidst the clatter of dishes, the breakfast chef was cracking eggs on to the griddle, flipping them with a slice and singing to Radio One. Radio One was always on in here; it had been in the last hotel, too. 'Radio One!' was one of the first things she'd picked up: it used to ring in her head as she yawned her way through breakfast; now it was just part of the background. Over the last couple of weeks, talk of Poland and Solidarity had been part of the background, too, in the news bulletins – a lot had been happening. In the first days of December, helicopters had landed on the roof of the Fire Officers' Academy in Warsaw, occupied for days by cadets trying to press the government to 'demilitarize' the college. A thousand riot police had stormed the building, evicting them with a brutality worse than at Bydgoszcz. Wałęsa had put the whole union on strike alert, then,

543

but the last thing he'd said, a couple of days ago in Gdańsk, had been: 'We do *not* want confrontation.'

Danuta had listened to most of this in a blur. She had saved and saved, and spent every hour of free time shopping, and packing an enormous parcel to send home for Christmas, sending it off just before the last date. She tried not to think of the reality of Christmas for her parents without her, or of herself, here, probably working, without them. All the Polish girls were planning to spend *Wigilia* together, perhaps going out to a Polish restaurant, or maybe Basia's Frenchman would let her have them back to his Knightsbridge apartment.

'And I'm saving a *lot*,' Danuta had told her mother on the phone last Sunday. 'I'll be able to come home next spring, I'm sure, for a visit, or you could come here, I'll be much more settled by then.'

'Wait and see,' said her mother. 'Don't hope for too much.'

'Do you think – ' she hadn't wanted to ask it. 'Are you all right, Mama? You don't think anything – '

'I don't think anything,' said her mother. 'I just say again – don't hope for too much.'

Since then, Danuta had tried not to think anything, either. She'd phone Mama today, when breakfast was finished: now, she had twelve tables to look after. She heaped brown and white triangles of toast on to a plate; there were baskets of butter and marmalade and mixed fruit jam in little packets with peel-off tops. The men in suits probably saw a lot of those. She covered the plate with a napkin, and made her way to the swing doors.

'*Ra*-dio One! And the latest news, on the half hour. A state of emergency has been declared in Poland. The country's leader, General Jaruzelski, said the country was at the edge of an abyss . . .'

Danuta stood stock still, holding the plate of toast. Then the swing doors were flung open, and one of the English waitresses sang out:

'Egg and bacon twi-ice! And one with beans.'

'Sssh!' said Danuta. 'Listen!'

'You what?'

'The news . . . the news . . .' She began to cry.

'Here, give us the toast . . .'

' . . . It's thought a number of Solidarity leaders have been arrested – and at the moment the whereabouts of the Union's leader, Lech Wałesa, are not known . . .'

'Is it something about Poland, then? Carlo, turn that radio up, will you?'

'All the telephone links with the outside world have been cut off, and within the country itself . . .'

'Oh, my God, I don't believe it. I must try . . . Can you look after my tables . . .'

Danuta pushed through the swing doors, and out into the foyer. She wasn't supposed to use the phone booth on duty, ever, and off duty she wasn't supposed to stay on for more than a few minutes, in case guests needed it. She didn't care. She ran over to the girl on the newspaper desk.

'Please – can you lend me some change, just for a few minutes? For the phone? It's very urgent.'

The girl turned from the rack of postcards. 'How much do you want?'

'A pound or two, in tens. I'll pay you back, but . . .' She was crying so much she couldn't explain about her bag being locked in her room downstairs.

'Here . . .' The girl rang up twenty pence on the till. 'That's for a paper, all right, pay me back, or I'll be short. Are you all right?'

Danuta shook her head. 'Just – the money, please.'

The girl counted out two pounds in tens; Danuta ran across the foyer to the booth by the door. She stood in it, crying and dialling, and waited. A high-pitched single tone. She dialled again. The same, dead, horrible sound. She thought of her parents, waking up to discover the streets full of armed police, not able to phone, worrying about her worrying. She tried once more, then banged down the receiver, and leaned against the side of the phone booth, sobbing. She felt herself begin to panic. Suppose I can never go back. Suppose I never see them again. I should never have come, never. I'll be a skivvy here for the rest of my life, and my parents will die without me.

'Hey, hey, come on, love, what's up?' The girl from the desk was patting her arm. 'Come on, come on.'

'Poland . . . Poland is under martial law. I can't get through, no one can get through, it's all cut off . . .'

'Oh, you poor thing. Come on, let's get away from here, okay, there's people looking . . .' She led Danuta into the Ladies', where she cried and cried.

'Come on, cheer up, it can't be as bad as all that. What's happened exactly?'

'Poland has been taken over, by the military, in the middle of the night, and I might never be able to go back. I want to talk to my mother . . .'

The girl from reception gave her a box of tissues. 'I expect it'll be all right in the end, I'm ever so sorry. I must get back to the desk or they'll kill me, all right? You stay here till you feel better.'

Danuta blew her nose. 'And I must get back to my tables.' She splashed her face with water, and dried it on the roll-on towel. 'Here . . .' She gave the girl the money from the till. 'Thank you.'

'That's all right. See you later, okay?'

They went out into the foyer. In the kitchens, Danuta found the three other Polish girls, just on duty, crying, too. The chef flipped eggs, and regarded them.

'Come on, you lot, you'll have to pull yourselves together, there's twenty-eight breakfasts!'

Danuta, red-eyed, hurried out to the dining room, where the men in suits were waiting for more coffee.

Anna drew back the curtains of the living room and looked out. It was grey and very cold, snow falling lightly on the rooftops, not thick enough to settle. Many of the curtains at the windows of the houses opposite were still drawn; on Sundays almost everyone slept in. In another week there would be Christmas trees in almost every window, lit up from first thing in the morning. Anna was going to buy theirs this week: she knew Jerzy and Elizabeth had their own, but Ewa didn't usually bother, and to have everyone home for *Wigilia* without a tree was unthinkable – especially this year, with the wedding to celebrate. Only another few days. She wondered if Ewa wanted to bring Stefan to the wedding, if she wanted to bring him home for *Wigilia*. She liked Stefan, from their few meetings; it was impossible not to; but to think that he had a wife and child in Warsaw! However – to discuss that, or anything about him with Ewa was impossible. She had tried, once, and seen the familiar, unbreachable expression: I know what I'm doing, and no one is going to stop me – and given up.

Anna went over to the next window, drew back the curtain and looked down the street. Even in winter, Dziadek and Babcia sometimes went to early mass; then walked home slowly along the uneven pavement, arm in arm, but she couldn't see them now, and she hoped they hadn't gone, it was much too cold. She went across the room and lit the fire. Above, on the mantelpiece, among the Christmas cards, was one from Wiktoria, the Solidarność logo cut out and pasted on. In the first, dramatic days of the Polish August last year, she had remembered standing in front of the Katyń memorial, and wondering: where is the spirit of Poland now? There was the answer.

Anna went back to the kitchen, to make tea. Jan was still asleep, after working late: she usually left him to have his one rest of the week like everyone else – for herself, she could never sleep very late, and she liked the quietness of early morning, with no train to catch to work, no shopping to do. She made herself tea and toast, and went to sit by the fire.

'Anna! Anna!'

Babcia was calling, urgently rattling the letter box. Anna got up and hurried out to the hall; she opened the door and saw her frail little mother-in-law white and shaken on the doormat. It's Dziadek, something has happened to Dziadek, she thought at once, and prepared herself.

'You've heard the news?'

'No?' said Anna. 'I've only just got up. What is it?'

'There's been . . . a crisis . . .' Babcia burst into tears. Behind her, Anna could hear the radio, and then Dziadek appeared, pulling open their door very slowly, and standing there, absolutely still.

'They have imposed martial law in Poland,' he said slowly. 'My wife is rather upset.'

He spoke as if to a stranger, and for a moment Anna was so shocked by this that she could not take in what he had said. 'Martial law . . .'

'Warsaw is full of soldiers,' Babcia sobbed. 'The whole country is cut off from the rest of the world – can you imagine? Arrests in the night . . . it is the Gestapo all over again. We must warn Jan . . .'

'Warn Jan . . . Mama, he's here, he's asleep, come on inside, both of you, come in, I'll wake him.'

She led them slowly into the living room, and sat them down by the fire. They were both in their Sunday clothes. She made them tea, went to the cupboard and took out a small bottle of brandy. She poured a good nip into each cup, and took it through.

'Here . . . This'll help.'

They sipped, shaking their heads, moving closer to the fire.

'I never, never really believed that this would happen,' Babcia said. 'It is like hearing of a death. Worse.'

Dziadek said nothing. He sat holding his cup and saucer and staring at the popping gas fire. Anna watched them and thought:

They are two creatures washed up on the shore. She got up and patted their shoulders, kissing Babcia on the cheek.

'I'll go and wake Jan, all right? You stay here. You'll feel better in a little while.'

Babcia nodded uncertainly, and Anna went out and along to the bedroom. And what will become of Stefan now, she wondered. And his poor wife, and my poor daughter. She felt suddenly so angry she wanted to kick the wall, and shout – and then she thought of telling Jan, and wished she could be telling him almost anything but this.

She went into the bedroom, which was still dark. She stood by the bed, seeing him in the crack of light through the curtains so deeply asleep, so tired, in sleep more profoundly lost to her than ever. She thought of how since last summer he had followed the news from Poland, for a while more interested than he had been for years in anything. He had sometimes mocked – Solidarity's demands were endless, their politics naive, the young 'Poles from Poland' over here, like Stefan, were riding on a bandwagon – but he had changed. He still came home late, but he talked when he came home, and he talked to the children when they did. He had come alive.

Anna slowly drew back the curtains, and saw the fine snowflakes whirling wetly on to the railway line. Then she turned back to the bed, and sat on the edge, and gently shook her husband's shoulder.

'Jan? Jan? Wake up.'

He turned, and woke instantly, as if on duty.

'What is it? God, what time is it, Anna?'

'It's just after nine – ssh, I know you wanted to sleep, but – but I'm afraid there's been some bad news. Your parents came in, they heard it on the radio . . .'

Jan sat up, frowning. 'They've invaded. They've invaded.'

'No, no – but almost. The country's under martial law, a take-over in the middle of the night. That's all I know, I haven't heard it.' She put her hand on his arm. 'Your parents are very shaken, I think they're a little better now, your mother was talking about the Gestapo, as if we were all still under the occupation – she wanted to warn you . . .' She was babbling, gabbling, she could hear herself, waiting for the shutters to come down.

The phone began to ring, and she jumped. 'I'd better answer it, the parents aren't in any fit state . . . I'll bring you some tea in a minute.'

'I don't want any.' He lay back on the pillows, and he looked as though someone had drawn a black sheet of silk over his face. Anna watched him, hesitating, and the phone went on ringing.

'I'll come back.'

He didn't answer. She heard the phone being lifted, and Babcia saying hesitantly: '*Słucham?* Jerzy?' and she hurried out of the room, and went to talk to him.

Ewa and Stefan were walking to the Embassy. It was bitterly cold, thin snowflakes settling briefly on their faces as they went quickly under the Christmas lights past the closed shops in Oxford Street, where the models in winter coats and skiing clothes stared out, unsmiling. They had caught an empty train from Blackheath, and walked from Charing Cross along streets which were almost deserted: they passed a figure huddled in a doorway; lit-up buses with a few stray passengers went by, and taxis, speeding.

'Do you want to get one?' asked Ewa. 'I'll pay.'

Stefan shook his head. 'Unless you are very cold? I feel like walking.'

When there were no buses, they could hear their footsteps on the pavement, Ewa in boots from Ravel, Stefan in boots from Poland. They walked arm in arm, their breath coming quickly.

At Oxford Circus they turned right, walking up towards Portland Place.

'Do you remember when we came here, the first evening?' Ewa asked. 'We had to wait to cross, and we realized we were near the embassy.'

Stefan frowned. 'Yes, I think so.' He was looking along the pavement. 'Do you see that?'

A little group of people were standing outside the embassy; there were placards, and black umbrellas. As Ewa and Stefan drew near they saw an elderly man in a hat and heavy coat holding a placard: *Polski Sierpień* – Polish August – 1980–81. From beneath the Solidarność logo rose a fist. There were Solidarność badges, and more placards and posters – Free Poland: Army Out! A cordon had been run round the building. Ewa and Stefan stood at the edge of the group, and waited.

'Can you see anything?' Stefan asked.

Ewa craned her neck towards the unlit windows. 'No.' She turned to the woman next to her. 'Has anyone come out?'

The woman shook her head. 'What do you expect? But I think

there is to be a deputation, from the Polish Solidarity Campaign. Eric Heffer, he is coming, I think.'

They waited, stamping their feet. After a while, journalists and cameramen appeared. Photographs were taken – the elderly man with the placard, a beautiful girl in a headscarf holding another. 'Jerzy should be here,' Ewa said suddenly. 'This is exactly what he should be doing, photographing this.' Someone moved to take a picture of her and Stefan, arm in arm, and Stefan moved abruptly away, putting his hand up to his face.

'What?' she asked. 'Are you really afraid?'

'I just don't want my picture in the paper,' he said, and waved the photographer away. 'No – please.'

A car drew up: heads turned. Two men got out and walked through the crowd; they crossed the cordon, went up to the door, and knocked loudly. 'That's Eric Heffer,' said Ewa to Stefan. 'The great big guy – he's a Labour MP.'

Heffer and the other man knocked again, and peered into the windows on the ground floor. Ewa pressed forward as they turned away, and spoke to the journalists.

'They say they can see people moving about inside,' she told Stefan.

After a while, the two men drove away again.

'What do you want to do?'

'I want to break the fucking door down,' said Stefan. 'Excuse me. I don't know.' He lit a cigarette. 'We can wait a bit longer, I suppose, just to see.'

They waited, and once they saw a face at an upper window, looking down, just for a moment. Then it disappeared, and after that nothing happened.

'Let's go,' said Ewa. 'We can go and have a coffee, or a drink. We can go home and have lunch with my mother, would you like that? She always cooks Sunday lunch, and we can hear the news there . . .'

Stefan shut his eyes. 'I don't know,' he said again. 'Perhaps.' He opened them again. 'You decide. I can't think properly.'

Ewa hesitated. 'Let's . . . let's go and find a pub and have a drink, and take it from there.'

'Sure.' Stefan was pale again; he looked blank and cold. Ewa put her arm through his again.

'Come on.'

They walked back into Oxford Street, and turned to walk the way they had come, crossing into Wardour Street. 'We'll find somewhere along here, or in Soho,' said Ewa. They began to smell Chinese food, wafting on the cold air, and an amusement arcade whined and banged, lights flashing. They passed a little alleyway, with a phone box, and Stefan stopped.

'I have to try again,' he said. 'I know there's no chance, but I have to, okay?'

'All right. Have you got enough change?'

'I think so. Can you wait? Do you mind?'

'No, of course not.'

He lightly brushed the melting snow from her hair. 'I'm sorry – I know it's difficult . . . Wait here, okay?'

She stood on the corner of the alleyway, and watched him walk to the phone box, feeling in his pocket for change. I love his back, she thought; I love the way he walks. I love him, I love him. What are we going to do? People were hurrying past the alleyway, on their way to a Chinese lunch, or Christmas shopping in Chinatown. Ewa stood huddled into her coat, feeling her feet aching with cold; she paced up and down, and waited, watching Stefan in the call box dial and dial and dial.

Suddenly he turned and flung back the door, coming out shouting. 'Bastards! Fucking miserable bastards.' The door swung to, and he began to kick it, in a frenzy. He flung himself against it, pounding on the glass, kicking and swearing. Ewa had never seen Stefan angry, barely even irritated; she stood for a moment, frozen. Then she ran down the alleyway towards him.

'Stop it! Stop it!'

'Bastards! Pigs!' He drew back and flung himself on the door again, beating it so hard with his fist she thought he would break the glass, or break his fingers.

'Stefan!' She grabbed him, trying to pull him away. 'Stefan, please . . .'

He began to cry, covering his face with his hands. 'I can't get through, I can't get through. My poor Krysia! What have I done, what the hell have I done?'

Ewa drew back. 'I love you,' she said helplessly, knowing that this was the last of last moments she should be telling him. 'I love you. I'll try to help you – '

Stefan went on sobbing, kicking the box again. 'I'm sorry, Ewa, forgive me, forgive me, it's not you. I just want to go home, do you understand?'

'Yes,' she said bleakly. 'I understand.'

*

They had lunch in Chinatown because to face the family seemed impossible. Stefan was calmer, and better after they had eaten, but he said simply: 'I don't know what to do,' and because there was nothing he could do, they wandered, past the open supermarkets selling noodles, soy sauce, tins of water chestnuts, thin china bowls and plastic chopsticks. After a while, they walked back to Charing Cross. Carol singers in the concourse rattled tins for the blind. None of the newspapers on the stall had headlines about Poland yet. Travelling on the stuffy train back to Blackheath, over the Thames where the fine snow fell on to the riverboats, it was as if nothing had happened at all.

Back at the house, they found Jane decorating the tree in the hall. They could smell mince pies from the kitchen, and hear an old movie on the television in the sitting room. Through the open door they glimpsed the boys, sprawled on the sofa, and Stuart, reading the paper by the fire.

Jane smiled at them as they went towards the stairs. 'Would you like to come and have a drink with us, tonight?'

'Oh – ' Ewa hesitated, looking at Stefan. From the sitting room they could hear Stuart calling:

'Is that them?' Then he got up, and came out. 'Sorry to hear the news,' he said. 'Must be a bit of a shock for you both.'

Stefan shrugged, half-smiling. 'They are bastards,' he said, in his slow English. 'Excuse me.'

'Come and have a drink,' Jane said again. 'Do. We never see you, Ewa, or – Stefan? Is that right?'

He nodded, holding out his hand. For a flicker, Ewa felt she should be saying: 'You don't mind him staying here, do you?' as if she were an au pair, or something, not a grown-up who had purchased her own flat. Then they were all shaking hands, and she and Stefan agreeing to come down about six, for a drink.

Upstairs, she switched on the lights, lit the fire, quickly, and went into the kitchen to make coffee, hearing him pick up the telephone again, and dial, and put it down again, defeatedly. They drank their coffee, and watched the old movie, too, and Ewa rang Jerzy, and got Elizabeth, who said that he was very low.

'I'm not sure this is the right time to have a wedding,' she said lightly.

'Oh?' But Ewa didn't ask more. 'Can you tell Jerzy to ring me when he feels like it?'

'All right. How's Stefan?'

'Much as you would expect,' said Ewa, and said goodbye. She didn't ring her mother, because she thought she would start crying, but Mama rang her anyway, and she forced herself not to, talking in monosyllables. Stefan paced, smoking. Before they went down, they switched on the television again, for the early evening news, where Michael Buerk's voice could be heard, behind his photograph.

'Warsaw tonight has been sealed off by troops. Scores of armoured personnel carriers are patrolling the roads, the soldiers inside carrying automatic weapons with fixed bayonets. Hundreds of police with riot shields and truncheons ring important buildings. Strict censorship has been imposed. There's a curfew. Anybody breaking the emergency regulations, according to the new "military council for national salvation", will be shot. During the night all Solidarity's offices were raided, its leaders and officials under arrest. All except one . . .'
Wałęsa's picture flashed on to the screen.

' . . . Lech Wałęsa, who's said to have avoided immediate imprisonment, by agreeing to "negotiate" with the government.

'Poland's Prime Minister, General Jaruzelski'
– flash to his photograph, in uniform and the inexplicable dark glasses –

'in his message to the Polish people, said "Our country is on the edge of an abyss. We are not days, but hours away from catastrophe." '

Ewa reached out to Stefan, and took his hand. He squeezed it, then took it away, and lit another cigarette. She got up, and went to the bathroom, brushing her hair, doing her face, spraying on scent. She did these things because that was what you did, before you went to parties, but she was scarcely aware of doing any of them.

While she was gone, Stefan sat watching the second lead item, about a car bomb explosion in the West End today. How had that happened, and they knew nothing about it? Then he got up and switched off the television, and stood by the fire, smoking. He thought about Krysia, who did not even have a proper address for him in London, just a pigeon hole in a post office. He had sent her and Olek, and the parents, a Christmas parcel two weeks ago, with the snowsuit in it: would it ever reach her now? He tried to imagine her, watching Jaruzelski on the television in their apartment, holding Olek on her lap, and crying, and he realized that thinking of Poland now was as if he were watching a film whose sound track had been ripped out without warning, leaving only silently mouthing figures, trapped in silent apartments, silently arrested and interned, or

553

walking through silent, snow-filled streets, past soundless men with bayonets. He closed his eyes, thinking again: What have I done?

Then Ewa was back in the room, lightly touching his arm and asking gently: 'Are you all right?'

He opened his eyes, and nodded. 'Sure. Should we go down now?'

'If you're really up to it.'

'Sure,' he said again. 'They're nice people, aren't they?'

'Very nice,' said Ewa, as if she were speaking to a stranger, and they went out of the flat and down the stairs, for drinks and mince pies.

Sunday 20 December

The afternoon was cold and damp. Drizzle clung to the winter coats and anoraks of the crowds making their way across Park Lane and over the muddy grass in Hyde Park, towards the raised platform of the Polish Solidarity Campaign. Jostled along the underpass from the tube station, Anna and Jan found themselves met by a forest of hands giving out leaflets and magazines.

Anna looked at a copy of *Socialist Worker*, thrust at her by a young man in a donkey jacket.

'What is this?'

'It doesn't have to be like it is in Poland,' he said. 'Take it – go on, please take it.'

Anna hesitated, aware of Jan, dark-faced, beside her.

'What does he say?'

'That . . .' she faltered. 'I think he means that what has happened in Poland is not the true socialism . . .'

Jan looked the boy in the donkey jacket up and down. 'You know nothing,' he said in slow English. 'Nothing.' He strode off towards the steps, and Anna hurried after him.

Behind them, Ewa, arm in arm with Stefan, was calling: 'Wait for us!'

When they came up through the exit by the park, they saw at once that already it would be hard to get anywhere near the platform.

'But there are thousands,' said Stefan, alongside Anna.

'Did you think no one cared?' she asked. 'Didn't you think there would be thousands here?'

He shook his head, bemused, reaching for his cigarettes. 'I don't know . . . the last time I was in a crowd like this was . . . when? Waiting to hear that Solidarność had been registered? I think so. Incredible to see all these people now.'

Anna looked at his pale face, filmed with sweat. Ever since last weekend, he'd had a permanent air of confusion. Beside him, Ewa looked tense, protective, gloved hand slipped through his arm. Stefan was probably about the same age as the *Socialist Worker* fellow – Anna wanted to ask him what he thought about . . . all that, but she didn't want to distract him any more, and anyway, Jan . . .

Jan looked grim. As they walked slowly with the crowd towards the platform, she said carefully: 'I'm glad you've come. I think Stefan is a little overwhelmed.'

He shrugged.

Damp grey mist clung to the bare trees on the edge of the park; Anna slipped suddenly in the mud, and reached for Jan's arm, automatically. He did not ask if she was all right, he did not take her arm; he simply stood, like a dead thing, waiting until she had recovered her balance. Then they walked on, separately.

The megaphone on the platform was being tested: hollow shouting echoed over the crowd. After a while, Ewa said: 'Mama? Let's stop, shall we? We can hear.'

'All right.' They came to a halt next to a little group of two or three families, the men in heavy coats and fur hats, the women in hats. The air was full of Polish voices, but there were plenty of English ones, too – how many were there here? Ten thousand? Fifteen thousand? Clouds of breath streamed out on to the air. Beside her, Anna could hear Ewa trying to identify for Stefan some of the people up on the distant platform. Shirley Williams . . . Peter Shore . . . Lord Bethell . . . E. P. Thompson . . .

A dark man had taken the microphone and announced himself as Tadek Jarski, chairing the platform: the speakers were to have five minutes each.

Then the speeches began: passionate declarations of allegiance, passionate pleas that Poland should not once again, as at Yalta, be abandoned by the British, that British trade unions should show real, practical solidarity with Solidarity. Food aid was to be sent through the Church. Piotr Iglikowski, Secretary of the Polish Solidarity Campaign, described how he had been in Poland last week, at the time of the coup; he spoke of the fascist-style terror, and of how he only just managed to get out before the borders were closed.

Collection tins rattled. 'Medical Aid for Poland . . . Medical Aid for Poland . . .' The collectors were moving through the crowd; everyone was feeling in pockets, getting out purses. 'Thank you, thank you . . .' On the lapels of the dark winter coats and anoraks, in the greyness of the winter afternoon, the white and red Solidarność badge shone. PSC leaflets were being passed out everywhere.

Anna's feet were getting cold. Dziadek and Babcia had talked after mass this morning about coming here, but she was glad they hadn't – it would have been far too much for them. There was to be a march, soon, down Oxford Street, and up to the Embassy. She turned to look at Jan, standing impassively. Ewa and Stefan had their arms round each other; Anna felt suddenly so lonely, and so sad, that she thought she was going to cry. I wish Jerzy had come, she thought. I know he's unhappy, but even so . . .

The wedding had been cancelled within days of martial law, and it had been Elizabeth who rang, and told her.

'Jerzy doesn't feel he can celebrate anything at the moment,' she said lightly. 'It's better we postpone it, just until he's feeling better.'

'Are you very upset?'

'No, no, it's all right. What about you, Anna? This must have been a shock – to all of you. How are the grandparents? How is your husband?'

'The grandparents spend all day watching the news. My husband – well, he is very angry, and frustrated . . .'

He doesn't know what to do with himself. I had to force him to come here, to try to make him see that people are fighting, that you don't have to be alone. But he is . . . unreachable.

'Mama? Are you coming on the march?'

'What – oh yes. Yes, my feet are frozen, I need to walk.'

'What about Tata?'

Anna shook her head. 'You ask him.'

Ewa hesitated.

'Oh, go on!' Anna snapped. 'I can't do everything.'

Ewa frowned. Then she leaned forward, and kissed her. 'Of course you can. You're my *Mamusia*, my little Mummy.'

Anna smiled, and patted her cold cheek. 'Thank you, darling. You're a good girl.'

'No, I'm not. You know I'm not.'

'Well . . .'

Around them people were turning, beginning to make their way back towards the park gates.

'Come on.' Ewa moved over to Jan. 'Tata? Are you coming with us? To the Embassy?'

'To the Embassy . . .' Jan said slowly.

'Tata! Wake up! They're delivering a petition.'

Jan looked at her. Ewa looked at Anna. Anna moved quickly towards him.

'Jan? What is it? Are you ill?'

With the same, half-dead slowness, he shook his head. 'No. No. Just . . . I want to be by myself for a while. I've had enough.'

'All right.' She wanted to say: I'll come with you, I'll be with you, let me look after you. She said: 'We'll see you back at home, then.'

'All right. Or – I might go back to work for a bit.'

'Tata!' Ewa said again. 'For heaven's *sake*. Don't go back to work, go home. Have a rest, you look terrible.'

He nodded distantly, and then the crowd round them was so large that they all had to turn round and walk with them to the open iron gates and out on to Park Lane. Ahead, a great long river of people, with banners held high way up at the front, was moving, flanked by police, towards Marble Arch.

Anna took Jan's hand. 'See you soon.'

'Yes.' He dropped her hand, nodded to Ewa and Stefan, and walked away from them, down into the underpass.

Ewa put her other arm through Anna's. 'Come on, Mama. Don't let him upset you.'

Anna's eyes filled with tears. 'I wish . . . I wish . . .'

Stefan coughed, and lit a cigarette.

Then they all followed the endless river of people. There was no shouting, no chanting, not even for the television cameras mounted high up on the buildings at Oxford Circus.

'It must be the quietest demonstration in London for years,' said Ewa.

A petition was to be delivered at the Embassy, demanding the release of the detainees – four thousand people arrested and interned. The petition demanded an end to martial law, and the restoration of trade union rights, according to the Gdańsk Agreements.

It took almost an hour to walk the mile or so to the Embassy; on the way, they passed a little group of people, waiting in the cold with placards: 'Czechs support the Poles!' Ewa remembered, suddenly, the long-ago summer afternoon when she had watched the Russian tanks moving into Prague, and she looked at Stefan, and looked away.

By the time they all got near the Embassy, and found the streets cordoned off by police, the petition had long since been coldly refused. Those who presented it were told by the officials who appeared at the door, for just a few minutes, that the 'state of war' had been declared in order to prevent a coup by Solidarity.

In a mine near Katowice, in western Poland, thirteen hundred miners were refusing to come to the surface until martial law was lifted, and the interned Solidarity leaders freed. They had been down there for a week, supplied at first with food by their families and supporters; now, the police had stopped all that. Four days ago, seven striking miners, at the pit head of another colliery nearby, armed with crowbars and pickaxes, had been shot by the police, in 'self-defence'. It was freezing cold down the occupied mine, the men huddling together at night, but they weren't coming up.

Elizabeth, in her studio, with the radio on all day, heard about the occupation at Katowice almost every hour. At first she had stood listening, imagining the darkness, the cold, the wives talking to the men down the pit telephone, the circle of police at the top of the shafts, waiting. Now she was aware of it as a background, much as individual killings over months in Northern Ireland blurred into a single death: a nineteen-year-old private from Glasgow; or a man in his forties, with a wife and two children, driving along a country road home after visiting his brother, stopped, dragged out, murdered, his body left in the long grass on the verge. They had become archetypes. Elizabeth switched back and forth between Radio Three and Radio Four, filling the studio with the news, the *World at One*, concerts from Manchester, the afternoon play, carols, *The Archers*, Bach and Haydn. She took in hardly any of it.

Yesterday, she and Jerzy had been going to get married.

Today, she had left the house when he was still asleep, when it was still dark. Tonight, she supposed she was going back there.

The wedding had been called off in a very low key. It had, after all, been only a quiet one planned – her parents and family down, meeting all Jerzy's family in the register office, and Stefan, perhaps, and Delia, who rented out the studio. It was intended to be small, but a celebration, nonetheless, going out for a meal afterwards, and a honeymoon planned for New Year.

'How can we celebrate anything?' Jerzy had asked, on the night of the thirteenth. In Poland they were calling it not martial law, nor a state of emergency, but *stan wojenny* – state of war. Jerzy was in his own state of war, restless and withdrawn, suffering from nightmares. Fifteen thousand people had attended a rally in Hyde Park today, and marched to the Polish Embassy. Anna had gone, and Ewa, and

Stefan. Even Jan was there. Why hadn't Jerzy gone? She would have gone with him. He wouldn't talk to her, so she came down here and painted, half-listening to the radio.

She was painting a sickbed, it made her feel as if she were living a hundred years ago. She had sketched in a child, half-propped up against the pillows, her eyes closed. The room was very dark – you were to see the curtained windows, and fire, and a woman moving towards the bed, holding a glass. By the bed was a table, and on the table a night-light burned.

Elizabeth had never been close to anyone who had died. But there had been, years ago, the sitter at art school, the woman whose portrait they had all wanted to paint, and who had died of cancer. Elizabeth had known for a long time that the woman was ill, she had been expecting to hear of her death – but still, when she did hear the shock was as great as if she had been run over by a bus. It was as if a night-light had been burning very dimly for a long time, getting lower and lower, the wax almost gone – when at last, in a single moment, it went out, you realized that what you had thought of as darkness had been lit up, always. Now, there was nothing.

Elizabeth knew the night-light in the painting was going to go out, and that the little girl was going to die. She was painting it because of what had happened in Poland, whose life seemed as if it were always going to be bound up with Jerzy's, and therefore hers. They had all known that something terrible was going to happen – and still, when it came, the shock was as great as a death. You could never, really, prepare yourself for a death.

Outside the studio windows it had been dark for a long time. The concert on Radio Three came to an end, and the quiet voice of the announcer began to speak. Elizabeth looked at her watch and found it was after six. She was hungry, nothing but coffee and cheese all day; she wanted to go home and find Jerzy recovering, the fire on and the table laid for supper. She packed up her paints and brushes, pulled on her coat and turned out the lights, calling goodbye to Delia as she went down the stairs.

Delia appeared in her upstairs sitting room doorway, dark hair done up in a knot, earrings swinging. 'Come and have a drink.'

'I ought to get back.'

'Oh, for God's sake. It's almost Christmas, forget about the Poles for a minute and have a drink. I've been wrapping presents all afternoon while the kids are out, I need a bit of sanity.'

Elizabeth took off her coat and went into the sitting room. There was a pile of exquisitely wrapped presents on the table, and the room was very warm, all faded pink sofas and beige carpet, and prints and oils by friends on the walls. The kids weren't really allowed in here.

'Where are they?' asked Elizabeth, watching Delia pour out whisky.

'With their father, having a pre-Christmas treat before he abandons us all for the south of France and his new lady.'

'You didn't tell me there was a new lady.'

'There's always a new lady. Here.' Delia passed her a cut-glass tumbler and flopped on to the sofa. 'Cheers. Happy Christmas. What are you painting?'

Elizabeth hesitated.

'That means it's something dark and meaningful. Don't tell me, I don't want to hear. How's Jerzy? Do I want to hear how he is? Are you feeling bloody?'

Elizabeth drank. 'Not as bloody as I was, thanks. Cheers.'

'Are you going to leave him?'

'Delia . . . No, of course not.'

'Why?'

'How can I?'

'Well, I don't mean just before Christmas.'

'Christmas hasn't got anything to do with it. I don't want to leave him.'

'In spite of everything, you love him still.' Delia had lit a cigarette; she described an elaborate gesture with it in the air.

'Yes, I suppose that's just sentimental nonsense to a hardened cynic like you.'

'You mean crap. On the contrary, I find it deeply touching.' She took another puff and eyed Elizabeth. 'And what about Ewa? Isn't her lover from Poland? What's going to happen to them?'

Elizabeth sipped her whisky. 'I don't know. You know he's married.'

'The nice ones always are.'

'Well – I expect they're going through hell. It isn't really so funny, Delia.'

'Don't be so bloody pi, I never said it was. It's all highly . . . operatic. Have another.'

'No, thanks.'

'Cow.'

Elizabeth got up. 'Have you been drinking all afternoon?'

'I can't remember, Probably. Oh, well, off you go, darling. Will you be dropping in on us again before Christmas?'

Elizabeth pulled on her coat and bent down to kiss her. 'You know I will. Who else brings me down to earth like you?'

'There's plenty of us about,' said Delia. 'Christmas is full of us. Oh, well, bugger off then, the kids'll be back any minute anyway, I must be turning my mind to din-dins. Any ideas?'

'Not really,' said Elizabeth, 'but I'm starving. Thanks for the drink.'

'Any time.'

'Bye.'

'Bye.'

She ran down the stairs and out into the street, pulling out her woolly hat from her pocket, pulling on her gloves. She hurried to the main road, looking for a bus, but there wasn't one, so she walked, very fast, thinking about Delia, and her divorce, and Christmas with the kids. She turned into their street, and found herself thinking of the night Danuta had come to supper. She must be dreading Christmas now, too. They ought to ring her. Then she remembered standing at the window of their flat, watching for her and Jerzy, walking together down the road to the station, and found herself wondering, as she had briefly wondered then.

She reached their front door, and pulled out her key, fumbling with it in her woollen gloves. The hall was unlit. She felt for the time switch and went quickly upstairs. What had Jerzy been doing all day, without her? At the top, she unlocked their own front door, and opened it on to darkness.

'Jerzy?'

There was no answer.

'Jerzy!' She switched on the hall light, and felt how cold the flat was. She went to the bedroom, found the curtains drawn, with a look about them as if they hadn't been pulled back all day, and the bed unmade. She went to the sitting room, still calling.

The lights were off, the curtains drawn, she could see that from the hall light. Jerzy was sitting in an armchair by the unlit fire, wrapped in a blanket.

'Jerzy!'

'What?' he said flatly, and did not look up.

Elizabeth almost hit him. 'What do you mean, "what"? Didn't you hear me calling you? Of course you did.'

He shrugged.

'What's the matter?'

He shook his head.

Elizabeth crossed the room, and lit the fire, shivering. 'You gave me a terrible fright,' she said angrily. 'What are you playing at? I thought something – something had happened.'

'Well it hasn't. I just feel bloody awful, that's all. Don't you ever feel bloody awful?'

Elizabeth sat by the fire in her coat and closed her eyes. I can't live with this any more, she thought. I just can't, and that's all there is to it. She knew, then, that the best thing was to say nothing, but she was so angry, and so hungry, and Delia's mocking tone was still ringing in her ears, and she said:

'How do you think Stefan is feeling now? Don't you think that perhaps he has just a tiny bit more right to indulge in all this melancholia and self-pity?'

'Don't preach! I do not want to have a bloody sermon.'

'Why didn't you answer me? Why? Didn't you think for even a minute of what I might be thinking?'

'I didn't answer because I knew you were going to come in here and preach.'

'Oh, my God.' Elizabeth got up, and went out to the kitchen. Still in her coat, because the kitchen was always cold, she lit the oven, and turned it up to 9 and left the door open. She banged furiously in drawers and cupboards, and threw together a meal of sweet corn and scrambled eggs on toast and coffee. She ate it alone at the kitchen table, reading yesterday's paper, and then she went to run a bath, and make the bed, and fill a hot-water bottle. She lay in the bath, waiting for Jerzy to come in from the sitting room and say he was sorry, and make it up, but he didn't come, and she went to bed alone and fell asleep almost at once.

In the light from the platform, in the lights along the track, the rails gleamed, wet with frost melted by the last train, already beginning to freeze again, crystals glistening. In the watery yellow lakes of light along the embankment he could see stiff grass and weeds, rime-encrusted, winter's graveyard, then darkness. His breath streamed into the cold as he paced up and down, past the damp wooden seats, the posters, the graffiti.

In Warsaw, in Gdańsk, in Kraków and Bydgoszcz, in cities and obscure small towns all over Poland, they were creeping out at night with hoarded paint, and secretly printed, thin posters, as they had done in the war. Then, they had scrawled an anchor out of the letters PW – ⚓ – you could do that at lightning speed and run, leaving the message: *Polska Walcząca*. Fighting Poland. Now, the anchor swung from beneath the S of Solidarność. To chalk or paint that on a street corner wall, to scribble swiftly: Winter is yours, spring will be ours – just to do that, they were risking everything.

Here, there was nothing to risk, no freedom to lose or fight for, and they played with aerosols, spraying the wall with obscenities, the phone numbers of prostitutes. No – sometimes there was something else, another two letters: NF. Once, a swastika. He had tried to cross that out, but it was done in thick black spray, and was impossible. Let it stay – let them find out here what it was like to live in an occupied country, to wake to find the phone lines cut, hear of arrests in the night, see from your window the tanks, crawling down the street.

He was at the foot of the steps leading up to the bridge, the ticket office and the Christmas lights in the shop windows beyond, and he heard voices. He turned abruptly, walked for the hundredth time back towards the end of the platform, and the warning: Passengers Must Not Go Beyond This Point. The last train of the evening was due in a few minutes: then they would close the barrier at the top of the steps, and no one else would come down.

He had been here for perhaps an hour. The raw air had seeped into his shoes, his coat and gloves; his feet and his face were almost numb, and he was glad. Over there, they had been herded into camps by the thousand; they stood stamping frantically in the snow, interned like criminals, like cattle, all the energy and hope of the summer of 1980 crushed and spat upon. Why should he be spared?

The line hummed, and he heard behind him the rattle of the southbound train. More footsteps came pounding down the steps, doors slammed, the train moved slowly past him and swung, carriage by carriage, into the distance. The last alighted passenger walked away; on the bridge, someone was drunkenly singing 'Jingle Bells'. Then there was only the sound of the traffic, and no voices. He stood looking along the gleaming rails, and saw again the thousands of figures, stamping behind snow-covered barbed wire, and himself outside it, free, undeserving of freedom, belonging neither with them, in a doomed country, nor here, in a country of exile.

Above him the barrier creaked, and was slammed shut. The neon strips over the platform flickered and went out; then the light in the ticket office. A few stinging flakes of snow began to fall into the blackness – it did not feel as if it were going to be a generous fall, but perhaps, by tomorrow, the heath would be blanketed. He walked slowly along the platform, hearing his own steps as if, already, they did not matter, or were made by someone else who did not matter, and he made out the telegraph pole, and the outline of the notice. When he reached it, he used it to hold on to for a moment, to feel his way on to the slope of concrete leading down. It was only a short slope, and then he could feel gravel and frozen earth, before he stumbled over the first rail, and out on to the track.

Stefan? No.
Jerzy? No.
Jan.

For a while he just picked his way over the cold concrete sleepers between the first two rails. Within yards of leaving the platform, the track was lit only intermittently, by the street lamps and houses in the roads running between South Hampstead and Gospel Oak; he could hear himself panting, as he negotiated each sleeper, as if he were afraid, though he didn't feel afraid, not out here. He felt driven. Beside him, the electrified rail stretched out like an uncoiled snake, a companion, ready for him when he chose. He didn't choose yet. He stopped and felt in his pocket for his cigarettes and lit one, the tiny flame of the lighter very bright. He snapped it shut, and stood smoking, and went slowly on.

After the rally, unable to bear his wife and daughter watching him, worrying about him, any longer: unable to stand Stefan, the Pole from Poland who was sleeping with his daughter, observing him, baffled; unable to bear his own feelings, or to be among the crowd, with anyone, any longer, he had gone down into the tube and found a press of people queuing up at the ticket machines, pouring on to the platforms. He almost turned back, then, but there were people everywhere, above, below. He bought a fifty-pence ticket, just to get through the barrier, and walked blindly in the crush to a platform, he didn't notice which.

He thought: I don't have to go home, I don't have to go to the office, I don't have to go anywhere. But he had to go somewhere. He thought: I have no one to talk to, not without frightening them, or seeing them pity me. He caught the first train that came into the platform.

He stood in a smoker, jammed up against the handrail, dozens of people all round him, as the train moved into the tunnel. It was very hot, the heating on full blast, and airless, and the train moved slowly, creaking. Everyone was talking about the rally: why weren't they all on the march? He strained to hear a Polish voice, and could not.

At Bond Street, more got on, forcing him back and away from the doors. If he wanted to get out now in a hurry, he couldn't. He began to sweat. At Oxford Circus the doors could hardly open for the people already in the carriage: on the platform, another wave surged forward, pushing and elbowing – people who'd already been to the Embassy, perhaps, and who now were going home. Jan coughed thickly, feeling for his cigarettes, just to be sure. The train moved off again, even more slowly; it felt as if it were being dragged down by the weight of all the passengers, too many, far too many; if there were an accident, or if for some reason they simply had to stop . . .

Jan had not been on the tube for over twenty years.

The carriage swayed, creaking. The carriage lights flickered, briefly, once, then again. The train went still more slowly, and then it stopped, juddering.

For a minute or two, it was as if no one had noticed. People went on talking, awkwardly turning the pages of the Sunday papers in the crush. Gradually, the talking stopped. Throats were cleared. The lights in the carriage flickered again, and for a terrifying second went out altogether. Then they were on again, dimly.

Jan felt sweat pour down him.

'Excuse me . . .' He pushed and shoved his way towards the windows, leaning across the people sitting down, fumbling with the catch. Further along, a woman was trying to do the same.

'Mind out, mate,' said the man below him.

'Excuse me . . .' He pulled and tugged, and at last got it free, and slammed the upper window down. A pitiful waft of stale air came in and was lost among the smoke, the breathing passengers. Jan was panting. He leaned right over the people sitting before him, whose knees were pressed into his and peered through the open gap, trying to see anything, up ahead.

Distantly, a red light glowed.

Then it was just a signal. Thank Christ. They'd be moving again in a minute.

Unless it had failed. If there was a signal failure, they could be down here another half hour, another hour.

He got out his cigarettes and lit one, quickly.

'Hey!'

'Not now, mate.'

'For God's sake put it out.' That was the woman, further down, her voice rising as he felt his voice would rise, hysterically, if he tried to speak. He took a long, frantic puff, and dropped the butt, stubbing it out. He thought: I was half-mad before I came down here. If we don't move soon . . .

The train creaked, and stumbled forward. They were moving, they were moving. Jan felt his whole body tremble as the train gathered speed, and then it slowed again, and drew into Tottenham Court Road station. The doors opened, and Jan pushed his way through and out on to the platform. He moved quickly through the passengers waiting there, and almost ran up the stairs and out of the station to the blessed freedom of the open air.

For a while he just stood there, by the news stand, as the crowds milled round Macdonald's, opposite, brightly lit. Then he crossed over, and stood at the bus stop, waiting for the number 24, which would take him to South Hampstead, and to Jerzy and Elizabeth, who had not got married yesterday. When the bus came, he climbed to the top deck, and sat smoking as they stopped and started in the traffic, and the winter afternoon light in Camden Town began to fade. I'll go and see my son, he thought, I never see him.

But when the bus eventually stopped at the terminus beneath the trees of South End Green, and he climbed down the stairs and got off, he knew at once that he wouldn't. He couldn't. He paced up and down beneath the trees, and depression gnawed at his stomach like a rat, as it had for years.

Across the road from the trees was a café, but that was closed. There was a row of brightly lit little shops, also closed, with Christmas decorations and snow sprayed on to the window panes. There was a pub, and that was open. He went in and had a whisky, and then another, but he wasn't used to it and he didn't want to get drunk. He wanted to die.

A winking fruit machine thumped and rattled; he sat and watched a couple collect a shower of ten-pence pieces. Across the bar a television hung on the wall was roaring; the bar was strung with Christmas cards and fairy lights, with a plastic Father Christmas in the middle. Jan finished his drink and got up and went outside. He stood wondering where to go next, heard the banging doors of a railway carriage, and knew. The tube was out of the question, for every reason. An empty railway track was fine. He walked to the station and bought a ticket to Gospel Oak because it was the nearest and the only name he could remember anyway. Then he went down, and waited . . .

He finished his cigarette, and found he was near another bridge. For a moment he hesitated; it was absolutely dark under there. He didn't want to slip and fall, he wanted to know exactly what he was doing. He felt in his pocket again, brought out the lighter, and snapped it on. It shone like a little life, as he went carefully over the sleepers under the bridge.

'I said pass on the fucking candle!' It was snatched away from him, and went out. He could hear himself panting hard again as he came out and realized like an animal, from the smell of cold grass and earth, that on the left the track was now running right next to the heath. A few lights from the upper windows of houses on the long road on the right were just enough to see by, but the snow was beginning to fall more thickly. He brushed flakes off his face, stood still, and made out the distance between here and the third rail. He only had to take a few steps. He only had to bend down and touch it. He stepped forward, and stopped. He took off his gloves, and lifted his foot, to cross the second rail, and almost overbalanced, and heard himself shout. He stumbled back, and stood between the two safe rails, shaking. The snow whirled.

He put his head in his hands and howled.

There was a bell ringing somewhere. It pierced Elizabeth's sleep like an arrow, and she woke, or rather half-woke, and listened. She heard the sitting room door open, and Jerzy go to the front door of the flat, and she knew without opening her eyes that it was very late. Flat 2 are locked out again, she thought, or half-thought, and turned over and fell deeply asleep again, very warm.

'Elizabeth! Wake up! Elizabeth!'

She rolled over and opened her eyes. Jerzy had switched on the bedside lamp and was leaning over her. He looked tense, almost panicky.

'What? What is it?'

'My father's here.'

'Your *father?* What? It's the middle of the night.' She sat up, and peered at the clock: it was after one. 'I don't understand.'

'He's in the sitting room. Something's happened to him, he looks terrible, but I don't know what to do with him. He's just – here.'

Elizabeth got out of bed and put on her dressing gown and followed Jerzy to the sitting room. Jan was standing in his coat in front of the fire, his face deathly white, and even from here she could feel how cold he was.

'Jan?' She went quickly over to him and touched his arm. His coat was wet from melted snow, smelling of raw air. 'What's happened? What's happened to you?'

He shook his head, staring at the fire.

'Get him a drink,' she said to Jerzy. 'A brandy, there's some in the kitchen, I'm sure there is.' She led Jan slowly to the chair by the fire and sat him down. Jerzy came back with a bottle of brandy and a glass; he poured out a drink, his hand shaking.

'Here you are, Tata.'

Jan took it, and drank. 'Thank you. Please forgive me, I – ' He broke off, and took another sip. He lit a cigarette.

'You don't have to talk,' Jerzy said, awkwardly. 'You can just stay here and sleep. We can make up a bed on the sofa for you.' He turned to Elizabeth. 'Can't we?'

'Of course.' She went to the door. 'I'll get some bedclothes.'

She went to the kitchen and put on the kettle for another hot-water bottle, and in the bedroom she pulled out sheets, a pillowcase, blankets and an old eiderdown from the cupboard. She found a pair of Jerzy's pyjamas, and she took the whole pile back to the sitting room, where she found Jerzy on the floor, on the opposite side of the fire from Jan, hugging his knees. He looked very young; because he was so thin you might have thought from the back that he was still in his teens, just sitting with his father in the evening. There was only one lamp on; the room looked warm and friendly.

Jan coughed; Jerzy jumped.

Elizabeth put down the pile of bedding on the sofa, and went to fill the hot-water bottle. She stood for a moment looking across the kitchen table at the black, uncurtained windows, where snow was falling. In the daytime and early evening you could hear the trains go past the heath from here, it was one of the reasons Jerzy had liked this flat, and they didn't run too late, so she didn't mind. She thought suddenly: How on earth did Jan get here? And then: I wonder if I do know what happened, and she sat down quickly.

When she went back into the sitting room again, she found that Jerzy had made up the bed on the sofa. Jan was still by the fire, still in his coat, and Jerzy was on the floor again, but next to him now. Elizabeth slipped the bottle between the sheets, and picked up the brandy.

'I'm going to have one,' she said. 'I think I need it. Jan? Do you want another? Jerzy?'

They all sat drinking round the fire.

'Have you eaten, Jan?' Elizabeth asked. 'Can I get you anything?'

'No, no thank you. I don't want anything.' The colour was back in his face; he stood up, and took off the heavy damp coat. Jerzy took it from him, and went to hang it in the hall. Elizabeth and Jan looked at each other, and looked away. When Jerzy came back, Jan said to him, very slowly:

'I tried to kill myself tonight, but I didn't have the courage.'

Jerzy stared at him.

Jan held out his hand, and Jerzy hesitated, then came and took it. There was silence. Ash from Jan's cigarette fell on to the carpet. After a while Jerzy took his hand away, and they both just stood there.

'Jan? Would you like to go to bed now?' Elizabeth asked carefully. 'We can talk in the morning.'

He nodded, looking utterly drained. They left him to undress.

In the kitchen, Jerzy began to cry.

'I can't believe it, I can't believe it.' He put his arms round Elizabeth and held her. 'Do you forgive me?'

'Yes. Yes.' She stroked his hair.

When he had stopped, they switched off the kitchen light, and then he went out to the sitting room door and knocked. There was no answer. He pushed the door open and went inside. Jan was in the made-up bed, asleep. Jerzy went over and turned out the fire. He bent and kissed his father on the forehead, and then he switched out the lamp and came out. He and Elizabeth went back to bed, and fell asleep in each other's arms.

Perhaps an hour later, the telephone rang and rang. Jerzy stumbled out of bed. Lying there, listening, Elizabeth heard him push open the sitting room door, and mutter: 'It's all right, Tata, stay there.'

She heard him pick up the ringing phone and say, automatically, for who else but the family would be ringing in the middle of the night: '*Słucham?*' And then, his voice croaking with sleep: 'No, no, it's all right, Mama, he's here, he's fine.'

Monday 21 December

It was late morning, as cold as yesterday; last night's snow had not settled but melted, soon after first light, leaving the grass wet, and drops of water clinging to every bare branch of the trees. Pale cloud hung above the heath, where a handful of people were out walking – people with dogs, mothers with children on the first day of the Christmas holidays, watching them run up and down the sloping path to the hill where the kite flyers came.

'Race you to the bottom – come on!'

'No – no, wait! *Wait!*'

Jerzy and Jan were walking up the path in silence. Jerzy's camera bumped against his chest. Jan was smoking; every now and then he coughed. After a while he dropped the cigarette and stubbed it out with his heel. They walked on, past the dodging children, scarves flying.

Someone had approached the top of the hill from the other side; he stood unwinding a long kite string, a slightly built young man in corduroy jacket and knitted hat. The jacket looked like a very old cast-off, something from an Oxfam shop. The kite lay on the ground beside him, in a supermarket carrier bag; the string seemed endless, wound on to a stick, not a proper handle. He nodded to them as they approached; Jerzy nodded back. It was much colder up here, the wind cutting across the wet grass from the lake below. He turned to look at his father, as a train rattled past the heath towards Gospel Oak station.

'Tata? All right? Are you cold?'

'I'm all right,' said Jan, 'but let's keep walking.'

They passed the young man, who had heard them, and who gave them a fleeting, hesitant smile, as if he wanted to speak. Then they went down to where the path branched to the right, leading to a clump of tall, misty-topped trees. They could see one or two figures in dark coats walking away through them, like distant ghosts.

Jan said: 'I want to talk to you, Jerzy, but I don't know where to start.' He felt in his pocket and lit another cigarette. A waft of smoke drifted on the cold damp air into Jerzy's face, and he coughed.

'I'm sorry.' He said it automatically.

'No,' said Jan. 'It is I who should be sorry. For everything.'

Jerzy looked down across the long stretch of grass to the trees.

Jan said slowly: 'I told you last night that I lacked the courage to – to do what I intended. I've lacked courage in a lot of things, perhaps, and it is something I valued above everything.'

'I know,' said Jerzy. 'You were a hero. And I never had enough courage.'

Jan took a deep breath. 'I wasn't a hero, I simply did what I wanted to do. And as for you – I was very hard on you, Jerzy. On everyone, but especially you.'

'It's all right,' Jerzy said uneasily. 'It's all right, Tata. I'm sorry you've been feeling so . . .'

So low, so miserable, so bleak and lonely and bitter. None of the words was enough for what his father must have been feeling last night.

'Last night,' said Jan, 'I wanted to – to die, because I felt guilty for being free. Well . . . that is what I told myself.'

Jerzy turned to look at him. 'That's how I've felt, ever since martial law. That I'd done nothing to deserve what everyone over there has been fighting for. And they've been punished for it. But you fought, Tata, you fought . . .'

'And we were punished, too. Well . . .' He put out his hand, as he had done last night, and Jerzy took it, and gripped it hard. Then they went on, down towards the misty trees, where the figures had walked through, and vanished.

'Hey! You two – you are Poles, yes?'

They swung round and saw the young man on the hill above them, waving and calling in Polish: 'Watch this!'

His kite lay beside him, out of the bag, but still in the grass, where they couldn't see it.

'I made it!' he shouted, and tugged at the string and began to run. The kite lifted, and they caught a glimpse of red and white. The young man tugged, it lifted higher, and fell, bumping along the grass. Then the wind blew, and it began to rise again, and they saw it was a banner, two bands roughly stitched together. Across the white, the letters of *Solidarność* had been painted in dripping red.

Jan shook his head, smiling. 'I don't believe it.'

Beside him, Jerzy was snapping open his camera case.

The young man had stopped running; the wind was working for him, now, and the kite was rising faster and faster into the sky, tugging at the taut string. Jerzy was looking through the viewfinder, focusing. He snapped and snapped again: the kite and the kite flyer, in his scruffy old jacket and knitted hat, raising his hand to steady it aloft; and then just the banner itself, floating full out, *Solidarność* billowing against the cloud.

'Poland is not yet lost!' the young man yelled, in an accent just like Stefan's.

Jan and Jerzy stood next to each other, watching the banner soar into the winter sky.

New Year's Eve

Outside the Embassy, candles burned. Three large crosses, modelled on the martyrs' memorial in Gdańsk, were hung with black, and with Polish flags; there were flowers and candles at their feet, stretching for yards along the centre of the road. There had been a vigil here for fourteen days, beginning on the eleventh anniversary of the 1970 shootings in Gdańsk.

It was cold, but there was no snow; the candles flickered, and the air smelt of burning wax. The whole family had come tonight, and Danuta, whom Jerzy had telephoned. Babcia had brought candles for everyone; they stood in a little knot among the small crowd and she passed them round, as Dziadek had passed round the host at *Wigilia*. Then Babcia bent down and lit her candle from one on the ground; she stood up slowly, leaning on Dziadek's arm, and he lit his candle from hers, and turned to Jan, who lit his own. Flame lit flame, all through the family – Jan to Anna, Anna to Jerzy, Jerzy to Elizabeth, Elizabeth to Ewa, Ewa to Stefan, who passed his to Danuta, and then they all bent down to put theirs among the others. There was a path of perhaps two hundred little lights, and each time one burnt low another one was lit.

Anna stood next to Jan, watching the illuminated faces of the people in the crowd. There weren't so many, probably less than a hundred: grave old men and women in hats, with wrinkled faces, who like Dziadek and Babcia had left Poland in their thirties and forties, here after the war for a 'temporary sojourn' which had lasted almost forty years. There were couples like her and Jan, almost children when they left, whose own children had been born and brought up in this country – there were quite a number of Ewa's and Jerzy's contemporaries here: how had they lived their lives among the British? And there were the new arrivals, the young ones like Stefan and Danuta – and the kite flyer Jan and Jerzy had told them about. Most of them had thought their sojourn was going to be temporary, too, and now what was going to become of them?

Anna watched Ewa, standing with her arm through Stefan's looking down at the burning candles, and ached for her. She turned to Jan, who was looking straight ahead. He had cried when he told her about the night on the track, the first time she had ever seen him cry. Since then, he hadn't spoken about it; she knew he would never want to again. She said carefully: 'Jan?'

He turned and looked at her, still guarded, but no longer cold.

She slipped her arm through his, and he didn't draw away.

Ewa looked up from the candles and saw them, arm in arm. She looked at Stefan, and said: 'I want to wish you a Happy New Year, but I can't. I just want to say – I'll try to help you. I won't make it difficult, I'll try not to.'

Stefan put his arm round her. 'I know, Ewa, I know. You don't have to say these things. And – and I will try to be the same. Whatever happens.' He kissed her lightly on the cheek, and she said: 'You are the dearest person I have ever known. Whatever happens.'

Beside them, Danuta stood feeling horribly alone. The people in the hotel had been very sympathetic. That is to say they had all said how sorry they were, and that it must be awful. Every time she turned on the radio, every time the television in the hotel lounge was on, there was talk of Poland, or a film by Wajda, or clips from the summer of last year. The whole world was watching Poland – but who was watching her? If she hadn't met Jerzy and Elizabeth, who would she turn to now? No one knew what the Home Office was going to do. The Poles trapped in this country by martial law could stay for the moment, that was all they could say, but their status was unchanged. Danuta was still not allowed to work.

She turned to Jerzy, and said: 'Thank you for phoning me. It was very kind.'

He smiled down at her. 'I'm glad you came. And don't worry too much, all right? We'll work something out.'

Elizabeth was bending down to tend a candle. She stood up and said to Jerzy: 'Aren't you going to take any photographs?'

'Yes,' he said, and snapped open his camera case, slung round his neck. He set the flash and raised it, and looked through his view-finder. He saw his grandparents, standing close to each other, but not touching, because that was not quite dignified. Babcia said something to Dziadek, and Dziadek bent his head to hear her, attentive, courteous, very old. Jerzy snapped. He took a photograph of his parents, arm in arm, and Jan looked up at the flash and waved him away, but as if to a friend. He took Ewa, looking at Stefan, and Stefan, looking out over the candles, and he took Danuta, very pale, who wasn't looking at anyone. On the other side of the crowd, people were beginning to sing carols. He found himself humming, and he took a photograph of Elizabeth, who didn't know the words. He moved through the crowd, photographing the candlelit faces.

Someone began singing softly the refrain of the song that Solidarity had made its own.

'*Żeby Polską była Polską*

573

Żeby Polską była Polską . . .
So that Poland shall be Poland
So that Poland shall be Poland . . .'
They all sang it, over and over again, words and music floating out in the cold air above the candles, burning before the dark and shuttered Embassy, beneath the towering crosses.

Jerzy lowered his camera, and looked up at them.

13
Warsaw, January 1982

Krystyna stood with Olek in her arms, looking out of the window at the little park. The silver birches were bare, the swings at the far end empty, the ground thick with snow. Olek was pointing.

'Park! Park!'

'It's cold, Olek, it's very cold out there.'

'Park!'

She put him down, and he began to cry. 'Park! Go park!'

She picked him up again, and he squirmed. 'Park!'

'Oh, stop it!' she snapped, and put him down. 'Come on, *maleńki*, we'll go later, all right? You'll freeze out there.' He toddled off to the kitchen; she could hear him opening cupboards, banging saucepans.

If Stefan had sent the snowsuit, it hadn't arrived. Nothing had arrived for Christmas – no snowsuit, no food parcel, no letter. No letter. Everyone she knew with relatives in the West was waiting for letters. She didn't actually know anyone whose husband was there.

Outside in the street a patrol of the *milicja* went by, stamping. She wanted to open the window and spit at them. She hadn't taken down any of the posters on the wall, and she wasn't going to. The offices of Solidarność in Szpitalna Street were locked and boarded; she knew plenty of people whose husbands had been arrested and interned. If Stefan had been here, he would almost certainly have been among them. If he ever got back here, he would almost certainly be among them. Hadn't he stood outside his factory holding the Polish flag on the day of the one-hour strike? Hadn't he delivered leaflets and flysheets, and plastered posters all over Warsaw?

Hadn't everyone?

There was a joke going round, there was always a joke. The television news had gone down the drain again, and now there was a useful TV Dictionary:

2 Poles: an illegal gathering

3 Poles: an illegal demonstration

10 million Poles: a handful of extremists

Stefan would like it. She didn't know if she was ever going to see

Stefan again. There wasn't a day she didn't pick up the telephone and see if it was working. It wasn't. None of them were working, she couldn't even phone her mother. She knew Stefan would be trying to phone her, but beyond that she knew nothing. She didn't even know his address.

Condensation had misted the window. She rubbed it, and went on standing there. From here you could see not just the park but other apartment blocks on the estate: she and Stefan used to watch the graffiti change. *SOLIDARNOŚĆ!* STRIKE! WE DEMAND REGISTRATION . . . THE RELEASE OF NAROŻNIAK . . . ACCESS TO THE MEDIA. BREZHNEV: STAY HOME!

When the state of war was declared, the graffiti stopped, but only for a few days. They were soon out with paint pots, defying the curfew, defying the proclamations, with their lists of punishments. *GESTAPO!* was scrawled over most of those. *BEKANNTMACHUNG!* WARNING! The *milicja* went round painting it all out, but they did it very badly, like everything else.

There was a slogan all over Warsaw, probably all over the country. It had been on the wall of the block across the path, hastily written in dripping paint: WINTER IS YOURS, BUT SPRING WILL BE OURS. The pigs had tried to paint it out, but they'd obviously been in a hurry. You could still read what it said.